I0592393

M. Guizot

Monk

Or the Fall of the Republic and the Restoration of the Monarchy in England, in 1660

M. Guizot

Monk
Or the Fall of the Republic and the Restoration of the Monarchy in England, in 1660

ISBN/EAN: 9783744622264

Printed in Europe, USA, Canada, Australia, Japan

Cover: Foto ©Raphael Reischuk / pixelio.de

More available books at **www.hansebooks.com**

M O N K :

OR THE

FALL OF THE REPUBLIC

AND THE

RESTORATION OF THE MONARCH'

IN ENGLAND, IN 1660.

BY

M. GUIZOT.

Translated from the French,

BY

ANDREW R. SCOBLE

LONDON:
BELL & DALDY, 6, YORK STREET, COVENT GARDEN,
AND 186, FLEET STREET.
1866.

TRANSLATOR'S PREFACE.

MANY of the readers of M. Guizot's admirable History of the English Revolution have, no doubt, regretted that no account is given therein of the Restoration of the Monarchy under Charles II. This deficiency is amply supplied in the present work. In it, M. Guizot has pourtrayed, with a master's hand, the character of the man by whom the reactionary tendencies of the English people were guided to a successful issue; and has narrated, with brevity and clearness, the course of events which ultimated in the recall of the Stuart dynasty. Notwithstanding the interest and importance of the subject, no trustworthy life of Monk had previously been published ; and we cannot therefore be surprised, when the high reputation of its author is considered, that the present biography should at once have become an authority, and assumed a permanent position in the historical library.

In preparing the present edition for the press, no pains have been spared to render it as accurate and complete as possible. The quotations have, in almost every case, been verified by reference to the originals. The valuable collection of diplomatic correspondence, inserted by M. Guizot in the

Appendix to his work, is now presented for the first time to the British public, and will be found to contribute largely to our previous knowledge of the subject. A portrait, and an analytical table of contents, have also been added, and will, it is hoped, somewhat enhance the value of this edition.

A. R. S.

London, *February*, 1851.

ANALYTICAL TABLE OF CONTENTS.

AUTHOR'S PREFACE.

The present work was not written with a view to publication. It was intended to be nothing more than an historical study, prepared for my own use, in order that I might clearly understand the causes of the Restoration of the Monarchy in England, in 1660, and accurately estimate the character of the man who brought about that great event. In 1837, some friends who had read my sketch, requested me to allow its insertion in the *Revue Française;* and I consented. It has never before been published either separately or completely.

In 1837, it had a purely historical interest; at the present day, it evidently possesses a value of an altogether different nature. France is indeed in a strange position ! Anxious to avoid another revolution, all she desires is stability; and four or five questions, which all imply a revolution, afford an increasing theme of reflection and conversation to all her citizens :—

Can the Republic be consolidated ?

Can the Monarchy be restored ?

Which Monarchy shall we have ? The Empire or the House of Bourbon ?

Which branch of the House of Bourbon shall we choose ? the elder or the younger ? or both together, and in concert ?

If France desires nothing but stability, why are all these questions continually under discussion ? Let her put an end to all further debate, and remain *in statu quo.* If she does not believe in the stability of her present position, why does she not make choice of some solution to the questions at issue ? Is it that these questions can be neither suppressed nor resolved ? Such a state of affairs would ‚be the worst imagin-

able ; for, in that case, we should be condemned to passive
anxiety—having no confidence in the present, and no hope
for the future.   I cannot, and will not, believe that this is the
state of my country.

The France of 1850 and the England of 1660 bear but very
slight resemblance to each other, and I have no intention,
although this has been sometimes laid to my charge, of pro-
posing the one as a model for the other's imitation.   France
has her own peculiar genius and destiny; let her preserve and
trust to them.   But there is a something which rises above
all diversities of destiny and of national genius,—a something
which is equally necessary everywhere and at all times : I
refer to the *esprit politique*, or that good sense which in politics, as in everything else, and for nations as well as for individuals, can alone ensure definite and lasting success.

The good sense of two parties united to restore the English
Monarchy in 1660.   These were, the good sense of a man and
the good sense of the country, or, to speak more exactly, of
the Monarchical party in the country.   In England, two hundred years ago, it was said, as it is now said in France, that
the Monarchy had been irrevocably abolished, and that the
Republic alone was possible.   Monk perceived that this was a
false notion.   He believed in the Monarchy during the existence of the republic, when all around him, and himself among
the number, were talking, either sincerely or hypocritically,
of nothing but the Republic.   And when, after the death of
Cromwell, and the fall of his son Richard, the nation was
really called on to choose between the two forms of government, Monk decided in favour of the Monarchy.

This merit has been denied him ; and Monk, in pursuing
the object he had in view, made so great use and abuse of
falsehood, that men of prejudiced or superficial minds have
doubted whether his resolution was early adopted and constantly maintained.   But when we closely and thoroughly
study documents and events, doubt is no longer possible. From
the very first day, Monk was decided ; and whatever he did

or said, he was decided on every day, even to the last. He had a fixed resolution and plan of action, whilst every one else was doubting and hesitating. This was his first act of political good sense.

But although Monk was determined, he was also patient. He could wait until due time for success. A soldier, and acting by means of his army, he was firmly and constantly resolved not to recommence violent measures and a civil war. He understood that, to be securely established, the Monarchy must be restored pacifically and naturally, as a national necessity and the last refuge of the country. Disregarding the impatience and mistrust of others, he restrained, dissimulated, delayed, and waited, until the event took place, as it were, of itself. And when the event had taken place, Monk desired that, in the letters patent which were destined to commemorate his good fortune and glory, the words, *Victor sine sanguine* (a bloodless conqueror) should be inserted, to show that his prudence had been the result of reflection and of choice.

The monarchical party, also, acted sensibly. It occupied a less difficult position then, than it does in France at the present day. It was not wavering between two or three monarchies ; all were in favour of one and the same aspirant to the throne. The party was nevertheless composed of very different elements. Some had caused the revolution, while others had opposed it. They had fought boldly with each other, either for or against the King whose son they now proposed to restore. Opposite ideas, passions, and interests separated them ; but they postponed their dissensions. Until their success was complete, they made their opposite ideas, passions, and interests give way before the idea, the passion, and the interest which they had in common. They subordinated that which they would have preferred to that which they desired. This is the touchstone of the political intelligence of parties.

The English Royalists did even more than this. They confided the execution of their design to a man whom they distrusted, and whom they had good reason to distrust. Monk had served the King, the Revolution, the Republic, Cromwell, and the Parliament. He was utterly incomprehensible and obscure. He frequently said one thing and did another ; and he lied with a cool audacity which startled his most intimate confidants. As far as he was concerned, the Monarchical party was full of doubt and disquietude, passing alternately from hope to fear, and from glimpses of light to thick darkness. But neither their doubts, fears, and desires, nor the obscurities of Monk, could mislead the Royalists. Monk was the man whom the crisis at once offered to them and forced upon them. Altogether, they had more reasons to hope from him than to distrust him ; and, moreover, they were compelled to accept him. The Royalists felt this and acted accordingly. They did not repose blind confidence in Monk, but they discreetly supported his views, drawing him on without compromising him, obedient to his advice, and watching quietly, but vigilantly, behind him, as behind a leader of their choice. For a leader there must be. to execute plans of this kind ; and no leader can be of real service who is not allowed to choose his own method of proceeding, and vigorously sustained in all he undertakes. Success rewarded the good conduct of the Monarchical party and their leader.

Peoples, parties, or individuals, indeed, men in general, at the great turning-points of their destiny, may be deceived in two different, but equally fatal ways. Sometimes, undecided and discouraged, they give up all hope, remain as inactive as unconcerned spectators, and resign their fate to that unknown Power which, according to, their faith or their impiety, they call Providence, fatality, or chance. Sometimes, blindly confident and heedless, they act according to the caprices of their imagination or desires, believing that everything is possible to them, and that nothing will prevent them from succeeding in the way they wish and hope. God does not tolerate or leave unpunished either of these errors. He wills that men should take their share in the management of their own business, and should accept its toil as well as its chances. And, at the same time, he does not suffer men to imagine that they can dispose of events at their will, and that all circumstances will bend to their interests or caprices. With regard to those who will do nothing for themselves, but wait until God shall deliver them from their troubles, God also waits and lets them suffer. To those, whose presumption leads them to think they can obtain all that they desire, God sends obstacles and hindrances which compel them to acknowledge that there are around them forces, rights, and interests, other than their own, and with which they must make terms. Good policy consists in recognising beforehand these natural necessities, which, if disregarded, would presently become Divine lessons, and in ordering our conduct with due regard to their existence.

I do not wish to say anything about the Revolution of February. I am not the man whom it behoves to speak of that occurrence at the present time. But I cannot believe, and there is not a single Frenchman who can be satisfied to believe, that that revolution was the crowning event of the glorious history of France. It suits the daring disposition of my country to plunge, no matter at what cost or peril, into vast and unheard-of experiments. France, we may say, seems to consider herself the grand laboratory of the civilisation of the world. But if she is quick to run into danger, she is also quick to bethink herself and retrace her steps, when she perceives that she has taken the wrong road, and is about to fall. Already has she stayed her progress under the shadow of a great name ; but a salutary halt is not safety. It is not enough that France is prevented from falling into the abyss : the abyss must be filled up, and France recover herself. To effect this, she needs the assistance of a Washington or a Monk. Which of the two will Providence grant us ?

I am anxious to throw upon the event which forms the subject of this sketch, all the light that can be collected, so as to render it more comprehensible to us. With this view, I publish, in continuation of my narrative, seventy-one despatches or fragments of despatches, addressed, in 1659 and 1660, to

Cardinal Mazarin, and M. de Brienne, by M. de Bourdeaux, at that time French ambassador at London. These documents have been taken from the archives of the department of Foreign Affairs at Paris. It is curious to notice how the representative of Louis XIV. at Cromwell's court daily collected information, and strove to influence the progress of Monk towards the restoration of the Stuart dynasty.

I also publish a letter addressed to Monk by Richard Cromwell, fifteen days before the restoration of Charles II., in order that, as he says, "when the Parliament shall be met, you would make use of your interest on my behalf, that I be not left liable to debts which, I am confident, neither God nor conscience can ever reckon mine . . . having this persuasion of you that, as I cannot but think myself unworthy of great things, so you will not think me worthy of utter ruin." This is, indeed, a singular mixture of humble modesty and recollections of former greatness.

In 1838, shortly after the publication of my first essay on Monk in the *Revue Française*, the Hon. J. Stuart Wortley, then a member of the House of Commons, but who now sits as Lord Wharncliffe in the House of Lords, translated and published it in London. To his translation he added an introduction and notes replete with historic interest and value. In revising and recasting my essay at the present time, I have made use of Lord Wharncliffe's work, both to correct some inaccuracies which had crept into my own sketch, and to borrow some notes which either explain or complete the statements I have made.

GUIZOT.

Val Richer, *October*, 1850.

MONK:

AN HISTORICAL STUDY.

1608—1670.

AMONG the men who have played a part upon the great stage of history, the fate of Monk has been remarkable. At once celebrated and obscure, he has connected his name with the restoration of the Stuarts, but has left us almost no other memorial of himself. On one day, we behold him distinguished above all others, and disposing of a throne and a people; on the days which precede and follow it, we can scarcely catch a glimpse of him in the crowd with which he mingles. He is one of those men whose lives contain only a single day upon which their character and faculties, their virtues or vices, can display themselves in their full energy and imperiousness; yet these are men whom it is important to study closely, for it is only when we know them thoroughly that we can rightly understand the rapid drama in which they performed the leading part, and the event which they alone were able to accomplish.

George Monk, second son of Sir Thomas Monk, a gentleman of the county of Devon, was born on the 6th of December, 1608, at the manor-house of Potheridge, the hereditary residence of his family, which was one of the most ancient and respectable in the county. But the estate had long been in great disorder, and Sir Thomas, like many other gentlemen at that period, was able to maintain his rank only by ruinous expedients. George Monk was under seventeen years of age when Charles I. visited Plymouth, in 1625, the very year of his accession to the throne, to superintend the equipment of the expedition which he intended to send against Spain. The gentlemen of the county assembled round the king, anxious to appear before his eyes with a splendour befitting the occasion. Sir Thomas Monk, among others, made preparations for going; but, alarmed by the proceedings of a creditor

who threatened to arrest him, he sent his son George to
Exeter, to persuade the under-sheriff, by the offer of a small
sum, to delay the execution of the writ. The under-sheriff
accepted the money, promised what was asked, and, a few
days afterwards, having probably received a larger bribe
from the other side, had Sir Thomas publicly arrested, in the
midst of the gentlemen who had assembled to meet the king.
Indignant at this treachery, young Monk hastened to Exeter,
and, had he not been rescued by some neighbours, the man
of law, whom he stoutly belaboured, would have had great
difficulty in escaping from his hands. It now became necessary for our hero to evade the probable consequences of his
adventure. The squadron destined to cruize before Cadiz, in
the hope of intercepting the Spanish galleons, was just ready
to set sail; Sir Richard Greenville, Monk's near relative,
served with it; and George Monk, intrusted to his care,
found a refuge on board his ship, and was enrolled as a
volunteer; thus cast by chance, and when he had only just
emerged from childhood, into a career to which he was
destined both by his parents and his inclination.

Fortune proved unfavourable to him in the choice of his
first campaign and his first patron. Although Sir Richard
Greenville had not yet found an opportunity for displaying
that harsh and imperious rapacity which he subsequently
manifested during the civil war, he was ill adapted to exercise
a salutary influence over his cousin; and the example of the
dashing young courtiers, who had embarked on board the
fleet to seek, in a hazardous expedition, some diversion from
their frivolous pleasures, might be dangerous to the younger
son of a ruined family, whose only wealth was his economy,
and whose prospects in life depended entirely upon his good
conduct. But George Monk already felt that firm and decided
bent, which evil example strengthens instead of destroying;
and amid the disorder of his father's house, and the licence of
his first companions, he contracted those tastes and habits
of order which, in after-times, contributed so greatly to ensure
his success in life. The enterprise against Cadiz, as ill-
conducted as it was ill-conceived, failed under the most disastrous circumstances; and the next year, Monk enlisted as an
ensign in the expedition of the Duke of Buckingham against
the Isle de Rhé, and witnessed a second time the spectacle of
shame and misfortune which the presumptuous ignorance of a

favourite may occasion. Of this event he retained a bitter recollection, which he frequently expressed when relating the occurrences of his youth. In 1629, a year after his return from the Isle de Rhé, he went to Holland, where he entered the regiment of the Earl of Oxford.

Germany and the Low Countries were, at this period, the resort of those young Englishmen whose taste, or the state of whose fortunes, led them to embrace the profession of arms, as well as of those whose activity languished in their own country, which was at peace with Europe, and had not yet begun to struggle for its own liberty. Whoever was tormented by a desire for action, went to satisfy it in distant wars, which had no other attraction for him than the game of war, with its emotions and its chances. Whoever felt that he was capable of gaining renown by his valour, went to dispose of it in the best market. Thus was formed a race of men inured to danger, watchful over their own interests, imperturbable in those habits of calculation which made their very lives a merchandise, uniting brilliant actions with vulgar feelings, indifferent to moral maxims, yet attached to certain duties, and trained by their occupation to dispense with virtues, and at the same time to keep themselves from many vices. Such were the greater number of those officers whom England then sent abroad to gain instruction and advancement in foreign wars, and who, at a later period, under the name of soldiers of fortune, played an important part in her civil wars. Although devoid of principle, they were not wanting in a certain kind of honour; and when fortune plunged them into the midst of the vicissitudes of political parties, they resigned themselves to their fate with a coolness not unmingled with repugnance, never breaking without pain the engagement which they had first contracted, and rarely determining to quit, before their time, the standard to which they had temporarily hired their courage and fidelity. Caring little for their country, they entertained warm feelings of brotherhood towards the men whose dangers they had shared; and thus, though doubtful citizens, they were excellent comrades. Indifferent to the sufferings of the people, they knew how to spare those of the soldier; and, orderly even in their violence, they did not aggravate it by the evil of confusion. Their brutality was harsh, but not ferocious; their rapacity was subject to the laws of discipline; and that disgraceful

B 2

love of pillage, which made the noble Cavaliers* the terror of
England, has rarely been charged upon the soldiers of fortune.
Monk was one of them, superior to all in talent, but similar
to all in his tastes and necessities; his genius rose with circumstances, but his sentiments remained unchanged. He
did great things without conferring great lustre upon himself,
and carried into the destiny of the man who changed the face
of an empire, some of those habits of mind and heart which
had been formed in him by the obscure fortune of a mercenary
soldier.

After several years of service, he obtained a company in
the regiment of Lord Goring, which was almost exclusively
composed of volunteers, for the most part rich and of high
birth, and consequently but ill-disposed to submit to the
rigours of discipline. Monk arrived among them, the only
one who thoroughly understood his profession; invested with
that authority which remarkable and marked courage gives
among men of spirit: grave, exact, regular in his manners—
at least for a soldier; and, according to the statement of
Gumble, his chaplain, punctual in the fulfilment of the duties
of his religion, which he respected as much as his military
duties. He soon gained over those whom he commanded that
ascendancy which belongs to the man who has in himself a
natural right to command; he made himself at once loved
and obeyed, and many of his subordinates, in the course of
their after-lives, thanked him for the benefit which they had
derived from his severity.

He had served in Holland for nearly ten years, when,
towards the end of the year 1638, he was placed in winter-
quarters at Dort. His soldiers committed some disorders,
and the magistrates of the town wished to take cognizance of
the offence. Monk maintained that a court-martial alone
had any right to try the case. The matter was referred to
Frederic Henry, Prince of Orange, who was at that time
stadtholder. In a previous case of a similar nature, he had
decided in favour of military authority; but this time, either
out of respect for the privileges of the town of Dort, or
because his opinions had changed, judgment was pronounced
in favour of the magistrates, and Monk was obliged to leave

---

* This name, as my readers are doubtless aware, was given to those
gentlemen who, during the civil war, took arms to support Charles I.
against the parliament.

Dort for much less comfortable quarters. Wounded in his honour as a soldier, he forthwith determined to leave the service of Holland; and the more willingly, because England was on the point of offering him useful employment for his talents and courage.

The religious differences which, for more than a year, had revolted Scotland against the government of Charles I., were already approaching their crisis—the prelude to so many others. On both sides, active preparations for attack or defence were being made; and to maintain a war which was detested by his people, and disdained by his courtiers, whom it would merely annoy without enriching, Charles was obliged to seek the assistance of those officers who, trained to arms in foreign lands, were indifferent to the opinions of their countrymen, and accustomed even to set little value upon their own. They flocked in great numbers to his army, which had also been recruited by a considerable number of country gentlemen, who were eager and proud to approach the court. Monk had, in his childhood, imbibed some presbyterian notions; but, as he was not greatly troubled with religious scruples, he entered without repugnance into the service of Anglican intolerance against the liberty of conscience then demanded by the Scotch presbyterians*; and, full of zeal for the cause which offered him employment, he obtained, through the good offices of the Earl of Leicester—a connexion of his family—the rank of lieutenant-colonel, in the regiment of the Earl of Newport, general of the ordnance.

The people of England were opposed to the war with Scotland; public aversion delayed its first blows; and before any blood had been shed, the treaty of Berwick, concluded on the 18th of June, 1639, declared that the campaign was over, but without putting an end to the animosities which had caused its commencement. The English and Scotch armies, which, according to the terms of the treaty, had both been disbanded within forty-eight hours, remained ready to re-assemble at the first order. It was not long before a fresh outburst took place; and, on the 1st of August, 1640, Monk, at his post on the Scottish frontier, by the banks of the Tyne,

---

* The presbyterians were that party who wished to introduce a democratic revolution into the Anglican church; and who, in the state, sustained the parliament against the king, although they wished for the maintenance of royalty.

took part in the affair of Newburne, an engagement unique
in this war, and for a moment saved the English from some
of its disastrous results. The Scotch, after having crossed
the Tyne almost without opposition, marched towards the
quarters of the Earl of Newport, in order to gain possession
of the artillery; for in the royal army, disorder had not
waited for the enemy. Monk, still at the head of his regiment,
had for each of his own guns only one ball and one charge of
powder; he sent to major-general Astley for some ammunition, and was told, in reply, that there was no more. Upon
this, placing his soldiers, armed with their muskets, along
the hedges, he presented such an imposing front to the
Scotch, that they did not dare to attack him, but allowed
him to convey the English artillery to Newcastle, where,
together with the place itself, it soon fell into their hands.

Public opinion had prevailed; England refused to defend
herself, and the war with Scotland became impossible. In
vain did Strafford attempt to influence the army by caresses,
threats, and punishments; in vain did he strive to surround
himself with men whose views were the same as his own.
Monk, summoned to the council, maintained that it was
necessary to fight. Strafford was unwilling to suppose that
authority could meet with any obstacles; and Monk would
not admit that the opinion of the soldiery could affect the
fate of a battle, for he had not yet learned to doubt the power
of discipline. Their advice was rejected; peace was resolved
upon; and long afterwards, when Monk had become the
faithful servant of the parliament, he never spoke without
indignation of the craven counsels which, in 1640, had rendered useless an army, "fitted," as he said, "to reduce very
different troops from those of the covenanters,* and a very
different kingdom from that of Scotland."

It appears that at this period, either through discontent at
the turn which affairs had taken, or through a desire to try
his fortune in a country more tranquil than his own, and in a
career more profitable than that of arms, Monk listened to a
proposition for founding a colony in Madagascar. The plan,
however, failed. The Long parliament had met, and its
quarrel with the king daily grew more violent; the insurrec-

* This was the name given to the presbyterians, and especially to those
of Scotland, because when they first revolted, they, on the 1st of March,
1638, bound themselves to support each other, by a civil and religious
compact, known by the name of the *covenant.*

tion of Catholic Ireland* offered every Englishman a national
cause to defend, and every soldier a war to wage, without
pledging himself to either party. The recent execution of
Strafford† had left the government of Ireland vacant; and
this office was conferred upon the Earl of Leicester, together
with the command of the troops destined to quell the revolt.
Every commander of an army had his own regiment; and
Monk was appointed colonel of that of Leicester.

The parliament, about to engage in the civil war, had at
that time too urgent need in England of its troops and money,
to employ them in succouring the Irish Protestants, whose
misfortunes they could so easily and so profitably impute to
the king. Though supplies were continually promised and
voted, they were never ready; or else they were diverted
from their destination, or appropriated by Charles himself,
who, whilst he complained of the indifference of the parliament to the deplorable situation of the Anglo-Irish, did not
scruple to apply to his own use their powder and muskets,
even taking them from the arsenal of Dublin. Some regiments were at length sent over, and among others that of the
Earl of Leicester; but the earl himself stayed at home; not
being at all eager to place himself at the head of a government without resources, of a wasted country, and of an army
scarcely formed, and worse paid, he remained in London,
leaving the command in Ireland to the Earl of Ormonde, lieutenant-general *ad interim*. Ormonde was a royalist, and,
though himself a Protestant, belonged to a Catholic family;
but he was one of the chief nobility of Ireland, and the only
man with sufficient influence to counterbalance the formidable
popular power which the insurrection had called into existence. On the first news of the rebellion, the king had
appointed Ormonde commander-in-chief of the army, as being
a man upon whose fidelity he could depend; the lords-justices,
who were invested with the civil authority at Dublin, had
had recourse to him, seeing that they could hope for assistance from no other person near them; and the parliament
had accepted him, because they could not do otherwise.

It was on the 21st of February, 1642, that Monk dis-

* On the 23rd of October, 1641.
† Eight days after the re-assembling of the Long parliament, on the
11th of November, 1640, this great and despotic minister of Charles I.
was impeached by the House of Commons, revolutionarily condemned on
the 21st of April following, and executed on the 12th of May.

embarked at the port of Dublin at the head of a regiment of fifteen hundred infantry, and accompanied by four hundred cavalry under the command of Sir Richard Greenville. These troops had been preceded, about six weeks before, by the arrival of fourteen hundred men, the first whom England had sent to Ireland since the commencement of the rebellion. Of these fourteen hundred men, three hundred had arrived unprovided with arms, and all were without provisions, without ammunition, and without money, in a country exposed to the ravages of two rival parties. The most pressing necessity was not to lead these troops to battle, but to provide them with the means of subsistence. The forced supplies had been quickly exhausted, and the contractors, who received no pay, did not again make their appearance. In vain were the most lamentable supplications daily addressed to the king and the parliament; neither parliament nor king were willing to spare anything from what barely sufficed for their own wants. Inadequate supplies of money, provisions, ammunition, and accoutrements, arrived occasionally, and though always long expected, always fell far short of what was required and hoped, and being generally composed of damaged or inferior articles, served only to irritate the despair of the soldiers, thus abandoned in their distress to the cupidity of contractors.

To these causes of disorder was added the uncertainty of the measures of the Irish government; the inevitable vice of a council composed of two hostile parties, who, though obliged to act in concert, laboured only to destroy each other, and were careful merely to maintain a semblance of unanimity until the time when one should feel itself strong enough to dislodge the other. Ormonde was a zealous royalist; the lords justices were zealous parliamentarians. Leicester held his commission from the king, and inactive in London, commanded in the name of the parliament; Ormonde, established in Dublin, asserted the right of the king to appoint to public employments and to decide affairs of war. Conflicts of authority were frequently, and terminated always in favour of the party which at the moment happened to be most powerful. In general the adherents of the king had the advantage. In spite of the pretensions of Leicester, Ormonde, active and present, disposed of most appointments. The army, originally organized by Strafford, had lately received into its ranks the greater number of those officers whom the distrust of the parliament had deemed it wise to remove from England; and

the state of destitution in which it was left was not calculated
to calm its discontent. It naturally turned to the two Houses,
which were responsible for the evil, as they were in possession
of the power. This power, however, itself restrained the
feelings which it aroused; and the arrears of pay, as they
accumulated, only bound the officers more and more closely to
the cause which alone could pay them. Thus suspended
between opposite inclinations and interests, and at the same
time pressed by common dangers and enemies, the army, in
presence of the revolted Irish, felt rather English than parliamentarian or royalist; and the lukewarmness of their political
opinions afforded the leaders great latitude in gaining pro-
selytes, and the inferiors much facility in maintaining a good
understanding with both parties.

Monk, the most skilful of all, thenceforth began his
apprenticeship to that art which he afterwards so dexterously
practised,—the art of pushing his fortunes with the dominant
party, without losing the confidence of that which might one
day prevail. The absence of all passion, an apparent languor of
mind, produced by the circumspection of his character, and a
natural taciturnity preserved him from the snares of speech;
he made little use of it in the conduct of life, except to ascertain the opinions of others, by giving a false account of his
own. But his silence was active; with an assiduous but
tranquil diligence he maintained relations everywhere that his
situation permitted; and without ever appearing to have
pledged himself, every one thought they had gained, or could
gain him, if necessary. Besides, devoted with indefatigable
activity to the difficult duties of the administration which had
been intrusted to him, he appeared to be exclusively occupied
by it; and the bitterness or distrust of political opinions could
hardly reach a man with whom some special and urgent
business was always to be transacted.

The military renown of a commander had little to gain in
this sad and perilous war, almost always directed against
enemies more easy to disperse than to reach, and from whom
surprise was more to be feared than resistance. Monk rarely
had an opportunity of distinguishing himself, but he never let
one escape, and he always displayed, as at Tymochoe and
Castle Jordan, the utmost skill and bravery in routing enemies
much more numerous than his own troops. The greater
number of these expeditions were confined to rapid incursions,

of which the object was devastation, the result pillage, and the march the greatest danger. These incursions were designedly multiplied; since, while they kept the troops employed, they supplied them with provisions for several days at least; but on each occasion it was necessary to go further to find some district to ravage, and the enterprise became every time more difficult for soldiers worn out by fatigue and unprovided with clothes or shoes. Many sank down by the road-side, incapable of proceeding further: more than once they refused to commence their march; and it was often to be feared that an announcement of departure would become the signal for a mutiny. Monk alone knew how to induce them to follow him. As skilful as he was bold, his presence always assured his men of success. "There was not," it was said, " a soldier ever so sick or so ill-shod, who would not make an effort to follow George Monk,"—a familiar name given him by the affection of the soldiers, who are always more disposed to obey when they have in some sort appropriated their commander to themselves, and can recognize a comrade in their leader. Monk, a soldier like themselves, with no other interest but theirs, was to them the object of that confidence which men, in pressing extremities, unreservedly repose in him on whom they think they can depend. Attentive to their wants, careful to remove from them those hardships which he could spare them, as regular in his communications with them as the irregularity of the circumstances in which they were placed would permit, he maintained in their minds that idea of justice which calms the impatience of subordinates, by tranquillizing their imagination, and strengthens the authority of the chief, because it leaves no ground for complaint against him.

Repulsed by degrees, and compelled to concentrate their forces, the Irish insurgents had left at the disposition of the government a large extent of land which, though waste and uncultivated, was likely soon to become fertile. It was at length determined to take advantage of this, and these estates became at once a resource to the army, and to the government a means of still retaining some influence. The privy council gave these lands in custodiam to commanders of corps, who had them cultivated by their soldiers, and derived from them a profit which was partially devoted to obtaining the means of subsistence for those who served under their orders. Favouritism usually presided in these distributions. Monk contrived to obtain a good share, and turned it to advantage with that spirit of order and economy which was natural to him. The habits of labour which was destined to render their condition more endurable maintained obedience and gaiety among his soldiers; and without troubling themselves about the political coquetry to which their leader might be indebted for his credit, they attached themselves to him because he knew how to manage both for himself and for them. The royalist party did not take offence at it. Among men daily exposed to the extremest misery, opinion yielded to more pressing necessities; and few people thought of finding fault with the prudent dissimulation of a general anxious to obtain the arrears of his pay, or to obtain some equivalent which would enable him to wait.

It was not from the king that Monk could then expect the advancement and the favours reserved for men of higher rank and more ardent zeal. The post of governor of the town of Dublin fell vacant. Lord Leicester, immediately informed of it in London, appointed Monk to the office; but a nomination from the king arrived from Oxford a few days after, and it was for Lord Lambert. In vain did the lords-justices of Ireland strive to elude this decision : the preponderance of the royalists daily became more irresistible; and Monk, avoiding this perilous contest, contrived to retire so soon, and with such good grace, as not to compromise himself with the party which had thus disobliged him.

For an instant only he seemed to forget his ordinary circumspection. The pay of the army in Ireland had not been forthcoming since the commencement of the war. The parliament, to appease the dissatisfaction of the officers, and keep them under its power, proposed to fund a portion of their arrears, which it engaged to pay them in lands confiscated from the rebels as soon as by their vote the Houses had declared the subjection of Ireland. A register was to be opened, in which those who consented to the arrangement were to inscribe their names. The officers, who were mostly royalists, and moreover but little convinced that the parliament wished to put an end to this war, objected to this engagement. Some, however, subscribed; and Monk was one of the first to be drawn into the scheme. Reynolds, one of the Westminster commissioners, had offered to him, as well as to some others, to make himself personally responsible to them for the fidelity of the

parliament in fulfilling its promises. Indu
the fear of losing all if he refused this offer,]
but when the names were once inscribed
Reynolds was in no hurry to give his bond
those to whom it was to serve as a security.
made public, caused Monk some trouble, a
beware of precipitation even in an act of pri

The power of the parliament in Ireland was,
near its close. Evidently, it was not desirou
there to an end, and it was unable to sustai
principal members of the Committee for
London, had answered Major Warren, wh
Dublin to ask assistance, that " if only fiv
were wanted to save Ireland, they would no!
The officers at length resolved to address the
to the king; and at the end of that petitio
tined to bring about definitively a royalist
government of Ireland, figured the name of
during the month of February 1643, the p
missioners had left Dublin, where their posi
tenable. At length, on the 1st of August, 1
Oxford an order for the imprisonment of th
William Parsons, the leader of the parliam
of those members of the privy council who
Charles wished, by means of this measure,
conclude with the Irish insurgents a suspen
which they, as well as himself, had long
signed on the 15th of September; and imme
Ormonde prepared to send a portion of the
assistance of the king. He chose, for the
transferred to England, those regiments of
himself most sure, and made them take ar
king against the army of the Earl of Esse:
parliamentary commander. Two officers o
it: Monk was one of them. His politica
more towards the king than towards his en
been absent from England for more than ei
could not, without some investigation, d
between the two parties: he had, besides, oth
sider; and the hope of obtaining his pay fr
before he took service against it, was, it app
and even avowed reason of his refusal.

accepted, and Ormonde consented to let him leave for London; but an incident occurred to derange Monk's plans, and constrain him to decide more promptly than he wished.

There are occasions when even circumspection compromises, and when carefulness to displease neither party exposes a man to the suspicions of all. The parliament, incensed at the suspension of hostilities which Charles had just concluded with the Irish insurgents, had resolved openly to separate, in Ireland as elsewhere, its interests from those of the king. They deliberated on the choice of a lieutenant-general whom they could effectively oppose to the earl, recently created marquis, of Ormonde. Lord Lisle, eldest son of the Earl of Leicester, was proposed, and declared that he was sure to be joined by Monk and some other colonels of the army. The king was informed of Lord Lisle's promises, and Lord Digby reported them to Ormonde, but without attaching importance to them; for he said he had always heard those officers spoken of as men of honour. Digby at the same time wrote a persuasive letter to Monk, in which, treating him as an affectionate servant of the king, he pressed him to come and devote to him his services. The suspicion excited at Oxford with regard to Monk would therefore have produced no effect, if it had not been confirmed by another report. A person named Johnson, coming from London, declared that at the committee, while he was waiting for his passport to be signed, Mr. Pym, after having questioned him about the state of the army in Ireland, charged him to seek out Colonel Monk on his behalf, and to persuade him to use his influence with the soldiers, so as to divert them from serving the king, promising him all the assistance he might require, and a reward proportionate to the good offices which were expected from him. This language of Pym proved that, even if Monk had not yet entered into any engagement with the parliamentarians, they at least believed him disposed to be gained over by their favours. This was enough to make the royalists consider it prudent to preserve him from temptation. Instead of allowing him to embark with the troops, Ormonde sent him under a strong guard to Bristol; accompanying this act, however, with a pressing recommendation to the governor of that place to treat Monk well, so long as he was obliged to detain him, while awaiting orders from the king.

There was no longer room for deliberation; Monk arrived

at Bristol a decided royalist; and he soon inspired the governor, Lord Hawley, with so much confidence, that the latter sent him on his parole to Oxford, addressing him directly to the king, and charging him at the same time with letters for Lord Digby. He was received as a man of importance; the king consulted him on several occasions; and Monk, who was better skilled in commanding an army than in governing a party, advised him, if he wished to derive any advantage from his, to reduce it to 10,000 men, well-disciplined, and well-officered. His services appeared more useful than his advice; it was known that " of all the officers in the army, none was so dear to the soldiers;" and it was judged that he would nowhere be so serviceable as in the midst of those whom he had lately commanded. His regiment had been taken from him at the time of his arrest; but the king appointed him major-general of the troops which had come from Ireland, and were then engaged in the siege of Nantwich, under the command of Lord Byron. Monk had scarcely arrived at his post, when Fairfax, by the extraordinary rapidity of his march, surprised Lord Byron, defeated him at Nantwich, on the 25th of January, 1644, and forced him to raise the siege, leaving in the enemy's hands a large number of prisoners, and amongst others, the major-general, who, in the absence of the new colonel, had placed himself at the head of his old regiment. Monk was sent first to Hull, from whence he was, by order of the parliament, immediately transferred to London and confined in the Tower.

There he passed rather more than two years, faithful to the engagement which he had first contracted with the king, and obstinately rejecting the offers of the parliament. He several times solicited his exchange, but in vain; for, in London, they were aware of his importance as a military leader, and were desirous to detain him; whilst, at Oxford, men of a higher rank obtained the preference over him; and he languished in the Tower, a prey to all those miseries which can assail a prisoner without fortune. His father was dead; his elder brother, embarrassed in his affairs, and busily engaged in serving the king, wherever the chances of war might lead him, had but little leisure or means to send him his very moderate allowance. But Monk's connexion with the family of the Earl of Leicester, who had always been devoted to the

parliament, had never been broken off; from them he received some assistance; and at the same time, the king, more
constant in remembering him than powerful to serve him,
sent him a hundred pounds; a remarkable proof of interest
and consideration, when we regard the state of penury in
which the court at Oxford were obliged to live.

Meanwhile, events pursued their course. In 1646, the king
was a prisoner in the hands of the parliament, and the civil
war seemed decidedly at an end. Monk no longer had any
choice to make; and, ceasing to be dangerous to the revolutionary party, might become useful to it. Lord Lisle,
appointed lieutenant-general of Ireland for one year, was at
length thinking of going thither; and Monk was considered a
fit person to act as his second. The efforts to gain him over,
which now probably became more active, were also more
effective. "Money, which he loved dearly," says Clarendon,* " aided Cromwell not a little in obtaining his decision."
The necessity, however, of swearing to the covenant still presented an obstacle. Monk's whole life attests the repugnance
which he felt for oaths; and this was considering them of
some importance. Besides, he was not fond of extreme parties,
and an ardently parliamentarian army doubtless appeared to
him a bad means for pacifying Ireland. Numerous conferences with men, who being, like himself, prisoners in the Tower,
could influence his conscience and his politics, at length
determined him to accept the proffered conditions ; and on
the 13th of November, 1646, a message from the House of
Lords informed the House of Commons of Colonel Monk's
submission, and requested that, on account of his military
talents, he should be employed in the Irish war. The Commons consented to this, induced by Monk's popularity in the
army. One member only, Mr. Cawley, opposed it; for what
reason we do not know. Monk left his prison to go and
serve the parliament, leaving in the Tower the royalists, his
companions in misfortune, who notwithstanding his desertion
of their cause, never ceased, in their private conversations, to
flatter themselves that he would one day be useful to the
king.

The king's party was at that time overcome in Ireland, as

* This phrase, which we find in the manuscripts of Clarendon's History of the Rebellion, was omitted in the early editions: it has, however,
been restored in the last edition published at Oxford.

elsewhere. The truce concluded with the Catholic insurgents had not effected a sincere and effectual union between them and the Protestant royalists. Without hope that Charles could send him any succour, and stripped of all resources, Ormonde, who would not, at any price, deliver the fate of the Irish Protestants into the hands of the Catholics, had entered into a negociation with the English parliament, to place Dublin and the shattered remains of the government in their possession. The negociation was prolonged very greatly. Parliamentary commissioners and Lord Lisle came successively, the former to Dublin, the latter to Cork, without effecting anything; and Monk had returned to England two months, before the treaty was finally signed on the 19th of June, 1647.

By this treaty, the parliament entered into possession of the government of Ireland, with the exception of the districts occupied by the rebels. It was judged more prudent to divide this government, than to place such great power in the hands of one man. Colonel Jones had the command in Leinster, and Monk in Ulster, a province from which James I. had expelled the inhabitants, that he might establish Scottish colonists there. Resentment and interest had made the dispossessed proprietors the most irreconcileable enemies of the English dominion. Assembled under the leadership of Owen O'Neill, the ablest and boldest of the insurgent chieftains, the *old Irish* (so the exiles of Ulster named themselves) wandered incessantly in arms around their former dwellings, and sometimes penetrated into the very heart of the province; always beaten, but always returning to the charge, and collecting again in one point almost as soon as they were dispersed in another. It was impossible to come to a regular action with them; O'Neill carefully avoided such encounters, and would not have been able to sustain them. It was not so difficult to repel his attacks as to prevent them. Monk succeeded in this by dint of vigilance; and by setting spies to follow O'Neill's footsteps, and taking care to cut off his supplies of provisions and to ravage the neighbourhood of his encampments, he was soon in a condition to fear little from him.

But, in the interior of his government, he had to struggle against graver difficulties. At the commencement of the Irish rebellion, Scotland had sent to the aid of the Scottish colonists who were settled in Ulster, a body of troops which, under the command of Robert Monroe, had taken possession of the country, and for six years had done with it as they pleased. The *new Scotch* had become an object of hatred to their fellow-countrymen, the *old Scotch*, and all were sufficiently ill-disposed towards the English troops. Monk already excelled in keeping parties at peace, by taking advantage of their hostilities. Under his administration, all recognized his authority; an arbitrary, but generally equitable kind of justice was dispensed; the land was cultivated; and, by his economy in the distribution of booty, and of the small produce of the land, he contrived to maintain the war without assistance, and almost to make his soldiers forget that they were receiving none of their pay; whilst his table, always abundantly supplied, was ever open to his officers, who had scarcely any other means of subsistence.

To the personal animosities which divided the two Scottish populations of Ulster, political dissensions were soon added. The second civil war was breaking out in England;* the parliament of Scotland had declared for the king; its army was already in the field; and Sir George Monroe, a nephew of Robert Monroe, had received a command in it. For some time past, Robert had been requested to join his nephew; and he must have been the more inclined to do this, because the English parliament had of late caused great discontent among the Scottish troops stationed in Ulster, by insisting, though unsuccessfully, that they should return to Scotland, and return without being paid. Distrust of each other daily increased: Monk judged it prudent to end this by a single stroke; and in concert with the old Scotch, towards the middle of September 1648, at the time when Cromwell, victorious at Preston, was crossing the Tweed at the head of the parliamentary army, he fell unexpectedly upon the quarters of Robert Monroe, took possession of Belfast and Carrickfergus, and sent the Scottish army and its general prisoners to England. It was stated, not without some foundation, that Robert Monroe was actually preparing to go and join his nephew, George, in order to serve the royal cause with him; according to some even, his project was to carry off Monk, who had only been beforehand with him. However this may be, the discovery was opportune, and no service

* This was in 1648.

C

could have been more agreeable to the parliament, and especially to Cromwell, whom this stroke delivered from a portion of his enemies whom he might have feared would cause him trouble. A Thanksgiving service was celebrated at London; Monk received a gratuity of five hundred pounds; a letter of thanks was addressed to him; he was appointed governor of Belfast, and consulted on the choice of the governor of Carrickfergus; and an order was given to propose means for ensuring the payment of his soldiers.

It was urgently necessary to provide for this, for the Marquis of Ormonde had just returned to Ireland to place himself at the head of the Protestant royalists, and conclude a new alliance with most of the Catholic leaders. O'Neill was almost the only one not included in this treaty. The *old Irish*, victims of the government of James I., were bound by no tie to a Protestant dynasty, and their secret wish was to make Ireland an independent kingdom, under the protection of the Pope. Around O'Neill rallied the fanatical Catholics, blindly obedient to the directions of the nuncio Rinuccini. O'Neill had always opposed hindrances to the attempts of the Marquis of Ormonde to reduce all the Irish to obedience to Charles; and he was at that time equally at war with both the royalists and the parliamentarians. But the latter did not cause him much uneasiness, for they were not able to do him much harm. The promises made to Monk for the payment of his troops had not been performed; his soldiers, in their distress, heard that Ormonde's army was well fed and well paid; their affection for their commander was not sufficient to resist so great a seduction; and they deserted in troops, to swell the ranks of the royalists. On their side, the *old Scotch* of Ulster, after having helped Monk against their fellow-countrymen, the soldiers of Monroe, had in their turn abandoned him to join Ormonde. The government at London, then in the hands of the Independents,* and under the influence of Cromwell, was not ignorant of the distress of its army in Ireland, but was not as yet in a position to succour it. To prevent its expulsion or total destruction, by opposing some obstacle to the progress of the royalists, was all that could be

---

* Such was the name of that religious and political sect which, in 1645, took the empire of the English revolution from the Presbyterians, and, in 1649, decided the execution of Charles I. and the proclamation of a Republic.

attempted. It listened, therefore, to the propositions of the
old Irish and of Owen O'Neill, who, himself reduced to the
most pressing extremities, was ready to treat with either
party, according as he might find it his interest and safety to
do so. His inclination led him towards the Independents,
who were predominant at London, but too weak in Ireland to
give him the law, and who, on their side, were rather inclined
to show momentary favour to O'Neill and the Irish fanatics,
looking upon them as a party whom it would be easy to
destroy after they had been made use of to arrest the progress
of Ormonde and the Irish royalists, who were much more dangerous enemies. O'Neill had entered into negociations with
the Independent leaders by means of the Abbé O'Reilly, his
agent in London; and he maintained at the same time, in
Leinster and Ulster, a very active intercourse with the parliamentary governors, Jones and Monk. They had been authorized to furnish him secretly with small supplies of money and
ammunition, which were always to be paid for by some enterprise against their common enemies. These attacks of a bandit
chieftain were insignificant against the powerful royalist con-
federation which then overspread Ireland, and his alliance
compromised instead of serving. The time, however, arrived
when Monk had no other resource but to call in and avow
this dangerous ally. Of seven hundred men whom he had
retained, five hundred left him to pass over to the enemy,
" who had money." Meanwhile, Cromwell, appointed lieutenant-general of Ireland, and provided with all the means of
success which had until then been refused to his predecessors,
had left London on the 10th of July, 1649, with a pompous
retinue, on his way to Bristol, where he was to embark with
his army. The hope of a speedy deliverance still sustained
the last efforts of the parliamentary leaders, when Monk
learned that a body of royalists, under the command of Lord
Inchiquin, was advancing to besiege Dundalk. Most of the
other places held by the parliament were alike besieged or
taken: and all intercommunication was cut off. Certain that
he would not be relieved, and unable to reckon surely upon
the small number of men who surrounded him, Monk demanded of O'Neill that, in virtue of the agreements which
had previously been made between them, he should assemble
his forces to fall on the royalists as soon as they should
approach the town. O'Neill replies that he is ready, but in

c 2

want of ammunition. Nevertheless, he sets out on his march;
and, on the 25th of July, having arrived with his troops at
Glassdromore, about seven miles from Dundalk, he detaches
a body of twelve hundred infantry and two hundred cavalry,
to escort the ammunition with which Monk was to supply
him. The old *Irish* were returning joyfully, conveying the
ammunition which they had received from Monk, when they
learned that Inchiquin was advancing towards them; they
hastened their progress to endeavour to regain the main body
of their army, but in vain. Inchiquin came up with them,
and carried off their ammunition after a sanguinary conflict,
in which five hundred of them were left dead upon the
field. The remainder were taken or dispersed; and, says
Whitelocke, "few of them escaped without their death-
wounds." At the news of this disaster, O'Neill's army,
panic-stricken, took to flight, and retired into the county of
Longford.

The effect of this check was not less terrible in the little
camp of the English attached to the service of the parliament. To behold themselves the allies of the papist O'Neill
and of the defeated O'Neill, was a disgrace for which they
could not forgive their general. Indignation was now added
to the alarm caused by the approach of danger. Monk saw
his situation; but, determined to keep it up to the end, he
assembled his soldiers, and with that tone of military bluntness which, in him, accompanied the authority of command,
inquired of them if they still consented to follow him. " If
any one of you," he said, "is averse to fighting in this
quarrel, let him speak; he shall receive a pass from me." A
single soldier advanced, declaring that his conscience did not
permit him to remain in the same cause with O'Neill; and
the pass was delivered to him. The others, yielding to the
enthusiasm excited by the presence of a leader whom they
had not yet learned to disobey, swore with loud shouts
to remain faithful to him, and Monk shut himself up with
them within the walls of Dundalk. The town was well
provisioned; Cromwell was on his way; a few days more,
and fortune might again declare for the parliamentarians. Monk hoped to hold out long enough to await
the success of his party; but the town was speedily invested
by Inchiquin. The enthusiasm now cooled down; both soldiers and officers ran to the ramparts, and, shouting from

thence to Inchiquin's troops, that they would never consent
to fight under the orders of O'Neill's ally, they forced Monk
to surrender Dundalk. As calm in his disappointment as he
had been in his resolution, he did not forget to make his own
conditions, and departed with permission to take away what
belonged to him.

He was returning to England, tranquilly confident that he
had well served those from whom he received his orders,
when he met at Bristol, Cromwell, just ready to embark, who
informed him of the excitement which the report of his alliance with O'Neill had produced in London. The Protestant
feeling of the nation had burst out with an angry energy
which it would have been useless to attempt to check. The
Independents, whom Monk had obeyed, far from avowing
their share in the matter, left him to bear the whole fury of
the storm, and, without exactly wishing to sacrifice him to
public opinion, refused to expose themselves in his defence.
At this news, Monk manifested no indignation,—did not
reject the burden thus cast upon him,—but continued his
journey to London, bearing with him, besides certain sums of
money furnished to him by Cromwell, some pressing letters
to the principal leaders.

He found them little disposed to compromise the secret of
their own connexion with O'Neill, by giving him hearty support. Among the Presbyterian party, which was passionately
opposed to the Independents, the men of ability, persuaded
that Monk had not acted without orders, were eagerly pursuing the discovery of a fact so well calculated to injure in
popular estimation those who could be convicted of having
participated in it. Monk, when interrogated by the council
of state and the parliament, took all the blame to himself,
without alleging any other excuse than necessity. Long and
violent debates took place in the house; some one proposed
to commit Monk to the Tower, whereupon another answered,
that "it would be better to commit the Tower to him."
However, some satisfaction was due to public opinion; it was
necessary to divert suspicions of alliance with the Irish
papists, or at least to deprive them of all grounds of justification. The Independent party did not hesitate to give
itself the lie, by agreeing to a vote that "the government
disapproved of Major-general Monk having made peace with
the great and sanguinary Irish rebel, Owen Roe O'Neill, and

abhorred all participation in that act." But, having allowed
their adversaries this little triumph, the Independents, careful
also not to discourage their friends, had a vote passed, that
"the parliament, persuaded that Major-general Monk had no
object in this but the advantage of the English cause in
Ireland, discharged him from any further question in the
matter." Monk had reckoned on more sincere and decisive
efforts; he was deeply hurt at the turn which the debate had
taken, and the accusations which had been allowed to rest
upon him unanswered. Prudent men thought that either too
much or too little had been done for him; and they blamed
the policy, which, says Whitelocke, had been "to beat him,
and to stroak him afterwards; and some believe," he adds,
"that he never forgot it." Attempts were also made to
extenuate the effect of this unfortunate affair on the public;
the Independent party printed the articles of Monk's treaty
with O'Neill, adding thereto a declaration of the reasons
which had led Monk to enter into it; but the public suspected
the truth, and were only the more vehement in anathe-
matizing any partisan of the parliament capable of treating
with the execrated enemies of the English.

About this period, Monk's elder brother died of a fall from
his horse, leaving only daughters. The family property thus
devolved upon the major-general, and, under his skilful
management, soon recovered from its disorder. Power, at
this time, even in its inferior ranks, led constantly to wealth;
no service rendered to the dominant party went without its
reward. Much has been said of Monk's avarice, and much
of his economy; but it does not appear that any one has ever
attacked his probity. But when a government becomes a
party to venality, legal probity is easy to its agents; and
without incurring any accusation, or even any reproach,
a commander-in-chief of the army in Ireland might very
well make his fortune, if not at the expense, at least in the
midst, of soldiers without pay, without shoes, and without
clothes.

Cromwell, at the head of the first army which the parliament had sent into Ireland, had quickly subjugated the country
by dint of victories and massacres. He had just met with
equal success in alarming the conscience of Fairfax about the
war which the parliament was meditating against Scotland,
then revolted in favour of Charles II.; he had, as it were,

thrust Fairfax out of the command of the troops intended for that expedition, and was proceeding alone to this new triumph. Monk had acquired Cromwell's entire confidence; there was as close an intimacy between them as there can be between two clever and ambitious men, one of whom consents to make his fortune by helping the other on to greatness. Determined to employ Monk near himself, Cromwell first organized a regiment for him, and then appointed him lieutenant-general of the artillery. Monk's military talents assumed in this war the rank which belonged to them. At Dunbar, on the 3rd of September, 1650, Cromwell, hard-pressed by the Scotch, who were superior in numbers, had imprudently brought his army into a confined position, between the sea and the heights occupied by the enemy. There was no other way of retreat than a narrow passage, guarded by a strong body of troops. The general assembled his council; terror had seized all minds; and few officers gave their opinion in favour of an engagement. "Sir," said Monk, " the Scots have numbers and the hills: these are their advantages. We have discipline and despair, two things that will make soldiers fight! these are ours. My advice, therefore, is to attack them immediately, which if you follow, I am ready to command the van." These words put an end to all opposition; and Monk, pike in hand, at the head of his soldiers, forced the passage, which the Scotch, surprised at so vigorous a charge, did not long defend. This success decided the victory.

When Cromwell was obliged to return to England to pursue and attack Charles II. at Worcester,* he left Monk, with six thousand men, to complete the reduction of Scotland; he also left him the example of his conduct in Ireland, and probably some instructions to follow. Monk was persuaded that men constitute the strength of a place; "neither bulwarks nor rocks," he used to say, " are such fortifications as man's flesh." He determined to crush entirely the courage of the enemy. Rapid attacks and sanguinary executions everywhere intimidated resistance. Weakness did not always save, nor was valour always respected. Monk laid siege to Dundee, where all the wealth of southern Scotland had been

* On the 3rd of September, 1651. About a month before, Charles had suddenly determined to transfer the war from Scotland to England, and Cromwell had hastened to follow him.

deposited, as in a place of safety. Lumsden, the governor of the place, a man remarkable for his bravery, was summoned to surrender. His only answer was to offer the besiegers, if they would surrender themselves with their arms and baggage, passes to return home. The town, bravely defended, but ill guarded by the soldiers, who were invariably drunk, was taken by assault, after some resistance, and Monk put to the sword in cold blood, Lumsden and eight hundred of the garrison.* A general outcry was raised against this bar. barity. Even his panegyrists appear to have thought that a violent malady, under which Monk nearly sank some time afterwards, might be regarded as a chastisement for the terrible services which he had rendered in this war. It was remarked also, that sixty vessels, laden with the booty obtained at Dundee, perished in sight of port, and almost without a storm, with the treasures which they were conveying to England; as if Providence had at least wished to mark by some sign of its anger, the odious success which it had resolved to permit. The indifferent policy which had combined such cruelties, succeeded in Scotland as in Ireland; all submitted. The Edinburgh road was infested with brigands, known by the name of "moss-troopers;" Monk pursued them, and captured them in their retreat at Dirlton; and to disorder succeeded at last the appearance of peace.

After a short sojourn in England, for the restoration of his health, Monk, at the commencement of 1652, returned to Scotland with St. John, Vane, Lambert, and some other commissioners, who had been sent, with himself, to forward the union of the two nations. Specially charged, as it would appear, with secret instructions from Cromwell, Monk showed himself vigilant and rigorous against the Presbyterians in Scotland, and favourable to the royalist remnants of the party of Montrose; and, in spite of the recollection of his recent cruelties, he laid from thenceforward the foundation of that monarchical popularity, which, notwithstanding contrary appearances, constantly directed towards him the hopes of the Stuarts and their party.

War had now broken out between England and Holland. The two republics had not been able to live in peace for two

* There is much reason to doubt the truth of this statement; it is supported by only one authority, and unmentioned by other writers, both royalists and parliamentarians.

years. In 1653, Monk was appointed to the command of the fleet, in conjunction with Admirals Blake and Dean. On the 2nd of June, the English with ninety-five vessels, and the Dutch with ninety-eight, met and attacked each other off the coast of Flanders. Blake was separated from the main body of the fleet with a squadron of eighteen vessels. Tromp commanded the Dutch fleet. Dean was killed close by Monk at the first broadside; Monk threw his cloak over the admiral's body, forbade his men to haul down their colours, forced the Dutch to retreat, and pursued them during the whole night. The next morning, reinforced by the junction of Blake, he attacked the enemy, captured eleven of their ships, sank six, and compelled the rest to fly. The report became current through Europe, that he had been killed in the action. On July 31, the two fleets again joined battle. The Dutch, who had retreated to their harbours to refit, had the advantage of numbers. Monk, so as not to employ his vessels in guarding prizes, ordered that every vessel captured should be sunk. Thirty perished with their crews, and Tromp was killed in the action at the moment when, sword in hand upon the deck of his ship, he was encouraging his men to fight. The Dutch took to flight, and sued for peace. The English admirals returned to London, to reap the reward of their triumph. The parliament voted them, as marks of honour, golden chains and medals; and, on the day of the dinner given in the city in celebration of the victory, Cromwell himself placed the chain round Monk's neck, and forced him to wear it during the whole festival.

The return of the new admiral was marked by a domestic event which was not without its influence upon his conduct and reputation. Unrefined tastes, and that need of repose in private life which frequently accompanies activity in business, had brought him under the power of a woman of vulgar manners, destitute even of the charms which can seduce, and whose behaviour did not contradict the rumour which placed her origin in a shop, or according to some, in a much less honest profession. She had lived for a long while with Monk, and joined to the power of habit, the authority conferred by an impetuosity of will and words, which disturbed, and sometimes overcame, the cool circumspection of her lover. It has been said that she succeeded, in 1649, in inducing him to marry her; but it is certain that this marriage was not

declared until 1653, for a letter from London, dated on the
19th of September in that year, thus announced the news:—
" Our Admiral Monk hath lately declared an ugly common
[prostitute] his wife, and legitimated three or four bastards
he hath had by her during his growth in grace and saint-
ship." The newsmonger, according to all appearance, had
amused himself by adding to the scandal, for Monk is not known
to have had a child older than his son Christopher, after him
Duke of Albemarle, and born in the course of this same year,
1653.   There is, therefore, room for supposing that the birth
of this son was the cause of his marriage.   Monk, besides,
either from sincerity or prudence, maintained that devout
appearance which was then indispensable to fortune; and,
without falling into the hypocritical jargon of the times, he
thought it right to keep his conduct free from all irregu-
larities which might be hurtful to him, even in eyes less
severe than those of the saints.   It appears certain that his
wife used, if not the influence of religion, at least the discourses of its ministers, to induce him to marry her.   " Taking
no care for any other part of herself," says Clarendon, " she
had deposited her soul with some Presbyterian ministers."
They declared the necessity of the marriage, and perhaps
employed, to decide the general, some of those sermons which
his wife, in the course of their union, was careful to use whenever she wanted to tire out his resistance.   She was one of
the rather ignoble causes, which, at a later period, urged
Monk to display his superior faculties, at a great crisis;
and she subsequently became, when he had attained high
rank, a striking proof of the vulgarity of his habits and
tastes.*

But all was then lost sight of in the popularity of Monk's
naval victories, the first which, for eleven years, had given
the English the pleasure of triumphing over a foreign enemy.
To the violently-dissolved Long parliament, the Barebone
parliament had succeeded; an assembly of fanatical bigots,
who believed their success certain when they had repented
over their reverses.   Monk was in their eyes the favourite of'
the Lord.   For a moment, their enthusiasm about him disturbed Cromwell.   Tired of being incessantly obliged to
deceive without ever being able to lead them, Cromwell soon

* This is another of the passages suppressed in the early editions of
Clarendon, and restored in that of Oxford.

discovered that he would find only unteachable and unskilful
instruments of his will in men who possessed faith, but no
knowledge. Resolved to bring them to resign the power of
which he was not willing to deprive them, he feared lest they
should make Monk a support against his insinuations, and a
power against his designs; but he was speedily reassured.
Monk accepted the high station offered to him, but without
pretending to aim higher; and after a short conference,
Cromwell, skilful in discovering weaknesses of which he stood
in need, understood that, too much attached to the fortune he
had already made to risk it by seeking to increase it, Monk
was a sure man so long as he felt himself sure. Cromwell,
therefore, pursued his course, without fearing any hindrance
on his part. The Barebone parliament allowed itself to be
thrust out; and, four days afterwards, on the 16th of December, 1653, a council of officers appointed Cromwell
Protector.

Free to choose henceforward between peace and war,
Cromwell thought it advantageous to his new dignity to treat
with the Dutch upon more favourable conditions than had
been granted them by the republican parliament and council
of state. Monk disapproved of peace: he did not like the
Dutch, who had formerly offended him; participated in the
popular prejudices of an Englishman against them; and, as
enemies, despised them with all the boldness of a soldier and
a conqueror. Besides, he held sway of the sea, and did not
expect to be so soon deprived of it. He shared in the public
indignation against a treaty which wounded the national
pride, as well as injured a great many private interests; and
his vehemence in this respect added to his popularity in the
country without at all diminishing his credit with the Protector. Appointed to regulate the navy accounts, Monk
acquired new titles to popular favour by his proceedings: his
protection was granted to all who had justice on their side,
or who could plead the services they had rendered; wounded
men, widows, and orphans, obtained, by his assistance, the aid
to which they were entitled; and those who had been his
comrades in danger learned to depend on him in peace as well
as in the hour of conflict. One morning, whilst he was sitting
at the Admiralty, some thousands of sailors came tumultuously
to complain of the delay which occurred before they were paid
their share of the prize-money. Monk went out, and pro-

mised them that they should be paid as soon as all the captured
ships had been sold. They retired apparently satisfied with
this promise. In the afternoon Monk went to Whitehall,*
and was relating what had occurred to the Protector, when a
messenger came to inform him that a troop more numerous
than that which had assembled in the morning was advancing
towards the palace, armed with swords, pistols, and bludgeons,
and that it had already nearly reached Charing Cross. Monk
had given to the sailors one of those promises which he never
failed to perform. Indignant that it had not been sufficient,
he rushed out of Whitehall, and, followed by Cromwell and
some others who hastened after him, ran to meet the mutineers,
fell upon them sword in hand, and hitting both right and left,
dispersed them even more by his presence than by his blows.
In the confusion he had wounded in the nose a man who was
there only by chance : he directed that ten pounds should be
given to him; " But," said he, " what business had that rook
in the midst of a crowd of birds of prey ?"

New storms were rising in Scotland. Cromwell now had
to defend, instead of achieving his greatness. He could not
leave England, and he looked around him for some one to
whom he could confide the dangerous power of representing
him among the Scotch. Fleetwood, his son-in-law, and
Desborough, his brother-in-law, were both incompetent. He
did not dare to entrust Lambert with such a mission at a distance from him; for, though ill-adapted to succeed, he was
ready to undertake much. He resolved to confide it to Monk
with all the precautions of distrust. The body of troops
which he gave him was composed of the most restless and
fanatical soldiers in the army. He was aware of Monk's
aversion to such men ; and knowing also that Monk was in a
certain degree suspected by them, he calculated that they
would mutually watch over each other.

Monk arrived in Scotland on the 23rd of April, 1654.
Everywhere he found ferment and trouble : on one side,
Middleton, at the head of the insurgent royalists in the Highlands ; on the other, the people discontented and ready for
sedition ; the army, without discipline, abandoned to all sorts
of religious folly, and at open war with the presbyterian

* The palace of Charles I., built by the celebrated architect, Inigo Jones,
and in which Cromwell resided. This palace was twice destroyed by fire,
viz., in 1691 and 1698.

clergy, whom it had driven from the churches and the pulpit. Monk thought that there was an urgent necessity for employing their ardent imaginations in works of greater difficulty; and having quickly made his preparations, he left some troops to keep the Lowlands in order, and entered the Highlands with the rest of his army. Here they found, if not many enemies to combat, at least fatigues enough to make them daily feel in need of repose. He had divided his forces into two bodies, one commanded by himself, and the other by General Morgan, in order to harass the enemy on all sides. His first care was to possess himself, as he advanced through the country, of every post capable of defence. Having one day arrived at the house of one Campbell, laird of Glenorchie, he found it fitted to receive a small garrison. The laird refused to yield it up. " Well," said Monk, " I will not violate hospitality;" and he immediately ordered the officers who accompanied him to evacuate the house. " Now," said he to the laird, " look to the defence, for we are about to attack." The laird, although surrounded by a considerable number of his friends and relations, judged it prudent to treat, and consented to receive a garrison, on condition that a portion of his house should remain at his own service.

Monk had established large magazines of fodder and biscuit at Leith, St. Johnstoun, and Inverness; from whence he drew provisions for all his small posts, and thus always had the necessary supplies within his reach. He made each soldier take with him provisions for six days; and laden only with this light baggage, he was able to penetrate into fastnesses which until then the Highlanders had considered inaccessible. The horses were not always able to follow him: many fell among the precipices; and one day he lost forty-one in a morass. But in these unknown districts, in the midst of enemies ambushed everywhere along his route, his vigilance never allowed the foe to gain the slightest advantage over him. Informed by the spies whom he maintained in all quarters, he regulated his marches by certain information. They were short. Arriving almost always by mid-day at the place where he intended to encamp, he himself chose the position, marked the enclosure, posted the sentinels, looked to everything, and sent out foraging or exploring parties ; then seating himself on the ground, in the midst of his officers, he took a repast of cold meat,—a species of provision which

always followed him in abundance, and which he almost invariably shared with them.   During the evening he received
them in his tent, at a table covered with everything that the
country could furnish.   His soldiers relied as much upon his
active vigilance as upon the walls of a citadel.   He attended
to their supply of food, provided as he best could for their
lodging, watched over them in difficult circumstances; and
even had, in cases of necessity, recipes and remedies for their
ailments.   He thus in every sense overran the enemy's
country, restraining some, and making others fly before him;
perplexing and starving Middleton, who, destitute of magazines
and strongholds, had reckoned upon finding the means of subsistence and defence in the country itself, his possession of
which would, he thought, be disputed by none.   Neither
party were desirous to come to an engagement.   Middleton
did not think himself strong enough to sustain a battle, and
Monk was sure that he could do without one.   The secret
communications kept up by Cromwell in the country, and the
pardon promised to those who submitted, had weakened the
resolution of the Scottish chiefs; and rendering it impossible
for Middleton to risk an engagement, constrained him to allow
his forces to be destroyed in detail.   However, Morgan having
surprised and defeated him at Loch Garry, that check destroyed at a blow the languishing remnant of the party.
Middleton retired into the island of Skye, from whence he
passed into Holland.   The country submitted.   The army did
not, however, retire until it had, by the establishment of a
certain number of garrisons, ensured the payment of the taxes,
which up to that time the inhabitants of the Highlands had
thought they could refuse with impunity; and order was established in these refuges of robbers to so great an extent, that
it is said the proprietor of a strayed horse sent the crier round
the country to recover it.

   Monk returned to Edinburgh towards the end of August 1654.
Armed with the power of a conqueror, he used it with severity.
The Anabaptists were repressed; the Presbyterians received
full liberty to exercise their worship, but were forbidden to
interfere in civil affairs with the arm of excommunication, and
to manifest their opinions of the measures of the government.
The conventicles were strictly sought after, and dispersed of
their own accord at the sight of a squadron.   A Scottish
gentleman no longer had permission to wear a sword, to ride

a horse of more than a certain value, to raise his banner against his personal enemies, or to exercise arbitrary jurisdiction over his vassals and domestics. All had to yield to a yoke which, though harsh, was equitable; rendered tolerable by regularity, and not aggravated by insolence. The army was kept in as much subjection as the country. No disorder was permitted, no injustice tolerated, either on the part of the officer towards the soldier, or of the soldier towards the citizen. The troops, well paid, brought prosperity to trade and repose to the country. Quiet but indefatigable in his activity, the general had fixed his residence at Dalkeith, a mansion belonging to the Earls of Buccleugh, which he had taken on lease, and where he spent the five years of his command in Scotland. There, always at work or in his plantations, which he was fond of as a recreation and employment, he gave access to all, listened to everything they had to say; had a language for all ranks, all classes, and all parties; kept himself well acquainted with all occurrences; and learning what he had to fear or watch, directed, by his own personal knowledge, the numerous spies whose reports never reached any other ears or hands than his own. He thus spared himself those useless vexations which excite even more hatred against a suspicious government than the rigour of its proceedings.

Towards the month of June 1655, when Scotland was completely subjugated, Cromwell appointed for its government a commission composed of Lord Broghill, as president, Monk, Desborough, and Colonels Howard, Lockhart, Scroop, and Wetham. Their powers were very extensive; and the majority which Monk constantly had in this council placed them nearly all in his hands. Dalkeith was really the centre of the government; and the Scottish nobility, Monk's obsequious politeness towards whom palliated the harshness of his authority, learned to approach him, and to derive, from his feelings with regard to the proscribed dynasty, a confidence which he never authorized in such a manner as to be afterwards obliged to discourage it.

A servant of Cromwell, but the hope of the royalist party, and inflexible in denying any immediate intervention of the Lord in public affairs, Monk was necessarily an object of hatred to all religious and political fanatics. This hatred had burst out during the early part of his residence in Scotland. Overton, the major-general of his infantry, a millenarian enthusiast and leader of the malcontents, had formed the plan of seizing the command of the troops and declaring against Cromwell. The conspirators intended to surprise Monk at Dalkeith on the 1st of January, 1656. Some wished that he should be killed; but Samuel Oates,* a minister, opposed this, threatening to reveal all, if his murder were contemplated. This opposition caused the postponement of the conference to another day. Monk, informed of the plot, towards the end of December, arrested Overton and several of his accomplices, and sent them to London. A great many others were cashiered; and Monk took advantage of this occurrence to be more stringent in his army against that fanaticism and independence which were so obnoxious to him.

This conspiracy was the only one which he had to guard against during his stay in Scotland. Royalist plots became at this period more numerous. They multiplied around Cromwell; but with respect to Monk, the efforts of the party took another direction. As early as the year 1655, he had received the following letter from Charles II. :—

"Cologne, Aug. 12, 1655.

" One who believes he knows your nature and inclinations very well assures me, that notwithstanding all ill accidents and misfortunes, you retain still your old affection to me, and resolve to express it upon the seasonable opportunity, which is as much as I look for from you. We must all patiently wait for that opportunity, which may be offered sooner than we expect. When it is, let it find you ready; and in the meantime have a care to keep yourself out of their hands, who know the hurt you can do them in a good conjuncture; and can never but suspect your affection to be as I am confident it is towards your, &c.   " CHARLES REX."

Monk sent a copy of this letter to Cromwell. Whatever

---

* Mr. Maseres, in his *Select Tracts*, has supposed that this Oates, whose Christian name is not given by Price, who relates the occurrence, was the famous Titus Oates. I had expressed doubts of the correctness of this assertion, in my *Collection of Memoirs relative to the English Revolution* (Memoirs of Price, p. 148, note), but without alleging any other reasons than the impossibility of the fact. The error is now demonstrated. The Oates here mentioned is Samuel Oates or Otes, chaplain of Colonel Pride's regiment, as we see by his signature at the end of a letter addressed by several members of the party to Major Holmes, of Monk's regiment. (Intercepted Letter of December 18, 1644. Thurloe, State Papers, vol. iii. p. 30.)

might be his bias or anticipation, he never forestalled the future : and always solely occupied in securing his present position, he left time to decide what he might have to do. Already too powerful not to give umbrage to the power which he served, he was sufficiently strong to render it dangerous to attack him, unless he supplied weapons against himself. By avoiding the least pretext for suspicion, he derived strength from the very fears which he inspired ; and Cromwell, now able only to watch him, felt that he was escaping from his hands.

During the last years of Cromwell's protectorate and Monk's residence in Scotland, we may observe the growth, on the one side, of disquietude, and, on the other, of assurance and power, although always accompanied by forms of unlimited respect, and appearances of unbounded devotedness. If Monk congratulates the protector on the resolution he has taken to convoke a parliament, the special advantage which he perceives in such a step is, that if this new assembly behaves badly, no one can blame his highness for transacting the business of the nation without it.* In 1657 he requests that the taxation of Scotland may be diminished, and insists upon the motives of justice which ordain that, as that country had been united to England, it should be placed upon a footing of real equality with her; " then," he adds, " in case they be not quiet, I think it were just reason to plant it with English."† But he nevertheless pursues his demands with firmness. During the same year, being consulted, as it appears, by Cromwell, about the plan which the government had formed of interfering in the appointment of the magistrates of Glasgow, he exhibits in forcible terms the illegality and danger of such an attempt.‡ The next year he solicits assistance for the city of Edinburgh, which had been reduced to extreme difficulty by its debts and poverty.§ Monk is no longer the mere man of power, busied in restraining and subduing; he is a man of the country, touched by its interests, careful of its rights, and attentive to its wants. Cromwell is uneasy, and fears to displease him, but would willingly weaken him; he withdraws from him those officers and regiments upon whom he can reckon most surely,

* Monk to Thurloe, July 1, 1656.
† Monk to Thurloe, June 4, 1657.
‡ Monk to Thurloe, September 24, 1657.
§ Monk to Thurloe, March 17, 1658.

D

to replace them by the most restless of that party over which
Monk has no power, and against which he has always practised
and recommended severity. An order from the council of
state directs a reduction of the number of troops stationed in
Scotland. Monk represents the folly of such a step; Cromwell
recalls the order, but with so much delay, that Monk, who is
desirous to maintain himself, and not to quarrel, regretfully
announces that he has obeyed. About this same time the
hopes of the royalists revive in Scotland; a descent is talked
of; the whole nation becomes agitated. "They are as
malignant," writes Monk, "as ever I knew them. But," he
adds, elsewhere, "I do not see them look so much after Charles
Stuart's business, but the hopes they have of discontent among
ourselves."* It is under such circumstances that Monk is
summoned to London to form a part of Cromwell's new House
of Lords, which, ashamed and embarrassed at its own existence,
timidly announced itself as the *other House.* Monk represents
the necessity of his remaining in Scotland;† and whether or
not Cromwell had the intention of withdrawing him from
thence, he yields to his arguments, and Monk remains at
Dalkeith, whence it was perhaps difficult to dislodge him, but
whither it would have been easy not to send him back.

Meanwhile the rumours, which are the precursors of
tempests, spread on all sides: the presentiment of another
revolution fills all minds; the eyes of Europe are fixed upon
England, and Monk is the object of all conjectures. Thurloe,
the secretary of state, warns Lockhart, Cromwell's ambassador
in France, against the report that Monk has refused to obey
the protector; and he assures Downing, the resident in Holland,
of the falsity of the same rumour. Finally, Cromwell writes
thus to Monk, in the postscript of a letter: "There be that
tell me that there is a certain cunning fellow in Scotland,
called George Monk, who is said to lie in wait there to introduce Charles Stuart. I pray use your diligence to apprehend
him, and send him up to me;"—a joke doubtless destined to
inform Monk that Cromwell was upon his guard.

The genius of one man was being wasted in maintaining his
power, without succeeding in establishing it, when Cromwell
died on the 3rd of September, 1658. The last breath of his
influence lifted his son to the protectorate for a few days.

* Monk to Thurloe, June 13, 1658.
† Monk to Thurloe, January 9, 1658.

Monk did not refuse to join in this movement, but he took in it the position which befitted him; and the remonstrance which, when he recognized Richard Cromwell, he addressed to him by means of his brother-in-law, Dr. Clarges, is written in the tone of a man whose advice must be listened to. In his opinion, Richard can be securely established only by means of the Presbyterian party, which he (Monk) regards as the national party; and in doing this, Richard will have more facilities than his father, "having not the same obligations to many disquieted spirits." He recommends the new authority to establish unity of religion in essential points, and liberty in all those which are not essential; he insists upon the necessity of reducing the army, and withdrawing all fanatical sectaries from it—a measure which would be unattended by danger, whatever might be said about it; for "there is not," he writes, "an officer in the army, upon any discontent, that has interest enough to draw two men after him, if he be out of place." Finally, he recommends Richard, when he convokes a parliament, to introduce into his House of Lords all the old nobility upon whom he can reckon, and some of the influential gentlemen of the different counties, amongst whom he mentions Sir George Booth.

The new protector was proclaimed at Edinburgh, coldly, and with the indifference attaching to an insignificant ceremony. People there felt themselves out of the reach of the power which was then endeavouring to establish itself in England, and without any interest in its destinies. "Why not rather old George?" said the soldiers and subalterns: "he would be fitter for a protector than Dick Cromwell." After this act of adhesion, Monk, sheltered from the storms which were gathering at a distance, resolved to await the moment when the safest course should present itself to him, and meanwhile not to adopt or reject either.

Richard was in want of money; to obtain it, it was necessary to assemble a parliament. It was filled, as much as possible, with the creatures of Cromwell. But a parliament, of whatever kind, was incompatible with the government of the army, the sole support of the protectoral power: and the republican party, the only one which then dared to stir, had entered into the House of Commons in sufficiently large numbers to hamper at least the measures of the protector and his court. Richard liked neither the republicans, who were

D 2

troublesome to an authority which he little cared to exercise, but which he wished to possess at his ease, nor the fanatical Independents, who formed the active portion of the army, and whose enthusiasm was repugnant to his natural good sense and the levity of his disposition. The army was soon almost as discontented with Richard Cromwell as with the parliaments; and its principal leaders, with Lambert and Fleetwood at their head, met at Wallingford House, and consulted together as to how they could undo what they had done. To these revolutionary soldiers, no task could have been less difficult; for they only needed to substitute a phantom of a government in the place of the phantom they had driven away. The Long parliament, or at least that remnant of the Long parliament which has since been called the *Rump*, offered itself, and was accepted. Already reduced, by various exclusions, to a number far inferior to that of which i' was originally composed, it had finally, in the year 1648, and under the influence of Cromwell, been *purged*, by the army, of all the Presbyterian party. Out of seventy-eight members who remained present after the purification had taken place, twenty-eight had retired, protesting against the violence; and the fifty or sixty members who remained at Westminster, had sanctioned the measures of the army, and alone formed the parliament during the six weeks which preceded the death of the king.

After this act, and when the republic had once been proclaimed, several of those who had withdrawn in disgust or fear, had successively returned to their seats, and a house of between one hundred and sixty and one hundred and eighty members had been reconstituted, and was almost exclusively occupied in perpetuating itself in power, by virtue of the bill which, in 1640, had declared that this parliament could not be dissolved except by its own consent. Tired of fruitlessly demanding its dissolution, Cromwell, who wished to reign in his turn, had forcibly ejected the members on the 19th of April, 1653, entering, himself, into their place of assemblage at the head of his troops. Thus violated, but not dissolved, the *Rump* had remained, in its own opinion, the only legal parliament of England; and formed in the country a small faction of fanatical egotists, more important from their passionate activity than from their reputation or talents. Some distinguished men, however, were to be met with among their ranks; Sir Harry Vane, for example, a man of vast but chimerical mind, who remained among them because he found elsewhere neither room nor instruments for his ideas and plans; and Ludlow, a clever man of business, rather than an enlightened politician, and too honest a man ever to resign himself to the belief that he had done anything against his conscience. But the true representatives of the party were Sir Arthur Haslerig, a rapacious, headstrong, and conceited agitator; Scott, almost as vain, and even more obstinate and blind; and some others, the dupes of their interest as much as of their faith, always ready to govern whenever they were permitted to do so, and uniting to fondness for power and fanaticism of opinions, the absurdity of impotence and the infatuation of pretended legitimacy.

It was to this assembly, only forty-two members of which were in London, that, on the 7th of May, 1659, the army resolved to intrust the government, which it did not know how else to dispose of. After Richard had been compelled to dissolve his parliament, the *Rump* was re-installed, and with it the good old cause, that is, the republic, of which the *Rump* was declared the only true support; "for," it was said, "it had been ever favoured in this work with the special presence of God, and with his signal blessing." Richard yielded to his fall without resistance, and without any one making an attempt to save him. Some time before, his friends had offered Monk 20,000*l.* a-year, if he would take up his cause. Monk allowed them to hope everything, but gave no pledge, and answered, "The said revenue will do Richard more good than my sticking to him."* When Richard fell, Monk received the news with his usual tranquillity; congratulated the new authorities, entertained the advances of Fleetwood and Lambert, and the assurances of favour from the

* Manuscript Journal of Sir Edward Montague, afterwards Lord Sandwich; Harris, Life of Charles II., p. 194, note. A year after this, upon the eve of the return of Charles II., Richard Cromwell again addressed himself to Monk, in the distress of his private life, begging him to obtain, from the royalist convention then about to meet, the payment of his debts. The letter which Richard wrote to Monk on this subject on the 18th of April, 1660, will be found among the documents inserted at the end of this volume. I am indebted for this curious and hitherto unpublished document to the kindness of my learned friend, Dr. Travers Twiss, who obligingly copied it for me from the original, contained among the archives of Admiral Popham's family, at Littlecott Castle.

Rump, which however would continue, as Cromwell had done, to deprive of their employments in the army of Scotland, those officers who were most devoted to their general. Monk remonstrated; and meanwhile, by the consent of the parliament itself, retained his officers in their commissions until the arrival of those who were to replace them, but who never arrived.

Matters were, however, rapidly proceeding towards a crisis: the time for decision was at hand, and the circumspection of Monk himself was near allowing itself to be taken by surprise. The greater number of the counties of England were preparing to support Sir George Booth, who, at the head of the Presbyterian party, had taken up arms in Cheshire on the 1st of August, 1659, apparently to obtain the election of a free parliament, or at least the restoration of the parliament in its integrity, by the re-admission of the members whom Cromwell had excluded. The royalists were not to appear at all; but the leaders of the two parties were acting in concert; and among the agents there were very few whose illusion was not the fruit of great complacency in allowing themselves to be deceived. The eyes of both parties were turned towards Monk, as the man they needed; around him different interests were in agitation, striving to shake his apparent immoveableness. Even in his private circle, either by chance or skill, the different parties had their representatives: Price, the general's chaplain, a royalist and Anglican at heart, his intermediary with the Scottish cavaliers, and who, though daily urging him to aid the good cause, took care never to utter the words *king* and *kingdom;* Gumble, another chaplain, of Presbyterian opinions, but a man of talent and intrigue, Monk's principal agent, and devoted to all his projects; and lastly, Monk's wife, an ardent Presbyterian, and as much attached to the king as she was opposed to episcopacy. Possessed of a liberty of speech of which it would have been difficult to deprive her, she forced her husband to listen to what others would not have dared to say to him, and by her impetuosity accelerated the rather tardy progression of his circumspect character. Others also, in their different degrees, attempted to learn his views, and act accordingly; some secretly, others more openly; and in the midst of them all, the general, calm, taciturn, and too good-tempered to be displeased at what he was determined not to understand, quieted and contented each in particular, by some concession to the views of his interrogator, or by some half-confidence intended as much to conceal what he did not say, as to insinuate what he wished to have believed. Every one had his distinct part to play, and, on some given occasion, each might consider himself the nominal confidant; " that is," to use the language of Price, " him who had the post of first dupe to the general." Beyond this intimate circle, exposed to the efforts or curiosity of all those who sought to gain him over or to learn his views, Monk's taciturnity provided him with a rampart which he seldom allowed to be forced. But his very silence was significant, and he made use of it to maintain at once both reserve and confidence. As soon as an appearance of insinuation, or the utterance of a few preliminary ideas, announced the intention of introducing an overture, Monk, with an air of profound attention, gave scarcely any answers, offered still less opposition, opened no field for discussion, and no channel for indiscretion; after having exhausted the first attack, it was unavoidable to drop the subject; and each went away persuaded that he had either shaken his resolution, or found him in a favourable mood, but without having received the least encouragement to venture upon using more explicit language.

Meanwhile, in proportion as the decisive moment advanced, and circumstances became pressing, the object of these attacks also became more evident, and Monk found it necessary to contrive to repel without preventing them, or to inspire hopes without giving pledges. Persuaded that Sir George Booth's insurrection must decide everything, Charles Stuart and his partisans redoubled their efforts to insure its success. Sir Stephen Fox arrived, bearing a letter in which Charles besought Monk to march with his army against the parliament. Monk received it coldly, making no promises, and giving no answer; but he allowed the messenger full liberty to return. This was saying that he did not refuse to receive such messages. Colonel Atkins, deputed by the Presbyterians to urge him to support the insurrection which was about to break out in the north of England, pressed him as to what they might expect from him. " I shall send a force against them," bluntly replied the general; " by the duty of my place, I can do no less:" and Price, his chaplain, when interrogated in his turn by Atkins, seemed to think that there was nothing to be done, " unless," he added, carelessly, " the city of London would rise, and shut up its gates."

At length a direct negociator arrived, charged with positive proposals. Sir John Greenville, nephew of Sir Richard, and one of the most active cavaliers in the king's service, had carefully kept up a close connexion with his relative, Nicholas Monk, brother to the general; and had presented him to a valuable living in his gift, in the county of Cornwall. Sir John had, moreover, induced the king to send him with more extensive powers to treat with Monk, and endeavour to make him join the royal cause. At the moment of Sir George Booth's insurrection, he sent off the clergyman to Dalkeith, charged with his instructions, and the promises of the king.

Nicholas Monk arrived at Dalkeith in the month of August, 1659, two days after the visit of Colonel Atkins, and found his brother disposed to listen to his proposals. Monk feared and expected little from those ephemeral governments which were already falling to pieces, one after the other, in London; the parties of Richard Cromwell, Haslerig, and Lambert, might agitate around him, without affecting him; he was more securely established than any of them. As for the Presbyterians, even supposing that they obtained the upper hand, they could never be so strong as that Monk would not always be sure of treating with them upon whatever terms he pleased. But this was not the case as regarded the royalists, towards whom the chances of the future were beginning to incline. All the other parties had tried their hand at government; and all, alternately powerful and over-thrown, had exposed the secret of their errors, violence, and weakness. Royalty alone, for twenty years, had not been put to the test; it alone had yet to make promises which had not been already broken; good was expected from it, because it had not recently inflicted any evil; and finally, the nation returned to it, after so many years of agitation, as a son returns to the paternal roof, which he left in hope, but returns to in fatigue. The restoration of the Stuarts was then the hope and desire of that numerous but nameless class of the people, who, except in a few moments of excitement, gene-rally long after political repose, that they may devote them-selves uninterruptedly to the affairs of civil life. The desires of the multitude are rarely restrained by foresight; and if, when taking up the royal cause, the Presbyterians wished to prevent its triumphing without conditions and guarantees, there was reason to expect that they would not succeed in thus measuring success at their will, and that, when they had opened the door to the king, the people, having only to choose between them and him, would not leave them time to settle the price of their victory.

Monk could not but believe that such would be the course of events, and rejoice at it. Caring little for the rights or necessities of liberty, but greatly injured by the inconveniences of anarchy, he never considered either the nature or the exact limits of power, whether he exercised or obeyed it. He believed that a country was quite happy enough when it was quiet, and under government; and he knew very well, as far as he was himself concerned, that the fortune of the servant depends upon the power of the master. He was in a position to become the most useful and best recompensed servant of Charles Stuart; and it therefore was to his advantage to treat singly and directly with the king, with the sole intention of properly establishing his own personal position, and leaving others to contend for the interests of the country. His foresight had always made him secretly favourable to the royalists; and as soon as they addressed themselves to him with any hope of success, they must have been promptly received. Monk never treated frankly with any but them; and during his progress towards the restoration of the monarchy, one single sentiment is conspicuous and predominant—the desire to withdraw that great event from every other influence than his own, in order that he might deliver it, complete and unshackled, into the hands of the prince from whom he was to receive its price.

But, in the state of affairs in 1659, the assistance of the Presbyterians was the most useful which the cunning general could call in to his aid; and consequently, while entertaining the communications of his brother, he appeared specially influenced by the Presbyterian standard of Booth's insurrection, and by the certainty of Fairfax's co-operation. When his resolution was once taken, he began to appear undecided to those by whom he was surrounded; while he was making promises on one side, he pointed out difficulties on the other, in his usual manner, without expressing his opinion on the manner of surmounting them. He confided to each that which he intended each to know or believe of his plans;

needed solicitation to undertake what he had resolved upon
doing; examined the state of his exchequer; and finally
directed his agents to sound the feelings of his troops, and
learn to what degree they might be irritated against a
government imposed on them by the army in England.
The soldiers were found less angry than uncertain about their
position, and depending entirely upon their general. "Why
will not old George do something?" they asked; "it is not
in our power." But at the idea of putting themselves in
motion under his orders, they grew animated, and manifested
their readiness to follow him; " for," said they, " we may
march safely behind George Monk."

Thus assured of his means, Monk thought that there was
no more time to be lost. Sir George Booth, at the head of
the county of Cheshire, was on the point of coming to an
engagement with the parliamentary army, under the command
of Lambert; the other counties were about to rise; and he
must not be among the last. It was now Saturday evening;*
the night was spent in drawing up a letter to the parliament,
in which, with all due forms of respect, and even of praise,
the army declared against the perpetuity of power which it
seemed to arrogate to itself; not being able in conscience, as
they said, to consent that so much blood had been shed
merely to place the sovereignty in the hands of a few men.
They therefore demanded that, conformably with its promises,
the parliament should complete itself, and regulate the mode
of election and convocation of the parliaments destined to
succeed it; and, in conclusion, announced their intention of
maintaining their demand by arms. This letter was to be
presented, on Monday, for the signature of the principal
officers; and it was intended at the same time to take possession of the castle of Edinburgh and the citadel of Leith.
All was ready on Sunday evening; at one o'clock in the
morning, Monk, still in the room in which the oaths of
secrecy had been taken, and the last conferences held, gives
orders to his aide-de-camp, Smith, to get ready to take his

* We have ascertained, by comparing the days of the week and the
dates of the events in the month of August, 1659, that this Saturday must
have been Saturday, August 23rd. Sir George Booth was defeated by
Lambert, on the 18th and 19th of August, at Winnington and Nantwich.
This news would not be known at Dalkeith on the 23rd, but would reach
that place by Monday the 25th of August.

ɔrders to the commanders at Leith and the castle of Edinburgh, of whom he was sure; and then goes down to give
audience to other agents already in motion on all sides. But
a moment afterwards, he returns: "Smith," he says, "will
not set out yet; Booth and Lambert are on the brink of an
engagement; to-morrow is the post-day; we shall know how
things stand, what is Booth's force, and how far we may hope
to secure his success by our help. The delay of one day
cannot do much harm. We will wait." These words fell
like an icy shower in the midst of men already intoxicated
with hope, and ready to enter upon action; but they must
obey, they must even be silent. However, the general
having again left the room, his chaplain, Price, the most
ardent of all, followed him, to try and shake his resolution;
he found him in conference with a Scotchman of Montrose's
party, and did not thence augur ill for the success of the
efforts he was about to make. Monk came to him; but
scarcely had Price opened his mouth, when his patron, who
never grew angry except when persons wished him to go
faster than he intended, exclaimed in a passion, "Would you
have me ruin all, then, and bring my neck to the block, for
love of the king?" "Sir, I have never named the king to
you, either now or at any other time," replied the chaplain,
in a submissive tone. "Well, I know you have not; but I
know you, and have understood your meaning." This was
the general's first declaration to Price. At six o'clock the
next morning, a courier brought the news of Sir George
Booth's complete defeat. The conspirators shuddered at the
danger they had run. "What would have become of us,"
Price one day asked of Monk, "if the tidings of Booth's
defeat had arrived a day too late?" "I doubt not but I
should have secured to myself the castle of Edinburgh and
citadel of Leith," replied the general; "some officers and
many soldiers would have followed me; and then I would
have commissioned the whole Scottish nation to rise." Slow
to involve himself in peril, he never entered upon any undertaking without having made up his mind to brave every risk.

No sooner had the news of Lambert's victory become
known, than numbers flocked from all quarters to Dalkeith;
and at dinner the general's table was crowded by officers,
Independents, Anabaptists, and other sectaries, whose gaiety
and imagination were excited by this triumph over their

principal enemies, the Presbyterians. Th
freely in their mirth, and having more to co
greater openness. Some one having spok
which the insurgents certainly entertained of
Stuart, "My opinion is," said Monk, witho
chaplain, "that the parliament should make
ever should but mention the restoring of him
be hanged." The discussion hereupon gre
one Captain Poole declared that the nation v
peace and quietness so long as there was ei
steeple left. At these words the old gener
tone to which they were not accustomed,
softly, Captain Poole; if you and your pa
pluck there, I will pluck with you." A
immediately ensued, and whatever distrust
felt of the intentions of the general, all at
that he did not consider himself vanquished.

His position, however, might become
whatever pretexts Nicholas Monk had take
his journey, it had excited suspicion; and t
man, assailed by questioners on all sides, ha
enough to escape from their hands. Monk,
indiscretions, reproached his brother with th
him a new oath that he would not commu
not even to Sir John Greenville, what had
them; adding, with unfeigned anger, that
transpired by either one or the other, he
means untried to ruin them both. Then, ad
never again to meddle with intrigue, so
sacred profession, he appeared so disguste
affair, that Nicholas, on his return, assured
ville that, for the present at least, it was us
further attempt.

For a moment, in fact, Monk seemed to
royal cause was irretrievably lost; and, i
parliament from all distrust, or to make kno
or rather because, yielding to his natural bia
strongest party, he really wished to retire,
opposition to the advice of all his friend
resignation. And, on the 3rd of Septembe
to the parliament that, feeling the approach
of old age, he desired to be discharged fro

that he might quietly end his days at home. He took care not to send his letter by means of his brother-in-law, Clarges, a physician by profession, but recently appointed an army commissary, and almost always intrusted with the general's secret business in London—a trust of which he acquitted himself with boldness and address. Monk knew very well that Clarges would disapprove of his step, and was much afraid of his influence, which he exercised, according to all appearance, by the imperious agency of Mrs. Monk. But his own brother, Nicholas Monk, informed of the arrival of the letter, succeeded in getting possession of it, and gave it to Clarges, who in his turn carried it to Lenthall, who was still speaker of the parliament.

Two principal parties were at that time contending at Westminster; that of Lambert and the army, with which were connected those men who, like Vane, thought their situation was desperate, and did not fear to apply the most violent remedies; and that of the moderate men of all classes, and the blind apostles of the legitimacy of the *Rump*, who, seeing that they had most to fear from the army, directed all their efforts against it. Lenthall was one of this latter party, all whose hopes centred upon Monk, as the only champion who could be opposed to Lambert; and Clarges easily persuaded him to make no mention of Monk's resignation, for fear lest the party of the army should hasten to profit by it, and send out his successor. Lenthall and his friends, in fact, eluded all the questions of Vane, who, having got wind of Monk's letter, on several occasions demanded that it should be read; but, before ten days had elapsed, Clarges received orders from the general to withdraw it.

Whatever may have been the motives and means employed to bring Monk to this resolution, as soon as he had afresh incurred danger, he set to work that he might place himself in a position to face it. He applied himself to sounding, more closely than he had hitherto done, the dispositions of all the officers in his army, and opened a correspondence with Fairfax, from whom he had received overtures at the time of Sir George Booth's insurrection. Clarges was directed to assure the principal members of the parliament that they would have the support of the general of the Scottish army against the projects of the English army, whose insolence had not been long in manifesting itself. At the same time, trustworthy agents, unknown to one another, informed Monk of the state of London, and of the progress of the misunderstanding between the two parties. Anonymous letters, or letters signed with false names, were despatched to increase animosities or to thwart plans, by revealing to one party what it had been possible to learn of the intentions of the other. The quarrel grew warmer every day. "I see now that I shall have a better game to play than I had before," said Monk; "I know Lambert so well, that I am sure he will not let those people at Westminster sit till Christmas Day." In fact, on the 13th of October, 1659, the avenues of Westminster were occupied by troops; the *Rump* was compelled to abdicate its power; Lambert and his adherents constituted themselves a government, under the name of the Committee of Safety, and Fleetwood figured at their head. This news arrived at Dalkeith on the 17th; all was ready, and all was set in motion. After reading his despatches, Monk declared to those of his officers who were around him, his resolution to support the parliament—stopped all the letters to London —and immediately summoned to Dalkeith the officers of the garrisons of Edinburgh and Leith; and, having assured himself of their co-operation, marched the next day to Edinburgh at the head of his guards. Two regiments were quartered in the town; he cashiered those officers who he knew were opposed to his design, arrested those whom he most distrusted; and, having assembled the troops, declared to them, in a firm and animated tone, the reasons for his determination. "The army in England," said he, "has broken up the parliament. Incapable of rest, it is determined to invade all authority, and will not suffer the nation to arrive at a lasting settlement. Its insolent extravagance will presently rise so as to grasp at the command of the army in Scotland, which is neither subordinate nor inferior. For my own part, I think it the duty of my place to keep the military power in obedience to the civil. It is the duty of us all to defend the parliament, from which you receive your pay and commissions. I rely, therefore, on your obedience. If, however, any one of you dissents from this resolution, he shall have full liberty to quit the service, and receive his pass."

This speech was received with the liveliest acclamations by the soldiers, to which were added the cheers of the Scotch, rendered happy by the hope of liberty which the dissensions of their masters afforded them. During the night, Captain Johnson set off, with a detachment of cavalry, to assist the commandant of Berwick, of whom Monk was sure, in getting rid of the officers of his garrison, who were all Anabaptists and Independents; they were arrested and superseded. At the very moment when Johnson had completed his operation, Colonel Cobbett entered Berwick for the purpose of securing the town in the name of the army of England and its leaders. Cobbett was arrested, and conducted to Edinburgh castle. The same step had been taken at Ayr and St. Johnstoun, but with less difficulty, because the dissidents there were fewer in number. Newcastle was lost; for Colonel Lilburne, who happened to be at York, had taken possession of it on behalf of the Committee of Safety. In the distant garrisons, the commandants of Monk's party were directed to perform the above operation immediately; those who were suspected received orders to proceed to Dalkeith, to confer with the general upon affairs of importance; and hardly had they left their fortresses before they were arrested by agents posted on their route, and forthwith conducted to prison in Edinburgh. At the same time, Monk wrote to Lenthall, the speaker of the parliament, to Fleetwood, and to Lambert, to announce the resolution taken by the army in Scotland to defend against violence the laws and liberties of England. Several of his officers had demanded that, before they drew their swords and were exposed to shed the blood of their brethren in England, an attempt should be made to reclaim them by at least some warning. Monk was not in a position to refuse such a demand; and besides, was not afraid of allowing time to pass, which he was sure of employing better than his adversaries. He had no desire or intention to come to an engagement with the English army; he had witnessed a civil war, and was aware of its chances; and no man ever was more careful than himself to avoid chances, until he perceived that the safest course was to encounter them. With the habits and profession of a soldier, he was a man of business, and loved peace. Among the predictions which had long ago marked him out as the restorer of the monarchy, he used to relate that of an old Earl of Nithsdale who had come to see him, to tell him that the king would be restored before many months had elapsed; that he, Monk, would be the principal instrument of this revolution, and that not even a finger would be cut in the affair. "In that case," Monk added gaily, "I am assured of my share in it." Besides, although he set little value on Lambert's military talents, he was no strong enough to engage him with an equal force. On the standard which he had just raised, he inscribed two principles which he was careful to indite with great precision, that they might on all occasions furnish him with an answer:—" The government cannot stand without the entire subjection of the military to the civil power."—" The commonwealth must be administered by parliament." These were the two civil truths which he undertook to render triumphant by the aid of an army of which he had made himself master only by banishing from its ranks every man disposed to act in virtue of a political idea, and by reducing it to a purely military spirit and interest.

It was easy to foresee that such soldiers would agree better with other soldiers than with a parliament; and it was impossible to doubt that when in presence of Lambert's army, one-half, at least, of Monk's forces would go over to the side on which it would recognize its own cause. Monk had therefore resolved to keep them constantly at a distance from each other, and to let time do what it necessarily would effect. Well informed of what was passing among his enemies, he knew that Lambert's army, much more numerous than his own, but destitute alike of order and money, would soon be forced to disband. The parliament, when it saw that its fall was inevitable, had striven to deprive its oppressors of the power of profiting by it; and its last signs of life had been a prohibition to pay the taxes, the disorganization of the military authorities then in power, and the nomination of seven commissioners charged with the government of the army, among whom they had taken care to include Monk, the faithful friend of the parliament, according to the assurances of Scott, one of the most ardent members of the republican party, but the complete dupe of Chaplain Gumble, with whom he had long kept up a correspondence. Of these two votes, the first, very willingly adopted by the English people, compelled Lambert to obtain the means of subsistence for his troops by the use of violent measures, which no one was now in a position to employ; and the second gave an appearance of legality to the arbitrary power exercised by Monk in the disposal of military employments, which, in the part he had taken, it was important for him to retain. As for the payment and maintenance of his army, although he had not for a long while received any money from England, Monk, by his provident economy, had supplied himself with ample resources. The state of his exchequer even permitted him to order the payment of the arrears due to the officers whom he cashiered. But as, before they had received their money, their discontent was imprudent enough to break out in words and plans to debauch the soldiers, it was considered both just and advantageous to dismiss them unpaid; and, banished from Scotland under penalty of death, they went to swell the troops, and add to the embarrassment of Lambert.

In spite of all this purging, and of the material means of which he could dispose, Monk felt that his military authority was no longer sufficient to lead an army whose views he had been obliged to consult. It had become a political party, and it was necessary to give it the movements and interests of one. All the officers were assembled in a great council presided over by the general, and in which the affairs of the cause were discussed. There Monk, patient and imperturbable, allowed free course to the pretensions of subaltern wit, to the coarse distrust of ignorance, and to the diffuse language of the soldier raised from the ranks, and anxious to gain further distinction. All was listened to, and disposed of by the adroitness of some confidant, whose logic easily confuted his unskilful antagonists. Monk spoke but little, except when it was necessary to give the authority of his assent to the opinion of which he approved; and, almost without making his influence felt, he governed the resolutions of an assembly destined to serve as his instrument. At the same time, intelligent non-commissioned officers, carefully instructed in the ideas which they were to disseminate or destroy, in the opinions they were to ascertain, and the sentiments they were to encourage, applied themselves to gain the confidence of the soldiers; and, actuated by promises of promotion, zealously seconded the designs of their general. A weekly gazette, and occasionally flying tracts, artfully drawn up, were diffused, read, and commented upon in the mess-rooms. On all sides began to be displayed that activity of mind, and importance of individual opinions, which, though alarming to unskilful authority, are powerful though inconvenient instruments in the hands of all who can wield them.

E

One regiment, abandoned by its officers, threatened to desert if not allowed to choose those who were to replace them: means were first found to limit the pretensions of the soldiers to the choice of their subaltern officers, and then to prevent their coming to an agreement, and oblige them to have recourse to the wisdom of their superiors. The whole of this interior and concealed government was carried on by a certain number of officers who were devoted to Monk, and allied to his plans. At the head of the intrigues and internal affairs of the party was Chaplain Gumble, ever active, persuasive, full of invention, and almost the only agent to be seen. "George Monk would not have stirred without that man," angrily remarked the agents of the opposite party. To these subterraneous intrigues were added public declarations: Monk's letters to Fleetwood, Lambert, and Lenthall, were printed and distributed at Edinburgh, as well as a declaration of the great council of officers to this effect: "That they had taken up arms to defend the freedom and privilege of parliaments, and to vindicate the rights and liberties of the people against all opposition whatever." The arrival of these letters in London had excited a deep feeling of joy in the public mind, and occasioned great surprise to those officers who were in possession of power. Imprudent and thoughtless, they had never once doubted but that the whole of the army in Scotland would acknowledge their government; and Colonel Cobbett, whom Monk had just arrested at Berwick, had been sent thither to ascertain the feelings of the troops, and if it were necessary, to secure the person of the general. It is even related, that on a certain post-day, one of Monk's guards, walking along the Edinburgh road, met the courier, who, instead of calling first at Dalkeith, according to his usual custom, was going direct to the town. Indignant at this want of respect, the soldier brought him, in spite of his resistance, to the general, who at once took possession of all the letters, and found among them an order for his own arrest, addressed by the Committee of Safety to an officer of his army, who was immediately to take the command in his place. But this circumstance, which will be found materially impossible, if we examine its various particulars, is moreover mentioned by neither of Monk's biographers, and appears to be one of those dramatic touches by which the human imagination delights to embellish great events.

Whatever may have been the intentions of Lambert and his party with regard to Monk, they had feared his rivalry, but not his patriotism, and they quickly perceived the discredit into which the cause he had embraced would throw their own. Besides they learned at the same time as his resolution the measures already taken to support it ; and the officer charged with Monk's despatches had augmented their fears by betraying what he knew or suspected of his general's secrets. Undeceived as to the vain idea of their power over the army in Scotland, the leaders of the English army suddenly beheld the appearance of a force ready to attack them before they had dreamt of suspecting its existence. They resolved to attempt an accommodation, were it only to gain time for putting themselves in a position of defence; and whilst Lambert, appointed general of the troops in the North, was marching at their head towards Newcastle, Dr. Clarges, and Talbot, one of the colonels of Monk's army, who happened to be just then in London, were sent to explain what was called a misunderstanding, and to propose negociations.

Nothing could have been more favourable to Monk's plans. He had just failed in his attempts to draw over the army in Ireland to his side, and had reason to fear that it would declare against him. His efforts had not been more successful in the fleet ; and Overton, the governor of Hull, as well as some other commandants of fortresses in England, whose republican opinions seemed likely to array them on the side of the parliament, had shown themselves mistrustful of Monk's intentions, and had given no other answer to his overtures than an offer to use their influence to effect his reconciliation with the Committee of Safety. Thus reduced to his own resources, Monk nevertheless did not contemplate further hesitation. When he was engaged in action a singular sagacity in discerning the true state of affairs preserved him from all uncertainty regarding his immediate conduct. Solely occupied in accomplishing that which was required by his actual situation, he took a complete view of it, and allowed nothing to escape him which might compromise the future. He was one of those practical men in whom reflection does not precede experience, but whom experience gradually enlightens, and whose mind, though inaccessible to every truth which does not come under their notice in a tangible form, yet recognizes and seizes it as soon as it assumes in their eyes a place in the affairs and interests of this world. Incapable perhaps of forming a complete preconception of himself, Monk never failed himself in any emergency; his mind, rather penetrating than vast, and more firm than enterprising, could not embrace the entire scope of a great project while it was yet unprepared for execution; his placid character was little exposed to the temptations of rash enterprise; but boldness, when occasion required it, was as familiar to him as prudence; and when, after advancing step by step, he arrived at one of those dangerous passages where it became necessary that great resolution should suddenly surmount great obstacles, his quick and sure good sense proceeded straight towards the difficulty, of whatever magnitude it might be; and the boldest course became to him the simplest as soon as he perceived it was the most advantageous.

At this period his position compelled him at once to act and to temporize. He paid great attention to the envoys of the London Committee. Talbot effected no change in his plans, and Clarges only endeavoured to promote them. The officers, being consulted on the message, agreed to a proposition to appoint three commissioners to treat with their brethren of the army in England. The choice of these was left to the general, who nominated two, and allowed the officers to elect the third. They named Colonel Wilks, a not very trustworthy agent, and whose fidelity was perhaps the more shaken by his discontent at not having been chosen first. The negociators set out at the commencement of November, 1659, charged with the public instructions of the council, and the secret orders of the general. The principal point was to gain time, and not to conclude any arrangement, except at the last extremity, and then only upon condition of the restoration of the old parliament. If they could not obtain this, they were at least to require that a new parliament, freely elected, should be convoked forthwith. But as the committee of officers in London would necessarily prefer the convocation of a new parliament to the restoration of the one they had ejected, the commissioners were ordered to keep them in ignorance of their power to consent to it, until the time when a longer resistance might compromise the popularity of their mission. They were finally charged to ascertain what assistance might be expected from the opinion of the city of London, which had already declared in favour of Monk's plans, and to regulate their conduct accordingly.

Whilst Monk's envoys were proceeding to London, and Lambert was marching upon Newcastle, other negociations and other intrigues were following their course. Fleetwood, already alarmed at Lambert's ambition, was seeking to secure to himself some private resource on Monk's side, and sent to him, on his own account, Dean, one of the treasurers of the army. But at the same time he declared to the Common Council of the city that it was Monk's intention to restore the king by warlike means; and Dean, less anxious to gain the general than to alienate his army, openly made mention, even at Monk's table, of the royalist projects imputed to him ; and strove by his speeches, and by widely-diffused tracts, to seduce or alarm the soldiers. One day, when passing in front of a company of infantry, " My lord Lambert," he said, " is coming upon you; and all Monk's army will not be enough for a breakfast for him." " Lambert must have a very good stomach this cold weather," replied a soldier, " if he can eat pikes and swallow bullets."

Lambert attempted, like Fleetwood, and by the same means, to make his own private arrangement. He tried to persuade Monk's commissioners, who were obliged to pass through his army, that he had power to treat with them; but as they insisted on repairing to London, unless Lambert would consent to restore the parliament, he allowed them to continue their journey, after having agreed with them upon a suspension of hostilities as long as the negociations lasted ; and he intrusted the management of his private interests to Morgan, a major-general of Monk's army, whom he had found at York, where Morgan, detained by the effects of a violent attack of gout, and in the midst of Lambert's army, declared himself vehemently against the plans of his general. As soon as his health permitted, Morgan set out for Edinburgh, directed, as the rest had been, to try his influence over the general, but even more to employ his credit in the army against him. On the other hand, some congregations of Independents and other sectaries, moved by the declarations of Monk, and the care which he took to re-assure them, had thought it their duty to present him with their thanks; but others, more prudent or more suspicious, had distrusted the intentions of a man so little advanced in the ways of the Lord. Three ministers and two colonels arrived in their name at Edinburgh,—the men of peace to speak of an accommodation,—the colonels to tamper

with the soldiers, and lead them to desert to Lambert's army.
At the same time Fairfax informed Monk that he and his
adherents in the county of York, who had been ready to rise
ever since Sir George Booth's insurrection, were willing to
join their forces to his, if, instead of constituting himself the
protector of a phantom parliament, he would declare himself
for the re-admission of the members excluded by Cromwell
and the army, or for the convocation of a new parliament.
This latter proposition made peace far too easy to please
Monk; and the other could not yet be even hinted to his
troops without danger. The envoy from Fairfax was made to
understand the necessity for further patience; the ministers
and colonels were dismissed after some sharp words and many
pacific demonstrations; and Morgan, as soon as he found
himself beyond the reach of Lambert, became, in military
affairs, the most important agent of the designs of Monk, whose
entire confidence he possessed.

All this movement of intrigue and seduction was not, however, entirely without result. Some alarm as to the ulterior
projects of the general began to be felt, both in and out of the
army, by men who, either from interest or opinion, were
strongly opposed to the return of the Stuarts; and also by
those timid spirits who are frightened by every idea of change.
In the same proportion the hopes of the royalist party increased. Monk's confidants were besieged by questions; and
even Monk had to defend himself against the indiscreet pre-
cipitancy of the Cavaliers, the suspicious watchfulness of their
enemies, and the imprudence of his household. " Mr. Monk,"
his wife used to say, " is a Presbyterian, and my son Kit (he
was then six years of age) is for the Long parliament and the
good old cause ;" and in the midst of the insults to which the
cause which he cherished was exposed in the general's house,
Chaplain Price could not always restrain the outbursts of his
royalist anger. " I can be undone by none," Monk said to
him one day, " but you and my wife." Several of those who
had at first served him with zeal were not slow to abandon
him now. His cavalry, already far from numerous, deserted
him almost entirely; but the infantry only manifested firmer
attachment, and Monk, after this movement of desertion,
thought he could rely upon what remained.

A month had elapsed in preparations when he judged that
the time was come to enter upon the campaign, and sustain

his declarations by some unequivocal measure. During the early part of November he had assembled at Edinburgh the principal nobility of Scotland, and the deputies of the boroughs and counties, had announced to them that he intended to march into England for the defence of the laws and liberty, and had asked them to support his plans, first by maintaining tranquillity in Scotland whilst he was occupied elsewhere, and, secondly, by handing over to him the arrear of the taxes necessary for the payment of his troops. The Scotch, unprovided with weapons, could do little to preserve public order; but they promised the money, and kept their word. To settle the other interests which they might have to discuss, they requested Monk to give them a second conference, which he fixed for the 13th of December, at Berwick. Finally, on the 18th of November, 1659, he gave orders to march, set out himself on the same day, with his staff, in advance of his army, and proceeded to Haddington, on the road to Berwick.

His commissioners had arrived in London on the 12th of November. They immediately found themselves artfully surrounded and persecuted by the caresses and advances of the officers of the army, and quite unable to communicate with any one, to receive a visit or a message from their friends, and almost to confer amongst themselves. Around them everything breathed strength and confidence; from a distance nothing reached them but terror and discouragement. From hour to hour the most disastrous news accumulated; one body after another of Monk's army had deserted; soon their general would be left alone, and out of a position to treat; and they would find themselves defenceless in the hands of their enemies. They were at a loss what to do. Wilks, having been deceived or gained over, led the others astray; and on the evening of the 15th of November a treaty of nine articles was signed, agreeing to the convocation of a new parliament, the displacement of the officers of the two armies, and some other analogous measures; that is to say, the ruin of Monk, of his party, and of his projects. And in order to prevent any change of mind, or to hasten the effect of their victory, the government of London, without waiting for the departure of the commissioners, sent two officers to carry to Monk with all diligence the articles which had been signed, and to request their ratification.

Monk was leaving the dinner-table, on the 18th of November,

when the two officers arrived at Haddington and presented him with the treaty. He read it, gave it for perusal to those who were present, and, according to his usual custom, without saying a word, retired immediately to his own room.

The next day he returned to Edinburgh. The news of the treaty had preceded him thither. The first consternation had already given way to anger; and the irritation was increasing. The sixth article of the treaty especially roused all interests against this imprudent transaction. It prescribed the nomination of a committee of fourteen officers, half of whom were to be chosen from each army, and who were to meet at Newcastle to decide upon the claims of the officers whom Monk had deprived of their commissions, or who had resigned since the 7th of October. Thus all the promotions obtained in Monk's army, in consequence of the purging it had undergone, were called in question. At the same time they must renounce all hope of returning into their native country, whither their imagination had already transported them; and instead of the long-promised participation in those advantages which the English army alone had enjoyed for such a length of time, they would have to return to their exile in Scotland, with its poverty, and wild and cheerless garrisons.

The reception-room was full of officers, on all whose countenances agitation was plainly visible. Monk was walking up and down in their midst, sombre, pensive, and without addressing a word to any one. Around him were heard murmurs of discontent; and all eyes followed his movements. Chaplain Gumble enters the hall; the general goes towards him, and asks him, " How now? What say you to this agreement?" " Truly, sir, I have not seen it; but I hear so well of it, that I am come to make a little request to you this morning." " What is that, I wonder?" " Even that you would sign me a pass to go into Holland; yonder is a ship at Leith that is ready to set sail." " What! will you now leave me?" " I know not how you may shift for yourself by your greatness, but be confident that they will never be at rest till they have torn you from your command; and what they will do with you then it concerns you to consider: but for my part, though I am a poor man, I will never put myself into their power, for I know it will not be for my safety." " Will you lay the blame upon me?" cried the general. " If the army will stick to me, I will stick to them." At these words a shout of satisfaction burst

forth on all sides; protestations and transports of joy succeeded to silence and consternation; serenity was restored to
the countenance of the general, and the preparations for
departure were completed with cheerful activity.

During the first moments of their exasperation, Monk's
officers demanded that the commissioners who had been sent
to London should be disavowed as traitors; but it was judged
more prudent to take advantage of the treaty they had concluded, for the purpose of prolonging the negociation. Answer
was made to the Committee of Safety that, although they had
no objection to offer against any of the articles, yet, as several
important ones had been omitted, the ratification of the treaty
was delayed until new conferences should have taken place.
To these they demanded that two new commissioners should
be admitted, who, with the former envoys, and an equal
number of English commissioners, should meet at Alnwick, or
in any other place beyond the power of either army, in order
to settle definitively the conditions of peace. The envoys of
the Committee of Safety returned to London on the 20th of
November with this message; and Monk intrusted the further
management of the affair to the confidential committee which
conducted all his political correspondence, and upon which
he devolved the task of maintaining this paper war, as well
as of drawing up such proclamations, protests, and declarations of principles, as he wished to be able to set aside or
disavow, according to circumstances. His own commissioners
soon returned from London, and made what excuses they
could. Wilks, whose reasons were not deemed satisfactory,
was arrested, but afterwards released. The refusal to ratify
the treaty redoubled the fears of that little knot of politicians
in London, whom the officers of the English army had thought
it prudent to associate with themselves in their strange government. Too clear-sighted to allow themselves to be deceived
by artifices intended only to dupe soldiers, they perceived with
anxiety that they were becoming entangled in a net the meshes
of which it was still easy to break. Vainly had they insisted
that, from the very first, setting aside all delay, and, if necessary, all hope of negociation, Lambert's army should hasten to
seize the moment favourable for victory. The heedless faction
which then held the reins of government at London having
gained its power by violent measures, thought it could dispense
with all foresight, banished every unpleasant reflection, and

slumbered in the security of its triumph, until the moment when it was destined to awake and find itself deceived and conquered.

Monk marched towards Berwick at the head of six good regiments of infantry and four of cavalry, the latter incompletely equipped and badly mounted; in all six or seven thousand men, well paid, well disciplined, inured to labour to fatigue, and to the severity of the Scottish climate. Lambert had at Newcastle eight or ten thousand men, well mounted and well-equipped, but without money, and without discipline, accustomed to ease, and unused to war; many of them were well-disposed towards the expelled parliament. and unfavourable to the cause they were about to defend; while others were attached to Fleetwood's party, and felt little zeal in promoting the success of Lambert. The news of Monk's refusal to ratify the treaty produced upon them so injurious an effect that Lambert felt it imperatively necessary to hasten the negotiations, if possible; and on his arrival at Berwick, on the 6th of December, Monk was met by Colonel Zanchey, who came, on the part of the general of the English army, to press the nomination of the two new commissioners, and to demand that the treaty should at once be adopted, without waiting until the new articles should be added. Referred to Monk's committee of correspondence, Zanchey received from them nothing but a positive refusal to depart from their original resolutions; and the banter of some of the officers gave him to understand that there remained to him few means of influencing persons who no longer feared him enough to take the trouble to deceive him. During the afternoon, intelligence arrived that Lambert's dragoons, urged by want of money, had made an incursion into Northumberland, in the hope of getting possession of a considerable sum belonging to Lord Grey of Wark, but which had been prudently removed some days before. At the news of this violation of the truce, Zanchey was arrested, which caused the gain of a few more days, before an answer was returned to Lambert. On the 8th of December, Monk marched forward, and established his head-quarters on the banks of the Tweed, at Coldstream, a wretched position, which seemed for a moment to startle the courage of the chaplains, but which was more favourable than any other locality for fording the Tweed, and whither, in case of alarm, Monk could in four hours muster all his troops, who were stationed in the neighbouring villages.

The crisis was now at hand: at Coldstream must be decided the question of victory or retreat. Careful to secure some support upon which he could fall back, Monk had not forgotten the promise he had made to meet the Scotch on the 13th of December, at Berwick. He found there a portion of the chief of the royalist nobility, who, full of zeal and hope, had come to request a supply of arms, and to offer such levies of men as the exigency of the cause might require; and who proposed at the outset to place under Monk's command six thousand infantry, and fifteen hundred horse. However useful such support might appear, Monk thought it even more dangerous. Scarcely had he, by admitting several English officers to the conferences held with the Scotch, succeeded in appeasing the disdainful discontent which they manifested at beholding subjects, whom they claimed to govern by right of conquest, interfere in their affairs: and the army had displayed great indignation because some Scots had been introduced into it, in order to complete the ranks. It was necessary carefully to avoid all causes of distrust; the Scotch were supplied with arms; but Monk declined their assistance, promising to have recourse to it in case of need; while, to compensate for this refusal, he took pains to inspire them with confidence in a future, which it was not difficult for them to foresee.

From hour to hour, so to speak, it became more necessary to Lambert and the London government to obtain a prompt decision—which it was the constant policy of Monk and his committee to avoid. A few days more, and from all quarters Monk would receive assistance, or promises, which, against a disheartened enemy, are perhaps of even more value than assistance. London was in a ferment; the members of the Long parliament had taken fresh courage; the city, though not very favourable to their pretensions, nevertheless united with them in opposing the government of the army. Informed of this state of feeling, Monk wrote to the Common Council, that, at the very first moment, he had addressed letters to it, as well as to all the other great bodies of the state, but that they must certainly have been intercepted. He was lavish in his protestations of devotion; and exhorted

the citizens of London to use every effort to free themselve
from their servitude.

Delighted at his promises, they displayed a strong incli
nation to follow his advice. The garrisons of London and it
neighbourhood did not highly estimate the honours of frater
nity with a power which could not pay them, and began to
regret the abolition of the power of the parliament which
alone had been able to vote and enforce the payment of the
taxes. The fleet, upon receiving more correct information
declared in favour of the parliament. The same party had
prevailed in the army in Ireland. Fairfax, with whom Monk
maintained a very active correspondence, by means of the
ministers who transmitted news to each other from parish to
parish, promised to be ready, in the early part of January, to
fall upon the rear of Lambert's army. Finally, Colonel
Wetham, governor of Portsmouth, and an old connection
of Monk's, had willingly listened to the persuasions of Haslerig, Morley, and Walton, who begged him to unite in the
efforts which Monk was making in their favour. In concert
with them, the garrison of Portsmouth had unanimously proclaimed the parliament: and the troops sent by Fleetwood to
besiege the town, had arrived under its walls only to declare
the same views.

On hearing this last piece of news, Monk hastened to write
to Lambert to inform him of his readiness to resume the
negociations; but as Haslerig and the other parliamentarians,
then masters of Portsmouth, had been of the number of the
commissioners whom the parliament, just before its fall, had
appointed to the government of the army, Monk, as their colleague, thought that he could not treat without their concurrence, and requested Lambert to send him a pass, that he
might despatch a messenger to Portsmouth to obtain their
instructions.

Lambert could not fail to perceive that he had been
tricked: he grew angry, refused the passport, and understood
that a treaty was now out of the question. But it was no
longer a time for action. Snow, several feet in depth, covered
the forty miles of precipitous country which separated Lambert from Monk and the Tweed; and he was obliged to
abandon all hope of getting at his enemy until that not far
distant period when his army would have exhausted its last

resources. But Lambert was destined soon to have not even a cause to support. The feeble hands of Fleetwood had not been able to retain the reins of government in London; and on the 25th of December, 1659, the *Rump*, accepting the submissive excuses of the humbled general, entered for the last time into possession of Westminster. Its first care was to direct that both armies should return to their quarters; and to vote the army of Scotland, as a mark of its approbation, chains and medals of gold.

The same messenger who brought to Monk the intelligence of the change which had just taken place in London, informed him that Fairfax had taken arms, having been forced to declare himself sooner than he intended through fear of being discovered and prevented. Monk did not hesitate about what course to take. To go to the assistance of Fairfax, now in danger of being attacked and overwhelmed by Lambert—to hasten to forestall by marching onwards, the official order to retreat, which they were determined not to obey—such was the unanimous movement of the Scottish army, which, during the last few days, had been wonderfully reinforced by the friends whom the aspect of affairs brought to it from all quarters. On the 1st of January, 1660, during a sharp frost, it crossed the Tweed, and joyfully set foot upon the soil of England. At Wooler, his first halting-place, Monk received a letter from Speaker Lenthall, informing him, in cold and constrained terms, of the restoration of the parliament, adding scarcely any thanks for his services, and not even inviting him to come to London. However, the same messenger took to Lambert orders to disband his troops, but brought no such directions to Monk. This was sufficient to inform Monk, that to the distrust with which he was regarded there was already added as much fear as it was necessary that he should inspire, in order to remain master. On the morning of the next day, Lenthall's letter was read at the head of each regiment. The soldiers, buried up to their knees in the snow, but consoled for the fatigues which awaited them by the hope of arriving at length at a resting-place, unanimously exclaimed that they would go to London to see the parliament assembled.

The impulse was given, and no further obstacle presented itself to arrest it. Lambert, on hearing of the restoration and vote of the parliament, had withdrawn by flight from the danger of being left at the mercy of those whom he had offended. His troops had submitted and dispersed. Monk remained alone, and his army, having now no choice to make, returned to its dependence upon him. From this time forth, there was an end of general councils of officers, political assemblies, votes, and remonstrances. The most intelligent were able to perceive that Lambert's army was not the only one vanquished by recent events, but to submit was unavoidable; and Monk, restored to possession of his liberty, which had been infringed upon by all those liberties with which he was not accustomed to treat, could henceforward singly, or with the concurrence of a few confidants, more or less in the dark regarding his ulterior intentions, pursue that active, covert, and silent policy which suited at once his taste and his situation.

He had also contrived to escape the danger and importunity of family indiscretions. When his wife, without asking his sanction, came to join him at Coldstream, the general, who had now abandoned home duties to enter upon the activity of public life and the authority of a commander, sent her back with a rather severe reprimand to Berwick, whence he afterwards had her conveyed by sea to England. As for chaplain Price, as soon as ever Monk had determined upon the course he was to take, he had informed him: "I shall not employ you in this business; and be not discontented with it, for you know not these people as well as I do, and cannot dissemble with them." Price was struck, as he informs us himself, with the general's frankness, and from that moment kept himself aloof, contented with maintaining a careful watch, and hastening by a few solicitations the accomplishment of the tacit promises upon which he thought he could already reckon.

Relieved of his fears respecting Fairfax, Monk slackened his march, leaving to time to dispel the obscurities of his new situation, but without losing an instant in turning against the parliament those methods of cunning and activity which had rid him of Lambert's army. Always occupied by the enterprise of the moment, after he had finished in one quarter, he directed all his strength to enable him to triumph in the other. Gumble, despatched to London to examine into the state of affairs, and learn something about the men with whom the general would have to deal, conveyed to the *Rump* the most solemn promises of his devotedness; and laid before it, as a pledge of his fidelity, a letter in which the Common Council of the city requested Monk to aid them in obtaining the re-admission of the members who had been excluded from the Long parliament, or the convocation of a free and complete parliament. The same wish, expressed all along his route by a multitude of addresses and felicitations, was met by the most humble protestations of obedience to the civil authority. Declarations against Charles Stuart and his family were multiplied daily, and were the stronger and more explicit, because, upon this point, men's hopes and suspicions began to be manifested more undisguisedly. Monk publicly caned, and probably with real anger, an officer who had said, "This Monk will at last bring back Charles Stuart." His language was in conformity with his actions, and was accompanied by such appearances of military frankness and heartfelt emotion that Price felt it necessary to obtain some new assurance, and crept one night into the room of his master, whom he found, during a brief interval of toil, asleep in his clothes upon two chairs, with his head resting upon the edge of his bed. The chaplain, in the ardour of his zeal, awoke him to express his fears. Monk, always equable, and always ready, re-assured him in words which were the more positive because they entailed no consequences, and conjured him to think nothing of all those engagements which it was impossible for him to decline, "for," said he, "they are distrustful enough of me already;" and Price, tranquillized once more by this proof of the sincerity of his general's intentions, quietly resumed his character of a mere spectator.

Although careful not to belie for an instant the respectful language he had used, Monk continued to advance without orders, or rather in opposition to the orders which the *Rump* had not had the courage to make known to him. His arrival was everywhere hailed by the ringing of bells, and the joyful shouts of the multitude, as he marched forward, receiving the homage and requests of a population eager to gain hopes from him, cashiering the officers of the regiments which he met, and replacing them by men devoted to his service. When he reached York, however, he thought it proper to wait for some indication of the intentions of the parliament. The county of Yorkshire, where predominated the influence of Fairfax

(then resolved to restore the monarchy which he had formerly
overthrown, almost without intending it,) offered Monk an
advantageous position, which he was unwilling to abandon,
until he was sure of London. Fairfax even urged him to remain
at York, and declare at once for the king. His officers were
surrounded; some began to settle the price of their adhesion
to the royal cause, and carried it so high that one of them, it
is said, refused to have anything to do with them unless they
promised to make him Lord Chancellor. But Monk never
advanced openly when he could proceed as effectually in
secret; and the chances of war in Yorkshire were not so
good as those of armed intrigue, such as he intended to carry
on in London, as soon as he had established his head-
quarters there. Resolved to try his best to reach the
metropolis without striking a blow, he had even provided
for the case in which he might have finally received at York
formal orders to retreat: he would then have had means of
forcing the parliament to reflect upon its imprudence, and
he intended to obey so slowly as to leave it time for so
doing.

But already the unfortunate *Rump*, re-established only to
be driven from suspicion to suspicion, possessed merely a
choice of dangers; and Monk's presence in London appeared
less alarming than the junction of his forces with those of
Fairfax in Yorkshire. On the 6th of January, 1660, a vote
was passed, requesting Monk to come to London " as speedily
as he could." On the 12th, in consequence of the letters
presented by Gumble, another vote was carried, approving of
all that Monk had done up to that time. Finally, on the
16th, a tardy vote of thanks bestowed upon him a perpetual
annuity of one thousand pounds sterling; and the Speaker
was directed to write to him, that the House, impressed with
a sense of his great services, would endeavour to provide for
the payment of his soldiers, and was glad to learn that,
" according to the desire of the parliament, he purposed to
come to London." It was also voted that two parliamentary
commissioners should be sent to meet him, to do him honour.
Scott and Robinson, two of the most hot-headed of that
infatuated party which was hurrying to its ruin through its
precautions to avert it, were proposed for this mission by the
Presbyterians, to whom they had become troublesome in
Westminster, and accepted by the Independents as trust-

vorthy and faithful spies, well qualified to inform them of the
proceedings of the enemy.

Monk arrived at York on the 11th of January, and left it
on the 16th, on his way to London, taking with him only four
thousand infantry and eighteen hundred horse — an army
sufficient to overawe, without exciting suspicion. To give
positive proof of the purity of his designs, he sent back
Morgan with two regiments of cavalry into Scotland; thus
strengthening his party there, and ensuring his retreat in case
of misfortune. Another regiment was left at York, under
the command of Colonel Fairfax, a nephew of Sir Thomas,
and one of the officers of the Scottish army, who, from the
first, had co-operated most usefully with his general's measures. Careful not to be burdensome to the county of York,
Monk had dispersed his troops in distant quarters; so that,
when he arrived at Nottingham on the 19th of January, he
was obliged to remain there for two days, to collect together his
forces. There he found Dr. Clarges, and Gumble had rejoined
him on the previous evening. Both brought him news of
the state of London. Monk was loudly summoned thither
by a portion of the people, and by the leading men of the
city. Among the lower classes, a considerable party still
preferred Lambert and the Independents; but the parliament
was regarded by all with aversion and contempt. The troops
quartered in London and its neighbourhood were hardly able
to restrain the popular outbreaks, which were always ready
to burst forth against it. The last resource of that government which they had overthrown two months before, these
troops became once more the hope of some who were disposed,
if their courage had not failed them, to throw themselves
again into the arms of Lambert, that they might escape
falling into the power of Monk.

It was necessary to deprive them of this last refuge. Some
of the members of Monk's political committee—either because
they did not yet suspect intentions which they continued to
serve, or because they were desirous to obtain some assurance
of them—proposed to cut short all distrust, by making the
army sign an engagement to obey all that the parliament
should command, except the restoration of Charles Stuart.
This proposition was set aside out of respect to the parliament, and in order not to fall into the error committed by the
English army, in presuming to prescribe laws to it. The

F

principle of submission to the civil authority was of the mo
service upon this occasion, because there was no time
admit of discussion.   Scott and Robinson were to arrive t
next day, and all freedom of conference would then be at i
end.   It was, therefore, necessary to be contented with
letter.   Monk, much less scrupulous about his own engag
ments than about those which his army was wished to mak
allowed them to write in his name to his fellow-countrymei
the gentry of Devonshire, to destroy, by arguments and pro
testations, the hopes which they were beginning to base upo
him for the return of the king.   The committee also employe
itself, in its last moments, in drawing up a letter to deman
that the troops then quartered in London should be dismissed
and those of Monk allowed the honour of guarding the par
liament.   But it was considered prudent not to despatch thi
letter until the approach of the army should render its praye
more efficacious.

Scott and Robinson arrived, in fact, on the next day
Orders had been given, and the highest honours awaited thei
advent.   Monk spared none of those demonstrations of humility which befitted the most obsequious servant of the parliament; and his officers, who had been carefully instructed
and perhaps felt a malicious pleasure in thus duping thei
temporary masters, made such an overwhelming display of
their homage and respect, that the commissioners, and especially Scott, intoxicated by their importance, took the greatest
pains to extol, in their reports, the general's affection for the
parliament, and the respectful discipline of his army.   They
did not, however, feel secure enough to neglect any precautions of the most minute and even most ignoble inspection.   Until the last halting-place, close by London, they
arranged so as always to lodge in the same house as the
general, and were careful to discover or to contrive secretly
in the walls and partitions some opening through which they
might observe what was going on in his room.   Alarmed and
mortified at that unanimous concurrence of prayers which
from the Scottish frontiers to London, had unceasingly pronounced against the everlasting domination of the *Rump*, they
angrily repelled even the slightest attack; so angrily, indeed
that Scott one day declared that, if it were proposed to
re-admit the excluded members, or to convoke a new parliament, he, old as he was, would take arms, and defend the

loors of the house by open force against the intruders. Thus osing by their ill-temper any advantage that might otherwise lave accrued from their importunate assiduity, they freed Monk from the greatest inconvenience of their presence; and by their impetuosity in seizing every opportunity for making ι speech, spared him the embarrassment he would have felt n giving a reply in their presence. Almost always confining limself to the part of a passive or docile spectator, the general seemed, by his silence, to approve, or rather to submit. A few words upon the obedience due to superiors, an nclination of the head, or a knitting of the brows, which each could interpret as he pleased, were ordinarily the only share which he took in the conversation. At the same time he was as anxious as he could be, without compromising himself, o modify, by the modest affability of his deportment, the harshness of the reception given by the commissioners; and, on their leaving the hall of audience, his confidants were careful not to let any petitioner depart discontented, or uncertain as to the intentions in which he had come to confide. Particular care was taken to calm the displeasure of the Aldermen of London, who, on the faith of the letters which Monk had written to them, had come to meet him at Harborough, reckoning upon a more friendly reception. The tone of freedom and boldness which characterized their address displeased the commissioners of the *Rump* to such a degree, that Monk was compelled to appear cold when Scott and Robinson appeared irritated. The aldermen retired deeply offended, and the report of their misadventure seemed for a moment to discourage other petitioners; but all were soon given to understand that the presentation of their petitions possessed far more importance than the answers which were given to them.

Meanwhile, the Cavaliers, faithful to their system of prudence, forbore to swell the triumphal procession of the restorer of republican laws and liberty. Some even began to change their impatient hopes into suspicions; and their alarm suspended the progress of distrust in Monk's army. At St. Albans, the famous Independent preacher, Hugh Peters, came to congratulate Monk, in a long sermon upon the text, "He led them forth by the right way;" and tracing with his finger on the cushion before him the windings of the course pursued by the Israelites in the desert, he showed that

F 2

they wandered forty years to reach the land of Canaan, which was situated at only forty days journey from Egypt; but that, nevertheless, they were always led in "the Lord's way." The application was deemed ingenious; and several of the hearers smiled as they thought that the road might be longer and lead farther than Hugh Peters expected.

From St. Albans, Monk, without informing the commissioners, despatched to the parliament the letter which he had prepared at Nottingham, to request the dismissal of the regiments quartered in London and its neighbourhood, with the exception of those of Morley and Fagg, which had remained faithful to their duty towards the parliament. He feared, he said, to expose the discipline of his army to contact with troops which had so recently been in rebellion, and were always ready to revolt again. Whatever suspicions such a request might arouse in the men to whom it was addressed, the time for resistance was passed. In vain did some strive to obtain that only half of the old regiments should be dismissed, to make room for half of Monk's troops; the movement could no longer be arrested; and Haslerig, in order to baffle his personal enemies, who, he said, that they might cause a quarrel, had suggested to Monk to demand the removal of his regiment, lost no time in soliciting it himself. The order for departure was given; only, as a mark of regret, and to calm the discontent of the soldiers, a month's pay was voted them.

This was not enough to compensate for such an affront, and a very poor amends for the power which these troops had lately exercised, and the pleasures of a London life, to which they were accustomed. At the moment for quitting their quarters, two regiments of infantry mutinied, declaring that they would not consent to depart until they had been paid what was due to them. The cavalry seemed disposed to follow their example. At the same time, the apprentices took arms, and began to parade the city, loudly demanding a free parliament, in the hope that the discontented soldiers would join them in opposing the *Rump*. The news of this outbreak arrived at midnight at Barnet, whence Monk's troops had received orders to march towards the city on the following day. Scott, in alarm, left his house in his nightcap, dressing-gown, and slippers, to go and intreat the general to proceed to London forthwith. "I will answer for this night's dis-

turbance," Monk calmly replied, " and be early enough
in the morning to prevent any mischief." Determined to
prevent the two armies from coming to blows with each
other, he felt little uneasiness about the harm which the
soldiers and the parliament might mutually inflict. He soon
learned that order had been completely restored. The officers
of the mutinous regiments were for the most part new, and
chosen by the parliament; and the soldiers, without leaders,
had allowed themselves to be pacified by the hope of being
paid at their first halting-place. They had marched off
quietly, and a few squadrons of cavalry had easily dispersed
the apprentices. On the next day, the 3rd of February, 1660,
Monk entered London on horseback, at the head of his troops,
accompanied by the commissioners of the *Rump*, his principal
officers, and a rather numerous cavalcade of persons of more
or less rank, who had come to meet him at different parts of
his route. The bells rang as he passed; but the people appeared unenthusiastic, and the troops were astonished at
meeting with so different a reception to that which they had
everywhere received during their march. London had not
yet recovered from the emotion of the previous evening : the
hatred which was felt to the *Rump* disposed many minds in
favour of those who had overthrown it, and against those
who had restored it; and Monk's soldiers, emaciated and
fatigued by their long and painful march, were a poor substitute, in the eyes of the people, for Cromwell's brilliant and
daring army, which had so long held sway over the country.
The procession marched towards the residence of the Speaker
of the parliament. He had not yet returned from the House,
but they met him soon afterwards in his carriage, with the
mace, the emblem of his sovereignty. The general dismounted from his horse, and complimented him in a few
words ; after which he proceeded to Whitehall, where a
lodging had been assigned him in the apartments of the Prince
of Wales.

The next day, Monk, whom the parliament had appointed
a member of the Council of State, which was charged with
the executive power, was invited to assume his seat therein,
and take the oath of abjuration of royalty. Seven members
of the council had refused to take it. Monk said that he
could not in conscience decide until he had heard the reasons
of both parties, and desired that they might be discussed in a

conference; adding that his army felt great delicacy with regard
to oaths, and that he could not bind himself by this one before
he had informed it of his intention. The struggle was beginning
again: it was now his object gradually to render his army
hostile to that parliament which it had come to support. On
the second day, Monk, summoned to Westminster to receive
the thanks of the parliament, declined to sit down upon the
arm-chair which had been placed for him at the bar, and
standing up, with his arm resting merely upon the back of the
chair, he gave the parliament, in the most modest terms, and
with the most submissive tone, a series of counsels, which his
position rendered very much like orders. He represented
the inconvenience of multiplying oaths and engagements;
insisted upon their removing from public employments all
Cavaliers and fanatics—a name which the sectaries, whom
Cromwell had made the instruments of his power, had never
before heard openly applied to themselves. He related how,
when assailed upon his journey by a multitude of petitions,
expressing the wish to behold the termination of the session
of parliament, he had replied that it was his duty to preserve
the parliament from all violence; pacifying them, however,
by the promise which the parliament had itself given of
speedily putting an end to its power. He spoke of Scotland
and of Ireland; neglected none of the points which he thought
it necessary to settle without delay; and displeased many
persons, who, however, did not dare to show that they were
offended, so great need had they of holding fast to the last
hope.

It was not yet time to disabuse them; and yet it was
becoming difficult to deceive them any longer. Now placed
upon the stage, and surrounded on all sides by impatient
spectators, Monk could no longer make use of his favourite
resource of silence. Exposed to suspicion if he did not
openly declare his intentions, his taciturnity ceased to be a
sufficient disguise, and falsehood became necessary. He
adopted this new course of action with all the indifference of
a soldier, who considers lying a mere stratagem of war. His
pledges daily became more positive. He said to Ludlow,
" We must live and die for and with a commonwealth;" and
declared that, notwithstanding his respect for the parliament,
he would never allow the re-admission of any one of the
excluded members. He calmed the irritation of the turbu-

lent Haslerig, who was greatly incensed because the Speaker had treated Monk as a general, instead of calling him Commissioner Monk; dissipated the constantly reviving fears of Scott, and staggered the most resolute distrust by the solemnity of his protestations. Admiral Lawson, who felt little confidence in Monk's principles, said to Ludlow, as he left the house, " The Levite and the priest have passed by and would not help us; I hope we have now found the Samaritan who will save us." At the same time, Mrs. Monk, whom he directed to receive the wives of the members of parliament, overwhelmed them with the attentions of her talkative civility; and with a politeness which, in the eyes of the London ladies, savoured somewhat of vulgarity, she herself poured out wine for them, and went to fetch the sweetmeats which it was then the custom to offer to visitors.

These demonstrations did not, however, shake the confidence which the city had resolved to repose in Monk. His friends and confidants zealously laboured to maintain it. His officers, who were most of them natives of London, diffused among their families and acquaintances the most favourable ideas concerning the general who had restored them to their homes. The people felt a liking for his soldiers, who were modest, orderly, and peaceable, who paid with punctuality, and caused neither disturbance nor fear. The apprentices began to have strong suspicions of the attachment of the Scottish army to the parliament which it had restored. Cries of " A free parliament! Down with the *Rump!*" began to break out in all quarters, and were scarcely repressed, and almost authorized, by the acquiescence of the city magistrates. At length the common council, losing all patience, refused to levy a tax which the *Rump* had attempted to impose upon it; and voted, on the 8th of February, that no more should be collected until the nation was represented by a freely-elected parliament.

The Council of State hastily assembled to deliberate on the measures which they should take against such an act of rebellion. There were two parties in the council: the more moderate ventured to speak only of the danger of the enterprise; Scott opposed and pacified them: " Monk," said he, " has pronounced against the insolence of the city, and has declared that he will defend the parliament." Being invited to attend the council, Monk found that they had already settled the matter, and that orders to compel the city to obedience were already signed and addressed to the seven commissioners who had been appointed to the government of the army. He had to choose one of three things—either to let the measure be executed by some one else and thus nullify himself; or to oppose it, and compromise himself; or to undertake it, and remain the master. Whether by instinct, or by predetermination, he joined the extreme party, exaggerated the necessity for rigorous measures, offered to do what was required, and answered for his success. At length, it was agreed that on the next day he should enter the city with his army, to demolish the gates and portcullises; to remove and break the chains which blocked up the entrance to the streets, as well as the posts to which they were fastened; to arrest eleven of the most resolute and influential members of the common council; and to quarter his troops in the city, until it should return to its obedience. He returned at two o'clock in the morning to his house, where his friends and domestics were waiting for him in the greatest anxiety. Some days before, they had been informed that Scott's son had confided to the man in whose house he lodged that a plan had been formed, and would soon be executed, for imprisoning Monk in the Tower, and instituting against him a criminal process, by means of which they would speedily get rid of him. His friends thought him lost, but when they saw him return, their grief quickly changed its object. In consternation at the order which Monk had received, and at his resolution to execute it, they vainly sought to dissuade him from his purpose; but he remained inflexible, retired to escape from their importunities, and was just going to bed, when those councillors of state who, like himself, had refused to take the oath of abjuration, arrived to endeavour to divert him from his resolution. Profiting by the lateness of the hour, he would hardly listen to them, and they were obliged to retire.

Monk could not hesitate. His own safety, which had been in danger ever since Sir George Booth's insurrection, was daily becoming more precarious. The disclosures made by Scott's son, even had they merely indicated the fleeting ideas of a moment of ill-humour and suspicion, warned him of the dangers by which he was surrounded; and if the parliament

plucked up courage to accuse him, he was not altogether sure
that his army would disbelieve the accusation. But the service which he was about to render the *Rump* could not fail
to remove, at least for some time, every pretext for distrust;
and perhaps he thought it would be advantageous to take
possession of the city in the name of the parliament, that he
might afterwards dispose of it at his will. The next morning,
on the 9th of February, 1660, without giving any explanation
to any one, and before there existed in the city the slightest
suspicion of what was contemplated, Monk entered it at the
head of his troops, stationed his detachments at their different
posts, and established himself in a tavern in the neighbourhood of Guildhall. Surprised at this military parade, the
citizens fluctuated between alarm and confidence, and awaited
with anxiety the termination of this strange scene. For a
moment the report spread that Monk had declared for the
king; but this error was not of long duration, and indignation soon succeeded to surprise. The army resented his
conduct as much as the citizens. The superior officers, when
Monk communicated to them the orders which they were to
execute, exclaimed against an act of such ingratitude towards
the city, refused to lend themselves to it, and tendered their
resignation. The general, while listening to them, chewed
his tobacco, and knit his brows; he saw that events were
ripening, and learned how much he might risk. "What!
will you not obey the parliament?" he asked them , in an
abrupt tone, and with a gloomy look; and it was clear that
his ill-temper was not directed against them. They withdrew; and Monk only pursued more vigorously those measures which could not fail soon to turn against his adversaries.
Upon the refusal of the superior officers, the duty was
entrusted to the subalterns. No sooner had the work commenced, than a kind of stupor seized the inhabitants of the
city. Their ideas became confused; they did not know what
to believe, and could understand nothing of what they saw.
"Is this," they said, " that Monk that would bring in the king?
This is a Scottish devil. To what shall we come?" In
terror they beheld the men who were most beloved in the
city arrested and conducted to the Tower. Surprise had
banished all ideas of resistance ; the people ran in alarm
through the streets; and one might have fancied oneself in a
a town just taken by storm. The parliamentary party

triumphed, and Haslerig exclaimed: "Now, George, we have thee for ever, body and soul!"

The principal men of the city, however, had not yet lost courage: uncertain as to what to think, they went to Monk, and endeavoured to treat with him on a footing of good-will. They offered him a dinner in the name of the city; he declined, and still retained a gloomy and severe countenance. From all quarters, the most notable citizens came to complain, some in a moderate tone, and others with vehemence, of the indignity of such an affront. Monk was astonished at the warmth of their resentment, and the menaces of their despair; then, towards the end of the day, tired of the part he was playing, or thinking he had done enough, or fearing that it might be dangerous to do more, he gave orders to suspend operations, although only the chains and posts had as yet been removed, and wrote to the parliament that he was in want of tools, as those which he had brought were worn out; but that he did not think it necessary to do any thing further, that the city appeared disposed to submit, and that a common council had been summoned for the next day, when he did not doubt that resolutions of obedience would be passed. From this moment, softening his manner, he received with his accustomed courtesy all the citizens who, during the evening, flocked around him, excusing himself to some by the urgency of the orders which had been given him, and letting others perceive that he entertained a deeper design; "in short," says Whitelocke, "hardly giving the same account to two men."

His language was of little importance; he was the most powerful; they were obliged to believe in him, in order to hope anything at all. Colonel Morley offered to place the Tower in his hands, and promised him the assistance of his own regiment and that of his brother-in-law, Colonel Fagg. The parliament had heard the report of the council of state upon what had passed in the morning. The moderate party were silent in consternation; the triumphant republicans had just voted Monk fifty pounds sterling for the expenses of his table, when they received the letter which he had written from the city. A feeling of violent displeasure seized the victorious party; the common council had been forbidden to meet; its dissolution was now directed; the order for the demolition of the gates and chains was renewed with greater strictness, and Monk thought that obedience was still his safest course. The same operations were, therefore, recommenced on the morning of the next day; but under an altogether different aspect; the citizens began to resume confidence; the soldiers, now better informed and under little constraint, openly expressed their indignation at the part they were obliged to enact; each blow was accompanied by expressions of anger and insult against those who had given the orders; and the officers, picking up the fragments of the chains, said: "These are the medals and chains of gold that the parliament promised us at Coldstream."

Towards the evening, the troops evacuated the city, and Monk returned to Whitehall. Fresh reason for discontent was thereby excited against him in Westminster; he had received orders to remain in the city, and the parliament began to feel astonished at being so ill obeyed. The republican party was not yet undeceived as to its victory. Resolved to push it still further, it had caused a petition to be presented to the *Rump*, on that very morning, praying that none should be admitted to public employments who had not taken the oath of abjuration of royalty; and this petition had been favourably received. At the same time, Lambert's adherents began to raise their heads; Lambert himself was undisturbed in London, although he had received orders to depart. Monk's army became disturbed and excited; events seemed about to take their course independently of the hand which had directed them up to that point with so much circumspection. It was necessary to yield to them, in order to continue to direct them. On the evening of the 10th, a certain number of officers of his army came to Monk, and told him that, after having dishonoured them in the eyes of the nation, the parliament only sought an opportunity for sacrificing them to Lambert's army; and that it was time to break with a party which, by employing them in its service, had deprived them of all their old friends, without supplying them with new ones. Monk appeared to hesitate, or perhaps really did hesitate, to decide so quickly; at length, after some entreaty, he yielded; and, acting for the first time without the co-operation of the other commissioners, who, with himself, had been entrusted with the government of the army, he gave orders for his troops to march the next day towards the city, directed that his principal officers should be summoned to Whitehall at an early hour, and during the night had a letter to the parliament prepared. The next day, the officers, whom he had convoked, signed it after him. This letter, perhaps the harshest ever received by that parliament which had already endured so many insults, began by stating the grievances of the army, amongst which the city affair figured in the first rank; and ended by declaring that it was indispensable that, before the following Friday, the parliament should have issued its writs for the election of the members destined to fill the vacant seats, and that it should fix the 6th of May as the day upon which it would finally retire, to give place to a freely-elected parliament. As soon as the letter had been dispatched, Monk placed himself at the head of his troops, and marched towards Finsbury Fields, from whence he sent to the lord-mayor, to request him to provide quarters for his soldiers. Surprised, and not very much pleased at this fresh visit, the lord-mayor, Sir Thomas Allen, evading a direct answer, sent to invite the general to dine with him, when they would confer about his request. Monk went to him immediately, and noticing the constrained behaviour of the lord-mayor, said, " How is this? your lordship does not receive me in the same manner as usually!" The lord-mayor alleged as his reason the occurrences of the preceding days. " My return," said Monk, " is for the very purpose of rectifying all our misunderstandings; will your lordship convoke a common council this afternoon in the Guildhall?" This was the very council which the parliament had dissolved. Nothing further was required to indicate his change of purpose. Besides, some friends had been informed of it, and the general's suite, which had entered London, had begun to diffuse new hopes. After a splendid dinner, which announced a day of rejoicing, Monk was preparing to accompany the lord-mayor to Guildhall—where the common council had hastened to assemble, and which was surrounded on every side by the people, impatient for the news they were about to learn—when the arrival of two parliamentary commissioners, Scott and Robinson, was announced.

Upon receiving Monk's letter, the parliament, informed of his march to the city, and of the movement which seemed to be preparing there, had judged that it was most urgent to induce him to withdraw from thence, if it were possible, and had sent to him Scott and Robinson, thinking they would be

agreeable to him, with orders to inform him that at the moment
when his letter arrived, the parliament was engaged in considering the measures to be taken for the elections, and that
they would settle that affair as soon as they had regulated
certain others. The two deputies were to press Monk to
return to Whitehall, where he would be able to satisfy himself more closely, and with his own eyes, of the good intentions of the parliament; whereas by remaining in the city,
he exposed the fidelity of his soldiers to the influence of a
disaffected populace. Scott and Robinson, who had with
difficulty got through the crowd, which felt alarmed at their
arrival, were furthermore obliged, in order to reach the
general, to pass through the midst of a hundred of those
officers who had lately appeared so respectful, but who now,
rude and irritated, loaded them with reproaches of ingratitude
and perfidy. Monk received them coldly, answered them by
bitter complaints of the conduct of the parliament, and, when
the commissioners desired to express to him the fears which
were occasioned them by his sojourn in the city, "If the
parliament," said he, "will do as I desire them in my letter,
they have nothing to fear; all will go well." The deputies
were in consternation; Scott himself, for the first time,
acknowledged that no further reliance could be placed upon
Monk's respect for the parliament. Both retired, and had
great difficulty in escaping from the search of the apprentices,
who examined every carriage, and covered with mud those in
which they suspected the commissioners might be.

Monk, on his part, proceeded to Guildhall, and without
appearing embarrassed at disavowing his previous conduct,
spoke as follows: "The last time I was among you, it was
for the most disagreeable matter I have been engaged in
during my whole life; the execution of which was as contrary
to my own inclinations as to the obligations I have to the
city. But since what is done, is done, I can only be sorry
for those affronts which have been put upon you against my
will; and I have come to London, in order to render a fuller
answer to your letters than I was able to do at Morpeth,
where I received them. In compliance with your desires, I
have this morning written to the parliament to issue out their
writs, within seven days, for filling up the vacant seats; and
to fix on the 6th of May next as the day on which to dissolve;
and thereby to give place to a full and free parliament. In

the interim, I am resolved to quarter my army in the city,
and to continue myself among you, till I see the contents of
my letter, and the desires of the city and nation, accomplished."

At these words, the hall re-echoed with acclamations; and
the people answered them from without. Already Monk's
letter to the parliament had been printed, and distributed in
the city; the bells began to ring; bonfires were lighted, and,
in joy at the dissolution of the *Rump*, all the hind-quarters of
animals which were to be found in the butchers' shops were
thrown into them. Lodgings were assigned to the soldiers,
who up to that time had remained under arms, and without
taking any food. All their wants were forthwith supplied;
wine and money was lavished upon them, and the whole
night was passed in a disorderly freedom, which continually
increasing, began soon to threaten the safety of the vanquished. It was in accordance with neither Monk's taste
nor intentions to leave the field open to popular violence;
and these dangerous outbreaks were repressed. Precautions
taken at the post-offices prevented the transmission from
London on the next day of any other accounts but those
likely to favour the propagation of the movement; and over
the whole face of England, on the arrival of the mails, the
Rump was burnt by the youth of the towns, who, on this
occasion, received but little blame from sensible people.

The 11th of February, 1660, was one of those decisive days
which Providence marks as final, and which men on reaching
boast of having brought about. "This was a trick you
knew not of," said Monk laughingly to Price, when after
his success the latter respectfully inquired what motive could
have induced him to undertake the unworthy part which he
had played for some hours. Monk himself had, probably,
neither combined nor foreseen long beforehand the effect of
that series of treacheries, which were continually ready, and
so admirably adapted to the moment which rendered them
useful ; but he had learned daily, and with a singular mixture
of artifice and good sense, of prudence and boldness, how to
unravel and complete the movement which was destined to
carry him forward to his object. He became, from that day
forth, the sole power in England, for there no longer existed
in the country any other force, but that of public opinion,
which Monk had first taken as his ally. It still remained

to be seen what use he would make of his power. Careful
to maintain uncertainty, he always reserved to himself liberty
to decide, at the last moment, for one of the two parties to
which he had supplied equal motives for hope and fear. For
a long while the excluded members had been begging him to
favour their re-admission into the parliament; he was engaged
in secret negotiations with them, whilst he continued to protest loudly against their pretensions. He had at first been
inclined to take some more direct way for arriving at his
definitive object, which now, in his opinion at least, had ceased
to be problematical, but public opinion proved to him the
necessity for another circuit. The excluded members, for the
most part, possessed of that importance which attaches to long
participation in public affairs, influential in their counties, and
restored to popularity by their disgrace, would have had it in
their power to embarrass any man who attempted to pass
them over. Their re-admission was moreover the only prompt
means of modifying this parliament, which, though now quite
prostrate, might rally, and inflict a dangerous blow in its
dying moments. On the 11th of February, the moderate
party in the House had tried to profit so far by the consternation of their adversaries as to obtain that, instead of renewing Monk's appointment as one of the seven commissioners of
the army, they should name him general-in-chief. This proposition had awakened the energy of despair among the vanquished; they had voted that the number of the Commissioners
should be reduced to five, that three of them should suffice to
constitute a quorum, and some one having demanded that
Monk must necessarily belong to this quorum, the motion had
been rejected; so that the majority of this commission, who
belonged to the party opposed to Monk, might, at any given
moment, use against him the military authority with which
they were invested. Arms taken from the government arse-
nals had been distributed amongst the numerous sectaries
whom their common interests rallied against a Presbyterian
parliament. Lambert's army began to move about in its
quarters; and even Monk's troops, who, during the last few
days, had again been called upon to deliberate and act according to their own opinions, seemed to assume a less submissive
aspect. It was necessary, before the spirit of resistance had
begun to appear, to hasten to deprive it of all support; and if
the officers could not be induced to consent to the re-admission

of the excluded members into the parliament, they must at
least be prevented from opposing it.

The head-quarters still remained in the city; vainly had
Monk been urged to return to Whitehall, and resume his seat
at the council of state; he had distinctly refused to do so
until the oath of abjuration had been dispensed with; and as
for his stay in the city, it was indispensable, he said, to allay
disquietude, and restrain the discontent excited by the distribution of arms among the fanatics. There, receiving daily
visits from such of the excluded members as happened to be in
London,—Annesley, Pierrepont, Holles, Grimstone,—Monk
admitted them to interviews in presence of several of his
officers; and nearly all of them, surprised at the moderation
and urbanity of those men whom they had ever before regarded
as enemies, yielded to the ascendancy which is exercised by
superior powers over coarse and unreflecting minds, seldom
accustomed to distinguish their opinions from their impressions. At these conferences there were present some of the
moderate members of the *Rump*, who were disposed, if they
could venture to do it without endangering any vital point, to
favour the re-admission of the excluded members. Monk, in
his conversations with Haslerig, Ludlow, and their adherents,
always declared such a measure impossible; but to free himself, as he said, from the importunities of Annesley and Pierrepont, he requested Scott and Haslerig to consent to a parley.
The latter were no longer in a condition to refuse to negotiate,
they repaired to Monk's lodging, where they found twelve of
the excluded members and several officers. At Annesley's
first words Haslerig grew angry, and would have left the room.
Monk prevented him, saying, with a laugh, " Let Annesley
alone; I know well how to moderate him." Haslerig resumed
his seat; and Annesley continued without further interruption. Haslerig, unable to endure any more, at length went out;
and, after his departure, the conference was brought to a
peaceable conclusion. The great objection urged by the
members of the *Rump* was the disorder which would be caused
by revoking all the sales of property, and all the acts which
had been passed in favour of liberty of conscience. The
excluded members promised not to interfere with these interests, or to turn their attention to the past, but to labour only
to establish the future well-being of the country upon more
lawful and secure foundations. No disagreement took place,

yet no decision was arrived at; and, when the sitting was over, the officers, left alone with their general, declared that, in order to come to any determination, something more than mere conferences was required. Two or three, however, less headstrong than the others, demanded that the excluded members should bind themselves to pass a fresh vote in parliament for a republican government, and the confirmation of the sales of the public lands. In opposition to this, it was urged that the writs for the elections would necessarily be issued in the name of the " keepers of the liberties of the commonwealth of England ;" and that the sales of land had been confirmed as much as it was possible for them to be. In order not to leave time for new objections to be raised, all the excluded members who were in London met together on the evening of the 20th of February, and made a definitive arrangement by promising, amongst other things, to vote, immediately after their readmission, that a tax should be levied sufficient to discharge the pay of the troops, including their arrears; to convoke a new parliament for the 20th of April following, and to appoint Monk commander-in-chief of the forces both by land and sea. On his part he promised to require nothing more from them during the continuance of their session; and they separated, leaving it to a future period, which seemed very near at hand, to unfold what it was not yet necessary to discuss.

Early the next morning Monk left the city, and transferred his head-quarters again to Whitehall, where he had directed the excluded members to meet him. On their arrival, there was read to them in his name a speech which, he said, he had committed to writing through fear of being misunderstood or deceived, as had recently been the case. Reasons against the restoration of the Stuarts and of episcopacy, and upon the necessity of their either withdrawing and preparing the way for new parliaments, or of convoking one for the 20th of April, constituted the principal topics of this speech, which, on the same day, was printed by Monk's orders, with the title of a *Declaration*, and afterwards sent by him to the parliament, in the form of a letter*. Thus fortified, Monk directed his guards to conduct the excluded members to Westminster,

---

* Lord Wharncliffe is of opinion that the speech published by Monk's orders was not the same as that which he had had read to the excluded members.

where several officers were at the door to receive them. Some
of the peers wished to profit by this opportunity to resume
possession of their house,* but the time had not yet arrived;
the attempt had been foreseen, and Colonel Miller, in command of the guard on duty there, who had his orders, executed
them like a soldier, in such a manner as to give great offence
to those who had endeavoured to obtain admission.

, The republicans, still blind and deceived, were completely
ignorant of what was in preparation. On beholding the men,
whom they had expelled so long before, return and take their
seats in their old places, their uneasiness was equal to their
anger. Several, and amongst others Haslerig, left the house,
exclaiming that Monk was a traitor. Ludlow refused to enter
it again; resolved not to sanction, as he said, the illegal
readmission of one hundred and fifty-seven members who had
been expelled by seventy others, legally elected, and constituting a number competent to vote. Some of the malcontents
subsequently returned; others remained, for they began to
take thought for the morrow on their own account. The
parliament, thus completed, hastened to fulfil its promise, by
appointing Monk general-in-chief of the troops in England,
Scotland, and Ireland. The command of the fleet was given
to Admiral Montague; and as if to assert its independence,
the convocation of the new parliament was postponed to the
25th of April. It was voted that its chains and gates should
be restored to the city; the liberation of those persons who
had been imprisoned on account of the transactions of the
9th of February was ordered, and an inquiry was instituted
into the causes of the arrest of Sir George Booth. On the
same day Monk caused a letter to be drawn up, addressed to
all the garrisons, that it might be sent off on the next morning, simultaneously with the news of the restoration of the
excluded members, explaining the necessity which had compelled him to place the parliament in a condition to vote the
taxes requisite for the payment of the troops, and concluding
with the strictest injunctions to watch and publicly denounce
all who should attempt to stir in favour of Charles Stuart.

* William, Earl of Strafford, son of the great Earl of Strafford, who
was executed in 1641, appeared on this day as one of the most eager to
resume possession of his seat in the House of Lords. He died, without
issue, in 1695, and the title, won by his illustrious father, thus became
extinct.

Everything, however, was in obedience to those beginnings of re-action which are followed up and favoured by a government ready to alter its course. A new Council of State had been appointed, composed principally of the members who had just been readmitted into the parliament. Lambert was arrested; Sir George Booth and his adherents were released, without submitting to the conditions which had at first been required of them; and the Bishop of Ely, after twenty years of imprisonment in the Tower, was permitted once more to behold the light of liberty. The militia was organized, and its command entrusted to men whose views could no longer be doubtful. Old officers were dismissed, and replaced by royalist gentlemen. Haslerig and several of his party went once more to see Monk, and remind him of his promises; upon which the general, taking off his glove, placed his hand in that of Haslerig, and said, in a solemn tone, " I protest to you that I will oppose with my utmost strength the setting up of Charles Stuart, and the government of a single person, or a house of peers." He added immediately, "What then have I done to give you disquiet in bringing these members into the house? If others cut off the king's head, and that justly, are not these the same that brought him to the scaffold?" Haslerig left him once more reassured. Ludlow, no less ardent, attempted to raise a conspiracy, trusting to the promise which Colonel Morley had made to give him possession of the Tower; but, fortunately for himself, he met with a thousand hindrances to the execution of his project. Overton was striving to induce Hull and some other English garrisons to revolt; but, being prevented in time, he gave up the town to Colonel Fairfax, who was appointed to supersede him. The Irish army had declared for a free and full parliament; and Scotland, where Morgan had received fresh reinforcements, was ready to obey at the slightest signal.

The republicans, reduced to Monk's fidelity as their last resource, neglected no means to restrain and secure him. A few days after the restoration of the excluded members, they had proposed to give in perpetuity, to Monk and his heirs, the royal domain of Hampton Court, which Oliver Cromwell had reserved to himself out of the property of the crown. The restored members had not dared to oppose this grant; but Monk himself, embarrassed by such a favour, declared that the house was too large for him. His friends, therefore, on

G 2

the third reading of the bill, proposed to substitute for the title of proprietor that of steward for life of the domains and manors of Hampton Court; and Monk, by accepting a gratuity of twenty thousand pounds sterling instead of the property, clearly showed the slight dependence which he placed upon the stability of the then existing government. The alarm was great among those persons whose fortune and existence were connected with it. The army especially observed with uneasiness that it was imperceptibly withdrawn from all participation in public affairs, and felt that whatever was done without it, might be done against it. Already had the officers complained of the plan for the reorganization of the militia, and particularly that this duty had been entrusted to men notoriously infected with royalism. Monk appeared surprised; and wishing, as he said, to have the thing explained to him, he demanded that a conference should be held between his officers and some members of the different parties in the parliament. Several were held, in which Haslerig supported the wishes of the army, and Monk the supremacy of the parliament. Finally, when the dispute had lasted a considerable time, they declared that it was time to have done with these parleys, which had become useless, as the result could not be brought before the parliament, now on the point of dissolution.

Men do not quietly consent to continue without any influence over the decision of their own fate. The republican party, considering its defeat inevitable, was desirous to take part in it, were it only in the hope of rendering its downfall more gentle. It felt less alarmed at a new protectorate than at the restoration of royalty. Those men especially who, either in the parliament or in the army, had contributed to the death of the king, would have esteemed themselves fortunate if they could at any price have got rid of his son. They resolved, therefore, to offer Monk the supreme power for himself; and the parliament having, on the 13th of March, 1660, effaced from its journals the pledge of fidelity to the republic in its actually existing form, without a king or house of lords, Scott, Haslerig, and some others, members of parliament, or officers of their party, approached Monk at Whitehall, whither he had come to attend the Council of State, and began by expressing to him the apprehensions excited in them by the proceedings of the parliament, and particularly by the vote of the preceding evening. " It is visible enough," said Haslerig, "that they want to bring back the king." "If he were to come in again, general," said another, "you would be lost; you would have contributed too much to it to make it possible to reward you; you would be put out of the way, like Stanley, when he placed Henry VII. on the throne. It was but a frivolous pretext: but his real crime was an excess of merit." Monk showed little emotion at this. "I have not either," said he, "been much pleased with the late unnecessary vote. I have mentioned it to some of the most reasonable; and they have told me that since the case of finally modelling the form of government was referred to the parliament now about to meet, they would not encroach on its authority, nor encumber themselves with an engagement made beforehand. But there is nothing to be afraid of," he added; "the writs of election will fix the limits of discussion." His audience did not appear satisfied. "The people," they said, "are always bad judges of what is best for themselves; and therefore, since a single person is necessary, there cannot be one fitter than yourself for the office; and in this we have good grounds to believe all the good people of the nation will concur with us." Monk continued calm. "I have the example of Cromwell before me," he said; "and I have reasons to avoid the rock on which that family was split." It was urged in reply that Cromwell had usurped the sovereignty against the will of the army and of the respectable classes. "You, on the contrary," they said, "will have their unanimous consent, and under what name and title you please to accept it." "We will give you a hundred thousand signatures," cried Haselrig, with his usual impetuosity. Monk persevered in rejecting with indifference the offer of a fortune which was not solid enough to tempt him. His ambition was neither unbounded nor unreflecting, and he possessed no quality likely to make him disregard the precautions of good sense and the calculations of probability. The baffled negotiators left him, in order, without loss of time, to try other measures, and Monk repaired to the Council. It is said that his brother-in-law, Clarges, to whom the republican deputies had at first made some overtures, seeing them call afterwards upon Monk, and apparently presuming upon the intentions of the general, had immediately informed Sir Anthony Ashley Cooper, who was then in the Council, of what was going forward. Eager to find their enemies in fault, the presbyterian members of the Council had

decided that, as soon as the conference was over, and the
general had taken his seat, Clarges should be summoned to
depose what he knew, and that Monk should be requested to
give the necessary information to prevent such mischievous
designs. Monk arrived, and thought that there was no reason
for such agitation. "It is true," he said, "that some have
been with me to be resolved in scruples concerning the past
transactions of parliament, but they went away well satisfied."
It was equally opposed to Monk's inclinations to destroy
persons from whom he had nothing to fear, to break with
those whom he still hoped to deceive, and to hasten by
violence that which might be peaceably accomplished.

One more effort to thwart his views was, however, in preparation for him. When the conference broke up, the principal leaders among the officers had met together, and determined
to compel the parliament, before its dissolution, to constitute
the country a republic for evermore, in such a manner that no
subsequent parliament could have any right to alter that form
of government. A declaration was accordingly drawn up for
the army to sign; and the meeting separated after having
appointed a general council of officers for the next day.

Clarges was with Monk when they brought him the declaration for his signature at the head of the army. He saw that
the general was disquieted, and proposed to adjourn its signature till the next day, at the general council of officers. Monk
was present; and Colonel Okey, one of the king's judges, and
more bold in action than able in discussion, spoke in the name
of the malcontents, saying that the good old cause was lost,
unless a remedy were applied, and that the surest remedy
would be the proposed declaration. "If the parliament should
refuse to subscribe it," he added, "we must take such other
methods to save the nation as the Lord may inspire." Clarges,
who followed him, asked his auditors what means they could
use for imposing their will upon the parliament, which was
strong in the concurrence of the people, who would not fail to
assist it with all their strength in repelling the despotism of
the army. "To succeed formerly," he said, "you found it
necessary to impeach at different times, fourteen of its members,
and to exclude two hundred; and now what will it do if you
should resort to violence again? It will dissolve itself without
issuing the writs of election, and will leave you without a
government and without pay; unless, after having treated as

you have with Richard Cromwell, you should have recourse to his favour. There would be one resource remaining," added he, turning towards Monk, " that his Excellency should undertake the government, but he has refused."

" I had rather be torn to pieces by wild horses," said Monk, " than be so treacherous to the country's freedom."

Clarges resumed; a reply ensued; the debate was long and animated; and Monk, according to his custom, taking up the discussion when the embarrassment felt at answering questions began to leave the field open to authority, gravely admonished the officers of their duty, prohibited such assemblies for the future, remarked who were the boldest and most rebellious, that he might quickly get rid of them, and the next day wrote to the parliament.

The approaching dissolution was about to free him from several of those parties which he had to humour or to lead. None at this moment gave him more trouble than his own, or at least, that which he had temporarily adopted for the purpose of arriving at his definitive object. With satisfaction he beheld the Presbyterians daily advancing further and further along the road to royalty; but he would neither advance along with them, nor on any account allow them to get before him. The difficulty was to keep them back. Once restored to possession of their seats in parliament, the leaders of this party, consulting their own interest as well as that of the country, had thought that they ought to make use of this restoration to power in order to secure their share in the great event which was in preparation, and to establish finally, by the restoration of the king, the essential results of the revolution they had accomplished twenty years before. Prynne was the first to say, " If the king must come in, it is safest for those who made war against his father that he should come in by their votes;" and with this view, many seemed disposed still to defer the dissolution of the parliament. Monk, careful to prevent any fresh combination, actively employed for that purpose during three weeks the dexterity of Morrice, his surest and most useful confidant among the Presbyterians. Silence was imposed on Prynne; the severe republicanism of the general repressed all premature confidence; the most obstinate were reminded of their promise and of the necessity of a dissolution. At length they decided upon it on the 16th of March, and that

Long Parliament which, though convoked for the purpose of supporting liberty, had practised itself in the exercise of tyranny, found that, after having survived so many defeats, it did not possess sufficient strength to exist a few weeks longer, and complete its work. In vain did they, by a vote passed before their separation, prohibit the employment of any officer unless he declared in writing that he approved of the war waged by the Houses against the late king; in vain did they desire to exclude from the next parliament those who had taken arms against the one about to dissolve, together with their sons: the *Rump* was no longer in a condition to survive, and no one was deceived with regard to the nullity of its testamentary dispositions.

On the day of its last sitting, Monk, urged no doubt by his officers, wrote to the House to request it to revoke the act concerning the militia, the organization of which being entrusted, as he said, to suspected persons, might, in spite of the army, lead to the return of Charles Stuart. Some, disturbed and embarrassed by this message, apprehended a snare; but others had received secret instructions. Prynne went immediately to the printer to hasten the publication of the act, which, in fact, appeared the same evening; and a large number of gentlemen set out for their counties to realize the fears of the army.

Everything was rapidly advancing towards an appointed end. Royalist opinions, if they did not yet pretend to rule, at least were no longer concealed. The people, always bolder than their leaders, because they reflect less, and have much less to lose, cried out on all sides, "The king! the king!" Royalist songs echoed freely through the streets; and two days before the dissolution of the parliament, a painter, accompanied by some soldiers*, came to the Royal Exchange,

---

* This fact is related by Clarendon in a letter to Sir Henry Bennet, dated April 10, 1660, (Clarendon, *State Papers*, vol. iii., p. 725,) and confirmed by Pepys, in his *Journal*, from 1659 to 1669, (vol. i., p. 46, of the 8vo edition of 1828); but neither make any mention of soldiers having taken part in it, and Lord Wharncliffe, in his translation of this work, asks how I managed to introduce them into my narrative, and endeavours to explain the addition by a mistake. The presence of the soldiers is expressly mentioned in a letter addressed from London to M. de Brienne, on the 25th of March, 1660, which runs thus: " I will tell you an occurrence, which I saw with my own eyes; namely that, about seven o'clock in the evening, some soldiers, accompanied by other

ad effaced the inscription placed there on the spot formerly occupied by the statue of Charles I.: *Exit tyrannus, regum ultimus, anno libertatis Angliæ restitutæ primo, annoque Domini*, 1648. No one asked the painter for his orders, and no one doubted that they came from the general. As for Monk, always the same, that is to say, constant in varying his language according to the person to whom he spoke, he gave no ground for forming a definite opinion regarding himself. The movement went on increasing, while the man who directed it did not seem to advance a single step, unless it were to recede the instant after. One of the king's agents in London, wrote on the 10th of March: " On Wednesday Monk declared himself to my friend that he would acquiesce in the judgment of the parliament both in relation to your Majesty and the House of Lords; and yet yesterday he told him, in great passion, he would spend the last drop of his blood, rather than the Stuarts should ever come into England; though I hear from other hands he was in good temper again the same night." His slightest expressions, carefully gathered up, and repeated from mouth to mouth, only served, by their variety, to maintain the prevailing uncertainty. It was known, however, that Mrs. Monk, in her impertinent gaiety, had asked Hugh Peters, who had grown rich upon confiscated property, if he were not for the restoration; and little Kit, her son, being tormented with questions and presents, had avowed that one morning, in bed, his father and mother had talked about the return of the king. The Republicans could deceive themselves no longer. Henry Martin, with whom Monk had been intimate, one day asked him what he finally intended to establish. " A commonwealth," said Monk; " I have always desired it, and desire it still." " I ought to

persons, came to the Exchange, with ladders, and then effaced what was written beneath the statue of the defunct king, to the effect that he, that is, his statue, had been cast out of that place, as a tyrant. This action took place very peaceably, and with great acclamations of the people there assembled, who were in great numbers, indeed, almost as many as if it had been at full Exchange ; moreover bonfires were lighted in the midst of the said Exchange, where the shouts were of nothing but *Long live the King !* as I remained till the last moment to try and learn something worthy of being communicated to you." (*Archives des Affaires Etrangères de France;* Angleterre, reg. 58, No. 135.) This narrative of an eye-witness is moreover conformable to probability. If, as all who mention this fact seem to think, Monk was no stranger to it, there is reason to believe that he sent some soldiers to accompany the painter who was directed to efface the inscription.

believe your excellency," replied Martin; " but will you give me leave to tell you a story? A city tailor was met one evening in the country with implements of husbandry, and was asked what he was going to do with them. 'To take measure for a new suit,' he answered. 'What! with a spade and a pickaxe.' 'Yes, these are the measures used now-a-days.'"

However, that which alarmed some was not sufficient entirely to satisfy others. The cavaliers did not yet dare to approach Monk; one alone, Sir John Greenville, knew that he was accessible, and began to seek for means of communicating with him.

The very evening of the return of the excluded members to Westminster, Monk went to establish himself at St. James's, where, at a greater distance from the city and less exposed to observation, he expected to be able to conduct with more secresy the new affairs in which he foresaw he would soon have to engage. Sir John, in quality of a relation, often went to see him there, like many others; but he was always received in the midst of a crowd, and vainly prolonged his visits beyond their due limits, in order to contrive to be alone with the general. As soon, however, as the apartments began to empty, and Monk foresaw a *tête-à-tête*, he used to say, " It is late; good night, cousin;" or else, at other times, he was called away by business. Desperate at not being able to find a favourable moment, Sir John at length addressed himself to Morrice, one of the restored members, a friend and relation of the general, who lodged in his house, and who, since the affair had increased, had supplied the place of the political committee and of Chaplain Gumble, in its confidential direction. Greenville conjured him to obtain for him an interview with the general, to whom he had to communicate some matters of the highest importance. Monk sent him word to confide them to Morrice. Greenville absolutely refused to divulge them to any other than the general himself, and declared that, if he could not obtain an audience, he would speak to him the very next time he met him, no matter in what place. Monk gave him an interview on the next evening in Morrice's apartments. Greenville began by congratulating himself that he was at length able to place in the general's hands a deposit which had been for a long while in his own, and to fulfil the orders of the king his master

egarding him; at the same time he presented to him the
etters written by the king at the time of Sir George Booth's
nsurrection. Monk, casting his eye over the papers, receded
few steps, and asked his cousin, in an angry tone, how it
vas that he had not feared the danger to which he exposed
imself by undertaking such a mission to him. Greenville
eplied that he willingly ran the risk, as he had often done
efore, for the king's service. " But in this case, general,"
e added, " I am the more encouraged in regard that your
Excellency cannot but remember the message you received in
Scotland by your brother."

Disguise was no longer seasonable: Monk suddenly
changed his tactics, and advancing with open arms towards
his cousin, thanked him for having kept his secret so well,
and assured him that there was no man in the world with
whom he would have preferred to treat in this great matter.
He then read the letter. " I cannot," wrote the king,
' think you wish me ill, for you have no reason so to do; and
the good I expect from you will bring so great a benefit to
your country and to yourself, that I cannot think you will
decline my interest." In the powers given to Greenville,
Charles thus expressed himself: " I am confident that George
Monk can have no malice in his heart against me, nor hath
done anything against me which I cannot easily pardon; and
it is in his power to do me so great service, that I cannot
easily reward; but I will do all I can."

He then authorized Greenville to treat with Monk on the
conditions which the general should ask, either for himself, or
for his army, the command of which the king promised to
continue to him. According to his secret instructions, however, Greenville was to confine himself to promising, in the
king's name, a grant of one hundred thousand pounds sterling,
to be distributed between Monk and his army, as the general
should please. But since the 21st of July, 1659, when these
letters were dated, times and situations had greatly changed;
and Greenville did not think he exceeded his powers by
offering to Monk, with the title of Lord High Constable, the
choice of any of the great offices of the crown. Too well
assured of his market to spoil it by making his bargains too
soon, Monk refused every condition for himself; and, lying
even when he was treating sincerely, he disavowed, in terms
of the most humble and submissive loyalty, all that part of

his past conduct which had been in oppositi
which, he said, he had always preserved in
have never," added he, " been in a condit
king till the present time; I am now not on
his commands, but to sacrifice my life an
service." And then calling Morrice, " This
said, " shall witness my promise." Everyth
arranged between them. Monk was dispe
least as much for his country as for himsel
intentions of his Majesty; but in order
obstacle to his return, he required, first, a
except for those whom the parliament shoul
to exclude; secondly, a promise to conse
judged necessary to confirm the sales of]
the payment of the arrears of the army; t]
liberty of conscience, as far as it should be
the tranquillity of the civil government. :
treated the king at once to leave the Spanisl
whence, when he was once acknowleged as
he would probably find it difficult to esca
troublesome condition. Monk, not wishing
letter to the king, requested Sir John to be]
of his answer, read his instructions to him :
then burnt the paper, exacting a promise t
re-write it, but confide the secret of his m
alone, without any intermediary. This prec
had particular reference to the Chancellor
of Monk's special antipathy, which he ampl
    Greenville made his passage in the same
Mordaunt, who was going to Brussels on his
who had not the slightest suspicion of the mi
ling companion. Every one at that moment
his own account, and to secure his own sh;
sequel. There was not a single interest, or
which had not its agent at Brussels or
ordinarily in both quarters at once; all se
and deceive each other; and entertaining
without being able to divine the views of
Among the most important, Hollis and the
leaders, on some occasions, flattered then
were directing the course of events. The
sincere and patriotic, but their obstinacy ha

from experience. After so many reverses which they had
not been able to avoid, and after so long impotency, they
thought they were restored by events, which had taken their
course independently of them, to the same point which they
had occupied before their fall; and did not perceive that the
power just restored to them was but one of the first steps in
the reaction which raised them up for a moment, in order
subsequently to proceed much farther. In possession of the
government, which was then entirely vested in the Council
of State, these former leaders of the Long Parliament, considered themselves still the masters of the country, of whose
opinions they were ignorant, and whose army was against
them, and they prepared to contest with the king the conditions which they desired to impose upon his restoration.
These were rigorous; his father had accepted them only when
reduced to the last extremity, when the moment for obtaining
them had already elapsed. What appeared to them their
greatest difficulty was to gain Monk, who daily grew more
strict in his presbyterian republicanism. It only remained
for him to deceive these men, and to this task he diligently
applied himself. They approached him with caution, and
were at first repulsed by his unshakeable attachment to the
republic. Their arguments, however, were powerful; the
men by whom he was addressed were worthy of consideration; he appeared to allow himself to be convinced; then he
suddenly hesitated, and seemed to fear to meddle with a difficult negociation, which it would be better to leave to the
parliament. The Presbyterians attached only the more value
to the victory which Monk seemed to grant them with regret;
and a messenger was hastily despatched on their part to
inform Charles II. that they had at length induced the general
to recognize him upon the same conditions as had been proposed to his father in the Isle of Wight, but upon those conditions alone. They conjured his majesty not to reject this
means, perhaps the only one, of regaining his crown. Sir
John Greenville had just arrived, and had seen the king,
when the presbyterian envoy brought these propositions.
Charles and his advisers, whom, notwithstanding Monk's
repugnance, it had been found necessary to inform of the
general's offers, experienced a moment's uneasiness; but,
being quickly reassured by Sir John, the king smiled at the
tardy service which Monk's messenger had just taught him

to despise, and refused to enter into negociations with the Presbyterian leaders.

All were anxious, at this last moment, to regain the time they had lost, and were alarmed at seeing events hasten onwards before they had taken their position in them. The French ambassador, M. de Bourdeaux, entreated Clarges, with whom he had some acquaintance, to procure him an interview with the general. Clarges called upon him, and the ambassador, having taken him alone into his study, commenced, with his Gascon vivacity, a conversation, the burden of which Clarges willingly allowed him to bear. "The general," said Bourdeaux, "has some great design; everybody can see that this is the case. Without any doubt, he wishes either to make himself king, or to bring the king back. Well! in either of these cases, no one can render him greater service than myself. An Englishman would compromise his safety, but I run no risk. But what I propose is not merely in reference to myself, but to the cardinal. He will be delighted to have the honour of his Excellency's friendship, and is ready to assist him in all his plans." Then resuming his own discourse, he added, "I would not say which would be best for the general, whether to establish the sovereignty of his own family, or to bring back the king. Both would raise him to great honour, and the latter would not be less glorious because it is more easy. But in every case, he may reckon upon the cardinal; for you should know, the cardinal was the close ally of Oliver Cromwell. Cromwell did not seize upon the sovereignty without his concurrence, and it was the cardinal who directed him, step by step, in all that business." And continuing to offer his services, he assured Clarges that, if it were the general's intention to restore the king, the best thing he could do would be to advise Charles to pass over into France, and place the whole negociation in the cardinal's hands, in which case there was nothing that Monk might not expect from the court of France.

Clarges received these overtures coldly, and, anxious to relieve himself from a useless and dangerous confidence, declared himself much too insignificant a person to enter into such great affairs, and contented himself with assuring the ambassador that his brother-in-law had no such ambition for himself, and was even determined to submit to the decision of parliament. "Your parliaments," said Bourdeaux, "are such

multuary and changeable assemblies, that no reliance can
e placed upon them. If the general does not do what I
advise, they may hurry him into some measure which will
ruin both himself and his family." Clarges withdrew, promising the ambassador that he would sound his brother-in-law
in order to ascertain how far such a proposition could be
opened to him, and would inform Bourdeaux thereof, that he
might treat in his own person, knowing, as he said, enough
English to make himself understood by the general, who did
not know a word of French.

Monk would listen to nothing of the kind; but, so as not
to offend the ambassador, he consented to receive from him a
simple visit which, on Bourdeaux's part, was confined to
general offers of service, and ended in nothing more.[*]

Charles, by the advice of Monk, had immediately left Brussels, and taken up his residence at Breda, from whence
Greenville soon after set out again, bearing letters and declarations from the king, addressed to the new parliament,
the army, and the city; others were for Monk, of which one
in particular was written with Charles's own hand; a commission of generalissimo of all the forces by sea and land in the
three kingdoms; and finally, a blank appointment of a secretary of state, which Monk destined for Morrice. But for the
moment, keeping only the king's letter, and true to his habits
of precaution, Monk would not take possession of the other
papers, which Greenville locked up, until the day arrived for
using them, in a secret receptacle which had long been appropriated to such purposes.

The month of April was approaching, and with it the elec-

* This is the account which Clarges himself gives of his and Monk's
relations with the French ambassador, in the *Continuation of Baker's
Chronicle*, of which he is the author. This account is completed and
almost entirely confirmed by the documents published at the end of this
volume, which contain the whole of that part of M. de Bourdeaux's
correspondence with Cardinal Mazarin and M. de Brienne, which has
reference to the progressive conduct of Monk, both in Scotland and England, from the death of Cromwell to the restoration of Charles II. The
publication of these documents relieves me from the necessity of again
refuting the anecdote related by Locke, on the authority of his friend
Ashley Cooper, the celebrated Earl of Shaftesbury, who boasted of having
baffled Monk in his design for assuming the sovereignty of England, with
the aid of Cardinal Mazarin. It will there be seen with what good reason
Hume, Hallam, and Lord Wharncliffe, have refused credence to this

tions. No doubt was felt as to the majority which they would indicate; and Monk, who refused no request, having written to the municipal officers of Bridgnorth to recommend to the choice of the electors Thurloe, Cromwell's secretary, they replied, that they had not ventured to make use of his letter, and added, "We jointly conclude that the general's writing would be so far from speeding your election, that his standing would not have carried his own at Bridgnorth, except he would have declared himself absolutely for the king, and without any such terms as they hear are about to be offered to him." The militia was organized everywhere in the same spirit. The army, discontented but subdued, offered no further resistance, although it was still held in dread. Severe penalties were enacted against any who should endeavour to excite disturbance or alarm among the soldiers or officers, and ten pounds reward was promised to any who should give information of such an attempt. The officers were induced to sign an address to the general, in which they promised, for themselves and their soldiers, to render implicit obedience to the orders of his Excellency, of the Council of State, or of the parliament about to assemble; and to abstain from all meetings and remonstrances. Those who refused were cashiered, and replaced by royalist gentlemen or nobles.

All seemed ready, and they waited for nothing more than the arrival of the 25th of April, 1660, the day on which the new parliament was to open, when it was ascertained that Lambert had escaped from the Tower. He was missed for a short time in London, where he concealed himself at first; but they soon learned that he had arrived in the county of Warwick, where he had previously appointed some of his friends to meet him, and was beginning to draw around him the troops of the neighbourhood. The disaffection appeared general; to make sure of the soldiers, an attempt was made to oblige them to sign the address of the officers, but they deserted in troops. The army in London alone remained entire, or at least had lost only two soldiers; but it would not have been safe to trust to it; and Monk was careful to be dissuaded from the resolution which he had announced of marching in person against Lambert. He sent Ingoldsby in pursuit of him, and remained in London, where the crisis required other cares of him. Resuming, in this moment of danger, the decision which was natural to him whenever it

ecame necessary, he sent for Sir John Greenville, and said
him, "If Ingoldsby is beaten, and the army revolts to
ambert, I shall declare for the king, publish my commission,
d raise all the royalists to arms in England, Scotland, and
eland; be in readiness to receive orders." It was at this
me also that he wrote to the king to thank him, and to
gage himself formally in his service. His letter was forth-
ith conveyed to Breda, by Bernard Greenville, Sir John's
ephew.

On Easter eve, the 21st of April, 1660,* four days after
ambert's escape, Ingoldsby was at Northampton, with what-
ver faithful troops he could muster, the county militia, and a
undred royalist gentlemen, under the command of the Earl of
xeter. The next day they marched on Daventry, where they
ad learned that Lambert was, surrounded by people who had
astily gathered round him; a disorderly troop, who were still
ndecided as to the course they were to take. Whilst Lam-
ert was retreating, and Ingoldsby hastening to come up with
im, some scouts met Captain Haslerig, son of Sir Arthur,
ho, either discontented with Lambert, or despairing of the
uccess of his undertaking, had just quitted him, but alone, and
eaving his company with Lambert. He was taken prisoner,
ut afterwards released upon promising to make his company
esert. At length they overtook Lambert, posted behind a
mall brook, which separated the two armies. He had only
even ill-formed squadrons of cavalry, and a very small body
f infantry. Some of his men advanced, but singly, and
ithout any intention of making an attack. Ingoldsby forbade
is men to quit their ranks, and mingling with those of Lam-
ert in the garb of a simple horse-soldier, and without being
ecognized by any of them, he spoke to them of the danger
o which they were exposing themselves. Twenty-five of
Lambert's cavalry, with a quartermaster at their head, passed
over to Ingoldsby's side, but refused to take part with him:
they were deprived for the moment of their horses and arms,
which were afterwards returned to them. This sort of parley
lasted for nearly four hours; neither were desirous to begin
the action. At length, Ingoldsby gave the order to charge;
his infantry fired, and wounded two of Lambert's men. The
latter advanced at a quick march, ordering his men not to fire
until they were close upon the enemy; but when they arrived

* According to the old style, still in use in England at that period.

H

within pistol shot, they halted and lowerec
company of Haslerig's son passed over
under the command of a quartermaster, wl
he had directed to execute the promised tre
another company followed his example.
irresolution which precedes flight, Ingoldsb
bert and said, "You are my prisoner."
treat, but was refused; he then solicited
escape. "Do what you like with us, but
Axtell, Okey, and the other officers who stil
"What will it serve you to destroy him !
Lambert put his horse to a gallop to esca]
dashing off in pursuit, soon was close u]
hand, calling on him to surrender, or he
Lambert had too often failed of success,
sustained him; his courage abandoned
vainly demanded his liberty, then surr
brought back to the Tower, in less than a '
quitted it.

About this time, several officers came tc
to accomplish themselves what he was abor
them. They engaged to make the army de
and thus to render their part more honoura
dition better. Monk no longer had nee(
not wish to make use of them; so he r(
declarations of submission to the decision
At length, on the 25th of April, the parl
House of Lords also assembled, compose
former members who had sat until the
Monk received from both houses the title
of the land forces, and also solemn tha
replied by recommending them to attend les:
the future. The 1st of May was the day fiɔ
upon the government which it was best tc
nations; and, in the interval. Greenville pɪ
the door of the Council of State, demand
General Monk. Monk, informed of this
one of the members of the council, went ɪ
Greenville gave into his hands the official
been addressed to him by the king, to be
cated to the Council of State and the off

* Monk took his seat as member for D

Monk scarcely looked at Greenville, cast his eyes upon the seal of the letter, feigned surprise, and returned to the council, commanding Greenville, in a severe tone, to wait, and ordering his guards to watch that he did not escape. The council, more surprised than Monk had been, had an animated debate about the course they should take in reference to this letter. Birch, in alarm, protested that he had informed the general without suspecting anything of the kind. Greenville, on being introduced and questioned as to the origin of this letter, replied that he had received it at Breda, from the king his master. They were about to commit him to prison, but Monk answered for his safe-keeping, and it was decided that the letter should not be opened until the meeting of parliament.

At length, on the 1st of May, 1660, this long-continued farce, which had ceased to deceive any one, came to an end. Greenville appeared successively before both houses, as bearer of the king's letters and of the declaration of Breda, drawn up on the basis which Monk had indicated in his instructions to Sir John. The king, immediately acknowledged with eagerness in both houses, was proclaimed at London on the 8th of May, in the midst of shouts, bonfires, and all that uproar of victory which, for a moment, scarcely permits us to suspect the existence of a vanquished and discontented party. But already Monk, anxious to get rid of the burden with which he felt himself laden, had despatched Sir John Greenville back to Breda. By his exertions, the sum of fifty thousand pounds sterling, which had been voted to the king for the expenses of his journey home, and borrowed of the city, was furnished within two days; ten thousand in gold, and the rest in bills of exchange on Amsterdam, payable at sight. Greenville took them with him, and Monk secretly directed Admiral Montague to cruise off the coast of Holland with his fleet. The parliamentary commissioners, when they set out on the 13th of May, to convey to the king the vote of the two houses, were rather offended because the Admiral had only left a convoy to escort them across; and, in order to pacify their ill-humour, it was necessary to produce an antedated order from the king to Montague. As early as the 5th of May, an address from the army had been entrusted to Clarges to convey it to Breda, from whence he returned with the title of Sir Thomas Clarges, the first

H 2

of the numerous promotions which were to accompany the restoration.

Every one now hurried towards the new fountain of fortune. The roads were thronged by Cavaliers, hastening to demand the reward of their constant services; by royalists of a later date, who were anxious to make the king forget their recent adhesion to his cause; and by men of all sorts, who had a fortune either to make or to preserve. Every imagination was in movement, every hope was entertained, and every means attempted. Ten thousand pounds sterling were offered to Monk, in exchange for the appointment of a Secretary of State, reserved for Morrice. Lenthall, the speaker of the Long Parliament, who had made his power subservient to his fortune, sent the king a present of three thousand pounds sterling, with a request that he would continue him in the office of Master of the Rolls; but he soon after learned that he had been already deprived of it, and that the place was promised to another. In this active competition, everything became a marketable commodity; and cupidity, party spirit, and popular improvidence, vied with each other in setting aside all regard for public interests, so as to give free course to the torrent of new pretensions which was on the point of inundating all beside. In vain did the men who had begun the revolution and had just contributed towards terminating it, although rather more quickly than they wished, endeavour to obtain some of its fruits; in vain, while representing the return of the king as the restoration of the laws and liberties of the land, did they attempt to call attention to the securities of which these stood in need; their efforts daily became more timid, and their own passions plunged them into the current which they wished to stem. Hollis, Maynard, Annesley, and all the leaders of the Presbyterian party had, like the Cavaliers, personal injuries to avenge; and of all the feelings which then animated them, the most violent was their hatred for the republicans and Independents, those last enemies, whose outrages they had so recently experienced. By their carefulness to renounce all connexion with them, they deprived themselves of the remnant of strength which might have been afforded them by a conquered but obstinate party, and retained only power enough to crush it. The Presbyterians, in the early days of the restoration, distinguished themselves only by their bitterness in pursuing the

regicides, and by the futility of their efforts to rally a party
in opposition to the reaction of the Cavaliers. Some few,
during the time which elapsed before the return of the king,
attempted to induce Monk to use, for the liberty of his
country, the power which still remained entire in his hands.
But it was difficult to offer him advantages superior to those
which he had reason to expect from complete submission, and
which he had determined to deserve. He resolutely declined
their proposal, and in the House of Commons opposed every
attempt of the kind. At the time of the debate on the instructions to the commissioners whom the parliament was to
send to the king, he had strongly advised them to merit his
majesty's favour by trusting to his generosity. The commissioners were despatched with no other mission than to invite
Charles to resume his royal functions; and the opposition,
thus informed of its powerlessness, had consented to avoid
the danger of a useless defence. But, when from general
they passed to personal questions, when they began to deliberate upon the list of those who were to be excepted from
the amnesty, Monk, as little influenced by party hatred as by
patriotic anxiety, strove to moderate the fury of vengeance
or of meanness, and succeeded in reducing the exceptions to
seven instead of the larger number which his opponents
endeavoured to make it. He had, it it said, pledged himself
to obtain an absolute pardon; and when Lord Say spoke to
him of the necessity for an act of amnesty, from which some
of the king's judges alone should be excepted, " Not a man!"
Monk exclaimed in an angry tone; "for if I should suffer
such a thing, I should be the arrantest rogue that ever lived."
"Let me be damned body and soul," likewise said Sir Anthony
Ashley Cooper to Colonel Hutchinson, "if ever I see a hair of
any man's head touched, or a penny of any man's estate, upon
this quarrel." But supposing that such declarations were
sincere, Monk and Ashley Cooper soon found themselves in
presence of a reaction too powerful to be resisted by their
cautious and egotistical wisdom.*

* Monk had been reproached for his acquiescence in the vengeance
taken at the restoration, and especially for his participation in the condemnation of the regicides who were excepted from the amnesty. My
excellent friend, Mr. Hallam, with his ordinary impartiality and high-
mindedness, has reduced this accusation to its true worth. "Monk," he
says, "certainly did not satisfy the king, even in his first promises of
support, when he advised an absolute indemnity, and the preservation of

Monk had not yet reached his last sacrifice. On the 23rd of May he received the king on the beach at Dover; and, notwithstanding the grateful reception given him by Charles, who embraced him, and called him his father, such was the humility of his deportment at this first meeting, that, according to the panegyric of one of his biographers, he seemed rather to be imploring his pardon than receiving thanks. However, in spite of these external forms, Monk was conscious of the authority vested in him by his position, and while relinquishing the power into hands so unused to its management, he thought it right to give some advice, or at least, some information. Accordingly, when on the same day the king had arrived at Canterbury, and was delivered from the selfish crowds to whose demands rather than congratulations he had to listen, Monk entered, and, without imagining that he ought to excuse himself to his majesty for so great presumption, told him that he thought he could not do him a better service than by pointing out to him the men who were best adapted to serve the country. He thereupon presented him with a list which Charles, in surprise and alarm, put into his pocket, without venturing to discuss a piece of advice which he was disposed to consider in the light of an order. Terrified by the torrent of royalist pretensions which had just burst upon him without either modesty or restraint, he thought himself besieged at the same time by the exactions of the revolutionists, and a prey to all the embarrassments of royalty. Hyde, afterwards Lord Clarendon, arrived; and Charles read the list with him. The chancellor was in even greater consternation than his master; for there

actual interests in the lands of the crown and church. In the first debates on the bill of indemnity, when the case of the regicides came into discussion, he pressed for the smallest number of exceptions from pardon." (Hallam, Constitutional History of England, ed. 1827, vol. ii. p. 161.) Lord Wharncliffe, in his translation of this work, adopts and confirms Mr. Hallam's opinion by many irrefragable proofs. Among others, he quotes Ludlow, who, in spite of his hatred of Monk, specially says, in reference to the debate which arose in the parliament on the question of the regicides, " Some proposed that all might be excepted, others would be contented with twenty, and many with thirteen; but Monk, who had betrayed them all, expressing his desires to be for moderation, they were reduced to nine, which that *boute-feu* Prynne, contrary to the orders of the House, undertook to name. Yet I was so far obliged to him, that my name was not upon his list. Monk at last prevailed with the House to bring the number to seven." (Ludlow's Memoirs, ed. 1751, p. 346.)

as not a man upon this list who had served the king, except the Marquis of Hertford and the Earl of Southampton, both nown to have no need of recommendation to his favour. Beside them were placed the Presbyterian leaders, and almost all the notable men of that national party which had been ormed, during the early years of the revolution, by a hatred of despotism and the necessity of resisting it. Monk had added to these a few of those men whom the course of events ad raised from an inferior station to the management of public affairs. These men had governed the country; they ad shared in its fortunes; they knew it, and were known by t. It was to these, in his opinion, that a new king should address himself, as he was surrounded by advisers as foreign as himself to the interests which had for twenty years agitated the nation. Monk did not anticipate the ridiculous difficulties which would enter into public affairs in the train of a king and court which had long been absent from the country, any more than the king and his minister, Hyde, could comprehend a man so careless of what was due to royalty, and of the ancient usages of the monarchy. But they still feared the old general; and the greater was his power, the more did it appear dangerous either to submit to it or to reject it. After some deliberation, it was resolved that the chancellor should seek out Morrice, Monk's principal confidant, with whom he was not yet acquainted, and represent to him the great discredit which such strange selections would do to the king's judgment or dignity, if it were imagined that he had allowed them to be imposed upon him by the general. Morrice, surprised in his turn at the effect produced by this list, which had been written by his hand, and probably at his suggestion, protested the innocence of the general's intentions, and speedily returned, on his part, to beg the king to attach no importance to these recommendations, the majority of which were destined merely to fulfil Monk's word towards persons to whom he had not been able to avoid promising his services; and to protest that from that day forth his chief desire, in all the propositions which he might venture to make, would be, that they should in no wise interfere with his majesty's freedom of choice. Charles and his minister began to perceive that they had not much to fear from a tutelage which had at first alarmed them. Meanwhile a little more knowledge of the country soon taught them to pay less attention to their aversions; and Monk's recommendation obtained all the weight that could be granted it by aristocratic pride and the dignity of royal rancour. As for himself, he received on the following day the order of the garter, and was admitted to the council; soon after, he was invested with the rank of lieutenant-general of the armies of the three kingdoms; and from among the offices under the crown offered to his choice he took that of Master of the Horse. Lastly, he was created Duke of Albemarle, Earl of, Torrington, Baron Monk of Potheridge, Beauchamp, and Tees; and to the pensions annexed by his letters patent* to these high dignities, there was added a perpetual annuity of seven thousand pounds sterling, in lands taken from the domains of the crown; while, in order to retain him more continually near the king, he was appointed a gentleman of the bedchamber.

Charles had strongly felt the necessity of attaching to himself the only man capable of restraining the army, which was still on foot, and more discontented than ever. Amid the din of acclamations, the review of the troops at Blackheath had not presented a very encouraging aspect. Those veteran soldiers, and those officers of the old army, whose frozen demeanour announced only obedience, presented to the king's eyes an immoveable but irreconcileable body, which could awake from its coldness only to turn against him. In reality this apparent calmness concealed a deep-seated anger, which daily became more violent. An army which had ever been victorious, and but lately had ruled the country, did not yield without murmuring to that vanquished party which suddenly reappeared on all sides to occupy the first ranks. The soldiers thought they were humiliated, and felt they were disdained. The aristocratic pride of that swarm of royalists, who had been transformed by the restoration into courtiers, thrust back into obscurity those men who had lately obtained or hoped for some renown. The free and noisy manners of the Cavaliers was an insult to the rather awkward stiffness of

---

* In these letters patent, which were drawn up in Latin, after a pompous enumeration of all the services rendered by Monk to England and to the king, we read this characteristic phrase : " Hæc omnia, prudentiâ ac felicitate summâ, *victor sine sanguine*, perfecit.'' It was Monk's dominant thought to accomplish the restoration of the monarchy *without bloodshed ;* and this phrase in his letters-patent proves that this was also his principal title to glory in the eyes of his contemporaries.

ic old officers, who felt embarrassed by their situation, and restrained by their habits; and the disorders gloried in by these licentious youths were the scandal of a party who were edate even in their follies. On the day of the king's arrival, ome one, seeing a brilliant troop of volunteers pass by, who, ecorated with feathers and scarfs, were going to meet him, aid to Monk, "You had none of these at Coldstream; but rasshoppers and butterflies never come abroad in frosty eather." The soldiers held in contempt the new officers rhom Monk during the last few days had placed at the head f several regiments. Their meetings became frequent, and heir language violent; but Monk overawed them, and no eader was in a position to raise against him even an inconsiderable force. The malcontents several times formed plans or assassinating him, or at least were suspected of doing so. Vothing but plots was talked of. Spies were dispersed in all quarters, and paid at once by both parties, whom they betrayed like.

Charles, alarmed at this temper of the troops, and weary of he circumspection he was compelled to use by a power not ret entirely within his hands, longed for the time when he could disband the army; and Monk, ready for everything, carefully avoided any suspicion of the least repugnance to a measure which would put an end to his importance. At ength the disbanding was voted, and accomplished without difficulty. Before it was quite completed, there broke out in London the insurrection of Venner, a fifth-monarchy-man, who, at the head of some fifty enthusiasts, rushed at midnight into the street, crying as a watchword, "God and Gideon," and calling to the citizens, in the full persuasion that all would follow him, and re-establish the reign of the Lord. The boldness of these men and their heroic resistance struck the court with alarm, and appeared to the general's friends a good reason why he should at least demand the maintenance of his regiment of guards, which had shown great zeal on the occasion. He refused to concur in a demand which he said would be wrongly interpreted; and all they could obtain from him was, that he would not oppose their solicitations, which, in fact, saved the regiment. Monk declared to the parliament that he had already given his orders that, until the disbanding was entirely accomplished, no soldier should be enlisted into any corps, and no officers commissioned, to replace those who might die

or be discharged.   He obtained, for all those who were disbanded, the right of entering into such commercial corporations
as they might choose.   But though he thus insured to them
some means of subsistence, which they nearly all adopted
with remarkable resignation and fortitude, he could not appease
the bitter feelings of their hearts against a general who had so
ostentatiously renounced them.

After the disbanding of the army, Monk retained no influence beyond that which he derived from his aptitude to
business, and from a devotedness, the humble reserve of which
rendered his counsels as convenient as they might sometimes
be useful.   During the earlier years, his knowledge of men
and things contributed, in as great a degree as his power, to
insure him a considerable share in the government; and the
Secretary of State, Nicolas, a man of business, who had been
attached to his royal masters for thirty years, said, " That if
the general had not been an instrument in the king's restoration, yet he deserved all the bounties his majesty had bestowed
upon him, for his services after the king's return."   He declined no proof of devotedness.   Being appointed one of the
commissioners charged to try the regicides, he did nothing
either to aggravate or to moderate the severity of the prosecutions; and co-operated shortly after in the condemnation of
the Marquis of Argyll, with a disgraceful abandonment of his
own honour.   He felt no partiality for the marquis, whose
skill in intrigue had been constantly employed for the purpose
of disturbing the tranquillity of his administration in Scotland;
and he had injured him more than once with Cromwell.   But
between these two cautious men the mutual wish to do each
other mischief was rarely displayed; and the letters of the
marquis to Monk in particular were full of protestations of
attachment to the government of the Protector.   When, after
the restoration in 1661, Argyll was arrested in London, and
taken back to Scotland, to be there tried on a charge of high
treason, he was accused of participation in the death of
Charles I., and of a formal and active adhesion to Cromwell's
government.   The proofs did not appear sufficient, and the
party who were anxious to destroy Argyll feared they would
lose their victim.   The Earls of Glencairn and Rothes repaired to London with all speed, to excite Monk and Clarendon
in the affair, and deprive the marquis of the support given
him by the Earl of Lauderdale.   The Scottish parliament was

session for the trial, and on the point of proceeding to discuss the evidence, when a loud knock at the door announced some important messenger. It was a courier from London, bearing a packet for the parliament. By the haste of the messenger, who moreover happened to belong to the Campbell clan, it was thought that he brought either a pardon or a reprieve; but when the packet was opened, it was found to contain Argyll's letters to Monk—an evidence of the inefficiency of human prudence. Monk, on being intreated to give them up, had desired to wait until they should appear absolutely necessary; and "having been informed," as he said, of the want of proofs," he had hastened to forward them to the parliament. They dispelled all hesitation. Argyll was condemned on the next day, and Monk received, doubtless with his habitual humility, the congratulations and thanks of the court.*

Henceforward the court was too sure of Monk to think it necessary to treat him with deference. His advice, though generally good, was seldom followed; he withdrew it without ill-temper or persistence, and, though never eager to offer, never refused to give it. Careful not to encroach upon the jurisdiction of others, he took no pains to defend his own against the inroads of any man who was powerful or in favour. His behaviour was that of a courtier who has his fortune to make with everybody; and everybody knew that money could atone for many wrongs, with the Duke of Albemarle. He was even accused of allowing himself to be too easily blinded with regard to the profits derived by his wife from the nomination to appointments in the royal tables, of which he had the disposal. The manners and habits of the duchess, more vulgar and less simple than those of her husband, were the laughing-stock of a witty and jocular court, and cast a shade of ridicule over the life of the old general, which a person held in far greater respect would have found considerable difficulty in resisting.

Though he was always constant in his attendance at the

* Lord Wharncliffe, who had quoted and discussed the various testimonies upon which is based this account of Monk's conduct in Argyll's trial, has attempted, though with some timidity, to lessen their value, and to exculpate, or at least excuse, Monk. But his reasonings do not appear to me conclusive; and the unworthiness of Monk's procedure in this case remains, in my opinion, undeniable.

Privy Council and the House of Lords, Monk was imperceptibly disappearing from public life, when at the end of
1661, he fell dangerously ill. Such had been the strength of
his constitution that, in his younger days, he had been seen,
during a campaign, to recover from the small-pox, almost
without being absent for a single day from his place at the
head of his company. But for some time past he had
appeared to become prematurely feeble, and this first attack
of a disease under which he was destined to sink, a few years
after, left him subject to painful infirmities. Attacked by
asthma, and disposed to lethargy and drowsiness, he seemed,
to have abandoned the activity which was, perhaps, necessary
to him, when an unforeseen occurrence revived the energy
which still lay hid in his heavy and failing body. In 1664,
England declared war against Holland, and the 'Duke of
York, Lord High Admiral, when he left to take command of
the fleet, had placed the administration of the Admiralty in
Monk's hands. He devoted himself to his new employment
with all his natural taste for business; but, almost contem-
poraneously with the war, another scourge had begun its
ravages in London—the plague, which, taken little notice of
at its outset, and suspended by the cold of winter, broke out
in the spring of 1665 with so much violence, that an inex-
pressible terror seized upon all the inhabitants. The rich
fled; the poor died, to the number of from six to ten thousand a-week. The royal family left London; the parliament
was summoned to Oxford; the courts of justice were also
transferred thither; and the greater number of men in
authority abandoned all to escape from contagion. Monk
remained, and having been invested by the king with the
government of the town, he provided for all wants, and
braved all dangers, receiving at any hour and without difficulty all who had business with him; and seconded by the
courageous charity of the Archbishop of Canterbury and the
Earl of Craven, who, like himself, had devoted themselves to
the service of the desolated populace, he established order
amidst this terrible confusion, saved deserted property from
pillage, rescued from famine those unfortunates whose destitution prevented them from going to die of hunger elsewhere,
and was, in fine, the preserver of London. He thus regained
that popularity which he well knew how to deserve whenever,
liberated from all temptation to be complaisant to power, he

ound himself, influenced only by his reason and his love of order, in presence of the rights and wants of men.

In the midst of this activity, new exigencies claimed his assistance. The war with Holland still continued, but the Duke of York was no longer in command of the British forces. After a brilliant affair and a doubtful adventure, he had been withdrawn from command of the fleet, under the pretext of fraternal apprehension of the dangers to which the presumptive heir to the crown was exposed. The Earl of Sandwich, who had succeeded him, had just been disgraced for an irregularity greatly aggravated by the profit which he had derived from it. Admiral Lawson was dead. There remained none but Monk, to whom the honour of the English navy could be confided. The king resolved to divide the command between him and Prince Rupert. Some doubt was felt whether Monk would consent to this association; and Clarendon, who was directed to communicate to him the king's intentions, mentioned them at first with some timidity. Monk, in fact, appeared disturbed and uncertain; he even observed that, if the plague continued, he would, perhaps, be more useful in London than anywhere else. Clarendon insisted; Monk withdrew every objection; and they went together to the king. Monk still retained his thoughtful and embarrassed air, and suddenly said to the chancellor that " he would tell him now what the true cause was that had made that pause in him upon the first discourse of the business, and that it would be necessary for him, after all things should be adjusted with the king. and duke, and Prince Rupert, that what concerned him should still remain a secret, and Prince Rupert be understood to command alone; for if his wife should come to know it before he had by degrees prepared her for it, she would break out into such passions as would be very uneasy to him ; but he would in a short time dispose her well enough: and in the mean time nothing should be omitted on his part that was necessary for the advancement of the service."

His wish was complied with, and his appointment remained for some days a secret; but as soon as it became known, as soon as he was seen, with his quiet and indefatigable activity, surveying the preparations for the cruise, providing rigging, provisions, and ammunition, the sailors came in crowds to offer their services; " for they were sure," they said, " that

honest George would see them well fed and justly paid."
The fleet put to sea at the end of April, 1665, and, one
month afterwards, during three consecutive days, Monk, first
alone, and afterwards in conjunction with Prince Rupert,
engaged the Dutch, under the command of Ruyter, in the
most furious actions ever sustained by either nation. The
issue remained doubtful, although, on the whole, more
unfavourable to the English than to their adversaries; but
Monk's bravery was displayed in so brilliant a manner as to
strike with admiration, and even with some fear, the nearest
spectators.   On the first appearance of the Dutch fleet,
Monk had only a portion of his own with him, and some of
his officers seemed not altogether devoid of doubt with
regard to the consequences of an abrupt engagement: " At
least," said he, " I am sure of one thing, that I will not be
taken;" and, says the young Duke of Buckingham, who
served on board his ship, " when we spied him charging a
very little pistol and putting it in his pocket, we could
imagine no reason for it except his having taken a resolution
of going down into the powder-room to blow up the ship in
case at any time it should be in danger of being taken; and
therefore we, in a laughing way, most meritoriously resolved
to throw him overboard in case we should ever catch him
going down to the powder-room."

After four months' cruise, however, it became necessary
to put back to the coast of England, to refit the disabled
fleet, and Monk was at anchor in St. Helen's Bay, near
Spithead, when he received the news of the terrible fire
which, on the 2nd of September, 1666, reduced nearly the
whole of the city of London to ashes.   The king, the court,
the magistrates, and the people, were all panic-stricken and
stupified; the most absurd suspicions and strangest rumours
were circulated and believed with reference to the causes of
this disaster, and in the midst of the extravagant ravings of
the popular imagination and displeasure, which ascribed all
their misfortunes to the carelessness or incapacity of the
government, the exclamation was heard, " Ah! if old George
had been here, the city would not have been burnt."   The
king hastened to recall him to employ him in repairing the
effects of the catastrophe; and in the following year when
the Dutch, who had learned to despise, if not the English
people, at least their masters, made a descent upon Chatham,

urnt nineteen vessels, and threatened London itself, it was
Monk again who set out immediately, at the head of a few
ompanies, to repel this audacious aggression. The Dutch
e-embarked, but not, however, so soon but that the Duke of
Albemarle, who had advanced to their out-posts, heard their
alls whistle past his ears, One of his officers besought him
o retreat a little. " Sir," said Monk, " if I had been afraid
f bullets, I should have quitted this trade of a soldier long
go."

He had, however, made his last campaign, On his return
rom this expedition, his infirmities, and especially his asthma
nd threatenings of dropsy, redoubled in violence; he felt
imself incapable of exertion, and retired to his property of
New Hall, in Essex, rather to die in the peaceful repose of
he country than with the hope of obtaining any alleviation
f his sufferings. He paid little attention to his physicians,
efused to use their remedies, and having for some years been
melancholy without mentioning it or explaining its causes to
ny one, he merely replied to Gumble, who was still his
haplain, and who exhorted him to take care of his health,
' Why should I desire to live?" However, while at New
Hall, one of his neighbours, formerly an officer in his army,
ecommended him to take some pills, which, it was said,
vere a sovereign cure for dropsy, and which were sold at
Bristol by a man named Salmon, who also had served under
us orders in Scotland as a private soldier. This advice and
emedy from old comrades inspired the old general with more
onfidence than the knowledge of the doctors. He sent for
ome of Salmon's pills, and for some time found them so
)eneficial, that he returned to London towards the end of the
ummer. But not long after his arrival, during the latter
)art of December, 1669, the dropsy made alarming progress,
nd Monk, too intrepid to lose on this occasion his habit of
eeing things as they were, announced himself that he had
)nly a short time to live. One last piece of business he had
much at heart: the marriage of his son Christopher with
Lady Elizabeth Cavendish, grand-daughter of the Duke of
Newcastle. He hastened its completion with the same
ctivity, and the same minute solicitude, that he would have
levoted to it in perfect health, and on the 30th of December
he marriage was actually celebrated in his room, which he
vas no longer able to leave. Nothing thenceforward could

rouse him from his indifference to others as well as to himself; his friends tried to induce him to recommend his family to the favour of the king, who came to see him almost daily. " It is useless," he said; " I do not doubt the kindness of the king for me and mine." He listened apathetically to the discourses of Gumble, who took pains to prepare him for his approaching end, and spoke of his death with great composure to his friends, whom he still continued to receive. At length, on the 3rd of January, 1670, about nine o'clock in the morning, while he was sitting silently in his chair, he sighed, turned his head aside, and expired. He was a man capable of great things, although he possessed no greatness of soul; born at once to command and to serve; sensible, patient, and bold; attached to his own interest, but devoted also, on every great occasion, to his duty as a soldier and an Englishman; and who, devoid of political ambition and with no pretensions to govern his country, was able to recognize and restore to it that government with which it could not dispense.

He was buried at Westminster, among the tombs of the kings, in Henry the Seventh's Chapel. Charles II. in person accompanied his funeral procession. No monument was erected to his memory; the effigy used at his funeral is, however, still in existence, clothed in his armour, and preserved in a wooden case. His son Christopher, after having wasted, in a life of scandalous profligacy, the immense fortune* left him by his father, and lost the credit which he owed to his name, died childless, in 1688, at Jamaica, of which island he was governor.

* Besides his great possessions in landed and personal property, Monk, it is said, left his son 400,000l. sterling in money.

APPENDIX.

(1.)—RICHARD CROMWELL TO MONK.
(With this superscription : *For His Excellency the Lord General Monk.*)

My Lord,   April 18, 1660.

ALTHOUGH I cannot suppose you altogether unacquainted with my present condition, nor insensible to what my friends have represented to you concerning it; but being urged by my present exigencies, and necessitated for some time of late to retire into hiding-places to avoid arrests for debts contracted upon the public account, I have been encouraged from the persuasion I have had of your affection to me, and the opportunities you now have to show me kindness, to add this request to the former solicitations of my friends, that, when the parliament shall be met, you would make use of your interest on my behalf, that I be not left liable to debts which, I am confident, neither God nor conscience can ever reckon mine. I cannot but promise myself that, when it shall be seasonable, I shall not want a faithful friend in you to take effectual care of my concernments; having this persuasion of you, that as I cannot but think myself unworthy of great things, so you will not think me worthy of utter ruin.

My Lord, I am your affectionate friend to serve you,

R. CROMWELL.

(2.)—M. DE BOURDEAUX TO CARDINAL MAZARIN.

My Lord,   London, May 5, 1659.

IF my last letters have not been detained in England, they will have prepared your Eminence to receive without surprise some news of what has happened here since the first of this month. It is true that the evil did not appear so pressing, and that it was still hoped, on that very day, to find some way of accommodation; but the leaders of the army, finding that they were being amused by negociations, whilst the friends of the Protector* were pressing the parlia-

* Richard Cromwell.

I

ment to take resolutions tending to his establishment and
their ruin, judged it fitting to provide for their own safety,
and to do by force what they could not obtain by fair means.
With this intent, on Thursday, at midnight, they placed the
troops under arms in the neighbourhood of Whitehall; and the
principal men among them having met together in St. James's,
without admitting to their council those who were known to
be well intentioned to the court, they sent Major-General
Desborough, with a dozen officers, to demand of the Protector
that he should himself dissolve the parliament on the next
day. These deputies found him with a few officers who were
his friends, and already informed of the resolution taken by
the council of war, but also deprived of the confidence which
he had had in some regiments, all the subordinate officers of
which had abandoned their colonels to join other corps; to
that degree even, that a squadron of cavalry refused to follow
their captain, who was leading them to Whitehall. Although
the Protector was aware of this general alienation, and that
his friends had scarcely been able to find two hundred men,
in all the troops, willing to follow them, he did not cease to
display boldness, and to declare that he would suffer all kinds
of violence rather than grant the request which had been made
to him. This refusal obliged the said General Desborough
to come to threats, and to let him know that he was not in a
position to defer, even for an hour, the resolution which the
army had taken; leaving him, nevertheless, the liberty, if he
would not go in person to dissolve the parliament, to grant a
commission, for that purpose, to some member of his council.
His Highness, seeing the necessity inevitable, and those who
were with him having agreed that they must submit to force,
after having given some signs of his displeasure and repugnance, promised that which he could not refuse. The said
General Desborough and the other deputies retired upon this
promise, and went to await its performance in a neighbouring
house, where the Secretary of State brought to them, between
two and three o'clock in the morning, the orders addressed
to the Keeper of the Seal. In the meanwhile, some companies of cavalry and infantry entered into the courtyard of
Whitehall, and there conducted themselves with considerable
license, especially in the cellars, and there were also many
comings and goings; and they say that it was agreed not
entirely to destroy the Protector, but to let him govern with

the council which will be given to him, without however allowing him to meddle with the army, which remains in London
and near Whitehall, opposite to which there was a body of
guards, who arrested some officers and soldiers, considered
to be partisans of the court, who wished to enter. This great
movement did not prevent the members of parliament from
repairing to Westminster at the accustomed hour; so, when
they were seated, the chief Keeper of the Seals, the president
of the new House, declared the intention of His Highness
and it was resolved to call in the Commons, to read to them
the letters of the great seal announcing the dissolution of the
parliament. But this message being sent to them by the
usher of the black rod, as it had been previously determined not
to receive any message from that chamber, except from one
of its members, and that moreover the invitation was not very
agreeable, after a debate of two hours, it was resolved to
take no notice of it; and to prevent the order of dissolution
being notified to them in some other way, they adjourned
the assembly to this day, and separated immediately. In this
deliberation the violence of the officers of the army was
greatly reprehended; some proposed to declare them all
traitors, and others to request the concurrence of the town of
London, and to assemble there. The Presbyterians, among
others, appeared very animated, and General Fairfax was
malignant. Some republicans also affected discontent. Nevertheless, no conclusion was arrived at; many of the deputies
wishing, and having underhand fomented, the dissolution of
the parliament, because they saw it was too blindly attached
to the interest of the Protector.

    *   *   *   *   *   *

Some also apprehend that the troops in Scotland and Ireland disapprove of the conduct of those in England, and that
my Lord Henry* and General Monk are fomenting division
among them.

(3.)—M. DE BOURDEAUX TO CARDINAL MAZARIN.
MY LORD,   London, May 8, 1659.
    *   *   * You may still wait for the news of the next
post, before you judge of the government which is to be set
up in England, and of the fate of the Protector, to whom

* Henry Cromwell, Richard's younger brother, who commanded in
Ireland.

these divisions leave some hope : if the army of Ireland or of Scotland were to declare in his favour, it would be better founded. The officers here are persuaded that neither the one nor the other, and especially the latter, will take up his quarrel; and, nevertheless, the courtiers expect much from General Monk. * * * *

(4.)—M. DE BOURDEAUX TO CARDINAL MAZARIN.
MY LORD, London, May 12, 1659.
* * * THE sentiments of the troops in Scotland and Ireland will decide the question. It is still spoken about with uncertainty, and no one can yet have received any news, although these last few days a report has been current that my Lord Henry was in the same condition as the Protector, that is, under a species of arrest. The royalists are, meanwhile, full of great hopes, and it is true that a little assistance would be sufficient to secure their success. Some of them flatter themselves that the Protector and his party are not far removed from joining them. * * *

(5.)—M. DE BOURDEAUX TO CARDINAL MAZARIN.
MY LORD, London, August 25, 1659.
* * * THE tranquillity of Scotland is complete, and General Monk has been ordered to send two regiments into England. * * *

(6.)—M. DE BOURDEAUX TO CARDINAL MAZARIN.
MY LORD, London, September 29, 1659.
* * * GENERAL MONK, esteemed one of the best officers in the army, has lately requested permission to retire, under the pretext of business and ill-health, but, in all probability, because he is not well satisfied. His friends have prevented his letter from being read in the parliament, and wish to retain him in the service. * * *

(7.)—M. DE BOURDEAUX TO CARDINAL MAZARIN.
MY LORD, London, October 13, 1659.
* * * THE officers will no longer be dependent upon the parliament, but upon a Council of War : this was the subject of their quarrel with the last Protector, and the cause of his ruin. No doubt is felt but that the troops in Scotland and Ireland enter into the feelings of those in England; and

General Monk has yielded to the request of Lieutenant-General Fleetwood, that he should remain in the service. * *

(8.)—M. DE BOURDEAUX TO CARDINAL MAZARIN.
MY LORD, London, October 20, 1659.
* * * THE republicans have striven all these days to gain over some officers to their side, to make them sign a declaration contrary to that of the Council of War, composed of 230 officers of all ranks; and some, among others the colonels recently restored, have shown themselves sufficiently disposed to disavow the proceedings of the majority. They even reckon upon the army in Scotland, because two days ago General Monk wrote to the parliament that he had prevented the requisition of the Northern brigade from being subscribed by the troops under his command; and it is said that both parties have dispatched messengers into Scotland to gain over this leader, and to get the officers either to approve or disavow the last propositions. * * *

(9.)—M. DE BOURDEAUX TO CARDINAL MAZARIN.
MY LORD, London, October 30, 1659.
THERE is as yet no Government established in England, notwithstanding the attempts which have been made for this long while by the leaders of the army, and some ministers of the Council of State, to agree to one. They had indeed projected to form a secret council, with a senate of seventy, and to recall the parliament to make it authorize this establishment, revoke the acts of the 21st, 22nd, and 23rd of September, provide for the payment of the troops, and pass some regulations. But at the meeting which was held yesterday evening at the house of the Speaker of this body, for the purpose of concerting these propositions with the deputies, before restoring the power into their hands, they could not agree, the greater number refusing to receive orders from the army: already even many of them have retired, as well as nine members of the Council. The others continue to meet: one of their principal cares has been to dispose the judges to perform their functions, and they must sit until the twentieth of next month, parliament having given them commission only until that time. The Council of War has, meanwhile, made Lambert major-general of all the forces, and Colonel Desborough, the uncle of the last Protector, commissary-

general of the cavalry; it has also sent messengers on its
part into Scotland, Ireland, and all the garrisons, to make
sure of the commanders, or to dispose of them. Some doub
whether Generals Monk and Ludlow will change their view
so easily, and there even appears to be considerable difference
of opinion among the officers who are in London; one
party is inclined to maintain the republican government
and opposes the resolutions which Lambert wishes to have
adopted. *   *   *   _____

(10.)—M. DE BOURDEAUX TO CARDINAL MAZARIN.
MY LORD,   London, November 3, 1659.
     *   *   * IT remains for me, in order to satisfy the
wish that your Eminence has to be exactly informed of the state
of England, to report to you that the principal officers of the
army, and some ministers of the Council of State. after different propositions and overtures of accommodation with the
parliament, which met with no success, have at last resolved
on the day before yesterday, to establish a council of twenty-
three persons, of whom ten are colonels, three citizens of
London, and the rest members of the preceding council or of
that of the Protector. Lieutenant-General Fleetwood, Lambert, Desborough, and Sir Harry Vane, are the most distinguished members of this body, and those who apparently will
have all the authority, the others being persons neither possessed of a talent for governing. nor even summoned for that purpose, but only to make up the number. It is said that their
establishment is merely provisional, and until they have chosen
a larger number. This small body might easily continue to
govern, if it is approved of by all the troops; it was to be recognized to-day by the Council of War of the officers who are
in London, and in all probability the others will follow this
example, although Monk, who is not one of these new ministers, has latterly again renewed the assurance of his fidelity
to the parliament, which he believed still existed. and at the
same time replied to Major-General Lambert, that he could
not make the officers under his command subscribe to the
propositions which those in England had presented to the
parliament, as they were more fitted to cause division than to
maintain union in the army. His letters were immediately
published, and seem to have hastened the establishment of
this Senate, in order that the officers in Scotland, seeing a

government constituted and the parliament dissolved, may give up the idea of taking its part. * * *

——————

(11.)—M. DE BOURDEAUX TO CARDINAL MAZARIN.

MY LORD,   London, November 6, 1659.

SINCE the letter which I did myself the honour to write to your Eminence on the 3rd of this month, no great progress has been made in the establishment of the gove nment of England, and we can still speak of it with only very little certainty, since the letters which arrived from Scotland on the evening of the day before yesterday, assure us that General Monk persists in his resolution in favour of the parliament, and that the news of its dissolution had no sooner reached him than he assembled the officers of his troops, declared to them his intentions, and, having found that their opinions were conformable to his own, ordered them to hold themselves in readiness to march. It is even said that he arrested some Anabaptist officers less inclined to follow him than to accommo- date themselves to the desires of the army. This information caused the despatch from hence yesterday morning of his brother-in-law and a colonel with some propositions, and in the evening another messenger was sent to declare to him that it had been determined to give him battle if he cannot be brought to hear reason; it has already been even proposed to go and meet him, and decide the quarrel promptly; but he is too far advanced to draw back, and threats do not seem to be able to alarm him, as he is a very determined man. His troops may be more tractable, and prefer reconciliation to the uncertain success of a battle; this is also the principal reliance of the army in England. * * * * The cabal of the Millenarians prevails in the army, among whom Mr. Lambert is greatly decried for having no religion, or show of it, in which last alone he differs from the most of them. His reputation still maintains him in credit in the minds of the soldiers, and most honest persons in the army; and the number of these being small, his position is tolerably precarious, as well as is that of the republic, the forces of which are divided into two parties, some being friends of the parliament, and the others of those who dissolved it. These last are again very different in their sentiments. The Millenarians and Anabaptists wish to keep the government to themselves, and Fleetwood inclines to their side; Lambert and his faction, perceiving that they are lost if the executive authority falls into the hands of these sectaries, and being no less ambitious, are striving to render themselves the masters. Until this moment this has only been done by means of intrigue; but if the army of Scotland came to an accommodation, probably there would occur some other division, and many imagine that Lambert will at length, if he loses all hope of prevailing, treat with the king of England. Others think that Monk is not less disposed to take this side, and even that, unless he had already entered into some engagement, he would not so freely have declared himself, or have left Scotland, his departure with the troops giving that nation every facility for revolt. It is further remarked that his last letter speaks, indeed, of shedding his blood, even to the last drop, for the parliament of England, but without indicating whether he means that one which has just been dissolved. These are reflections upon which no very positive measures should be taken, and we can only state that circumstances remain very favourable for the return of the prince to that army, whose leaders are least opposed to a monarchical government, and who, as they took no part in the death of the defunct king, will more easily put confidence in the promises which may be made them on the part of the present sovereign. Their greatest difficulty would be, if they were willing to embrace his cause, to influence in his favour the troops under their command, and this is not to be hoped for until they are thoroughly engaged, the one against the other; to which they have hitherto shown so much repugnance, that a reconciliation might even take place' at the expense of their leaders.

(12.)—M. DE BOURDEAUX TO CARDINAL MAZARIN.

MY LORD,   London, November, 10, 1659.
    I SHALL continue to inform your Eminence of the sequel of the divisions of England. Since the letter which I did myself the honour to write to you by the preceding post, news have come from Scotland which confirm the report that Monk persists in his intention to re-establish the parliament; that he has arrested all the officers of his troops who held other views, even a colonel who had been sent to him from hence; that the garrisons of Berwick, Carlisle, and another fortified

castle on the frontier of England have declared for him; and that finally, he is taking every measure to strengthen himself. Lieutenant-General Fleetwood has, at the same time, received his declaration in conformity to these advices; he has also written to the churches in the same terms, promising them assistance for the maintenance of their prerogatives. This proceeding has caused the Council of War to come to a resolution to send an army of eight thousand men to give him battle, or at least to arrest his progress; and on this very day there have left London a body of infantry and cavalry drawn from the veteran troops, whose place will be supplied by new levies. Major-General Lambert will again command in this expedition, it having been judged that General Fleetwood was more necessary in the town to maintain peace. Monk having in all Scotland only nine regiments of infantry and three of cavalry, will not be able to bring so many forces into the field as will be sent against him, unless he makes new levies or ungarrisons all the towns of Scotland; which would make him suspected by his troops of an understanding with the king of England, and would entirely alienate them, their inclination tending more towards the Republic than towards any other form of government. Mild measures are at the same time being practised to influence them, and there took place yesterday, at the instance of the officers here, a meeting of ministers, which resulted in their sending them four deputies, two of whom are colonels, who were cashiered when the parliament was restored. It is not an easy thing to divine what will be the success of this deputation, as this leader is very popular, and has now advanced too far to draw back. It is feared here that he will join the king's party if he does not feel himself strong enough, and that he has even already formed the plan of doing so, and only makes use of the name of the parliament to secure his troops, for he cannot have the preservation of that body so much at heart as to go to war on its account. Besides that, it is not so agreeable a cause that he must wait until no one is willing to authorize it, or he alone is able to defend it, the army in England being united, as it now appears, and having only the governor of Hull, whose inclinations are doubtful. Great umbrage has been caused by the conduct of the commandant of Ireland; he has arrived in London, and he will not be permitted to leave again. If the troops in Ireland do not follow his inclinations, and if those in England

remain constant to those which they at present exhibit, it
will be necessary for Monk either to come to an accommodation or to seek assistance elsewhere. This last step would
be very easy to him, the Scotch and English being quite
disposed to revolt, but he must use great address in order to
deceive his troops and although, according to public report,
they are said to be very averse to a reconciliation, they will with
difficulty be induced to fight against each other. It is also
hoped here, that, Lambert being on the spot, his presence
will give courage to those whom the fear of evil treatment
prevents from declaring themselves in favour of the army;
otherwise the war will be indefinitely prolonged, as neither
the season nor the forces of England permit the undertaking
of sieges in a very wild country, although some artillery has
been embarked upon the Thames I have thought it right,
in this doubtful conjuncture, to inform General Fleetwood
that if my intervention could possibly contribute to reunion,
I would exert myself with all the zeal which might be expected
from the known affection of his Majesty to England He has
this evening sent to thank me for this offer, without either
declining or accepting it, excusing himself by the great perplexity of affairs for not having come in person to express to
me the gratitude which the government could not but feel
for a civility which it has not received from any other foreign
minister. There is no inconvenience connected with being
the first to take such a step as cannot fail to obtain the thanks
of both parties; I nevertheless did not address myself to the
Committee, so that my offer might not be made public; and,
up to this hour, no notification has been sent to me of its establishment, which took place at the end of last week without
much ceremony. Part of the ministers chosen having met in
the room generally used by the council, a colonel brought and
read to them the act of the army. Sir Harry Vane and two
others asked time to consider if they should act, taking as a
pretext for this postponement that this commission gave them
a legislative power which belonged only to the parliament.
Lambert wished to remove this scruple ; but his reasons did
not prevent them from retiring, and they have not presented
themselves again to-day; whence we may infer that they are
in doubt about the stability of the present government, and
apprehend that Monk will prevail; it being certain that these
same persons were at first for the dissolution of the parlia-

ment, and that they would not now make any difficulty about
taking their seats, unless they apprehended its return, or the
establishment of some authority which would prosecute them
for having taken part in the government without any legitimate title for so doing. By the retirement of Sir H. Vane,
this assembly finds itself greatly destitute of capable persons,
and there only remains Lambert, who must set out in two
days, probably not to return very soon. * * *

(13.)—M. DE BOURDEAUX TO CARDINAL MAZARIN.

MY LORD,   London, November 17, 1659.

I SHALL not have to write to you to-day of the reunion
of the army; there appears rather a disposition to an entire
rupture, as the last advices received here state that the troops
in Scotland have, with great demonstrations of joy, promised
Monk to live and die with him, and that on his part he has
given them reason to hope for the payment of their arrears,
and has since detached some troops to take possession of
Newcastle, a large town without fortifications, from whence is
obtained all the coal used in England, which would render its
capture very prejudicial, especially to London. Some of his
letters to other towns have also been intercepted, in which
he invited them to join his party, and represented London to
be well-disposed towards him. To counteract these measures,
Major-General Lambert set out post-haste three days ago,
leaving the army in march, but without hoping that it could
make haste enough to secure the frontier towns, if they had
any inclination to join the said General Monk. In order to
divert them from this by the example of the London militia,
this body has also been requested to write a letter to that leader,
inviting him to peace. But the greater part of the assembly
have not yet judged it fitting to show any partiality, and seem
desirous to put off a declaration until it shall more certainly
appear what is his design. The public voice has maintained,
during the last few days, that he is in communication with
the king of England, and his enemies affect to fear something
of the kind. Nevertheless, the Republicans defend him from
this charge, and declare that his sole object is to re-establish
the parliament. He has moreover written to the army here,
in conformity with this statement. Nevertheless, whether his
words do not meet with credence, or whether he judges that

necessity may lead him to adopt other sentiments, and that
if the war continues, a third party may be formed in England
new levies are being made. This precaution is the more
necessary, because the city of London is beginning to hold
the same views as the militia, and to change the officers
whom the parliament appointed; and some of the most influential citizens even talk of having a free parliament.
If Monk used the same language, he would be more readily
supported; whence it follows that all sorts of means are
employed to gain either him or his troops. With this
view, the Committee has appointed a sub-committee to form a
a government which shall meet the wishes of all parties, and
disengage them honourably from the step they have taken. Sir
Harry Vane has consented to be of the number of these subde-
legated commissioners, although he does not publicly engage
in other matters of state; but some others who had felt scruples about acting in virtue of a commission given them by
the army, have become more bold; and last week there was
published an act of this assembly, which continues all the
officers and civil magistrates in the performance of their
duties, and orders the payment of the taxes already imposed,
under penalty of having to give free quarters to the soldiers.
This threat has been considered extraordinary, and has given
the discontented a pretext for finding fault with the present
condition of England. But the Council of War feels no alarm
at this, and has lately even been upon the point of suppressing
tithes and the Court of Chancery, as being both a burden to
the people and very unnecessary; if the wishes of the subaltern officers had been attended to, this reform would have
been accomplished. The leaders must find it inconvenient to
offend so many people at the present conjuncture, the sequel
of which cannot clearly be foreseen; only it is probable that,
if there is no secret understanding with the King of England,
the quarrel will soon come to an end, and the troops will
reunite, as neither are at all desirous to come to conflict with
each other, and those in England have been entirely at
union since the governor of Hull rejected the propositions
made him by Monk, to which rejection their private enmity
greatly contributed. There is nothing said about Ireland
which should excite jealousy, nor about the affairs of England; and it only remains for me to subscribe myself,
&c., &c., &c.

(14.)—M. DE BOURDEAUX TO CARDINAL MAZARIN.

MY LORD, London, November 20, 1659.

THE general feeling to-day appears very different to that which I described in my preceding letters. At the beginning of the week, the city of London seemed very discontented, and even inclined to press the army for a free parliament: it had also refused to write the letter to General Monk which it was requested to send, and the people daily insulted the troops, and particularly some regiments of sectaries who went on guard every night. These bad humours are now dissipated, and it is said that the mayor has promised to permit nothing that may disturb the public tranquillity, or prejudice the present government; and that this agreement has been made upon condition that those sectaries, against whom the people are greatly enraged, shall no longer be employed to guard the town; the council of citizens adopted this resolution yesterday, and having communicated it to the Committee, its terms were agreed to. At the very moment when the affair was being deliberated, there arrived letters from Monk which caused no less joy; they represent him to be disposed to treat, and he is to send four officers to manage this negociation, of the success of which no one doubts. There is also news that his troops have not presented themselves before Newcastle, and that those which had approached that town retired to Berwick, where the garrison declared in Monk's favour; as regards Carlisle and Tynemouth, which it was thought had followed the same example, because Haslerig's regiment was in garrison there, they have not yet declared themselves; and there appears to be complete union among the troops in England, which will doubtless abate the confidence of the others, founded upon the conviction which they entertained that some regiments here were in favour of restoring the parliament. Mention has been again made of this, in the Council of War, during the last few days, as a means for settling all differences, and it would have been resolved upon if forty members of that body had been found well-intentioned towards the army. Now that Monk has changed his views, this idea will be rejected, and the Committee will complete the work it has begun. It is even asserted that it has already determined on a form of government composed of a council of fifty, which will summon another of two hundred, and name the members to the people, leaving them only liberty to choose them out of four hundred candidates who will be brought forward; this second body i to be changed once in every three years, and every year ten of the council of fifty will go out of office to make room for ten others to be chosen from among the two hundred. This plan has not yet been published, and before it appears, there may probably be some changes introduced into it, as the reunion or division of the army cannot but serve as a rule for the resolutions of the present government.

(15.)—M. DE BOURDEAUX TO CARDINAL MAZARIN.
MY LORD,   London, November 24, 1659.
THE letters which General Monk wrote last week, were followed, three days afterwards, by his officers: these are three officers of different corps who arrived in London the day before yesterday, and have to-day begun their conferences with the leaders of the army. They had, on their way, seen my lord General Lambert, and their propositions must have appeared reasonable to him, as he immediately halted his troops, according to their desire. It is said that they are charged to insist principally upon the recall of the old parliament, or the convocation of a new one, on the maintenance of the ancient laws of the nation, and on the support of the ministers by the ordinary mode, that is, by tithes. The last two points seem to be ill-received by the sectaries, who wish to employ the tithes for other purposes, and establish another fund for the support of the ministers. They also have it very much at heart to change many of the laws; but as for the parliament, there will be no difficulty in obtaining it, provided that it be with such restrictions that the people shall not be able to elect persons opposed to the republican government, and that there shall also be established, at the same time, a senate with equal power in some cases; it is even said that the Committee resolved to convoke this body instead of the assembly of two hundred which was projected, and it is not probable that any of these conditions will be refused to the troops in Scotland, if they can thereby be brought to union. Some are persuaded that Monk is not treating in good faith, and that he is advancing his demand in order to gain time, and to render his cause more popular, in the hope that they will not be granted; nevertheless, the most general opinion is that he really intends to come to an accommo-

lation, seeing no likelihood of success for the cause which he
maintains, since the army in Ireland has refused to join him :
besides he is not a man to pursue a course of conduct so
utterly at variance with his views, and his troops would
quickly abandon him if they had the least suspicion of any
understanding with the king's party, without whose assistance
he cannot maintain himself against the whole army. It is
true that the Presbyterians would readily join him, if the
existing authorities were to persecute them; but whatever
their inclination may be, it will not be manifested in the present conjuncture, and it was only three days ago that, in
order to calm the minds of the citizens of London, who
appeared still to apprehend a change in religion, General
Fleetwood, Colonel Desborough, and Mr. Whitelocke went to
he town-hall, and delivered three harangues in different
style. The first professed entire disinterestedness of the
army, and promised that no prejudice should be done to
either the liberties of the nation or the government of religion. The second spoke in terms more military, and more in
conformity with his rather stern character, declaring that
hey had not come to flatter the town, that the army would
never put itself in a position of dependence upon those whom
t had conquered, and that it would rather support the sec-
aries than suffer the adoption of any resolution to its pre-
udice. The last, who is now keeper of the seal, exhorted
he company to union and peace, for the maintenance of which
are posted, in the principal places, troops, but not sectaries.
The mayor is very active, manifesting by his conduct his
wish that no tumult should take place; for such would be
doubtless followed by great confusion, as the people are not
of the same mind, and the sectaries find themselves sufficiently numerous, together with the rest of the army, to
balance the power of the other citizens; a state of things
which will keep the former in their duty until the negociation
has met with some success; but if fortune decreed that it
should not produce an accommodation, the town would probably give some trouble to the present government, which is
still occupied with home affairs.   *   *   *

(16.)—ABBE MONTAGUE* TO CARDINAL MAZARIN.

Bourdeaux, November 25, 165!

YOUR's of the 22nd, from Auch, was received on ou arrival at Bourdeaux on the 25th, the bad weather and th roads not permitting us to make greater speed. The kin received here letters from England which give nearly the sam news as the letter of M. de Bourdeaux; but the resolutio to reduce Monk by force was one of the best pieces of new we could expect in order to begin to work in consequenc I could not adequately express to you the joy which the kin manifested at your letter, for he said immediately that th proof it afforded him of the interest which you take in h affairs was even more valuable than the news it commun cated; for the success of these petty movements is uncertai but the good effect of your interest is infallible. He h therefore commanded me to inform you that, from to-morrov he will begin to follow your views, and will take post t proceed to the frontier as quickly as possible, after havin seen the queen his mother at Colombe. He has alread commenced overtures to Monk, and he is assured that he ca send messages to him in safety; but besides the person who he has on the spot, who will not fail to act according to h first commission, he will despatch an express, and will begi also to have Lambert sounded by an envoy whom he think sufficiently trustworthy to be able to make overtures to hi without their ever being turned to his prejudice. At th worst, he will inform us of the result of all to communicate to you, protesting to you that he shall do nothing withou your concurrence, or otherwise than in conformity with you advice, which he urgently begs you to be so kind as continu to him, assuring you that he will keep the secret so well th appearances shall always accord with your sentiments, an that he will derive all the advantage from this correspondenc without the possibility of any inconvenience occurring to yo This is what he has commanded me to tell you, and beg o you on his behalf, expressing to you all possible gratitude fo this very opportune proof of your friendship; and I assure yo that from day to day I become more bold to offer myself as guarantee for all that he promises you, for I am more an more persuaded of his talents and ingenuity; and as for th Marquis of Ormonde, he seems to me a man of great probit;

* Abbé Montague was chaplain to Queen Henrietta Maria.

remains very well satisfied with the con-
c had with you.

MONTAGUE TO CARDINAL MAZARIN.
Bourdeaux, November 26, 1659.
England left this morning by post, as I in-
day that he would: this morning he has had
ed expressly to bring him the declaration of
g against the London army, and the march
t them with some four thousand men. The
ater force, according to all accounts; and
he entrances into Scotland on both sides;
towns of Berwick and Carlisle, and some
f this be so, the English will have difficulty
king of England hopes that they will come
est thing for him would be that the war
that it should not be finished immediately
; for, if one or the other party remained the
e would have greater difficulty in making
with the master. The king has commanded
incture to propose to you the consideration of
er, in case of some sure opening for the town of
itself in the absence of the army, you would
hat he should pass into England with the
Spaniards might give him of their subjects;
t, if you approve of the plan, you will assist
holds himself quite ready to do whatsoever
at to him, being determined to undertake
our advice. We shall from day to day see
the consequences of these alarms; and I will
lf well informed of all things on arriving at
ill be in ten days, if it please God. The
greatly desired to write to you, to thank you
which you have given to his interests, but I
om doing so, foreseeing the consequence of
might embarrass you. You can send it to
sily; and I shall expect it from M. Colbert

CURDEAUX TO CARDINAL MAZARIN.
London, November 27, 1659.
ers which I had the honour to write to your
re informed you of the dispositions which pre-

K

vailed here with regard to an accommodation between the troops. These appearances were not deceitful, for a treaty was concluded twenty-four hours after. The deputies from Scotland were from the first so well satisfied with the government which the Committee had projected, that they no longer insisted upon the recall of the old parliament, and immediately agreed to forget all causes of discontent, to pass an act of indemnity for all that had been done on either side, to set at liberty the officers whom Monk had arrested, and to assemble at New-castle fourteen deputies of the two armies to settle the claims of those who have lately been cashiered or suspended, both in England and Scotland; that the pretended rights of the king of England and his family shall be disclaimed; that the three nations shall be governed in the form of a free state, or of a republic without either a king, a House of Lords, or any single ruler; that there shall be established a Council of nineteen persons, ten of whom shall be moderate Presbyterians, nominated by Monk's deputies and the army here, and the other nine chosen from the three armies in England, Scotland, and Ireland; that all together, or at least nine of them, shall regulate the qualifications of those who may be elected by the people to hold the parliament; that there shall also be convoked an assembly of two officers from each regiment, one from each garrison, and ten from the navy, to whom the proposed form of government shall be presented for deliberation on the 16th of next month. It has also been resolved that the Universities shall be so well maintained and reformed that they may become schools of learning and piety. These are the articles which appear. As for the model of the government, although it is said to have been approved of, it has not yet been published. The agreement had no sooner been signed by the Commissioners of the two armies than it was presented to the general Council of officers, and, after some discussion, confirmed. Two copies of it were forthwith despatched yesterday to Generals Lambert and Monk, who had begun their march; and during the evening the cannon of the Tower of London solemnized this reconciliation, which many thought would have been more difficult than it has proved; but they had little reason for such an opinion, there being no likelihood that the interest of the old parliament could maintain a division which would undoubtedly have ruined both partes, even though it had lasted only a short time. The

people of London were daily becoming more arrogant—even
to refusing the payment of the ordinary taxes—under pretext
that the parliament had revoked them all two days before its
dissolution. This refusal obliged the army to send soldiers
with the collectors, and no disorder ensued therefrom. It has
also been found necessary to change the greater number of the
officers of the city militia, as the old ones were not found to
be well-disposed; and the militia of Westminster refused to
arm at the orders of the Committee. If the army here met
with some opposition, Monk was not exempt from trouble and
mistrust of the constancy of his troops, several companies of
which have disbanded: thus both were in some degree compelled to an agreement; and by their treaty the power will
remain in the hands of the leaders, since the government is to
be composed of a Senate which they will choose; that this
body will convoke parliaments when they are needed; will
have a *veto* upon them, in regard to affairs of religion and government, and will even propose to them the matters upon which
they will have to deliberate. It is also said that the tithes will
be employed for other purposes than the support of ministers,
for whom another provision will be made, and that many other
regulations are to be introduced into the administration of
justice. As the people of England are greatly displeased with
all the revolutions which have happened, and as the new
project in some measure preserves their prerogatives, in that
it leaves to the parliaments the powers which they possessed
under the kings, whom the Senate will represent, we have
reason to believe that the present establishment will be stable,
although the sectaries have more share in it than the Presbyterians, whom they will doubtless try to keep out of the
parliament. It will not, nevertheless, be easy to stifle the
jealousies of the leaders; and if fear of the royal family, or the
impressions which are prevalent that France and Spain have
resolved to undertake its restoration, have caused union at the
present moment, as soon as these fears are dissipated new
causes of disunion will very probably arise.

I saw Mr. Lockhart to-day, and he appeared to me persuaded
that the king had no intention of interfering in the affairs of
England; he will doubtless have spoken in the same strain to
the heads of the government, and dissipated their suspicions,
if they are real. The said general ambassador has also returned me thanks, on the part of Mr. Fleetwood, for the

K 2

mediation which I offered him at the time when the success
of the negociation was very uncertain.   I did not think it my
duty, in the present conjuncture, to change my tone, neither
did I think fit to discuss any other affair.   *   *   *   *

(19.)—M. DE BOURDEAUX TO CARDINAL MAZARIN.
MY LORD,   London, December 5, 1659.
    *   *   * My preceding despatches will have in-
formed your Eminence with tolerable exactness of the state
of affairs in England during last week, and led you to expect
a complete reunion of all the forces after the accommodation
upon which the deputies of both parties had agreed; this is
still the wish and the hope of the leaders of the army. Nevertheless, a short time after that treaty had been signed, the
deputies from Scotland received orders to insist upon the
recall of the old parliament, and to demand that the command
in Scotland should be separated from that in England.   It
has also become known that Monk has called together deputies from all the provinces and towns which are under his
government.   Some of his letters furthermore represent him
as resolved to prolong rather than to conclude the war; and
one was delivered yesterday to the city of London on his
behalf, in which he professed that his sole intention was to
have a free parliament, and to deliver the nation from its
present state of slavery, and invited the people to assist him.
Some of the company wished to prevent its being opened;
but, as they were in a minority, the letter was read, and
immediately the mayor, under pretext that it was late, adjourned the meeting.   He has also written to other towns in
the same terms; and although this was done before the
General had been informed of the treaty, his conduct has
not failed to excite apprehensions that he has changed his
views, that the English Presbyterians have given him fresh
courage, and that, flattered with the hope of becoming the
leader of this most considerable party, he will reject the
agreement, the retardation of which can produce none but
bad consequences, as the mind of the whole nation is strongly
inclined to throw off the yoke of the army, and the people
are excited, as much by the old parliamentarians as by the
other factions, to refuse to pay the taxes, in order to compel
the soldiers, by want of pay, to mutiny and join Monk. The
Presbyterians are, at the same time, striving to gain over the

others; and I learn that, during the last few days, their principal men have held some meetings in London, in order to seek out some way of accommodation which will be advantageous to the king. Besides the cabals of the enemies of the present government, there are, in the army, several conflicting interests. Fleetwood, Lambert, and the sectaries, who are headed by Vane, are each desirous of obtaining the chief power. The first party is now the strongest. Sir Harry Vane talks of retiring from public affairs, as his advice is no longer followed. Lambert will not leave so easily : he is reputed to have credit enough to draw over to his side a portion of the army, and to be ambitious enough to seek his aggrandizement from the king, if he cannot see his way clear to become, in time, the head of the republic, or at least of all its forces; he is, therefore, greatly caressed by the royalists, whom he has latterly treated with great consideration. Those of them whom I have seen are more full of hope than they have ever before appeared, and flatter themselves that the accommodation will be rejected. The opposite party has also taken the alarm, and does not deny that present appearances are very bad; and the principal reliance here is in the fear which Monk's officers will entertain lest their division should restore the king. It is even said that many have abandoned him since Lambert's troops approached the frontier; and they must now be near Newcastle, and Monk between Edinburgh and Berwick. Public rumour asserts that there has been some engagement between their parties, but this is without foundation, for it is not to be supposed that they are so desirous to destroy each other, that they have sought each other out before receiving news about the negociation from London, where the deputies from Scotland are still expecting the ratification of the treaty. It is no easy matter to foresee what will be the end of these movements. Reason ordains that both parties should come to a speedy accommodation, upon any conditions whatever; but Monk may persuade himself that, by remaining firm, all the Presbyterians will favour him, and that with their support he will become the master. Up to this hour, it is not asserted that any other project is entertained by him, or that he has any understanding with the king of England : his answer about the treaty will, ere long, develop his plans. Meanwhile, all is in suspense ; even the Courts of Justice are closed, because the judges had been commissioned by parliament only until the 20th of last month. The tallages were ordered only for the same term, and by the end of the present month all other taxes will cease, although the Committee has directed their continuation: the levy will not be effected without the aid of soldiers. I have already informed your Eminence that Mr. Lockhart had visited me, and appeared persuaded that the passage of the king of England through France did not proceed from any intention on our part to support his plans: he has doubtless spoken to the Committee in the same terms. It still continues to affect great jealousy of his Majesty's inclinations—a feeling partly originated by the royalists, although it would be the means of bringing the minds of the army into greater unanimity. *   *   *

(20.)—M. DE BOURDEAUX TO CARDINAL MAZARIN.
MY LORD,   London, December 8, 1659.
THE affairs of England remain in the state which I described to you in my preceding letter. The ratification of the agreement between the two armies has not yet arrived, and it was not expected until to-day or to-morrow. However, it appears that General Monk has declared to the Assembly of Scotland, which was held in the ordinary place of meeting of the parliaments, that God and men summoned him to England to re-establish the parliament; and that he exhorted the deputies to do their duty in maintaining public tranquillity during his brief absence, and requested some pecuniary assistance. The said deputies professed that they did not wish to interfere in the quarrel, as its termination could not be advantageous to their country, and that as their country was disarmed, nothing was to be apprehended from it; that, nevertheless, they would not fail to do their best to keep it in peace, and would give a subsidy. This strong disposition to open their purse casts greater suspicion upon the inclinations of this general, there being little likelihood that the Scotch, who are not very rich, and still less fond of their governor, would grant him assistance so readily, unless they saw their way clear to gain him over to the interest of the king, for whom he formerly fought. Besides that he has at present no other object than the one he professes, this distrust is augmented by the changes he is making in his troops while the deputies are negociating; and although they still hope not to be disavowed, recruitments and new levies are being

made all over England, either in order to reduce it to reason, or to overcome the resistance which will be opposed to the levying of the taxes, for the people daily become more determined, insomuch that an artisan in London sorely maltreated some soldiers who were assisting the collectors. The difficulty will not be less in the country, and fear alone will be able to extract money, so long as the taxes are not enacted by the parliament. The Committee is working at the same time to place the new form of government in a fit state to be presented to the officers of all the armies who are to assemble on the 16th of this month, and the Council of War has appointed twenty-seven commissioners to examine it. It has also had some debate about recalling the old parliament, or at least forty members of it. * * * The city of London has not yet deliberated upon Monk's letters; they are even suspected of being supposititious, and the bearers have been arrested since they were disowned by the deputies from Scotland. A report has been very prevalent that some troops of both parties had encountered each other, and the disadvantage was on the side of Lambert's men, but it has no foundation, and up to the present time no act of hostility has taken place on either side; and it is probable that, even if the accommodation is not approved of, the assembly of officers will take place notwithstanding on the 16th, and that meanwhile all things will remain in their present state. * * *

(21.)—M. DE BOURDEAUX TO CARDINAL MAZARIN.
MY LORD, London, December 11, 1659.
I THINK I have fulfilled the order which your Eminence gives me in your letter of the 27th of November, not having allowed any post to leave without informing you of what had come to my knowledge regarding the affairs of England, and it was not until after I had performed this duty that I wrote to M. de Turenne on public affairs; but some of my letters, and among others, that in which I relate the dissolution of the parliament, have been suppressed, and no restitution of them has been made, notwithstanding my complaints. I should be deceived if the present had the same fortune, since it informs you of Monk's answer to the treaty which his Commissioners had signed at London. I send a copy of it, that you may judge from it what are his intentions. This despatch had no sooner arrived yesterday evening at London,

than a resolution was taken to send back the deputies from Scotland to Newcastle to-day, and to give General Lambert power to treat, on the spot, about the differences which may remain. The royalists do not think that these can be settled so easily, and are persuaded that Monk still claims independence of the general who commands in England, and will never allow the officers whom he has cashiered to be restored; their hope is, moreover, founded upon the fact, that three additional regiments have been commanded to march to the frontier since this news, and that the leaders of the army speak with uncertainty about the success of this negociation. Nevertheless, as it does not appear that Monk has any understanding with the king of England, and as his troops are considerably weakened by the continual withdrawal of the officers, and further, as neither the English army, nor the city of London, have declared for him, according to the assurance which had been given him,—it is not to be presumed that the division will continue; and the English army is so well aware of the ill effect which war would produce, not to grant the greater part of the demands that will be made, excepting the separation of the forces. It is said that the despatch from hence will find the Scottish army on the march with its artillery and baggage; that, on the same day, Monk had dismounted three companies of cavalry which were with him, and that the goodwill of his troops towards him was beginning to subside; and that thus the evil would not be so great if he should be very much opposed to the accommodation, in reliance upon which the regiments are naming their deputies to proceed to London on the 16th, and form a government there. Mr. Lockhart returned to Dunkirk to-day, after having obtained that the regiments of his garrison should belong to the main body of the army, but having failed to procure the restoration of the officers cashiered during his absence. The letter which he gave me to forward to your Eminence will, doubtless, inform you of the object of his journey, and of the resolution here regarding the continuation of the truce between England and Spain : he entered into no explanations with me; but he strongly assured me of having done all in his power to dispel the jealousy felt here in regard to France: I shall not fail to see some member of the government upon this matter, and diligence is very necessary now that the king of England is staying in France ; for his party have published some propositions which he made to induce the king and your Eminence to undertake his restoration, which will be difficult if his ill-fortune decrees that the troops should come to an agreement; it is, however, true that even if they become reconciled now, there will always remain seeds of dissension for the future.   *   *   *

(22.)—M. DE BOURDEAUX TO CARDINAL MAZARIN.
MY LORD,   London, December 15, 1669.
THE news to-day will represent the condition of England, as rather different from what it has been of late ; and if my letters by the preceding post led you to expect the reunion of the troops, you will now doubtless judge that this is still very remote, as the people of London are inclined to favour the designs of General Monk. About the end of last week, it was discovered that, at the instigation of some Presbyterian ministers, royalists, and old parliamentarians, some apprentices of this town proposed to get up a requisition tending to the convocation of a free parliament, or to the recall of the last, and to the maintenance of the churches. The Committee, upon hearing this, directed the mayor of London, on the 12th inst., to publish on the following day, a prohibition to proceed further in the matter, on pain of indictment for treason. He did not refuse to obey ; nevertheless, under the pretext of indisposition and fear of the people, the officers whose duty it is to perform this act refused to do it, and the mayor being again called upon, asked time to confer on the subject with the Common Council, which met at eight o'clock this morning. But, without waiting until its deliberations were over, a company of cavalry proceeded to the front of the Exchange, and attempted to make the proclamation. The apprentices did not fail to gather around, and to interrupt it by yells, even to maltreat the trumpeters and mingle among the horsemen, who not finding themselves strong enough to withstand the populace, retired in disorder, and were pursued as far as St. Paul's Church, where there is a garrison. Immediately, all the cavalry and infantry which had been posted in different parts of the town took arms, and marched through the streets in order of battle, and one regiment went to take possession of the neighbourhood of the Exchange. The apprentices having continued still to irritate them with words, and even with stones, the soldiers fired upon the people, only two of whom were killed and several

wounded; the rest dispersed, having no arms wherewith
to defend themselves. At the same time the shops were
shut. Some cried to arms, and six apprentices went to the
Guildhall, where the citizens were assembled, and presented
their requisition, signed by a large number of others ; it was
immediately read, and a committee of twelve appointed to
examine and report upon it to the assembly. It was also
resolved immediately to request General Fleetwood to withdraw his soldiers, and to order the heads of families to keep
their apprentices and servants at home, that peace might be
preserved. Before this deliberation was finished, the troops
had several skirmishes in the streets with the citizens : some
more of the latter were killed and wounded, and one artisan
was obliged, in order to escape having his house burnt
down, to give up his apprentice, who had thrown stones at
the soldiers. The disturbance continued until the evening,
when the deputies from the citizens went to General Fleetwood, and informed him of the resolution of the town-council,
assuring him that the magistrates would do their best to
repress insurrection, if he would withdraw his troops into
their quarters. He accepted this offer, and Colonel Desborough, at the head of three companies of cavalry, with
drawn swords and pistols in hand, went to the mayor to
request him to order the people to retire, which was immediately done. The soldiers at the same time evacuated
the streets, and returned to their ordinary posts : and tranquillity seems now to be fully restored, although the ill-feeling
is not extinguished, and the citizens declare that they will
not suffer the army to be in the town. It is not, however,
probable, that the guard will be entrusted to them; this
would be affording the ill-intentioned, the number of whom
is considerable, facilities for promoting their very different
design ; many of them aim only at restoring the king, and
amuse the populace under the name of liberty ; others hope to
have a free parliament, and believe that they will succeed, if
Monk joins them; and the old parliamentarians hope that
the confusion will force the army to recall them. The latter
have, during the last two days, made themselves masters of
Portsmouth, and the governor whom they had established
there, has received Sir Arthur Haslerig, and three others of
his faction ; the news arrived yesterday in time to give free
course to the malcontents, and some say that Hull and
Plymouth have joined the same party. Letters from Monk

lso arrived the day before yesterday, which represent him
o be very arrogant. He requires that Lambert shall with-
lraw his troops, which have approached too near his quarters,
f they have any desire to treat, and avows the letters which
ave been presented to the city of London, by demanding the
iberation of the bearers; from whence it is judged that
ais former dispositions to an accommodation have greatly
altered, and that the progress of his party will render it still
nore difficult, although the prolongation of this quarrel must,
according to all appearance, turn to the advantage of the king
of England. Those, therefore, who desire his return are full
of hope, and leave no means untried to excite the people of
London, who are ill-disposed to insurrection on account of
he injury done to trade by domestic disorders; it is not that
he principal inhabitants do not apprehend a tumult, and that
his fear cannot prevent them from following their inclina-
ions, and that there are not many of them very much opposed
o the return of the king, through being in possession of con-
iscated property. This diversity of interests does not permit
ne as yet to form a solid judgment about the future, and I
an only promise to write by every post the consequences of
o-day's action, and if the ports are closed, as there is reason
o believe they are, to send an express messenger to France,
hat your Eminence may be as fully persuaded of my diligence
'n the execution of your last orders, as I beseech you to be of
he affection and respect with which I am, &c.

(23.)—M. DE BOURDEAUX TO CARDINAL MAZARIN.
MY LORD,   London, December 18, 1659.
    *   *   *   SINCE the 15th, the ill-feeling between the
city and the army has augmented rather than diminished;
the mayor has refused to wait upon the Committee, who had
summoned him to attend, and the Common council declares,
that in an interregnum like the present, their chief magistrate ought rather to give than receive the law from any
other authority. This same body appears greatly inclined to
press for the convocation of a free parliament, and I have
been told that a requisition to this effect is now being signed
by the principal citizens, the number of apprentices not being
capable to authorize a demand of this nature. The citizens
profess also that they cannot allow the town to be guarded
by the army, and they have received orders to hold them-

selves ready to arm the militia; besides their natural aver
sion to the soldiery, the people are instigated by the royalis
and old parliamentarians to insist upon this last point, whic
they think will not be granted by the government, and failir
to obtain which, they would immediately declare themselve,
These unfriendly feelings have as yet produced no hostilit;
and the troops remain in their posts with as much arrogancc
as ever. It is even said that, within the last twenty-fou
hours, they have been supplied with a quantity of ammu
nition, and among other things, with grenades, in order tha
fear of pillage and fire may keep the wealthy citizens in the
allegiance, and without their assistance the common peopl,
can effect nothing. * * * But if the state of London i
doubtful, that of the country is far from being certain. Th
news of the defection of Portsmouth has been found to b
true, and eight companies of infantry have set out, in th
belief that a portion of the garrison is disposed to open th
gates to them; some vessels have also left the Downs to pro
ceed thither, and keep in obedience those which are at Ports
mouth. Fears are also entertained about the Isle of Wight
and some other places on the same coast; but Colchester i
said to have declared in favour of the parliament, and wha
has taken place in London will give so much courage to al
people, that a reunion with Monk can alone dispel all thes
storms. I do not learn that any news from him has been
received here of late, and a colonel has been despatched to
Newcastle to hasten the accommodation, the delay of whicl
cannot but be very favourable to the king of England; whicl
leads people to believe that this general will become mor
tractable, unless he has more plans than one. Some report
affirmed that he had armed the Scotch, and placed severa
fortresses in their hands; but apparently his troops would no
have suffered him to do this: he has paid them two months
wages out of the ordinary taxes of the country, and give
liberty to all those officers and soldiers whose views are con
trary to his own to retire. * * *

(24.)—M. DE BOURDEAUX TO CARDINAL MAZARIN.
MY LORD,   London, December 25, 1659.
     * * * IF my preceding letter represented the city c
London to be agitated, tranquillity now appears to be some
what restored; and either because the leading citizens hav

)st courage, on seeing the failure of the design on the Tower,
r because the mayor and citizens foresee the inconveniences
f domestic warfare, the people have not yet taken arms,
either has the militia guard left London; and to-day orders
ave been given on the part of the mayor to all the heads of
imilies to keep strict watch over their children, apprentices,
nd servants, so that the public peace may not be disturbed.
his order is based upon the convocation, which has just been
ublished in front of the Exchange, of a parliament on the
th of February, in conformity with the answer which Ge-
eral Fleetwood gave on the day before yesterday to the
eputies from the city; he communicated to them at the same
ime the resolution taken by the council of officers regarding
he form of the government. * * * Even if the expec-
ition of parliament should put a stop to these disorders, still,
,' it is ill-intentioned, which we must presume it will be, the
rmy will have some trouble to maintain the establishment
/hich it contemplates, and still more to destroy a body whom
he whole nation will have chosen: it might even happen
hat the proposed restrictions will serve only to rekindle the
re, which is not thoroughly extinguished. The common
eople of London seemed very disposed to insurrection, to
rhich they are instigated by the royalists, among whose
anks we may include a portion of the Presbyterians, some of
vhose ministers have of late spoken openly of the king of
England in their sermons and prayers; and in all proba-
iility, if the mayor of London had not been a man of peace,
ve should already have beheld many disorders here. The
langer is not yet past, and there is still great reason to fear
o long as the troops are disunited. The letters which have
irrived from Scotland, and the report of the deputies whom a
iongregation of ministers had sent to Monk, in order to dis-
iose him to a treaty, represent him as far removed from such
i step; instead of hastening the meeting at Newcastle which
ie had demanded, before he will send his new deputies, he
wishes to see those who signed the treaty at London; and
:his conduct is attributed to be a design for gaining time.
Some of his troops, in violation of the negociation, have also
marched towards England; and moreover all the speeches of
this general tend only to war, under the specious pretext of
restoring the parliament. He might probably have pursued
this course of conduct in the hope that the city and Tower of

London would support his plans; but if he does not change
his tactics, now that he knows that one has entirely failed
and that the leading citizens are opposed to the other, there
will be no reason to doubt the existence of a perfect under
standing between him and the royalists. * * *

(25.)—M. DE BOURDEAUX TO M. DE BRIENNE.
SIR,   London, December 29, 1659.
    * * * I WILL not fail to comply as quickly as pos-
sible with the order which your Excellency has given me to
inform this government of the peace of France, and of the
dispositions of his Majesty towards England, which are in
conformity with the language which, on different occasions,
I have had to use to the ministers here in order to dispel the
distrust produced by the letters written by the royalists on
the continent to those in England, to encourage them by the
hope of strong assistance from France, and in order to contradict the reports which have consequently prevailed, without giving rise to any complaints against me on the part of
the royalists. But the most considerate have remained. of
opinion that it would cause the entire ruin of their affairs, if
the people apprehended the return of the king of England
with foreign troops; for the parties which are now in arms
are not so embittered against each other, but that the slightest
likelihood of this prince's return would reunite them; the
greater number even of those who wish him back do not
desire to see him in a position to exercise absolute authority,
but rather necessitated to grant them all the conditions they
may desire. This capitulation can be made only by a free
parliament; this is, therefore, the object aimed at by the
Presbyterians, and generally by all the nobility, who are confident that, if the votes of this body are not influenced by
violence, they will restore the monarchy, and that not only
the town of London, but all the people of England would
arm to prevent the army from treating this parliament as it
did the former one. Whether these measures are true or
false, prudence will not permit me to declare too openly for
either one or the other party just now; and, with great
reasonableness, I am directed to regulate my language according to the condition of the present government, so as not to
offend those into whose hands it may ere long fall. My conduct will continue to be conformable to this advice, until I

perceive on which side fortune will turn. Although, at the present, the king's name is mentioned in the declarations of Monk and the other malcontents only to express entire alienation from his interests, he nevertheless has never yet had such great cause for hope—as the present confusion makes those who destroyed the monarchy desire its return, and there is moreover considerable room for the presumption that, if the present ill-will between the leaders of the army continues to increase, some of them will be forced to seek safety in the royalist party. There is no news yet whether Monk is disposed to peace, and if the ill-success of the design of the old parliament upon the Tower of London, and the orders of the mayor of London to keep the people in peace, had rendered this general more tractable, he will have had reason to return to his former views after having been informed that, notwithstanding the convocation of a parliament was proclaimed on the 25th of this month, Lawson, the admiral in command of the Channel fleet, has openly declared for the recall of the old parliament, and that, on the 26th, he entered the river with thirteen vessels, in order to favour those in the city who have the same inclinations, and to intimidate the others. * * * *

(26.)—M. DE BOURDEAUX TO CARDINAL MAZARIN.
MY LORD,   London, December 29, 1659.
    *   *   * IT appears to me that there is a great cabal of the nobles and principal Presbyterians; their design is to induce the town-council, in spite of the mayor, to demand the restoration of the Long Parliament, but with all the members who were excluded from it before the death of the king, feeling sure that they will recall his son on the conditions which he granted in the Isle of Wight. They had expected that the people would take arms on the preceding night; and they are striving to excite an outbreak by all sorts of ways. I have besides had conversation with one of the near relations of General Fleetwood, and have given him strong assurances that his Majesty, notwithstanding any reports to the contrary, had contracted no engagement in favour of the king of England, did not contemplate assisting him with his troops, and would not meddle with domestic divisions of this nature, except in order to appease them, if his intervention were desired. He greatly exaggerated to me the present state of

affairs, representing Monk as already engaged with the king, or very disposed to take up his cause ; the city of London as ill-disposed, although the principal citizens profess to desire to maintain peace ; and the generality of the officers as incapable of taking any resolution.   He even went so far as to give me to understand that if his relative and the members of his party could find safety in an accommodation with the king, they would not refuse it, but that such a proposition was too dangerous to be hazarded, and that distrust alone would lead many other principal officers to take the initiative in order to make more favorable conditions for themselves.   I judged it advisable to state that his Majesty would hear with regret of this bad state of things, that he had hoped soon to be informed of the reconciliation of the troops, and that the king of England was so much attached to Spain, that his restoration could not but be one day prejudicial to France, unless those who restored him should request his Majesty to be their arbiter and warrant for the conditions of the treaty ; that this was the greatest safety which they could find, and also a very proper deference to exhibit, in order that the royal family, returning by the intervention of France, might feel no more resentment at the close connexion which has existed between our two countries of late.   This speech was well received and followed up, without, however, my inviting them to an accommodation so long as any other resource was left ; consequently, I was merely informed that, according to the course of affairs, Mr. Fleetwood would take his resolution, and that he would doubtless avail himself of this opening, which cannot give umbrage, but must, on the contrary, produce some advantage.   Monk's brother-in-law also saw me not long since, and represented the general to have no other design than the restoration of the parliament. Nevertheless, he does not answer for the future, and if the movement which is taking place in London does not decide him to make peace, he must have some understanding with the English Presbyterians ; in which case the army would not be able to maintain itself long, and the king of England would return upon the conditions of the Isle of Wight.   The Catholics are in great apprehension, and hope that France and Spain will take part in this revolution, fearing that otherwise their condition will be worse than it is under the present government.   The hopes of the one party and the fears of the other may both be ill-grounded, and the Council of War, now

n session, may take resolutions which will reunite all minds.
There is much talk of recalling the last parliament, although
he convocation of another has been proclaimed; as for the
onservators of the principles,* they will, to all appearances,
e suppressed if the misunderstanding continues. And if your
Eminence judges it advisable that I should make advances to
my party, you will, if you please, let me know : meanwhile,
n order to disoblige none, I shall continue to speak fair
rords to all.   *   *   *

_____

(27.)—M. DE BOURDEAUX TO CARDINAL MAZARIN.

MY LORD,   London, January 1, 1660.

THE city-watch so often arrested the bearer of my letters
)y the preceding post, that they arrived too late at the office;
shall therefore join them to my present letter, in order that
our Eminence may be informed of what had taken place up
o the first day of the week, although affairs seem to have
ntirely changed their appearance within the last hour.   On
he 30th of last month, two very similar resolutions were
adopted by the town council, and by that of the officers of
he army.   In the first of these assemblies, after the mayor
had cleared himself from the public reproach which had been
ast upon him of having abandoned the interests of the town
o support the designs of the army; and after he had also
disavowed that he had approved of the establishment of the
onservators of the principles of the republic, it was determined to use every effort with the army, in order that a free
parliament might assemble as quickly as possible, notwithstanding the letter which, during this deliberation, was presented on the part of Admiral Lawson in favour of the last
hat had separated.   Some of the citizens coincided in this
opinion ; others, also, held up their hands in its favour, but
on condition that all the members excluded from their seats
n 1648 should be readmitted; and many were for a new
election.   This diversity of opinions resulted in the company
agreeing to general terms which, in some sort, left the army
iberty to choose whichever it should please.   The council of
officers was, at the same time, deliberating upon the report
of the deputies who had been sent to the fleet, the Vice-
Admiral of which would not depart from his original resolu-
ion, and had only offered to agree upon some articles for the

* The keepers of the liberties of the republic of England.

L

security and indemnity of the principal officers of the arm
provided that, before they entered on a treaty, they shoul
agree to recall the old parliament. The firmness of this leade:
and the difficulties which are met with in all the other estat
lishments, had so greatly shaken the subaltern officers, the
their superiors had some trouble to prevent them from revok
ing their resolution of the preceding week in conformity wit
that of the city. But the conservators of the principles wer
destroyed, and it was found more advisable to form a com
mittee of officers who should take care that no attack wa
made upon either liberty of conscience, the support of th
army, or the republican form of government. It seeme
likely that these two deliberations would restrain for som
time the violence of the parties, each being full of hope tha
the parliament would be favourable to it ; the royalists per
suading themselves that they would be able to recall the king upon
certain conditions, and the army that neither Monk, nor the
fleet, could refuse to submit to it. * * * * Yesterday
occurred the election of a new common council for next year
from which all those sectaries who lean towards the army
were excluded, and Sir Harry Vane returned to Lawson, who
was near Gravesend with twenty-one vessels, and whose fleet
is daily increasing, only two vessels remaining in the Channel
to cruise before Dunkirk, although he has been pressed to
send more thither, out of fear lest the king of England should
undertake to transport foreign troops into England or Scotland. But, contrary to all expectation, upon the news that
Sir Arthur Haslerig, who had been joined by the troops sent
from hence against him, was preparing to march towards
London with fifteen hundred horse, it being proposed to the
Council of War to send some troops to give him battle, the
greater number of officers opposed it. At the same time,
two regiments which are on guard near Whitehall declared
for the old parliament, although their colonels are opposed
to it. The other corps are disposed to follow this example,
and this general alienation seems to leave no other course
open to General Fleetwood, than to join the city with the
rest of his faction, and summon a new parliament ; indeed,
I am told that he has sent to make this offer, which will be
very agreeable to the royalists ; but it will come very late, and
it has even been reported to me that news has arrived this
evening of an accommodation signed on board the fleet, which

ecalls the parliament, and assures an act of indemnity to all
he officers and others who have taken part in public affairs
f late, with the exception of Lambert, of Whitelocke, the
eeper of the seals, and of Lord Warrenstowne, a Scotchman,
nd member of the committee. If this report be true, we
hall speedily see this treaty carried into effect, and the praise
r blame attaching to it will be due to Vane, who is accused
f having excited the fleet when he saw that he had lost his
redit with the army. Reports are also current that some
ssemblages have taken place in the country, and even that
he cavalry are in a state of excitement at Oxford; but no
redit can be given to them, and what now appears most
ertain is the return of the parliament, to the great prejudice
f the royalists. Nothing is said about Monk, except that
e is at Berwick with his troops, waiting for news of what is
oing on here. The intelligence of the accommodation of
he Dutch with the king of Sweden is not confirmed, and
ven their ministers who had communicated it to me, beg me
) make offers here in their favour, which I shall not fail to do
s soon as the present storm is dispelled; it is also for this
eason that I defer giving information of the peace between
rance and Spain. I am, &c.

<hr>

(28.)—M. DE BOURDEAUX TO CARDINAL MAZARIN.
Iy LORD, London, January 5, 1660.
THE information which I gave you on the 1st of this
month regarding the disposition of the troops has proved so
orrect that, although on that same day, in the general
ouncil of officers, their leaders had taken a resolu ion to inst strongly upon certain principles which, in part, tended to
heir own preservation, nevertheless, on leaving the assembly,
ach one had no thought but how he should make his own
rivate arrangement with the old parliamentarians; and on
he following day, there was not found a single company in all
he regiments of either Fleetwood or Lambert which had not
hanged sides, some without taking any precautions, others
fter having bid good-bye to their leaders, and excused them-
elves on the ground of the necessity to which they were re-
uced of conforming to the views of the troops in general.
he members of parliament who were on board the fleet re-
urned at the same time to London, and met, together with the
thers who were in the city, at the house of the Speaker, in

L 2

whose name they sent to Mr. Fleetwood to demand the ke'
of the parliament. He delivered them into their hands, an
shortly after, upon the refusal of some corps to obey his order
he resigned to them also the direction of the army, and pro
pared for retirement. Nevertheless, either because they hav
assured him of good treatment, or because he would rathe
expose himself to the rigour of the parliament than take t
flight, he has not yet quitted London. But Colonel Des
borough and all the other leaders have retired, and the troop
have received their orders from the Speaker, in front of whos
house they assembled the day before yesterday. He cam
down to the threshold of his door, in his robes of ceremony
and received from the officers an assurance of their futur
fidelity, which assurance the soldiers accompanied with joyft
acclamations : they afterwards marched in bodies through th
streets of Westminster without entering the city until th
evening, when a portion of the infantry returned thither t
their ordinary posts. The Speaker, accompanied by some c
the deputies, then went to take possession of the Tower c
London ; and, although the garrison had previously refused t
recognize the government which the army had decreed, the'
made no difficulty about receiving him, and submitting to th
parliament ; and three commissioners were left there to giv
them orders until the session, which commenced this afternoon
Before entering their house, the deputies proceeded to White
hall, to ascertain their number, and having found that it wa
sixty, among whom are those very persons who compose th
Committee, no one besides Mr. Whitelocke, the Keeper of th
Seals, having absented himself, they went and took thei
places without any ceremony or guard ; the Speaker only wa
between the two earls who conducted me to the audience
Their first deliberation was to order a month's pay to th
troops, and to decide upon the provisional government of th
troops, which has been given to some colonels whom the army
had cashiered. The company of guards came afterwards t
take its post before Westminster Hall, commanded by th
same officers whom Lambert had dismounted on the day when th
parliament was broken up, and all things are returned to th
state in which they were before this revolution. There is no
doubt felt but that the other troops will follow the example
of those in London. Already Desborough's regiment, which
had been recalled from the Scottish frontier, has sent it
major to give assurance of its fidelity. There is here also, c

colonel from the garrison of Dunkirk who speaks no less positively, and there is no reason to distrust the troops sent
against Monk, since they were detached from the regiments
which are in London. It is not that Lambert, believing
himself lost, cannot take the king's side, under the pretext of
favouring a free parliament, which the people greatly desire ;
but the English generals have little authority with the officers,
who see that the convocation of such a body entails the return of the king, and consequently, their entire destruction.
As for the Irish army, the greater part of it had already
mutinied and had arrested two of its leaders, so that the
commander, a staunch republican who had been detained here,
was obliged to return thither last week in all haste, to ex-
tinguish the fire which is thought to have been partly
kindled by the friends of the last Protector, who desire to
recall his brother,* their former leader. The city of London
alone appears to entertain sentiments not very favourable to
the present government. It was, perhaps, remarked in my
preceding letter, that, last week, the citizens elected a new
council, composed of persons well-affectioned towards the
king. The day after its establishment, letters were presented
to it from Monk, Lawson, and Haslerig, all tending to induce
the city to join them in re-establishing the old parliament.
This incitement, and the pretext of present danger in a time
of division among the troops, gave rise, during all the latter
days of last week, to different resolutions. It was at first
determined to send a deputation to the last two of these
leaders, to inform them of the resolution which had already
been adopted to convoke a free parliament, without explaining
whether it had reference to a new one, or to the old one
together with the members excluded in 1648. It then became necessary to change the militia, to hold it in readiness,
to restore the chains to all the streets, and to demand their
restoration by the governor of the Tower, in whose custody
they are kept. These decrees obliged the Speaker to call upon
the mayor on the day before yesterday, to represent to him that
these precautions were now very unnecessary, since the army
had returned to obedience to the parliament; and the result
was, that this magistrate, who is naturally very pacific, promised to continue his cares to prevent any interruption of the

* Henry Cromwell, Richard's younger brother, and for a long time the
governor of Ireland.

public tranquillity. Nevertheless, 'the main reliance of the royalists, and their only resource, is that the town-council will not agree to this, that it will persist in its resolution to arm the people under the officers already selected, and to insist upon the convocation of another parliament, if the excluded members are not recalled: that even the city train-bands would put an end to the sessions of the present parliament, that all the people of England will support them, and that Lambert and the other officers ruined by its return will embrace the same cause. This is, in effect, the only resource that remains to the royalists, and I am persuaded that if the wishes of the people were attended to, their projects would succeed. But as there is now no established and respected authority, it is doubtful whether the wealthy citizens who remained peaceful in more favourable times, would be willing to engage in a war which would be unsuccessful if the army remained united. The most disinterested are of opinion that their division alone can encourage the people to arm, and that after having had a good grumble they will be appeased, unless Lambert succeeds in gaining over some corps. Fleetwood made an offer in writing, on the day that he was abandoned, to join with the city in favour of a free parliament; but on the next day, having been summoned to keep his word, his sentiments were changed. Even though it be unfounded, there is a report that Sir Harry Vane had agreed with the commander of the fleet upon an indemnity for the leaders of the army, who make bitter complaints of him, and say that he is in part the author of this unexpected change, which may be attributed to the resolutions of the Council of War, to the necessities of the troops who were not paid, to their fatigues, and the continual dangers to which they were exposed during the interregnum, without any hope of seeing its termination except by their total ruin, if a free parliament were called—while, on the other hand, this parliament, not being able to maintain itself without the army, will pay them, and dissipate all the factions which may arise. These weighty considerations may also have been supported by the intrigues of the parliamentarians, who during all this time have had liberty to act, and by others who did not see that their authority would be so much augmented by the ruin of the parliament as they had hoped. This is, my lord, the present state of England. My next letters will give even more certain information of its

ondition. Meanwhile, I have only to beg you to allow me
to sign myself with respect, &c.

(29.)—M. DE BOURDEAUX TO CARDINAL MAZARIN.
MY LORD, London, January 8, 1660.
My last letter informed you of the resolutions of the
parliament at its first session; on the next day, the 6th, they
passed an act for the continuation of the customs and excise
duties until the 10th of March: liberated those who had been
imprisoned by their predecessors in power, disbanded all the
troops levied without authority, ordered that the troops in the
North should retire to the quarters which would be assigned them
by the directors of the army, without mentioning Lambert, their
commander, and voted that the Speaker should present the
thanks of the house to General Monk, Admiral Lawson, and
the commissioners who were at Portsmouth. During the time
that these deliberations were proceeding, about thirty of the
members, whom the army expelled from the parliament in
1648 for having advocated an accommodation with the King,
presented themselves at the door to resume their seats, presupposing that as violence, and not any just cause, had deprived them of their rights, they would meet with no opposition,
now that the army was subjected to the parliament. It was
not, however, thought desirable to admit them, but only to
resolve that the matter should be taken into consideration on
the 15th of the month; that they should also deliberate upon
the means of filling up the vacant seats; that meanwhile a
committee should examine the proceedings, orders, and reasons
concerning the absent members, who were obliged to be
satisfied with this answer, although it appears to them an
amusement until news shall arrive from the troops in the
North. The debates yesterday were of no importance; it was
only resolved to pass an act of indemnity for the soldiers who
had returned to obedience to the parliament, that a loan of
£20,000 sterling should be raised, and that a review should
be held only of the subaltern officers and soldiers. To-day,
the act of indemnity occupied their attention, and their minds
appeared somewhat excited when, upon this subject Sir Harry
Vane spoke of Lambert, some of the assembly having called
him a traitor. The town-council has, on its part, continued
to carry out its former resolutions touching the establishment
of the militia, which is to consist of six infantry regiments, of

3,000 men each, under very royalist colonels, to the exclusio
even of the Presbyterians, who are not considered sufficientl
zealous. It was also resolved yesterday, to present a requi
sition to the parliament to the effect that that body may b
free, which imports the recall of the excluded members, and i
general there appears to be great disposition to press upon
this point. Some even flatter themselves that, if the city i
not satisfied, it will receive these deputies, and that they wil
compose a parliament more considerable than the present
both in rank, fortune, and number. But to all appearance
the one party will not have courage to sit, or the other to exclude, unless Lambert has formed a faction in the army; no
one doubts his good-will, and despatches have been sent to
him from hence to invite him to do so. The difficulty is about
his credit among the troops, who are by no means accustomed
blindly to follow their leaders, and who are sufficiently enlightened to perceive that they must either conform to the views
of the others, or support the interest of the King, although
they talk of nothing but a free parliament. As the number
of discontented officers is very great, and moreover the English
government shows no wish to arrange with them, despair may
make them act in opposition to their own inclinations: in
this case, the confusion would be as great as it ever has been
of late, London and the country having no more affection for
the parliament than for the army. It is to be believed that
expectation of what Lambert may have done will keep men's
minds in suspense. The last news received about him states,
that he was preparing to march against Monk on the 2nd of
this month, because the latter general had refused to treat
without the sanction of those of his party who are in Portsmouth; but the country, the season, and the retreats possessed
by the latter general, give him great facility for avoiding an
engagement as long as he may please, and orders will arrive
from hence before the two armies will have been able to approach each other. It is also said that a brigade of the troops
from Ireland, who were serving under Lambert, has abandoned
him, not being persuaded of the justice of his cause, and that
the others will hear with joy of the re-establishment of the
parliament, in favour of which a part of the Irish army had
declared, and had surprised Dublin. These dispositions leave
room for belief that, if prosperity does not render it too
haughty, its establishment will be consolidated, notwith-

landing the opposition of the Presbyterians, whose leaders
re coming round. Liberty to return has been granted to
hose who retired voluntarily; and it might also be granted
) the others if they would enter into an engagement against
he king; otherwise their places will be quickly filled up by
ew elections, as it had been already proposed before the last
interruption. * * *

(30.)—M. DE BOURDEAUX TO CARDINAL MAZARIN.

Iy LORD,   London, January 12, 1660.
  THE debates of the parliament during the last few days
o not furnish matter for a long narrative: it has been occu-
ied chiefly with the act of oblivion, and with the organiza-
on of the Council of State which, like the preceding one, is
omposed of twenty-one deputies, among whom Sir Harry
'ane is not included, and ten others; the remaining resolu-
ons authorize all that have been done during the interruption
y Monk and the others, manifest gratitude for their services,
nd give power to the directors of the army to appoint officers.
A new form of oath has also been projected, and a deputation
has been sent to the Guildhall to persuade the citizens not to alter
he course of conduct they have pursued in all previous years.
The commissioners who were sent the day before yesterday
eceived a very vague answer, and there still appears a great
disposition on the part of the common council to insist upon
he readmission of the members excluded in 1648. Although
he requisition to this effect, which was to be presented to
parliament, has been suppressed, it has been only in order not
o recognize its authority; and instead of sending him an
address, an express has been despatched to Monk to invite him
n the name of the city, to defend the same cause. But after
he declaration which he has lately again renewed of his
obedience to the parliament, and the oath which his troops
have taken against the royal family, it is not to be expected
that this general will support the wishes of the people; it is
rather from Lambert that the evil is likely to come. The
news from the Scottish frontier is that, having been informed
of the revolution which has taken place in London, he made
his troops determine to go thither, and set out on his march
immediately with his cavalry and all his infantry for whom
he could find horses; that a portion of the remainder has been
left at Newcastle, or its neighbourhood, and that he has given

liberty to withdraw to all who were not willing to follow him before they knew what was passing in London. The same leader had sent some troops to York, and others against General Fairfax, around whom a number of gentlemen had gathered, but who immediately retired; but some accounts assure us that they have reassembled, and even that that brigade of the Irish army which had deserted Lambert had offered their services to Fairfax, if he would declare in favour of a free parliament, and that he is now at their head. Reports about Monk are very contradictory, and some say that he is on the march hither to defend the parliament; but in all probability the preservation of Scotland will have appeared to him of too much importance to be neglected in such a doubtful conjuncture as this, which has encouraged the town of Exeter to expel its garrison. Public rumours affirm that other towns have followed this example, and that in some counties mobs have gathered together under the pretext of having a free parliament. I nevertheless know of nothing very certain, except the march of Lambert, who aims at strengthening himself with the sectaries, who are dissatisfied with the parliament, the condition of which is rather precarious; having no longer their support, and the Presbyterians being so hostile to it, it will be indispensable for it to make an accommodation with one or the other party; and if the latter will enter into an arrangement against the royal family, the doors of parliament will be opened to them. As this news only arrived this afternoon, it cannot yet be foreseen what resolutions it will produce; but a few days will clear up these uncertainties.   *   *   *

(31.)—M. DE BOURDEAUX TO CARDINAL MAZARIN.
MY LORD,   London, January 15, 1660. '
    IT will not be without some surprise that your Eminence will learn the great change which has taken place here since my last. If its contents led you to apprehend that England would relapse into a civil war, my news of to-day will produce other feelings, and you will judge from it that we shall soon behold the entire re-establishment of public tranquillity. The day before yesterday conversation ran extremely upon the approach of Lambert with four thousand horse, upon the letters he has written to some sectaries, whose interest he professed to support, and upon the disposition of the city of London to favour him. Letters from the northern counties, moreover, assured

·; that General Fairfax was in arms at the head of all the
ɔbility of the country, and of a brigade which had deserted
ɔm the army under Lambert's command; it was also very
ɛrtain that many very considerable towns had expelled their
ɪrrisons and declared for a free parliament. The city of
ɔndon threatened, on its side, to take some very bold resolu-
ɔn, if the excluded members were not readmitted, and it has
ɔt yet consented to recognize the authority of the parliament.
know even that of late many assemblies of the principal
ɔblemen and Presbyterians have been held, and that they
ave spoken of nothing but the conditions upon which the
ing should be recalled, flattering themselves that the different
ɪrties could no longer come to a reconciliation, that the
ɛakest would be constrained to join them, and that the peo-
le having so strong a disposition to return to a monarchical
ɔvernment, the parliament would not be able to prevent it.
ut, contrary to all these appearances, there arrived yesterday
ɛvening intelligence that Lambert had submitted to the parlia-
ɩent, and had already retired with some of his friends, per-
ɛeiving that his troops wished to prevent him. At the same
ɩme, there arrived assurances that Fairfax had returned to his
ɔuse, and had no other intention but to oppose the violence
ɔmmitted by the army in his county, and to support the
ɪterests of the parliament. All the towns which were thought
o be in insurrection have made similar declarations, and there
ɔes not now appear to be any body in the army or among
he people, who do not profess entire obedience to the parlia-
ɩent, except the council of the citizens of London, which is
ɔmposed of royalists, who had flattered themselves up to this
ɩour that they could have their own way so long as the
ɩivisions continued in the army. As these measures are
ɔroved to be without foundation, the citizens of their own
ɪccord, or by force, will follow the example of the rest of
ɩhe country, and not suffer their dissatisfaction to break out,.
ɩnless some more favourable conjuncture presents itself for
ɛxecuting their designs, which they would cover with the
ɔretext of public liberty, wounded by the exclusion of the
ɩajority of the members of parliament by the minority, which
ɩhas now the good fortune to behold all its enemies vanquished
ɩnd their army in subjection; the glory of which is chiefly
attributed to the firmness of General Monk in supporting their
interest. His friends here affirm that he has greatly contri-

butcd by his intrigues to withdraw the troops from Lambert,
and that he has no less a share in the reduction of the Irish
army. In gratitude for these services, there has been forwarded to him the commission of Licutenant-General of all
the forces of the republic, with very ample authority, and he
is now the most powerful subject in the whole nation.
Fleetwood, Desborough, and all the others of the same faction
are entirely out of employment, and it was only with some
trouble that they were comprehended in the act of indemnity
passed by parliament on the first day of this week. Lambert
has not been excepted from it, provided that he submits within
nine days; and an express had been despatched to inform him
of this. His fall entails that of Vane, and there has been some
talk during the last few days, of putting him in the Tower, it
having been discovered by one of his intercepted letters that
they kept up an extensive correspondence. The Protector's
family also is entirely cast down by this change, not one of
them remaining in authority. Those who possess it are not
men of great name, nor are they sufficiently moderate to preserve themselves from all the dangers to which vengeance,
passion, violence, and private interests will expose them.
Moreover, they do not act with all that unanimity which is
necessary, and on the day before yesterday, the principal of
them indulged in such very bitter language on the subject of
the oath against the royal family, that the Speaker threatened
to leave his chair. On the same day it was enacted that the
places of the definitive deputies should be filled up by new elections, and Mr. Lockhart's letter was read; but although it was
submissive to excess, and expressed extraordinary joy at the
return of the parliament, thanks were ordered only to the
soldiers and officers of the garrison, without mentioning the
government which Fleetwood, Desborough, and Vane, had
maintained. Yesterday's session was spent in devotions, and
to-day the act of abjuration of the royal family was passed, as
well as the re-exclusion of the members excluded in 1648.
These questions would not have been decided so speedily, but
for the reunion of the troops ; and the recommendations of
the common council would have met with greater attention
than they have now experienced; it had resolved upon arming
its militia, but this warmth will soon cool down. * * *

(32.)—M. DE BOURDEAUX TO CARDINAL MAZARIN.

MY LORD,   London, January 26, 1660.

I DID not do myself the honour to write to your Eminence by the preceding post, because I had nothing of importance to communicate; this barrenness of news will continue until the arrival of General Monk, who still pursues his march towards London with five or six thousand men of the Scottish army, and will probably arrive here about the end of the week. All parties now cast their eyes upon him, and each fancies that he is favourable to it; to which his answer to the city has not slightly contributed; he approves and praises its conduct of late, and the declarations that it has made in favour of a free parliament. But he also professes to hold his commission from the parliament, and to desire to support liberty of conscience and a free republic, deferring further explanations until after his arrival in London. The perusal of this letter in the common-council was not followed by any debate, because they had not been able to discover what his sentiments were, and there was no room for taking any decided measures without his assistance. At the same time the parliament received a copy, not only of his letter to the city, but of the answer thereto, by the hands of a messenger whom General Monk despatched express. Thus, up to this time, he has kept on good terms with both these bodies, and the parliament does not manifest less impatience in expecting him than the city; it has even been determined to-day, that two of the members should go to meet him, and invite him to hasten his march, and that an annuity of one thousand pounds sterling should be given him in landed property, as a mark of gratitude for his services. Moreover, all possible complacency is shown to him by authorizing the changes he has made in the army and the establishments in Scotland, where Major-General Morgan commands the troops which he has left here, and a brigade of those from Ireland, which had at first deserted Lambert. Nevertheless, whatever caresses are lavished on him, it is certain that his credit excites great jealousy and that the republicans will give him, if they can, coadjutors in the command of the army, so as to weaken his authority, which they think is incompatible with the safety of their government; this may, perhaps, produce some discontent, upon which the city and the royalists partly found their hopes. The Presbyterians excluded from

the parliament also think him disposed to restore them, and
to favour the design which they have of recalling the king,
of England, upon conditions which will not destroy the
liberty of the people of England ; and I see that very enlightened persons hold these sentiments, which he will be
moreover led to embrace, however little he may be inclined
to do so, by the great divisions by which the parliament is
now agitated.   Never has the misunderstanding been greater
between the few deputies of whom it is composed ; and the
expulsion of Sir Harry Vane, which it was thought would
unite all minds, has only served to bring new factions to light.
Sir Arthur Haslerig, who had greatly distinguished himself
of late, and had appeared to be opposed to the sectaries,
declared for them when the presbyterian faction wished to
expel other deputies of Vane's party ; and their mutual
jealousies have risen so high, that they accuse each other of
wishing to recall the king of England.   This suspicion seems
to have more foundation in the case of the Presbyterians,
and they would otherwise have slight reason for discontent-
ing the sectarians, the staunchest supporters of the parliament, at a time when they are offending the people by the
exclusion of the members expelled in 1648.   There is much
talk of filling up their places by new elections, and this
would be giving some satisfaction to the people ; but as there
would be great difficulty in disposing them to depute persons
well-affectioned towards the republic. and the number of the
new comers would be greater by far than that of the members
now sitting, it is not presumable that their design is to fill
the parliament, unless they wish to favour the return of the
king.   The great opposition of some to the abjuration of the
royal family, also augments all these distrusts, and now it is
proposed to take an engagement in more moderate terms :
some wish to reject it entirely, and the retirement of the
Speaker of the parliament for some days, under the pretext of
indisposition, is considered a prognostic of some storm, it
being certain that he has intimate relations with Monk.   These
are the reflections of this time, their correctness will be ascertained in a few days.   Meanwhile the course of affairs is
arrested, and all that parliament did, last week, was to fill up
those places in the army which had become vacant by the
dismissal of a number of officers, to disband the regiments
of Vane and the sectaries, to give orders for the payment

)f the other troops, and to direct the Council to make sure)f those colonels who, eight days ago, were sentenced to confinement in their own houses, for being most of them, and among others Lambert, suspected of not having obeyed orders, and of caballing in the city. * * *

(33.)—M. DE BOURDEAUX TO CARDINAL MAZARIN.

MY LORD, London, February 2, 1660.

THE letter which your Eminence did me the honour to write to me on the 14th of last month, permits me only to continue my narration of what comes to my knowledge of the affairs of England, and I cannot better discharge this duty than by representing them in the same state which I described in my preceding letter. General Monk not having yet arrived, and his conduct continuing to keep up the hopes of all parties, the commissioners of the parliament set out at the commencement of last week, to convey to him the compliments and reward which have been assigned to him. London, a few days afterwards, followed this example, and deputed three citizens to congratulate him on his journey. The excluded members of parliament have also sent to him one of their number. The nobility of the country through which he passes, do not fail to do him all honour. The towns receive him with ringing of bells, and the people convey to him their complaints. He treats every one with great civility, discloses his feelings to none, and, whilst he is conferring appointments on persons suspected by the parliament, he assures it of his fidelity. The letters which have been received to-day, are again in these terms; they give no reason to expect him until the end of the week, with his army of four thousand infantry, in four regiments, and three of cavalry of about sixteen hundred men, the rest having returned to Scotland. This force would not be sufficient to overthrow the government, if he were not seconded by the city of London, the council of which persists in its refusal to recognize the parliament, and in desiring that the excluded members may be readmitted, or that another parliament shall be called. The city of Exeter, one of the most important in England, together with the county of which it is the capital, have declared themselves to hold the same opinions, and have sent a deputy to communicate their request to the Speaker of the parliament. Other counties have treated it

with still greater contempt, addressing thei
to the mayor of London; and there is a ge
to prevent the government from consolidatii
it therefore professes to have no intentic
itself, but to form a perfect republic, the c
shall be left to successive parliaments; ar
employed itself in drawing up a declaration
abuse the people of the impressions which
it, in order to render it favourable to the re
In addition to this precaution, a great p
has been posted in the city and its suburbs
arise only from discontent among the trooj
to satisfy them by promises of speedy r
gratuities to the leaders. Admiral Lawso
annuity of 500*l.* sterling, in landed prope1
had an idea of presenting a request on be
Vane, but their warmth produced no result
ment continues to seek out and punish othe1
same faction. One, a colonel and the gove
of Wight, has been deprived of his regime
has been suspended and sent to the Tower c
liament has also received the accusation
officers of the Irish armies against the co:
governed it during the interregnum, and
Ludlow, their leader, who had been detained
time, because he appeared too much attacl
ment, and who, a few days before its re-es
returned to his post; but, not having bec
had retired into one of the fortresses of tl
with some sectaries. He has been directe
the other accused persons, to come and give
actions; and, as peace now prevails, they
position to disobey this order. Other commis
sent in their stead, and parliament provid<
all the principal posts in connexion with the
justice in England, without exacting any pa1
also made Mr. Scott a Secretary of State, i
places of the cashiered officers, giving regi
their supporters who have never seen any
are, as nearly as I can tell, the doings of
end of which the old Speaker resumed his <
some draw inferences in favour of the pa1

assert that a great number of its members are well-disposed owards the king, that they encourage the disobedience of the hity, and only await Monk's arrival to declare themselves, as they think he will not fail to pay attention to the wishes of the whole nation, the great advantages which he will gain from it, the small amount of intelligence and stability displayed by the present government, its jealousies, and the bad fortune of all the generals who have served it. But, although all these considerations are weighty, we may, nevertheless, doubt whether they will make much impression upon a man of compact mind, who prides himself upon his great sincerity and firmness of purpose, who is moreover a republican, and whose conduct in domestic matters gives no great promise. It is not certain also whether his troops are entirely devoted to him; and if the royalists have made any arrangements with him, they are very secret, as he passes for impregnable among most of them, whom he has not yet made terms with. As the destiny of England partly depends upon his resolution, and as he himself may not yet have come to any determination, no solid judgment can be formed upon affairs here until we have a clearer insight into his views, and I should not deserve the confidence which your Eminence shows that you place in my opinion if, on the eve of so great a crisis, and at a time when those most passionately attached or opposed to the government, are not less agitated by hope and fear, I should presume to foretell the future. * * *

(34.)—M. DE BOURDEAUX TO CARDINAL MAZARIN.

MY LORD,   London, February 9, 1660.

THE last letter which I did myself the honour to write to your Eminence, informed you that the hopes of all parties in England were based upon General Monk, and that all were impatiently awaiting his arrival. He has not yet reached London, and will not arrive here for three days, during which his troops will refresh themselves in the environs. But his views have already been ascertained by the reception which he gave to the deputies from this city, and from many of the counties. He received the first in presence of the commissioners of the parliament, and replied to their compliments by demonstrations of astonishment that he should be thought capable of being unfaithful to the authorities from whom he held his commission, exhorted them to submit, and not inter-

M

fere with the measures which it would take to restore tran
quillity to the nation under a suitable form of government
but rather to second its good intentions by their prayers, an
meanwhile to have patience, the only services which the
parliament desired of the town.   He spoke with still greate
sharpness to the other deputies who came to request him, or
the part of the nobility of different counties, to support the
readmission of the excluded members without their taking
any oath, or the convocation of a free parliament.   Afte
having blamed their impatience and the demand which the
made, after the parliament had rejected it, he also gave
them to understand that it was not the custom to allow any
deputy to take his seat in such an assembly, before he had
entered into some obligation; he represented to them that
the present parliament was the freest that had ever been seen
in England; saying that it would fill up the vacant places as
soon as they should have decided upon the qualifications
necessary to prevent the ruin of a cause for which they had
fought so long; that, finally, they must submit to the present
government, and that he was bound to defend it.   Besides
these verbal declarations, he has made a similar one in writing,
in the form of a letter addressed to his own county, the
nobility of which had adopted the same opinions as the city
of London; he therein expressed at some length the reasons
which oppose the return of the royal family, and which ought
to dispose the whole nation to choose in preference a republican government.   The parliament received the news on the
5th instant, together with letters, both from its own deputies
and from the said General Monk, full of assurances of his
fidelity, in gratitude for which, the general's commission,
which had been given him during the interregnum by the
Council of State, was approved.   The post of Master of the
Rolls of his country was given him, and an act of approbation of all that he had done was read for the first time.
From this time forth also there began to appear a great
change in the disposition of the minds of this assembly, it
being even resolved immediately to levy a tax of one hundred
thousand pounds sterling per month; and search was afterwards made, in the houses of some citizens, for the money
which is said to be intended for the king of England.   A
considerable sum was, in fact, found in the house of one very
royalist merchant, but it is claimed by several individuals.

t is also now proposed to dissolve the common council, and
) compel the city to yield that obedience which it has up to
his hour refused. If, on the one side, their boldness has
ncreased, that of the people is not the less diminished, nor
o the royalists appear less downcast; their only resource is
ow in the general discontent of all the nobility, who are
eginning to assemble in different quarters. It is not,
moreover, to be presumed that the army will always remain
a such complete dependance upon the civil power; and,
lthough just now the condition of the government appears
dvantageous, though the troops are under no apprehension
ith regard to the return of the king, and though this fear may
e strong enough to keep them united, nevertheless, I cannot
ut concur in the opinion of those who think that there is yet
much progress to be made before the parliament will be con-
lidated, seeing the general alienation of all the people, and
he jealousies which some of the deputies were not able to
lissimulate to-day, when it was proposed to withdraw the
roops from the town to make way for those from Scotland,
according to Monk's desire, which has been complied with.
This request has reawakened some hopes and doubts, and it
may safely be stated that the least discontent of the army, or
assistance from without, would destroy all the existing establishments, unless the people were to change their humour.
a order to recover them from the great aversion which
hey appear to feel, the parliament decreed and published, at
he commencement of last week, a declaration in which it
rofesses its desire to establish a free government, without
ing or lords, under the direction of the parliament; and to
orm an army in such a manner that, so long as it shall be
ecessary to the safety of the republic, it shall obey the civil
uthority; that all questions and proceedings concerning the
ves, liberties, and conditions of the people, shall be regulated
ccording to the laws of the country, and that the parliament
hall not meddle either with the ordinary administration, or
ith the execution of the laws; that provision shall be made
or the maintenance of the ministers, that the tithes shall be
ontinued to them as the most convenient method of sup-
orting them, and that provision shall also be made for
liberty of conscience in matters of religion, in conformity with
he word of God; that the universities shall be kept up, even
vith an augmentation of their privileges, if it is necessary:

M 2

that the parliament shall turn its attention to means fo
restoring and increasing commerce, and that, finally, it shal
seek some method of relieving the people as quickly as pos
sible from the heavy taxes with which they were burdene(
by the bad councils and conduct of preceding governments
The other debates of this week are of less importance, and :
may merely remark, that two gentlemen who had presente(
a species of declaration in favour of a free parliament, fron
one of the counties of England, were sent to the Tower o
London, not so much because of the contents of this document, as of the address made to the Speaker of the parliament, and the gentlemen sitting at Westminster. This
treatment has not prevented other gentlemen from under.
taking similar commissions, and presenting to the Speaker, on
the day before yesterday, a request in the same style. A
debate again took place on the qualifications for the contemplated elections, but no decision was arrived at, and parliament has been employed in granting commissions, both to
civil and military officers; and a committee of twenty-one
persons has been appointed to administer the affairs of the
navy, the commander of which has gone with a large number
of his officers to meet Monk, who has, upon his march,
obtained a very express declaration from the governor of
Hull; after which there remain in England no troops, or garrisons to be reduced to obedience to the parliament, any more
than in Scotland and Ireland.   *   *   *

(35.)—M. DE BOURDEAUX TO CARDINAL MAZARIN.
MY LORD,   London, February 16, 1660.
    THE last posts having brought me no letter from your
Eminence, and as I have no other orders to execute, I have
only to inform you of what took place at the audience which
the council of state granted me last week, and of the internal
affairs of England. The duplicate of my despatch to M. de
Brienne will acquit me of this duty; and I have nothing to
add thereto, except that the Scottish general has declared
again to-day in parliament that he would remain constant to
its interests, and that he is reputed to be entirely opposed to
the interests of the king of England, although he refuses to
take any particular engagement against his whole family. The
Presbyterian faction of this same assembly holds similar
opinions; and finding itself sustained by the army, it will

revail over the sectaries, who remain few in number. The great business of the present moment is to fill up the vacant places by persons well-affectioned to the present government; and it is not easy to succeed in this, whatever precautions they may take, for the people are so alienated. Moreover, these new elections cannot long be deferred without great inconvenience, as the counties declare that they will pay no more until the parliament is free and complete, and the soldiers are beginning to lose patience. Those whom the Scottish general forced to withdraw from London appeared greatly discontented, and the 600 men who were ordered to proceed to Dunkirk were still more violent in their mutiny, in which their officers joined. The colonel having had some difficulty in preserving his life, it is proposed to decimate them. Mr. Lockhart is expected here this week, and it is contemplated to send him, or some one else, to France; but the government must be delivered from its present embarrassment before it can attend to any affairs abroad. * * *

(36.)—M. DE BOURDEAUX TO M. DE BRIENNE.

My Lord,   London, February 17, 1660.

* * * The heads of the English government declare that they will not support the interests of Portugal, and that it is necessary to make peace with Spain, in order to restore the commerce of England, the ruin of which is alienating the affection of the people. They are in fact necessitated to leave no means untried to overcome the aversion of the nation; and it is upon good grounds that the officers of the English army represent it to be so general. But it does not follow that a slight support from abroad would be able to restore the monarchy, there being little vigour among the nobility, and less disposition in the large towns to run any risk, since they have not availed themselves of the opportunities presented to them by the recent divisions; they confine their opposition to starving the army, by refusing to pay the taxes, and declare that the declarations of all the counties in favour of a free parliament will be followed by a resolution to close their purses, until their wishes have been complied with. But the sword usually can produce gold; and if the army remains united, the people will find it difficult to avoid supporting it. The orders for the levy of the taxes are therefore addressed to the troops quartered in the counties; and as their interest is

concerned, they will not fail to carry them into thorough exe
cution. The hopes which were still entertained of Monk are
daily proved to have been unfounded by the declarations which
he continued to make to numbers of deputies from the provinces
before he reached London. He arrived here on the morning
of the 13th, at the head of his troops, having been sent for on
the preceding night in great haste, because the infantry which
was in the city had mutinied, and part had installed themselves in Somerset House, after having driven away their
officers; they would not go to the quarters which had been
assigned them until they were paid, and the soldiers declared
themselves ready to serve any one who would pay them,
making mention of a free parliament and of Lambert. Neither
remonstrances nor the arrival of some cavalry were able either
to persuade or intimidate them; and it not being considered
advisable to proceed to extremities, the council made all haste
to give them a month's pay, which pacified them. Those at
Somerset House did not leave their post until they saw Monk,
and remained all night under arms. Propositions were meanwhile made to them in the name of the city, which they refused to believe; and some apprentices taking advantage of
the opportunity, assembled in considerable numbers; but the
mayor having given information of this, the cavalry marched
against them, dispersed them without much resistance, and
took fifty prisoners. The remainder of the night was spent
in continual alarms; and the evil would have been very great
but for the neighbourhood of the Scottish army, which deprived
of courage those who are believed to have excited this mutiny,
which produced consequences at Gravesend, the few men who
were sent to recruit the garrison of Dunkirk having on the
next day revolted against their officers, and even wished to
force their colonel. They also sent a deputation of two
soldiers to Monk, who represented to him the injustice done
them by sending them out of England unpaid ; he exhorted
them to return to their duty, and some squadrons of cavalry
forthwith marched against them to compel them to do so, and
succeeded without bloodshed. But it is proposed to punish
the most factious of the three hundred who have been arrested,
and to cashier all those who joined in the insurrection at
London. The whole army would incur the same fate if means
were not taken to appease these discontents, which have been
greatly increased by the order which Monk sent to the troops

a London to withdraw. The parliament did not wish to
ppose him, although this arrangement was considered rather
rbitrary. Nothing remarkable took place on the entry of
his general, except that the Speaker, who thought that he
would alight at his house, left the company to go to receive
him, and having met him on his road, the one got out of his
arriage. and the other off his horse, and they paid each other
great civilities; after which the general continued his march
as far as Whitehall, where the members of parliament presented him a complimentary address. The day after his arrival
he again made in their presence a solemn declaration of his
active and passive obedience, offering even to resign his commission if it should be judged necessary for the welfare of the
republic, and only excepting from this great obedience submission to a monarchical government. He was to-day conducted into this assembly by two of the members, his soldiers
lining the court-yard and hall of Westminster; and he gave
an account of his journey, represented the general desire of
the people for a free parliament without any oath, explained
himself against that which had been proposed to him, and
besought aid for Scotland and Ireland, which he represented
as very poor. His wishes were accompanied by so much submission that the parliament was greatly satisfied with him,
and bestowed upon him more honours than have been granted
to any other subject in the nation. Nevertheless, his appointment as general is not well established, and it is affirmed that
it ceased on the day of his arrival in London; that now he is
only one of the commissaries-general of the army, and that he
can take no important step without the consent of his colleagues. But if he shares this title with them, his power is
very different, as the troops recognize him as their only leader,
and all parties look upon him as the man upon whom depends
the establishment or the ruin of the government; consequently,
he has not time enough to receive all the visits that are paid
him. The ambassadors were not the last to seek him out.
The envoy from Holland sent his son to compliment him upon
his campaign, and the Portuguese minister requested an
audience. I made no such haste, not judging it compatible
with my dignity. But the correspondence which has taken
place between him and myself, on some matters of business,
gave me an excuse for calling on him to-day. During the last
few days the parliament has been chiefly occupied in settling

the qualifications for the new elections, which it can no longer
defer, whatever danger may arise from filling up the vacant
seats, as the people are so badly disposed towards it; it has
also given some commissions in the army, received with thanks
a declaration from the seamen, given orders for the recovery
of the money which certain individuals, under different pretexts, received from the state during the last interregnum, and
restored that which had been seized because it was supposed
to be intended for the king of England. For want of proofs,
it has deputed the Council of State to examine into the tumult
which has just occurred in London; and General Ludlow,
who was in Ireland, has arrived to give an account of his
actions. I am, &c.

(37.)—M. DE BOURDEAUX TO CARDINAL MAZARIN.
MY LORD,   London, February 19, 1660.
    IT seemed probable that the declarations made by General
Monk, before and after his arrival in London, would produce
some effect in that city and in the country to the advantage of
the parliament, and during some days there appeared to be
considerable despondency; nevertheless, the objections raised
by the general against taking a special oath against the royal
family having occasioned some to declare that he was inclined
to embrace the royal cause, and disposed others to take confidence, the town council yesterday made no difficulty about
receiving a deputation from one of the English counties, who
came to offer their assistance in obtaining the convocation of
a free parliament. It was also debated whether the city
should pay the taxes ordered by the parliament, and the
majority of votes seemed to be opposed to doing so. The
mayor, who held more moderate views, was hard pressed by
some citizens who talked of nothing but shedding the last
drop of their blood in defence of the liberties of the whole
nation and of the city. The Council of State, foreseeing that
longer toleration would end in destroying the authority of the
government, and that every other community would follow
this bad example, judged it necessary at once to disperse this
faction, and destroy the hopes which it centred on Monk, by
the orders which he executed this morning. At break of day
he entered the city at the head of all his troops, posted them
in the streets and at the gates, and then removed all the
chains and posts from the streets; seized six of the most

eminent citizens, and sent them to the Tower of London; some others fled. He also sent for the record of the deliberations of the common council, and ordered the town-clerk to present it to the parliament to-morrow; summoned the mayor and aldermen, and desired them to tell him precisely whether the city would pay the taxes or not; upon which no answer was given him, it being postponed until the council shall have met, which will be to-morrow. Meanwhile the troops remain in the same posts, and the general at an inn near the Guildhall. The parliament has authorized all these proceedings; and it is believed that, in order to make sure of the town, some other measures will be taken, as no good can be expected from it so long as it is governed by those who are now in office. The mayor and aldermen alone are well-intentioned; the others are entirely opposed to the parliament and devotedly attached to royalty. The tranquillity with which the action of to-day took place leaves no room to doubt that the people will suffer all establishments which may be considered necessary. They beheld without murmuring, and in great crowds, the removal of their chains and the imprisonment of the citizens, and the mildness with which General Monk spoke kept them still in some hope that he will contribute to their design of having a free parliament, without the deputies being obliged to enter into any engagement before admission. Orders have been issued for the arrest of twenty-six deputies from the provinces, and the government is persuaded that fear alone can prevent them from combining against the existing authorities. The town of Bristol, one of the most wealthy and populous in England, revolted under the same pretext; but the magistrates and leading citizens succeeded in appeasing the populace. Gloucester also has been rather agitated. The parliament has not yet decided upon the qualifications for the new elections, and great inconveniences are found to exist, whatever precautions they may take against having republican deputies, since the people are so badly intentioned. * * *

(38.)—M. DE BOURDEAUX TO CARDINAL MAZARIN.
MY LORD, London, February 22, 1660.
I SEND the present letter by an express courier, foreseeing that the post will be stopped, and it might be somewhat prejudicial, in the present conjuncture, if your Eminence were not promptly acquainted with what is taking place here

in London. My letter of the 19th of this month informed
you that the debates in the common council had obliged the
Council of State to send General Monk, with all his troops,
into the city, and that he had committed six citizens to the
Tower, removed the chains, and urged the payment of the
taxes : he was also ordered to break down the gates ; but,
upon being besought by the mayor not to commit such a
violence, he undertook to intercede with the parliament; and,
in fact, in the same letter in which he reported the performance of all his orders, he represented that it would be proceeding to too great extremities, and that the most respectable
inhabitants of the city appeared quite disposed to submit.
Instead of paying attention to his remonstrance, the parliament, without further delay, dissolved the common council,
and directed the general, in rather harsh terms, to do what
he was ordered.   He obeyed, the next morning, and had
some gates burned, without opposition by the people.   He
again sent to the mayor and citizens, in order to obtain some
money from them ; but some declared that they had no power
to determine upon anything without the concurrence of the
common council, and others answered that they would rather
consent to the pillage of their houses than to a tax, unless it
were levied by order of a free parliament.   Having been
unable to gain anything, either by threats or persuasion, the
general returned to Whitehall on the afternoon of the 20th,
leaving the greater part of his troops in the city, and being
much hurt at the bad reception which had been given to his
intercession.   The enemies of the government did not fail to
take advantage of his discontent; and, entirely to alienate
him, they suggested to him, by means of some ministers, and
other persons who have some credit with him, that the parliament had appointed him to act against the city, in order to
render him more odious, and afterwards to destroy him with
less trouble ; that a resolution had already been taken to
deprive him of his commission, as soon as the town was reduced; that Lambert was to be recalled, General Ludlow
sent back to take the command in Ireland, and Vane re-established in authority, as the latter had already obtained permission to remain in London, under the pretext of illness,
and the prosecutions instituted against the others had been
suspended ; and that, finally, the sectaries were going to
resume the government, since, when they had presented to

...arliament a requisition to the effect that no one should be admitted into that assembly, or into any public employment, unless he had taken the oath of abjuration of the royal family, which was refused by the Presbyterians, far from rejecting such a demand, they had received a vote of thanks, from which circumstance he might infer that the request was not disagreeable. Fate, or the design of some members of parliament, determined that on that same day a debate arose, and an act was passed, giving the command of the army to five commissioners, without taking Monk's services into particular consideration, or regarding the rank of commander-in-chief of all the forces of the republic, which had been conferred upon him during the interregnum, and afterwards confirmed, it being presupposed that the said rank came to an end on his arrival in London. This bad treatment, and their just reasons for jealousy, caused his officers to assemble around him on that very evening; and having found them all disposed to follow him, they resolved to repair the injury which they had just done, though with repugnance, to the city, and even to adopt its sentiments, and retire thither, in order to support them with greater security; which was done yesterday, at about eleven o'clock in the morning, the general having left Whitehall at the head of a few companies of cavalry to proceed to the mayor, whom he had shortly beforehand informed, that he might not take the alarm at his return into the city. As he mounted his horse, he dispatched two colonels with a letter to the parliament, in which—after having complained of the orders which he had been obliged to execute, of the measures which were being concerted with the sectaries, of the impunity of Lambert, Ludlow, and Vane, of the little inclination shown by the parliament to fill up the vacant seats, and of the position it has taken to force upon the people an oath against the royal family, which can be taken only by persons accustomed to perjure themselves—he summons them to issue writs, between to-day and Friday, for the election of new deputies in all the counties, without binding them by any fresh oath. . . . . He also desires that this body may not continue its session beyond the 16th of May, and that another free parliament may be convoked for the same time; and, in conclusion, he declares his resolution to wait in the city for an answer. The reading of this despatch caused no little surprise; and it was resolved to send immediately to the

general the same two deputies who had gone to meet him, to
endeavour to satisfy him. They found him with the mayor, and
expressed to him that the parliament had learned with regret
of his discontent, and did not think it had given him any
cause; they disavowed the pretended correspondence with
the sectaries, Lambert, and the others, and attributed the
delay of the proceedings which had commenced against them
to the difficulty they would find in convicting them. As to
the replacement of the excluded or deceased members, they
declared that the parliament warmly desired it, that the writs
would even have been issued long before, but for the frequent
interruptions occasioned by the general himself; and that,
finally, the parliament was disposed to do whatever he and
the city and the people might desire, with the single exception
of recalling the royal family. It is said that he declared that
he was equally opposed to this last step. This conference,
however, which took place in the presence of two citizens
and one colonel, did not produce a reunion, the general
remaining steadfast in his opinions; and the deputies retired,
after having ineffectually besought him not to press the parliament so hard, and returned to Westminster in the afternoon,
to make their report, upon which a resolution was taken to
issue the writs for the elections as speedily as possible. The
five commissioners who are to govern the army were next
chosen: General Monk is one, and with him are associated
Sir Arthur Haslerig, Colonel Morley, the governor of the
Tower, and two other colonels. While these deliberations
were going on at Westminster, the mayor and aldermen
assembled in the Guildhall, whither the general having
repaired, the advocate of the army spoke, as much in his
name as in that of the other officers, and represented them
all to be greatly grieved that they had been obliged to execute
such rigorous orders on the two preceding days. He attributed the burning of the gates to Haslerig's soldiers; and
declared that the army was resolved to unite with the city in
support of the convocation of a free parliament—praying
that, meanwhile, it might be furnished with quarters.

This speech was received with extraordinary demonstrations
of joy, and offers of their houses and their purses; the troops
were then distributed in their quarters, and during the evening the people manifested all imaginable public marks of
joy. Never were soldiers so greatly caressed, or so liberally

upplied with drink; bonfires were kept up all night long, in
ront of most houses, both in Westminster and in the city,
nd the bells contributed to express the general delight. In
ome places the king's health was publicly drunk; in others,
aany things were done in derision of the parliament, and the
ouses of several sectaries were in danger of being pillaged.
:his general inclination will doubtless lead to the supposition
hat the ancient form of government will be restored; and
he private statements of persons who take a leading part in
Monk's deliberations, give reason to believe that this is his
ntention, although he professes to be opposed to the monarchy,
ind that he uses this language through fear of being abandoned
)y his troops; if, before he had gained them thoroughly over,
ie should declare for the king. Yesterday's step, in fact,
eaves him no other course to take, as he cannot make friends
igain with the parliament, and as the forces which recognize
:his general's authority are too weak to maintain him, unless
ie is supported by London and the nobility, who are entirely
)ent upon restoring the monarchy. It is true that the ma-
ority, among others the Presbyterians, who are now predomi-
1ant, do not wish the king of England to return uncondition-
illy; being persuaded that, if he returned with unlimited
iuthority, their religion would suffer greatly under the bishops;
ind that, as the most influential of them contributed to the
overthrow of the deceased king, if the hands of the present
monarch were not tied, their whole cabal would be exposed
to great danger, especially as his ministers are considered
to be violent and vindictive. It cannot either be disavowed
that some of these very Presbyterians are inclined to a republican government; and that, if they found themselves excluded, the idea might occur to them of gaining the supreme
authority, by the assistance of Monk, who is believed to have
come to London with the ambition of raising himself to a
post similar to that held by the Prince of Orange. These
different plans cannot but throw obstacles in the way of the
royal family; but as all the people desire their return, and
have liberty to choose their deputies, it is not to be supposed
that their choice will fall upon persons suspected of holding
opposite views. It is even a well-founded opinion that some
of the members of the present parliament—among others,
the governor of the Tower and the Speaker—foment Monk's
jealousies, in order to detach him from the party he had em-

braced. This suspicion is not of recent date; the oath was proposed merely for the purpose of discovering these false brethren; and it is remarked that some of those who have refused to take it have always passed over the establishment of the republic, and kept on good terms with the royalists; and that these are also the least connected with the downfall of the deceased king, and the most wealthy. It does not yet appear what course will be pursued by the others, who cannot expect safety either for their lives or property if the king returns: they have perceived, but too late, the fault they committed in cashiering all the officers of the army, and abandoning the sectaries; and it is not without reason that they are accused of seeking to obtain a reconciliation with both. But they would have great difficulty in doing this now, being in the power of Monk, who will not fail to disperse them, and to substitute in their places the excluded members, whose numbers are three times as great as their own, if he sees troops approaching to their assistance; moreover, the people hold them in such great aversion, that, if they were once driven from Westminster, they would never return thither, unless they could conquer England. Thus their sole hope seems still to be Monk; and therefore they continue to humour him, through fear lest, raising the mask, he should summon back the king without waiting for a parliament, being persuaded that, when the parliament is assembled, they will be able to form factions to thwart the royalists, and, in time, to gain over the troops, who clearly see that they will fall with the republic, as the people desire the king, but no army; and that, in any case, they will be able to call back the king upon certain conditions, and thus provide for their own safety. I am not sufficiently well informed of his Majesty's intentions, to take much share in these domestic conflicts; nevertheless, according to the course which they take, I will do my best to secure his interests, which can be no other than to forward, in some manner, the return of the king of England, if it is inevitable, and I shall have sufficient facilities to insinuate to General Monk that which will probably be desired of him. Your Eminence will, if you please, let me know; and will consider that the election of the new deputies will require some time, and that affairs here might take such a course, that their assemblage may be prevented by some other change. If anything of importance occurs tonorrow, I will write it by the post. Meanwhile, it only remains for me to subscribe myself, &c.

(39.)—M. DE BOURDEAUX TO CARDINAL MAZARIN.

MY LORD, London, February 26, 1660.

THE letter which your Eminence did me the honour to write to me on the 3rd instant, directed me to inform you, with all possible exactitude, of what is taking place in England; I will not allow to-day's post to leave without executing this order, although I can as yet give no positive information. The parliament has continued to humour General Monk in all sorts of ways; and during the early part of the present week, it recommenced prosecuting those who excited his jealousy, ordering Sir Harry Vane to leave the city, and publishing a proclamation commanding Lambert to present himself before them within three days, on pain of confiscation of all his property; it also fixed a day for hearing those members of parliament who acted during the late interruption, and gave orders for the payment of the troops which have come from Scotland. The same and following days were employed in settling the qualifications for the ensuing elections; and the abjuration of the royal family, which some wished to render essential, has been changed into a simple promise to be faithful to the republic of England, and to its government in the form of a free state, without any single person as king, and without any House of Lords. The other restrictions are very inconsiderable, although very numerous, and this business is to be terminated to-day, in order that the writs may be issued by the end of the week, according to the desire of the general, in conformity with which declarations have arrived from different counties, and among others, from Yorkshire, where General Fairfax and all the nobility have entered into an engagement not to pay any tax, until the excluded members of the parliament are readmitted, or another free parliament is called. Although the latter course seems to be more agreeable, there have been some overtures of accommodation with the excluded members, and it is said, that ten of each party are to meet for conference this evening. If the excluded members were to take the oath in its original terms, and would bind themselves not to interfere with any acts passed since the year 1648, they would surmount the chief obstacles to their restoration, and,

in this case, it would not be proposed to summon another
parliament so soon. These propositions do not satisfy the
royalists, and they are beginning to doubt the intentions of
General Monk, since he has forbidden the town council
to meet, and to arm the militia before the parliament
has finished its deliberations upon the convocation of the
deputies, and has, as it were, approved of the engagement
against a royal government, which was communicated to him
before it was adopted, and against which he made no other
objection, than that the words *in the presence of God*, should
be left out, and they were accordingly omitted. This conduct still keeps men's minds in suspense, and some believe
him to be a republican, and that he will not favour any other
form of government, that he would not even have taken this
last step if the parliament would have given him some prerogative over the other four commissioners appointed to govern
the army, according to the opinion of some deputies of this
assembly who wished to render it necessary; and that he is
on the eve of quitting the city, notwithstanding the caresses
it has lavished upon him, and the money it has given to his
troops, and of entering into the Council of State with all those
whom the abjuration prevented from taking their places.
Others still persuade themselves that his real feelings are in
favour of a free parliament, and that whatever oath the
deputies may take, he will recall the king, to whom he gave
assurances of support, both before his departure from Scotland, and since his arrival in London, and that henceforward
he cannot be in safety with the parliament. Both these
opinions have some foundation, and it appears that this
general has kept up the hopes of all parties in order to
place himself in a position to support that one from which
he would derive most advantage, but that in reality, his
primary aim has been to consolidate the republic, and
make himself its general; that such alluring conditions may
have been offered him of late, that he has returned to his
first opinions, and will think that he has done his duty to
the city and the whole nation in reference to the promise
which he made them to act in concert with them so as to
obtain a free parliament, by obliging the present to fill up
the vacant seats, although it may be with an oath contrary to
the desires of all the people of England, which will not be
without effect if the armies are united to enforce its observ-

ance. We must wait a few days more before forming a decisive opinion. The Scotch have sent six deputies, with the Earl of Glencairn at their head, to watch over the interests, of their nation here, and this deputation is con- sidered to be a consequence of the fair words spoken to them by Monk. Mr. Lockhart has been in London for some days, out I have not yet seen him; his arrival and the embarrass- ments of the country have caused me up to the present time to postpone speaking to the Council of State about the differ- ences which have arisen between the garrisons of Dunkirk and Calais. As the important business now under discussion is to be brought to an end to-morrow, there will soon be an opportunity for treating of other affairs ; and I am conse- quently urged by the Swedish ministers to press the despatch of fresh orders to the British plenipotentiaries in Zealand. I have been informed that General Lambert sent to tell General Monk that, in order to heal the jealousies which his presence excites, he would enter into the service of the king of Sweden, if the parliament would give him liberty to do so and to take with him those soldiers who would be willing to follow him. This offer may, probably, be accepted , at least as far as concerns himself. I am, &c.

(40.)—M. DE BOURDEAUX TO CARDINAL MAZARIN.
MY LORD,   London, March 1, 1660.
    I SHALL not write to-day more positively of the affairs of this country than I did in my preceding letter, but, on the last day of last week, the parliament concluded its debates upon the elections, warned the people, under very severe penalties, not to give their votes unless they had all the requisite qualifications, and reserved to itself the power to de- cide in doubtful cases ; there has also taken place, in presence of General Monk, a conference between the excluded and actual members, without their coming to any resolution, the latter having offered to admit the former if they would take the oath against royalty, and these having refused to do so, not so much from conscientious scruples, as from fear of losing their credit. This negociation is not yet broken off, and there still remains hope of an accommodation upon con- ditions that will secure one party without pledging the others to any form of government, although up to the present time General Monk has professed that he desires a republic, and

N

most of his officers are of the same opinion. Meanwhile, the issue of the writs for the election is delayed. As it is of importance that the bailiffs who assemble the people and preside over them should be well-intentioned, the parliament has, according to custom, renewed the commissioners and appointed persons on whom it can rely. These are the principal occurrences of the last few days. Nothing of importance has taken place in the city, except that the Council of State having invited the general to come and take his seat to advise with them on the means of preserving Dunkirk, presupposing that the Spaniards were preparing to attack it, and Mr. Lockhart having come expressly to give his advice, the mayor and alderman begged the general not to leave the city or withdraw his soldiers, until some arrangement had been made for the safety of the town, which he promised he would do; and under this pretext he refused to go to the Council, but gave them to understand, that whatever might be the division of England, it would always be sufficiently at union to preserve the place, even if a hundred-and-fifty thousand men should attack it. I have been informed, that, in order to please the city still more, he has represented to parliament that peace with Spain is necessary. The provinces still profess to desire a free parliament, and the bonfires which were made in London, have caused others to be made in several towns, where there even occurred some tumult, to repress which Monk sent orders; from which we may conclude that the fate of the nation is now in his hands, as all parties caress him and do all in their power to gain him over to their side. Lambert even has addressed himself to him to obtain a mitigation of his prosecution by the parliament, and his recommendation produced an immediate effect. It is said that this great complaisance does not prevent them from taking underhand measures with the sectaries, and that a plan has been formed to place Lambert at their head, if Monk declares for the King; but the object of their efforts, would, in this case, be rather uncertain, as the nation is so disposed to favour his return. * * *

(41.)—M. DE BOURDEAUX TO CARDINAL MAZARIN.
MY LORD,   London, March 2, 1660.
    I SEND an express after yesterday's post to inform your Eminence that this morning, General Monk restored the old

members, having first agreed with them that they shall sit
only for four days, during which they shall despatch writs
into the provinces to cause the election of a new parliament,
excepting only royalists and sectaries, and without binding
them by any oath : all the troops are also to be disbanded,
with the exception of those under General Monk, and the
militia will be intrusted to the hands of the gentlemen of the
country. A new Council of State will be elected, and all that
has been done by the parliament since 1648 will be ratified.
Besides these conditions, a promise has been made to Monk
to constitute him General of all the forces in England, Scotland, and Ireland. I postpone until Thursday's post such
particulars of this important change as may come to my knowledge ; for I have now only time to subscribe myself with
respect, &c.

(42.)—M. DE BOURDEAUX TO CARDINAL MAZARIN.

MY LORD,   London, March 4, 1660.

THE letter which I wrote to your Eminence on the day
before yesterday, arrived at Dover in time enough to be taken
by the post of the 1st of this month, and will already have
informed you that General Monk has restored the members of
parliament who were excluded in 1648, and of the principal
conditions agreed on between them. This change, very important when we consider the consequences it may entail,
took place without any opposition or ceremony whatever, and
with such secresy that, although it had been concerted with
many persons on the 1st of this month, when the general returned, on the next day morning, from the City to Whitehall
with most of his troops, Sir Arthur Haslerig and those of his
faction went immediately to visit him, being persuaded that
he had returned with the intention of remaining steadfast in
their interests. He disabused them, and, after having communicated to them his resolution, invited them to continue
their session, professing that he still held the same views with
regard to the form of the government ; which occasioned them
urgently to request that he would at least oblige these members to take that oath against the monarchy which he himself
seemed to have approved. He declined to do so, saying that
it was an act of useless circumspection, as it had appeared to
him that most of them were well-intentioned towards the republic. They were obliged to be satisfied with this answer,

N 2

and just at that time, the excluded members having come to
wait upon the general, he told them that his cares had not
been able to arrest the course of the divisions which existed
amongst them, and that several conferences had been held to
that end without success, but that at last he had received
entire satisfaction from them, and had given them the trouble
to call upon him in order that he might declare his views to
them more freely than in past times ; and that, through fear
of being misunderstood, as he often had been before, he had
reduced to writing the heads of his speech, which he would
now have read to them.   At the commencement, he declares
that he has perceived that the peace and establishment of the
nation depended, after God, on their hands ; praises their
wisdom, piety, and disinterestedness ; and affirms that he has
entire confidence that they will show all necessary readiness
to repair past evils.   He next professes that he contemplates
nothing but the glory of God and the establishment of the
nation upon the foundation of a republic, and that he wishes
to impose nothing upon them likely to restrain their liberty
in making future establishments, but only represents to them,
that as the old government has been broken up, it can be re-
constructed only upon the ruins of the people, who have
pledged themselves in defence of the parliament and of religion,
and that, if the king returns, his power will become arbitrary.
He speaks afterwards of the City of London as the bulwark
of the parliaments, makes its happiness depend upon a republican government, and presupposes that under any other, it
cannot become the metropolis of the commerce of all Christendom, to which rank God and nature seem to have destined it.
He also proves to them that, upon religious grounds, the
monarchy cannot be introduced, because it would bring with
it that system of prelacy against which the nation has pledged
itself so solemnly ; and insinuates that a moderate Presbyterian government, with sufficient liberty for really tender
consciences, is the most suitable that can just now be established.   The interest of the nobles who have joined with the
people is not forgotten ; the general judges it advisable that
as the state of the three nations is such that another House of
Parliament cannot be suffered, some hereditary distinction
should be given them which may make them appear more
noble to posterity.   His conclusion of the whole speech is an
invitation to the members to go and promptly take their seats

in order to establish the conduct of the armies in such a manner that they may contribute to the peace and security of the
country, and not to its ruin; to provide for the future maintenance of all the forces both by land and sea, as well as for
the payment of their arrears and the other necessities of the
government; to form a Council of State, with authority to provide for the civil government and the administration of justice,
both in Ireland and Scotland, and also to issue writs for the
convocation of a parliament of the three united nations on the
30th of April next, with qualifications which shall assure the
safety of the cause in which he and the others are engaged,
and according to the division of the country effected in the
year 1654; which parliament, thus convoked, shall be able to
assemble and act with all liberty for a more perfect establishment of the republic, without a king, single ruler, or House
of Lords, and that finally the parliament shall legally dissolve
itself, in order to make way for others. He then finished by
an assurance that the guards would allow the excluded members to resume their seats, that himself and the officers under
his command and all the soldiers of the three nations would shed
their blood for them and the successive parliaments; but that
if their counsels tend to other objects, force and violence will
immediately return, and all hopes of the long-desired settlement will be buried in disorder. The members went, with
this mission, to resume their places before the others had taken
their seats, and found the infantry drawn up in line in Westmin-
ster-Hall, with crowds of people who expressed exceeding
joy. They found themselves to be sixty in number, and the
Speaker having arrived with twenty of the others, they
began by revoking all the acts passed against themselves
since their election, even the protest which they had entered
against the violence of the army, and the resolutions taken
subsequently to fill up their places by new elections. General Monk was afterwards declared Captain-general and Com-
mander-in chief under the parliament of all the forces of
England, Scotland, and Ireland; and Vice-admiral Lawson was
confirmed in the command of the fleet. The appointment of
the five commissioners, named a few days before to govern
the army, was also revoked; the deputies from some of the
counties, and the citizens of London were set at liberty; and
the governor of the Tower was ordered to give an account on
the next day of the reasons of the imprisonment of Sir George

Booth and another of the same party; all the orders given by
the Council of State or the commissioners of the army since
the last day of last week were suspended until they had been
communicated to General Monk; and the power of the Council
of State was also suspended until new orders should be received
from the parliament, which met in the afternoon, and restored
the town council which had been dissolved, permitted the
mayor of London to replace the city-gates and chains at the
public expense, and decided upon forming a new Council of
State, composed of thirty-one persons, of whom General Monk
was declared one, and the election of the others was deferred
until to-morrow morning. Orders were also given for the
liberation of several prisoners, among others, of three Scottish
earls who had been in confinement for ten years; and the
Speaker was directed to summon all the absent members to
come and take their places as quickly as possible. The acts
passed against Major-General Brown, a timber-merchant in
London, who has greatly distinguished himself of late, were
abrogated, and liberty was given him to resume his place in
the House. Sir George Booth was also set at liberty on giving
surety that he would answer to the charges brought against
him. An act was then passed for the continuation of the
customs and excise duties, another for the convocation of a
parliament on the 25th of April next, and commissioners were
appointed to decide on the qualifications of those who are
eligible for election; others were directed to confer with the
mayor of London about a loan for the payment of the army
and fleet, and to agree with him upon the securities for re-
payment. The majority of the acts proposed on the previous
evening were again read and approved, and the nomination of
the Council of State again deferred to this morning: it has,
nevertheless, not yet been completed, and it is said that
General Monk is desirous that the parliament should choose
some of the old members, among others, Haslerig and Mr.
Scott, who appeared to be his greatest opponents, and who
are very distinguished among the republicans. Deputies were
sent from the City to-day to congratulate and thank the parliament; they have also offered it a considerable sum of money,
and the people are for the present so well satisfied, that it will
have no difficulty in obtaining the necessary assistance from
them. Their joy did not appear to be less on the evening of
the day before yesterday than it was on the day when Monk

entered the City; during all the evening and night, bonfires and festivities were kept up, and in many places the king's health was not forgotten. Orders have been given to communicate this news without delay to the whole of the country, and, in order to retain the distant troops in obedience to the present authorities, a letter has been published from General Monk and all the officers under his command, giving reasons for the recent change, and assuring them that all the acts and ordinances of the parliament, in reference to the sale of lands confiscated or given in payment to the soldiers, will be confirmed; it further promises them prompt payment of that which is due to them, exhorts them to take care that the tranquillity of the republic is not disturbed by the partisans of Charles Stuart or any other authority, and invites them to send as soon as possible one of their number to give assurance of their acquiescence in the present government, the inclinations of which are nevertheless esteemed to be royalist. I know that some of the most active amongst them hold these views; and it is consequently the generally-received opinion, that if the declarations of General Monk and his officers are in conformity with their opinions, they will at some future time have great difficulty in preventing the return of the king upon the conditions which were formerly offered to his father in the Isle of Wight. It may, moreover, be presumed that General Monk intends to recall him, that all these demonstrations which he gives by word of mouth, by writing, and by the unfavourable reception of all who wish to treat upon this point with him, may be affected, through fear lest, if he should make known these views, the greater part of the forces both by land and sea would rise in opposition against him; the prolongation of the command of the vice-admiral cannot be attributed to any other cause, as he is a man greatly esteemed by the fleet, but a sectary, and in consequence not very agreeable to the Presbyterians, who are now in possession of the supreme power. These are reflections which are made upon the present condition of England, and nevertheless we must not yet form a decisive opinion upon the future, as there is so little clue in all the actions and words of those upon whom the fate of the government depends, and as it still appears that Monk intends to maintain the establishment of the republic. And if he thought to make himself commander of all the forces, he has now perfectly attained his object; but he will have

some difficulty to maintain himself against the general desire
and bent of the whole nation, as he does not possess so vigorous a mind as the deceased Protector, and has to do with
skilful adversaries who propose to place the militia in the
hands of the nobility of the country, who are all royalists, and
thus to strengthen them against the army, if it should attempt
to thwart their plans.   It was said that the parliament would
not sit longer than the end of the week, but a longer time is
now spoken of, as it is not possible to settle affairs in so short
a time, although the greatest diligence is displayed, and this
afternoon, the Council of State was elected, without attending
to the general's recommendation in favour of some of the old
members. The qualifications of the deputies to the parliament
have also been decided upon, without excepting the sectaries,
so as not to do them the honour of appearing to fear them.
Those who have been actually in arms against the parliament
are alone excepted. The Secretary of State has also been dismissed ; a proposition was made to call some of the nobles
into the Council, but they have given the government to understand that, without injuring their prerogative, they could
not form part of it, and this refusal is founded upon the hope
that their House will be re-established.   I am, &c.

(43.)—M. DE BOURDEAUX TO CARDINAL MAZARIN.
MY LORD,   London, March 5, 1660.
    THERE does not appear to me to be any change in the
inclinations of the government of England, and the duplicate
of my letter to M. de Brienne having informed you of what
has taken place during the last three days, it only remains for
me to add that Ireland has sent hither a declaration in entire
conformity with the course of conduct pursued by General
Monk.   It professes that the peace of the three nations cannot
be established without a free parliament, or the readmission
of the excluded members, and the terms of this document
show that still greater dispositions exist to return to the old
form of government.   The officers who held other views
retired into Dublin Castle, where they were besieged by the
others and taken without bloodshed, as the garrison made no
attempt to defend themselves.   This change is partly attributed to the news which the army had received of the restoration of the officers whom it had expelled, and among others
of Lieutenant-General Ludlow ; but if this declaration be an

ﾙtual one, it must have been projected with General Monk
ﾙfore his departure from Scotland, and expressions may be
ﾙmarked in it similar to his own on the subject of the sectaries.
ﾙ has also just been reported to me that the militia of London
ﾙs been countermanded this evening, which would afford
ﾙasons for believing that the troops gathered together by
ﾙme old colonels, great sectaries, had submitted, or that, as
ﾙe city has paid the money which was desired of it, the
ﾙneral is less careful to pleasure it. As the officers are not
ﾙminated by him but by commissioners approved by the
ﾙrliament, although he is Major-General of the militia, his
ﾙwer over it would not be very absolute. Preparations are
ﾙing made for arming that of the Lowlands, and placing it in
ﾙer hands than it has been in of late ; and all the officers of
ﾙlice whom the parliament had appointed before the admis-
ﾙn of the excluded members have been changed, and the new
ﾙes are said to be very much inclined towards the restoration
ﾙ the monarchy.* * * ──────

(44.)—M. DE BOURDEAUX TO CARDINAL MAZARIN.

MY LORD, London, March 8, 1660.

I WAS not surprised when I saw in the letter which it
ﾙased you to write to me on the 1st of this month, by my
ﾙurier, an account of the reports prevalent in France of the
ﾙoclamation of the King of England. The joy with which
ﾙeneral Monk was received in the city of London, and the
ﾙas exhibited by the people on that day, gave good reasons
ﾙ supposing that all was ready here for the reception of the
ﾙnce. Nothing has since occurred of a nature to change this
ﾙinion, and nevertheless we cannot but praise the moderation
ﾙth which the queen of England and her ministers receive
ﾙch news, when we consider the inconstancy of the people,
ﾙd the uncertainty of the real opinions of the army under the
ﾙmmand of General Monk. His officers are not so blindly
ﾙedient to him as to be willing to remain in ignorance of his
ﾙans, and, as early as last week, they manifested their dis-
ﾙprobation of the conduct of the parliament, because it tended
ﾙ the restoration of the monarchy. Their commander pacified
ﾙem with assurances that all the readmitted deputies had
ﾙedged themselves to act in conformity with the document
ﾙich he had delivered to them before they resumed their
ﾙits. This jealousy did not fail to excite the alarm of the
ﾙrliament, as it followed immediately after the advice given

them by the general to dissolve in a few days, and leave th
Council of State to govern until the 15th of April next, whe
other representatives of the people will commence the
sittings.   At the same time there also arose some disput
between the general and the city, because the former ha
opposed the establishment of the militia; but, on the evenin
of the day before yesterday, he was assured that he should b
its commander, which had at first been refused him, unde
the pretext that such an employment was beneath the dignit
of the general of all the forces of the republic.· In fact, thoug
it was not judged advisable to intrust so much power to th
hands of one single person, this scruple had to be over
come, in order not to displease the general, who had als
been obliged to consent to the wishes of the citizens, althoug
with some risk of his authority, in order to obtain from then
———— pounds sterling, which they would not advance unti
they received permission to organize their militia, Fate woul
have it that whilst this question was being treated, new
arrived from the country which made him decide in favour o
the citizens.   On the day before yesterday, certain intelli
gence came that one of the colonels of the army had gatheree
together some of the old troops at thirty leagues distance fron
London.   A regiment of cavalry, and the general's company
of guards set out yesterday to disperse these insurgents, whos
leader is not so rash or senseless as to have taken arms with
out feeling great confidence that many others would follow hi
example, and especially the sectaries, who are very discontented
with the present government.   Doubts are even entertained
about the general's own troops ; and if they failed him great
confusion would immediately prevail in England, whereas it
they remain devoted to his interests, and he to those of the
parliament, the nobility and the city of London, the party
of sectaries would not be able to rise again ; and their arming
will only serve to reduce the general to the necessity of making
an earlier accommodation with the royalists, unless he has
already made one, which his actions would lead us to believe,
although his declarations are of an opposite character. I saw
the general this morning, taking as a pretext for my visit, the
civilities which I have received from him on different occasions;
and after some general compliments, I informed him that the
court of France would be glad to hear that the forces of
England were under the command of a person of such great

ıerit and so well affectioned towards the nation; accompany-
ıg this compliment by personal offers. He began by referring
) matters of public interest, spoke to me of our peace with
pain, and of the affairs of Sweden, but from his whole dis-
ourse I can only gather that he is well-intentioned towards
ıis crown, that he would have wished England to have been
ıcluded in the treaty, and that he hopes that the next parlia-
ıent will establish a stable government here. Last week the
resent government approved of the commissioners pre-
ented to it to organize the London militia. It has also
uperseded a number of officers, and appointed others in their
tead ; and is still debating the qualifications for the next par-
.ament, as well as the form of the writs which are to be issued ;
pon which question some deputies discovered that in order to
ct legally they must convoke it in the name of the king.
With regard to the taxes, it has been resolved to invite the
>eople to pay them in accordance with the act passed before
he return of the excluded members. The general's commis-
ion has been approved, and accompanied by the gift of
Iampton-court, with the lands adjoining, for himself and his
ıeirs. The circuit which the judges usually make through
he provinces at this season has been postponed to another
.ime, and pardon granted to a number of condemned criminals.
The act establishing the Council of State and limiting their
)owers, was passed only the day before yesterday : it con-
:ains a very remarkable clause, authority being given it to
mprison even members of parliament, notwithstanding that
:his is contrary to all usage. The ministers of whom it is
:omposed will begin their sittings on this very day and will
:reate their officers. Mr. Thurloe has returned upon the
stage in the quality of Secretary of State, but with Thompson,
the auditor-general, for his colleague. This choice must not
surprise you, since the chief men of the council are the same
who had great share in the government under the deceased
Protector, whose son has again been proposed to General
Monk by the very persons who overthrew him, his restoration
appearing to them to be less injurious than that of the King ;
and in all probability, he would be preferred to him, however
little he may be esteemed, as the return of the latter is as
much apprehended by the Presbyterians as by those who have
been engaged in the recent movements in England. To-day
it will be determined upon what day the parliament will
dissolve, and all to-morrow will be passed in thanksgivings.

(45.)—M. DE BOURDEAUX TO CARDINAL MAZARIN.

MY LORD,   London, March 15, 1660\
    THE internal affairs of England are in the same state a\|
my preceding letter informed you they were, and the con\|
duct of General Monk continues to induce the belief that hi\|
inclinations are for the recall of the King, although his word\|
are opposed to it.   The troops in London and elsewhere als\(
profess to feel great repugnance thereto; and the officer\|
having a day or two since brought this question under discussion, they were of opinion that if the republic could not
be established, at least the King and the last Protector ought
to be excluded from the government, and they appeared more
inclined to raise their general to the throne than any other.
Although he has expressed his disapprobation of these consultations, people have not failed to entertain the idea that they may
be intended to suggest to the parliament what it ought to do;
but this body would with difficulty be led to place any other
but the legitimate sovereign upon the throne, as it perceives
that such a course would plunge the nation into continual
troubles, and its debates seem to be preparing the way for the
king's return.   A few days since it passed an act for the levy
of the militia of London and the country under the command
of General Monk, without, however, leaving him power to dispose of the commissions, which have all been given to royalists.
It has also declared him together with Colonel Montague,
colonel of the sea, and the latter has orders to proceed to the
fleet without delay.   Besides the establishment of the militia,
and the confirmation of the choice made by the Council of
State, of Messrs. Thompson and Thurloe as Secretaries of State,
the parliament further decided, last week, upon what shall be
the national religion : this will be a confession of faith which
was presented to it in 1646, in conformity with the opinions
of our Calvinists ; and in future no one will be admitted to a
living until he has subscribed to it.   This matter occasioned
them to speak of the Covenant, and to propose an order to
have it read in the parishes, so that the people may be reminded
of their engagements.   As mention is made therein of the
king and nobility, this will in some sort dispose the minds of
men to return to the old form of government.   It was also
determined last week that the parliament should dissolve at
the very latest on the 25th of this month, and a debate arose
on the form of the writs and on the qualifications of the representatives who are to succeed them, but was not brought to

conclusion. A number of prisoners were again liberated, r George Booth and all his party discharged from further osecution, and the city and county of Chester restored to icir privileges. As this act of indemnity extends also to iose who were then in the service of the parliament, General ambert has begun to re-appear in public. This morning an ·der was issued directing the Catholics to remain confined in icir houses, under the pretext that they are in correspondence ·ith the sectaries, some of whom have openly declared ;ainst this government, among others the garrison of Hull, nd Vice-admiral Lawson, who has been trying to alienate ie fleet; some of the old troops have also revolted in the ountry, and five companies of infantry have seized upon the)wn of Gloucester. But unless all the troops follow this bad xample, these movements will not have any results of im- ortance. The city of London continues to caress and humour he general, and last week deputies were sent by the citizens o present him with the command of the militia. Letters iave been received from the army in Ireland in conformity rith the declaration which appeared last week, and the latest iews from that country is, that on the 3rd inst. a meeting was ·o be held to consider what means they had of maintaining hemselves, in case England did not entertain the same views. ' .l'his is, my lord, all that I have to write of the actions and leliberations which have occurred here. *   *   *

(46.)—M. DE BOURDEAUX TO CARDINAL MAZARIN.
My LORD,   London, March 18, 1660.
I HAVE received to-day the two letters which your Eminence did me the honour to write to me on the 26th of last month and the 5th of the present. My previous letters will have informed you that I have forestalled the order which you give me in your first regarding General Monk, as I have already paid him a visit, and told him that the king and your Eminence would be delighted to hear that the forces of England were under his command, and that you would contribute to the furtherance of his plans. I will not fail to reiterate the same sentiments to him by means of a third person, if he ob- jects to receive a second visit. At my first interview I did not fail to touch upon all matters likely to discover his in- clinations towards France, and he seemed to me to speak reproachfully, although rather in raillery, of the peace between

France and Spain, because England had not been included i
it.   I however obliged him at last to confess that the foreig
affairs of the country were entirely new to him.   He the
referred to the wars of the North, and asked me whether w
should not continue to assist the king of Sweden; appearin
to advocate this monarch's interests with considerable warmtl
I pointed out to him that France alone had maintained thi
principle, and that, in order to secure it against all its enemies
it was necessary that England should speak and act in con
formity with what his Majesty had done both at Frankfort anc
at the Hague, in order to compel the Emperor and the States
general to take some measures for an accommodation; I ever
offered to have a private conference with the ministers of the
Council of State, in order to concert measures for its advancement.   This language cannot but be very agreeable to him, as
his hatred of the United Provinces has always been very
great—so great, indeed, that when the deceased Protector sent
him to command the fleet he was not contented with combating them on the sea, but wished to make a descent upon
the coast and attack Flushing, which he felt sure of capturing.
The Protector did not judge it advisable to go to such lengths
against the Provinces, but rather to make peace with them,
through fear of their maritime power; and so he sent the
general into Scotland, whence he was never afterwards able
to withdraw him, nor could the Protector Richard induce him
to take up his defence.   If your Eminence has anything to insinuate to him, I can easily do it through his confidants.   In
my previous letters I dwelt at considerable length upon the
conduct pursued by this general, and the opinions entertained
of it.   People are now beginning to think that his ambition
is not so limited, and that he aspires to the sovereignty; that, in
order to attain to it, he permits the restoration of the monarchy
to be spoken of in the parliament in very undisguised language,
and allows the militia both in London and the country to be
placed under the command of royalists, in order that the
troops, becoming jealous, may unite with him, and adopt his
interests, to which they have at first manifested considerable
aversion; but whatever may be the general's intentions, he is
allowing matters to take a very decided turn in favour of the
king.   And on the first day of this week the parliament decreed that the Covenant made at the commencement of the
wars in England should be read in all the parishes, and fixed

p in the House of Parliament. As this engagement speaks
ι very express terms of the defence of the king, and of his
ιst authority, the troops have immediately taken the alarm at
, and the officers at their meeting yesterday proposed a
:quisition tending to the suppression of the monarchy and
f the House of Lords. They went this morning to com-
ιunicate it to the general, in order to obtain his approbation
efore presenting it; but he opposed it, declaring that he
·ould not allow the parliament to be constrained in its votes;
e even treated some of the officers, who appeared to be more
nimated than the others, with harshness; but he nevertheless
:ated that the object of the requisition was a good and just
ne, and undertook to confer upon the matter with some
ιembers of parliament this evening. Many occasions have
ιken place of late on which this assembly has manifested its
ιclination towards the king, even so far as to receive with
ιanks addresses in which it was termed only the House of
'ommons, and to disapprove of others which gave it the title
f sovereign authority; it has even been declared that another
arliament could not legitimately be called without the Lords,
nd that, in consequence of the king's death, the present
arliament is at an end. These private opinions would be of
:ss weight if all the appointments, both in the militia and the
olice, were not given to royalists; and two days ago the
overnment of Hull, whose garrison has declared against the
resent authorities, was conferred by the general, on the re-
ommendation of the parliament, upon a person strongly
ιclined towards that party. The republicans have never-
ιeless resumed courage since the meeting of the officers; and
ow that all are entered into the parliament, their number is
ιther considerable. Yesterday Sir Arthur Haslerig and
·olonel Rich (who had tried to induce the sectaries to revolt),
fter having been heard in their own defence, were, the first
ischarged, and the other sent back to the Council, who put
im in arrest. As for General Lambert, his imprisonment
ι the Tower has been approved, although he is confined only
ι default of having given surety for his future conduct.
ome regulations concerning religion have also been made
uring the last few days, and debates will be permitted only
pon this matter, or the militia and the qualifications of the
nsuing parliament, until the day of the dissolution of the pre-
:nt, which will be in eight days, unless some change takes

place. The republicans will strive to prolong its session
and instead of convoking a new representative assembly, t'.
fill up the vacant places so as to perpetuate this one. Som
royalists appear to apprehend it, and others to be desirous t'
have the merit of making establishments instead of putting ther
off, although the excluded members pledged themselves, befor
their readmission, to introduce no changes into the govern
ment, but to convoke another free parliament, to whose enact
ments the general has promised and still professes that he wil
submit. There is no news from Ireland; and public rumou
still affirms that the army there is very well disposed toward
the king, and that it has even sent to treat with him. Scotland
is very tranquil, according to the promise which the principa
nobility made to the general before his departure, and the
resolution to restore the Covenant will give them great satisfaction. The movements which occurred at Gloucester and
some other places have subsided of themselves; and the troops
which the governor of Hull attempted to excite by his declaration, have continued in their obedience; the Vice-admiral, also,
as it was reported, raised the mask; but his intentions are still
suspected, as he is a great sectary. The city of London has
organized its militia without giving much consideration to the
persons whom the general had recommended; but it has nevertheless continued to caress and regale him very greatly. * * *

(47.)—M. DE BOURDEAUX TO CARDINAL MAZARIN.

MY LORD,　　　　　　　　London, March 22, 1660.

SINCE my letter of the 18th, the general and some
officers have had a conference with some members of parliament, in which the former demanded an act of indemnity for
all the past, that the sales of confiscated property shall be confirmed, that the government shall be constituted without a
king or House of Lords, and that the militia shall not be
organized. Nothing was granted to them, under the pretext
that the present parliament could not do it validly; and they
were referred to the next, with which they appeared satisfied.
Their general has not failed to remove most of them out of the
way, commanding them to withdraw each to his own quarters;
which order they obeyed to-day. Meanwhile the parliament
has continued its debates upon the establishment of the militia,
and this morning concluded this very important business,
notwithstanding the opposition of the republicans, who have

ily obtained that no one shall be employed therein before he
is acknowledged that the late wars were just and for the
good of the country. An act has also been passed approving
of all that the parliament had done from the commencement
of its session until 1648, when the members were excluded;
and now the universal talk is of the dissolution of this
assembly in three days, as the general hopes to execute his
designs more easily under a new one than with the present.
His conduct still confirms the king's return. The republicans
agree with the royalists in thinking so; and there does not
appear sufficient resolution among the troops to prevent him.
Some officers who attempted to excite them to mutiny have
been arrested, and the governor of Hull has received the law
from those whom the general had sent to him. There is no
news from either Scotland, Ireland, or abroad; and it only
remains for me to subscribe myself with respect, &c.

I learn that accounts have just arrived from Ireland which
declare that the army has proclaimed the king, and that
Colonel Cooke has gone over to Flanders. If this news is
true, the next post will bring its confirmation.

(48.)—M. DE BOURDEAUX TO CARDINAL MAZARIN.

MY LORD,   London, March 25, 1660.

THE news which I added to my last letter has proved
untrue; and although the army in Ireland appears inclined to
recall the king, it will probably postpone any declaration until
some government is established in England. You will judge
from my previous letters that everything concurs to the restoration of the monarchy. The parliament has, moreover,
lately erased from its journals the act of abjuration of a king
or any single ruler, and has appointed commissioners to
examine into what has passed against the House of Lords,
with some intention of restoring it to authority. Nevertheless,
for the last twenty-four hours, there has been much uncertainty
in the course of events, because the officers of the army in
London continue loudly to threaten, and propose a declaration
against the king, the nobility, and the levy of the militia. At
the present time, nine o'clock in the evening, they are assembled; and as hitherto the officers have never deferred
to their other commanders when once they have been aroused,
every one expects some great event before long; otherwise
the militia would be organized, and in a position to oppose

O

the designs of the army. On the other side, the parliament
assembled for a few hours more, part of the deputies bei
desirous to terminate their session to-day, and the others o
posing it. With this view different propositions are bei
made to gain time : the general presses their dissolution, a:
the royalists think it advantageous; but some of the 1
admitted members having changed sides and joined the o
parliamentarians, the House is nearly equally divided.
this night, which seems to be critical, produces any importa
resolution, I will send it by an express to Calais. I have on
time to add that the qualifications of the future parliame
were concluded yesterday evening. The most important
the exclusion of those who have been in arms against tl
parliament, and of their children. This morning, when tl
act conferring Hampton Court upon the general was read f
the last time, according to custom, objections were broug'
against it; and a proposition having been made to give hi
20,000l. sterling in money instead, the question was postpon
to another time. Some regulations were also made in referen
to religion. The same act which compels the officers of tl
militia to acknowledge that the war undertaken by the tv
Houses of Parliament to defend themselves against the forc
levied in the name of the king was just and legitimate, enac
also that they shall acknowledge the ministry and magistra
to be of God's appointment. I have nothing to communica
of a more positive character regarding the general than
wrote by my preceding letters; his conduct and words st
continue to be opposed to each other, and he keeps on go
terms with the city of London. The royalists hope that he
in their favour, and others that he intends to raise himself
the crown. Some members of parliament have the idea
placing the Duke of Gloucester upon the throne, and throu
him ensuring themselves against inquiries into the past.
is by no means easy to judge what will be the issue of all t
present intrigues. I am, &c.

(49.)—M. DE BOURDEAUX TO CARDINAL MAZARIN.
MY LORD,   London, March 29, 1660.
     I HAVE given so full an answer to what M. de Brien
wrote me on the 9th of this month by your Eminence's couri
that I have nothing to add thereto regarding the present co
dition of England, as nothing has occurred of any importan

since the 25th, except the voluntary dissolution of the parliament, after it had given the necessary orders for the convocation
of another, which is to commence its sittings on the 5th of
May next, and for the levy of the militia in all the counties,
under the command of the principal nobility and gentry,
without excluding those who took arms under Sir George
Booth. General Monk wrote to the parliament to suspend
this act; and whether because his officers were satisfied with
this diligence, or have been otherwise pacified, that great
murmuring, which exhibited itself among them three days ago,
has changed into complete silence and submission, although
the levy of the militia is considered as their ruin. The rest
of the people are very quiet; and all await the meeting of
parliament, in the hope of beholding a great revolution in the
government. It appears that the Council of State is desirous
also to make sure of the navy by the preparations which are
making; and Admiral Montague, who is restored to the command, is to proceed to the fleet without delay. The last
letters from Ireland represent that great uniformity of opinions
exists between the army and the assembly which was held in
Dublin, this last body having approved of the declaration of
the other in favour of a free parliament, and the readmission
of the excluded members; but both are desirous that in future
the Irish parliament may be held, and that no levy shall be
made in the country without its consent, as was the case in
past times. The great changes which this nation has of late
undergone, and its poverty through want of commerce, have
given rise to this desire. I have not yet performed what
your Eminence ordered me with regard to the general. I
shall do it to-morrow; and by the next post I shall answer the
letter which you did me the honour to write to me on the
13th, it having been delivered too late for me to discharge this
duty to-day. Meanwhile I have nothing to add, except that
I am, &c. ⸻

(50.)—M. DE BOURDEAUX TO M. DE BRIENNE.

SIR, London, March 29, 1660.

I ANNOUNCED by the previous mail, my reception of the
letter which it pleased you to write to me on the 9th of last
month, and reserved my answer until to-day; and in reply to
your question I must say that it is considered, and with great
reason, that England, after having made trial of so many
governments, none of which have been able to establish them-

selves, will prefer a monarchy to the others, and that the king has now great reason for strong hopes, as the nobles and the people desire his return with greater ardour than they formerly exhibited in overthrowing the authority of his predecessor. It is also no less certain that the actions of the general authorize the belief that his intentions are in conformity with the wishes of the nation, although he professes the contrary; and this unanimity having persuaded me that the king's return was, as it were, certain, the idea occurred to me, before I received any orders, to induce, if possible, the present government to invite the mediation of his Majesty, and to receive their sovereign from his hands rather than from those of Spain : to which it seemed to me that the Presbyterians, who are now in power, might be disposed, that they might have a powerful guarantee of all the conditions upon which they would admit their prince. The attempt, however, which I have made by means of persons interested in the success of this negociation, have not yet produced the desired effect, and this is an overture which could not be made without danger by a private person before the authorities had taken all the requisite precautions for changing the government without involving the country in a war. It is also to be feared that the party leaders who ought to support such a proposition will be diverted from it by the personal advantages which they will derive from private treaties. Already even, the principal posts under the crown are said to be destined for some of them, in which case it is not to be expected that they will take much care to provide for the public interests, or that they will have recourse to foreign mediation, which the king of England will endeavour to avoid so as not to be indebted to any other power for his restoration. The same opinion may be held regarding General Monk, it being to be presumed that he will not consent to give up the sovereignty which he now enjoys in all but the name, and become a subject, unless he is assured of all the advantages that the king can grant him, to deserve which he will desire alone to have the glory of replacing him on the throne, and will not avail himself of the offers of France except in case of extremity ; besides which, it being necessary for the accomplishment of such a design, that he should deceive his army and profess himself a republican, he will make great difficulties about listening to any proposition which may force him to declare himself. These difficulties will not prevent me from doing all in my power for the performance of my orders, and with this view, I shall avail myself of one of those most interested in the fortune of the general, who has already conveyed to him very obliging messages from me, even so far as to assure him that his Majesty would contribute to his elevation. It has seemed to him advisable to dispose him by these marks of esteem to give a better reception to the other propositions with which I might be charged; I am also making preparations for sounding some of the principal members of the Council who have, in former times, declared their intentions to me so openly in favour of the king that they will not take in bad part anything respecting him; and finally, Sir, it is enough to stimulate my little industry and all my cares to know that this service is so agreeable to the king, and so much desired by his Eminence. It may be effected during the interregnum, as it is not to be supposed that any government will be formed before the meeting of the next parliament; that one which dates its origin from 1640, has at last voluntarily dissolved upon the 26th of this month. Up to this moment every one had doubted its dissolution, and it was thought that the deputies of whom this assembly was composed would rather recall the king than leave the merit of that step to others, even if it would not besides have been to their interest to efface in this way the recollection of the evils which they have caused. The will of the general prevailed over these considerations, and there appeared only three voices against so violent a resolution, which was adopted, after having left the Council of State rather ample powers, and passed an act for the convocation of the new parliament, including the clause that it should not be prejudicial to the rights of the nobility, which some even wished to extend to the prerogatives of the king; the establishment of the militia was also determined upon, notwithstanding the letter which the general wrote on the same day to the Speaker to suspend it. He showed this zeal in order to satisfy his officers and some republicans; but the deputies whom the parliament sent to him induced him by their reasons to cease his opposition. It is affirmed, nevertheless, that he has promised to prevent its execution in order to appease the army, the intentions of which appear in a very different aspect from that which they exhibited last week. It is also stated as a fact that, on the evening before the parliament dissolved, the general made use of very precise language towards the·republicans, and some of them spoke against royalty with their last breath ; nevertheless, his conduct shows that he is more and more favourable to a monarchical government, and he has of late given the command of towns, vessels, and troops to notorious royalists. The greater part of the militia of the country has been placed in their hands ; Sir George Booth is even to command that of Cheshire ; and there arrive daily from Flanders persons known to be attached to the king, and no inquiries are made about their movements. No words could be capable of effacing the impression produced by this behaviour ; and consequently no one doubts that, unless the army revolts soon, it will be obliged to receive the law and consent to its own destruction, which is projected by changing the old officers, and re-organizing all the corps one after another. The Council of State began to meet on the day before yesterday, and its first step has been to issue, to-day, public prohibitions of all assemblies under any pretext whatever; a proclamation to send back the royalists and Catholics to their ordinary places of residence, and another to make the officers withdraw to their quarters. The first two seem to have been framed only with a view to give a colour to the last, as it is not a great mortification to send the nobility back to the country, whither they are, moreover, summoned by the election of the members of parliament, which now occupies all minds.   *   *   *

(51.)—M. DE BOURDEAUX TO CARDINAL MAZARIN.
MY LORD,   London, April 1, 1660.
    I HAD postponed until to-day writing an answer to the letter which it pleased your Eminence to write to me on the 13th of last month, in the hope of sending you at the same time an account of the success which might have attended my efforts to execute the orders sent me by M. de Brienne : but, not·having yet been able to obtain an interview with the general, or see that person who can give me most information about his views, I can only assure your Eminence of my entire devotedness to the service expected of me, and that I shall employ in it all the circumspection of which I am capable. I can also confirm all that my previous letters have stated regarding the present disposition of England to recall the king. The members of the Council openly profess that they have this intention, and although the general still keeps up the hopes

the republicans, he has nevertheless declared that he will submit to the resolutions of the ensuing parliament, and will do his best to keep the army in the same obedience and declare itself for the king, as it is not doubted for a moment that the nobility and people will elect deputies well-affectioned towards him. Words have also escaped from the general, in his family, which give reason to believe him altogether pledged to favour the king's return even if the parliament opposed it, and his actions are in great conformity with such a design. If it is already formed, the good offices of another power will not be necessary, and the steps I am taking will only manifest his Majesty's inclinations, of which the royalists appear to be fully persuaded since the journey of Lord Jermyn and Abbé Montague. If the general were still wavering between the recall of the king and acceptance of the sovereignty which has been offered him by the republicans, he might be determined to one or the other course by the dispositions of France ; but his ambition must be limited to the highest fortune of a subject, since he allows the whole nation to be armed under the command of nobles and gentlemen known to be passionately attached to the royal family. As for a republican government, it is no longer mentioned, except in the addresses of the regiments of the whole army, which the Council intends to disband as soon as the militia is organized, at which all parties are diligently labouring. Some are desirous that at the same time the heads of the government should propose the conditions upon which the king shall be received, and do not consider themselves safe if he is to dispose of the militia, money, commissions, appointments, and the choice of his Council. These limitations may nevertheless be proposed at first to appease those who apprehend the revolution, and it is deferred until the next parliament meets. This body will be composed of young persons who, not having been engaged in the war, will not make use of all these precautions ; preparations are also being made to regulate religion according to the example of the Protestant faith in France, both in doctrine and in ecclesiastical discipline; and, during the last few days the ministers have felt great grief because the king of England has made some bishops. As the Presbyterians, who are now in power, formerly appeared more inclined towards France than to Spain, I had the idea that they might be persuaded to seek the king from their friends rather than from their

enemies, and the overtures which were made to some of them
on this point were favourably received; but many others
judge it more advisable that he should retire into Holland or
to Cologne, that they may treat with him more conveniently,
and without exciting the jealousy of the two crowns. This
course will probably be pursued, and the reports which have
been spread of his retirement into Flanders seem rather to
have derived their foundation from this, than from any disposition to a peace between England and Spain.   It is very
true that the parliament, a few days before the readmission
of the excluded members had some thoughts of making an accommodation, and receiving money for Dunkirk and Jamaica:
if its administration had continued a little longer, it would
have depended upon Spain only to put an end to the war,
which we may say has largely contributed to the great animosity of the people, and particularly of the City of London,
against the last parliament, on account of the injury which it
has done to trade, and which has been attributed to the domestic divisions of the nations, since which this city has become more powerful than it ever was under the kings.   The
present government, in order to please it, has first professed
to be desirous of peace, and it will easily be perceived that the
king is under too great obligations to Spain to continue the
war.   Letters from Flanders even assure us that the Duke of
York has accepted the command of the naval forces of Spain,
with the title of Prince of the Sea, and the same prerogatives
as were enjoyed by Don John of Austria, under Philip II.
Nevertheless, during the last few days, the propositions of the
Portuguese ambassador have been more favourably listened
to, and there is a strong disposition not to enter into a league
with this prince, but to permit and assist him to levy all the
infantry that he may need, even to lend him vessels for their
transport, and to send others, at his cost, against the coast of
Spain, to thwart its designs against Portugal, the separation
of which is considered very necessary.   This good will, which
proceeds in part from a desire to remove the old troops from
England, would not be compatible with a treaty of peace, and
apparently the negociation will be put off until the government
is established.   I will not fail to make every effort to learn what
passes upon this subject, and give you an account of it.   I
have had occasion to speak at some length on behalf of the
Swedes, at a conference with some commissioners of the

'ouncil who paid me a visit: after having declared to them
hat the king would be glad to see the government of England
n the hands of those who at all times have shown themselves
o be well-intentioned towards France, I invited them to unite
,ith us in securing the preservation of the crown of Sweden
nd the advancement of the peace of the North, exaggerating
ts condition to them, and the steps which his Majesty had
;aken in order both to frustrate the Emperor's designs, and
;ring the United Provinces to an accommodation. In answer
o my civilities, they declared that it was their wish to fall in
with his Majesty's views, and to contribute by all means in
heir power to the maintenance of good feeling between the
,wo states : but their language with regard to the interests of
;jweden was not so decisive. I, nevertheless, remain per-
,;uaded that the Council is disposed to act in concert with
;?rance, and we agreed that, in that case, the English ministers
,esident at the Hague and in Zealand shall press the King of
,Denmark and the States-General to accept the treaties which
;:hey themselves proposed before the death of the king of
;weden, and which the governors of the kingdom have since
l)ffered to sign, abandoning their pretensions to the bailiwick of
,Drontheim, which seemed to form the chief difficulty. · But
'if the good offices of France and England produce no effect,
and if the king of Denmark resolves to take advantage of the
,present conjuncture to return into possession of the territory
,which he ceded by the treaty of Roskield, the said ministers
will declare their opposition to this step, and will accompany
their protest by some menaces; and we shall then advise upon
the means of forcing him to an accommodation, and this plan
will be communicated beforehand to the Dutch ambassador
resident here. I shall require to be still more particularly
assured of the sentiments of the Council. These commissioners
having affected to speak only on their own authority and
without orders, I reminded them of the entreaties which have
been made on the part of the United Provinces to induce
England not to pay the new tax of a crown for every ton of
freight; and they agreed that every state might act as it
pleased in regard to itself, and that no resolution should be
taken upon this subject before they had communicated it to
me. These are the principal points which we discussed. I
took care to let fall, when the conversation allowed it, some
words which gave them to understand that the king wished

that England might enjoy peace at home as well as abroad,
and was not less disposed than in past times to contribute to
both; but these expressions of good will were not taken up
and produced nothing but general thanks, and it is to be presumed that those who are in a position to contribute to the
king's restoration will think it more advantageous to treat
directly with him than to accept the mediation of France.
Nothing of importance has occurred during the last few days,
except that the officers of the army have drawn up a declaration conformable to their first propositions; but the general
has caused it to be suppressed, and they have not undertaken
anything since. The City of London has not failed to offer a
refuge both to the general and to the Council of State, to preserve them from the danger to which the discontent of the
army seemed to expose them: they have not considered it
right to accept this offer, and thus the evil has not been found
so great as the citizens thought it was. For greater precaution,
the Council had obtained parole from the principal reformed
officers, and those who refused to take this pledge have been
imprisoned. The parliament had instructed the Council of
State to take sureties from Lambert, but they have judged it
more advisable to keep him in confinement than to grant him
liberty. All the nobility have gone into the country to organize the militia and work in the elections. It only remains
for me, &c.   *   *   *

(52.)—M. DE BOURDEAUX TO CARDINAL MAZARIN.
MY LORD,   London, April 5, 1660.
    NOTHING of importance has occurred, to my knowledge,
since the 1st of this month; and all ideas seem now to run
on the establishment of the militia, and the election of the
parliament, which are drawing all persons into the country.
One regiment, at some considerable distance from London, is
said to have mutinied; but the others remain in obedience.
This is not a revolt worthy of much consideration. The General
has cashiered several colonels, and given their commissions to
gentlemen who are considered to be inclined towards royalty.
He is also preparing to disband four regiments, and by these
reforms to reduce the troops to that footing which they should
be on, in order to give no opposition to the establishments
which the new parliament may wish to make. The General
still declares that he will introduce no innovations until it

gins its session. I visited him on the day before yesterday, d conveyed to him the message with which your Eminence trusted me, without obtaining from him anything beyond neral thanks, notwithstanding the care that I took to induce m to be more explicit with regard to the offer of friendship, d the desire of your Eminence that he should repose as uch confidence in you as the deceased Protector had done: gave no further explanations on the subject of the government of England, and reiterated that it would be established ly by the new parliament. We next spoke of the affairs Sweden and Portugal; and I found him rather disposed to sist the former, if the King of Denmark refuses the accommodation which has been proposed to him. He confirmed to e what I had previously heard of the resolution adopted by e Council, to allow the ambassador of Portugal to levy all e infantry which his sovereign may require, and to lend m ships for their transport. This is all that I was able to rive from this visit, except excuses that he had not yet lled upon me. His wife's brother has since visited me, and gave him further explanations, assuring him that your Emi-nce would be very glad to make known to the General the teem which you feel for him: I even offered him your ediation, when he told me that the General had not taken any easures with the King of England, avowing, nevertheless, at if he becomes disposed to his return, he has taken upon mself to make the proposition spontaneously, and to see e again. But I cannot believe that they have waited until is time to make some private treaty. There are, at present, London, persons accredited on the part of the king. If that hich is reported is true, they insinuate that the Queen of ngland is excepted from the accommodation, together with l the English of her household. It is also to the interest of ose who are in Flanders to believe that they are exchanging ese good offices underhand, and the Presbyterians will easily e induced to humour them on this point. I have even heard tely that the Council, so as not to be obliged to grant the turn of the queen, will not seek the mediation of France. will remove these scruples, if possible; and will continue y endeavours to induce this government to do what his lajesty desires of it. *   *   *   There are news from reland, which represent the assembly of that country to be ery much at union with the army, to remain, in some method,

independent of England. Neither the Council nor the Genera
are satisfied with this proceeding, which may materially hasten
their determinations. It only remains for me to write that
General Montague has set out for the fleet; Vice-Admiral
Lawson, who is in command of it, does not appear very well
satisfied at the downfall of the sectaries; nevertheless, it is
not expected that he will refuse to obey. I am, &c.,

(53.)—M. DE BOURDEAUX TO CARDINAL MAZARIN.
MY LORD,   London, April 12, 1660.
    I HAVE not received any news for a long while, either from
the General or his wife's brother; it has, however, been
reported to me by another authority that the leaders of the
Council have of late discussed the proposition which I made,
of the mediation of France to reconcile the King of England
and the Parliament; and that they are divided in opinion,
some wishing to treat with him either in Flanders or some
neutral town, such as Cologne or Breda, and others that he
should proceed to France to receive their propositions. The
first wish is in conformity with the desire of the ministers of
this prince, who, by means of their friends, are straining
every nerve to prevent us from having any part in the accommodation, and also to exclude from it the Queen of England,
with all her household. To this end they make use of a
number of suppositions, and amongst others, in order to
excite the popular fury against France, they assert that the
king is willing to undertake to restore the monarch of England
with an army; that Abbé Montague has gone to give him
assurances of his purpose; that already even preparations are
being made in France for its performance; and that a marriage is projected, in consideration for which his Majesty will
spare no pains to make the enterprise succeed, in which case
the people of England will be deprived of all their prerogatives, and the authority of the parliaments will be destroyed;
whereas, by treating directly with the king, he will grant all
that may be judged necessary for the preservation of both.
It is even insinuated that Spain would keep the king back,
rather than allow France the glory of the treaty; and the
same persons also make use of the pretext of religion against
the Queen of England, representing that her return would
entail liberty of conscience for the Catholics; but their principal fear is, that she will gain possession of the king's mind,

from state affairs.   I see that some of the
nment are not much affected by these con-
in order to confirm them in their present
assure them that his Majesty would exact
ed either to the laws of England, or to the
10 have been mixed up in the recent com-
it would not be to his interest that they
fice, as he believes they are well-affectioned
I have also given some to understand that
rests might be attended to, and that your
feel obliged by the confidence reposed in
cture.   It cannot be predicted what will be
advances, so long as the General refuses to
I understand, his accommodation is already
g, he will conform to his intentions, which
: opposed to the mediation of any foreign
1 this matter at considerable length with
paid me a visit on the day before yesterday.
claration that he had come in his private
me for the politeness I have shown him
office ; nevertheless, after this compliment,
eak of public affairs, affecting to be ignorant
place of late between France and England.
hat the government was very jealous of us ;
i from Flanders and France declared that
f his Majesty's troops were destined to the
ig of England, and that his marriage was
at Abbé Montague had gone to Flanders
hence, and convey to him these resolutions,
re even confirmed by the agents of this
l that, although the people of England were
e him, neither the Council nor the army
with foreign troops, or without conditions,
e power might still remain in their hands ;
them, and attempted to come back by other
d all unite against his return, and would
in preventing it, as the army and part of
1uch opposed to it.   I assured the secretary
appear to me to be any foundation for all
that I had orders to declare that his Ma-
1intain perfect unanimity with the govern-
that I had been sent hither with very

precise instructions, and that nothing had occurred since to gi'
reason to believe that he had changed his views: that if an
individuals attempted to give contrary impressions, it was
prevent the government from remembering the good offic
which his Majesty formerly interposed to stop the course
divisions between the king and the people of England, and fro
having recourse to him on the present occasion; and I too
occasion to say that, far from any hostile measures being con
templated in France, I had been ordered to give them
understand that, if his mediation could contribute to the
welfare of the nation, he would gladly employ it, and woul
even receive with pleasure any request that might be mad
to him to intervene, as a very obliging token of the confidenc
which the government reposed in his friendship. I accom
panied this overture by every argument that was adapted t
render it agreeable, and to induce the secretary to support i
whenever occasion should offer; and he very solemnly pro
tested to me that he would do all in his power to cause mea
sures to be taken here, whether the king is recalled or th
republic established, which shall closely unite France an
England, repeating that, in either case, those who were now
in power would retain the chief authority; that the mos
zealous, who were in appearance for the king, will easil
change their minds when they find themselves in power; an
that he could not answer for the conduct of the next parlia
ment, as so numerous a body is subject to factions, and th
least division might restore the courage of the army, whicl
is as much opposed to the king as ever. Mr. Thurloe nex
passed from these general expressions to particulars, and aske
me how a negociation could be carried on through Franc
during the removal of the court, if the King of Englan
would repair thither, and if Spain did not arrest him as soo
as she suspected his intentions. I satisfied him on this point
by assuring him that, as soon as your Eminence was informe
of the desire which existed here, you would take care t
obtain a speedy resolution from the King of England, an
would take measures against the hindrances which migh
arise on the part of Spain. The conclusion of all this conver
sation was a promise from the secretary to think the matte
over, and to see me again in a few days. I gathered from hi
expressions, and from the warmth with which he spoke t
me, that the jealousies of the Council are great, and fomente

by the agents of the king of England, in order, perhaps, to
inspire alarm here, and thus to hasten his return upon more
advantageous terms; but this is a very dangerous policy, it
being presumable that the heads of the government will rather
adopt the views of the army than expose themselves to the
animosity of the royalists, whom they have offended. In
common with many others, I perceive less inconvenience in
acquiescence with the conditions which will be required here,
since, whatever they may be, if the parliament is once dissolved and the army disbanded, the king will meet with no
opposition to the re-establishment of the authority enjoyed
by his predecessors, as the militia is in the hands of nobles
and gentlemen, whose interest it is to diminish the power of
the people. I learn, also, from my conversation with the
secretary, that the English who are with the king, are not on
good terms with those of the queen's retinue, and that the
former, of their own accord or by order, are attempting to
prevent her from having any part in the accommodation; in
which they will probably succeed, notwithstanding the inclination of some who have of late written to Brussels, to complain in this respect of the conduct of Mr. Mordaunt, an
emissary of Chancellor Hyde. The former maintain no more
connection with me than the others, but all are trying to gain
over the general, who does not explain his views, but refers
them to the next parliament; whence it is supposed that his
private treaty is already made, there being otherwise no likelihood that he would leave all the glory to this assembly, as
well as the power which it might easily use to his prejudice
and that of the ministers of the present government. I have
no other part to take in all these intrigues, in order to perform
the last orders which were forwarded to me, except to assure
all of his Majesty's goodwill, to offer them my services both
with the general and my acquaintances in the Council, and to
propose an accommodation through the mediation of France,
without excluding the queen: to this work I have applied
myself for several days, and I shall continue to do so until
the conclusion of the business, which does not seem likely to
occur before the meeting of parliament. Secretary Thurloe
told me, in the course of our conversation, that as the letters
from the North have not brought certain intelligence of an
accommodation between the kings of Sweden and Denmark, the
Council of State had resolved to send, by the secretary of the

plenipotentiaries who are in Zealand, orders to them and to Mr.
Downing to speak at the Hague and to the king of Denmark,
in conformity with the proposition which I made at my last conference ; and I was requested to inform MM. de Thou and de
Terlon of this, that, on their side, they might continue to urge
both states as before; which I undertook to do, assuring them that
his Majesty would take in very good part the disposition which
exists here to act in concert with him for the reconciliation of
these two princes.   We also spoke of the affairs of Portugal,
and of the permission which the Council was going to grant it
to levy as many as twelve thousand infantry: and the Secretary
having given me to understand that England would take
charge of this crown if the interests of the North did not
divert her attention, I told him that France would discharge
her from the latter duty upon that condition, and undertake
single-handed, the defence of the Swedes, but that there was
no reason to hope that she would engage, before the return of
the King of England, in such an important enterprise, especially as I know that the inclinations of this prince would
tend rather to favour Spain than her enemies.   He again
repeated to me that they would tie his hands so as to take
from him the liberty of making peace and war, and that the
overture which I had made might be adopted without the appearance, or even, the intervention of any treaty; which. nevertheless, is not very likely.   I should rather think that foreign
affairs will be postponed until the King is established, and no
one can form a decisive judgment upon what will happen
when the supreme authority is in other hands.   The interests
of Denmark will then receive greater consideration than those
of the King of Sweden, and I have already informed his ministers of this, as they were flattering themselves that they should
be benefited by the revolution to which all things are tending.
The deputies, who have been elected in various places, and
among others in London, are very favourable to it, and the
commissioners for the establishment of the militia are giving
the command of it to the most qualified among the nobility.
The old troops clearly perceive that this tends to their destruction ; nevertheless, they do not dare to revolt, and a
Colonel who appeared discontented was not in a position to
disobey the orders of the General, who has cashiered him.
Some plots for debauching the soldiers in London, have also
been discovered ; and it has been found that some were pro-

ecting the appointment of agitators, as in past times, to take
are of their private interests. But this plan also has been
frustrated by the imprisonment of its projector, and by the
rohibitions of the Council. The sectaries have, at the same
me, been suspected of having contributed a large sum of
money to bribe the soldiers, and some pains have been
aken during the last few days to discover the depositories
of this collection, which is, perhaps, a supposition in order
to render them more odious, it being certain that their num-
er is not sufficient to prevent the projected establishments,
unless the whole of the old army should rise with them. Ireland is still in the same state, and the Council has despatched
rders for the dissolution of the assembly of Dublin, which
till continues to meet. Scotland is very tranquil under the
ommand of Major-General Morgan, who served formerly in
Flanders; and it only remains for me to subscribe myself, &c.

(54.)—M. DE BOURDEAUX TO CARDINAL MAZARIN.

MY LORD, London, April 19, 1660.

THE advances which I have made both to the General
nd to Mr. Thurloe, not having prevented the Council of State
rom inclining to treat with the King of England in Holland, and
by the mediation of the States-General, rather than by that of his
Majesty, I have, by other means, inspired the most influential
members of the Council and some of the chief nobles of the
Presbyterian faction, with the desired sentiments. One of the
ormer has just given me his word, that they will invite the
prince to pass into France, and there receive the propositions
f the parliament, and that, in case any difficulty arises
bout the accommodation, the mediation of France will be
solicited. They desire, nevertheless, that at the same time
his Majesty should make the offer to the King of England,
nd assure him that he shall be received in any maritime
town which may appear to him most convenient. I have
promised both, as soon as the present state of feeling becomes known in France, that his Majesty will take in good
part all the confidence reposed in him by the principal
ministers of the English government, that he will promote
a reconciliation by all means in his power, and that your
Eminence will take particular care of their interests. I
must not conceal from you that, in the various conferences
which I have had with several of them, they have questioned

P

me repeatedly about the marriage of the King of England,
and state that the nation felt great apprehensions respecting
that alliance which public report says has been negociated by
Abbé Montague; being persuaded that, besides the injury
which the Protestant religion would receive from such an
union, the counsels of your Eminence might tend to raise
too high the power of the English monarch.   I was not
sufficiently well informed to speak positively of the fact,
but I gave them clearly to understand that, even if the report
were well founded, neither the religion nor the prerogatives
of the people would, in consequence, be in a worse condition
than if under another queen; for the rest, they would find it
more advantageous to favour than to oppose it, since your
Eminence would in that case have more power to secure to
them all the public and private conventions which might be
stipulated in an accommodation.   One who came to see me
this afternoon, did not fail to refer to this subject in order to
inform me that the publication of this marriage should be
postponed, until the king of England has made an agreement
with the parliament, and to assure me that in the conditions
which will be presented to him, no mention will be made of
it, so that he may retain entire liberty to follow his inclinations
in the matter. I continued to declare that I had very little information on the subject, and did not fail to assure him, on the
other hand, that your Eminence would feel greatly obliged
by the good-will which they manifest towards you by their
resolutions, and by their wish to remove all obstacles calculated to overthrow an establishment in which you would be
so much interested.   I have also been visited, this afternoon,
by an English earl, who came to inform me that a resolution
had been adopted by some of his order, to despatch a gentleman this evening to the queen, to inform her that they wish
that the king of England would pass into France, to concert
measures with her for drawing him thither, and to take a
course which will be determined by the news which this
envoy brings back ; she will also contribute to induce them
to place entire confidence in me, which was necessary in
order to enable me to perform the service required of me.   I
have informed M. de Brienne of this, that he may announce
to the queen of England that I am acting by order, and that
she may not make this negociation take another course; from
which it will be perceived that, if no change takes place in
the present state of feeling, the king of England will be

bliged to repair to France, notwithstanding the repugnance
which his ministers feel to such a proceeding, and the media-
ion of his Majesty will be solicited, if any difficulty is
hrown in the way of the treaty : which I think will pro-
ably occur, as the rulers of the kingdom and all the Presby-
erians declare that they will not receive him without rather
igorous conditions, which the royalists affirm that he will
lever accept. I have communicated to the former, that we
hould not be opposed to any condition which had reference
o their safety, in order to remove the scruples which many
ntertained about trusting to France, through fear that your
Eminence would free the royal authority from all restraint;
and I may say that, in making this declaration, I have spoken
n accordance with the opinions of the wisest royalists, who
hink that the restoration of the monarchy is not to be
xpected without some limitation. If any advances are
found to be in conformity with his Majesty's intentions, I
shall continue to act and speak in the same manner, and it
will be necessary to perform what I have led them to hope
in reference to the offer of mediation, and the reception of
the king of England in some maritime town of Picardy. As
the approach of the parliament gives reason to believe that
the affairs of England will be brought to some issue before
his Majesty's return from the frontier, and the absence of
your Eminence will not enable me to receive your orders in
regard to any accidents that might arise, you will be pleased
also to let me know in advance what you think should be
done for the king's service in this conjuncture, and whether
the correspondence which I maintain with some of the
leaders of the government, might be made to contribute to
the advancement of his designs. When I am better informed,
I shall be better able to act. Nothing of any importance
has occurred abroad during the last few days. General
Monk continues to reform the army, and remove from it the
old officers and soldiers to fill up their places by men of more
obedient minds. He has presented an engagement, on his
own part, during the last few days, to those who remain in
office, by which they bind themselves to conform to whatever
the next parliament may judge advisable for the welfare of
the nation. The houses of some noted sectaries have been
searched, and some arms found ; and, under the pretext of
some apprehension of their ill-will, Colonel Lambert has been

imprisoned in the Tower of London. The elections are continued daily without paying much attention to the qualifications appointed by the late parliament, and in some localities royalists have been elected. Colonel Massey, one of the most zealous of this party, and who formerly did not dare to appear in England, has not scrupled to offer himself for election, and having found the people of Gloucester well-disposed towards him, some disorder arose between them and the soldiers, to appease which the Council sent for the colonel ; but after having heard him, he was set at liberty, and no one is refused permission either to enter or leave England. The secretary of the plenipotentiaries who are in Denmark, was sent off last week with the orders which I requested might be given him. The ministers of Sweden assured me that the States-General had disapproved of the cessation of hostilities, agreed upon by their ministers in Zealand, and the other mediators, because the king of Denmark had refused to accept the treaty which was offered to him ; but I do not see this news in the letters of M. de Thou, and the Dutch ambassador declares that his superiors desire nothing so ardently as peace in those quarters. He even came himself to read to me the answer of the States-General to his Majesty, accompanying it by many fine protestations, but without mentioning the speech of M. de Thou. There still appears to exist a favourable disposition towards Portugal, and the ambassador expects to-morrow to obtain a favourable resolution upon his propositions requesting permission to levy twelve thousand men for the service of his prince, without any limitation of time. The idea has occurred to obtain from him some advantages in return for this concession, such as liberty of conscience for the English residents in Portugal ; but he has no power to grant anything, and his predecessor in the embassy was disavowed for having given himself a little too much liberty in this respect. You will have learnt from other sources that the suspension of hostilities between Dunkirk and Flanders, is prorogued for six weeks. There is no news from Scotland ; Ireland still remains in the same state, and the assembly at Dublin has not dissolved, or given any heed to the orders sent from here : deputies are expected to arrive from that country in a few days, and it is generally believed that they have sent to the king of England, with propositions. The same report has lately been spread with regard to the General. I am, with respect, &c.

(55.)—M. DE BOURDEAUX TO CARDINAL MAZARIN.

MY LORD, London, April 22, 1660.

I HAVE been again assured, during the last few days, that the majority of the Council hold the same views as I stated in my preceding letter, and that the king of England will be invited to repair to France, in order to treat with the parliament through the mediation of his Majesty, if any difficulty arises respecting the accommodation. I observe also a great change of opinion with regard to the queen, and those who appeared most opposed to her return are now most favourable to it, having adopted this view together with the resolution to invite the king into France. Chancellor Hyde's agents continue to oppose it, and have already induced him to go to Breda, in order that, finding himself removed thither, the negociation may be opened there, and being continued there, that minister may have a greater share in it than if the treaty were made in France. As he proposes munificent rewards to everybody, and is considered to have great influence over his master, those who regard only their own private advantage will probably defer to this desire, without caring very much which course would be most honourable or most useful to the nation. It is, moreover, greatly to be feared that private accommodations, or the general inclination which now exists to recall the King without conditions, will frustrate the measures which the leaders of the Council are taking, and that the approaching parliament will disregard all the considerations which they may urge in order to restrain the youthful ardour of the members of that assembly. The General alone is capable of preventing these results, and he professes that he will not lay down his arms, until both public and private interests have been placed in entire safety. Nevertheless, complete belief is not given to his words, and he begins to be more reserved than before towards those ministers of the Council whom he once treated with the greatest confidence : which has led them to suspect the existence of some private treaty, especially since the journey which one of his relatives has made to Brussels. Some are even persuaded that he will recall the King before the parliament meets, in order to obtain for himself all the merit of the action, and the Council repents that it did not take this course; but it is now too late, as the session of the parliament is so near at hand, and the ministers of State hold too conflicting

opinions to come to an agreement in so short a time. Some
are desirous to follow exactly the treaty of the Isle of Wight,
others wish to append additional restrictions thereto, and some
are willing to content themselves with the safeguard of the
ancient laws of the realm : this last opinion is held in common
with the people. This diversity of opinions will not prevent
some resolution from being taken, perhaps even before I can
receive orders and instructions, with regard to the course
which I shall have to pursue in the event of the King's return
into England. His return may perhaps be hastened also by
the jealousy excited by Lambert's escape from the Tower of London. It is believed that he must have some plans in connexion
with the sectaries, and some of them have hinted to several discontented officers that in a few days they might be able to give
them employment. A proclamation was issued yesterday to
order the prisoner to surrender within twenty-four hours, and
100l. sterling were offered to any one who should apprehend him.
The danger does not, however, seem to be very great now that
the old troops have been reduced, by the change of officers, to
such a condition that they have presented to the General a
declaration assuring him of their submission to all that he,
the Council, or the Parliament may think it advisable to do for
the establishment of the civil government. Such obedience
does not exist in the army in Ireland. The assembly at
Dublin still continues to meet, and has ordered the arrest of
a number of the Catholic nobility, under the pretext of some
insurrection. It is confidently affirmed, that their deputies
have offered to receive the King of England, upon certain
conditions, the principal of which has reference to the disposal of the confiscated lands, which he has refused to confirm, as it would be to ruin those who have followed him ;
but the army will also have some difficulty in resolving to
leave go its hold. Scotland has of late talked of following
the example of Ireland, and it has been discovered that a
quantity of arms had been conveyed thither ; one of the
principal men of that country has, however, assured me that
no movement will take place until they see what England
will do ; and she will be obliged to go faster than the Council
and the Presbyterians wished, in order not to be anticipated.
The Presbyterians are beginning to be apprehensive of the
bishops, whose entire abolition they are determined to demand,
and some ministers, during the last few days, have preached

against the impiety of the royalists, as well as against the extravagance of the sectaries, not anticipating less danger from one party than from the other; and some have been so unrestrained in their discourse, that the General was yesterday, at his own table, compelled to maltreat a gentleman, formerly a colonel in the troops of the King of England, and afterwards to send him to prison, for having publicly made use of threats against those who have taken any part in the revolutions, without considering that they are the same persons who are now at the head of affairs. The people, in several counties, have appeared incensed against them, and have refused to vote for them. These are, my Lord, the present inclinations and actions of this country, my narration of which I will not fail to continue by every post. There is nothing from abroad, except the confirmation of what the Dutch ambassador told me regarding the peace with Denmark, which is advancing even more rapidly than it did in Poland. I am, &c.

(56.)—M. DE BOURDEAUX TO CARDINAL MAZARIN.

MY LORD,   London, April 26, 1660.

I CANNOT yet inform you of any progress in the affairs of this country, as nothing has occurred during the last few days; profession is still made to me of a great disposition to negociate in France, and at the present moment the principal members of the Council are assembled with the nobles who have taken part against the king, in order to settle the conditions, the manner, and the place of accommodation, so that the matter may be thoroughly digested when the parliament meets. It is also to be decided what noblemen shall take their seats in the Upper House, and although their decrees are not to be considered as laws, we may judge from this step what course the negociation will probably take. Chancellor Hyde's agents neglect no means of preventing France from having a share in it, and they accompany private offers by a declaration that the king will accede to whatever may be desired of him; this course appears more likely to be taken by the ministers than that of contesting anything, and thus giving a plea for demanding his withdrawal from affairs, as some desire, and among others those who are favourable to the queen. It has also been reported to me that offers of money are being made through the States-General, and that the princess-dowager proposes the marriage of her daughter to the king of England, and the pretext of religion would make such a marriage very agreeable here; nevertheless, those of the Council whom I know, are anxious to thwart the scheme, and with this view to withdraw the king from Holland, if possible. I left them again this morning, in the full intention of sending an accredited envoy to Breda; which would have been done before now, but for fear of giving umbrage to the general, whom they hope to gain over to their views. One of his relations has, however, conveyed propositions to the king on his behalf, and if they are well received, the others will have some difficulty to succeed in their plans, as the decision of affairs lies in his hands. The time for decision is not far off, and, according to some statements, it will be announced before I shall be able to receive letters of credence to the king of England. This is not an unfounded opinion, since, on one hand, those here are anxious to lose no time, and the interests of the king's ministers urge them to avoid all delays and interventions. There also appears to be a disposition to an insurrection among the sectaries, and since the escape of Lambert some of the old colonels are no longer to be found in their houses. The general's company of guards has been sent out of London to repress any tumult that may arise, and some of the most distinguished sectaries have already been arrested. Strict watch is also maintained every night in the city of London, and the general has changed the garrison of the Tower, under the pretext that some of the officers had favoured the escape of Lambert, to whom it was said that liberty would be granted upon his parole, but that his wife has declined the offer: he is not, however, in a position to do any mischief unless all the army revolts, and this is not at all to be feared now that all the suspected officers have been cashiered. To retain the soldiers in their obedience, they have been promised payment of their arrears, and, as they are so scattered, they would have great difficulty in uniting with one another before they were defeated by the militia of the country. I am, &c.

(57.)—M. DE BOURDEAUX TO CARDINAL MAZARIN.
MY LORD,   London, May 3, 1660.
    I HAD nothing to write by the preceding post, as the affairs of England were then in the same state as my last letter had informed you. Since then, great alarm has been

lt about an insurrection of sectaries in different localities;
)me had assembled in the neighbourhood of York, with the
htention of taking it by surprise; and, at the distance of
wenty leagues from London, Colonel Lambert had gathered
)gether a body of cavalry which the first accounts stated to
)nsist of three hundred men. Orders were immediately
iven to send against him most of the troops which are in
;ondon; the levy of the London militia was also directed to
old itself in readiness, and that of several counties, which has
ot been set on foot to be placed within the hands of persons
onsidered to be too violent royalists, was also ordered out.
,t the same time some of the most distinguished sectaries
oth in this city and in the country were arrested, and the
·eneral was making preparations to go and attack Lambert
efore he could increase his forces; but news arrived at the
nd of last week, that he had only two or three hundred men,
;nd this morning we were informed of his defeat by a party
f six hundred horse without much bloodshed; his troops
aving abandoned him one after another, he was taken pri-
oner with a few others who have been officers in the army,
nd they are on their way to London. The militia were im-
1ediately countermanded, and the universal topic of con-
ersation now is the punishment of the offenders, whose leader
7as proclaimed a traitor on the day before yesterday. His
apture seems entirely to ruin all his party, against which the
1eople entertain so great an aversion that unless the old troops
1ad mutinied, it could not have met with better fortune. Some
oyalists could have wished it to hold out a little longer, in
he hope that the present authorities would have been thereby
ompelled to hasten the return of the king upon more advan-
ageous conditions; whereas they will now have entire liberty
o act, and will perhaps impose harsher conditions, as they
1ave nothing to fear from the sectaries. There has been a
;reat contest of late between those noblemen who have been
·ngaged in the war since the year 1648, and the others, be-
:ause the former are desirous alone to constitute the Upper
Iouse; the general supports their design, and even presents
1is name to authorize it, professing that he would not be able
o restrain the army if those who have not been on the side
)f the parliament were admitted, as most of them would ad-
·ocate the recall of the king without any other limitation to
lis authority than that of the ancient laws. The question was

discussed at Whitehall, on the day before yesterday, betwee the general and some of the noblemen who are to take thei seats, and to-day, the others having gone to press him, the rather irritated than persuaded him; it is even proposed not to exclude from the House of Commons a hundred or si score members who are found not to possess the qualification fixed by the last act of the parliament, through fear that if the are allowed to enter, they will be too violent for the king, and that some question will arise in the assembly as to how the Upper House shall be constituted; which might very probably happen even if the exclusion took place, as there would remain enough other members equally opposed to all the projected limitations, of which those that are most difficult to digest have reference to the *veto* upon the parliaments, and the disposal of offices and places in the Council. It appears to me, nevertheless, that they will only be brought forward in order to obtain from the king some particular advantages in favour of the heads of the government and of the fifteen noblemen who compose the Upper House. There are none who do not neglect the public advantage in order to attend to their own private interests; but both good and evil are in the hands of the general, and all appearances indicate that he has resolved to please the king; at least it is certain that his family has particular connexion with the minister Morley, who has been sent here by Chancellor Hyde, to make terms with all parties, even the Tremblers (Quakers), in which he seems to be succeeding. But as he is not equally gracious to all, jealousies are beginning to be felt, which may be prejudicial to the affairs of the king, who I learn has not been again much pressed to proceed into France, according to the assurance which had been given me on the subject by some members of the Council. This resolution meets with considerable opposition, and, not being supported by any offer, cannot but be subjected to change. Some attempts to debauch the soldiers in Ireland have been made on the part of several cashiered officers, but the authors of them were immediately discovered and arrested; the same was attempted with the garrison of Hull with the same success. As for the troops in Scotland, they have sent a declaration, similar to that which the officers here presented to the general some days since, and which the soldiers were afterwards required to sign in order to make more sure of them in the recent conjuncture. All these movements have not prevented the Council of State from signing, three days ago, the treaty which its commissioners had agreed upon with the Portuguese ambassador. It gives his prince permission to raise as many as 12,000 infantry and 2,500 cavalry, without limitation as to time ; he may also hire vessels for his service, according to the necessity of his affairs, even against the king of Spain ; and the ambassador took his leave this morning in order to go and persuade his court to avail themselves of this permission. But it may be presumed that if the king of England returns, obstacles will be thrown in his way ; and the people are so persuaded that trade with Spain is of such importance that, with whatever limitations they may hamper the power of the king, he will be left at liberty to make peace with that crown. The affairs of the north leave me nothing to add.

(58.)—M. DE BOURDEAUX TO CARDINAL MAZARIN.

MY LORD, London, May 6, 1660.

THE letter which your Eminence did me the honour to write to me on the 16th of last month, gives me only instructions to inform you of what has come to my knowledge regarding the affairs of this country. The parliament began to assemble yesterday ; the Commons, after listening to an exhortation, went into their usual room, chose their Speaker and other officers, and then, upon an overture made by the general, appointed a committee to examine into the elections. At the same time the Lords of the year 1648 went also to take their seats and choose their officers ; some of the young ones presented themselves at the door in order to enter, affecting to be ignorant of the request which the general had made to two of them, who had visited him on the previous evening, not to take their seats for a few days, assuring them that no injury should accrue to them from this delay ; but they allowed themselves to be persuaded to yield to this desire, and retired. Nothing of importance has passed as yet this morning in either House, except that the Commons have recognized the Lords by sending an answer to a proposition for a fast-day made by the latter yesterday. This proceeding is much discussed, and was opposed only by one of the deputies who sat in the preceding parliament. It is also of some consequence that the general now consents to the admission of all the young peers, who will take their seats to-morrow, and

has ceased to talk of excluding from the House of Commons
those deputies who were elected in disregard of the qualifications. It is inferred from this, with much reason, that the
return of the king will take place more speedily, and on less
harsh conditions, and this matter will doubtless be soon
brought into consideration. There are still two parties,—one,
composed of those who favour Hyde, is anxious that the proposition shall be sent to Breda ; the other, devoted to the
interests of the Queen of England, desires that the King shall
be invited to carry on the negociation in some town in France ;
and the latter desire that I should continue to support their
plans, and this course seems to me to accord with the wish
felt by his Majesty to contribute to the restoration of the King
of England, which can never take place if he is not in France,
and if the parliament remains firm in its present determination
to allow no innovations upon the ancient laws of the country.
The Presbyterians are ill satisfied about it ; but if the general
does not keep his word to them, as there is reason to believe
he will not, the inclination of the people will be followed, and
before the month has elapsed, the King will be in England.
Your Eminence knows what it is necessary to prescribe to
me, and what course of conduct I shall have to pursue, and
whether I am to remain in England until the revolution is
completed, which I cannot do without new letters of credence.
The House of Commons has also this morning appointed some
committees, read an act against vagabonds, and voted thanks
both to the general and to the colonel who took General
Lambert prisoner without bloodshed ; this was not because
the latter had only about three or four hundred cavalry, but
having approached the troops of the State in the hope that
they would join him, his own men changed sides, and he was
not sufficiently well-mounted to escape being taken. Only
seventeen jacobuses were found upon him. Two of the principal officers of the army shared his fate, and they were all
brought to London on the day before yesterday. The Council
heard them in their defence immediately ; they acknowledged
that they had taken arms under the pretext of opposing the
royalists, and that if those who had pledged themselves to
assist them had performed their promises, a considerable army
would have been on foot in a few days. They were sent to
the Tower, and a proclamation has been issued against some
other officers, commanding them to surrender on pain of being

⸺clared traitors. Several citizens of London are also sus-
⸱rcted of being concerned in this conspiracy, and it is intended
⸱ extort large sums from the accomplices, although these ap-
ear as yet to be only disaffected officers. The London militia
⸱ict on the day before yesterday; the general was not present,
⸱aving been requested by the Council not to expose himself.
ome regiments shouted *God save the King!* and the tendency
⸱f all the people is not now more favourable to him than it
⸱as adverse to the deceased king at the beginning of the
⸱ar. I am, &c.

(59.)—M. DE BOURDEAUX TO CARDINAL MAZARIN.

⸱Iy LORD, London, May 10, 1660.

THE approbation with which your Eminence, in your
⸱tter of the 28th of last month, honours my conversation with
Ir. Thurloe, leaves me nothing more to desire than that all
⸱iy offers may produce their due effect. I thought this was
lmost certain a few days before the meeting of parliament,
nd the principal members of the Council then thought they
⸱ould be able to gain the general over to their views, what-
vcr efforts were made to induce him not to take any mea-
ures with France; but affairs have, it seems, changed their
⸱spect, and there now appears so strong a desire to recall the
⸱ing without conditions, that the offer of a place of meeting
⸱nd of mediators is altogether superfluous; it would not be
⸱vithout some difficulty, even if obstacles arose to an accom-
nodation, that France would be preferred to Breda, although
⸱verybody is of opinion that there is no reason to place the
⸱ne in the scale against the other, since the Chancellor's
⸱missaries declare that the King of England does not wish to
⸱reat anywhere else than in Holland or in London, by means
⸱f commissioners to whom he will give full powers. It was of
this minister, and of the Marquis of Ormonde, that I intended
to speak when I wrote that the English who were about the
person of the prince were attempting to prevent him from
passing into France; their aversion to France has been sufficiently displayed in the reports which they have spread, and
in their conduct with regard to me, for I have received no
civility from them, although I have communicated to them my
orders in respect to their master; they have also declared
themselves very strongly against the queen. Nevertheless,
if those who desire to see her in authority had been more
active, they might have frustrated all the measures of these
two ministers, who are generally disliked here, and prevented

the journey of the king to Breda, whither they are of opinion that the queen will proceed, if the negociations are of long continuance. There is no reason to believe this, and the Presbyterians are losing all hope of obtaining conditions now that they find themselves abandoned by the general, upon whom all their expectations were built. After having promised them not to allow any other lords to enter into the Upper House but those who have been engaged in the war against the King, he has contented himself with excluding the young peers for two days, and has declared to them that this was done only to satisfy the others; and those even who have borne arms against the parliament will take their seats. He has consented to the admission of all the members of the House of Commons without regard to qualifications; which leads the army to murmur, and weakens the credit of the Presbyterian party, the leaders of which accuse the general of having duped them. He is not also without cause of complaint against some of them, having discovered that they were making preparations for dividing among themselves all the offices under the crown, and that in order to effect this arrangement more conveniently, the old Lords were desirous alone to compose the Upper House, under the pretext that the others were too great royalists. Their prudence has been frustrated, and the votes of the young members will prevail in both Houses, which have not met since the 11th of the month. The Upper House determined, at its last session, to confer with the Commons upon the form of the government, and in order to prepare for so important a deliberation, to-day has been spent in prayers; to-morrow, therefore, those letters will be read which the King has written to the general, to the Council, and to the officers of the army, dated on the 14th of this (last?) month; they were presented by a gentleman who is a near relative of the general, and who it is said was sent into Flanders by him. He refused to open them except in the parliament; nevertheless, no one doubts but that he is acquainted with their contents, and neither he nor his wife scruple openly to declare their inclination for the restoration of the King. The only difficulty has reference to the conditions; to-morrow we shall hear whether the accommodation is capable of longer delay. As the revolution may occur in a few days, I cannot but await orders with some impatience; it would even have been advisable to send me letters of credence to the parliament, in order that, if the service his Majesty or of the King of England requires it, I might in a position to request an audience. I cannot otherwise t in public, as the House of Lords does not acknowledge my ters to the previous parliament. If it is judged advisable send me new credentials, let them be with the quality of bassador extraordinary, as there is no longer any necessity : me to make a protracted stay here, and moreover it will ince greater esteem towards the new government. The neral has been confirmed by the Upper House in his office r so long as may be considered necessary, and he continues change the old officers of the army. My Lord Falconbridge s obtained a regiment of cavalry from him. A number of ïcers of Lambert's party have been taken of late, and he has ade another attempt to escape from the Tower this afternoon. report is current that the troops in Ireland have been hting with each other, because one party desired to recall the ing with conditions, and the other without any, and that the tter had the advantage : the troops in London have appeared ther restless of late, and spoke of presenting some request r the confirmation of the confiscated lands, some titular pro- ietors of which have already taken possession without a legal der. This will be one of the principal questions of the commodation. I am, &c.

(60.)—M. DE BOURDEAUX TO CARDINAL MAZARIN.
Y LORD, London, May 11, 1660.
THE news which I wrote yesterday will have prepared our Eminence to receive that which I have to communicate -day, which I think it worth while to forward by an express. s soon as the parliament had met, the President of the ouncil laid before it the letter which the king had written to e general, but which neither he nor the Council had been illing to open ; one of the members at the same time in- rmed the House that a gentleman was at the door on behalf f the king. He was brought in forthwith, and presented nother letter, with a declaration, which, in substance, after an umeration of the evils which have afflicted England for so any years, invites the people to put an end to them by sub- itting to their old form of government, offers an amnesty r the past with no other exceptions than those whom the arliament shall judge right to exclude from it, refers to it the rrangement of the confiscated lands, appoints a national

council to settle differences of religion, and promises complet
satisfaction to the soldiers. The perusal of these letters wa;
followed by several harangues in praise of the king, and th;
general applause of the whole assembly, which immediatel'
resolved .to send deputies to thank him, and voted hin
50,000l. sterling. The same gentleman had presented to th(
House of Lords a letter containing the same declaration, an(
they had adopted a similar resolution of sending deputies t(
express their gratitude to the king, whom the Speaker calle(
" our sovereign lord." A conference was then held betweer
the commissioners of the two Houses, during which it wa!
determined that England should be governed as in formei
times, and that means should be taken for obtaining the king'!
return as quickly as possible. This result was approved of bj
both Houses, and they are now employed in drawing up ar
answer to his letter, which is to be presented to him by tw(
lords and four members of the House of Commons. Th(
general has requested permission to reply privately to his owr
letter, which has been granted him ; and the town council ha!
also received one this afternoon, which gave it great satis
faction. Their joy is now manifested by the great numbei
of bonfires which have been lighted, and the other tokens o
delight of which an enthusiastic populace are capable. Ther(
is no room for doubt but that by the end of this month, or th(
beginning of next, the business will be entirely settled
and the king in England. Not but that some are anxiousl\
desirous to take precautions for the future; but the excitemen
is too great, and no one would be willing to draw down upor
himself the resentment of the public by propositions whicl
cannot but be rejected, as the general is undoubtedly actin{
in concert with the king, and the declaration has been agreed or
between them. The bearer·of the letters is a relation of his
and the same who it is thought was sent into Flanders by him
I have to-day seen some Presbyterians who were greatly cas
down by this change without conditions, and they are unde
apprehensions that the general has stipulated to reserve ;
portion of the army under the pretext of keeping the sectarie
in order, but in reality to maintain the royal authority agains
the prerogatives of the people. We shall shortly be able t(
judge with greater certainty, and at present it only appears t(
me that no preparations are being made yet for disbanding th(
troops; that the king's declaration will be reduced to the forn

.f an act of parliament without addition or abridgment; that
no further proposition will be made for the exclusion of the
Chancellor; that the government will henceforth be administered according to the ancient laws; that the deputies
of both Houses will set out in two or three days to convey
he first submission of the parliament; and that they will
speedily be followed by another more solemn deputation to
accompany the king, whose return will take place, according
to all appearances, at the beginning of next month. It would
be desirable for me to be informed before that period of the
course of conduct which I am to pursue in this very extraordinary conjuncture; and this is the reason why I send the
present courier to the frontier, unless M. de Brienne judges it
more advisable to detain him at Paris. The post of the day after
to-morrow will inform you of the consequences of to-day's resolutions. Meanwhile I have only again to entreat your Eminence that if I am ordered to present the first compliments to
he King of England, it may be in some higher quality than I
have sustained towards the preceding governments, and that,
as this will oblige me to incur new expenses, I may receive the
necessary funds from the King. I shall expect both these favours
from the kindness with which you are pleased to honour, &c.

(61.)—M. DE BOURDEAUX TO CARDINAL MAZARIN.

My Lord,   London, May 13, 1660.

SINCE my letter of the day before yesterday, the army
has followed the example of the Parliament and city; and
when the general communicated the King's letters to the
officers, they assured him of their obedience by a declaration.
Some, however, had a little while before attempted to induce
the general's wife to prefer the advantages of sovereign authority to all those which the King of England will bestow upon
her family; but she rejected this proposition, and her inclinations have undoubtedly contributed largely to the revolution
in the government. Some soldiers were found among the
troops who preferred to leave the army rather than submit;
but their number is very inconsiderable, and the offer which
the King has made, in his declaration and letters to the
general, to retain the services of the army, will probably appease their discontent. The Parliament, in pursuance of its
resolutions of the day before yesterday, has appointed a Committee to draw up the acts which are to be passed by the

Q

King before his return, and to choose the deputies who are to convey to him the answers both of the Upper House and o the Commons. The anxiety manifested to belong to this deputation has caused the Lords to name six of their body with the Earl of Oxford at their head, and the Commons wil send twelve. The general will also send his answers by his brother-in-law, and the city by some citizens. This large deputation will not leave until the beginning of next week It has also been resolved by the Upper House that all the Lords shall be invited to take their seats, without excepting either those who have been in arms for the King, or the Catholics; and a proposition was also made to proclaim the King, but it was not adopted, any more than one to request the King not to leave Breda. Besides the present of 50,000*l.* sterling which the Parliament has sent him, and the 6000*l.* sterling which have also been voted for the repairs of Whitehall, the city of London has made him a present of 10,000*l.* sterling, and some private citizens are going to send him 16,000*l.* sterling. Although all vie with each other as to who shall manifest most zeal, there nevertheless exists some fear lest his power will remain too absolute, and will be maintained by an army, which he talks of keeping up. This distrust will probably give rise to some debate upon the proposed acts. No further propositions have been made for withdrawing the King from Breda, as there is no appearance of any negociation, for the voice of the people demands the return of the King, with no other limitation than that of the ancient laws; and in order to banish the idea which was entertained of drawing him into France, those who are acting for the King have published that the ministers of the King of Spain are very much displeased with him, because he refuses to return thither, on the invitation of the Marquis of Caracena. The bad offices which some have been anxious to render the Queen have produced no effect, and there is a strong disposition to grant her all that she can desire from England. I have been requested to convey to her a letter from the general's wife in answer to that which she had received from her; her return into England will, it is thought, balance the power of the Chancellor, and all the parties appear to be already formed; this will be something to occupy attention after the return of the court. Such, my lord, is all that present affairs give me occasion to write to-day.   *   *   *

(62.)—M. DE BOURDEAUX TO CARDINAL MAZARIN.

MY LORD, London, May 17, 1660.

I HAVE to-day merely to inform you of the progress of the general acquiescence which all England has given to the re-establishment of royalty. General Montague, having received a letter from the King containing the declaration which was read in the Parliament, communicated it to the principal commanders of the fleet, and it was forthwith made known in all the vessels with all the marks of joy which the officers and sailors were able to express. Ireland has displayed similar conduct, and has even gone so far as solemnly to proclaim the King, which seems to have given rise to the resolution adopted by the parliament to-day to perform the same ceremony in London to-morrow, with all the solemnities customary upon such an occasion. It has also been determined this afternoon, in the House of Lords, to invite the King to come to England as quickly as possible. This determination will be communicated to the House of Commons to-morrow, and if it concurs in it, as there is reason to believe it will, although some are not greatly disposed to urge his return, the King will soon be in England, as orders have already been sent to the fleet to hold itself in readiness to take him on board, and news has arrived that he has proceeded to Middleburg. The other debates in the House of Lords during the last few days are of less importance; they had resolved to invite all their members to come and take their seats; and since, under the pretext that this might give occasion for some discontent, they have excepted the Catholic peers from this invitation, without, however, refusing them admission. They have also, upon a complaint made by the sectaries, of some violence done them by the populace, directed the Mayor of London to prevent such disorders; granted to the Duke of Buckingham and three other individuals an act to deprive the possessors of their property, of liberty to dispose of it, or even to make use of the income derived from it; and the answers made by the two Houses to the King's letters have been read. They are worded with all the respect which could be expected from good subjects, and the death of the deceased King is disavowed therein, and even termed a horrible murder. The Commons have, on their side, laboured daily to complete the acts which are to be presented to the King by their deputies. These have reference to the general amnesty, from which all those will be excepted who acted as

judges of the late King, most of whom have already retired
from England; the second states that all confiscated property
shall remain in the same state as it is now, until new orders
are issued; the third sanctions the present Parliament,
although it was not, according to custom, summoned by the
King, but this is not to be taken as a precedent in future.
There is a fourth which relates to religion, and refers its
differences to a national synod.   The Commons have also consented to the restitution of the property of the Duke of Buckingham and the others; but a similar order having been
proposed in favour of another lord, the general put difficulties
in the way of granting it, pretending that such a step would
be likely to displease the army; which terminated the affair,
and even postponed until to-morrow the debate upon the
duke's case, most of whose property is in the hands of the
Protector's heirs.   There are a great many deputies who are
of opinion that the presentation of these acts should be deferred until the King's return; but those who are called *Old
Presbyterians* desire to have this security before receiving him;
and it is even said that some of them have reproached the
general because he has taken no precautions for the liberty of
the people.   Upon to-morrow's debate will depend the speedy
return of the King, which, at latest, cannot be deferred
beyond the commencement of next month.   The deputies of the
two Houses will set out in two or three days: the city will
send their representatives with them and will charge them
with a present of 2,000*l.* sterling for the Dukes of York
and Gloucester.   The general has already despatched his
brother-in-law with his answer and the declaration of the
army.   It is said that some movement has been executed in
Scotland by the sectaries and Presbyterians who were engaged
against the King during the late wars, and that even Major General Morgan, who is in command of the troops, supports them;
but this is not probable, and the number of those mal-contents
would not, moreover, be sufficient to prevent the arrangements which are being made.   Many other equally ill-founded
reports are current; among others that the King of England
is very much displeased with France, that we have a design
for supporting an insurrection of Lambert's party, and that I
have pressed the general to constitute himself Protector.   The
general's brother-in-law has undertaken to give testimony as
to what has passed on the latter point, and it will be shown

lat I have urged him to use language very far removed from
lch a proposition. The source of all these impressions which
is attempted to give, proceeds from the animosity felt
^ainst the Queen and France by some of those who enjoy the
.ing's confidence. It is also pretty openly declared that
Sweden has of late greatly disobliged England ; but I cannot
^elieve that the court which is about to return will entertain
,> much bitter feeling, and moreover it will not be in a posi-
, on to take offence at the past, especially against powerful
^tates. Mr. Lockhart has gone to Breda to make his peace,
^nd the news has been confirmed of late that the ministers of
^ie King of Spain have attempted to entice the English mon-
rch into Flanders, in order to oblige him to restore Dunkirk.
t only remains for me to subscribe myself, &c.

(63.)—M. DE BOURDEAUX TO CARDINAL MAZARIN.
IY LORD,   London, May 21, 1660.
THE narration of what has taken place since my last letter
rill inform your Eminence that the King of England was pro-
laimed on the day before yesterday, first at Westminster, and
hen in front of Whitehall and in the city of London, with all
he solemnities customary upon such occasions, which, how-
ver, are not worth relating. Nothing extraordinary occurred
xcept the demonstrations of joy given by the people. On
he same day, bonfires were again lighted in front of all the
louses, the Tower guns were fired, and all persons of respect-
ibility distributed wine among the people. I thought it right
o conform to this example, and advised all the other foreign
ministers who consulted me to do the same. It is also to be
emarked that the proclamation was made in terms which, it
s said, are not generally used, in that they declared that a pro-
:lamation is unnecessary, and that the king's right to the
:rown is indubitably acquired to him by his birth. The arms
)f the republic, which were in the House of Parliament, were,
ifter having been exposed some time, burned by one of the
members of that body who had taken a leading part in the
.first movements of England. And, in short, every one is
ittempting to display peculiar zeal, without considering
whether the prerogatives of the people, of which they were
formerly so jealous, are injured by it or not. The members
of parliament, who act with less vehemence, wished to postpone this proclamation ; but they did not see any chance of

succeeding, and confined their efforts to a proposition that after having done everything that had reference to the interest of the king, the popular acts should be taken into consideration : and during their last sessions strenuous efforts have been made to complete those which have reference to religion, the amnesty, the sales of confiscated property, and the payment of the arrears due both to the army and navy. In reference to the second point, it was proposed to shut up the ports in order to prevent the escape of those who had any share in the death of the king ; but it was judged more advisable to leave the door open, and all of them are not even excepted from pardon. It was also considered that those who have acted as Judges in the high Courts of Justice, or as members of the Committee of Safety, ought not to be admitted to the benefit of the act which confirms the sales or gifts of confiscated lands, from the number of which those of the Duke of Buckingham and three others have been excepted. The idea had occurred to some of the servants of the queen to except also the domains set apart for the dowry of the queen ; but others, with more foresight, are of opinion that it will be better not to mention the matter just now, lest Hyde's faction should take the opportunity of making some overture prejudicial to her interests : and the same do not doubt that after the king's return, unless he is opposed to it, she will have no difficulty in regaining possession of all her rights. The general also professes his willingness to act in her service ; and consequently no one doubts but that perfect liberty will be left her to return into England, and the jealousy which some entertain of the influence of Chancellor Hyde leads them to wish that she may come to England as quickly as possible. The Parliament has, by an express deliberation, decreed that the king shall be invited to come over without delay, and Admiral Montague has been ordered to proceed with all his fleet to the coast of Holland in order to receive the royal commands. The deputies of the parliament are also to set out to-morrow with a large retinue of noblemen, in addition to those who have already gone over to Flanders ; they were to be charged only with the answers of the two Houses ; but instructions will be given them in reference to all that is desired of the king, and they will accompany him on his journey, which cannot be postponed longer than twelve or fifteen days, as he has been advised by his most zealous servants to hasten it in order to revent the factions which might be formed, during his absence, against his authority, which some are greatly desirous of limiting; among others, they propose to present him with the great officers of the kingdom. A committee was established a few days ago, to regulate the ceremonies and manner of his reception; another is labouring to provide funds for the support of his household, and to obtain the income which is to be given him; and the general's wife is attending to the furniture. The parliament has to-day returned thanksgivings to God for the change which has taken place, and the ministers of religion have been ordered to pray in future for the King and the Dukes of York and Gloucester; but the queen is not included, which is contrary to the custom of past times. The reports which prevailed about an insurrection in Scotland have proved untrue, and all the advices which are received from the provinces announce entire submission. The garrison of Dunkirk has not failed to follow this example, and Mr. Lockhart has gone to the king by order of the Council of State. It is doubted whether he will be continued in the government of Dunkirk, and whether liberty will be left to the king to restore that place to Spain; but such affairs are not mentioned yet, but everything is deferred until his return. I have now only to sign myself, &c.

(64.)—M. DE BOURDEAUX TO CARDINAL MAZARIN.

MY LORD,   London, June 3, 1660.

THE letter which your Eminence did me the honour to write to me on the 29th of last month has just been delivered to me, and I have also received a despatch from M. de Brienne; but the course which the affairs of England have taken will not permit me to perform the services which they direct. You will already have remarked, from my previous letters, that the intrigues of the friends of Chancellor Hyde have met with more success than my efforts to induce the king of England to go into France, and that the excitement, both of the parliament and the people, has frustrated all the measures which were being taken for transferring thither the negociation of the treaty projected by the leading members of the Council of State, in the expectation that the general would remain true to the sentiments which he professed to them that he entertained. If the advantages which have been proposed to him have disposed him to abandon his friends, the lukewarm-

ness of the queen's partisans has been no less favourable to
the Chancellor's designs : they throw the blame upon the
court of the Palais Royal, and, in fact, Lord Jermyn did not
go into Flanders until after the arrival of a gentleman who
was despatched from hence to the queen, in order to learn her
intentions with regard to the overtures which I had made,
and which they did not think would be agreeable to her, as
she had not written to them on the subject.   Whilst this
explanation was awaited, the general pledged himself to support the retirement of the king to Breda, in preference to
any other place, unless he had any objection ; if the queen
had sent a messenger to him before, or if they had acted with
a little more spirit, this blow would have been prevented.
There now remains nothing to do but to thwart the designs
which the Chancellor may form to the prejudice of France ;
his ill-will is said to be undiminished ; but different reports
are current with regard to his influence, and many flatter
themselves that it will not be difficult to destroy it.   This
cannot, however, be done by the general ; he is not reputed
to be either a counsellor or a courtier ; and his relations, to
whose advice he yields great deference, are gained over, among
others his wife's brother, who claims the honour of having
disposed him to restore the king.   It was through him that I
kept up a correspondence with the general ; and since the
Chancellor's agents have won him over to their interests, he
has discontinued to see me.   The old Presbyterians are more
disposed to oppose the prime minister, and if the number of
young men with whom both Houses of parliament have been
filled had not made them lose courage, they would now have
stipulated for his removal.   As one party apprehends that
their efforts will be useless, and the others are buoyed up with
hopes, it is impossible to count on their inclinations.   I have
not neglected to enter into connection with some leading men,
who are most anxious for the return of the Queen of England,
that she may support them and combat the power of the
Chancellor before it is more strongly established.   Although
there appears to be no obstacle to her return, one cannot
answer for the sentiments which the King will entertain when
he is here, and perhaps difficulties will be raised on the part
of the parliament, in order to give him a pretext for post-
poning her return.   Already, even, it is said to be inoppor-
tune, before affairs are settled, that it will produce factions in

that religion will be prejudiced thereby.
ie considerations will have no weight unless
:d underhand by those who are known to
)f this court ; thus upon this depends the
.ve must form of this minister's credit : he
: to be offended if he is not capable of keep-
France, I have not failed to act in her
:he zeal which you prescribe ; and she, as
of England, will undoubtedly have been
erformance of the orders which have been
of the most distinguished members of her
I have been on intimate terms since my
itry have undertaken to bear this testimony
hey are even persuaded that, as early as the
e Booth's insurrection, France was ready to
: republic, as we then used language which
to be very positive propositions. The last
iich his Majesty has given of his good-will
ice the King of England that my conduct
and I entertain no doubts about presenting
a manner of which he will approve, if his
the orders which I am expecting by my
;o continue to humour the general, to whom
:rests of the queen at my last visit, inviting
lory of her restoration as well as of that of
whom he started yesterday, with no other
ompany of cavalry, in which a number of
rolled themselves. It has not been judged
: so much confidence in the old regiments,
:rs are well-intentioned ; and so some other
lemen have been formed, among others one
)f the general's lady, of which an English
ned to become the lieutenant. The citizens
formed others, and after having displayed
streets, they all set out yesterday on their
ence of the information given by the depu-
nent that the king intended to embark on
iterday, that he would land at Dover, and
y proceed to Canterbury, where he would
The two Houses of Parliament will await
nd, as they are making no preparations to
I have also thought it right to remain in
iuse of Commons has, during the last few

days, been engaged in hot debate upon a proposition made by one of the members to remove all Catholics from the court, according to the ancient laws. The pretext of this banishment is derived from some insurrection which has taken place in Ireland, and of which the Catholics are thought to be the principal authors. The question has not yet been decided, as part of the assembly did not think it advisable to enforce such rigorous measures at the present crisis. This proposition has not prevented all the Catholic peers from taking their seats in the Upper House, and up to this hour the others have not taken offence at their conduct; but if the proposed act is passed, they will probably be attacked. The two Houses have had some discussion in reference to their prerogatives; because the Commons having requested the concurrence of the Lords in the confiscation of the property of the king's judges, the latter readily gave their assent, but in their act treated the Commons as complainants and not as judges, and declare that they can act in no other capacity. The levying of money has also occupied this assembly, of which the general took leave before his departure. There is news from Ireland that the Irish Convention has sent a deputation to the king, and made him a present of 20,000l. sterling and 4000l. to the Dukes of York and Gloucester. Several of the officers of the Court of Justice which condemned the king, and one of his judges, have had the boldness to present themselves before the House of Lords, who sent them to the Tower. I cannot, my lord, behold without gratitude the approbation with which your Eminence honours my conduct, and the assurances of friendship which you renew to me; but when I consider, on the other hand, the state of my affairs and the advantages which most others derive from their services in various offices, I cannot but accuse my fate, and imagine that fortune is less favourable in England than in any other place. This reflection augments the desire which I feel to return into France, and I supplicate your Eminence for permission to do so, after I have executed the orders which will probably be forwarded to me by my courier. I hope that this favour will not exhaust your bounty towards him who has the honour to be, &c.

(65.)—M. DE BOURDEAUX TO CARDINAL MAZARIN.
MY LORD, London, June 7, 1660.
I ACKNOWLEDGED by last post the receipt of the letter which your Eminence did me the honour to write to me on

e 25th of last month, by the courier whom I had despatched; it having postponed my answer until to-day, I must, before speak of what has occurred in England during the last few ays, assure you that I will not fail to execute punctually our Eminence's commands, as well as the orders sent me by . de Brienne. Now that the King of England has returned his own country, they are reduced to my employing myself the queen's service, and against Chancellor Hyde, and to rming opinions in the parliament by which his Majesty may e able to profit. As it has not only just now appeared to e that these were the only services which could be expected om me, this has been my principal occupation ever since the ing's return has been certain, and I have treated of it with ifferent persons, among others with the most influential Pres- yterians, who have pretty openly declared themselves on the ueen's side, and against the Chancellor, whose credit gives them ffence; but they have almost entirely lost courage since the eneral acceded to the resolutions adopted by the parliament recall the king without conditions; and their only resource at resent is in his conduct with regard to the queen, it being cer- ain that, unless she can induce him to recall her into England, he Chancellor and the Marquis of Ormonde will easily raise p obstacles to her return under the pretext of religion. And he overtures which have been made of late against the Catho- ics do not seem to have any other object than her exclusion, t least this is the opinion of many persons, and that these two inisters are closely united against her return, foreseeing that heir credit would be injured by her presence; but as to the ecuniary interests which she may have, full satisfaction ill doubtless be given her. Lord Jermyn, the Earl of St. Albans, who arrived here yesterday evening, will have found ut what is to be expected from the king, and the review hich he has already made of his friends will have given him lenty of information upon which to take measures; and if ny assistance can contribute to the advancement of his designs, I will not fail to act with all the zeal which you prescribe. As far as the parliament is concerned, it is impossible to say of what use its inclinations will be. The king has returned into possession of such complete affection of his subjects that no- thing can now be contested with him, and the forces which have been placed in his hands by the general's entire resigna- tion place him in a very different position from that of his an-

cestors. The most clearsighted are of opinion that henceforward'
the prerogatives of the people will depend upon the will of
their sovereign; and although he is but slightly armed, nothing will be difficult to him if he follows the example of the
Protector, who governed England with an army of seven or
eight thousand men, although all the nobility and most of the
people detested his authority. It has already been proposed
to dissolve the present parliament because it was not convoked
in due form; and appearances clearly indicate, that if the
ministers do not find it well-intentioned, they will not leave it
long in existence. The House of Lords appears the strongest;
but those of whom it is composed are not capable of great
enterprise, and the veterans who have fought during the late
wars have lost nearly all their haughtiness. The Earl of Manchester belongs to this number; but he thinks he has deserved
much of late, and the hope of obtaining some high office will
render him very circumspect. I had formed an intimacy with
him some years since, and had even first addressed myself to
him in order to induce parties here to invite the king of England to pass into France, and he professed that he would labour
to that end; nevertheless, I have not seen that he has done
anything in the matter, and since his brother's letter has been
given to him, he has certainly been to see me, but in company
with others; and in answer to my questions, he deferred conversation on the matter to some other time. The Countess of
Carlisle is more disposed to enter into intrigues, and has appeared so for a long while; but her credit is greatly diminished, as is also that of her brother, the Earl of Northumberland. It is to be feared that the rest of the Presbyterian
party, who are well-disposed towards France, will have the
same fate. As for the general, I have kept on good terms
with him, having anticipated the orders which were sent me
to congratulate him upon the happy success of his enterprise;
but no one believes that his opinion has much influence in
deciding the questions discussed in the Council of England,
especially in reference to foreign affairs; moreover his confidants are entirely devoted to the interests of the Chancellor.
One of them, Mr. Morrice, has been made a minister and Secretary of State; the others have received other rewards in
the same way. Different opinions, nevertheless, prevail with
regard to the Chancellor's influence, and the King of England
does not wish it to be considered so great as many represent it;

me think that the Earl of St. Albans will have a great deal to
with affairs of state. These opinions need confirmation, and
is cannot be given until after the king's arrival in London.
e disembarked at Dover on the 4th of this month; the
neral received him on the beach kneeling, and surrounded
all his army. The king bestowed upon him all imaginable
resses, called him his father, and after a short conversation
private, and when he had received the homage of the no-
lity under a dais which had been erected, having at his sides
e Dukes of York and Gloucester, who received similar re-
ects at the same time and remained covered, the king en-
red his carriage, into which the two princes and the general
first took their seats; the Duke of Buckingham also got in
ithout being invited, and although he had met with a very
ol reception. The king took the road to Canterbury, along
hich having met all the companies of gentlemen in battle-array,
e mounted on horseback, and so entered into that city, where
e has remained up to this time; during his stay there he has
iven the order of the Garter to the general and to the Earl of
outhampton, with this difference, that the Dukes of York
nd Gloucester fastened the sash and garter on the first, and
e herald-at-arms performed the same office to the other. A
aper was also read containing the reasons for the general's
romotion, which were derived from his connection with the
oyal family, although only by way of bastardy, and from the
ervices he has rendered in liberating the three nations from
lavery. Mr. Morrice and Sir Ashley Cooper, who both be-
onged to the old parliament, have been also favoured for the
atter reason, and the Garter has been sent to General Monta-
ue, who commands the fleet under the Duke of York, who
as been appointed Lord High Admiral. All this company
ill leave Canterbury to-day on its way to London, into which
ity the king will enter to-morrow at the head of the nobility.
The brevity of the time allowed for preparation not permitting
reat magnificence, the two Houses of Parliament will await
im at Whitehall. Nothing of importance has occurred in
hese two bodies of late. The Lords have granted the Commons the liberty to put on their hats, which they formerly
lisputed, and the latter have resolved upon a law against the
Irish Catholics, together with a renewal of the laws which
banish from the court all who are of the same religion. The
king, when embarking, forbade the Catholics of his suite to

accompany him, from which we may infer that uniformity of opinion exists upon this point.   I am preparing to present th' letters of credence which have been sent me.   The ambassado from the States General who was here has been recalled in conformity with the desire which the king expressed when at the Hague, and the Portuguese envoy greatly apprehends that he will not be admitted to an audience after what has happened to his colleague resident in Holland.   *   *   *

(66.)—M. de Bourdeaux to Cardinal Mazarin.
My Lord,   London, June 10, 1660.
    I have nothing to communicate to-day, except the entrance of the king into London, as I have had no opportunity since his arrival, of presenting to him his Majesty's letter and no remarkable solemnity, or great magnificence wa displayed upon this occasion, but only great declamation and expressions of joy.   In the morning the king left Ro chester, which is distant about ten leagues from this city and mounted his horse when about two leagues off, when he was met by all the companies of the nobility, and by five regiments of the army ; he marched forwards in the midst of these corps, and was soon met by the Mayor of London, ac companied by the Sheriffs and a number of citizens on horse back, at the utmost confines of his jurisdiction.   The Mayo presented his sword to the king, who returned it into his hands, upon which he remounted his horse, and carried his sword before him, still remaining bareheaded, and having General Monk on his right hand, and the Duke of Bucking ham on his left.   The King rode immediately behind him having the Dukes of York and Gloucester on either side but a little behind him ; in this order he passed through the whole length of the city, through two ranks of pikemen of the city militia, and of the guilds of merchants who stood with their robes and banners in a hedge behind the barriers which had been fixed up in all the streets, in some of which the water-conduits were filled with wine. The king found the members of both Houses of Parliament at Whitehall according to the orders which had been given them on the preceding evening, and harangues were made in their name for the Upper House by the Earl of Manchester, and for the Commons by their Speaker.   The day was ended with the erection of bonfires in front of all the houses, and the boom-

g of the guns at the Tower of London. All day yesterday as employed in receiving all those who presented themselves, and to-day the Dukes of York and Gloucester, have taken their seats in parliament for the first time, in virtue of the patents granted them during the reign of the deceased ing, as the princes of the blood enjoy this prerogative only y commission. They advocated the desire which the king xpressed through the medium of one of the Lords, that some f those who were created peers by the deceased king should be admitted: and although the House of Commons had projected an act to annul all these titles, and the House of Lords was willing to ratify such a resolution, not one of them ventured to oppose the proposition, and this acquiescence opens the door to all those titles which have been created ince the commencement of the war, which will render the Upper House more august in numbers than it formerly was. This afternoon, the Council of State began its sessions, and Mr. Hollis and the President of the preceding Council, were admitted. The Earl of Manchester and Lord Robarts, considered to be two of the ablest men in the nation, are also to be added, although the latter was a most zealous opponent of the king, and his appointment is a cause of chagrin to some of the old royalists. It has been judged advisable by this junto, to publish three acts of parliament, the principal of which has reference to the confirmation of sales; the act which renews the ancient penal laws against the Catholics has been presented on the part of the Commons to the House of Lords; that enacting the imposition of taxes to the amount of three millions, payable in three months, has passed, as has also the prorogation of the sessions of the Courts of Justice; and these are the principal deliberations which have occurred of late. The affairs of the queen are soon to be brought under discussion. I informed the Secretary of State, this morning, that his Majesty had sent me letters of credence, and the Earl of St. Albans, who came to see me this evening, assures me that the king was, this afternoon, well-disposed to receive me, notwithstanding the impression which my enemies tried to convey to him that, instead of acting on his behalf I had pressed the General, of late, to constitute himself Protector. This is a report which was prevalent some time since, but which has no other foundation than the civilities and offers of friendship which your Eminence ordered me to make

to him a few days after his arrival in London. The author
of the rumours are those men who are desirous to irritate the
public mind against France, and reflectively against the
queen. I postpone until the next post further remarks
upon this subject, and upon the influence possessed by the
Chancellor, as I have no time to write more to-day; and after
having informed you of the excuses sent me by Mr. Lockhart
for not having visited me, and which he has based upon the
fact that his disgrace is partly owing to the great friendship
which he had displayed towards France, I will subscribe
myself, &c. ——————

(67.)—M. DE BOURDEAUX TO CARDINAL MAZARIN.
MY LORD,   London, June 14, 1660.
I WILL now satisfy the expectations which my previous
letter will have led your Eminence to form with regard to
Chancellor Hyde, by informing you that it is reported to me
in different quarters, that the King of England determines
upon no affair of importance without his concurrence, that he
has bestowed no high office on any one who is not on good
terms with this minister, that he attributes his restoration to
him, and that he is quite disposed to devolve the burden of
government on to his shoulders; but that nevertheless, he is
offended if he is termed the prime minister, and believed to
have so much influence. The Earl of St. Albans gave me to
understand, that the King's favour is divided between the
Chancellor and the Marquis of Ormonde, but that he thinks
that the former will prevail in the end; the one may be more
active and devoted to business, and the other very much beloved by the king; both are equally discontented with France
and attached to Spain, and the fear which they entertain
with regard to the return of the queen induces them to seek
opportunities for irritating the mind of their master against
France. If they had succeeded in this as well as in inspiring
the people with an aversion towards us, a war might be expected; since the return of the court nothing else is talked
about, and many are of opinion, that, as it is necessary to give
some occupation abroad to the English troops, this could not
be done less prejudicially than by employing them against
France. But I do not learn that the king coincides with
these views, and the reports which have reached me up to
this moment, represent him to be better acquainted with his
true interests than to entertain such an idea. Public rumour

Also asserts that he will not receive me, and I cannot but suspect that this report has some foundation, as I have received
no news from the Secretary of State, although when I informed
him that I had letters of credence, he promised to inform the
king thereof immediately, and to give me an answer without
delay. I sent to him this evening to inquire the reason of his
silence, and he deferred all explanations until to-morrow. As
regards the position of the Earl of St. Albans, by his own
avowal, when he came into England, he did not think himself
very much advanced in the king's good graces, and many had
confirmed me in this opinion ; but he has met with greater attention during the last few days, and he assures me that he
found the king inclined quite otherwise than he is represented to be, both with regard to France, and to myself in-
dividually : consequently he has no cause for complaint, after
that the General's brother-in-law has declared that I had
charged him with no proposition which could tend to destroy
the good-will of the General, whose influence it is not thought
will be of long duration ; for the Presbyterians whom he has
deceived (by recalling the king unconditionally, contrary to
his promise), will, if possible, urge him to extremities, and
the Chancellor is temporizing with him. Some of the leading
Presbyterians have been summoned to the Council ; most of
the others are the best qualified of the peers who discharged
the same duties under the deceased king, or under the present
monarch : the Duke of Buckingham is the only one rejected,
and it is reported that the king himself made him leave his
room, telling him that he would send for him when his services should become necessary. His past conduct is the
cause of this disgrace, and of late he has not behaved himself
in a manner calculated to efface the remembrance of it. Most
of the principal offices have also been filled up ; the Marquis
of Ormonde is Grand-Master, and aspires to be Viceroy of
Ireland ; the General also aspires to the same post, although
he has been appointed Master of the Horse ; the Earl of Manchester is Lord High Chamberlain ; the Chancellor has assumed his seat both in the Court of Chancery, and in the
House of Lords, of which he is the Speaker ; the office of
Postmaster-General, with a salary of 1,000l. per annum, has
been given to the Duke of Gloucester. It is proposed to
place upon a permanent footing a regiment of 1,200 cavalry ;
and although it is said that the General is opposed to the

R

plan, the king will doubtless decide the matter according to his own pleasure. He went to the Parliament, on the 11th instant, by water and without ceremony, to give his approbation to the acts which authorize the session of that body, the continuance of the sessions of the Courts of Justice, and the tax of three millions of pounds sterling, which the Council of State had examined on the previous evening. This was done after the King had made a rather short speech to the two Houses, in which he expressed his gratitude for the affection which they had lately manifested towards him, and assured them that he would carry into complete execution the declaration which he had sent to them from Breda: the Chancellor spoke after him, and—after having exaggerated the importance of the miraculous revolution which has just happened, praised the General and represented the King to be strongly desirous to observe the declaration of Breda—he pressed the Parliament to conclude the act of amnesty by naming those who are to be excepted from it, in order that the others may be not only exempted from danger, but also from fear. He also recommended the act which has reference to religion, and gave them to understand that regard must be had to tender consciences; and advised the satisfaction of the army by the payment of the arrears which are due to it. On the very next day measures were taken in reference to the first of these acts, and it was resolved that those of the king's judges who shall not surrender themselves within fifteen days, shall be declared traitors; two of them have been taken, and one of these is the brother-in-law of the deceased Protector, and was the main cause of the downfal of his son. Search has been made during the last few days for other criminals, namely, the men who betrayed the king, some of whom were found out by Mr. Thurloe's clerk when he was at Breda; and he himself, as I am told, has revealed the others; among others have been found one of the leaders of the party commanded by Sir George Booth, and another, a Colonel greatly esteemed by the King, who has been lodged in the Tower. Two gentlemen of the Duke of Buckingham's retinue belonged to this same cabal, and have taken flight. There was also arrested, this morning, at Whitehall, in consequence of information which has arrived from the country, a man who is suspected of entertaining designs upon the person of the King, the first act of whose reign, which has appeared in public un-

der his name, is a proclamation against drunkenness, a vice
to which his partisans are accused of being rather addicted.
Two other proclamations have been published since, in conformity with the resolutions of the parliament, which prohibit
the dispossession, without a justice's order, of the holders of
confiscated lands, both in England and Ireland; these are
orders chiefly agreeable to the people and the army. The act
renewing the laws against the Catholics has not yet passed
the House of Lords; and it was even resolved, at the time
when the Common Prayers were ordered to be read in the
House, that no one should be compelled to attend; for that
would have excluded the Catholics. This same body has to-
day taken the oath of fidelity to the King. Some members of
the Council of citizens on Saturday, took advantage of the
absence of several of their colleagues to resolve on a requisition to Parliament for the maintenance of the Covenant; but
this morning, the Council being full, this resolution was revoked; and the generality of the nation have no other thought
but how they may please the King. It only remains for me
to subscribe myself, &c.

(68.)—M. DE BOURDEAUX TO CARDINAL MAZARIN.
MY LORD, London, June 17, 1660.
    THE promise which the Secretary of State made to me,
on the 14th of this month, that he would give me a speedy
answer, has been duly performed. He sent a man yesterday
to me, who told me on his behalf that, although the King is
desirous to maintain a good understanding with all his neighbours, and particularly with France, and is disposed to receive
those envoys whom his Majesty may send to him, he nevertheless could not admit me to an audience to present my letters
of credence, because, in the course of my negociations, I have
acted in opposition to his interests, and that the King therefore desired that I should quit England. I professed to be
surprised at such a message, and that I expected to have found
more coincidence with the friendship of his Majesty, whose
assurances of good-will I was instructed to renew; that as for
my conduct, it had been in conformity with my orders, and
that if it were rightly understood, the King of England would
have more cause to praise me for it than to complain of it.
The messenger, taking no notice of this answer, asked me
what reply he should give with regard to my departure from
R 2

England. I told him that I would inform his Majesty of this desire without delay, as I could not withdraw without his permission. He reiterated that as the resolution which he had communicated to me had not been taken without mature deliberation, it would not be changed. I informed him that I should doubtless be directed to conform to it, as it was not his Majesty's custom either to send or to maintain ministers in any State where they were regarded with an evil eye, but that I hoped that until the arrival of such orders, the King of England would behave towards me in the way in which he* would wish his ambassadors to be treated in France. I thought it advisable to use these general terms, as they leave the door open to a change of opinion, if that of the King of England were founded only upon some particular dislike, as I was informed it was, and I thought I could not better disabuse his mind than by the mediation of the Earl of St. Albans, whom I had visited on the evening before I received this message, in the hope of discovering whether such an answer were meditated, as I had heard; but he would not enter into any explanations; he only desired that as soon as the Secretary of State had sent it to me, I should communicate it to him. This I did, and this morning he came to see me, and told me that he was not at the Council when it was resolved to refuse me an audience, but that, having inquired the reasons for this step, he had leared that the zeal which I had displayed under the deceased Protector, and the ambiguous language which I had used of late towards General Monk, (which might have inspired him with the idea of following Cromwell's example,) having persuaded the Council of my aversion to the restoration of the King of England, it had been considered prudent not to admit me. I stated in reply that I have executed the orders of his Majesty under all the governments of England with all the zeal which can be expected from a good servant; that nevertheless, my actions have never been intended to injure the interests of the King of England, but only to establish perfect harmony between the two nations according to the orders given me, and that I did not think that any one could find fault with me in this respect; that even if they would thoroughly examine into what had taken place in the different conjunctures of affairs, it would be observed that France had always guarded the interests of the King of England so far as to avoid, in treaties, the slightest expressions which could derogate from the rights which he possessed by birth : and as regarded my compliments to the General, they were not subject to any interpretation, especially after I had on the same day so distinctly expressed myself to his brother-in-law, who acknowledges the truth of my statement; that all my advances and offers tended to favour the restoration of the royal family by the intervention of France, and to contribute at the same time to the private advancement of the General; that for the rest, if the information which had been given to the King of England prevailed over these truths which I could easily corroborate by my orders and my despatches to the court, and if the ill-feeling which seemed to be excited against me would not allow the King of England to see me, his refusal ought at least to be signified in a less disobliging manner than that which had been employed; that it was merely necessary to defer the audience, and meanwhile to beg his Majesty to send some more agreeable person, and even to take a public resolution not to treat with those foreign ministers who were employed under the preceding governments, in order that the ill-treatment which I had experienced might not be attributed to any particular hostility to France, as public reports declared, or to the animosity of some of the members of the English Council, who, in this case, seemed to follow the dictates of their passions rather than those of propriety, and to desire to alienate rather than maintain friendship between the two monarchs; that as for myself, I should not act in this spirit, and that, very far from involving the nations in a quarrel, I should only strive to prevent it, and to induce his Majesty to consent to my withdrawal, as my residence in England could no longer conduce to his interest; that I only wished, (in order that it might not be brought as a reproach against me that, for want of explanation, I had allowed credit to be attached to such ill-founded reports,) that the King of England had sent to me the Secretary of State, or some other member of his Council to confer with me, it being sufficiently common among friendly princes to use this circumspection, and that doubtless he would have been satisfied with the interview; that I could also have wished that the character with which I am invested had been more respected, and that the message which had been sent me had been brought by some well-known person; that as I could not receive such a message from an unknown individual, I intended to request the

Secretary to communicate it to me in writing. I even communicated to the Earl the letter which I was prepared to send with a copy of his Majesty's, which, by justifying my conduct, removes all pretext for the resolution adopted here. Meanwhile, the Earl professed his disapprobation of their whole proceedings with regard to me ; he also entered into the overtures which I made to prevent any animosity being excited, and desired that I should postpone the dispatch both of my letter to the Secretary and of the present, until he had spoken to the King, undertaking to represent to him that as the information which has been given him may be incorrect, he should not take further proceedings until he had first entered into some explanations, and had sent to me the Secretary of State with this view; or, if he finds that the King cannot be induced to change his resolution, to suggest to him to take a general determination not to treat with the other ministers who were employed before his return. I did not request either one thing or the other, and so I did not think it right to refuse him a few hours' delay to give time for repentance, or at least for taking some course which may give his Majesty less cause for irritation : but as I am uncertain as to what he will do, and as he informed me that an express is to be dispatched from hence to France to-day, to inform you of the reasons of the refusal which has been given, I should fear that your Eminence would be uneasy, unless I informed you immediately of what had taken place. I will also add, that I have been assured, upon good authority, that the Chancellor and the Marquis of Ormonde, feeling hurt at the mortifications which they received in France, particularly during their master's last residence there, and at the attempts which have latterly been made on our part in order to remove them, and inspired still more with fear of the return of the Queen of England, have induced the king to act in this manner towards me, in order to sow the seeds of division between the two courts, and by taking their revenge thus easily, to free themselves from the danger they would incur from the presence of the queen. The Earl of St. Albans had given me this information at his first visit, and nevertheless persuaded himself that he had warded off the blow, as the King had charged him to tell me that I should be well received ; but although I requested an audience on that same day, it was not granted me, and the resolution which has been sent me

gives reason to believe that it was hoped that I should press
for an interview, in order that it might be refused ; whence
I infer that the Earl of St. Albans is not in the secret confidence of the King, and that the Chancellor's influence augments
daily. It has not appeared to me consistent with my dignity
to pay him a visit, as I know he is so ill-intentioned towards
France. I had, nevertheless, expressed myself clearly enough
to several who are strongly attached to his interests, to give
him reason to expect every civility from me; an intimate
friend of the Marquis of Ormonde has also informed him
that I should behave in the same manner towards him ; but
these advances were not sufficient to dissipate their ill-will,
or to change their policy. As for the General, his credit
appears rather in the distribution of gratuities and benefac-
tions than in the Cabinet, where he has quite ceased to carry
on any intrigues ; and I have not, therefore, thought it worth
while to call upon him in this emergency. I only intend to
convey to him some reproach for the interpretation which he
placed upon my civilities, and for the effect, at least, of the
pretext which it furnished ; but I do not expect that any of
the steps which I can with propriety take will be of any influence, and after the sensation which will be produced by the
answer which has been given me, this court will consider itself
no longer in a position to swerve from it ; wherefore I suppose
that it will be judged expedient to send me permission to withdraw as quickly as possible. If your Eminence should consider
it consistent with the dignity of France to manifest some discontent at these proceedings, and should wish at the same time
to punish their authors, it would only be necessary, instead of
sending extraordinary ambassadors forthwith, to induce the
Queen of England to come hither under the pretext of mediating a reconciliation. I have seen many persons who are of
opinion that she ought to be conveyed hither by France, lest
England should display no wish to recall her, and lest the
ministry should meanwhile strengthen themselves to her prejudice, as affairs could not be administered by persons more
badly-intentioned than those who have been called into the
Council by the Chancellor ; the others are noblemen whose
votes have not very much weight, or who like the Earl of
Manchester, are striving to gain a position. Some of the latter
would become bolder if they had the Queen to support them,
and there is no more certain means, than her presence, for

sowing division in this court. Measures may be taken upon the information which has been given me, and it must be admitted that I have pursued a course of conduct which leaves his Majesty room either to express his resentment or to accept the reasons which may be urged to justify their proceedings here; and I am persuaded that it will always be time to assume a tone of complaint and haughtiness, if it is judged more honorable than that of concession to the desire felt for my withdrawal, and that your Eminence will follow rather the dictates of moderation than those of anger. If I have mistaken your choice, it will be easy for me to retrace my steps, as I feel very much disposed to assert the dignity of France. I shall await orders on this point with considerable impatience, as I cannot henceforward remain in England with satisfaction, either in my public or private capacity, and I hope that your Eminence will speedily deliver me from this unpleasant position. You will be pleased to consider that as I cannot leave the country without paying my debts, which amount to twenty thousand pounds, and as I have no credit either at Paris or in London, I should be greatly embarrassed unless the court would supply me with means to liquidate them ; the appointments which are due to me amount to a larger sum, and they could not be paid more opportunely. I entreat your Eminence to be good enough to take this into consideration, and I hope that the same person who brings me orders will also supply me with the means of executing them. If I can execute any commission in your service, I shall consider myself very fortunate to end my residence in England in this way. I have no more news of any importance to write to you just now. The Upper House has been engaged during the last few days in a debate upon the question whether in the absence of the Chancellor, it could appoint a Speaker or receive one from the King, and the discussion has not yet terminated. The Commons have named the seven judges of the King who are to be excepted from the amnesty. Major-General Harrison, and Colonel Jones, the brother-in-law of the deceased Protector, are the only ones arrested. One of the others, named Scott, having taken refuge in Flanders, was captured by the English there ; but notwithstanding that the Marquis of Caracena was requested to give him up, his escape was connived at, and with some justice, as this unfortunate man, who was Secretary of State under the Republic, was a pensioner and a valuable

rvant of Spain. The English court continues to complain of
e favour which has been shown him. Yesterday the Earl of
anchester proposed, in the House of Lords, the payment of
ie Queen's dowry, which was granted without opposition,
id this morning the House of Commons acquiesced in it, and
ppointed Commissioners to confer with the Lords upon the
ibject. Nothing has as yet been said of her return, or of any
reign affairs; and it only remains for me, &c.

POSTSCRIPT, JUNE 18, 1660.—I delayed the departure of
ie present courier because the Earl of St. Albans sent yes-
rday evening to tell me that he would come and see me this
iorning. He has not failed to do so, and informed me that
ie King had told him that he was too fully persuaded that I
ad acted in opposition to his interests to be willing to enter
ito any explanation, and immediately spoke to me of the
ecret article which had caused his departure from France, in
rms which justify the belief that this act was employed to irri-
ite him. I informed the Earl that, after I had done my duty by
iving the King better information, I had nothing more to do
ut receive my dismissal, and that I should greatly regret
o see that resentment for a civility which necessity had ex-
orted had prevailed over the remembrance of all the benefits
vhich he had received from his Majesty's friendship. The
arl also told me that they intended to adopt the plan of not
dmitting any other foreign minister who had treated with the
receding governments; and I answered that his Majesty
vould not take into consideration anything which concerned
hem, as the treatment which they experienced could not serve
s a rule for that which he had a right to expect for his min-
ters. This is the present position of this matter. I feel
ersuaded that your Eminence will judge it necessary to with-
raw me from hence without delay. * * *

(62.)—M. DE BOURDEAUX TO CARDINAL MAZARIN.
IY LORD,   London, June 24, 1660.
No change has taken place in the resolutions adopted here
vith regard to me : I have not, therefore, judged it expedient
o make fresh attempts to disabuse the King of England, after
he answers brought to me on his behalf by the Earl of St.
Albans. My principal care of late has been to discover the
rigin of these untoward dispositions ; and I have been assured

by different persons, among others by a nobleman who r₁
quested that his name should not appear in my letters, tha
the discontent of the Chancellor and of the Marquis ₁
Ormonde are the real causes ; that they thought they woul
execute a tremendous vengeance by refusing me an audienc
in so disobliging a manner, and that in order to dispose the
master to this step, they made use of the confessions of M
Thurloe, who has revealed the secrets of foreign as well as ₁
domestic negociations.   The same person informed me tha
the King of England feels great irritation at the treatmer
which he received latterly in France, and is far from considei
ing himself under any obligations to us ; apprehension of th
return of the Queen of England has also something to do wit
their conduct here, and I may say that public rumour make
the aversion to be greater than it possibly can be : that man
even think they cannot pay court better than by speakin
against France, and that some members of the Council hav
given me to understand that it would be a crime for them t
hold any correspondence with me. ˙ Lord Berkley has no
ceased to visit me with the permission of the Duke of Yorl
and on the day before yesterday he told me that he had recei
ved orders to assure me that his master entertained a grateft
recollection of the favours which he had received from hi
Majesty ; he even paid me some compliments on his be
half, and the conversation which we had persuaded me tha
the remainder of the court are of very different opinions from
the Duke of York, that the General had joined the Chancellor
and that this cabal was all-powerful.   But their ill-will is no
to be feared, as the King of England appears disposed not t
follow blindly their dictates ; and moreover, his precariou
position renders the friendship of neighbouring princes ex
tremely necessary.   Although the Parliament is very submis
sive, and no one either in the Upper House or in the House ₁
Commons dares to speak against propositions which are sup
posed to originate with him, there are, nevertheless, man
malcontents already, and religion will probably soon increas
their number, if the King is bent, as it is said, on re-establish
ing the bishops.   Requisitions to this effect are being got u
in several counties, and attempts are being made to overcom
the repugnance of the troops to this establishment.   Nothin
has as yet been said about the matter in Parliament.   The ac
of amnesty is still under consideration, and within the la₁

↓w days the House of Commons has named several of those
ho are to be excepted from it, as far as their property is con-
rned. Sir Harry Vane is the first on the list, and the most
istinguished members of the preceding governments will have
ie same fortune. Attention has also been given to the affairs
l' Ireland, and according to the project of the Commons, the
ondition of the Catholics in that country will be worse than
l was during the disgrace of the King of England. The
House of Lords does not treat of matters of so much impor-
ance; it has during the last few days, resolved upon taking
a oath of fidelity which is very repugnant to the Catholics,
iasmuch as it obliges them to acknowledge the King as head
nd defender of the Church; but they hope that they will not
e forced to take it, and many noblemen of the Presbyterian
iction also are no less opposed to it. A resolution has been
iken by this House to pay the Queen's dowry; but there is
ome difficulty about deciding whether the lands which had
een allotted to her shall be withdrawn from the hands of
those to whom the State has sold them, and the General
eclares that such a proceeding would offend the army.
Ie has reduced the body of cavalry which was to be perma-
ently established, from 1,200 to 200 men; and still they are
ot positively certain whether they will be maintained by the
'arliament. The Scotch demand the evacuation of the
English garrisons which are kept up in their country, that
heir Parliament shall be re-established, and that the ancient
rerogatives of the Council of State which was appointed in
650 shall be confirmed. This is indirectly demanding the
naintenance of the Covenant, and there is very little disposi-
ion to please them by granting this point. It only remains
or me to assure you, my lord, that I am, &c.   *   *   *

(70.)—M. DE BOURDEAUX TO CARDINAL MAZARIN.
My LORD,   London, July 1, 1660.
   I AM still in expectation of those orders from the King with
which my courier must be charged, and his delay cannot but
ause me uneasiness, as I find I am useless as regards the ser-
ice of the public, and treated in a manner which plainly
ndicates that my departure from England is ardently desired.
During the last few days I have obtained tolerably evident
roofs of this in a domestic squabble: my steward took to
light when the time came for him to give an account of his

administration; he has not only excited all my creditors b
giving them the alarm of my departure, and induced some t
seize my horses, but even had the insolence to cause th
arrest of one of my secretaries in virtue of a warrant signe
by an ordinary justice. As the first action was brought b
Englishmen and for debt, I did not think I could obtain muc
satisfaction for their proceeding, and endeavoured to pacif
them; but it appeared to me that I should injure the preroga
tives of my character, if for a dispute between two of my ser
vants I addressed myself to an ordinary justice of the country
and so I had recourse to the King by means of the Earl of St
Albans, who had undertaken to have satisfaction given me ever
for the first injury; nevertheless, having mentioned the las
to the King, he found him quite astonished at my pretension:
to the character of an ambassador during the remainder of the
time that I may be in England; his answer, even before he
had heard the request, was uttered in a tone which completely
stopped the Earl's mouth. I did not fail, before I was informed
of it, to write to the Secretary of State a letter in which I de
manded that my secretary and steward should be restored to
me; and to strengthen this demand, I appended a copy d
my letters of credence. I also saw the Earl of Manchester, whose
office obliges him to protect the rights of the ambassadors, and
informed him that the injury which had been done me did no
regard me personally, but my character, and thus could no
but offend his Majesty; he was convinced of the truth o
what I said, and promised to speak to the King about it. Yes
terday evening, he called on me to tell me that he had per
formed his promise, and the King had charged him to assur
me that Monsieur de Bourdeaux should be treated with al
civility, but that as ambassador of France I must expec
nothing, and that my secretary should be restored to me
without making any mention of my steward. I declared t
him that I had claimed nothing in my own right, and tha
although the King of England was kind enough to treat me
with so much consideration, I would nevertheless not take ad
vantage of his kindness on the present occasion, but only
claim respect for the quality with which I was invested i
England, and which could not be contested me: I insisted
again that complete justice should be done me by the restora
tion of my two servants, who could not recognize any othe
jurisdiction but mine, and that of France after my return, i

·y had any disputes with one another; and I thanked the
rl for his good offices. He promised to use all his efforts
obtain for me entire satisfaction, and I do not doubt that he
ll meet with some success, but not such as I could wish,
.ce they persist in making a distinction between me and his
ljesty's ambassador, and by this declaration manifest more
limosity against France than against myself personally.
iis untoward disposition has been again confirmed to me by
ᵉ same Earl of St. Albans, who came to relate to me the
inner in which the king had received my complaint; he told
iᵉ in very precise language, that this proceeding had no re-
:ence to me, that it had a deeper meaning, and that the
iancellor's faction were strongly desirous to excite animosity
tween our two States, hoping thereby to raise obstacles to
e Queen's return; that even they might intend to obtain for
:r similar treatment in France to that which has been given
e here. It has also been reported to me that two hours be-
re he mentioned this incident to the King, he had had a long
inversation with him with regard to me, taking occasion to
ᵎ so from the information which General Monk's brother-in-
w had just given him that he had been urged to declare that
had charged him, on the part of his Majesty and your
minence, to induce the General to constitute himself Protector
: to maintain the republic; this has been imputed to me now
ir some time, and I was publicly justified from the charge at
iᵉ Hague by this same brother-in-law. He expressed his
ᵎy that the Earl of St. Albans had unmasked this knavery, and
evertheless his discontent did not break out a moment after;
·om which it may be inferred that my conduct has not caused
; this is the feeling both of this Earl and of Lord Berkley and
ther courtiers, who have borne testimony to the King, of their
wn free-will, that I had appeared very zealous in his service.
: is to be hoped that their judgment is ill-founded, and that
iy withdrawal may stifle these seeds of misunderstanding
efore they take deeper root. If my debts permitted me to
:ave London, I should be greatly tempted to forestall the
ermission which will doubtless be sent me; for I am no longer
i a position to negociate, as the ministers of the Council avoid
iceting me. I do not learn that any foreign affairs have as
et been discussed in the Council; it has only been reported
ᵎ me that the King will not ratify the treaty which has been
iade between the two Kings of the North, because he con-

siders it too disadvantageous to Denmark, whose interests ar
much more considerable than those of the Swedes. Its re
sident has even had an audience, although he acted under the
preceding governments; and we must expect that the Dutch
notwithstanding the peace, will foment the present inclinations
of this court, of which I have no important news to write.
The Parliament has at length finished naming those who are
to be excepted from the amnesty as far as their property is
concerned. Besides Vane and Haslerig, Fleetwood, Lambert,
and the Speaker of the preceding Parliament, a great friend
of General Monk, have had the same fortune; and they have
augmented the number of those sentenced to death by the
minister Peters, whom they have not yet caught, and by a
major whom they have brought from Ireland, who is accused
of having cut off the head of the deceased king, and who confesses that he was on the scaffold in a mask. Some of the
judges have surrendered themselves, and have been placed in
confinement. The Commons have also been occupied with
the regulation of the public revenue, and have granted the
King during his whole lifetime, a considerable tax upon the
markets, have continued the customs and excise-duties, suspended the payment of the public debts contracted since 1648,
with the exception of the arrears of the army, and assigned
10,000*l.* sterling for the support of the Queen of England,
out of the tax of 70,000*l.* sterling, which is to be levied on
the people within three months. All the lands mortgaged for
her dowry, which have not been sold will be restored to her,
and some means of accommodation will be sought for the others.
It was proposed in the House of Lords to take an oath of
fidelity, with which the Catholics could not agree, because it
contained expressions which entirely destroy the power which
the Church of Rome claims to possess with regard to the de-
position of kings and excommunicated States; but it is now
no longer mentioned, and it is even not very agreeable to the
rigid Presbyterians. This same oath has already been taken
by several regiments, and it is to be presented to all the old
troops, into the command of which persons of quality are being
introduced. The King has been feasted every day by different
noblemen, and the city is to give him a great dinner in a fortnight. The deputies from Ireland have brought him their
submission and 20,000*l.* It only remains for me to sign myself, &c.

(71.)—M. DE BOURDEAUX TO CARDINAL MAZARIN.

; LORD, London, July 4, 1660.

I DO myself the honour to write to your Eminence only order to inform you of the arrival of my courier on the day fore yesterday, with orders from the King permitting me to .ve England, and that I am making preparations to leave ndon to-morrow, so as to return to France as quickly as ssible. The Secretary of State has this evening given me a ssport, but not a vessel, for my passage; which does not prise me after the animosity which has been displayed of e days. My secretary has not been restored to me, although was promised that he should be; with this exception, I ve nothing to desire, as I am very happy that your Eminence proves of my past conduct, and remains persuaded that y actions as well as my words were in conformity with le orders which were sent me. I hope to be with you speedily as not to make it necessary to enter into any gthened justification at present, and I shall defer until that ne an account of what has passed since the return of my urier. Meanwhile, having nothing of importance to write th regard to the affairs of England, I must thank your ninence for the kindness you have shown in giving me the eans of leaving this country honourably, in order to render u in France all those services of which you may consider me pable. My confidence that you will continue to honour me ith your commands enables me patiently to endure the petty ortifications to which I have latterly been subjected; and I nnot but esteem myself happy so long as it shall please you believe that I am with affection and respect, &c.

(72.)—M. DE BOURDEAUX TO CARDINAL MAZARIN.

[Y LORD, London, July 6, 1660.

I HAVE been detained here until now by those who, de- rous to prevent a misunderstanding between the two king- oms, were straining every nerve to change the resolution hich has been adopted with regard to me. Yesterday even, ey felt entire confidence that they would succeed, and the ffair was strongly debated in the Council, the principal inisters of which were in favour of satisfying France. Never- ueless, this evening the King decided the question, and I shall tart to-morrow without further delay in order to return to rance as quickly as possible. A courier will be despatched

hence at the same time to inform the Queen of what has passed
I have no time now to give you a more exact report, and no
prejudice can arise to the public if I postpone the performance
of this duty until my return. There is also nothing of importance for me to write regarding the other affairs of England;
and I now have only to sign myself with respect, &c.

THE END.

LONDON:
PRINTED BY HARRISON AND SON, 45, ST. MARTIN'S LANE.

RICHARD BOYLE

EARL OF CLARENDON

p. 275

BIOGRAPHIC STUDIES

ON

THE ENGLISH REVOLUTION;

OR,

MONK'S CONTEMPORARIES.

BY

M. GUIZOT.

Translated from the French,

BY

A. R. S.

PREFACE.

In the English Revolution, two figures, Charles I. and
Cromwell, tower above all others, and fill the history. Among
the personages who, though they do not so largely occupy
the stage, took a considerable part in the scene, Monk is
not the only one who deserves to be closely studied and
intimately known. When I published my " Collection des
Mémoires relatifs à la Revolution d'Angleterre," I prepared
sketches of the principal actors, and particularly of those
who were at once actors and historians, similar to that which
I had already written of General Monk. I have now collected these biographic studies into a volume; all of them
have been carefully revised and completed, and some are
entirely new. They constitute, together with Monk, a sort
of gallery of portraits, in which personages of the most different character appear in juxtaposition—chiefs or cham-
ions of sects or parties, Parliamentarians, Cavaliers, Repub-
cans, Levellers,—who, either at the termination of the

political conflicts in which they were engaged, or when
retirement towards the close of their lives, resolved to d
scribe themselves, their own times, and the part they play
therein. In the drawing together of such men, and in t
mixture of truth and vanity which characterises such worl
there is, unless I am greatly mistaken, abundance to intere
persons of serious and curious minds, especially amongst
and in our times; for in spite of the great diversity of ma
ners, contemporary comparisons and applications will prese
themselves at every step, however careful we may be not
seek them.

GUIZOT.

Paris, March, 1851.

TRANSLATOR'S PREFACE.

To dilate upon the character of the present work, after the mple explanation given by M. Guizot in his own Preface, ould be superfluous; but a few words in reference to the ircumstances under which it was originally composed, may ot be out of place, as it belongs to a most interesting period f its distinguished author's career. About thirty years ago, rhilst M. Guizot was Professor of History at the Sorbonne, ie published some pamphlets on political questions, which ;ained for him the ill-will of the ministry of the day. Upon his, his enemies sought to drive him from the university, and o deprive him of bread; but their machinations only stimu- ated him to increased effort, and he nobly replied to their at- acks by the publication of his "Collection of Memoirs relating :o the History of the Revolution in England." This great vork, which extended to twenty-seven volumes, was enriched)y him with copious annotations, and biographical sketches of

the various authors whose works he had translated. These
sketches he has recently revised and enlarged; and they are
now presented to the British public, for the first time, in a
complete form.

It only remains for me to add, that I am indebted to my
friend Mr. R. M. Theobald for a translation of several of the
articles; and that an English version of M. Guizot's new
work on the History of Representative Government is in
active preparation, and will speedily be published.

A. R. SCOBLE.

London, July, 1851.

CONTENTS.

MONK'S CONTEMPORARIES.

DENZIL HOLLIS.

[1597—1681.]

In order properly to understand a revolution, we must con-
er it at its origin and termination—in the earliest plans
ich it puts forth, and in the definitive results which it
ains. In these its true character is revealed; by these we
y judge what were the real thoughts and wishes of the
ple among whom it took place. All that occurs between
se two periods is more or less factitious, transitory, and
ceptive. The stream winds and wanders in its course;
o points alone, its source and its mouth, determine its
ection.

Just in this manner, during the course of a revolution, par-
s are formed and transformed, divided and subdivided, and
ze the empire by turns, to lose it again each in its turn;
t that is really the national party which appears at the
gin and termination of the crisis—which, after having
gun the war and endured all its vicissitudes, finds itself, at
t, strong and wise enough to restore peace.

This honour belonged, in England, to the Presbyterian
rty, and to the political, rather than to the religious, re-
rmers of that party. The English revolution, in 1640, took
first steps, and committed its first faults, under the
idance of the Presbyterians; in 1688, it was accomplished
d concluded under the banner of the Whigs—a new party,
ry different from the Presbyterians, but inheriting their
sential principles of public liberty and national govern-
ent. They constituted, at that period, the national party in
agland.

Denzil Hollis, the younger son of the Earl of Clare, born
Haughton, Nottinghamshire, in 1597, was one of the most

B

important and honourable members of this party; we me
with him at every step in the events of his lifetime, and i
his contemporaries bear testimony to his worth. "He was
says Clarendon, "as much valued and esteemed by the who
party as any man; as he deserved to be, being of more accor
plished parts than any of them, and of great reputation l
the part he acted against the court and the Duke of Bucl
ingham, in the Parliament of 1628."* Burnet says, "E
was a man of great courage, and of as great pride; he wi
counted for many years the head of the Presbyterian part
He was faithful and firm to his side, and never change
through the whole course of his life. He was well versed i
the records of Parliament: and argued well, but too veh
mently; for he could not bear contradiction. He had tl
soul of an old stubborn Roman in him. He was a faithf
but a rough friend, and a severe but fair enemy. He had
true sense of religion: and was a man of an unblamab
course of life, and of a sound judgment when it was n
biassed by passion."†

Hollis's first steps in life seemed to destine him to f
vour rather than to opposition. When he left college, l
was attached to the person of the Duke of York, afterwar
Charles I., and lived for some time on terms of the most int
mate familiarity with that prince, accompanying him in tl
chase, partaking in his pleasures, and sometimes even sharin
his bed. But he had been brought up by a haughty fathe
who openly lamented the departed glories of Elizabeth's sple
did court, and despised James I., his timid pretensions, h
contemptible pride, his avaricious countrymen, and his sham
ful favourites. "He who fears his enemy does not love h
friend,"‡ was the device of the Earl of Clare, and his son r
mained faithful to the motto. In 1624, young Hollis wa
elected to represent a Cornish borough in the House (
Commons, during the last Parliament of King James, an
took an active part in the defence of the public liberties. I
the following year, on his accession to the throne, Charle
withdrew the seals from Williams, Bishop of Lincoln, a frien
of the Earl of Clare. The earl considered himself affrontec
The king informed his two sons that he would make ther

* Clarendon's History of the Rebellion (Oxford, 1819), vol. i., p. 276.
† Burnet's History of his own Time (Oxford, 1823), vol. i., pp. 166-167.
‡ "Qui inimicum timet, amicum non amat."

nights of the Bath at his coronation ; but both refused the
nour. Denzil even declined to take part in a brilliant
asquerade in which the king had assigned him a place.* In
atters both of business and festivity, in affairs which con-
rned either the interests of the state or his own personal
lations, he already displayed that passionate haughtiness,
at fidelity to his cause, his friendships and his enmities, that
ixture of popular principles and aristocratic feelings, which
ere destined subsequently to make him one of the most
tive founders of that great Whig party, which has done so
uch for the credit of the British nobility, and for the liberty
: the English people.

It was in 1628, during the Parliament rendered famous
y the Petition of Rights, that his political activity really
ommenced ; he was then one of the most ardent opponents
? the court, the Duke of Buckingham, and all the oppressive
easures under which the country groaned. On the 2nd of
March, 1629, the Speaker of the Commons, in obedience to
1e orders of the king, was about to declare the adjournment
f the House, and to leave his chair, when Mr. Hollis made
im resume his seat, and kept him there by force, saying :
God's wounds, Mr. Speaker, you shall sit still till it please
he House to rise."† Charles I. had overstepped his lawful
uthority ; the Opposition followed his example ; and both
arties hurried rapidly along this fearful road. After the
dissolution of the Parliament, Hollis and several others were
ited before the Privy Council, for what they had said and
one in the House. Hollis was the first interrogated.
" Wherefore," he was asked, " did you, contrary to your
former use, that morning that the tumult was in the lower
House of Parliament, place yourself above divers of the privy
councillors, by the chair ?"—" At some other times, as well
as then," he answered, " I have seated myself in that place ;
and as for my sitting above the privy councillors, I take it
to be my due in any place wheresoever, unless at the council-
board." In the course of his examination, he protested that
he came into the House with as great zeal for his majesty's
service as any one, but added, that as his majesty was
offended with him, he humbly desired that he might rather

* Biographia Britannica, in the life of his father, John Hollis, Earl of Clare,
vol. iv., p. 2641.
† Hansard's Parliamentary History, vol. ii., col. 490.

be the subject of his mercy than of his power.
rather of his majesty's mercy than of his just
Lord Treasurer.—"I said of his majesty's pow
replied Hollis.* He was condemned to pay a
thousand silver marks, and was sent to prison,
mained for more than a year. Nearly all his frie
the same fate, and Charles, thus freed from the
Opposition, reigned for twelve years with blind
if the day of retribution were never to arrive.

It came, however, and the Opposition re-ap
Parliament of 1640, much more exasperated
than it had ever been before. Charles found h
face with, and at the mercy of, those men whom
as insolent and impotent rebels. Hampden, Py
were, from the first, the declared leaders of th
and Presbyterian party, in whose train followed
factions, as yet unaware of their own existence
only to hasten forward the general movement
trial placed Hollis, for a short time, in a pai
Strafford had married his sister, Arabella Holli
ference of their political opinions had not in
their friendship. As a member of the commit
to examine into the charges brought against St
strove to save the head of his brother-in-law,
his conduct to the pressure of public violence.
tiations commenced between the king and the
reform party. A cabinet was projected of whi
were to form part, and, when in office, to refor
ment according to the wishes of the country.
be made Secretary of State. The life of Stra
maintenance of the Church were the price of th
The king assented to this plan, but soon grew
ear to other counsels, and conspired against th
while continuing to negotiate with it. Whilst
hesitating and deceiving, Strafford was accused
condemned. Another negotiation was then se
the Commons should rest satisfied with his
Hollis conducted it, it is said, with some succes
mons. The king promised to go in person, an
earl's petition to the Houses. Hollis had
speech which his majesty was to deliver. Bu

* Hansard's Parliamentary History, col. 504.

nise, though made sincerely, any more than
ich were forcibly extorted from him. Straf-
nd Hollis plunged into the whirlwind which
)untry.
e, resolute, and high-spirited. He asserted
liberties of England, just as a gentleman
defend his own personal rights. In his eyes
:as the people, and the House of Commons
To secure the decided and continual prepon-
[ouse of Commons in the Parliament, while
:t to the Crown and the House of Lords, was,
d in that of all the Presbyterian party, first,
)untry, and secondly, the only means of abo-
ly of the King, the Church, and the Court.
orward to this object, ever in the foremost
, over all obstacles, accepting, that he might
sometimes the assistance of an insurrection,
subtleties of legists. And when, after two
the parliamentary struggle ended in the
no more hesitated to maintain his rights
1ad formerly hesitated to assert and demand
l a regiment, took his position, as colonel,
r the command of the Earl of Essex, and on
mber, 1642, his regiment, though unassisted,
h of the royal army for some time at Brent-
from London, and prevented it from falling
)n the city.
) nor his party entertained any subversive
ainst royalty or English society; they merely
tain the legal government of their country;
: from suspecting what a difficult and dan-
ition that government would have to under-
ouse of Commons could become its main-
r error was to believe that, by appealing to
would be the gainers, and could measure
at their will. When force, however, has
ession of society, no one can tell what it
it will go, or who will make use of it, and
ions. There begins at once a series of un-
ire occurrences which surpass the foresight
, occurrences which sometimes ennoble na-
good governments, but from which contem-

poraries, very erroneously, hope to educe a success much moı|
prompt and personal than the advantage of their posterity. |
When the Presbyterians saw that their hopes were dı
ceived they were astounded, and quite unwilling to suppo
that their faults had anything to do with their reverses ; an
soon they found fresh cause for indignation, in the discover
that the Independents, the Republicans, the army, and Cron
well were employing against them the same artifices and th
same violence which they had themselves put in practic
against the king's partisans. What marvel that one portio
of the Parliament believed itself justified in making wa
against another, when the Parliament had itself made wa
against the king, an integral part of every parliament ! Wh
should not the Independents have eliminated the Presbɔ
terians from the House of Commons, when the Presbyteriar
had already eliminated therefrom so many royalists, for n
other reason than that they were hampered and hindered b
their resistance ? The design of the Independents was, it :
true, subversive of the entire fabric of English society, an
contrary to the wishes of the nation; that of the Presbɔ
terians was moderate and national : thus, one of the tw
parties passed by like a terrible accident, the other resume
vigour to oppose its enemies, and finally gained the victorɔ
But as for the means employed, as for the illegal and tyrar
nical use of force, one had opened out the way for the other
it was by walking in the footsteps of the Presbyterians tha
the Independents learned to tread them under foot.

Parties will never acknowledge such a similarity; and, c
his faction, Hollis would have been the last to recognise iſ
for he was the most passionate of all the moderate reformerı
But passion is full of both blindness and penetration. If i
conceals faults, it discovers perils. Hollis quickly perceive
the gravity of the dangers which the Independents and Crom
well were preparing for the Presbyterians. Peace and th
reconciliation of the king with the Parliament were the onl
sure means of averting them. Hollis was early favourabl
to peace, as he was wearied with embarrassment and anxietɔ
and weighed down by the shackles imposed upon him by hi
recent conduct, the still furious contest, and, above all, th
necessity of defending himself against the king even whils
becoming reconciled with him; but he was as ardent an
sincere in his efforts for reconciliation as he had been in hi

r. In 1644 he was sent to Oxford, with
iissioners, to attempt a negotiation; and
ing of his arrival he went, with the con-
igues, and in company with Whitelocke,
the Earl of Lindsey, a nobleman of the
and their mutual friend. The king came
suddenly, while they were there, and, ad-
them with great affability, said: "I am
that you could bring to me no better pro-
:e, nor more reasonable than these are."
ollis, "they are such as the Parliament
ree upon, and I hope a good issue may be
" "I know," continued the king, "you
er than what they would send. But I con-
ttle wonder at some of them; surely, you
think them to be reasonable or honourable
' "Truly, sir," said Hollis, "I could have
of them had been otherwise than they are,
knows that those things are all carried by
"I know they are," answered the king,
t that you who are here and your friends
four party) in the House endeavoured to
:herwise, for I know you are well-willers to
: had the honour," observed Whitelocke,
majesty often heretofore upon this errand,
was not to better effect." "I wish, Mr.
ied the king, "that others had been of your
Mr. Hollis's judgment, and then I believe
ppy end of our differences before now; for
ire peace, and, in order to it, and out of the
of you two that are here with me, I ask
advice what answer will be best for me to
to your propositions, which may probably
:e as all good men desire." "Your majesty
said Hollis, "if we are not capable in our
to advise your majesty." "We now by
Whitelocke, "have the honour to be in your
e, but our present employment disables us
ir majesty, if we were otherwise worthy to
:ular." "For your abilities," answered the
to judge, and I now look not on you in
s from the Parliament, but as friends and

my private subjects, I require your advice."
Hollis, " to speak in a private capacity, your
that we have been very free; and, touching yo
shall say further, that I think the best answer w
own coming amongst us." " How can I come
safety?" asked the king. " I am confident," re
lis, " there would be no danger to your person t
directly to your Parliament." " That may be
said the king; " but I suppose your principals v
hither will expect a present answer to your messe
best present and most satisfactory answer," u
locke, " would be your majesty's presence with
ment." " Let us pass by that," answered the ki
me desire you two, Mr. Hollis and Mr. Whitelock
the next room, and a little to confer togethei
down somewhat in writing which you apprehen
for me to return in answer to your message, and
judgments may facilitate and promote this ge
peace." " We shall obey your majesty's comman
Hollis.*

They went together into an adjoining room,
carefully disguised their handwriting, drew up a
taining the advice which the king had requested
good-will was as powerless as it was dangerous.
their advice produced no result. At London, d
Lord Savile, a courtier and traitor in both cam
this advice became the text of a serious accusatio
vigorously urged against them, in the House of C
the Independent party. Hollis was the speci
their abhorrence. They endeavoured to separate
from his companion, and promised to free him fi
consequences. Whitelocke had some dislike for I
first answers in the House had been, in his opini
and haughty. But, for a man like Whitelocke,
sensible even in his pusillanimity, the hour of d
not yet arrived. He continued faithful to Hol
fended their common cause, and after a long exa
spite of the efforts of the Independent party t
matter at least in suspense, the House decided
ceedings should be taken upon the accusation.†

* Whitelocke's Memorials, p. 113 (London, 1782).
† Ibid., p. 161.

From this moment Whitelocke retired from the struggle, and Hollis engaged in it with redoubled ardour. He became the declared and personal adversary of Cromwell, Ireton, and all the leading Independents, attacking them in the House, denouncing them to the people; incessantly employed in predicting their crimes and unveiling their plots; provoking against them sometimes secret conferences, and sometimes public resolutions; and caring little if he envenomed their hatred against himself, provided that his own antipathy, though powerless, had free course.

Accordingly, when the Independents triumphed, when Cromwell became supreme in the Parliament as well as in the army, Hollis was one of the first proscribed. In August, 1647, excluded from the House of Commons, and accused of high treason, he took refuge in France, at Sainte-Mère-Eglide, in Normandy, near the coast; as if he were still determined to watch, from the other side of the ocean, what was going on in his own country, and unable to detach his soul from the cause he was no longer able to defend. For one moment, the battle-field opened to him again; the Presbyterians regained their ascendancy in the House of Commons. Hollis crossed over to England immediately, and resumed, with his former earnestness, his conflict with the Independents and Cromwell, and his exertions for peace with the king. " One day, Commissary-General Ireton speaking something concerning the excluded members, Mr. Hollis thinking it to be injurious to them, passing by him in the House, whispered him in the ear, telling him it was false, and he would justify it to be so if he would follow him, and thereupon immediately went out of the House, with the other following him. Some members who had observed their passionate carriage to each other, and seen them hastily leaving the House, acquainted the Parliament with their apprehensions; whereupon they sent their serjeant-at-arms to command their attendance, which he letting them understand, as they were taking boat to go to the other side of the water, they returned; and the House taking notice of what they were informed concerning them, enjoined them to forbear all words or actions of enmity towards each other, and to carry themselves for the future as fellow-members of the same body, which they promised to do."*

This pacification was as false as Hollis's victory in a duel with

* Ludlow's Memoirs, pp. 94-95 (London, 1751).

Ireton would have been vain. These ardent attacks of the Presbyterian leaders were only a transient gleam, the last flickering light of an expiring party. The power had passed into the hands of the Independents; and Cromwell felt his confidence mount as high as his ambition. " What a sway Stapleton and Hollis had heretofore in the kingdom," he said; " I know nothing to the contrary but that I am as well able to govern the kingdom as either of them."* Four months after fortune had apparently smiled once more upon the Presbyterians, they were expelled *en masse* from the House of Commons; the king was brought to judgment, and Hollis resumed, at Sainte-Mère-Eglide, on the other side of the Channel, the melancholy and inactive life of an exile.

It was during his first sojourn in this retreat, that he wrote his Memoirs, to which he prefixed the following dedication:

" To the unparalleled couple, Mr. Oliver St. John, his Majesty's Solicitor-General, and Mr. Oliver Cromwell, the Parliament's Lieutenant-General, the two grand designers of the ruin of three kingdoms.

" GENTLEMEN,

" As you have been principal in ministering the matter of this discourse, and giving me the leisure of making it, by banishing me from my country and business, so is it reason I should particularly address it to you. You will find in it some representation of the grosser lines of your features, those outward and notorious enormities that make you remarkable, and your pictures easy to be known, which cannot be expected here so fully to the life as I could wish. He only can do that, whose eye and hand have been with you in your secret councils, who has seen you at your meetings, your Sabbaths, where you have laid by your assumed shapes (with which you covered the world) and resumed your own; imparting each to other, and both of you to your fellow-witches, the bottom of your designs, the policy of your actings, the turns of your contrivances, all your falsehoods, cozenings, villanies, and cruelties, with your full intentions to ruin the three kingdoms. All I will say to you is no more than what St. Peter said to Simon the Sorcerer, ' Repent therefore of this your wickedness, and pray God, if perhaps the thoughts of

* Major Huntington's Reasons for laying down his Commission; in Maseres Select Tracts, vol. ii., p. 405.

ir hearts may be forgiven you.' And if you have not grace
pray for yourselves (as it may be you have not), I have the
irity to do it for you, but not faith enough to trust you.
I remain, I, thank God, not in your power, and as little at
ir service."*

Hollis doubtless intended to publish his work, and at
st to curse the enemies whom he was no longer able to
mbat. But the trial of the king, the establishment of the
public, the empire of Cromwell, the rapid succession of
odigious events, removed this useless design far from his
n thoughts. He did not even continue his Memoirs, and
ey were not published until 1699, nearly twenty years
er his death.
The book is a historic dithyramb against the Independents,
itten as if the Presbyterians had never had any other ad-
rsaries, and had never themselves been conquerors and op-
essors. Not only does Hollis confine his narrative to the
nflicts of his party against the republicans, the fanatics,
d the army, but it appears as if this was all that he had any
collection of, and that the conduct of the Presbyterians, at
e commencement of the civil war, was altogether absent
om his thoughts. If this great omission be borne in mind,
ollis's narrative is true, of a striking moral truth; and, not-
ithstanding the vehemence of his resentment, the impetuo-
ty of his language, and the floods of invective which he pours
rth, without, however, giving vent at any time to all the
iger which he feels, he has not calumniated his enemies.
e has supplied us with the most faithful picture that has
en drawn of the insolent violence and imperturbable hypo-
isy of a party which was both military, demagogic, and de-
ut, animated and sustained by unbridled passions, blind
ith, and shameless personal interests.
This party derived a portion of its strength, it is true, from
purer source; for the Independents, and the various factions
hich were connected with them, had caught glimpses of
ome truths regarding social organisation and the rights of
ian, far superior to the political theories of the Presbyte-
ians. But the time was not ripe for the application, or even
omprehension, of these truths; they were confused, dis-
rdered, and stifled beneath monstrous absurdities, and were
s yet capable neither of forming a system, nor of founding a

* Memoirs of Denzil, Lord Hollis, pp. xiii.-xv. (London, 1699).

government.　Thus, although they powerfu
curing the momentary success of the Indepe
exercised no great or lasting influence upon
no one need be astonished that Hollis, in
noblest spirits of his time, could discern in t
save the passions of an ignorant multitude,
or avidity of its chiefs.

So long as Cromwell reigned, Hollis resic
in sad and dignified inaction, sometimes she
hopes and proceedings of the Royalist par
part in the intrigues of the Cavaliers of the
sighted and proud to lend himself to the f
subaltern schemes which ill-fortune suggest
nevertheless, one of those who, in their fran
courage, never renounced the idea of servin
combating its enemies.　When, in 1659,
Cromwell, England, restored to herself, was
on all sides for a government, in the mids
and impotent agitation of all the factions
tion had produced, Hollis re-appeared at the
byterians, who foresaw, and prepared the w
ration of Charles II.　He could labour in
out abandoning his principles, or belying, in
gree, his past life ; as a high-born gentlem
tisan of monarchy, far from having ever thou
the Stuarts, he had never ceased to protest
pulsion.　He was, however, one of those P
though desirous to recal Charles II., wishe
with him, and impose upon him some of
which his father had so often refused.　Bu
" The king ! the king !"　The Presbyterian
weary, and powerless to renew an energetic
Cavaliers.　Monk employed his taciturn abil
one from hindering the progress of events,
country from the course which it had resolver
II. returned unconditionally.　The Presby
silently to a defeat as inevitable as its conse
tain.　Hollis was one of the committee who p
to present the king with the homage of the H
He was specially appointed to be spokesman
when he was advancing towards the king, M
brother of the Earl of Arundel, roughly inte
ing that it was great insolence in him to pre

another commissioner, his relative. Hollis
ied his right; the quarrel grew warm; at
terfered, and requested Mr. Hollis to dis-
ssion.* His discourse was an effusion of
metimes rising into eloquence, interspersed
eflections upon the fallen authorities and
d breathing a deep, though repressed, feel-
r of the Parliament.† When Hollis had
lon with the king, some complaints were
se against the language he had used; the
public and of Cromwell, lately so powerful,
ble, and persons had not yet lost the habit
The House, however, supported Hollis, and
print his speech.‡
not elapsed from this period, and Hollis
High Court appointed to judge twenty-nine
) had lately been judges of the king and
intry, but who now no longer inspired fear,
become objects of commiseration. As it
, vengeance smote the most courageous and
o neither denied their actions, nor would
es before their conquerors. Hollis con-
iout scruple or hesitation. They were the
e had zealously opposed when at the height
ing in judgment upon them even then, and
ilty of the public misfortunes and the ruin
ever occurred to him that the justice of the
) reach them, or that they could be bound
of the liberties of England. However, his
he discussion of the bill of amnesty proved
irst heat of triumph, he was not favourable
es, or to a spirit of reaction.§
opening of the Royalist Long Parliament,
ouse of Commons in which he had fought
tles, and was created a peer of the realm
rd Hollis, Baron of Isfield.
as now about to open before him. He had
nd was well acquainted with the French lan-
[ouse of Commons, whenever any despatch

's Memoirs, p. 346.
d's Parliamentary History, vol. iv., col. 36.
ls of the House of Commons, vol. x., p. 57.
d's Parliamentary History, vol. iv., col. 78.

or document in that language had to be explained, it was h
who generally undertook to act as interpreter.* He pos
sessed the esteem and confidence of that national party whic
the new reign was careful to conciliate. In June, 1663,
Charles II. appointed him his ambassador at the court o
Louis XIV.

The mission was a difficult one. At the beginning of tha
year, the Count de Comenge, French ambassador at London
had received orders to negotiate a treaty of alliance with th
English court, for the purpose of terminating the dispute o
the two monarchs about the possession of Acadie, regulating
freedom of trade between their subjects, and abolishing re
spectively the rights of escheat. The secret and specia
object of Louis XIV. was to prevent Charles II. from form
ing an alliance with Spain. But no satisfactory agreemen
could be arrived at regarding the conditions of the propose
alliance. The cabinet at London thought that the fault la
with the Count de Comenge, and hoped to gain better suc
cess by transferring the negotiation to Paris.

Lord Hollis was not well adapted to bring such a matter
to a successful issue. He entertained against Louis XIV
and his government all the prejudices of an Englishman, a
member of the House of Commons, and a Protestant. He
was naturally high-spirited, taciturn, and susceptible; and
he thus added the asperities of his own character to the
difficulties of the existing political juncture. He arrived a
Paris in September, 1663, and had first of all a private
audience "to greet the king." But when his first public
audience was being arranged, he mooted a question of eti
quette with so much obstinacy, that he delayed his audience
for six months. M. de Lionne, then minister of foreign
affairs, gives the following account of the matter to M. de
Comenge, in a despatch dated December 30, 1663 :—

"In order to perform at once the orders which the king
has given me, and to fulfil your wishes as expressed in you
last despatch, I shall be careful to inform you that there i
no truth in the statement that we desired to impose on Mr
Hollis any conditions at all disgraceful to the crown of Eng
land, and that he has been personally ill-treated, as you
inform me that the Spaniards and their partisans have sprea

---

* Whitelocke's Memorials, p. 118.
† Lord Hollis's letters of credence are dated Whitehall, June 21, 1663.

report throughout London. On the contrary, it is but
.e to say that the king has every reason to complain
ough he has not yet done so) of the proceedings of Mr.
llis, in that he has taken it into his head to call in question
order which has existed for centuries in this court, and
ich, as he very well knows, is practised daily by all the
bassadors of crowned heads. This order is that the car-
ges, which the princes of the blood are accustomed to send
honour their entrance, should precede those of the am-
ssadors in the procession ; whereas Mr. Hollis claims that
s carriage should have the precedence. In other words, he
sires that his majesty, in order to please him, should in
me measure degrade the princes of the blood, by depriving
em of a right which they have possessed from time imme-
rial ; and also that he should, at the same time, offend all
her crowns, or at least declare that their ministers have all
en in error, and have failed to maintain, as he has done,
e dignity of their masters.

" As recent examples are less likely to be contested or dis-
lieved, he has been duly informed of the conduct of the Count
Fuensaldagna, the Marquis de la Fuente, the Count de Tott,
e ambassador-extraordinary of Denmark, and MM. Nani,
rimani, and Sagredo, the Venetian ambassadors, who are
ually most exact in all matters of ceremony, that they may
us maintain themselves in the same rank as the representa-
es of crowns. Mr. Hollis admits the truth of these ex-
ples, but he says that they cannot serve as a rule for the
bassador of England ; to which objection we have the
ility to make no answer, though there are many things
ich we could easily urge against him on this point. The
ng ordered me to pay him a visit yesterday on his behalf, to
y and induce him to hear reason ; but as his majesty himself,
he had undertaken the task, would never have succeeded,
u will readily imagine that my mission failed entirely of
ccess.

" I remarked that he rested his claim principally upon three
rticular cases, and I will tell you my answer to each of his
guments.

" The first was, that in the year 1564 (if I mistake not) an
nglish ambassador came to swear to a treaty of alliance, and
as accompanied at his entrance by a Marshal of France (*quod
tandum*) ; but on the day upon which the treaty was sworn,

the king sent M. de la Roche-sur-Yon, a prince of the royal
race, of the branch of Montpensier, to fetch him from his
lodging; and Mr. Hollis deduces this consequence, that the
prince thus gave precedence to the ambassador, because, he
says, it is not likely that the king, being desirous to honour
the said ambassador, would have sent to him any one who
would afterwards have taken precedence of him.

"I urged two things in reply to this : first, that before the
time of Henry III., the princes of the blood in France held
no rank unless they were peers, and took precedence only
according to the date of their peerage, so that other princes
frequently preceded them; secondly, that his authority does
not state that the Prince de la Roche-sur-Yon walked after
the ambassador; and that, in order to show him that his argument of likelihood might very probably be false, only six
weeks ago, the Prince de Condé and Monseigneur le Duc
were sent by the king to conduct the Swiss ambassadors to
his presence, but that they, nevertheless, preceded the ambassadors, although his majesty desired to do them all honour.

"The second instance that he alleged was that one of our
kings, I do not remember whether it was Henry IV. or Louis
XIII. that he mentioned, on another similar occasion of
swearing to an alliance, being accompanied by all the princes
and others, took the English ambassador by the hand, and
made him walk by his side to the church, where he afterwards
sat down .on the king's right hand, while the princes and
other nobles of the kingdom remained standing on his left
hand.

"I replied to this, that when a reason proves too much, it
is of no force ; and that, if the English ambassador were
seated and the princes of the blood standing, it is evident, if
the thing be true, as it possibly may be, that the ceremony
occurred in honour of the ambassador alone, and that the
princes did not claim to take any part in it. As in fact, when
the king is in any place, and all pay their court to him, there
is no regular rank maintained ; otherwise it would be requisite
that the greatest and most considerable nobles should always
be nearest the person of his majesty, which is not the case ;
that the ambassador, therefore, could not gain any advantage
from the fact that the king, being perhaps desirous to converse
with him, had taken him by the hand, and talked with him as
they walked to the church.

The third instance was that he read me a letter from a
?etary, whom he did not name, who informs him that
?ng, by order of the King of Great Britain, inquired of
?d Leicester how matters had been arranged here during
? embassy which he and Lord Scudamore undertook in the
?n of the late king, that lord had told him that at his en-
?ce he rode in the king's carriage, which was followed by
? queen's carriage, and immediately after by his own and
?d Scudamore's; and that a Swedish ambassador had con-
?ed his place with Lord Scudamore, but after some dis-
?es the Swede had given way.

I replied to this that there were either no princes of the
?d at Paris, at that time, or that Lord Leicester had not a
?d memory, or that he was not well informed of what was
?ng on behind him and out of his sight.

? There was undoubtedly no necessity for me to enter into
? discussion, and it would have been sufficient for me to
?e informed him that he was opposing a privilege which
? princes of the blood have possessed from time immemo-
?, and to which all the other ambassadors of crowned heads
?lded daily without any difficulty.

' He then told me that he had hit upon the expedient of
? king no public entrance, and tried to persuade me that
?h a course would prejudice no one. I could not agree
?h him, but maintained, on the contrary, that, with the ex-
?tion of himself, all others who had any interest in mat-
?s of this kind would be placed at a very notable disadvan-
?e;—for the princes of the blood would be degraded from
?ir privilege, all the other ambassadors would be obliged to
?fess that they had hitherto been in error, and the king
?uld be injured most of all; for the other ambassadors
?uld not fail immediately to put forward the same claims,
?, if his desire was granted, it would be impossible to
?y them their request of making no public entry, after the
?el precedent which he would have established. That not
?y would the suppression of this ceremony abolish for ever
?ustom which is of some lustre in the courts of princes (as
? example would be infallibly followed in all other courts),
? it would finally appear that this expedient had ended
?y in doing the king one of the greatest injuries it is pos-
?le for him to receive, by depriving him of the means of
?uming and continuing in possession of the precedence

C

which has been yielded to him by the King of Spain; and 1
begged Mr. Hollis to infer from hence whether his expedient
were practicable, and whether the king could accede to it.

"The conclusion was, that Mr. Hollis told me that he
greatly desired that I would show him a single instance in
which an ambassador of England had given place to the
princes of the blood, as he would be glad to have good cause
for abandoning his claim. This morning I have sent to him
MM. de Berlize and de Bonneuil, who will prove to him
from a book printed a long while ago,* that at the marriage
of Louis XII. with Mary, the sister of the King of England
in 1514, all the princes of the blood were seated above the
Dukes of Norfolk and Suffolk, the English ambassadors. 1
do not know whether, after the promise he has given me, he
will be satisfied with this example, although it is so conclu
sive, and occurred at a time when the princes of the blood
royal in France did not hold so high a rank as they do now
Besides, the English ambassadors always pay the first visit
to the princes of the blood."†

Business matters were as difficult to arrange as questions
of etiquette. "I cannot believe," wrote M. de Lionne to
the Count de Comenge, "that the Chancellor (Lord Claren
don) can consider Lord Hollis capable of conducting any im
portant negotiation, and much less of arranging and con
cluding a treaty between two crowns. As soon as he has
had his public audience it will quickly be perceived, by the
course which he will adopt, what kind of orders he is com
missioned to execute."‡

Hollis was not wanting in capacity; but no one had less
disposition than he felt to make England a satellite of France
and he displayed with haughty stiffness his aversion to a policy
which he could find no means of eluding. In April, 1664
he submitted to M. de Lionne a draft of a treaty very similar
to that which had just begun to be discussed in England
"I can already perceive plainly, by the proceedings of Lord
Hollis," wrote Louis XIV. himself to the Count de Comenge
"that the negotiation will make no quicker progress here
than it did in London."§   This was, in fact, the case; it

* Cérémonial Français, by Godefroy, p. 745.
† This inedited despatch is printed from the original in the archives of the
French Foreign Office.
‡ Despatch of 26th December, 1663; French Foreign Office.
§ Letter of 25th June, 1664; French Foreign Office.

gered on, but no tangible results appeared; Hollis had
splendid house in Paris, arranged and kept in the Eng-
h fashion, as he would, in no respect, conform to the
nners and usages of France.*   It was not long before the
itical relations of the two courts escaped from his hands.
arles II.'s sister, Henrietta Duchess of Orleans, became
e real ambassadress of her brother to Louis XIV., and of
uis XIV. to her brother.   On the 22nd of November,
64, M. de Lionne wrote to the Count de Comenge :—" His
jesty has not forgotten to give his best thanks to Madame
r the kind reception and good treatment which you ex-
rience from the King of Great Britain and all his ministers ;
d his majesty gave her to understand that he would be
ry glad if she would convey his acknowledgments to the
ng her brother.   He considered that it would be better for
e thing to pass through this channel than by the medium
Lord Hollis, whom we see, by the way, about once a
ar."†
Hollis was held in no greater consideration at Whitehall
an at the Louvre, and, while Louis XIV. would hardly
ten to him, his own king seized the slightest pretext for
ughing at him.   On the 1st of December, 1664, M. de
omenge wrote from London to M. de Lionne :—" You will
doubtless be as much surprised as I was to learn that a man
f high rank, of mature age, and of exalted office, has written
the king of England that the queen, our mistress, has
een brought to bed of a *black (more)* daughter.   Be not
stonished that I have not yet told you his name; I cannot
take up my mind to do so, and I must break the matter to
ou gently, lest you should fall down in a fainting fit at the
ame of Lord Hollis.   I am not the author of this bit of news.
t has been related by the whole court of England, and by
ne king himself.   If the story be true, which is hardly cre-
ible, it must of necessity be that the slight acquaintance
hich that nobleman has with the French language has
ade him commit this gross—I don't know what to call it ;
nd that the first news he received was that the queen had
een brought to bed with a *dead (morte)* daughter, and that,
y a play upon the words, he manufactured this piece of in-
elligence ; or that his secretary did not rightly understand

* Biographia Britannica, vol. iv., p. 2650.
† Archives of the French Foreign Office.

him, and has improperly expressed his intentions; for, witl
out malice it is impossible to believe that a sensible ma
could have made so gross a mistake, though it is attribute
to him even by the king, his master; and although he blame
him greatly, I cannot but think it would have been better t
conceal such a misapprehension on the part of his ministe
than to publish it."*

Hollis soon perceived that he had lost all his influence, an
his correspondence with the English court became as melar
choly as his relations with the court of France were unplea
sant. "I have received yours of June 27th, most welcom
to me," he wrote in confidence, on the 19th of July, 1664, t
his friend Sir William Morrice, then Secretary of State; "an
I give you my humble thanks for it, be the contents wha
they will, which must be what the complexion of the tim
affords, and not always what you and I would desire. Cloud
enough it is for the poor Protestants, methinks, in all quarter:
and nowhere worse than here. The poor people of Priva:
that are forced from their lands and houses, are not suffere
to carry away their moveable goods with them, but are robbe
of it as they go; and the country of Gex, by Geneva, whic
the Duke of Savoy passed over to the King of France upo
an exchange, but with that condition for the freedom of thei
religion, which they have ever since enjoyed from the time c
Henry IV., being all Protestants : now all their temples ar
every one pulled down to the number of three-and-twenty
and the exercise of their religion suffered but in two place:
where they are glad to make use of barns; and no reaso:
given for it to such as have been deputed hither, both from
them and from the canton of Berne, to endeavour to obtai
some favour in it, but Le Roy le veut..... All seems to mak
for the greatness of France. The weakness, and division:
and ill counsels, and ill successes of the undertakings of a
the other Christian princes and states, are the elevation c
this young king, who may be raised so high that his brain
may turn, and he may *suis viribus ruere*—commonly the fat
of human greatness. Yet he hath certainly great advantage
of his own, besides what his neighbours contribute to mak
him great; a clear understanding, a good judgment, an inde
fatigable industry; then a vast treasure and absolute powe
within his kingdom. ..... If once he can get to be consider

* Archives of the French Foreign Office.

ole at sea, he will be formidable indeed; and yet need not
ur master fear him except he will; and he only of all the
rinces of Christendom is out of his reach, who can prejudice
im, and receive no prejudice from him; except it be that
he other plow with his heifer, get within his councils; so
rill he unriddle his riddles, and I doubt not doth now. . . . .
ir, it makes me mad, that I wish myself ten thousand miles
ff, to be the unhappy man that must be forced to deliver up
he honour of my king and nation. Oh! that I had never
ome hither, or that I might soon be suffered to return from
hence, where I shall be ashamed hereafter to show my face,
which hitherto I could hold up with some comfort, though I
received no favour or kindness from them." *

Hollis's wish was soon granted. The assistance which,
during the year 1665, in virtue of the treaty of defensive alliance made in 1662, Louis XIV. gave to the Dutch in their
war against England, induced the recal of the ambassador,
who had long been almost as disagreeable to his own court,
which he enlightened in spite of itself, as he was to the French
king, whose policy he watched with the most hostile sagacity.
Though recalled in December, 1665, a violent attack of gout
detained Hollis in Paris until May, 1666; and, during this interval, the two courts renewed their endeavours to treat of
peace. Louis XIV. has himself transmitted to us, in his
Memoirs, the details of this futile attempt:

"The Queen of England,"† he says, " continuing to manifest
a strong desire for peace, I was wishful to make use of this
means to defend myself against the pretentions of the King
of England, who maintained that, as he had been the first to
declare war, I ought to be the first to send an envoy into his
kingdom to negotiate peace. For I represented to him that
the house in which that princess resided ought to be considered by us both as neutral ground; that the respect due to
her dignity would in a moment settle all those preliminary questions of etiquette, which frequently cause as much difficulty as
the substantial provisions of treaties; that the anxiety which
that queen manifested for peace might at any hour furnish him
with expedients for clearing away all the difficulties that pre-

* This letter is printed at length in Collins's "Historical Collections of the
Noble Families of Hollis, Cavendish, &c.," p. 159 (London, 1752).
† The Queen Dowager Henrietta Maria, widow of Charles I. See "Œuvres de
Louis XIV.," vol. ii., p. 107 (Paris, 1806).

sented themselves ; and that lastly, as she h
position, it would not be reasonable to nego
concurrence, and thus deprive her of the ho
. "But the principal reason which made
this place, was the advantage which I there
of being able to give instructions to all the
employ, about every matter that occurred
of the negotiation.

"The King of England, who seemed at fii
my design, for some time was disposed to in
trary; but at length, having become more
powered his ambassador, Lord Hollis, to a
proceeded on the —th of April to the reside
of England, where Lionne was present on m
ambassador Van Beuninghen on behalf of the
At first all parties were very courteous to es
pressed, in the strongest terms, their hope t
agreement might be come to; but when 1
upon the business, the English ambassac
nothing was proposed to him but what had
suggested, intimated that he could not concl
ment, and, 'a few days afterwards, received oi
from my court, where he had remained unt
war had been declared. Meanwhile, the Q
found it necessary to take her departure fc
fore Lord Hollis had received final instri
master; she begged me, that if the treaty we
negotiation might still be carried on in her
she were still present. But whilst these 1
neighbours were being broken off, others wei
more distant nations."

Towards the end of May, 1666, Lord
Paris to return to England; and M. de Gom
puted by M. de Lionne to accompany him
gives an account of his journey and embar
following despatches:

"Di

"In obedience to the orders of the king
pleased to convey to me, I have accompanied
bassador to this place, where he arrived yi
and where I shall remain with him until his
order to give you an exact account, I have to

Monday, the 24th instant, he left Paris, and, proceeding his journey, dined at Pontoise, and slept at Magny the me night. On Tuesday, the 25th, at about five o'clock in the morning, his secretary-of-legation arrived, together with person named Petit; who brought several letters to the ambassador, and, among others, I know that there was one from Madame. The secretary-of-legation remained in his suite, and Petit posted back to Paris. He is the man who was formerly secretary to the ambassador, Lockhart, and afterwards in the service of the Earl of St. Albans. From Magny, my ambassador went forward, dined at Ecouy, and slept at Rouen, where he remained on Wednesday. On his arrival at Rouen, M. de Montausier paid him a visit, which the ambassador returned on the following day; and, besides these civilities, very few people have seen him, except one Madame le Cambremont, of Lower Normandy, who has been with him nearly all the time. Some merchants have visited him, by means of whom he received his money; and also one M. le Saint-Simon, Grand Provost of Normandy. On Thursday, the 27th, he left Rouen and proceeded to Toste, where he dined and slept that night. M. de Montigny, the commandant, came to pay his respects to him; and, after I had informed the said M. de Montigny of the king's intentions, and as there was nothing to be done for the ambassador, except to pay him private civilities, he desired. that the mayors and sheriffs of the town might pay him their respects in a body, as they had done when he passed through the town three years before. I represented to him that circumstances had changed since then. He then told me that what induced him, as well as the corporation of the town, to desire to pay him this compliment was, that as several sailors from this place are prisoners in England, he hoped that the ambassador would use his influence to obtain their liberation. As I did not think the matter was of any consequence, I allowed them to do as they wished.

" There are in the roadstead here a frigate of thirty guns, and a yacht belonging to the Duke of York, which have been sent for the use of the ambassador. There is also a French vessel in the port, which the ambassador wishes to hire to carry over his baggage. This vessel cannot leave the harbour until high tide, which will not be until Tuesday, the 1st of June. And as I perceive that my lord the ambassador is not

disposed to leave without his luggage, I do not think that l
will embark until Wednesday, the 2nd of June; although l
might start this very day if he pleased, as the time is favou
able for the frigate and yacht. He has, moreover, told n
several times, that he was anxious to present himself befol
his master, the King of England, as quickly as possible. H
present conduct makes me doubtful of this, for his luggage
not a matter worthy of any consideration, if he is really d
sirous to obey his master's orders with all diligence.

"I have gathered from his conversation that he never wi
of opinion that the king his master would treat with th
Bishop of Munster. He says that if the said bishop had n
begun to arm, the king would perhaps not have sent any c
his troops to the Dutch; and that up to that time thei
would not have been any rupture; and that by the account
which he will give to the King of England and his Council c
State, it will not be his fault if they interpret matters moi
favourably than they have hitherto done; and that he coul
easily conceive that each had manifested considerable warmt
in his turn. He tells me all that he pleases; I listen a
tentively and think myself bound to report it to you, tha
you may attach to it such belief as you please. I find hii
extremely polite and civil, but I remark that he is not devoi
of anxiety. I learn from a small barque, which arrived hei
this morning from Holland, that nearly all the Dutch fleet i
collected together to the number of one hundred and thirt
sail; and the master of this barque tells me that it is ri
moured that Admiral Ruyter is to pass by the north, to joi
M. de Beaufort at La Rochelle."

The second despatch is as follows :—

"Dieppe, June 1, 1666.

"I have just witnessed the embarkation of the Englis
ambassador, who will have the finest possible weather for hi
passage. He desired me to present his very humble thanks t
the king for the honour which his majesty has done him, an
to assure you, sir, of his good offices. He pressed me to accep
a present of two hundred silver crowns, which he had lodge
with a merchant to be employed as I might desire. I neithe
wished, nor thought it right, to receive it, as I thought nei
ther the king nor yourself would wish me to do so. He ha
many times assured me that, by the course of conduct h
would pursue, it should be clearly perceived that it was no

fault that matters had not been brought to a good accom-
odation, although perhaps such might not be the opinion
tertained of him ; and that what might have given rise to
is opinion was, because he had plainly expressed his views
on the novel conduct pursued towards the ambassadors,
d upon the little attention which had been given to that
hich was done by the servants of the Princess de Carignan to
s own servants, of which he had complained only by order
the king his master and the Council of State ; and which had
en considered an extraordinary proceeding, and was the
ason why he had not accepted his majesty's present. I ob-
rve by his conduct that he is not at ease, but full of anxiety.
seems that his return to England is not agreeable to him;
d, when on the point of embarking, he received information
om a merchant that the Dutch fleet had sailed out, to the
umber of one hundred and five vessels. He expressed his
stonishment at this, and told me that he had no Dutch
assport, and that if any of their vessels should come up with
is ship, his voyage might be retarded. I replied that I
hought it my duty to inform him that the vessels of the States
ould assuredly manifest great respect for his majesty's pass-
orts. He answered that he had no doubt of it, but that he
oped, nevertheless, that he would have no occasion to make
he experiment. On taking leave of him I wished him a
peedy return into France to negotiate a peace. He told me
e did not think he should return, but that it might very pro-
ably come to pass that, in a short time, the king his master
vould send some other ambassador."*

In 1667, the year after his return to his native land, Hollis
eft it once more to go and negotiate the peace of Breda. This
vas his last diplomatic act. The foreign policy of Charles II.
gave just offence to his honesty and manly pride. He ab-
ented himself almost entirely from the court, was assiduous
n the discharge of his duties in the House of Lords, and ever
proved himself one of the firmest supporters of the national
party. But he had fallen into a state of profound melancholy ;
n 1676, writing, in the unreserve of friendship, to M. Van
Beuninghen, the ambassador of the States-General in England,
he bitterly deplored the state of dependence and humiliation
nto which his country was falling, ascribed it chiefly to the
ad government of James I., Charles I., and Charles II. ; and

* Archives of the French Foreign Office.

concluded with these remarkable words: "I make no doul to affirm that if the government of the Parliament had n(been interposed in the middle, the government must hav sunk ere now; for save what they did, we have not taken on true step, nor struck one true stroke, since Queen Eliza beth's time."*

By an unexpected incident, this haughty Englishman, s thoroughly imbued with the spirit of nationality, and s hostile to all foreign influence, was one day publicly accusec before a Court of Justice, of manifesting too great com plaisance and fondness for foreigners. In 1669, he had take: as his third wife a Frenchwoman, Esther de Lou, widow c Jacques Richer, Lord of Cambernon, in Normandy. Hi marriage and residence at Sainte-Mère-Eglide had obtaine for him many connexions in that province. In 1671, tw young Norman gentlemen, who had unfortunately becom implicated in a criminal prosecution at London, wrote fror their prison to entreat the aid of Lady Hollis, with whor they claimed relationship. Hollis took up their defence wit characteristic ardour, obtained numerous witnesses to thei innocence, accompanied them to the Court of King's Bench and was about to speak on their behalf, when Lord Chie Justice Keeling stopped him, saying that he must not inter rupt the court. Lord Hollis replied that "it was neither t interrupt the court, nor to do them any wrong, to inforn them of what had passed." "My Lord," answered Keeling very angrily, "it is not the first time you have been observed to appear too much for strangers."† This was, perhaps, ir allusion to the secret, though justifiable, connexion whicl Lord Hollis, as well as Lord William Russell, maintainec with Louis XIV. by means of Barillon and Ruvigny, the French ambassadors at London.‡ However this may be Hollis did not patiently endure this uncalled-for reproach he repelled the charge, before the public, in a pamphlet ir which he defended both his own cause and that of the two young Frenchmen, and before the House of Lords, in a petition in which he complained of the indignity which had been put upon him, and demanded satisfaction. The Lord Chief Justice was brought before the House, and obliged to

* Collins's Historical Collections, pp. 152-157.
† Biographia Britannica, vol. iv., p. 2650.
‡ Dalrymple's Memoirs, vol. ii., pp. 131, 134, 146.

DENZIL HOLLIS. 27

knowledge his error, and to ask pardon of the House and
Lord Hollis.* The old Baron, of Isfield, on his seat in the
pper House, was as warm a friend and as untractable an
nemy, as Denzil Hollis had been, forty years before, on the
enches of the House of Commons.
He continued to live in noble repose, taking scarcely any
art either in public business or parliamentary debates, resting the bad policy of the times by silent reprobation, and
hat only when resistance was a duty. Charles II. was in the
abit of attending, in the most familiar manner, at the de-
berations of the House of Lords: "The king's going thi-
her," says Burnet, "had a much worse effect; for he became
common solicitor, not only on public affairs, but even on
rivate matters of justice. And he was apt to do this upon
he solicitation of any of the ladies in favour, or of any that
ad credit with them. He knew well on whom he could
revail: so being once in a matter of justice desired to speak
o the Earl of Essex and the Lord Hollis, he said they were
tiff and sullen men; but when he was next desired to solicit
wo others, he undertook to do it, and said, 'they are men of
o conscience, so I will take the government of their conscience into my own hands.' "†
Hollis well deserved the honour done to his old age by
his avowal of a corrupt monarch; for he would yield neither
to popular passion nor to royal solicitation. In 1679, during
the great debate which was carried on in Parliament for the
exclusion of the Duke of York from the succession to the
crown, he joined the moderate party, who desired to impose
conditions on the Duke of York but not to exclude him entirely. And in 1680, at that odious trial which terminated
in the condemnation of Lord Stafford, he was one of those
who did not hesitate to acquit that victim of the fanatical
frenzy of the people and the cowardice of the Lords.
It is a great happiness for a man, in a shameless and
wrong-headed age, to close his life by an act of courage and
virtue. Lord Hollis died on the 17th of February, 1681, at
nearly eighty-three years of age. Though he had been married three times, he left only one son, Sir Francis Hollis,
and his race became extinct in the third generation. His
property then passed to his grand-nephew, John Hollis, Duke

* Biographia Britannica, vol. iv., pp. 2649-2650.
† Burnet's History of his own Time, vol. i., p. 473.

of Newcastle, who erected a monument to his memory
Dorchester church, where he was buried.

The inscription on this tomb is said to contain so exact a
particular an account of Lord Hollis's character, that we a
induced to quote it, as a pendant to M. Guizot's biograph
It is as follows :—

To eternise the name and honour of Denzil, Lord Holl
BARON OF ISFIELD.

His birth was equal to his virtues, being the second son
John the first Earl of Clare, who, by sea and land, at hon
and abroad, did not more signalise himself in the service
his country than he was meritoriously distinguished and r
warded by Queen Elizabeth and King James. All that De
zil's wit or courage, probity or industry, presaged in h
youth, he made good and exceeded when a man. For as h
excellent endowments and abilities made him early known :
his prince and country, so he could, by his eloquence a
valour, intrepidly defend the liberty of the last, without r
fusing the obedience that was due to the former. When tl
rights of the nation were barbarously invaded by that arn
which the Parliament levied to secure them, he bore the vi
lence and injustice of his enemies as it became a finishe
hero; nor could losses, exile, or his hatred to the factiou
make him forget him the love that he owed to Englan
After the restoration of monarchy he was created Baron
Isfield by King Charles II., and had the honour of repr
senting him in two extraordinary embassies—the one t
Louis the French king, who no less admired the generosit
whereby he maintained so high a character, than he dreade
that virtue he was not able to corrupt by his magnificer
presents, which were more princely refused than offere
No part of his reputation was diminished when he went afte
wards plenipotentiary to the treaty at Breda. His learnin
was unaffected, useful, and general; but not to be exceede
by any in the knowledge of the ancient records of the kin
dom, and the distinct powers of the several parts of the a
ministration. So true a friend, that none could exceed o
equal him. He was as great a patron to religious as to civ
liberty, which made him universally beloved and lamente
when he peaceably ended a long and glorious life the seven

nth of February, in the year of Christ, one thousand six
ndred and seventy-nine, and in the eighty-second year
his age. This monument is therefore dedicated to his
mory, for the honour of the present age, as well as an
mple to posterity, by his nephew's son and heir, John,
Duke of Newcastle.

MDCXCIX.

EDMUND LUDLOW.

[1620—1693.]

WHEN Pascal is depicting the misery of human nature,
appears to triumph in his task, as if the sight of so many
ntrasts, obscurities, and eccentricities, made him feel a
nd of sombre joy, and as if he consoled himself for the
ep imperfection of humanity by the honour of being able
contemplate it with steady gaze, and boldly to strip off its
stments of disguise.

This arises from the fact that Pascal always considered
an in an abstract and general light; in his unshackled and
litary meditations he was never under the necessity of
pplying to individuals the terrible judgment which he had
onounced upon the whole race. When we have to speak
f one particular man, instead of mankind at large; when
'e are compelled to recognise and acknowledge, in the cha-
acter of the same individual, in the narrow compass of a
ingle life, all the contradictions and miseries of humanity,
hen it is that the task becomes difficult, and that the strongest
mind, constrained to take a close survey of this moral chaos,
eels ready to succumb under the difficulty, I do not say, of
understanding what he sees, but of believing it.

Whoever is desirous thoroughly to know, and equitably to
udge Edmund Ludlow, will be condemned to this painful
eeling. Providence seemed to have prepared for him an
asy and pleasant destiny. He was endowed with an upright
heart, a resolute character, a robust body, an active and ingenious mind. He was born in 1620, among the best gentlemen
f Wiltshire, of an ancient and wealthy family, devoted to
hose interests of landed property and agricultural life which

are the soundest of all social interests, and accustomed to re
ceive the esteem of the people and the consideration of me
in authority. His was a position at once comfortable an
strong, adapted to inculcate wisdom, and conduct to happiness

But men introduce disturbance into positions which Provi
dence had consecrated to order. The arrogant and foolis
despotism of James I. and Charles I. deeply irritated a larg
number of those country gentlemen who are the natural, bu
independent allies of power. Attacked in their rights, a
well as in their dignity, they became alienated from the Crow:
and attached to the people, who were as greatly irritated a
themselves, and under the influence of a violent fermentatior
The ancient religious society—the Catholic Church—was dis
solved; the new Anglican Church was not sufficient to occup
the vacant place, and around it, in spite of its efforts, spran
up a variety of sects, which it oppressed, but could not crush
In matters of faith, the minds of the people were unfettered
their consciences would be free. The civil power united wit
the ecclesiastical authority to refuse the liberty demanded
The Crown placed itself at the service of the despotism o
the Church, and the Church lent its aid to the despotism o
the Crown. In consequence, to secure its defence in religior
the spirit of liberty invaded the political arena; need o
safety urged it onward to the conquest of power; what men
desired in spiritual matters, they demanded in temporal mat
ters also; and thus Sectaries became Republicans. The
ambition of the people, as it thus rose higher and higher
chimed in with the anger of the offended gentlemen, who
came forward to meet it. From the very outset of civil dis
cord, the republican party had allies and leaders from among
their ranks.

Ludlow had not attained his twentieth year when he be
came involved in this quarrel. His father, Sir Henry Ludlow
not only sat in the Long Parliament, among the members o
the extremest opposition, but he was the intimate friend o
Henry Martyn, a cynical and bold republican, the first who
dared to say in the House of Commons, " That it were better
one family should be destroyed than many." Sir Nevil Poole
moved that Mr. Martyn might explain what one family he
meant. " The king and his children," answered Martyn
boldly.* Ludlow was educated in these opinions; while a

* Whitelocke's Memorials, p. 71.

mple, he made preparations to engage in the
anded of his young companions the reason of
the Parliament. No sooner had the war com-
lunged enthusiastically into it. His conduct
is father, and imitated by his two brothers,
nas Ludlow, and his two cousins, Gabriel
ɔw. The whole family, so to speak, became
ır. Before it had lasted two years, Edmund
his brother Robert, who had died while a
ıvaliers, and in consequence of the bad treat-
ced from them; his father, who had died of
te of his children, and alarm at the state of
d his cousin Gabriel, who had expired in his
of battle, of wounds received near Newbury.
rth, two feelings held sway in his soul; in-
d with surprise at the obstacles raised up
cause; hateful distrust of the king, as prin-
ɔse obstacles, and unalterable conviction that
r safety would be obtained by a treaty with
feelings determined his conduct and ruled

the war, however, like a gentleman, and not
rave, ardent, impregnably faithful, and inde-
to his cause, but at the same time exempt
r vengeance, and all disloyal or passionate
and humane, he treated with consideration,
ttle, those same enemies whom he detested
. the arena of political debate. When he
l republican, he did not lay aside either the
nce of his feelings and manners. In spite of
ice to the opinions he had adopted, some
iscence occasionally appears in him. For
res to express his contempt for Colonel
ted to the king's party. "His low and ab-
:ducation," he says, "became so prevalent
nsform him into an agent and spy for the
uly strange language for the friend of Har-
l many other valiant and fanatical sectaries,
rom the most obscure ranks of life.
, from 1643 to 1645, Ludlow's life was en-
rrying on the war, but his passion was not

* Ludlow's Memoirs, p. 69.

satisfied, and his plans were not executed. The Presbyterians while making war, desired peace. Ludlow, who had taken service in their army, in the company of guards commanded by their general, the Earl of Essex, soon left them to follow some more resolute leader, Waller first, and afterwards Fairfax. At the end of 1645, the House of Commons determined to fill up the places of those of its members who had left it to join the king, and form another Parliament at Oxford. During that election, which returned one hundred and forty-six new members to take their seats at Westminster, Ludlow was chosen by his county, and entered the House at the same time with Robert Blake, the greatest seaman of his age, and a stanch republican. "We went into the House together," says Ludlow, "which I chose to do, assuring myself, he having been faithful and active in the public service abroad, that we should be as unanimous in the carrying it on within doors."[*]

From that day, until the death of Charles I., Ludlow's work was more political than military; and, in politics, he was guided by one fixed idea: to prevent the king's restoration at any price. In his eyes this was the right of defence and the duty of justice; it was required for the safety of his party, and for his own safety; the blood shed in defence of oppressed liberty cried for vengeance. Moreover, this was the means of establishing the Republic, and ensuring the government of the people by the House of Commons, the only legitimate form of government.

Ludlow had not been many months a member of that House which he desired to render the sovereign authority in the country, when, one morning, as he was walking with Cromwell in Sir Robert Cotton's garden, Cromwell told him "That it was a miserable thing to serve a Parliament, to whom let a man be never so faithful, if one pragmatical fellow amongst them rise up and asperse him, he shall never wipe it off. Whereas, when one serves under a general, he may do as much service, and yet be free from all blame and envy. If thy father were alive," he added, "he would let some of them hear what they deserve."[†] And not long afterwards, in the midst of a violent tumult which the Presbyterians had raised in the House, Cromwell turned towards Ludlow, who was sitting by his side, and whispered to him, "These men will never leave till the army pull them out by the ears."[‡]

* Ludlow's Memoirs, p. 66.   † Ibid., p. 72.   ‡ Ibid., p. 73.

Ludlow was surprised and disturbed, but not enlightened Cromwell's rough confidences; his position combined with passion to conceal from him their full meaning. He re-ued his hopes and pursued his plans without caring for yalists or Presbyterians, Cromwell or Cromwell's party in ; Parliament and the army.

About nine months afterwards, during the winter of 1648, ilst the king was a prisoner in the Isle of Wight, Crom-ll, feeling that the crisis was at hand—and being more-?r convinced that this crisis was uncertain, in spite of his orts to foresee and guard all its issues—desired that a con-ence might be held between some of his party and the republican leaders, Vane, Hutchinson, Sidney, Haslerig, and dlow. These latter unhesitatingly declared their views, d absolutely proscribed a monarchical government, in the me of the Bible, of reason, of history, and of their own ?ent experience. They strongly urged the generals, and ?ecially Cromwell, to declare themselves, and act in concert th them. Cromwell evaded, sneered; till at last, being ry hard pressed, he extricated himself from his embarrass-?nt by a piece of buffoonery. Having gained the door of the om, he took up a cushion, flung it at Ludlow's head, and en ran down stairs; but Ludlow "overtook him with an-her, which made him hasten down faster than he desired."*

Cromwell was not so easily defeated; he demanded another inference with the Republican leaders. Hearing of this, idlow told him, "That he knew how to cajole and give 'em good words, when he had occasion to make use of em." Cromwell broke out into a rage, and said, "They ?re a proud sort of people, and only considerable in their ,n conceits." "It is no new thing," answered Ludlow, :o hear truth calumniated, and though the commonwealth's-?n are fallen under your displeasure, I will take the liberty say that they have always been and ever will be consider-le, where there is not a total defection from honesty, nerosity, and all true virtue, which I hope is not yet our se."†

Cromwell's ill-temper was not of long continuance; he 'ood in absolute need of the Republicans, and found it necessary either to seduce or deceive them. With Ludlow, e latter method alone was practicable. "Mine is an un-ppy condition," said Cromwell to him one day during the

* Ludlow's Memoirs, p. 93.　　　　† Ibid.

D

month of April, 1648; " I have made the greatest part of t
nation my enemies by adhering to a just cause. But n
greatest trouble is, that many who are engaged in the sar
cause with me, have entertained a jealousy and suspicion
me. This is a great discouragement to me. What meth
is best for me to take?" " I could not but acknowledge
says Ludlow, in relating the conversation, " that he had man
enemies for the sake of the cause in which he stood engage
and also that many who were friends to that cause had co
ceived · suspicions of him; but I observed to him that I
could never oblige the former, without betraying that cau
wherein he was engaged; which if he should do upon th
account of an empty title, riches, or any other advantage
how those contracts would be kept with him, was uncertai
but most certain it was, that his name would be abominat
by all good men, and his memory be abhorred by posterit
On the other side, if he persisted in the prosecution of o
just intentions, it was the most probable way to subdue h
enemies, to rectify the mistakes of those that had conceiv
a jealousy of him, and to convince his friends of his integrit
that if he should fall in the attempt, yet his loss would I
lamented by all good men, and his name be transmitted
future ages with honour."*

Cromwell appeared moved by this language, and dispose
to adopt the course recommended. Three months afterward
a common danger came to the aid of his skilful policy; th
second civil war broke out, and twenty thousand Scotch ei
tered England in support of the king. Cromwell was sei
off to oppose them, and the republican leaders laid aside the
distrust. " We writ a letter to him," says Ludlow, " to ei
courage him, from the consideration of the justice of the caus
wherein he was engaged, and the wickedness of those wit
whom he was to encounter, to proceed with cheerfulnes
assuring him, that notwithstanding our discouragements, w
would readily give him all the assistance we could."†

Cromwell had no need of this assurance; he knew he coul
command danger and victory. Whilst he was engaged in th
conquest of Scotland, the Republican party, of which Ludlo
was ever one of the most zealous and active members, ha
summoned Fairfax's troops to London, conducted the kin
in captivity to Windsor, forcibly expelled the Presbyteria

* Ludlow's Memoirs, p. 95.   † Ibid., p. 100.

ɘ House of Commons, and, thus left master
no rival to its sway in the political arena,
ʒht to Hugh Peters, exclaiming in the midst
ɪons, " Now I have it by revelation, now I
ɪis army must root up monarchy, not only
ɘ, and other kingdoms round about ; this is
of Egypt! This army is that corner-stone
ɔuntain, which must dash the powers of the
But it is objected, the way we walk in is
ɪt. What think you of the Virgin Mary ?
ɪny precedent before, that a woman should
ɪthout the company of a man ? This is an
ɪples and precedents in."*
f these outbursts of joy and pride, on the
ɪ the last remnant of the Presbyterians re-
ɔuse of Commons, Cromwell resumed his
ɪbly. " God is my witness," said he, " that
ɪted with what has been done in this House
ɪe it is done, I am glad of it, and will en-
ɪin it."† Before two months had elapsed,
ɪpleted ; the king had been judged, and the
ɪed. Ludlow had sat in the High Court of
still sat in the republican Council of State,
ɪh as much confidence as disinterestedness,
tle order and probity into the new form of
ɪh had at length been conquered for his

ɪiably sat by Ludlow's side in the House of
day, he said to him, " I have observed an
looks and carriage towards me, and I appre-
ɪertain some suspicions of me. Now, being
tendency of the designs of us both to the
ɪe public service, I am desirous that a meet-
ɪted, wherein we may with freedom discover
ɪr mistakes and misapprehensions, and create
ɪding between us for the future." " You
ɪn me," answered Ludlow, " what I have
ɪ myself. If I trouble you not so frequently
ɪither because I am conscious of that weight
ɪes upon you, or that I have nothing to ɪm-
ɪl, upon my own or any other account ; but,

ɘr's History of Independency, part 2, p. 50. ＼ˏ
ɪw's Memoirs, p. 105.

D 2

since you are pleased to do me the honour to desire a fre
conversation with me, I am ready at any time."

During the afternoon of the same day, on leaving th
Council of State, they went into a room which had formerl
been used as the queen's guard-chamber. Cromwell the
entered into an explanation of his past conduct, his secre
negotiations with the king, and his severity towards some r
publican soldiers. "It has been a necessity incumbent upo
me," he said, "to do several things that appear extraordinar
in the judgment of some men, who, in opposition to me, tak
such courses as would bring ruin upon themselves, as well s
upon me and the public cause ; but my intentions are directe
entirely to the good of the people, and I am ready to sacrific
my life in their service. I desire nothing more than that th
government of the nation may be settled in a free and equ
commonwealth. There is no other probable means to kee
out the old family and government from returning upon us
and I look upon the design of the Lord in this day to be th
freeing of his people from every burden. I believe that H
is now accomplishing what is prophesied in the 110th Psalm
and am often encouraged from the consideration of it to a
tend the effecting of those ends." He then spent about a
hour in repeating and commenting upon the 110th Psaln
alternately receiving and refuting Ludlow's observations, an
his persevering, but timid references to the past. At lengt
changing the subject, he said, "I intend to contribute the u
most of my endeavours to make a thorough reformation i
the clergy and law ; but the sons of Zeruiah are yet too stron
for us, and we cannot mention the reformation of the law bi
they presently cry out that we design to destroy property
whereas the law, as it is now constituted, serves only to mai
tain the lawyers, and to encourage the rich to oppress th
poor. Mr. Coke, now Justice of Ireland, by proceeding in
summary and expeditious way, determines more causes in
week than Westminster Hall in a year. Ireland is as a clea
paper in this particular, and capable of being governed b
such laws as should be found most agreeable to justice; whic
may be so impartially administered, as to be a good precede
even to England itself. When the English once perceive th
property is preserved at an easy and cheap rate in Irelan
they will never permit themselves to be so cheated and abuse
as now they are."

From the administration of justice in Ireland, Cromwe

tary government. "The whole weight of it,"
on Major-General Ireton, and, if he should
ther accident, be removed from that station,
hat part would probably fall into the hands
ther by principle or interest, are not proper
nd of whom I have no certain assurance.
eputation and known fidelity should be sent
the horse there, and to assist Ireton in the
ublic. Can you name any one who you
ly qualified for that station ?" Ludlow pro-
gernon Sidney. "No," said Cromwell, "he
ay who are in the king's interest ; Colonel
nond would do better ; but Hammond, by
ent with relation to the king, has so dis-
that I apprehend he would not be acceptable
d is a fine country ; try and think of some
' that employment."*
egan to comprehend his meaning, and made
fuse the offer. He had just married a wife,
. estate ; his private affairs required his per-
lence. But the Council of State interfered ;
nmons commanded. Ludlow was appointed
ral of the Horse in Ireland. He had an
romwell himself, explained to him his situa-
ated the immense injury which this appoint-
e him. "Men's private affairs," said Crom-
place to those of the public ; I have seriously
atter, and I cannot find a person so fit for the
urself."† Ludlow yielded, and left England ;
1651, less than two months after the esta-
Republic, Cromwell had decently removed,
nent and from England, that Republican
red the most troublesome of his opponents.
e elapsed, and the Republic had ceased to
ad served it valiantly and honestly. With
and uncommon capacity, he had carried on
lancholy war, which had been equally ruinous
ais fortune. He had narrowly escaped dying
: besieging Castle Clare ; and he had ex-
is own resources, 4500*l.* sterling, besides his
luct was guided by a disinterestedness even
ecuniary liberality—the disinterestedness of

lemoirs, pp. 122-123. † Ibid., p. 124.

self-love. Though possessed of the chief command in Irelan
for more than six months after the death of Ireton,* he ha
yielded it up without a murmur to Fleetwood, who wa
sent out in distrust of him,† and had served under his order
with the same zeal as if he had been himself in command
More than this, when Cromwell, in 1653, expelled the Lon
Parliament, Ludlow, notwithstanding his indignation, re
mained at his post, partly out of fidelity to the Republica
cause, partly out of consideration to some of his friends wh
had not yet separated from Cromwell, but chiefly in obedienc
to that irresistible bias which urges even the purest partisan
from concession to concession, when they feel they are gravel
compromised. But, in 1654, when the news arrived at Cor
that the Barebones Parliament had been dissolved,‡ and tha
Cromwell had been proclaimed Protector,§ Ludlow's patienc
came to an end. He stoutly opposed the proclamation of th
Protector in Ireland,‖ and resigned all participation in th
civil administration of the country, as he was determined no
to recognise the new power.

He attempted, however, to retain his military functions
He held his command from the Republican Parliament, an
might employ his authority for its restoration. It cost hin
a great deal also to separate himself entirely from a govern
ment for which he had fought so long, and to believe irre
mediable an evil which he had so little foreseen. The Protecto
sent his son Henry into Ireland to observe persons and things
and inform him of the result.¶ Ludlow received him wit
many marks of attention, placed his house and horses at hi
disposal; and when talking with him in his garden, on th
day that Henry Cromwell was to return to England, "
acquainted him," says Ludlow, "with the grounds of m
dissatisfaction with the present state of affairs in England
which I assured him was in no sort personal, but would b
the same were my own father alive, and in the place of his
He told me that his father looked upon me to be dissatisfied
upon a distinct account from most men in the three nations
and thereupon affirmed that he knew it to be his resolution
to carry himself with all tenderness towards me. I told him
that I ought to have so much charity for his father, to believe
that he apprehended his late undertaking to have been abso-

---

* Ireton died on November 27th, 1651.   † On the 9th of July, 1652.
‡ On the 12th of December, 1653.   § On the 16th of December, 1653.
‖ In January, 1654.   ¶ He arrived in Ireland on the 4th of March, 1654.

ely necessary, being well assured that he was not so weak man to decline his former station, wherein his power was great, and his wealth as much as any rational man could sh, to procure to himself nothing but envy and trouble. I pposed he would have agreed with me in these sentiments; it he, instead of that, acknowledged the ambition of his ther in these words: 'You, that are here, may think he d power, but they made a very kickshaw of him at London.' replied that, if it were so, they did ill, for he had deserved uch from them. Then I proceeded to acquaint him with y resolution not to act in any civil employment, and my rpectation not to be permitted to continue in my military mmand; to which he answered, that he was confident I would receive no interruption therein. I told him I could ot foresee what his father would do; but inclined to think at no other man in his case would permit it. To this I dded, that the reason of my drawing a sword in this war, as to remove those obstructions that the civil magistrate et with in the discharge of his duty; which being now ccomplished, I could not but think that all things ought for he future to run in their proper and genuine channel; for s the extraordinary remedy is not to be used till the ordinary ail to work its proper effect, so ought it to be continued no onger than the necessity of using it subsists; whereas, this hat they called a government, had no other means to preserve tself but such as were violent, which, not being natural, could not be lasting. 'Would you, then,' said he, 'have the sword laid down? I cannot but think you believe it to be as much your interest to have it kept up as any man.' I confessed I had been of that opinion whilst I was persuaded there was a necessity of it, which seeming to me to be now over, I accounted it to be much more my interest to see it well laid down, there being a vast difference between using the sword to restore the people to their rights and privileges, and the keeping it up for the robbing and despoiling them of the same. But company coming in, we could not be permitted to continue our discourse."*

Henry Cromwell left Ireland; and, on his arrival at Chester, being questioned as to the state in which he had left affairs in Ireland, "Very well," he answered; "only some who are in love with their power must be removed."†

Next year Ludlow arrived in London, stripped of all em-

* Ludlow's Memoirs, p. 187.   † Thurloe's State Papers, vol. ii., p. 150.

ployment, civil as well as military, and almo
of a prisoner. On disembarking at Beaun
arrested, and the governor of the town had
sign an engagement, by which he promi
against the existing government. Ludlow
but in order to obtain permission to contin
signed it at length, with this reservation, wh
his own hand: " I look upon this engageme
to me for my subscription by the governor
order from, &c., to be no longer of any forc
rendered myself a prisoner at Whitehall; a
only I subscribe it."* He was then allowe
arrived in London on the 10th of Decembe

On the Wednesday following, at about e:
evening, the Protector sent for him. Ludlo
hall, where he found him in his bed-chambe
general officers, Lambert, Sydenham, Walter
tague, and Fleetwood.

" The first salute I received from him," s:
to tell me, that I had not dealt fairly with hi
to believe I had signed an engagement not t
and yet reserving an explanation whereby
engagement; which if it had not been mad
he might have relied upon my promise, and
gaged in blood before he was aware. I tolc
why he should look upon me to be so con
could I apprehend how it had been possible fc
fairly and openly with him than I had done ;
governor at Beaumaris, that if my life as well
been at stake, I could not sign the engage
therefore had resolved to continue there, had
himself expressed a desire to accept of my
that explanation. And because I accounte
a repeal of the engagement, I had told him s
to do nothing out of respect to me that cons
duty; notwithstanding which, the governo
free to accept my subscription, so that I
might have received instructions so to do.
well, ' he had none from me.' ' That was m
I knew; and if you had not notice as well
other, it was not my fault, for I had acquai
ther; and those who informed you of the
had made you acquainted with the other al:

* Ludlow's Memoirs, p. 209.

" He next asked me wherefore I would not engage not to
t against the present government, telling me, that if Nero
re in power, it would be my duty to submit. To which I
plied, that I was ready to submit, and could truly say, that
knew not of any design against him. 'But,' said I, 'if Pro-
lence open a way and give an opportunity of appearing in
half of the people, I cannot consent to tie my own hands
forehand, and oblige myself not to lay hold on it.' 'How-
er,' said he, 'it is not reasonable to suffer one that I distrust
come within my house, till he assure me he will do me no
ischief.' I told him, I was not accustomed to go to any
ouse unless I expected to be welcome; neither had I come
ther but upon a message from him, and that I desired no-
ling but a little liberty to breathe in the air, to which I
onceived I had an equal right with other men. I told him
so, I had gone as far as I could in that engagement which I
ad given to Lieutenant-General Fleetwood,* and if that were
ot thought sufficient, I was resolved with God's assistance to
iffer any extremities that might be imposed upon me. 'Yes,'
aid he, 'we know your resolution well enough, and we have
ause to be as stout as you; but, I pray, who spoke of your
uffering?' 'Sir,' said I, 'if I am not deceived, you mentioned
ne securing my person.' 'Yea,' said he, 'and great reason
nere is why we should do so; for I am ashamed to see that
ngagement which you have given to the Lieutenant-General,
which would be more fit for a general who should be taken
risoner, and that hath yet an army of thirty thousand men
n the field, than for one in your condition.' I answered, that
is was as much as I could consent to give, and what Lieutenant-General Fleetwood thought fit to expect. Then beginning to carry himself more calmly, he said, that he had been
lways ready to do me what good offices he could, and that
le wished me as well as he did any one of his Council, desir-
ng me to make choice of some place to be in, where I might
lave good air. I assured him, that my dissatisfactions were
not grounded upon any animosity against his person; and
hat if my own father were alive, and in his place, they would,
I doubted not, be altogether as great. He acknowledged
that I had always carried myself fairly and openly to him

* Before leaving Ireland, and out of regard for Fleetwood, who treated him with
great consideration, Ludlow had promised to do nothing for six months against
the established government, unless he had previously surrendered himself into the
hands of the Lieutenant-General, or of Cromwell himself, and had begged them
to free him from that engagement.

and protested that he had never given me
otherwise."*

Here the conversation ceased.   Ludlow
into the next room, where Fleetwood soon
renewed his entreaties that he would sign th
ment, were it only for a week.

"Not for an hour," replied Ludlow; and

Cromwell left him for some time undisturb
ing year, he resolved to make a last attempt t
A Parliament was indispensable, but it was
all events it should be submissive and docile
fore, above all things, desirable to exclude
who were neither to be intimidated, deceived
Vane, Bradshaw, Rich, and Ludlow.   Towa
of the summer of 1656, Cromwell cited then
himself and his council. Ludlow presented hi
Cromwell "then said that he was not igno
plots that were on foot to disturb the presen
he thought it his duty to secure such as he
'I would have you know,' said he, 'that w
not from a motive of fear, but from a timely
see and prevent danger; that if I had dor
ought to have secured you immediately u
into England, or at least when you desired
the engagement you had given after your ar
now require you to give assurance not to
government.' I desired to be excused in th
minding him of the reasons I had formerly
refusal, adding that I was in his power, a
use me as he thought fit. 'Pray, then,' sa
that you would have? May not every man
will? What can you desire more than you
easy,' said I, 'to tell what we would have.'
pray?' said he. 'That which we sought for,'
nation might be governed by its own consei
he, 'as much for a government by consent
where shall we find that consent?—amon
presbyterian, independent, anabaptist, or
I answered, 'Amongst those of all sorts wl
fidelity and affection for the public.' The
commendation of his own government, bo
tection and quiet which the people enjoyed

* Ludlow's Memoirs, pp. 210-211.

ed to keep the nation from being imbrued
that I was of opinion too much blood had
unless there were a better account of it.
d he, ' to charge us with the guilt of blood ;
ɔ is a good return for what hath been shed ;
ɪd what clandestine correspondences are
s time between the Spaniard and those of
ake use of your name, and affirm that you
assist them.' ' I know not,' said I, ' what
party, and can truly say, that if any men
an engagement with Spain, they have had
so to do, and that if they will use my name
Then, in a softer way, he told me that he
any more hardships on me than on himself ;
ɪs been ready to do me all the good offices
wer, and that he aimed at nothing by this
public quiet and security. ' Truly, sir,' said
y you should be an enemy to me, who have
ɔu in all your difficulties.' ' I understand
ɪt you mean by my difficulties. I am sure
roperly mine as those of the public ; for, in
ward condition, I have not much improved
men,' pointing to his council, ' well know.'
med to assent, by rising from their chairs ;
ɔught not fit to insist further on that point,
to say, that it was from that duty which I
c, whereof he expressed such a peculiar
t not give the security he desired, because I
gainst the liberty of the people, and contrary
of England. For proof of this I produced
ɪt for restraining the council-table from im-
ɪe free-born people of England ; and in case
requiring the justices of the upper bench,
ion of the aggrieved party, to grant his
to give him considerable damages. To this
gave his free vote, assuring him that, for
st not do anything that should tend to the
ut,' said he, ' did not the army and Council
ɔersons to prison ?' I answered, that the
ɪd so, but it was by virtue of an authority
by the Parliament ; and if the army had
ɪ that manner, it had been in time of war,
bring the persons secured to a legal trial ;

whereas it is now pretended that we live in a time of peac
and are to be governed by the known laws of the land. '
justice of peace,' said he, 'may commit, and shall not I
'He is,' said I, 'a legal officer, and authorised by the law t
do so, which you could not be, though you were king; b
cause, if you do wrong therein, no remedy can be had again
you.' "*

The discussion on both sides was evidently useless. Lu
low was a second time directed to withdraw into an adjoi
ing room. The council grew animated, the members·spol
loudly, and Ludlow listened attentively. Presently he hea
Major-General Lambert advise that he might be "perem
torily required to give the security demanded. But Cromw
said that the air of Ireland was good, that I had a house the
and therefore he thought it best to send me thither." Imm
diately after, Mr. Scobel, one of the clerks of the counc
came and told him that he might retire.†

Indirect attempts were frequently renewed to induce Lu
low to give the required security. Its amount was mention
to him, 5000l. sterling, payable in three days. The order f
his arrest, issued by the council, was also shown to him. I
obstinately refused to comply. He was not arrested; he w
·not even sent to Ireland. It was Cromwell's policy never
urge either men or circumstances to extremes. Ludlow, (
his side, had no wish either ridiculously to brave a victorio
power, or to overthrow, at all risks, a man who, like himse
had combated and condemned the king. Having saved l
honour, he lived quietly in the country for two years.

In August, 1658, Cromwell was confined to his bed
severe gout and fever, and was grieving intensely for the dea
of his dearest daughter, Elizabeth Claypole. He was told th
Ludlow had just arrived in London. He 'immediately se
for Fleetwood, and ordered him to ascertain why Ludlow h
come to town so suddenly, at such a conjuncture. Ludl
explained his journey for family reasons, and protested th
he had no wish or intention to excite any commotion in t
army, or elsewhere.‡ Two days afterwards, on the 3rd
September, Cromwell was dead; and his son, Richard, h
succeeded him, without the least opposition. Four mont
afterwards, a Parliament was sitting at Westminster; Lu
low took his seat therein, and refused to swear obedience
the new Protector.

* Ludlow's Memoirs, pp. 217-218.   † Ibid., p. 218.   ‡ Ibid., p. 232.

This was not in consequence of any preconceived plan for rthrowing Richard Cromwell and the Protectorate. Perps even, he was desirous to conciliate their existence with theories of republican organisation. But on recovering a le power, he fell once more under the sway of all his pasns and prejudices. Blinded by the least chance of success, resumed his endeavours to secure the triumph of his old ise with the most untractable obstinacy, rejecting all the titutions and combinations which were likely to destroy e absolute empire of the House of Commons in the government, and the absolute empire of the party which had conered and condemned the king in the House of Commons. erein alone, in his opinion, consisted legitimate power; yond, all was suspicious and unendurable; he opposed ery obnoxious proposition with that exclusive, distrustful, d fractious spirit, which, even though it have no destructive sign, is sure to cripple, to enervate, and ere long to dissolve y government. While the Act which recognised Richard omwell as Protector was under discussion, some one prosed to insert the words, "that he shall govern according to w." "The term is ambiguous," said Ludlow, "to rule cording to law. I would have you first determine what you ean by law. The great quarrel between the king and us as the militia. Either he or we were guilty. I look on ayself as guiltless of that blood. My conscience went along ith the Parliament after the king was brought to justice. . . . honour his Highness as much as any man that speaks here. would have things settled for his honour and safety; but if e take the people's liberties from them, they will scratch hem back again."* In Ludlow's eyes, there never was any ther danger but the danger of the republic, and no other uestion than the question of life or death which had been ought out between Charles I. and the Long Parliament.

Richard Cromwell fell. The Long Parliament re-appeared, nd fell once more. The army, after having raised up and verthrown the Protector and the Long Parliament, attempted o stand alone, and fell. In eighteen months, all powers, arties, and men, had been put to the test, and had all been onvicted of incompetence. During this period, Ludlow led wretched life, passing and repassing from the Parliament to he army, from the army to the Parliament, from Haslerig to leetwood, from Lambert to Monk, from England to Ireland:

* Burton's Parliamentary Diary, vol. iii., p. 145.

a little less credulous and senseless than t
his fate, he endeavoured, but in vain, to c
mutilated limbs of the republican party, a:
attempts he not merely lost all credit with
perilled his ancient reputation for firmness

Meanwhile the restoration of Charles II
out resistance, and in presence of his adveri
it unmoved. On the 29th of May, 1660, f
which he was concealed, Ludlow saw the ii
of troops and people pass by, which had acc
on his entrance into London: and shortly aft
a proclamation published under his window
judges of Charles I. to surrender themselvei
fifteen days, on pain of being excluded f
which the Parliament had just voted.

Ludlow was one of those men who bear
than prosperity; and who are more exalte
than by power. No sooner had the eighte
he had spent in unproductive and paltry a
than he at once regained, under the rule
enemies, tranquil firmness of soul and cond
wantonly expose himself, like a hair-braine
hatred and their power; but he did not beli
of his life, or neglect any duty of his positio
himself at first; but when the elections fo
ment of Charles II. began, he resolved to ac
the nomination, for his own county, of or
Mr. Bainton. This gentleman, however, w
he had resolved not to put his friends t
appearing for him, judging it the best wa
with the stream than to be borne down by
bitants of the borough of Hinden offered
himself. "Though I durst not desire any
a trust on me, yet I confess it was no smal
me, that they would manifest their respecl
and their remembrances of my services, wh:
been, in such a conjuncture, when the Ca
what design may be easily conjectured, had j
of the late king's judges, of which number
to be one."†

Ludlow was, in fact, elected. He returne
took his seat in the House of Commons wit

* Ludlow's Memoirs, p. 332.

ostentation, but refusing to give his sanction to acts
ich implied the voluntary recal of the restored king, and
wering to those persons who advised him not to say a
rd in justification of the High Court against the late king,
hat unless I was constrained, I saw no reason to mention
t matter; but, in that case, though it should cost me my
, I could not prevaricate."*
Silence even would not suffice. The storm arose; the regi-
es were summoned to deliver themselves up as prisoners.
dlow surrendered himself, but remained free on giving
urity. The peril increased daily; new exceptions were
de to the amnesty; several even of those regicides who
d surrendered themselves were assailed. Ludlow sought
hin to conceal himself. Among the Presbyterians, even
se of them who were Cavaliers, several esteemed him, and
d kept up a courteous bearing to him. "Let him take care,"
d Sir William Morrice, Secretary of State to Charles II., to
e of Ludlow's friends, "if he is apprehended, he is a dead
an." A short time after, Lord Ossory, eldest son of the
arquis of Ormonde, advised him to quit the kingdom.
dlow, while incapable of feebleness, had no wish to be-
me a martyr. In the beginning of September, 1660, he
parted, and remained two days concealed at the bottom
a small vessel in the port of Lewes, on the coast of Sussex.
The master, among other things, inquired if Lieutenant-
eneral Ludlow were not imprisoned with the rest of the
ng's judges; to which I answered, that I had not heard of
ny such thing."† The next evening he was at Dieppe;
d, towards the end of the month of October, after having
ssed through Rouen, Paris, and Lyons, he arrived at
eneva, the first place where he thought himself in safety.
Geneva even appeared to him too near to monarchical
d Catholic France, which was governed by a despotic
vereign, intimately allied to the English king. He left it
the summer of 1662, and fixed his residence first at
ausanne, then at Vevey, under the protection of the can-
n of Berne, which displayed to him, and not to him only,
ut to nine other regicides who sought a similar refuge, the
ost constant hospitality.
It is a remarkable fact, and one that is not wanting in
oral grandeur, that this official and avowed protection was
eadily maintained for more than twenty years, by a small

* Ludlow's Memoirs, p. 343.   † Ibid., p. 360.

state, on behalf of men condemned by a king and proscribe
by his son and successor. Not only did the senators of Bern
allow Ludlow and his companions to reside in their territory,
but they gave them a formal reception, invited them to din
at their houses, made presents to them, gave them guards
—in fine, treated them, as far as their power allowed, with
the same regard, the same public and continued kindness
which Louis XIV. was to show in after time to the second
son (in his turn a royal fugitive) of that king whom Ludlow
had condemned.

Europe was then in its unreformed state. The different
states, monarchical or republican, powerful or weak, governed
and conducted themselves, each according to its own maxims
with an almost complete independence of one another, little
caring for their neighbours when not attacked by them. They
did not feel themselves all attacked by the same evils, and
threatened by the same dangers; and the lords of Berne pro-
tected, without any fear of embroiling themselves with the
Emperor of Austria or the King of France, those English regicides who, in their turn, did not for a moment dream of con-
spiring, in their retreat, against any one of the governments,
monarchical or otherwise, by which they were surrounded.

Such a protection was very necessary for the English refugees; and even this was not always sufficient for their safety.
Assassination was not, in the seventeenth century, the instrument only of anarchy and passion; royal hatred still resorted to it sometimes, though cautiously. Charles II. and
his sister, Henrietta, Duchess of Orleans, even more than
he, pursued the outlawed regicides with the utmost animosity,
as far as the borders of the Lake of Geneva. Perhaps these,
in spite of their distance from home and their impotence, were
not ignorant of the plots which were continually being carried
on or meditated in England by their fallen party. Perhaps
fear had as much to do as hatred with the obstinate attempts
of the Stuarts to rid themselves of their ancient enemies.
On looking more closely, we can detect, in these attempts, a
busy use of police agency and espionage, as well as an intention to assassinate. Whether this was the case or not, Ludlow and his companions lived, from 1662 to 1668, whether at
Geneva, at Lausanne, or at Vevey, in a state of continual
anxiety; obliged to keep a strict watch on their food; to for-
tify themselves in their houses; to be attended by an escort
in going to church; continually being warned that new as-

ins threatened them, that they had arrived on the other
of the Lake, were in the same town, and had con-
ed themselves at the bottom of their boat. Much false
m was, doubtless, given them, which occasioned ground-
fears. However, those who were credulous, were soon
eceived by fact. On the 11th of August, 1664, Mr.
e was assassinated at Lausanne. We shall see, by the fol-
ing letter, how the fact was communicated by a French
dent in Switzerland in his correspondence. The writer
ot be suspected of partiality, and his account agrees sub-
tially with that given by Ludlow.

"Soleure, August 26th, 1664.

On Thursday last, Cromwell's chancellor, who was living
er the protection of the lords of Berne in Lausanne,
re he has been for three years, was killed by a musket-
t fired by an unknown Cavalier, who, with a comrade, had
n for eight days in the town. They payed their score
er every meal, and every morning, at the time of service,
of these Cavaliers posted himself at the churchyard, with
musket concealed under his jacket, waiting till the chan-
or should come to attend service. The other, meanwhile,
t horses at the gate of the town, near a fountain, under
pretence of watering them, in order to make their escape,
ich they did when they had accomplished their purpose.
ey have left a letter with a large seal for the mayor of the
vn; it is thought to be a safeguard or some letter of the
ng of England."*

The success of crime multiplied its attempts: they were es-
cially directed against Ludlow, the most famous and resolute
the refugees. Warnings were sent to him from all parts.
ie of these documents runs thus: "You are hated and
ured more than all the rest of your companions. Your
ad is set at a great price; 'tis against you they take all
is pains to find assassins, and 'twas on your account they
ntrived the late attempt; so that upon the whole matter I
nnot but advise that you would resolve to retire to some
ace where you may be unknown; there being, in my opinion,
other way left to secure you from the rage of your ene-
ies."† However, he refused to move. The magistrates of
evey watched over him with the greatest care; the people

* Archives du département des affaires étrangères.
† Ludlow's Memoirs, p. 394.

E

were fond of him; and he was directly authorised, in case (f danger, to ring the alarum-bell. He remained at Vevey, guarding himself carefully in his house, but in no other respec changing his habits.

Meanwhile, war broke out: first between England an. Holland, and, a short time after, between France and Eng. land. A great man and a great king—John de Witt in th Hague, and Louis XIV. in Paris—formed the design of re viving in England the republican party, always agitated an unsettled. The disclosures relating to this subject are au thentic and personal. "On the one hand," says Louis XIV, himself, in his Mémoires,* "I made use of the remnant of Cromwell's faction, to raise, under their name, some new broil in London; and, on the other hand, I began communi cations with the Irish Catholics, who, being always very dis satisfied with their condition, seemed also to be always read to make an effort for its improvement.

" With these different intentions I listened to the proposal which were made to me by an English gentleman of the nam of Sidney, who promised that he would soon cause a tumult t break out if I furnished him with a hundred thousand crowns but I thought this sum rather too large for it thus to be riske upon the promise of a fugitive, unless I saw some proba bility in the things which he led me to expect. I therefor offered to give him only twenty thousand crowns, with th promise of sending afterwards to the insurgents all the as sistance which was necessary for them, as soon as they ap peared in a condition to avail themselves of it with success.'

About the same time, the 11th and 14th of March, 1666 the Comte d'Estrades, French ambassador in Holland, wrote thus to Louis XIV. :

" M. de Witt has requested me to supply a passport to Messrs. Sidney and Ludlow, enabling them to go into France These are two individuals of great merit. They are at Frank fort, and have expressed a desire of waiting upon your Majesty on important business. M. de Witt has not told me anything further about them."†

And to M. de Lionne he writes : " Mr. Sidney, a person of quality and of great desert, who was employed on im portant embassies by the late Protector, having informed me that, at this crisis, now that the king has declared war against

* In the year 1666. Œuvres de Louis XIV., vol. ii., p. 203.
† Archives du département des affaires étrangères.

land, he desires to place himself under the protection of
Majesty, and to go himself to France to offer his services,
ccasion should present itself for their exercise. I have
ned it right to give him my passport in order that no
ortunity which may arise for his serving his Majesty in
conjuncture may be delayed, leaving it, sir, for you to
sider what may be best, after having had an interview with
Sidney."

The passport sent to Ludlow was couched in these terms:
We require all governors, commanders, captains, lieu-
ants, mayors, sheriffs, judges, and other officers to whom
may belong, as well by sea as by land, to permit Mr.
mund Ludlow, with four servants, to pass freely and safely
ough the places of their respective powers and jurisdic-
ns, without any trouble or impediment, but rather with
manner of favour, aid, and assistance, and thus fulfil our
cial pleasure.

Given at the Hague, the 2nd of March, 1666.

" D'ESTRADES."*

At the same time, Sidney, Say, Colonel Bisco, and several
ers besides, proscribed regicides, or Republicans in volun-
y exile, wrote to Ludlow, some from Frankfort, others
m Amsterdam, entreating him to come to Holland and
them in their patriotic enterprise, and assuring him that
cess was certain, since they were supported by such power-
sovereigns.

Ludlow at first refused. Passion admonished him as well
wisdom. He distrusted Holland since it had delivered up
Charles II. two of the judges of Charles I.; he detested
uis XIV., and could not believe that any trustworthy sup-
rt would be given by him in aid of Republicans. He con-
ed to his friends these misgivings, but they were unmoved.
yet hesitated, and events soon showed that his refusal
d not been unreasonable. The negotiations entered into
st between France and England, then between England
d Holland, and, in 1667, the peace of Breda, put an end to
y hopes which the English Republicans might entertain of
sistance from foreign rulers.

Louis XIV., even during the war, had always retained
wer over Charles II., whose most precious secrets were
own to him, and he never intended to give any serious
pport to Sidney and his friends. The Count d'Estrades

* Ludlow's Memoirs, p. 412.

E 2

was even blamed, for a moment, for his eagerness in doing what John de Witt had requested from him. "We shall endeavour," writes M. de Lionne to him on the 2nd of April 1666, "to regain here the passports which you have given to Messrs. Sidney and Ludlow. At all events, it is not the same thing that they should have been forwarded by a minister believing that he would thus serve his master better and that they should have had them from his Majesty himself."*

At the latter part of this period Ludlow lived at Vevey obscure but not tranquil, forgotten by nearly all except the assassins who were lying in wait for him, earnestly endeavouring to defend his life against the poniards of his enemies and, we must confess it, against the anathemas of the greater part of his fellow-citizens,—a situation the more deplorable in that his mind could not discover any legitimate ground for it, and because all the want of success that befel his party all the misfortunes of his own lot, were, in his eyes, nothing but an unreasonable and inexplicable iniquity.

The composition of his Memoirs was, doubtless, a source of consolation and hope for him at this period. He took pleasure in retracing the past, the time of his youth, strength and glory, and in promising for himself justice from the future. Nevertheless there is ground to believe that he ended with despairing both of his work and of himself, for his Memoirs were closed in 1668, and during the twenty years he afterwards spent at Vevey, he did not take the trouble to continue the narrative of his monotonous existence.†

The revolution of 1688 came by surprise on Ludlow, and showed him that his country had not renounced the intention of being free, that its ancient enemies were vanquished and driven out. The old man did not doubt that the ideas of his youth were now again to be appreciated, and that the actions of his life would at length be treated with that justice which had been so long denied them. He left Vevey and returned to England: at the age of sixty-nine, after twenty-nine years of exile, he offered himself to fight again in Ireland with "the tyrant," as he said, "who has abdicated." Meanwhile, until they should accept his services, he walked about the streets of London, with a joy mingled with anger, delighted once more to behold the good people of England, and to show himself to them as one of their ancient de-

* Archives du département des affaires étrangères.
† See Note at p. 58.

ders. On the 7th of November, 1689, Sir Edward Sey-
ur, one of the leaders of that patriotic party which had
; expelled James II., presented to King William an ad-
ss from the House of Commons, entreating him to cause
onel Ludlow to be arrested as one of the murderers of
arles I.*

Sad and inexplicable disappointment! The old man took
flight, and hid himself on the sea-shore, as he had before
l and hid himself thirty years previously, to escape from
: restored monarch Charles II. He waited with anxiety
a favourable wind should once more transport him—always
scribed—far from his country, which had become free
iin. He arrived at Vevey, humbled, shattered, unable to
nprehend, and still less able to endure this new turn of
tune, and died four years afterwards, in 1693, with no
ier consolation than the esteem of some foreigners, who
d him buried in their church, and the affection of his wife,
io raised a small monument to his memory.†

How are we to account for this sad destiny? Was it then

* Biographia Britannica, article " Ludlow," vol. v., p. 3032.
† This monument still remains in the church of St. Martin, at Vevey. A Latin
cription is engraved upon it, which records the principal events of Ludlow's life,
: offices which he filled, and the constant affection of his widow, Elizabeth Olds-
rth. Another inscription had been placed, at Vevey, over the door of the house
which Ludlow lived. It is as follows: " Omne solum forti patria, quia patris:"
Every soil is a country for the brave, because it is the soil of his father." This
cription was purchased, eighteen years ago, by an Englishman, who caused it
be removed. We are not aware whether he was prompted to this by enthusiasm
by indignation.

The following is the translation of the Latin inscription on Ludlow's monu-
nt:—" Stop and consider. Here rests Edmund Ludlow, an Englishman,
the county of Wiltshire; son of Henry Ludlow, knight, and member of Par-
ment, as he was also himself; he was honourable by his birth, but still
ore so by his virtue; in religion a Protestant, and of eminent piety. In the
enty-third year of his age he was made colonel of a regiment, and soon after
utenant-general of the army. In this post he helped to subdue Ireland. He
as intrepid, and regardless of life in battle; clement and humane in victory; the
fender of his country's freedom, and the firm opponent of absolute power.
anished on this account from his native country, though worthy of a better lot,
: took refuge in Switzerland for thirty-two years, and died in the sixty-third year
his age, regretted by his friends, but gaining a dwelling amidst eternal joys.
" His beloved, courageous, and bereaved companion in misfortune, as in marriage,
lizabeth, prompted by her devotedness, and the strength of conjugal affection,
llowed him in his exile until his death, and has caused this monument to be
used, to retain in perpetual remembrance her true and sincere affection for her
eceased husband, in the year of our Lord 1693."—(Biographia Britannica, vol. v.,
. 3033.)

What is most remarkable in this inscription, is the absolute silence it maintains
ith reference to the trial and condemnation of Charles I., whose name is not even
entioned.

without reason—without justice; was it onl
hibit, as Ludlow must have thought, a new i
ingratitude of peoples: one of those severe s
which man knows not how to explain? I ci

When the Parliament of 1640 opened, the
reform was general in England. The me
progress produced by the religious reforn
desire a moral necessity; the absurd and ui
of Charles I. made it a practical necessity.
of national thought and the safety of ini
required that this end should be attained.
cipitated itself, without forethought, into
promised to conduct it thither.

But if, in the midst of this first spring o
future which was awaiting it could have beer
to this generation as it was buoyed up witl
had been able to see itself tormented, oppi
by its chiefs as well as by its enemies, the s
the personal interest of factions, as it had be
of the court; if it could have anticipated all
crimes which it would have to undergo, in oi
ing generations might enjoy a day of better
we believe that it would have entered upo
with so much gaiety—can we even think it
sented to enter upon it at all?

Happily for the moral dignity and progri
race, Providence does not entrust in this
generation the knowledge of, and control
which belongs also to others: when it desigi
one of those convulsions by which society ci
and commences a new era, it avails itseli
daring of men in order to spur them onwai
movement. But who can doubt that they w
such an advance if they foreknew all the n
that must attend it? Who can imagine t
English people would have consented to t
condemnation of Charles I., the anarchy of i
tyranny of Cromwell, and the corruption of th
the price with which it was to purchase, in 16
and the Bill of Rights? Assuredly Englan
tionary enthusiasm, did not anticipate any o

When such crises as these break out, men
found who not only do not foresee more

lic the terrible consequences which will follow, but who
so constituted that, when these results appear, they will
see them or accept them as perfectly legitimate. These
ı—and I now speak only of those who are sincere and dis-
·rested—are called to present a singular spectacle and
·er a strange destiny. They have proclaimed more con-
·ntly, more unreservedly than any others, the principles ot
)rm ; while, in fact, none forget and violate those principles
re than themselves. They are, more than any others,
·ently bent upon that general welfare which is the end
·ich reform proposes for itself; and, in their efforts to at-
·a it, they completely lose sight of it. The country stirs
·elf without foreseeing what will happen; they do more, they
·ance onwards without ever seeing what has already hap-
·ıed. Their actions belie their principles, and events con-
·dict their hopes ; they care not, they accept everything,
·lividual crimes, public calamities ; they call them necessi-
·s, and firmly believe that the country ought to receive them
·such. It cannot be so ; their blindness outlasts and sur-
·es the recklessness of the people ; as they are gradually
·saken they become successively a party, a faction, a coterie ;
·ll they are unconcerned ; at first they refuse to believe in
·eir isolation, and, when they believe it, they will not under-
·ınd it ; they have sacrificed all, even their fellow-country-
·en, and their own principles to the necessity of success ;
·ccess also forsakes them, they are yet unenlightened as to
·eir moral discredit and reverses.

·Such were, in the English revolution, almost all the honest
·aders of the Republican party ; such, among others, was
·dmund Ludlow. He was one of those limited and unbend-
·g spirits who are unable to admit more than one ruling
·ea ; and who, when they have received this idea, are pos-
··ssed by it, and allow it first to rule their conscience and
·ıen to acquire the undisputed sway of their whole being.
·o destroy the king and found the Republic, this was, I re-
·eat, the fixed idea that governed his life. The despotism of
·ıe Long Parliament, first over the king's party, then over
·ıe nation when it desired to come to terms with the king ;
·ıe despotism of the army over the Long Parliament, when
·ıis in its turn was desirous of peace ; lastly, the despotism
·f the Rump over the army and nation when, after the death
·f Cromwell, all England demanded a full and free Parliament,
·hich could not fail to recal Charles II. ; all these violent

and conflicting powers appeared to Ludlow just and neces
sary, because he expected they would issue, first in the down
fal of Charles I., then in the success of the Republican go
vernment. To this name alone he successively surrendered
the laws, liberties, and happiness of his contemporaries, and
remained firmly convinced that the perfidy, first of the king,
then of the Parliament, then of the army, then of Cromwell
and finally of Monk, had alone made him and his faithful
friends miscarry in their patriotic designs.

Ludlow was mistaken : the Republican party had brought
its misfortunes entirely upon itself, by its own errors, its own
unreasonableness, its own iniquities, and the evils which itself
had caused to the country. It had aimed at imposing the
Republic on England as Charles I. had aimed at imposing
absolute power ; it had not taken into consideration either
existing interests, national feelings, the immediate results of
its enterprise, or the justice of the means it adopted. It
had obstinately shut its eyes to the rights which it violated,
the resistance which it encountered, the reverses which it experienced, and to its own corruption, which soon came, and
ended by bringing pretended Republicans into contempt, then
over, into ridicule. Blinded by his infatuation, Ludlow, as long
as he remained in active life, saw nothing of all this ; when he
wrote his Memoirs in the seclusion of his retreat, his infatuation was the same ; in reviewing the past he perceived in it
nothing which he could not have observed while mingling in
its scenes, and his recollections were as confined as had been
his judgment while the events were actually occurring around
him.   But England had seen and judged all ; the antipathy
and scorn which, in 1688, it again felt for the Stuarts, had
not served to excuse, in public opinion, the former revolutionary factions ; and when, at that period, Ludlow returned
to his country, he did not find there any of the old prejudices
which he took back with him ; he was only recognised as one
of the abettors of the absurd tyranny of the Rump, and one
of the judges of Charles I. These were not the colours around
which England was then rallying, and which were to be the
heralds of the new revolution.

If Ludlow had known himself better, if he had been able to
analyse with impartiality what was passing in his own mind
when, proscribed and solitary, he was writing his Memoirs,
he might have foreseen his unhappy disappointment. In vain
is it that men mistake and elude the truth ; it acts upon them

ile they fail to recognise it; it appears even in the efforts
ich they make to keep it from their sight, and the blind-
ss of the most obstinate is never exempt from a kind of be-
derment which betrays a secret apprehension of blame and
or. Nothing could avail to enlighten Ludlow as to the
ilts of his party; he did not disapprove in his conscience,
disavow by his words, any of the acts to which it had given
concurrence. Nevertheless, we have only to read his
emoirs in order to be convinced that the remembrance of
ese acts, especially the condemnation of Charles I., was a
urce of regret and disquietude to him. He has defended,
d wished to justify his conduct, but he constantly felt the
sence of more solid grounds of justification. This is the
ought from which all else in his Memoirs proceeded, and to
nich all is related; we are conscious that it pursues and
noys him; in spite of his patriotic disinterestedness he is
pressed by a peculiar position, in which he was especially
volved; while he relates how the liberty of his country has
en wrested from it, he is continually engaged in his own
fence. This accounts for so many facts being unfaithfully
presented, so much omission and reserve which it is difficult
t to believe to be half-intended. Not only did not Ludlow
e, in events, all that he might have seen, but he did not tell
l that he had actually seen; he did not dare to relate in de-
il the death of the king, nor the resistance of the Presby-
rian party in Parliament to the tyranny of the army, nor
number of the acts of the Republican party which his own
rinciples condemned. He finds it necessary to dissimulate,
omit, or to pass rapidly over various circumstances, which
ere, nevertheless, weighty and important. In one word, his
ind is naturally limited and obtuse, and even in its own
here it is not free; blinded as he is, he is constrained to
fuse admittance to the few rays of light which he cannot
it see.

I have now said with reference to Ludlow all that I think;
have shown in him an example, among others, of the de-
orable consequences of that spirit of faction, and that pas-
onate adherence to one fixed idea which, in advancing to its
al, has regard neither to the laws of morality nor to the
ssons of experience. His was a sad lot; we cannot say
iat it was an unjust one; nevertheless he had a certain right
regard it as such, since he had been ever sincere. A friend
truth, and desirous of the general welfare of the commu-

nity, his actions were disinterested, and he steadily followed
his convictions, while but little enlightened as to what was
passing around him, and incapable of comprehending events
and men, he had impulses to justice and liberty often superior
to the enlightenment of his age. Easily beguiled by his
hopes, he remained constantly inaccessible to fear; if the
extent of his attachment to his party was blameable, Cromwell was never able to intimidate or corrupt him. He learnt
nothing by experience; but he was not overcome by it. As
a Republican he entered Parliament, and he died a Republican on the borders of the Lake of Geneva. In his judgment we can find little to esteem, and in his life there is
much which we must blame; but his name deserves our
respect; and among those of his time who judged it with
rigour, certainly the greater part had no proper appreciation
of him.*

THOMAS MAY.

[1595—1656.]

ENGLAND has enjoyed its season of national gaiety and
pleasure. This was during the reign of Elizabeth, when
religious excitement, occasioned by fear of foreign invasion,
arose in the very midst of the English Reformation. The
condition of the people was still one of difficulty and agitation—liberty was far from complete, public prospects were
uncertain; nevertheless the country was free from civil war,
and seemed to be preparing itself for approaching prosperity.
The government possessed the confidence of the nation : the
queen, though often tyrannical, was popular and respected.
In a time of such tranquillity there was no lack either of
employment or of recreation. With the exception of the
Puritans, then a small and obscure sect, the minds of the
people, although active, were not absorbed by any one passion, nor committed to any regular system. They gave a
ready reception to ideas and adventures, from whatever source
they might be derived. In the pursuit of fame, wealth, or

* The Memoirs of Ludlow were first published at Vevey in 1698, in two
volumes 8vo. A third volume appeared, also at Vevey, in 1699; and, in the
same year, a French translation of the first two volumes was published at Amsterdam. The original text was reprinted in England, in 1751, in one volume folio,
and has, since that time, passed through several editions.

asure, no expense was spared, no difficulty seemed insur-
untable. At court and among the people, alike in the
tages of the poor and the mansions of the rich, there was
fused a general taste for society, whether festive or serious;
peasant had his rustic, the noble his sumptuous, festivals.
uxury with the great was gay, though pompous; the poor
o found their circumstances no hindrance to mirth. In
ndon, both the higher and lower orders flocked to the
eatres to witness the performance of Shakspeare's dramas;
the country, they listened to the strains of wandering min-
rels. Banquets and games almost daily relieved the mono-
ny of labour and the constraint of religious solemnities. It
as a time of great moral and political turmoil, but of free
d happy movement, in which all seemed young and fresh;—
time at once peaceable and threatening, when society, as
it exacting little, was nevertheless full of ambition, curiosity,
id hope.

When Charles I. ascended the throne the stream of pro-
ess had increased, and England was much changed. The
ligious spirit had extended itself, and had become excited
id gloomy. The spirit of liberty, gathering intelligence
id vigour, sought to express itself, and spoke loudly of its
ghts and expectations. In the place of that unsettled and
to speak, floating activity, ready to recognise, and even to
rve, without any consideration of payment, a glorious and
rmidable national power, there arose on all sides determi-
ate ideas, ardent passions, undeveloped factions, a tendency
b scorn and oppose King James and his ignoble government.
n proportion as the country had become exacting in its re-
uirements, and severe in its habits, power had become arro-
ant in its pretensions, and dissipated in its morals; and the
ourt pageantry which, under Elizabeth, had so greatly ex-
ited popular curiosity and admiration, was, under her suc-
essor, an object only of reprehension and disgust.

Charles I. invested royalty and its adjuncts with an im-
osing exterior. His character was dignified, his manners
rave, and his morals pure. But things remained, in all
ssential respects, the same. The court, always brilliant, be-
ame more and more estranged from the country. The
aughty nobility, indolent and impoverished, thronged round
he prince, seeking only advancement and pleasure. The
ing's favourite, the Duke of Buckingham—an arrogant,
aughty, pompous, frivolous man—trafficked with the power

and wealth of office, as if they were only va
of purchasing the subserviency of his creat
ing his individual caprices. The queen, He
sirous of preserving unaltered the habits i
been nurtured, busied herself in the endea
at Whitehall the customs, pastimes, and id
of France ; considering absolute power ne
dignity, and Catholicism the only religion b
Poets, literary men, and wits, frequented tl
of opportunities of display for their talen
their vanity, and pensions for their po\
cuse may be found for these than for otl
the tastes and pleasures of intellect creat
and gentle fascination, which severs the
from the citizen, and fills his fancy with v
cupations alone which charm, and those pro
encourage. In the midst of spectacles, ele{
festivities, masquerades in which all the co
mated and brilliant clubs, where the succes{
met, and where Ben Jonson still presided,
the ship-money, the controversies of the Pi
bishop Laud, and the just though gloomy
the country.

There was a young man who, at this {
the court and the literary gatherings of tl
der resources and retiring disposition, al
with an impediment in his speech, which c
conversation, he was yet animated, accomp
pride but considerable susceptibility, and 1
stores of his mind and the generosity of his
mote the interests of his friends. Thomas
Sussex, in the year 1595, of an ancient and I
His early prospects of wealth were disapp{
of his father, who could bestow upon his
heritance than a liberal education, and the
his way by the assistance of that classic l
cultivated at the University of Cambridge
success. On leaving college, towards the
of James I., he came to London, and join
congenial literary circle of those who we1
drama, to books, and to such diversions as
cealed the threatening approach of serious
ing liberty and the stern experiences of civ

Five dramatic compositions, which were favourably re-
ved,* a translation into verse of the Georgics and some of
artial's Epigrams, two historical poems—one relating to
e reign of Henry II.,† the other to that of Edward III.‡—
itly, a translation of Lucan's Pharsalia, and the continua-
bn of that poem, in Latin and English, up to the death of
esar, soon procured for him a brilliant reputation.
None of these works displayed great or original talent;
ne addressed themselves to the general public, or were
ely to secure popularity. But they were acceptable to
e literary world, which delights, while enjoying its own
easures, to contemplate also its privileges; and to the
urt, which prides itself on according a willing admiration
those who amuse it. May's last work, the "Pharsalia,"
as regarded as a masterpiece, and it is still received with
vour. In reading it, we are struck with the intimate ac-
aintance with the sentiments and manners of ancient
ome which it displays, and with the rare felicity of its
yle. Charles I. treated May with distinction; frequently
lled him his poet; and it was at the king's request that he
mposed his two poems on the reigns of Henry II. and Ed-
ard III.

At this time Charles I. was oppressing his subjects, and
elings of distrust and anger had begun to brood in their
inds. But neither the king nor the poet had then the
ast suspicion of the alteration that was soon to occur in
eir sentiments towards each other, when the king would
ke up arms against his subjects, and the poet would enlist
the service of the enemies of his former patron.

Nevertheless, the relationship between men of letters and
heir superiors in station was not entirely of a pleasurable
haracter, as May soon learnt by sad experience. The students
f the Temple and their jovial associates, on one occasion,
xhibited before the court one of the masquerades then in
ogue. "They were," says an eye-witness, "well used at
ourt by the king and queen; no disgust given them, only
his one accident fell: Mr. May of Gray's Inn, a fine poet,

* These five pieces are: "The Heir," a comedy, performed in 1620; "Cleo-
atra," a tragedy, 1626; "Agrippina," a tragedy, 1628; "Antigone," a tragedy,
631; and "The Old Couple," a comedy. None of these remain on the stage.
† "The reign of King Henry the Second, written in seven books, by his Ma-
ssty's command." 1633.
‡ "The victorious reign of Edward the Third, in seven books, by his Majesty's

he who translated *Lucan*, came athwart my lord chamberlain in the banqueting-house, and he broke his staff over his shoulders, not knowing who he was; the king present, who knew him, for he called him 'his poet,' told the chamberlain of it, who sent for him the next morning, and fairly excused himself to him, and gave him fifty pounds in pieces. I believe he was the more indulgent for his name-sake."*

We find here a remarkable illustration of the coarseness of the manners then allowed at court, and of the humiliating position it assigned to literary men, whom it yet carefully sought after, and who were the chief ministers to its gratification.

A circumstance, if not more offensive, yet more serious soon after occurred, which altered the position of May, and gave a new direction both to his opinions and to his works. In 1637, Ben Jonson having died, the title and emoluments of poet-laureate, which had belonged to him, became vacant. May desired and solicited for the appointment, but a more fortunate candidate, Sir William Davenant, obtained it. Whether May had already formed connexions with the adversaries of the court, by which he had forfeited the royal favour, does not appear ; it would be better for his reputation if this had been the case, but there is nothing to indicate that it was. Royalist writers attribute his desertion of their cause to the vexation which he experienced on this defeat. "Since his fortune," says Clarendon, "could not raise his mind, he brought his mind down to his fortune."† May could be satisfied with a court life only as it procured him success and advancement ; the court had offended his pride and injured his fortune ; accordingly the poet, filled with mortification and disgust, suddenly changed his party and sought patronage elsewhere.

It was not by his verses that May could find acceptance with the Long Parliament ; the Presbyterian party expected other service from him than the composition of odes and tragedies. What offices were entrusted to him, and what recompense he received, is not known. We only find that he took the title of Clerk of the Parliament, that he was attached to Fairfax, and frequently took up military quarters during the civil war. There is no reason for believing that he ever

---

* See a letter of the 27th of February, 1634, addressed to the Earl of Strafford, then Lord-Lieutenant of Ireland.—(Biographia Britannica, art. May, vol. v., p. 3067, note E.)

† Life of Clarendon, vol. i., p. 39. Oxford ed.

inent part in political transactions. The
t him for the same reason that Charles had,
talent and literary renown, and accordingly
) struggle of political passions as he had in
the court. At the request of Charles I. he
)ems; at the request of the Commons, or
its political leaders, he wrote the history of
ime under his observation, and developed
ignificance. His " History of the Parlia-
in May, 1647, while the king was in cap-
) books of it which he published proceeded
le of Newbury, fought on the 23rd of Sep-

e more adventurous than to write the his-
ile they are actually transpiring; and, above
in the camp of one of the opposing parties,
important revolution, which every year, or
inth, appears under different leaders, and is
ierent principles, aims, and professions. It
i pamphlet, devoted to the consideration of.
f one circumstance which May had to com-
pen chronicles intended for publication after
ch he could record, with or without impar-
erfect freedom, whatever he had seen, heard,
) had an immediate end prescribed for him,
is he might not and would not bring into
ad long passed since the Parliament met
idence of the entire nation. Even the most
in can never perform all the promises which
intemporaries, and must inevitably produce
it could not anticipate. England became
issatisfied with its new masters. Oppressed
m, distracted by their factions, desolated by
n to reproach the dominant party for hav-
hort-comings, caused the evils under which
groaning. The Parliament had to struggle
, attempting at once to justify what it had
it its own course when the impetus urging it
me irresistible. It was, we cannot doubt,
ind imperious emergency that May under-
" Perchance," he himself says, in the preface,
iay be put in mind of their own thoughts
i thoughts have since, like Nebuchadnezzar's

dream, departed from them. An English gentleman, who went to travel when this Parliament was called, and returned when these differences were grown among us, hearing what discourses were daily made, affirmed that the Parliament of England, in his opinion, was more misunderstood in England than at Rome; and that there was greater need to remember our own countrymen, than to inform strangers of what was past; so much, said he, have they seemed to forget the things themselves, and their own notions concerning them."

Such being the disposition of the people, a treatise which should present itself as apologetic might expect instant condemnation; it was necessary that a work of a more grave and calm bearing, written as if addressed only to posterity, should bring back fresh to the minds of the people the corrupt state of Charles's government before the assembling of the Long Parliament, and should exhibit the conduct of the House since that time as uniformly patriotic, as dictated by a necessity imposed upon it solely by the evil practices of the king and by his obstinate refusal of the only guarantees which could secure permanence for their liberty. It was required that, in such a work, the passions of the Parliamentary party, its intrigues, its illegal practices, the personal aims of its chiefs, whatever had tended to reflect a slight on the power residing in the popular will, should be absolutely omitted and ignored, as if nothing of the kind had influenced the course of events; as if all the transactions of the House, and the consequences flowing from them, were traceable solely to the malicious designs of their adversaries and the necessities of their position. Such is the true character of May's "History of the Long Parliament," a work at once official and literary, written by a man naturally moderate, and careful to preserve, in the tone of his work at least, that impartiality which the mission of the historian seemed to him to demand, but engaged in the service of a power embarrassed by its own existence, regarded with coldness by the public, and which, feeling itself unsustained by any popular enthusiasm, wished at least to show that it had only acted from necessity and duty.

While with these intentions May was composing and publishing his book, a new power arose, less scrupulous, more energetic, more aggressive; this was the Republican party and the army. That which had sufficed as an apology for the Presbyterians would not satisfy Cromwell and the Independents. May abandoned his history. How, indeed, could

have continued it? In passing on to the next chapter he
uld have been compelled to change his principles and his
oes, abjure the Earl of Essex, Hollis, and all the claims of
eration in its treatment of the king which he had made
behalf of the Parliament. The transition would have been
abrupt, and the contrast too palpable. May probably
ceived this, for he ceased to write for some time. 1 find
n, in Whitelocke's "Memorials," a fact stated which seems
ndicate that he allowed a disposition very much like oppo-
on to manifest itself against Cromwell and the Inde-
dents. Whitelocke, under date of February 5, 1650,
tes, "that one Mr. Thomas May was secured by the gover-
there (at Weymouth), and to be sent up in custody to
ndon, for raising false rumours concerning the Parliament
d the general."* May attempted, doubtless verbally, to
end his Presbyterian patrons; but Cromwell was as skilful
winning over his adversaries, as he was vigorous in crushing
m. There is no indication of what became of May after he
d been conveyed in custody to London, nor what was the
ure of the relationship established between him and the
ublican general. Only we find him again at liberty
wards the close of the year 1650, and publishing first in
tin, then in English, a "Breviary of the History of the Par-
ment of England; expressed in three Parts: 1. The Causes
d Beginnings of the Civil War of England; 2. A short
ntion of the Progress of the Civil War; 3. A compendious
ation of the Original and Progress of the Second Civil War."
this new work the revolution was entirely retraced up to
e trial of Charles, and matters were placed in such a light
would be most agreeable to Cromwell, and to the party
ich Cromwell was endeavouring to corrupt, and which he
eanwhile deceived.

Whoever, after having witnessed a revolution, will take the
ouble of comparing the two works of Thomas May, will be
ruck with the great difference between them. There is no
oss and palpable contradiction; the historian, deficient
either in moderation nor in the art of presenting facts so as
serve the end he had in view, has yet been careful to pre-
rve the appearance of impartiality. But the circumstances
his position determine his conclusions, and show themselves
the incidental reflections, the groundless insinuations, the

* Whitelocke's Memorials of English Affairs. 1684. Folio, p. 440.

F

general colouring, which characterise his narrative. In 164h
the cause of the king did not seem utterly lost; that of the
Parliament was still merely an opposition fundamentally leg|
timate, though already sustained by much fraud and iniqui|
Most good citizens still hoped for peace, and the revolutic|
was desirous merely of justifying itself for not having befo|
concluded it. It had not been able to do this, although |
had constantly desired it, and this is what May had unde|
taken to prove for the Parliament; he had addressed himsel|
chiefly to that enlightened and moderate portion of the publ|
from whom the Parliament had received, in 1640, its force an|
impulse. In 1650, on the other hand, the revolution had push|
its violence to the last extreme; the final, irrevocable act la
been consummated, to the great dissatisfaction of the city o|
London, of a large number of the country gentlemen, and o|
honest townsmen who were but a short time before activel|
engaged in promoting the Parliamentary cause. The Inde|
pendents, who were now the sole rulers, neither attempte|
nor wished to rally these classes; it was to the lower order|
that they looked for support, and even among them thei|
credit began to wane. The king became popular as soon a|
he died, and the restoration of those Presbyterian member|
who had been excluded from the Parliament was constantl|
demanded by enraged mobs. Now, therefore, was it neces|
sary to address the inferior classes, and to revive in them|
those interests and prejudices which might serve the revolu
tion, by reaffirming old suspicions and distrust, and exhibiting
as alone faithful to the national cause, those men who ha|
either urged on or followed the revolution to its extrem|
limit, whatever might be the real wish or ultimate fate of th|
country.

It was with this design that May, with prudent conformity
to circumstances, instead of continuing his history wrote hi|
breviary, in which the narrative is recast and completed
His tone is bitter and sarcastic, not only towards the king
and the Royalists, but towards all parties, all sections, all individuals, who believed that the revolution should have been
arrested in its course. Different opinions are no longer, as
in the former work, presented with that apparent impartiality
which seems to leave the verdict concerning them to be pronounced by the reader. The author limits himself to the
relation of such facts as reflect favourably on the revolution

its last stage, introducing, wherever an opportunity is pre-
nted, reflections and insinuations most calculated to bring
to odium or suspicion, in the eyes of the people, every
nion, and all conduct, except that of Cromwell and his ad-
rents.

But in imposing upon himself this task, the historian
d undertaken more than his personal feelings, and perps, also, those of the public, would allow him to exe-
te. Presbyterian in his opinions and moderate in his
aracter, May felt himself obliged to halt in the new course
had undertaken. After having written so as to serve the
terests of Cromwell and the Independents, the history of
e civil war, and of the internal dissensions of the Parlia-
nt, after having palliated the despotism of the army and
e violent expulsions from the House of Commons, he did
t dare to relate, as without doubt his patrons wished, the
ial and death of Charles I. The "Breviary" finishes abruptly
the brink of this terrible fact, which, says the author,
would make a history by itself." It is something that party
irit and subservience to authority should recognise some
nit, whatever it be.

May did not long survive the publication of his last work.
n the 13th of November, 1650, after having, say his bio-
raphers, gaily quaffed his accustomed bottle of wine, he re-
red to rest without displaying any symptom of disease, and
e next morning was found dead in his bed. His literary
nown was great; he had served well the sect which then
resided alone in the House of Commons; they granted him
stately funeral and a tomb in Westminster Abbey, where a
monument in white marble, adorned with a long inscription,
as erected to his memory. Ten years after, Charles II. had
scended the throne, and political reactions, like revolutions,
id not respect even the resting-places of the dead; on the
2th and 14th of September, 1661, the bodies of Admiral
Blake, of Pym, of the mother of Cromwell, of his daughter,
Lady Claypole, and of Thomas May, were exhumed from
Westminster and removed pell-mell, says a Puritan historian,*
to the burying-ground of St. Margaret's Church, and, as long
as the Stuarts reigned, the memory and the writings of the
poet-historian were treated with as little consideration as his
mortal remains.

* Neal's History of the Puritans, vol. iv., pp. 317-318.

I will not use the language of Clarendon, who, leagued with May at first, afterwards accused him of " prostituting himself to the vile office of celebrating the infamous acts of those who were in rebellion against the king; which he did so meanly that he seemed to all men to have lost his wits when he left his honesty."* A more impartial writer than Clarendon, who, under Charles I., had sympathised with the Reformers, but who, after the Restoration, almost always sided with the Opposition, and whom Charles II. several times ineffectually attempted to seduce—Andrew Marvell—has written a short poem against May, in which he reproaches " his mercenary pen," ridicules the truckling subservience which led him to speak of one man of his party as " a Cato," of another as " a Cicero," and maintains that the errors of his history have originated, " not by ignorance, or seeming good, but malice."

A century had not passed away before Lord Chatham,† the father of Mr. Pitt, and himself one of the greatest states-men who ever ruled England, writing to his nephew, Lord Camelford, then studying at the University of Cambridge, uses the following language :‡

" I desired you some time since to read ' Lord Clarendon's History of the Civil Wars.' I have lately read a much honester and more instructive book, of the same period of history: it is the History of the Parliament, by Thomas May, Esq."

About the same time,§ the learned and ingenious Bishop Warburton writes thus to Dr. Hurd: " ' May's History of Parliament ' is a just composition, according to the rules of history. It is written with much judgment, penetration, manliness, and spirit; and with a candour that will greatly increase your esteem, when you understand that he wrote by order of his masters, the Parliament."

Thus, the man whom, a little after his death, a patriotic Independent charged with venality and perfidy, was con-sidered eighty years later, and perhaps is still considered by modern patriots, as the most impartial and faithful narrator of that great crisis to which England owes its liberties.

Neither the predilections of party, nor the fickleness of

---

* Memoirs of the Private Life of Clarendon, vol. i., p. 40. Oxford, 1827.
† Biographia Britannica, article "May," vol. v., p. 3070. Edition of 1760.
    ‡ September 5th, 1754.   § August 16th, 1753.

man judgments, will suffice to explain these differences of
nion; they must be traced to more general causes. The
imate of that revolution which Thomas May has related
s changed as well as the repute of his book; and it is be-
se the events themselves present a different aspect that
historian is judged so differently.

May has in his "History," if not in his "Breviary," seized
on those truths, the recollection of which is still cherished,
d which alone, after the lapse of a hundred and fifty years,
n retain their importance in the eyes of Englishmen.
ents do not present themselves in their completeness, nor
their full realisation, to the eyes of those living subse-
ently to the epoch in which they occurred. Men of an after
e look for and regard that only which still interests them-
lves, whatever has influenced their own destiny, whatever
rresponds to their particular impressions, notions, and wants.
ne Long Parliament, and all the parties which it engen-
red, notwithstanding the original justice of their cause, be-
me violent, deceitful, unjust, tyrannical; England suffered
ring its continuance all the evils of civil war and sectarian
le; these sufferings were followed by reactions, which in
eir turn produced new reactions; for fifty years public con-
lence and hope passed alternately from kings to parliaments,
d from parliaments to kings, wandering from one name to
other; from system to system, from power to power, find-
g nowhere any settlement or repose. All this is now past
d forgotten, and all that remains of the Revolution of 1640,
the general principles which it proclaimed, and the salutary
sults which it secured for the country; these are the asso-
ations that win for it the continued attachment and remem-
ance of the English people; no one now cares to weigh
rupulously the merits of particular acts, nor to ascertain
hat deductions are to be made for individual sins. We do
t expect that a reader of the history of that period should
mpathise with all the impressions which were natural to a
ntemporary, and kindle into anger at the mention of wrongs
d iniquities which he has neither seen nor suffered. Each
ge has its own destiny and its own life; only that can affect
vividly of which it bears the pain or gathers the fruit; and
ut few men possess that judicial firmness and disinterested-
ess which will move them to disentangle the entire truth out
f facts which do not press upon themselves. Here, then, we

see why it is that Thomas May is held in such high esteem
by English patriots; he has presented the revolution as it
appears in fact to them, showing its aims and real causes.
What he has said of it—the value which he attributes to it—
is just that which remains now, and still answers to the ideas
and sentiments of his modern readers.   What he has mis-
represented, or omitted, is that which no personal feelings
will lead them to inquire into, and no consideration prompts
them to make a rigorous investigation.   There are truths
which die with the age that witnessed them, and the world
would become too wise if it had collected, without any dimi-
nution, all those verities which have come to light since men
and events have existed.

I do not, therefore, wonder that the Whigs of our own
day should be so little struck with the adroit partiality which
characterises the writings of Thomas May, and eulogise him
as a "candid and upright" historian.   It is even honourable
to his intellect, if not to his character, that, writing the history of events which were passing under his eye, he has
exhibited an impartiality that belongs to posterity.   In no
case, has he done violent outrage to truth; he has apologised
for no crime, nor for any great disorder; he has not wantonly
insulted his adversaries.   Omission, palliation, dissimulation,
is his method and aim; his reason never allows him to attempt
more; and if, in his "Breviary," he is more completely chained
to a violent faction, I am constrained to believe that it was
not without perplexity nor without regret.

Nevertheless, thus much having been said, and this allowance having been made in accommodation to the egoism of
men and of ages—an allowance which it were unreasonable
to refuse—the higher tribunal of truth and justice remains,
to which we must finally refer—justice, which in the rigour
of its verdict has no respect for persons; truth, knowing
neither compromise nor limitation.   This is at once the prerogative and the duty of history; only thus can it acquire a
moral element.   It may hear, understand, and explain all—
the empire of circumstance and of passion, the rival claims of
conflicting interests, the success or failure of political combinations, and that irresistible current of events which urges
men along its course, and exerts so mighty an influence on
their conduct and destiny.   But history, which must traverse
all these paths, must not stop in any—it has a goal to which it

st direct itself. It must determine and judge. In the
ons and events which it relates there is good and evil,
ice and injustice, wisdom and folly. They have a meaning
. a worth; they are either consonant with, or contrary to,
universal order of things, and the eternal laws of the
son. In that valley of Jehoshaphat, where all must de-
nd as they quit the scene, there is a judgment which
its those who have been the actors, and, in a measure,
authors of history—a judgment supremely wise and
itable, which knows and measures all, determines the
ere of each, and the part which each shall perform—a
gment, in fine, which decides and declares, and illumines
h the torch of truth the complicated web of human action
l destiny. If history does not light this torch—if, on
iving at its goal, it has no decision to offer, no verdict to
ng, it loses its intellectual worth and its moral dignity; it
nought but a frivolous display of empty trifling.
At the same time it loses its practical importance. History
l offer to us serious lessons only in so far as it determines
d judges. If it merely aims to bring before our eyes the
ectacle of human activity without disclosing its meaning
d results, it may indeed pretend to amuse us, but it is no
ger the lamp of experience guiding our steps onwards into
e future by a light reflected from the past.
But to accomplish so lofty an end, to become at once
oral and instructive, the virtue of sincerity is pre-eminently
cessary. When the lives and liberties of our fellow-men
e concerned, the law justly requires a scrupulous exactness
the collection of facts, and in securing at every step of the
ocess publicity and certainty. And history is the tribunal
which the honour and the moral life of men are brought
receive a lasting sentence: its aim is to teach; its voice
ronounces a verdict. Conscientiousness, impartiality, per-
ct ingenuousness, and publicity, are here sacred duties;—
much the more sacred, inasmuch as history speaks of
ose who are departed, and addresses itself to the public,
hich is more easily duped.
When our civilisation shall have become more diffused and
levated, that public which must finally test those who serve
, which guides and gives morality to the time, will, I doubt
ot, show itself especially severe and unrelenting towards
istorians. It will demand from them a due regard to the

morality of their mission, and will inflict a just reprobatio[*
on those who perpetuate through ages the illusions of a tim[*
of civil discord and faction.

Here it is that we discover the error of Thomas May an[*
his "History of the Long Parliament." We must accord t[*
his work the merit of being important and curious, as i[*
could not fail of being when we consider that it is almost a[*
official history, written as the events which it records occurre[*
under the direction of the chief actors, and with the desig[*
of keeping or regaining the attachment of the English t[*
that cause which was, on the whole, the cause of the country[*
but it has the vices of hypocrisy and partiality—a culture[*
partiality, which veils itself under the guise of truth, an[*
avails itself, for purposes of deception, of that uninquirin[*
facility with which even earnest minds often form the[*
opinions when the full and exact knowledge of the truth i[*
no longer for them a matter of immediate and practica[*
interest.

SIR PHILIP WARWICK.
[1608—1683.]

GREAT revolutions meet with a double opposition from
enemies to their nature and their mode of development:
from those who condemn the end which they pursue, and
from those who object to the means which they employ.
They concern themselves only with the first, but the second
soon become their most formidable adversaries, and it is in
the struggle with these that they betray their weakness, until
they have learnt to purify and moderate themselves.

We should bestow too much honour on Sir Philip Warwick did we class him with those men who were opposed only
to the hypocrisy, the perfidy, the tyranny, the violence of the
Revolution of 1640. He was no stranger to the false ideas
and unworthy interests of the court of the Stuarts; he did
not disapprove of all the illegitimate pretensions of power, and
he neither liked nor did he thoroughly understand the general
principles which were urged in support of political rights and
freedom. Nevertheless, he was not one of those who were

different to the injustice of Charles's government, who
tertained no respect for the time-honoured laws and cha-
cters of their country, and who adopted the maxims of
solute power with the flippancy of courtiers who expect to
in by it. He is the type and representative of a large
ass of men, numerous at that time in England, who, with-
t occupying a prominent place in history, yet exerted a
al influence on the events of their time; men devoted with
almost superstitious regard to Charles I., yet friends to
eir country which Charles oppressed; attached to the
urt, and to the last espousing its cause, yet without having
st all reverence for established laws, all respect for public
berty, never estranged from national interests nor insensible
patriotic emotions. These men constituted the main
rength of the Stuart party in England from 1640 to 1688.
Unenlightened, yet not servile, stationary rather than biassed
y interest, they mingled confusedly the old maxims of
Magna Charta with the recent maxims of the courts of Henry
VIII. and Elizabeth; they regarded sovereignty as belong-
ng to the king alone, a sovereignty independent of the Par-
iament; and yet they considered the pretensions of a monarch
o rule without a Parliament as dangerous and illegitimate.
They repudiated the natural consequences of the Reforma-
ion, yet they detested the papacy. They fondly wished to
reconcile the royal prerogative carried out according to the
pattern of Elizabeth, and the incomplete and compromising
revolution as accomplished by Henry VIII., with the down-
al of Catholicism and the constitutional liberties handed
lown from their ancestors. Vain attempt! which led its
partisans to shake hands with despotism and imperil the
reformation, but which, by a marvel of human inconsistency,
lid not prevent them from maintaining the independence of
their character, the patriotism of their sentiments, and their
influence on the nation, with which they could not but
identify themselves.

Sir Philip Warwick was one of these men: if his obscure
political life gives but little indication of this, his writings,
and especially his "Memoirs," do not allow us to doubt it.
He was born at London in 1608, and descended from a
respectable family of the county of Cumberland. He was
brought up at Eton,—afterwards he travelled in France, and
resided some time at Geneva. On his return to England he

became private secretary to Juxon, Bishop of London, then Lord Treasurer, and obtained the office of Clerk of the Signet.* Bishop Juxon was, as Warwick says in his Memoirs, one of the most respected and learned men attached to the royal cause. As Lord Treasurer he acted with wisdom and economy, opposing to abuses the honourable though ineffectual resistance of an upright minister, who has only his own virtue to defend him from the feebleness of the monarch and the greediness of courtiers. Young Warwick had at least the advantage of not being connected with a personally vicious administration, and of not himself having formed that habit of misapplying the power conferred by office which so soon corrupts those who are its instruments. Although his post was an unimportant one, it established him at court, where he formed those social connexions which determine both the lot and the opinions of most men, and was sometimes the medium of communication between the minister and the king, whose good-will he thus obtained. In 1640 the borough of Radnor, in Wales, appointed him its representative in the Long Parliament, where he uniformly sided with the Royalist party—conduct which would have earned for him no praise were it not for the displays of courage which it involved, and which he constantly manifested. On the 21st of April, 1641, he was one of the fifty-six members who voted against the bill of attainder by which the Parliament, without the formality of a trial, sent the Earl of Strafford to the scaffold. All the chronicles of the time testify to the danger which was incurred by those who refused thus to lend their assent to a public injustice, the clamour which attended their entrance into or departure from the House, the fury of the mobs by whom they were baited and reviled, and who denounced them by name on placards as "Straffordians, traitors to their country." Such a courage is less rare at the commencement of a revolution than at its close, before character has suffered in the violent shock of untoward experience. Nevertheless it is always difficult and noble to confront a triumphant party, and resist the intimidations of the multi-

---

* The signet is one of the seals of the King of England, and is affixed to letters which the king addresses to private individuals and to certain other documents. This seal is always under the guardianship of one of the royal secretaries, and there are four clerks of the signet. By a statute of the 57th year of George the Third (1817), they have been declared ineligible to a seat in Parliament. (See Tomlins's " Dictionary of English Law," 3rd edit., London, 1820.)

e. Sir Philip Warwick never yielded. When war was
lared, he was one of the first to quit the House of Com-
ns and join the king, and on the 5th of February, 1643,
Parliament dismissed him from their number. At that
ie he had already borne arms against the Parliament; he
iself tells us that, at the battle of Edgehill (23rd of Octo-
:, 1642), he was one of a party of gentlemen who formed
mselves into a squadron and were the first to charge the
emy.
Nothing remarkable is related of him during the civil war;
find only that Charles I. entrusted him with his confi-
nce, often asked his advice, and employed him in several
ficult missions, in which, however, Warwick was for the
ist part unsuccessful; not so much through any mistake of
i own, as through the dissensions of the Royalist party, which
oved itself as ungovernable in misfortune as it had been in-
pable of rule in prosperity. Warwick was fully awake to
e interior vices of his party, and to the fatal consequences
iich must result from them. He did not write his "Memoirs"
1 a time when experience ought to have revealed to him that
iich perhaps he had not anticipated; nevertheless the cha-
cter of his mind gives ground for believing that he was
ver the dupe of his position; his reason, wanting in depth
id culture, was yet upright, simple, practical, and quickly
llightened by facts as to the errors in conduct and the ex-
avagant expectations of his friends. Though little qualified
/ his situation and capacity to view comprehensively and
dge impartially the cause he had embraced, he was not so
arped by passion, or deficient in sagacity, as to fail to see
iat it was ruined long before the event justified the opinion.
When Charles I., brought to that extremity in which every
ew step involved him in fresh and inextricable difficulties,
ed from Hampton Court, and took refuge in a worse prison,
ie Isle of Wight, Warwick followed him, in the capacity of
scretary. The "Memoirs" which he has left relating to this
eriod are full of a deep and pressing interest; they not only
bound with curious information, but the narrative is per-
aded by profound—albeit undiscriminating—feeling. This is
ot merely a general expression of that loyalty which neces-
arily arose in the mind of Warwick from the position which
e occupied,—it is rather the utterance of an unrestrained
nd indomitable will. It is a sincere, pensive, tender exhibi-

tion of personal affection, which survived the
and led Warwick to say, thirty years afterw;
ing emotion, " I am comforted in the approa
the hope of again seeing my king in heaven.'
this character are generally attributable to t
by the imagination on men who have endur
of fortune, and been led to contemplate t
suggested between the greatness of the worl
of humanity. There is yet another cause. 1
influence of calamity awakens, in natures su
generous emotions, feeling, impulses, virtue
were before strangers, which had been hidc
and which suddenly burst, as a simple dignit
the man, instead of an artificial majesty tl
the king. This was the case with Charles
who had been so haughty—at once self-c
fickle—pompous in show and frivolous in re
both his friends and enemies by his unpret
misfortune, his reverence for religious obliga
ness and calmness in discussion. " The king
improved," said, in 1648, the Earl of Salist
of the Parliament, to Warwick, in one of th
the Isle of Wight. " Your lordship is mi
reply; " the king has been always the same,
has perceived it too late." It was Warw
taken : Charles had become what he had not
it is chiefly to this display of moral greatnes
the fallen king, this sudden appearance of p
ous sentiments which had been stifled unde:
royalty, that we must ascribe that real tende
compassion which was entertained for the k
unreflectingly saw in Charles a prince mc
throne in proportion as he receded from it.

At the close of his life, one circumstance
removing Warwick from Charles I. It ap
the death of the king, he suddenly left
he returned, Cromwell was reigning, and c
at, once precarious and despotic, such as
restrain or dared to oppose, but such as
should be permanently established. In th
Protector to conciliate the Royalists, Warw
not forgotten. " I have no mind," he say

aracter of Cromwell, for in his conversation towards me he as ever friendly; though at the latter end of the day, find-g me ever incorrigible, and having some inducements to spect me a tamperer, he was sufficiently rigid. The first me I ever took notice of him was in the very beginning f the Parliament held in November, 1640, when I vainly ought myself a courtly young gentleman—for we courtiers lued ourselves much upon our good clothes! I came into he House one morning, well clad, and perceived a gentleman eaking, whom I knew not, very ordinarily apparelled; for was a plain cloth suit, which seemed to have been made by n ill country tailor; his linen was plain, and not very clean; d I remember a speck or two of blood upon his little band, hich was not much larger than his collar; his hat was with-ut a hatband; his stature was of a good size; his sword tuck close to his side; his countenance swollen and reddish; is voice sharp and untuneable, and his eloquence full of ervour; for the subject-matter would not bear much of *eason*, it being on behalf of a servant of Mr. Prynne's, who ad dispersed libels against the queen for her dancing, and uch like innocent and courtly sports; and he aggravated he imprisonment of this man by the council-table unto that eight, that one would have believed the very government tself had been in great danger by it. I sincerely profess it essened much my reverence unto that great council, for he was very much hearkened unto. And yet I lived to see this very gentleman—whom out of no ill-will to him I thus lescribe—by multiplied good success, and by real (but usurped) power (having had a good tailor, and more con-verse among good company), in my own eye, when for six weeks together I was a prisoner in his sergeant's hands, and daily waited at Whitehall, appear of a great and majestic deportment and comely presence. Of him, therefore, I will say no more, but that verily I believe he was extraordinarily designed for those extraordinary things, which one while most wickedly and facinorously he acted, and at another as successfully and greatly performed."

Warwick, however, was not to be won by the attentions of the new master of Whitehall. Doubtless his attachment to the Stuarts would have prevented his forming any such new con-nexion; but, apart from this, he had a sufficiently accurate dis-cernment of the real position of Cromwell to prevent him

from despairing of the ultimate reinstalment of the Cavalien
From his retirement in the county of Kent, Warwick ob
served, with a rare sagacity, that strange exercise of autho
rity, vigorous and glorious, but always unsteady and insecure
permitted and recognised by all, but regarded as final b
neither Presbyterians, Independents, nor Royalists, and sue
that no one wished it to receive the sanction of law. Th
authority expired with the man who had held it as his pa
sonal possession, and then appeared a far different scene, h
which the weakness of the contending parties who succes
sively composed the Long Parliament became evident. J
was soon obvious that these were no longer political partis
but rather revolutionary factions, who had sunk into th
condition of miserable coteries; separated from the nation
which no longer granted them any confidence or support
busy only in advancing their own personal interests, an
preventing the restoration of Charles II., which becam
daily more inevitable. Warwick, in the last part of hi
Memoirs, has given a graphic picture of this languishing
and contemptible anarchy, to which no party, not even the
Royalist, condescended an active opposition, because all Eng
land foresaw that it must soon die a natural death. At an
early period he commenced negotiations, whose object, as was
evident to all, though avowed by none, was the restoration of
Charles II. When events thus accomplish themselves, individuals play but a secondary part in them. Monk alone
signed the deed of restoration; but Warwick was one of
those who, in his private conferences, forwarded to the utmost
the general movement.

After the return of Charles II. he was chosen member
for Westminster, in the first Parliament called by the king.
on the 8th of May, 1661; a Parliament which continued, as
we know, till 1679. Warwick appears forty times in the
collection of the debates of this protracted assembly, almost
always confining his remarks to a few sentences, and seldom
indulging in lengthened speeches. There is no indication
that he had any share in those shameful intrigues which so
often disgraced the court and Parliament. He had resumed
the office of Clerk of the Signet; the estimable Earl of Southampton had confided to him the post of Secretary to the
Treasury, and he had thus the happiness of again becoming
connected with the only minister who never lost the esteem

ıd good-will of the people. On the death of the Earl of
outhampton, in 1667, Warwick retired from office, but still
tained his seat in Parliament. As far as we can gather
om the fragmentary notices of him which remain in the
arliamentary debates,* he voted constantly in favour of the
ourt party; and his every word betrays that dread of inno-
ation, that horror of all opposition, that haunting appre-
ension of new revolutions, which, after long-continued politi-
al disorder, takes possession of most peaceably-disposed men,
nd leads them into a kind of disinterested servility, not less
tal to that government which they wish to defend than are
he assaults of its most determined foes.

Warwick's leisure hours were more usefully employed than
hose which he spent in the House. Married twice, pos-
essed of a comfortable fortune, and respected by his neigh-
ours, he wrote, in his retirement at Frognal, a " Discourse
n Government †" and his " Memoirs,"‡ which he finished,
s he himself informs us, in 1677. Neither of these works
as published during his life. He died the 15th of January,
683, and the Discourse on Government appeared in
694, under the editorship of Dr. Smith. The Memoirs did
ot make their appearance till 1701. In subsequent editions
he Discourse on Government has frequently followed the
Memoirs.

The first of these works contains nothing remarkable.
Like the author's mind, it wants definiteness and grasp; it
s much more favourable to absolute power than to liberty,
ınd yet it shows that Warwick shrank from both the first
principles and the legitimate consequences of his own ideas.
Theories of despotism found in Hobbes, at that time, a far
more powerful, and in Filmer a far more consistent, advocate.

As to the Memoirs, they are the expressions of an
opinion which, though uninfluential at the commencement of
a revolution, become general and powerful through its excesses; an opinion which, above everything, wishes for order,
and thinks that only the strong arm of power can secure it;

---

* Cobbett's Parliamentary History, vol. iv., pp. 414, 522, 536, 540, 574, 844,
865, 925, 938, 954, 1033, 1043.
† A Discourse of Government, as examined by Reason, Scripture, and the Law
of the Land. A small volume in 12mo.
‡ Memoirs of the Reign of Charles the First, with a Continuation to the Restoration. One vol. 8vo. London, 1701.

which loves justice and dreads freedom, the only real guardian of justice; which only concerns itself about the present, and remains ever blind to the future; which, while sincere, is incapable of foresight, and, with upright intentions, gives its assent to maxims which encourage the approach of corrupting influences to the government, and then gazes with blank astonishment at the revolutions which these corruptions have produced.

As a historian, Warwick is frigid and diffuse. This is the fault of most English writers at that time; one would think that they wrote for themselves and not for the public, and they report facts or develop ideas as they are presented to their minds, without troubling themselves to exhibit them to their readers in the clearest and most attractive form. The last chapters of Warwick's Memoirs, however, are exempt from this fault,—those which relate to the residence of Charles I. in the Isle of Wight; they give a vivid description of that exciting period, and several of the anecdotes related by Warwick are not to be found in any other records of the time.

JOHN LILBURNE.

[1618—1657.]

In 1647, the civil war seemed to have reached its termination. Charles I. was in the hands of his conquerors. In the Parliament and country generally, the Presbyterians and Independents vied with each other with that passionate vehemence and regard for personal interests which is ever excited in revolutionary factions by the possession or expectation of power. "At that time," says Mr. Hutchinson, "a certain sort of public-spirited men stood up in the Parliament and the army, declaring against these factions and the ambition of the grandees of both, and the partiality that was in these days practised, by which great men were privileged to do those things which meaner men were punished for, and the injustice and other crimes of particular members of Parliament, were rather covered than punished, to the scandal of the whole House. . . The lords claimed many preroga-

es, which set them out of the reach of common justice,
ich these good-hearted people would have equally to belong
the poorest as well as to the mighty; and for this and such
icr honest declarations, they were nicknamed *Levellers.*
deed, as all virtues are mediums, and have their extremes,
ere rose up afterwards with that name a people, who en-
avoured the levelling of all estates and qualities, which
ese sober Levellers were never guilty of desiring, but were
m of just and sober principles, of honest and religious ends,
d therefore hated by all the designing, self-interested men
both factions."*

The revolution pursued its course, and Mrs. Hutchinson
r narrative. "After the death of the king," she says, "it
is debated and resolved to change the form of government
om a monarchy into a commonwealth. A council of state
is to be annually chosen for the management of affairs, ac-
untable to the Parliament. At that time almost every
an was fancying a form of government, and angry that his
vention took not place ; and, among these, John Lilburne,
turbulent-spirited man, who never was quiet with anything,
ablished libels ; and the Levellers made a disturbance with
kind of insurrection."†

The English government was then republican, and Colonel
utchinson had a seat in the Council of State. The honest
evellers of whom his wife spoke with so much sympathy in
547, were considered by her as ambitious meddlers in 1649.
Irs. Hutchinson's opinion was incorrect at both of these
eriods ; the Levellers, from their origin, were a turbulent
d quarrelsome faction, devoid of all political sense, and op-
osed to every form of government; and yet at the same
me, though passing through the corrupting phases of anarchy
ad despotism, many of them kept their faith and remained
nimpeachably honest. John Lilburne was at once the type
ad the hero of the party. He exercised no influence what-
ver upon the progress of the revolution in England, and,
evertheless, the part which he took in it is remarkable from
is unswerving attachment to certain ideas, from which the
reat revolutionary parties of that epoch by turns borrowed
heir means of attack, but which they never openly adopted
s their standard. Unable either to cause or permit the

* Memoirs of Colonel Hutchinson, p. 316 (Bohn's Standard Library).
† Ibid., p. 337.

G

foundation of any government, and an enei
tyranny, Lilburne attacked and endured the:
retire from the conflict until his wearied (
supply him with the weapons necessary for

He was born in 1618, of an ancient and r
in the county of Durham; and his pedigre(
to Sir John Lilburne, who was made prisoi
in 1375. As the youngest son, John was
prenticed to Thomas Hewson, a merchant-
of London. The city apprentices then for
class, who were rendered promptly accessibl
of all new ideas by their ancient habits of
the easy circumstances in which they wer
leisure which they enjoyed. Their politic
embarrassed by those doubts which are som
by superior knowledge; with more ardoui
they suffered themselves to be guided by g
and some few simple notions of natural
learned subtlety of jurisprudence, which
young students of the Temple to defend exi
an object of the special hatred of the app
Charles I., they raised the standard of refoi
the Parliament with some of its noisiest supp
while the army derived from their ranks, {
some of its bravest soldiers. But the app
too shrewd to be long deceived with reg
necessities, and when they saw that civil
them not liberty and improvement, but fett
taxation, they became as ardent for peace
viously been anxious for war; and as the
benefits of that liberty which they had hope
daily more apparent, they transferred to t
that hatred which had induced them to
against their old ones. In February, 166(
cleared the butchers' shops to celebrate th
Rump Parliament, and they soon aftei
Charles II. with acclamations, as loud as
which they had assailed his father.

Lilburne commenced his career among
but he soon became diverted from his fi
rather, he devoted himself with intense c
single interest of his own ideas. He wai

idst of all the factions of the revolution; some of which
d not scruple to exercise the greatest tyranny that they
ight realise their dreams of liberty, whilst others, in order
escape from the dominant form of despotism, consented
sacrifice all the guarantees of their future freedom. Lil-
urne made no sacrifices and accepted no compromises. Of
narrow but an ingenious mind, and of an indomitable
saracter, he remained firm at the post which he had chosen
r himself, and possessed no other influence but that which
ny man may gain over the multitude by an exhibition of
rtitude and intrepidity. Always in aggression against
ue ruling powers, and consequently in continual danger of
ssing his liberty, fortune, or life, he defended with the
tmost imperturbability his rights as an Englishman, or
ather as a freeman, and early acquired the nickname of
Free-born John. His first attempt at legal resistance was
iade against his master, the merchant-tailor; he obtained
atisfaction, and having, as it appears, been released from his
identures, he now followed no other vocation than that to
rhich he believed he had been specially called by the voice
f the Lord. He was habitually connected with the Puritans;
heir dogmatic principles, their enthusiasm, obstinacy, and
ourage, and the persecution to which they were subjected,
ll conspired to induce Lilburne to become one of their
ody, in which he soon attained considerable eminence. In
time of peril, inspiration belongs to fearlessness. Lilburne
ras recognised as one of the interpreters of the Lord's will.
While still an apprentice, he was consulted with regard to
he most dangerous undertakings, and he gladly made use of
is liberty to engage personally in them. The publication
f prohibited books was, at that time, almost the only danger
o which the enemies of episcopacy were free to expose them-
elves, and this danger was quite sufficient to tempt their
nthusiasm. Lilburne crossed over into Holland, where he
aused an edition to be printed of the works of Prynne
nd Bastwick, two celebrated Presbyterians of the time.
Ie then returned to circulate them in England. At the
eginning of 1638, before he was twenty years of age, he in-
urred the notice of the Star Chamber. Before this tribunal
ie began to display that intractability of character, and
anatical and sneering spirit of argument which, during the
rhole of Lilburne's life, carried him through the severest

G 2

trials, and more than once compelled the forms of justice to yield before the obstinacy of an individual man.

At his examination by Mr. Cockshey, the Attorney-General's clerk, Lilburne at first amused himself with disconcerting his interrogator by putting on an appearance of extreme simplicity, and feigning not to understand the purport of the questions asked him. " Where were you in Holland?" demanded Mr. Cockshey. " At Rotterdam." " And from thence you went to Amsterdam?" " Yes, I was at Amsterdam." " What books did you see in Holland?" " Great store of books; for in every bookseller's shop as I came in there were great store of books." " I know that; but I ask you if you did see Dr. Bastwick's ' Answer to my Master's Information,' and a book called his ' Litany?' " " Yes, I saw them there; and if you please to go thither, you may buy an hundred of them at the bookseller's, if you have a mind to them." " Who printed all those books?" " I do not know." " Who was at the charges of printing them?" " Of that I am ignorant." " But did you not send over some of these books?" " I sent not any of them over." " Do you know one Hargust there?" " Yes, I did see such a man." " Where did you see him?" " I met with him one day, accidentally, at Amsterdam." " How oft did you see him there?" " Twice upon one day." " But did he not send over books?" " If he did, it is nothing to me, for his doings are unknown to me."

The conversation continued for some time in this manner, when Lilburne suddenly exclaimed, " Why do you ask me all these questions? These are nothing pertinent to my imprisonment, for I am not imprisoned for knowing and talking with such and such men, but for sending over books; and therefore I am not willing to answer you to any more of these questions, because I see you go about by this examination to ensnare me: for seeing the things for which I am imprisoned cannot be proved against me, you will get other matter out of my examination. . . . And this is all the answer that for the present I am willing to make; and if you ask me of any more things, I shall answer you with silence."

From that moment the examination was nothing more than a dispute between Lilburne and the chief clerk, who at length grew angry, and sent him before the Attorney-General

nself. When there, Lilburne refused to sign his examina-
n, declared that he was made to say what he had never
d, and was again remanded by the magistrate, who had
mpletely failed to get anything out of him. Some days
er, he was taken to the Star Chamber office, and required,
cording to custom, to enter his appearance. "I am but
young man," said Lilburne, "and a prisoner, and money
not very plentiful with me; therefore I will not part with
y money upon such terms." Presently, an officer came
swear him on the Gospels, and said, "Pull off your glove
d lay your hand upon the book." "What to do, sir?"
id Lilburne. "You must swear," said he. "To what?"
That you shall make true answer to all things that are
ked you." "Must I so, sir? But before I swear, I will
low to what I must swear." "As soon as you have sworn,
u shall, but not before." "Sir, I am but a young man,
d do not well know what belongs to the nature of an oath,
d therefore, before I swear, I will be better advised."
How old are you?" "About twenty years old." "You
ve received the Sacrament, have you not?" "Yes, that
have." "And you have heard the ministers deliver God's
ord, have you not?" "I have heard sermons." "Well,
en, you know the Holy Evangelists?" "Yes, that I do:
ut, sir, though I have received the Sacrament, and have
eard sermons, yet it doth not therefore follow that I am
ound to take an oath, which I doubt of the lawfulness of."
Look you here," said he (and with that he opened the
ook), "we desire you to swear by no foreign thing, but to
wear by the Holy Evangelists." "Sir, I do not doubt or
uestion that; I question how lawful it is for me to swear to
do not know what." "But everybody takes this oath;
nd would you be wiser than all other men?" "It makes
o matter to me what other men do; but before I swear, I
rill know better grounds and reasons than other men's
ractices, to convince me of the lawfulness of such an oath."
"I am not to convince any man's conscience of the lawful-
ess of it, but only to offer and tender it: will you take it or
no?" "Sir, I will be better advised first."*
He was sent back to prison, and, some days afterwards
rought to the bar of the Star Chamber, to be tried both for
is original offence and the new misdemeanours of which he

* The Christian Man's Trial, by John Lilburne, London, 1641.

had been guilty during the course of the proceedings. A similar discussion now began; the court were unable to ex-tort the least submission either from Lilburne or from his fellow-prisoner, Wharton, an old printer, eighty-five years of age, who had already been imprisoned eight times for refusing to take the oath before the Star Chamber. Lilburne declared that he considered this oath to be contrary to the word of God; and old Wharton, who was allowed to explain his views in reference to the subject, inveighed with such violence against the bishops and the oaths required by them, that he was quickly silenced; " but," says Lilburne, " if they would have let him proceed, he would so have peppered the bishops as they were never in their lives in an open court of judica-ture." Wharton's speech, however, was not lost; on his return to prison he recited it to his gaoler, who, in conse-quence, kept Lilburne and himself in closer confinement. On leaving the bar, Lilburne said aloud to his judges, " My lords, I beseech God to bless your honours, and to discover and make known unto you the wickedness and cruelty of the prelates."

They were both condemned—Wharton, in consequence of his old age, to a fine of five hundred pounds, and the pillory only; Lilburne, to the additional penalty of a whipping. He underwent his punishment on the 18th of April, 1638, walk-ing at a cart's tail through the streets of Westminster, whilst an executioner beat him with knotted cords. During its in-fliction, Lilburne either sang psalms, or moved the multitude to anger and commiseration by his harangues. Crowds fol-lowed the young martyr on his way, praising his fortitude, and admiring his courage. When he arrived at the place where his punishment concluded, ready to faint with pain and fatigue, a messenger from the Star Chamber entered the room into which he had retired, and offered to remit the punish-ment of the pillory if he would acknowledge his error. This was not the time to yield; Lilburne remarked that it was rather late to expect that he would succumb now that the ad-vantages to be gained from submission were so much dimi-nished, and reminded the messenger that he had refused under circumstances far more favourable. When his wounds were healed, he was taken to the pillory. " When I was upon it," says Lilburne, " I made obeisance to the lords, some of them (as I suppose) looking out at the Star Chamber window

wards me." Of all the Christian virtues, humility is not
; one most easily practised by the man who believes him-
f specially endowed with heavenly graces; and to these
estial gifts Lilburne now added terrestrial glories. New
fferings awaited him to make still further trial of his con-
ncy. The pillory was too low for him, and his bent position
ded greatly to the pain of his wounds. The sun darted its
d-day beams upon his head, and he was not permitted to
elter himself by any means from its heat. But utterly in-
nsible to the tortures of his position, and animated by the
fferings he had undergone, Lilburne addressed the people,
nounced to them the tyranny of the bishops and their
ents, reproached them with their apathy, and urged them
throw off the yoke. In vain did his keepers attempt to
mpel him to silence; in vain did they threaten him with
other whipping; nothing would do but they must gag him,
d afterwards tie his hands, to prevent him from throwing
nong the people the pamphlets with which he had filled his
ckets. His courage was more than equal to his sufferings;
) sign of exhaustion betrayed a momentary weakness; but
hen the gag was removed, on his descent from the scaffold,
e shouted forth, " Now I am more than a conqueror through
im that hath loved me."
  Lilburne had, in fact, become a saint; the enthusiastic
omage which was henceforth rendered to him by the people
f London, resisted and survived all the revolutions which, in
he sequel, withdrew popular opinion far away from those
hannels in which it had flown at first. If, during the course
f civil dissensions, Lilburne did not share equally in all the
ishes of his fellow-citizens, he always struggled to remove
heir sufferings, and even when he would not acknowledge
heir allies, he continued to be the enemy of their oppressors.
  He was taken back to prison, and confined for nearly two
ears and a half in a dungeon, chained both hand and foot.
Iere he exercised his indefatigable activity, sometimes in
omposing and conveying to his friends outside writings
tamped with the spirit that possessed him, and sometimes
n putting to the test the patience or brutality of his keepers.
[n one of his conflicts with them he lost two of his fingers.
Once he set fire to his person at the risk of being burned
imself, and the cries of the other prisoners obtained the
emoval of Lilburne from the neighbourhood, as their lives,

they said, were endangered by his violence. Either from natural malice, or from vengeance, or in the hope of subduing him, his gaolers increased to the utmost the rigours of his captivity; they frequently refused to give him the food which was brought for him by his friends; and Lilburne, in one of his numerous auto-biographical publications, declares that he should more than once have been in danger of dying of hunger, had it not been for the active and ingenious zeal of his friends in conveying to him, at great expense, sometimes by one means and sometimes by another, the aliment necessary for his subsistence.

At last, in November, 1640, the convocation of the Long Parliament restored him to liberty; he was the first of the prisoners of the Star Chamber whose liberation was ordered by the Parliament. It was not to be expected that these two years of imprisonment would have calmed the mind and matured the reason of a man twenty years of age. In May, 1641, Lilburne appeared at the head of the tumults raised against the life of the Earl of Strafford; and, at a time when popular violence could go very far indeed without exhausting the patience of the Parliament, he managed to get himself arrested and brought to the bar of the House of Lords; it is true, he was acquitted, and, by a natural coincidence, the House of Commons voted him compensation for what he had suffered from the Star Chamber.

A more regular kind of warfare soon summoned to the standard of the Parliament all men of Lilburne's opinions. He entered the Earl of Essex's army as a volunteer; and on the 23rd October, 1642, he fought valiantly at Edgehill with the rank of a captain of infantry. Being made prisoner at Brentford on the 15th of November following, he was taken to Oxford, where Charles I. had established his head-quarters, and was brought before a council of war to be tried for high treason. "He behaved himself," says Clarendon, "with so great impudence, in extolling the power of the Parliament, that it was manifest he had an ambition to have been made a martyr for that cause."* But the Parliament interfered and declared that the lives of the prisoners whom they had in their hands should answer for Lilburne's safety. His trial was, therefore, suspended, and he soon found means to escape by bribing his gaoler. Such is, at all events, Clarendon's account, and he

Clarendon's History of the Rebellion, vol. iii., p. 671.

ds that, during Lilburne's imprisonment, his friends sup-
ed him abundantly with all the money he required. Lil-
rne, however, informs us that he was exchanged by the
rliament, "in a very honourable manner, and far above his
hk." However this may be, each account attests his im-
rtance at this period—an importance which ever attaches
the leaders of the multitude at the outset of a revolution.
1 his return to the Parliament quarters, " he was received,"
ys Clarendon, "with public joy, as a champion that had
fied the king in his own court."* He was offered an ap-
intment for his wife worth nearly a thousand pounds yearly;
t he refused it, to the great regret of Mrs. Lilburne, whom
told "that he must fight though it were for eightpence a
y, till he saw the liberties and peace of England settled,
her than set himself down in a rich place for his own ad-
ntage, in the midst of so many grand distractions of his
tive country."† Indeed, it is difficult to doubt that Lil-
urne might not, at this period, have made his fortune if he
d pleased, and had followed the example of many other less
nspicuous and popular than himself; but he was animated
7 the disinterestedness as well as the confidence of a
liever, and it would be difficult to determine whether he
usted most firmly in God, or in himself. " For about these
n years," he says, " an all-merciful God hath enabled me
carry my life in my hands, and to have it always in readi-
ess to lay it down in a quarter of an hour's warning, know-
ig that he has in store for me a mansion of eternal glory."‡
nd, on all occasions, fearless for his personal safety, he had
o more doubt of his knowledge than of his salvation, and
ever troubled himself about the dangers or miseries to
hich he might be exposed. He might have rested securely
pon the zeal of his friends, the sectaries, who never deserted
im; but it was because Lilburne never thought to secure
heir help beforehand that his party never failed to be ready
o assist him.

Divisions, however, began to arise in the army; the Earl
f Essex became the leader of the Presbyterian party, which
as more hateful to men of Lilburne's opinions than the
ourt party had ever been. In 1643, he took refuge in the

* Clarendon's History of the Rebellion, vol. iii., p. 671.
† Biographia Britannica, vol. v., p. 2940, note k.
‡ The Oppressed Man's Oppressions, p. 27.

army of the Earl of Manchester, which had been formed to serve as a nucleus for that new revolutionary party which was destined soon to rise on the ruins of the old one, and of which Cromwell was already the soul. Lilburne was too valuable an instrument to be neglected. Cromwell found no difficulty in gaining him over, for men of far greater ability had yielded to his seductive influence. Having made up his mind to ruin Colonel King, a man whom he suspected, but could not get rid of, he appointed Lilburne the major of his regiment, and directed him to watch his colonel's conduct, and report to head-quarters all that appeared injurious to the good of the commonwealth, that justice might be done. Lilburne did not fail to discharge the invidious mission which Cromwell had entrusted to him, and his colonel soon furnished him with ample cause for complaint. The major kept his eyes and ears open, and carefully collected facts prejudicial to the colonel, against whom he had a private grudge, because he had nearly caused his death or capture at the siege of Newark. At length he drew up his accusation, hastened to lay it before Cromwell, and demanded a court-martial. This was promised, but delayed from day to day; meanwhile, Colonel King was cashiered and deprived of all his employments. Cromwell required nothing further, but Lilburne would not be satisfied without a trial; he reiterated his demand for a court-martial, and not being able to obtain a satisfactory answer, he brought his accusation before the House of Commons, where he experienced a similar failure, for the trial was refused.

He met with a similar defeat in the case of the Earl of Manchester, against whom he had promised Cromwell that he would prefer an accusation, which Cromwell had abandoned when Manchester was set aside by the new organisation of the army, and had ceased to be obnoxious. These disappointments, his declared aversion to the Covenant, which it was necessary for him to subscribe in order to retain his commission, and the turbulent restlessness of his character, made Lilburne resolve to abandon a career in which his opinion and personal will could not be his sole law. His services had raised him to the rank of lieutenant-colonel; his bravery had gained him much notice at Marston Moor; an advantageous position was offered him in 1645, on the new organisation of the army; but he refused all these chances of promotion, and finding that he was never sufficient master of his blows un-

he fought alone and on his own account, he exchanged
sword for the pen, and warfare for polemics.
From this moment he was incessant in his attacks of every-
ng that excited his censure or displeasure; government
asures, party proceedings, individuals' actions, all fell
der his jurisdiction. To these general interests were soon
ded others of a more personal nature; for his indiscrimi-
te attacks and opposition gained for him enemies and em-
rrassments in all quarters. He had been applied to for the
counts of his administration of the different military offices
had held; these he had no objection to supply, as he
imed that large arrears were due to him from the State.
e Committee of Accounts desired him to swear to the
th of his statement. Lilburne refused to do so; the ac-
unts were not produced, and the committee prosecuted him
being accountable to the State for the sum of two thousand
unds. Lilburne, on his side, presented a petition to the
ouse of Lords, for the recovery of an equal sum, which had
en voted to him as compensation for his imprisonment by
e Star Chamber. Colonel King endeavoured to recover a
milar amount of damages from Lilburne, because he had
lled him a traitor; and Lilburne answered this charge by
cusing the colonel of treason before the House of Com-
ons. At the same time he was engaged in a suit with
rynne, his former associate, and now chairman of the Com-
ittee of Accounts, who had become Lilburne's inveterate
emy since the government had fallen into the hands of the
resbyterians. He was also busily pursuing his complaints
ainst Cromwell and the Earl of Manchester, the Speaker of
e House of Lords; and conducting an accusation against
enthall, the Speaker of the House of Commons. He had
gaged in this last quarrel in the capacity of an amateur.
Such occupations as these were not devoid of danger.
ilburne, when arrested at the suit of Colonel King, gave
il, but was summoned before the House of Lords for his
tacks upon the Earl of Manchester. When brought to the
r of the Lords he refused to recognise their jurisdiction;
peared before them with his hat on his head, would not
eel down, and stopped up his ears whilst his accusation was
ing read. He was reminded that he had not always been
refractory, and that in 1641, when prosecuted before that
me assembly, in connexion with the Strafford tumults, he had

not hesitated to defend himself. "When I was a child,"
answered Lilburne, "I spake as a child, and acted as a child
but as soon as I became a man, I put away childish things."
This was not considered a sufficient excuse; he was condemned to pay a fine, and in default, was committed to New-
gate, whence he was soon after transferred to the Tower, and
denied the use of pens and ink. He, however, contrived
some means to write, and almost every day there appeared a
new pamphlet of his, such as "The Anatomy of the Lords'
Tyranny," "The Just Man's Justification," "The Oppressed
Man's Oppression," "The Resolved Man's Resolution," &c.
This last title is so curious a specimen of the spirit of the
times and the spirit of Lilburne, that we are induced to
quote it entire:—"The Resolved Man's Resolution to maintain with the last drop of his heart's blood his civil liberties
and freedoms, granted unto him by the good, just, and honest
laws of England—his native country; and never to sit still
so long as he has a tongue to speak, or a hand to write, till
he hath either necessitated his adversaries, the House of
Lords, and their arbitrary assistants in the House of Commons, either to do him justice and right, by delivering him
from his cruel and illegal imprisonment, and holding out unto
him legal and ample reparation for all his unjust sufferings,
or else send him to Tyburn, of which he is not afraid; and
doubteth not, if they do it, but at and by his death to do
them, Samson-like, more mischief at his death than he did
them all his life. All which is expressed and declared in the
following epistle, written by Lieutenant-Colonel John Lilburne, prerogative prisoner in the Tower of London, to a
true friend of his, a citizen thereof; April, 1647."

To that singularity of style, which characterised his age
and sect, Lilburne added peculiarities of his own, and in him
the tone of a martyr combined with that of a bully. He
was continually offering his life as a sacrifice, and seemed dis-
appointed at his offer being rejected; and a vain-glorious
feeling of his own superiority may always be discerned in his
complaints against the iniquity of his adversaries. One of
his pamphlets against the Lords "will live," he says, "when
I am dead." He is continually speaking of what he has
written as "excellent, and to the purpose." Boasting appeared to be his prerogative; he could no more refrain from
praising himself, it was said, than "from eating when he was

ngry :" and probably he would have had less difficulty in
passing a day without eating than without disputing. "If
re were none living but himself," said his friend Henry
Martyn, "John would be against Lilburne, and Lilburne
inst John." In addition to the charms of martyrdom,
rsecution offered him the attractions of a quarrel.
If it be possible for an isolated and disarmed individual to
d delight in disturbing powerful adversaries, Lilburne's cup
enjoyment was full to overflowing. Whether free or in
ains, he was equally obnoxious to his enemies, and his
reat to arm the people on his behalf against those who re-
sed to do him justice was no rhodomontade. He had not
en many days in prison, before petitions signed by 8000 or
,000 persons were presented to Parliament, demanding the
ease of this friend of the people. The women especially,
aded by Lilburne's wife—a worthy companion of his ex-
its and afflictions—made the environs of Westminster re-
und with their cries in favour of the young champion of
erty. They were forced to depart unanswered ; but they
turned again and again, and were at last sent back to "wash
eir dishes ;" but in times of trouble, when petitions easily
anged into seditions, careful watch was kept against those
ich claimed Lilburne's liberation.
The interference of the people did not succeed in effecting
e emancipation of their champion ; and Lilburne thereupon
deavoured to obtain the more powerful intervention of the
my. He addressed himself to the popular leaders of those
giments which were known under the name of *agitators ;*
eir cause was his own ; from the confinement of his dun-
on he fomented their rebellion and associated himself in
eir projects, one of which was, it is said, to attempt the
erthrow of Cromwell. We are not, however, authorised in
lieving that this idea, though probably entertained by some
inds, ever assumed any definite form. Cromwell had already
come, in reference to the agitators, a sort of talisman with
hich the fate of their cause was indissolubly connected. If
ey were desirous to vanquish him, it was that they alone
ight possess him. Lilburne wrote a threatening letter to
romwell, which he signed thus: "John Lilburne, that
ither loves baseness, nor fears greatness." Cromwell was
en treating with the king. His position with regard to the
itators and the republican populace was not strong enough

to enable him to disregard such an adversary as Lilburne.
He went to see him in his prison, once more took the pain
of deceiving him by assurances and promises, and gave him to
understand how greatly the commonwealth might be injured
at that moment by an attack upon himself. Several of Lilburne's friends took the same tone, and he therefore contented
himself with asking for his liberty, promising to sell his goods
and leave the kingdom, where it had become impossible for
him to reside; "for," he said, "either I must follow my
trade, a clothier, which here I cannot do without taking oaths
which I cannot take; or else I must live in the country, and
there I neither can nor would pay tithes."

Meanwhile the star of Cromwell had for a moment waned.
In spite of the results of the meeting at Ware, on the 15th
of November, 1657, the popular party in the army had gained
the ascendancy over the adherents of the leaders, and the
reaction had begun to be felt in the House of Commons.
Lilburne received permission from the House to leave the
Tower during the day without his gaoler, on condition of
his returning thither in the evening; but soon a more active
spirit of sedition, diffused among the inferior officers, and
plans for petitioning the Parliament to bring its protracted
session to an end, revealed the presence of the new ferment
into which society had been thrown. The Lords complained
of Lilburne's liberty, and demanded the cause of his being at
large. They were told that the House of Commons had
given orders to that effect; and they accordingly requested
the Lower House to rescind their order, that a rupture
might be avoided. After lengthy debates the Commons
yielded. Lilburne, when brought to the bar, answered his
accusers by bringing a counter-accusation of high treason
against Cromwell and Ireton. He was again confined in the
Tower, and sent for trial to the court of King's Bench. He
wrote, pleaded, and petitioned against this treatment. Meanwhile the Scotch entered England; Cromwell was forced, as
it were, to fly to the army, and left the field open to his
enemies at London. Whether because Lilburne's implacable
hostility to him was a recommendation of the untractable
Leveller, whether it was out of esteem for his character and
pity for his sufferings, whether it was from a desire to conciliate the favour of the people, or simply to put an end to
that arbitrary government of which they had themselves

n victims,—the Presbyterians, when thus temporarily re-
red to power, took a favourable view of his case; and
ynard, one of the eleven members who were restored to
ir seats, obtained his liberation. The first use which
burne made of his freedom was to become reconciled with
omwell; for the danger of his cause led him to unite with
oppressor against his liberators, the Presbyterians. He
o declared himself against any personal treaty with the
g. But, when the army had regained its authority, Lil-
rne opposed the illegal form of the trial of Charles I. He
manded that the establishment of a system of regular go-
rnment should precede a process which would only be the
umph of the law. The leaders of the army desired the
ath of Charles that they might quietly enjoy their power;
lburne desired his judgment only as a striking proof that
ere was an equal law for all; and he, therefore, wished that
might be tried before an ordinary tribunal. The erection
a special court appeared to him an infraction of the rights
the accused person, and an insult to the nation, inasmuch
it indicated that a difference still existed between a cri-
inal king and a criminal subject.
It was at this time that the difference between the Inde-
ndents and the Levellers, between those who coveted em-
re and those who desired equality, became clearly marked.
ainly did they attempt a reconciliation at various conferences,
hich were incessantly interrupted, but frequently resumed,
twithstanding the bitterness which had caused their inter-
ption; and which, after most violent debates, often pro-
acted through the whole of the night, only led to an irre-
ediable rupture. When on the point of coming to blows,
e two parties separated, and Lilburne, "taking leave of
em," as he said, "for a pack of dissembling, juggling
aves," declared his resolution to abstain from "meddling
d making any more with so perfidious a generation of
en as the great ones of the army were, but especially the
nningest of Machiavellians, Commissary Henry Ireton."
He contented himself at first, however, with printing some
those maxims of government, the adoption of which he
d wished to secure, under the title of an "Agreement with
e People;" and having probably been abandoned by most
his adherents, who had either been frightened or persuaded
desert him, he temporarily suspended a struggle in which

he had never received assistance from any but the enemies o
his cause—the Presbyterians and the Cavaliers. He remove(
from London to take steps for the recovery of the sum whic[
had been assigned to him as damages and interest, and di(
not return until after the death of the king, one of who(
judges he had refused to be. On his return in February
1649, he found the High Court occupied with the trial o(
Lord Capel, Lord Goring, and their companions. He pro(
tested against this new piece of illegality, and being par(
ticularly touched by Lord Capel's intrepidity, he acte(
vigorously on their behalf, offering them his advice and the
assistance of his audacious practice in the art of resisting
judges; but they did not think it right to accept his aid.

The army was now the supreme authority, and the remnan(
of the Long Parliament, of which it made use as a phanton(
of representative government, consoled itself, under the nam(
of a Republic, with the subjugation of liberty. Where libert}
has ceased to exist, license only has free course; and it i(
possible to escape oppression by anarchy alone. Anarch}
and oppression now contested, or rather shared, the posses(
sion of England; beside a government of the most arbitrar}
and violent nature, which forcibly crushed its various ene(
mies in turn, the most impracticable principles of libert}
were sustained by armed Levellers of all sorts, scattere(
throughout the country, and raising upon the ruins of lega(
institutions the standard of natural law, explained in a hun
dred different ways, according to the turn of mind of the in
spired guide around whom the would-be legislators of the
country or district had gathered. It is impossible to cal(
Lilburne the leader of a party; the Levellers never were (
real party, acting conjointly and united together by positiv(
bonds. They were nothing but the spontaneous result of (
feeling which was very generally entertained in England a(
this period. They arose on every side by a species of move
ment analagous to that process of nature which, at the sprin(
of the year, produces simultaneously, from a thousand separate germs, a thousand similar or distinct plants. Lilburn(
was the representative and organ of whatever was mos(
honest, least unreasonable, and most consistent in the desig(
and desire of this party. In spite of the inflexibility of hi(
theories, the twelve years which he had passed in the mids(
of a revolution had introduced some just and practical idea(

o his head. Being always exposed, moreover, to the en-
rance of very positive evils from a very oppressive tyranny,
occupied himself less in establishing chimeras than in
nbating realities. Every one of his new plans of govern-
nt was based upon a violent attack on the established au-
rities; and his personal knowledge of the political leaders
the day, their intrigues, malversations, and perfidies, was
arsenal from whence he showered down upon them, with
ange energy, all the darts of public indignation.

Having learned that some threats had been uttered against
n in the council of war at Whitehall, he as usual endea-
ured to ward off the danger by braving it. On the 22nd
February, 1649, he published a pamphlet, entitled "Eng-
d's new Chains discovered;" and on the 26th, accompa-
d by Walwin, Prince, and Overton, three other Levellers,
laid before Parliament a new plan of government, in oppo-
ion to that which the army had prepared. Already, on the
blication of the first pamphlet by these four men, orders
d been given for their arrest; and Lilburne, in his speech at
e bar of the House, declared that if they presented them-
lves alone, and without bringing in support of their opinion
ose thousands of signatures which usually accompanied
em, it was because they had been informed that orders had
en issued for their arrest, two days before, by men who had
legal power over them, and into whose hands they feared, by
nger delay, to fall. Lilburne added, on behalf of his friends
d himself, that, in case of danger, they regretted that they
d not more than one life to sacrifice in support of "so gallant
piece."

They were dismissed unanswered; but either from fear or
oderation on the part of their enemies, or address on their
vn part, the order for their arrest was not carried into effect.
ilburne profited by this respite to publish the second part
t "England's new Chains discovered," in which he re-
rinted his plan of government, adding, that as no answer
ad been given to his proposition, he hoped that now a peti-
on, supported by several thousand signatures, would help
im to obtain "an effectual answer." He was hereupon
mmitted to the Tower with his associates, and a disavowal
f his last work was presented to the Parliament, in the name
f the Anabaptist congregations of London. More sponta-
eous petitions, however, rapidly multiplied in his favour.

H

One was sent in with ten thousand signatures; and a mult
tude of women drew up another, characterised by those livel
impressions which distinguish their sex.   They declared thei
conviction that Lilburne and his companions in misfortun
were to be taken from the Tower in the middle of the nigh
and shot at Whitehall; and they assured the Parliament tha
to condemn Lilburne's book would be to enslave all the peopl
since not a single conversation took place on public affaii
which did not discuss the contents of the pamphlet; an
that, therefore, all liberty of speech would be destroyed, whic
was the greatest of all servitudes. The petitioners were eithe
sent back without any answer, or repulsed with severe repr
mands; but they returned to the charge under a new forn
and among the grievances alleged by the leaders of th
Levellers, who sprang up on all sides, was the " barbarous an
unlawful" imprisonment of Lilburne and his friends.

The same spirit displayed itself in the army.   A revo.
broke out; five cavalry soldiers were condemned to death
four were pardoned, but notwithstanding the writings (
Lilburne and the efforts of his partisans, the fifth, name
Lockier, was shot on the 7th of April, 1649.   His comrade
celebrated his funeral with the greatest pomp; a hundre
horse soldiers opened the procession, followed by their horse
caparisoned in black; six trumpeters played a dead march
the coffin, surmounted by the dead man's sword and som
branches of rosemary dipped in blood, was followed by an ir
numerable crowd, marching in order, and wearing black an
green cockades; a number of women closed the procession
and several thousand citizens of a higher class, who had nc
thought it proper to follow the funeral through the streets c
London, awaited its arrival at the burial-ground.

In the midst of this active hostility, the Parliament, be
coming agitated in its terror and impotence, passed law
against the offences which menaced it on every side.   An ac
was proposed on the 1st of May, 1649, to declare every pei
son guilty of treason who should accuse the Parliament o
the Council of State of usurpation, or who should attempt t
change the existing form of government, or any soldier wh
should plot the death of his general or lieutenant-general,

* This clause, though originally proposed, was abandoned and omitted froi
the bill adopted on the 14th of May.

any person who should kill a member of Parliament or a
dge while in the exercise of his functions.

At the same time Lilburne issued a new pamphlet from his
nfinement in the Tower, presenting a summary of the
ishes of the people in reference to the changes to be intro-
uced into the existing form of government. This summary
as published under the name of the "Agreement of the
cople," and contains thirty propositions or articles, the most
mportant of which are as follows :—

"1. The supreme authority of this nation to be a repre-
entative of four hundred.

"2. That two hundred be a House, and the major voice
oncluding to the nation.

"3. All public officers to be capable of subjection; those of
alary not to be members.

"4. No members of one representative to be chosen of the
ext.

"5. This Parliament to end the first Wednesday in Au-
ust, 1649.

"6. If this omit to order it, that the people proceed to
lections.

"10. They not to make laws to compel in matters of
religion.

"11. None to be compelled to fight by sea or land against
his conscience.

"14. Not to give judgment against any, where no law was
provided before.

"15. Not to depend longer upon the incertain inclination
of Parliament.

"16. None to be punished for refusing to answer against
themselves.

"20. Men's persons not to be imprisoned for debt, nor
their estates free.

"21. Men's lives not to be taken away, but for murder and
the like.

"22. Men upon trials for life, liberty, &c., to have witnesses
heard.

"24. Every parish to choose their own minister, and to
force none to pay.

"25. Conviction for life, liberty, &c., to be by twelve neighbours sworn.

H 2

" 26. None to be exempted from offices for his religion only.

" 27. The people in all counties to choose all their public officers.

" 30. This agreement not to be nulled, no estates levelled, nor all things common."

The last two clauses of the thirtieth article are to be found only in Whitelocke's Memorials.*

To this formal attack upon an order of things which claimed to be considered a regular government, were soon added more violent onslaughts upon the heads of that government, and upon Cromwell in particular. Fresh severities followed these fresh aggressions. The Parliament ordered that the prisoners should be more closely confined, and deprived of all communication with each other. They were refused the pecuniary assistance frequently granted to captives; and the Lieutenant of the Tower was directed to provide them with sufficient sustenance. For three days Lilburne was put upon half rations. It was, however, impossible long to persist in these extreme measures; the anger and power of the Levellers became daily more threatening; and the prisoners were allowed twenty shillings a week. But at this time, on the 14th of May, 1649, the new act was passed, specifying cases of treason; and on the same day Lilburne was accused of high treason, and his property sequestrated.

The quarrel was a deadly one; men who had conquered power, and preserved it sword in hand, were indignant at finding that their strength was impotent against libels. The restrictions upon the liberty of the press, which were incessantly renewed, and as continually nullified by their rejection by public opinion, only presented an obstacle easily eluded or set at nought. The " Agreement of the People" appeared with the approbation of the censor, which was probably forged and the censor, Gilbert Mabbott, requested and obtained his dismissal from the office, on the 22nd of May, 1649, upon these grounds : " First, because many thousands of scandalous and malignant pamphlets had been published with his name thereunto, though he never saw them; and also because it was lawful, in his judgment, to print any book, sheet, &c. without licensing, so as the authors and printers do subscribe their true names thereunto, that so they may be liable to

* Whitelocke's Memorials, pp. 399-400.

swer the contents thereof; and if they offend therein, then be punished by such laws as are, or shall be, for those ses provided."* It was necessary to check, by some striking ample, an inundation which could not be restrained by so eble a dike as the censorship; and by making an example Lilburne, the most formidable source of the evil would be ied up. But such a proceeding would be attended with nsiderable danger. Six months were spent in consultations d deliberations upon the best method of attaining the de- red end; during this period the war of pamphlets raged as olently as ever, and Lilburne was incessant in his publica- ons. Indeed, pamphlets did not satisfy him; he offered, d begged to begin a war of public discussion. "Let the ouse of Commons," he says, in a letter to Cornelius Hol- nd, one of the members of the Council of State, "choose ro men, and let me choose other two, and let these four, if ey cannot agree, fix on a fifth. Let the debate be public, d let me have free leave to speak for myself: and if my nocency be not thus established, I will forfeit and lose all have, and my life to boot. If this proposition is not ac- epted within the next five days, I shall feel myself free to o what I can in anatomising what I know publicly or pri- ately of you and your associates."†

No answer was returned to this letter of Lilburne's, but gents were sent to seize a new pamphlet which he had just ad printed. His remonstrances, however, had such an effect pon the agents, that, as Whitelocke informs us, he persuaded hem "to look to their own liberties, and let the books alone."‡ hese illegal means were not persisted in, and Lilburne soon ad to defend himself against Thomas May, who accused him f complicity with Prince Charles Stuart, afterwards Charles II.

It was at last determined that he should be tried by a pecial commission of Oyer and Terminer, composed of forty ersons; and the jury was chosen with great care that they night give the desired verdict. Vainly did Lilburne's wife, nd his brother, Colonel Robert Lilburne, endeavour to ob- ain a suspension of his trial. They presented a petition, romising that he should leave England with his family, pro- ided the government would pay him what they owed him;

---

* Biographia Britannica, vol. v., p. 2955.
† Godwin's History of the Commonwealth, vol. iii., p. 166.
‡ Whitelocke's Memorials, p. 421.

but, on the same day (October 22nd, 1649), Lilburne published a pamphlet, in which he added to their proposal another
condition, "that all such as were willing to transport themselves with him to the West Indies, should be allowed that
liberty, and also have all their demands of monies in arrear
from the State paid to them; and further, that such as were
poor, and willing to attend him, should have some reasonable
allowance of money for that end ;"* because, he said, as it
was their right to live and claim subsistence in England, if
for the sake of peace, they consented to banish themselves, it
was only fair that they should be supplied with the means of
gaining a livelihood elsewhere. Another petition, in the form
of a remonstrance, was presented, signed as usual by large
numbers of his partisans. His brother Robert again attempted to obtain a delay of the trial, "till he should be able
to convince him of his mistakes, or, if not, prevail with him
to leave the kingdom." At length, overcome by the despair
of his wife, whose courage and tenderness deserved all his
affection, Lilburne himself consented to request a delay. But
the republican party had determined to decide the conflict;
and no delay could be obtained. The trial began at Guildhall on the 24th of October, 1649. It lasted for three days,
during which Lilburne made head against his judges, continually interrupting them, being put to silence, resuming his remarks, and finally overcoming all obstacles by dint of obstinacy ; and, using the advantage he had gained to point out
at every step, the illegality, usurpations, and tyranny of the
government by which he was oppressed. At the end of the
trial, he turned suddenly towards the jury, and said :

"Gentlemen of the jury, you are my sole judges, the
keepers of my life, at whose hands the Lord will require my
blood. And therefore I desire you to know your power, and
consider your duty, both to God, to me, to your own selves, and
to your country; and the gracious assisting spirit and presence
of the Lord God omnipotent, the governor of heaven and
earth, and all things therein contained, go along with you,
give counsel and direct you, to do that which is just and for
his glory!"

"Amen! amen!" cried the spectators with one voice.
The judges looked at each other with some uneasiness, and
requested Major-General Skippon to send for three more

* Biographia Britannica, vol. v., p. 2957.

mpanies of foot soldiers. The Attorney-General and the ord Chief Justice, who presided in the court, renewed their deavours to convince the jury that both justice and necessity quired the condemnation of the prisoner. After three ours' deliberation, the clerk of the court addressed the jury: "Gentlemen of the jury, are you agreed of your verdict?" "Yes." "Look upon the prisoner; is he guilty of the treasons harged upon him, or any of them, or not guilty?" "Not guilty of all of them." "Nor of all the treasons, or any of them that are laid to is charge?" "Not of all, nor of any one of them." At these words, Guildhall resounded "with such a loud nd unanimous shout, as is believed was never heard before." t lasted for half an hour, during which the judges sat pale nd trembling, exposed to this wild outburst of popular satis-action. The prisoner stood calmly at the bar, and it was ob-erved that he appeared rather less haughty and animated han before. When the tumult had subsided, the clerk re-umed: "Gentlemen of the jury, hearken to your verdict; the court has heard it: you say that John Lilburne is not guilty of all the treasons laid unto his charge, nor of any one of them; and so you say all?" "Yes, we do so."*

Lilburne was taken back to the Tower, followed by the ac-clamations of the multitude; and, during the whole of the night, bonfires were lighted in the streets. An attempt was made to detain him in prison; but, about a fortnight after-wards, on the 8th of November, 1649, the discontent of the people, and the efforts of the friends of the prisoner, amongst others, of Henry Martyn and Ludlow, obtained his libera-tion.†

Lilburne was no sooner at liberty, than he attempted to obtain from Sir Arthur Haslerig, the chairman of the Com-mittee of Sequestrations, the money which was due to him

* State Trials, vol. ii., pp. 77-79.
† In honour of this celebrated trial, Lilburne's friends had a medal struck, on one side of which he was represented standing at the bar, with this inscription: "John Lilburne, saved by the power of the Lord and the integrity of his jury, who are judge of law as well as fact." On the reverse were the names of the jury. —(Biographia Britannica, vol. x., p. 2958.)

from the State. Finding some difficulties i:
gentleman, he one day met Sir Arthur's clerl
and desired him, in the presence of witnesse
master's life and welfare, to tell him that h
wore a good dagger by his right side, and
his left; and if, within eight days, he d
all his money, or give him some rational
Arthur had better look to himself. "And,"
gets me committed to prison, and thereby tl
me to deal with him, he will be very mu
thereby the hand would only be changed."

The money was forthcoming on the ap:
Lilburne was not satisfied. Unhappily for ¦
rig, one of the numerous malversations '
singularly augmented his private fortune,
George Lilburne, John's uncle. John zeal
uncle's cause, collected witnesses, published
sented petitions: Sir Arthur's actions were
probably with that characteristic exaggeratic
employed, even when it was least necessary.
matter, in the opinion of the Parliament, co
ful; and the animosity it excited was so ¦
Lilburne, shortly after his acquittal, was ele
the common council of the city of London, t'
nulled the election;† a person named Ch¦
been active on Lilburne's behalf, was ser
deprived of his rights as a member of the
several others were subjected to prosecut
account. On the 15th of January, 165:
against Sir Arthur Haslerig was declared
burne was condemned to pay a fine of seven
and banished from the kingdom under pa:
champion of liberty had become troublesome
than one. Always active and ardent in his
existing despotism, Lilburne had begun to ¦
favourite system among the Royalists, wit
ments were easily made; and he had frequ
public that, if a master were indispensable
serve Prince Charles than any other, provi
could be made with him upon the basis of

* In August, 1651.
† On the 26th of December, 1649.

f the People." Neither the Royalists nor the Levellers, who
were more vigorously repressed by Cromwell in the army
than by Parliament in the nation, were in a condition to offer
any effectual resistance to the rapid increase of the new
power; but this power was glad to remove out of the way a
leader who was ever ready to foment discontent; and by one
of those tricks which were so largely employed in Cromwell's
policy, the Long Parliament, whose destruction he was mediating, was secretly urged by him to decree the banishment of
Lilburne, with whom he had just become reconciled. Such
is at least the fact attested in a letter which the undaunted
Leveller wrote to Cromwell from the place of his exile, and in
which he declares himself " as much honest John Lilburne as
ever I was in my life, that neither loves flattery nor fears
greatness or threatenings."*

However it may be, Lilburne then considered the Long
Parliament to be his real enemy. He retired to Holland, and
the ardour of his hostility led him, it is said, to enter into the
closest intimacy with several Royalists, proscribed like himself. He lived familiarly at Amsterdam with the Duke of
Buckingham, Sir John Colepepper, Sir Ralph Hopton, and
Bishop Bramhall, and even, according to certain reports,
offered to rid them in six months of Cromwell, the Council of
State, and the Parliament, if they would place ten thousand
pounds at his disposal. But the men who denounced Lilburne's plots were Cromwell's spies. In 1653, as soon as the
exiled Leveller heard of the expulsion of the Long Parliament,
he wrote a respectful letter to Cromwell to obtain permission
to return to England. Not having received an answer, he
returned without permission, about the middle of June, 1653.
He did not find more liberty in his native country than had
been allowed him by the Parliamentary Republic; the arbitrary exercise of power had only passed into stronger hands.
Lilburne was arrested soon after his arrival, and sentenced to
be tried for having broken his banishment. "Free-born
John," says a letter of this period, " has been sent to the Old
Bailey assizes, and I think he will soon be hung."
Lilburne was not a man to allow himself to be hanged so
easily. To ensure his condemnation, all those precautions
had been taken which could be invented by the subtle and
shameless dexterity of the servants of a powerful tyranny.

* Biographia Britannica, vol. v., p. 2960.

The trial was to be hurried through as quickly as possible; it commenced at the time when all the most celebrated lawyers, who might otherwise have aided Lilburne by their advice, had left London for their various circuits through the counties. The prisoner was refused a copy of his indictment, and his accusers would not read publicly the act of Parliament which had banished him, and upon which his indictment was founded. To give the jury an unfavourable impression of the case, the reports of the agents who had denounced his connexion with the Royalists in Holland were published. Lilburne struggled, with indomitable energy, against all these premeditated obstacles. Before their departure, he succeeded in procuring the written advice of two celebrated advocates one of whom was the learned Presbyterian Maynard. He compelled the court to give him a copy of the indictment and to promise that the act ordaining his banishment should be publicly read. He opposed obstinacy to obstinacy, and argument to argument. The Attorney-General Prideaux who had very irregularly taken his seat among the judges was very vehement against him. Lilburne immediately called to him to come down from his seat with that contemptuous energy which disturbs and weakens the boldest authority And when the court was inflexible, when all Lilburne's efforts failed to obtain what he demanded, he cried out, in passionate despair, "My Lord, rob me not of my birthright, the benefit of the law, which again and again I demand as my right and inheritance. And, my Lord, if you will be so audacious and unjust in the face of this great auditory of people, to deny me, and rob me of all the rules of justice and right, and will forcibly stop my mouth, and not suffer me freely to speak for my life according to law, I will cry out and appeal to the people that hear me this day, how that my Lord Mayor, and this court, by violence rob me of my birthright by law, and will not suffer me to speak for my life."

The audience were greatly moved by these words; Lilburne's relatives and friends, including his aged father and many brave soldiers who had been his companions in arms surrounded him continually, and lent him their support when ever he required it. The judges, in their anger, displayed their anxiety and displeasure; the accuser spoke in a low stuttering tone; and fresh reinforcements of guards were sent for. The trial, with all its incidents, lasted from the 13th o

ly to the 20th of August, 1653. At the last moment, Lil-
rne thus addressed the jury: "The act whereupon I am
licted, is a lie and a falsehood; an act that hath no reason
it, no law for it; it was done as Pharaoh did, resolved upon
e question that all the male children should be murdered.
nce the king's head was cut off, they could not make an
t of Parliament. By the same law they voted me to death,
ey might vote any of you honest jurymen. And I charge
u to consider, whether if I die on the Monday, the Parlia-
ent on Tuesday may not pass such a sentence against every
e of you twelve, and upon your wives and children, and all
ur relations; and then upon the rest of this city, and then
on the whole county of Middlesex, and then upon Hert-
rdshire, and so by degrees there be no people to inhabit
ngland but themselves."

Popular sympathy, and respect for the ancient laws of the
nd, overcame the efforts of all the Parliamentary and military
aders of the revolution; Lilburne was a second time acquitted
his jury.

Three days afterwards, on the 23rd of August, 1653, by
der of the Barebones Parliament, the Council of State sent
r the jury, and required them, with threat, to explain why
ey had pronounced such an acquittal. Seven of them for-
ally refused to answer, saying that they were accountable
r their verdict only to God and their conscience. Four
leged reasons for their vote, but maintained what they had
one, and stood by their colleagues. Against this firmness
n the part of obscure citizens, revolutionary tyranny could
ot venture to act; and they were allowed to return home.
But Lilburne was not set at liberty. On the recommendation
f Sir Anthony Ashley Cooper, who afterwards became the
elebrated Earl of Shaftesbury, the Parliament directed the
Council of State to take measures for preventing this mis-
hievous Leveller from disturbing the peace of the nation any
nore. He was accordingly imprisoned in the island of Jersey.
But there was no prison from which Lilburne could not make
his voice heard, and no distance which it could not traverse.
The report spread that he was making preparations for new
and more violent attacks. Tired of combating a popularity
which he could not vanquish, Cromwell attempted to neu-
ralise its influence. He excelled in the art of effecting compromises with even his most implacable enemies; and, it is

said, that he ordered that a pension should be paid to Lilburne, under the form of an indemnity, equal to his full salary
as a lieutenant-colonel.   Lilburne, on his part, had begun to
weary of a contest in which even success was useless.   The
negotiator of the treaty was his brother, Robert Lilburne, an
officer of distinction, and one of those honest men whom
military feeling had rendered a supporter and servant of
Cromwell.   John promised to live in quietness; and he was
restored to liberty and his native country.   He retired to
Eltham, in Kent, and amongst the Quakers, the gentlest but
most obstinate of sectaries, he passed the last four years of
a life of which it is impossible to say whether it was abridged
by his early fatigues or his subsequent tranquillity.   He died
on the 29th of August, 1657, still popular and powerless.[*]
He was a man of chimerical mind, without original or deep
views regarding general politics, and who would have been as
restless and discontented under a good government as he was
under a tyranny.   But his heart was honest and sincere; and
he was gifted, even to heroism, in the practical defence of his
rights, with that intelligent and indefatigable courage which
constitutes the best and most necessary guarantee of free
institutions.

Many years after his death, when the friends and the
memory of Cromwell and of Lilburne, of the Protector and
the Leveller, were subject to the same proscription, the
people used frequently to sing:

.

> John Lilburne is a stirring blade,
>   And understands the matter;
> He neither will king, bishops, lords,
>   Nor th' House of Commons flatter.
>
> John loves no power prerogatives,
>   But that derived from Sion;
> As for the mitre and the crown,
>   Those two he looks awry on.[†]

This song was composed and sung for the first time in
August, 1647,. in the Tower of London, by Sir Thomas
Wortley, at a banquet of Cavaliers and Levellers, who were
fellow-prisoners by the order of the Long Parliament.   The
people are frequently unjust and ungrateful towards their
living friends; but they are faithful to the memory of those
that are dead.

* Biographia Britannica, vol. v., p. 2961.
† Neal's History of the Puritans, vol. iv., p. 18.   (London, 1822.)

LORD THOMAS FAIRFAX.
[1611—1721.]

In every revolution, many ways for attaining power and
ory are sure to present themselves. Some men attain high
sitions by preserving a right judgment in the midst of
pular illusions, by their prudent foresight, or by their bold
rtility of mind and strength of character; others are
alted to dignities precisely because they are deficient in
ese qualities, because they are simple and credulous, inca-
ble of directing men and events, and capable only of
rving them. The heroes of revolutions are to be found in
o very dissimilar classes—ambitious politicians and sincere
pes.

Thomas Fairfax appears in the English revolution as a
ro of the latter class. Born on the 17th of January, 1611,
Denton Manor, in the parish of Otley, Yorkshire, he re-
ived his education at St. John's College, Cambridge; and
uring the whole of his life he was distinguished, if not for
eat erudition, at least for considerable taste for literature,
pecially for the history and antiquities of his native coun-
y. But he early manifested a greater predilection for arms
an for learning; and not finding sufficiently active service
England, he passed into Holland, and enrolled himself as
volunteer under the command of Lord Vere. On his
turn to England in 1637, he married Lady Anne Vere, his
eneral's daughter, and took up his residence in his father's
ouse, not mixing actively in public affairs, but sympathising
eeply with the general indignation excited by the maxims
nd actions of Charles I., the bishops, and the court. His
ife was a zealous Presbyterian; his father, Lord Fer-
inando Fairfax, a man of wealth and activity, was the leader
f the opposition in his county. Young Fairfax was con-
dent and generous; the cause which his family maintained
as the cause of his country and his faith; before the con-
ict had broken out between the king and the Parliament,
e had taken his resolution; and when Charles, having left
ondon, came into Yorkshire to attempt to raise a guard for
is person, Fairfax was commissioned to present to him, in
he name of the county, a petition imploring his Majesty to
bandon his design of raising forces, and to listen to the

wishes of the Parliament. The king was afraid of all suc[
manifestations of public opinion, and tried to avoid the re
ception of the petition; but on the 3rd of June, 1642,
large assemblage took place on Heyworth Moor: "Mor
than forty thousand men were there, gentlemen, freeholder[
farmers, citizens, mounted and on foot. The Cavaliers pe[
ceived that the petition was circulating among them. The
burst into invectives and menaces, rode violently among th
groups, snatched the copies of the petition from the hands c
those who were reading it, and declared that the king woul
never receive it. Charles arrived, annoyed and vexed, nc
knowing what to say to this multitude, whose presence an
turbulence had already offended his impolitic gravity. Aft[
having read an equivocal declaration, he was hastily retirin
in order to avoid any reply, when young Fairfax succeede
in getting near him, fell suddenly on one knee, and display[
the petition on the pommel of his saddle, thus braving, ev[
at his feet, the displeasure of the king, who immediate.
urged his horse against him, and pushed him violently, 1
force him to retire, but in vain."*

The civil war soon placed more effective weapons than pe[
tions in Fairfax's hands. From 1642 to 1644, he and h
father took part in the numerous skirmishes which occurr[
between the Parliamentarians and Cavaliers in Yorkshi[
In this local warfare he speedily acquired a great reputati[
for brilliant, intelligent, and commanding bravery; and wh[
the operations of the general war brought a large Parl[
mentary army into the north of England, young Thom[
Fairfax was at once invested with a high command. The
early adventures and exploits of his youth were replete wi[
lasting and cherished recollections; for many years aft[
wards, in the retirement of his country seat, he took delig
in relating them, with some detail, in a work which he e[
titled "A Short Memorial of the Northern Actions in whi[
I was engaged during the War there, from the year 1642
the year 1644."

In 1645, the first leaders of the revolution, both in t[
Parliament and the army, had been displaced; and the Ind[
pendents, at length masters of the field, had decreed t[
formation of a new army to complete a victory which the fir[
conquerors strove in vain to arrest. The military renov[

* Guizot's History of the English Revolution, vol. i., p. 287. (Paris, 1850.)

Fairfax, combined with Cromwell's recommendation, procured for him the chief command. From this time forward, his life is the history of the revolution itself; as a general, he was ever victorious on the battle-field; as a politician he was merely the tool of Cromwell and the army, whose designs he served, at first through ignorance, and afterwards through weakness and infatuation. In his old age, he wrote a second series of Memoirs on this second period of his life; but they are short and sad, and seem rather a sorrowful justification than a narrative of his actions. "When I bring to mind," he says, "the sad consequences that crafty and designing men have brought to pass since those first innocent undertakings, I am ready to let go that confidence I once had with God, when I could say with Job, *Till I die I will not remove my integrity from me*, nor *shall my heart reproach me so long as I live*: but I am now more fit to take up his complaint and say, *Why did I not die? why did I not give up the ghost when my life was on the confines of the grave?*"*

Fairfax's justification may easily be summed up in few words: he did not know what he was doing, and did not wish to do what he did; this is a fact attested by history, and proved by his own narrative.

When his blindness was in some measure dispelled, when his honesty had at last grown weary of that complicity from which it had not been able to withdraw him, after the death of the king and the subjugation of the Parliament by the army, Fairfax retired completely from public life. The measure by which the Republican Parliament, in 1650, ordered the English army to carry the war into Scotland, where Charles II. had just been crowned, was the pretext for this resolution; he declared that his fidelity to the Presbyterian covenant would not permit him to attack the Scotch in their own country, and he therefore resigned his command. The death of his father, on the 13th of March, 1648, had put him in possession of his title and fortune. Thenceforward he lived on his own estate of Nun-Appleton, in Yorkshire, greatly respected by the Presbyterian party, which more than once attempted to rally round him, but perfectly unconnected with the events which occurred until Cromwell's death. His relations with the Protector, during this period, were not of a very courteous nature. Cromwell rarely showed him any

* Maseres' Select Tracts, vol. ii., p. 443.

consideration, and sometimes treated him with mistrust and
ill-humour.   He seemed to hold him of no account, and
never entrusted him with any public duty, except some insignificant commissions regarding the local affairs of the
county. When Fairfax married his only daughter, Lady Mary
to the Duke of Buckingham, Cromwell was offended that his
permission had not previously been requested, as had been
the custom under the monarchy ; and he was, moreover, of
opinion that the Duke of Buckingham would have been a
suitable husband for one of his own daughters.   In paying
Fairfax his compliments on the occasion, he made use of language which deeply wounded the victor at Naseby. "I have
laid it up," said Fairfax to one of his friends, "and will remember it when there is occasion."*

This occasion did not occur during the lifetime of Cromwell, who had no fear of Fairfax's displeasure.   But after
the death of the Protector, and the rapid downfal of his son
Richard, when the eyes of all England were turned towards
the restoration of Charles II., the men who were preparing
for its consummation thought that Fairfax would willingly
help them, and they were not deceived.   Now, as clear-
sighted as he had formerly been credulous, the general of
the Parliamentary army hastened to place at the service of
Charles II. the popularity, consideration, and credit, which
he had gained by making war upon Charles I.   As soon as
he learned, by a message from Monk himself, that the general
of the Scottish army was preparing to march into England,
first to support the Rump against the London army, and probably afterwards to help the king against the Rump, he sent
his cousin, Brian Fairfax, to inform him that he was ready to
co-operate with him, and that he would appear in arms in a
few days, with such forces as he could collect.   He did appear
in arms, in fact, rather sooner than he had announced he
would, and Monk, on hearing this news, hastened forward to
assist him.   On his arrival at York, Monk was met by Bowles,
the chaplain and confidential adviser of Fairfax. "This gentleman," says Price, Monk's chaplain, in his Memoirs, "dealt
with the general about weighty and dangerous affairs.   One
night, above the rest, keeping him up so very late, that, upon
my entering the chamber to go to prayers, I found him and
Bowles in very private discourse, and the general ordered me

* The Fairfax Correspondence, first series, vol. i., p. cvi.

go out for a while, but not to bed. Some time after midnight Bowles went away, so that then our servants hoped to sleep; but the general sent for me into him, and commanded them to stay without, as before. He took me close to him, and said, "What do you think? Mr. Bowles has pressed me very hard to stay here, and declare for the king, assuring me that I shall have great assistance." I started at the boldness of the proposition, and asked him whether he had made Bowles any such promise. He answered me, "No; truly I have not, or I have not yet." For I found him a little perplexed in his thoughts, and I, myself, was as much; but, after a little pause, I spake to this effect: "That after the famous Gustavus, King of Sweedland, was slain in Germany,* his effigies in wax, with those of his queen and children, were carried up and down to be shown for twopence, the spectators being entertained with the story of his life, of which I remember this passage, that, when this king entered Germany, he said, ' *That if his shirt knew what he intended to do, he would tear it from his back, and burn it.*' My application of this saying to the general was designed to entreat him to keep between this and the walls of London; and when he came within them, which I doubted not but he would do very shortly, then to open his eyes and consider what he had to do."†

There was no need to press Monk to wait and be silent. He paid Fairfax a visit at his residence of Nun-Appleton, and Fairfax repeated to him what he had already stated, by means of his chaplain, Bowles; being perfectly convinced, he said, that there would be no peace in England until the nation were settled upon the old foundation of monarchy, and King Charles II. restored. "The general," says Brian Fairfax, "was more reserved than he needed to be upon this free discourse of my Lord Fairfax, being alone with him in his study, which gave my Lord occasion to suspect him ever after, till he declared himself the spring following to be of the same mind, having received another letter at London from my Lord Fairfax, accompanied with the address of all the gentlemen of Yorkshire for a free Parliament, and that they would pay no taxes till it met."‡

* Gustavus Adolphus was killed at the battle of Lutzen, on the 16th of November, 1633.
† Maseres' Select Tracts, vol. ii., pp. 731-752.
‡ The Fairfax Correspondence, first series, vol. i., p. cxi.

I.

114 MONK'S CONTEMPORARIES.

Events rapidly pursued their course. On the 29th
March, 1660, Fairfax was elected to represent Yorkshire i
the Healing Parliament; and on the 16th of May he pro
ceeded to the Hague, at the head of the deputies who ha
been sent by the House of Commons to recal Charles I
The king received him with marked distinction, sent Lor
Gerard to compliment him personally, and granted him
long private audience, to which his chaplain, Mr. Bowle
was also admitted; and when, after the Restoration, th
ceremony of the coronation took place, the king rode a hor
which Fairfax had given him, and to which the old warric
addressed some wretched verses, to congratulate him on th
great honour.

However, notwithstanding the ardour of his royalist zea
and the sincerity of his repentance, Fairfax did not abando
even those of his former associates whose actions he had no
approved. When the question of the amnesty, and the fat
of the regicides was discussed in Parliament, he oppose
their being brought to trial, saying that, if any one deserve
to be punished on that account, he was the greatest culpr
of all, for, at the time of the king's death, he had possesse
power enough to prevent his execution, and had not thougl
proper to employ it. But Fairfax, in 1660, was no mor
able to offer any effectual opposition to the trial of the reg
cides than he had been, in 1649, to prevent the judgment
Charles I. Shortly after the dissolution of the Healir
Parliament, in December, 1660, he left London for his sei
of Nun-Appleton, near York, which he had built some yea
before, and where he continued to reside until his deat
which occurred after a short illness, on the 12th of Noven
ber, 1671. He had long been a sufferer from gout and ston
which he endured with a patience equal to the courage
had displayed in battle. During the last few years of his li
he was deprived of the use of his lower limbs, and remaine
continually seated in his arm-chair, receiving with grave ar
unruffled countenance, from his family, his friends, his neig
bours, and his dependents, those testimonies of respect ar
affection which he had won by the simple austerity of h
manners, the sincerity of his convictions, the gentleness
his disposition, and the recollections of his former glor
which was daily heightened by the errors of the Restoratio
His religious duties occupied a large portion of his time.

w hours before his death he asked for a Bible. "My eyes
ow dim," he said, as he opened it; but, nevertheless, he
nd the 42nd Psalm: "As the hart panteth after the water
ooks, so panteth my soul after thee, O God! . . . When
all I come and appear before God?" He had scarcely read
us far when he fell into a mortal lethargy, and shortly after
pired.

His daughter, Lady Mary Fairfax, Duchess of Bucking-
m, was, next to God, his first and last thought. Her mar-
age was the occasion of his fulfilling a singular prediction
his grandfather, Lord Thomas Fairfax, the founder of the
litical fortune of his family, for he was the first of the name
ised to the peerage with the title of Baron Fairfax of
meron. "Not many months before his death, he, walking
his great parlour at Denton, I only then present," says one
his sons, Charles Fairfax of Wenston, younger brother of
rd Ferdinando Fairfax, and consequently uncle of the Par-
mentary general, "did seem much perplexed and troubled
his mind, but, after a few turns, broke out into these, or
e like expressions: 'Charles, I am thinking what will
come of my family when I am gone; I have added a title
the heir-male of my house, and shall leave a competent estate
support it. Ferdinando will keep it, and leave it to his son;
it such is Tom's pride, led by his wife, that he, not con-
nted to live in our rank, will destroy his house.' I then
fered something in vindication of both; yet, notwithstand-
g, he solemnly charged me upon his blessing to make known
hat he told me when I saw a probability that it might so
ll out. . . . . After some years, when I was informed
hat the now Lord Thomas had cut off the entail made by his
ther and grandfather for the settlement of the estate upon
e heir-male, charging the land with a complete provision
r a daughter or daughters; he, the now Lord Fairfax, being
hen at Denton, in the very same room where I received my
arge, I faithfully acquainted him with the passages, as above
id. He gave me my liberty, without words of impertinency,
any appearance of distaste, and made me (then) more than
erbal expressions of a kind acceptance."*

Lord Fairfax was attached to his uncle, and respectful to
e memory of his grandfather; but he nevertheless per-
sted in the determination which the latter had foreseen;

* The Fairfax Correspondence, first series, vol. i., pp. cvii.-cviii.

and, abolishing the entail of the estates up
left all his fortune to his daughter, the Duc
ham.   But his daughter was utterly ruined
of which Fairfax was so proud.   After ha
wife wretched during his lifetime, the Duk
left her, at his death, so overwhelmed wit
estate at Nun-Appleton was entirely absorl
of the creditors: and Fairfax's cherishec
Lady Mary whom he was so anxious to pla
tion, both for wealth and rank—died in Lo
of October, 1704, under circumstances of co:
and distress.

As for the title of Baron Fairfax of Cam
of the United Kingdom, it passed, at Fairl
cousin Henry, whose grandson Thomas, th
grated to Virginia, where he had immense e
he definitively established his family, thou
his rank and seat among the peers of En
still stands in the British peerage book, but
the family is thus indicated:—" Seat : W
land, United States of America."

In his retirement at Nun-Appleton, Fair
his death a strong taste for literary as we
pations.   He left manuscript translation
the Canticles, and some other portions of
tures, a short poem upon solitude, a numbe
sermons, written either by himself or by his
ter, and a treatise on the shortness of lif
scripts, with some others, are preserved; p
at Denton, and part in Mr. Thoresby's mu
than one occasion, while the civil war was a
fax afforded most useful protection to liters
institutions.   By his care, the libraries at
were, partially at least, preserved from p
contributed to the publication of the great
was the constant patron of the learned D
works upon British antiquities.

Epitaphs, and particularly family epitaphs
Nevertheless, that which the Duke of Buck
on Fairfax's tomb is worthy of remark.   H
picted in it with considerable truthfulness;
not merely the opinion entertained of his

also the brilliancy of his renown in his own country,
ι during the sway of the party which he had so long oped. It is entitled

PINDARIC POEM ON THE DEATH OF THE LORD FAIRFAX.

Under this stone does lie
One born for victory;
Fairfax the valiant, and the only he
Whoe'er for that alone a conqueror would be:
Both sexes' virtues were in him combined;
He had the fierceness of the manliest mind,
And yet the meekness, too, of womankind.
    He never knew what envy was, nor hate;
His soul was filled with truth and honesty,
And with another thing, quite out of date, called modesty.

He ne'er seemed impudent, but in the place
Where impudence itself dares seldom show its face;
Had any strangers spied him in the room
With some of those he had overcome,
    And had not heard their talk, but only seen
    Their gesture and their mien,
    They would have sworn he had the vanquished been:
For as they bragged, and dreadful would appear,
    While they their own ill-luck in war repeated,
His modesty still made him blush, to hear
    How often he had them defeated.

Through his whole life, the part he bore
    Was wonderful and great,
And yet it so appeared in nothing more
    Than in his private last retreat;
For 'tis a stranger thing to find
One man of such a worthy mind,
    As can dismiss the power which he has got;
Than millions of the polls and braves;
Those despicable fools and knaves,
Who such a pudder make,
Through dulness and mistake,
    In seeking after power, and get it not.

When all the nation he had won,
    And with expense of blood had bought
    Store great enough, he thought
Of glory and renown;
He then his arms laid down,
    With just as little pride
    As if he had been of his enemies' side,
Or one of them could do that were undone:
    He neither wealth nor places sought—
    He never for himself but others fought:
        He was content to know
        (For he had found it so)
That when he pleased to conquer, he was able,
And left the spoil and plunder to the rabble.

He might have been a king,
But that he understood
How much it was a meaner thing
To be unjustly great than honourably good.
This from the world did admiration draw,
And, from his friends, both love and awe,
    Rememb'ring what he did in fight before:
      And his foes loved him too,
      As they were bound to do,
    Because he was resolved to fight no more.
So, blessed by all, he died; but far more blest were we,
If we were sure to live till we could see
A man as great in war, as just in peace as he.[*]

Whatever latitude we may allow to the illusions of filial piety, and the eulogies of the deceased, such an epitaph could not have been inscribed, in the sight and knowledge of a whole people, of a free people, upon the tomb of a man whom public opinion had not greatly honoured. England really held Fairfax in high honour; and this not merely on account of his military glory, which was the more brilliant because his personal bravery and the enthusiasm with which he inspired his soldiers had always had a large share in his successes; Fairfax was also distinguished by the utmost frankness and disinterestedness, and these qualities, notwithstanding all faults and mistakes, strike the imagination and command the esteem of our fellow-men. He had been the dupe and the instrument of factions, but he was a perfect stranger to the spirit of faction; not only did he not seek his personal advantage in war and politics, he did not even seek to obtain the triumph of those party interests and passions which so frequently corrupt generous minds, when they have once fallen under their influence. Isolated in the midst of the Independents, the Republicans, and the army, who successively made use of him against the Presbyterians, the Parliament, and the monarchy, Fairfax lent his sanction to their actions, without sharing in their plans or associating himself with their intrigues; though continually deceived, he was never a deceiver; he was weak through his credulity, and credulous through his weakness; equally incapable of resisting the perverse and of being perverted by them. As long as he was concerned in public affairs, the clever men of all parties considered him a mere puppet; when the revolution appeared to be completed, his fellow-citizens were so convinced of his candour and rectitude, that they did not

---

[*] The works of George Villiers, Duke of Buckingham, vol. ii., pp. 135-137.

pute to him any of the evil that had been done under his
me.

In 1822, Mr. Fiennes Wykeham Martin, the proprietor
Leeds Castle, in the county of Kent, having occasion to
ake some alterations in the castle, set apart for sale a
uantity of useless furniture. Amongst the lumber which
as thus to be swept away was an old oaken chest, which
as purchased for a few shillings by Mr. Gooding, a shoe-
aker, in the neighbouring village of Lenham. Upon the
spection of its contents, Mr. Gooding found an enormous
uantity of manuscripts, carefully arranged. Not attaching
ny special value to treasures of this description, he con-
gned the papers to a cellar, to be destroyed, as occasion
erved, for waste paper. It was fortunately suggested to
Ir. Gooding, however, to offer them to Mr. Newington
Hughes, a banker at Maidstone, and well known as a col-
ctor of antiquities. Mr. Hughes bought them. Some of
he parchments had already been cut into strips for shoe-
akers' measures; others had been taken and dispersed
hrough the villages. Mr. Hughes and some of his fellow
ntiquaries instituted a diligent search for them, and they
ere nearly all recovered. These papers, originally de-
osited in one of Fairfax's residences in Yorkshire, had
oubtless been transferred to Leeds Castle on the marriage
f Thomas, fifth Lord Fairfax, to the daughter of Lord Cul-
epper, the owner of the latter estate. They contain
omestic documents and correspondence of the Fairfax
mily for two centuries, but chiefly concern the period of
he English revolution, from the accession of the Stuarts to
hat of the House of Hanover. Mr. Johnson, an eminent
awyer, commenced their publication three years ago. Two
olumes appeared in 1848, under the auspices of Mr. Bent-
y, the publisher, and were entitled, " The Fairfax Corre-
pondence: Memoirs of the Reign of Charles I." They
nly extend as far as the commencement of the civil war, in
642. It is much to be desired that this publication should
e completed; although it has hitherto revealed no new and
mportant facts, it contains many curious details respecting
he exact sequence of events, and the characters of the
rincipal personages who occur in the history.

In 1849, the second series of the "Fairfax Correspondence,"

relating to the period of the civil war and the Restoration, was
published under the editorship of Mr. Robert Bell.   " These
volumes," says the editor, "are crowded with minute details and
individual experiences, and bring us closer to the actual vicissitudes of the flying campaigns—from the hoisting of the roya
standard at Nottingham, to the imprisonment of the king a
Carisbrook—than any previous publication.   Written fo
the most part on the instant, under the walls of besieged
towns, in the committee-rooms of the House of Commons
on the field of battle, or in the midst of councils of war, they
are distinguished by a freshness and freedom seldom found
in documents of a more formal and elaborate character.'
Four volumes of this character must surely constitute a most
important addition to our historical literature.

MRS. HUTCHINSON.

[1620—1669.]

In the Tower of London, on the 29th of January, 1620,
five years before Charles I. ascended the throne, was born
Lucy Apsley, daughter of Sir Allen Apsley, Lieutenant of
the Tower—a devoted servant of the king, and whose sons,
when the war broke out between the king and the Parliament, were among the most faithful of the Cavaliers.   " My
mother," says Mrs. Hutchinson, in her Memoirs, " while she
was with child of me, dreamed that she was walking in the
garden with my father, and that a star came down into her hand,
with other circumstances, which, though I have often heard, I
minded not enough to remember perfectly; only my father told
her, her dream signified she should have a daughter of some
extraordinary eminency, which thing, like such vain prophe-
cies, wrought as far as it could its own accomplishment;
for my father and mother, fancying me then beautiful, and
more than ordinarily apprehensive (quick to learn), applied
all their cares and spared no cost to improve me in my education, which procured me the admiration of those that flattered
my parents. . . . . When I was about seven years of age, I
remember I had at one time eight tutors in several qualities,
languages, music, dancing, writing, and needlework ; but my

genius was quite averse from all but my book, and that I was so eager of, that every moment I could steal from my play, I would employ in any book I could find .... My father would have me learn Latin, and I was so apt that I outstripped my brothers who were at school, although my father's chaplain, that was my tutor, was a pitiful dull fellow. My mother would have been contented if I had not so wholly addicted myself to my learning as to neglect my other qualities. As for music and dancing, I profited very little in them, and I would never practise my lute or harpsichords but when my masters were with me; and for my needle, I absolutely hated it. Play among other children I despised, and when I was forced to entertain such as came to visit me, I tired them with more grave instructions than their mothers, and plucked all their babies to pieces, and kept the children in such awe, that they were glad when I entertained myself with graver company; to whom I was very acceptable, and living in the house with many persons that had a great deal of wit, and very profitable serious discourse, being frequent at my father's table, and in my mother's drawing-room, I was very attentive to all, and gathered up things that I would utter again, to great admiration of many that took my memory and imitation for wit. It pleased God that, through the good instructions of my mother, and the sermons she carried me to, I was convinced that the knowledge of God was the most excellent study, and accordingly applied myself to it, and to practise as I was taught. I used to exhort my mother's maids much, and to turn their idle discourses to good subjects; but I thought when I had done this on the Lord's Day, and every day performed my due tasks of reading and praying, that then I was free to anything that was not sin; for I was not at that time convinced of the vanity of conversation which was not scandalously wicked. I thought it no sin to learn or hear witty songs and amorous sonnets or poems, and twenty things of that kind, wherein I was so apt that I became the confidant in all the loves that were managed among my mother's young women; and there was none of them but had many lovers, and some particular friends beloved above the rest."*

Whilst Lucy Apsley was growing into womanhood, and dividing her time between learned studies, pious exercises,

* Memoirs of Colonel Hutchinson, pp. 16-18, in "Bohn's Standard Library."

and romantic sentiments, a young gentleman, named John Hutchinson, born in 1616, four years before her, at Owthorpe, in Nottinghamshire, was springing into manhood, unknown to Lucy and her parents, but addicted to the same feelings, habits, and tastes as herself. "He was of a middle stature, of a slender and exactly well-proportioned shape in all parts; his complexion fair; his hair of light brown, very thick set in his youth, softer than the finest silk, and curling into loose, great rings at the end; his eyes of a lively grey, well-shaped, and full of lively vigour, graced with many becoming motions; his visage thin; his mouth well made, and his lips very ruddy and graceful, although the nether chap shut over the upper, yet it was in such a manner as was not unbecoming; his teeth were even, and white as the purest ivory; his chin was something long, and the mould of his face; his forehead was not very high; his nose was ʳaised and sharp; but withal he had a most amiable countenance, which carried in it something of magnanimity and majesty mixed with sweetness, that at the same time bespoke love and awe in all that saw him."*

Then follows the moral portraiture of John Hutchinson, his fine natural disposition, his acquired virtues, his character and piety, his spiritual, temporal, political, and domestic merits; and at the conclusion of this long expression of her love, admiration, and respect, Mrs. Hutchinson has written: "All this, and more, is true; but I so much dislike the manner of relating it, that I will make another essay."† This, in fact, she did; but, in the opinion of the editor of her Memoirs, her second attempt to delineate the character of her husband was not equal to the first; and the first only has been published.

The acquaintance which led to the intimate union of these two persons could not fail to be accompanied by some of those singular incidents which strike lively imaginations and influence passionate wills. In 1637, Lucy Apsley's family was established for a time at Richmond, near London; and Mr. Hutchinson was invited by one of his friends to spend the summer at the same place, in a house where, he was told, he would find "very good company and recreations." He mentioned his plan to a gentleman of his acquaintance, and

* Memoirs of Colonel Hutchinson, p. 22, in " Bohn's Standard Library."
† Ibid., p. 35, note.

told him of the house whither he was going; but this friend
"bid him take heed of the place, for it was so fatal for love,
that never any young disengaged person went thither who
returned again free. Mr. Hutchinson laughed at him, and
went to Richmond, where he found a great deal of good
young company."* At this time, Miss Apsley was not there;
but Mr. Hutchinson heard a great deal about her. "One
day, when he was at her mother's house, some half a mile
from Richmond, looking upon an odd by-shelf in a closet, he
found a few Latin books; asking whose they were, he was
told they were Miss Lucy Apsley's; whereupon, inquiring
more after her, he began first to be sorry she was gone before he had seen her, and gone upon such an account that he
was not likely to see her. Then he grew to love to hear
mention of her, and the other gentlewomen who had been
her companions used to talk much to him of her, telling him
how reserved and studious she was, and other things which
they esteemed no advantage. But it so much inflamed Mr.
Hutchinson's desire of seeing her, that he began to wonder
at himself, that his heart, which had ever entertained so
much indifference for the most excellent of womankind,
should have such strong impulses towards a stranger he
never saw. One day there was a great deal of company at
Mr. Coleman's, the gentleman's house where he tabled, to
hear the music; and a certain song was sung which had been
lately set, and gave occasion to some of the company to mention an answer to it, which was in the house, and upon some
of their desires read. A gentleman saying it was believed
that a woman in the neighbourhood had made it, it was presently inquired who; whereupon a gentleman, then present,
who had made the first song, said there were but two women
that could be guilty of it; whereof one was a lady then
among them, the other Miss Apsley. Mr. Hutchinson, fancying something of rationality in the sonnet, beyond the
customary reach of a she-wit, addressed himself to the gentleman, and told him he could scarcely believe it was a
woman's; whereupon this gentleman, who was a man of
good understanding and expression, and inspired with some
passion for her himself, told Mr. Hutchinson that though,
for civility to the rest, he entitled another lady to the song,
yet he was confident it was Miss Apsley's only, for she had
* Memoirs of Colonel Hutchinson, p. 55.

sense above all the rest; and fell into such high praises of her, as might well have begotten those vehement desires of her acquaintance, which a strange sympathy in nature had before produced.

"Before many days had passed, a footboy of my lady her mother's came to young Miss Apsley as they were at dinner, bringing news that her mother and sister would in a few days return; and when they inquired of him whether Miss Apsley was married, having before been instructed to make them believe it, he smiled, and pulled out some bride-laces, which were given at a wedding in the house where she was, and gave them to the young gentlewoman and the gentleman's daughter of the house, and told them Miss Apsley bade him tell no news, but give them those tokens, and carried the matter so, that all the company believed she had been married. Mr. Hutchinson immediately turned pale as ashes, and felt a fainting to seize his spirits in that extraordinary manner, that he was fain to retire. When he was alone he began to recollect his wisdom and his reason, and to wonder at himself, why he should be so concerned in an unknown person; he then remembered the story that was told him when he came down, and began to believe there was some magic in the place, which enchanted men out of their right senses. Having fortified himself with resolution, he got up the next day; but yet could not quit himself of an extravagant perplexity of soul concerning this unknown gentlewoman, which had not been remarkable in another light person, but in him, who was from his childhood so serious and so rational in all his considerations, it was the effect of a miraculous power of Providence, leading him to her that was destined to make his future joy. While she so ran in his thoughts, meeting the boy again, he found out, upon a little stricter examination of him, that she was not married, and pleased himself in the hopes of her speedy return."*

Miss Apsley returned; Mr. Hutchinson saw her; they took much pleasure in each other's society, and soon gave expression to their mutual affection, with that combination of frankness and timidity which ever characterises the feelings of serious, virtuous, and enthusiastic youth. Various obstacles for some time thwarted the consummation of their happiness; their families hesitated, the young men were jealous, and the young ladies envious. Miss Apsley had an attack of

* Memoirs of Colonel Hutchinson, pp. 57-60.

small-pox, and fears were entertained, first for her life, and afterwards for her beauty. But she regained her health, and retained her charms. The constancy of Mr. Hutchinson overcame all obstacles. "I shall pass by," says Mrs. Hutchinson, "all the little amorous relations which, if I would take the pains to relate, would make a true history of a more handsome management of love than the best romances describe; but these are to be forgotten as the vanities of youth, not worthy of mention among the greater transactions of his life."*

Fortunately for us, Mrs. Hutchinson was not, when she began to write her Memoirs, under the influence of this Puritan rigidity with reference to the tender recollections of her youth; her first impulse was to allow herself to go on relating them with grave and touching sincerity, in which a little vain complacency sometimes appears, and even after she had prescribed herself silence upon this subject, her narrative of the great events in which her husband took a part continues to be much more of a biography than of a history. And this constitutes its peculiar merit and interest. In most of the memoirs relating to the English revolution, the narrator says very little about himself, and those matters which interested himself only. Royalists, Parliamentarians, and Republicans, all seem to forget themselves, and take heed only of the general fate of their cause; they relate the history of their own time, not of themselves; each man describes and judges facts according to the opinions and fashions of his party; but their only care is of the political interests which they maintain, and they seldom step aside to enter into details unconnected with the narrative of historical occurrences. In the Memoirs of Mrs. Hutchinson, on the contrary, the history of public affairs occupies only a secondary position; it was of Colonel Hutchinson himself, his position and actions, the incidents and experiences of his life, that his wife desired to perpetuate the remembrance. The part played by Sir John Hutchinson was not a conspicuous one; the trial of Charles I. was the only important act in which he shared; and yet he was a man of great activity; around him, in his county, within the walls of Nottingham (of which town he was governor), were displayed all the passions, and undergone all the vicissitudes, of the struggle which then convulsed England. The same cause

* Memoirs of Colonel Hutchinson, p. 62.

which, at London and in the Parliament, produced historical
events, led at Nottingham to municipal, or even simply domestic, occurrences, which excited as strong emotions, and
required from the men who wielded the local authority efforts
as numerous and vigorous, as were put forth at Westminster
by the leaders of the nation. These are the scenes which
Mrs. Hutchinson depicts; pictures of life, which constitute
an essential part of history, although history says very little
about them. Hampden, Pym, Strafford, Fairfax, Ireton, and
even Cromwell himself, only appear occasionally and dimly in
Mrs. Hutchinson's Memoirs; the persons who act, speak, and
occupy a prominent ʻposition in her work are Mr. Milling-
ton, the representative of Nottingham in Parliament; Dr.
Plumptre, a physician at Nottingham; Mr. Chadwick, a
lawyer; Mr. Hooper, an engineer; Mr. Palmer, a preacher;
and twenty others, as active as they were obscure, and who
really caused and guided, in their district or in their town,
that revolution from the history of which, a few years afterwards, their names had entirely disappeared. Mrs. Hutchinson
passed her life among these unknown revolutionaries; she describes their rivalries, their intrigues, their characters; and
relates the efforts made by the different parties, or fractions
of parties, to conquer, supplant, or injure each other. We
penetrate, under her guidance, into the midst of their families.
And whilst she brings before us these personages, true types
of the age in which they lived, but otherwise devoted to oblivion, she has this very rare merit, that neither the interests
of her cause nor her own passions can blind her with regard
to the vices or absurdities of the petty heroes and unworthy
servants of her party. As regards general events, she shares
in the prejudices and ignorance of the Puritan and Republican fanaticism of her times; but whenever she speaks of
events that have come under her own cognizance, that have occurred in her own neighbourhood, she rarely fails to manifest
independence and rectitude of mind; and she unhesitatingly
attacks and denounces anything that has excited her virtuous
indignation. In Derbyshire, which borders upon Nottinghamshire, Sir John Gell had raised a regiment of infantry on behalf of the Parliament. "These," says Mrs. Hutchinson,
"were good, stout, fighting-men, but the most licentious, ungovernable wretches that belonged to the Parliament. As
regards (Sir John Gell) himself, no man knew for what reason

he chose that side ; for he had not understanding enough to judge the equity of the cause, nor piety nor holiness ; being a foul adulterer all the time he served the Parliament, and so unjust that, without any remorse, he suffered his men indifferently to plunder both honest men and Cavaliers. . . . This man kept the journalists in pension, so that whatever was done in the neighbouring counties against the enemy was attributed to him ; and thus he hath indirectly purchased himself a name in story which he never merited. He was a very bad man, to sum up all in that word, yet an instrument of service to the Parliament in those parts."*

At Nottingham itself, Chadwick, the lawyer, and Palmer, the minister, were amongst the most important members of the Parliamentarian party. "Chadwick," says Mrs. Hutchinson, " was a fellow of a most pragmatical temper, and, to say truth, had strangely wrought himself into a station unfit for him. By flatteries and dissimulations he kept up his credit with the godly, cutting his hair, and taking up a form of godliness, the better to deceive. He was very poor, although he got abundance of money by a thousand cheats and other base ways, wherein he exercised all his life ; but he was as great a prodigal in spending as knave in getting. Among other villanies which he secretly practised, he was a libidinous goat, for which his wife, they say, paid him with making him a cuckold ; yet were there not two persons to be found that pretended more sanctity than these two."†

As for Palmer, the minister, " this man had a bold, ready, earnest way of preaching, and lived holily and regularly as to outward conversation, whereby he got a great reputation among the godly ; and this reputation swelled his spirit, which was very vain-glorious, covetous, contentious, and ambitious. The Newarkers plundered all the country even to the walls of Nottingham ; upon which some godly men offered themselves to bring in their horses, and form a troop for the defence of the country, and Mr. Palmer had a commission to be their captain. He would have it believed that it was rather pressed upon him, than he pressed into it ; and, therefore, being at that time in the castle, he came to the governor and his wife, telling them that these honest people pressed him very much to be their captain, and desiring their friendly and Christian

* Memoirs of Colonel Hutchinson, pp. 127-128.
† Ibid., pp. 134-136.

advice whether he should accept or refuse it. They freely
told him, that having entered into a charge of another kind,
they thought it not fit for him to engage in this; and that he
might as much advance the public service, and satisfy the
men, in marching with them in the nature of a chaplain as in
that of a captain. He, that asked not counsel to take any
contrary to his first resolve, went away confused when he
found he was not advised as he would have been, and said he
would endeavour to persuade them to be content; and afterwards said, they would not be otherwise satisfied, and so he
was forced to accept the commission."*

In view of the base and shameful practices of these subaltern
revolutionaries it is impossible not to feel a lively interest—
indeed, a kind of affection for Colonel Hutchinson and his
wife, in whose household piety mingled with nobility, and
gravity with tenderness, where the most hallowed domestic
feelings were united with the most sincere patriotism, and
where Puritan stiffness did not exclude either the passionate
enthusiasm of a wife's love for her husband, or the elegant
refinement of manners of a gentleman who devoted himself
to the popular cause without being influenced by the hatred,
the envy, the avarice, the thirst for vengeance, or any of the
passions of the multitude: passions as brutal as they are
hideous, even during those short and rare intervals when the
multitude is in the right. In 1646, Colonel Hutchinson,
though he did not entirely leave Nottingham, was transferred
to a wider sphere of action. He was elected a member of
the House of Commons, and his Parliamentary duties compelled him from that time forward to spend part of the year
in London. He found that the same egotistical passions, the
same absurd intrigues, and the same moral miseries as he had
deplored and combated in his county, existed in the capital;
but he and his wife were as uncorrupted at London as they
had been at Nottingham. In describing the scenes and actors
of the great theatre into which she had been introduced,
Mrs. Hutchinson displays the same sound and unbiassed
judgment as she had exhibited in relating the cabals and corruptions of the small town in which she had previously resided. "It was a misery to be bewailed in those days," she
says, "that many of the Parliamentary party exercised cruelty,

* Memoirs of Colonel Hutchinson, p. 175.

justice, and oppression to their conquered enemies.* . . . . .
lmost all the Parliament-garrisons were infected and dis-
rbed with factious little people, insomuch that many worthy
ntlemen were wearied out of their commands, and oppressed
a certain mean sort of people in the House, whom to dis-
nguish from the more honourable gentlemen, they called
Worsted-stocking Men.† . . . . . Cromwell's wife and children
ere setting up for principality, which suited no better with
ny of them than scarlet on the ape; only, to speak the truth
himself, he had much natural greatness, and well became
he place he had usurped. His daughter, Fleetwood, was
umbled, and not exalted with these things; but the rest
ere insolent fools. Claypole, who married his daughter,
nd his son, Henry, were two debauched, ungodly Cavaliers.
ichard was a peasant in his nature, yet gentle and virtuous,
ut became not greatness. His court was full of sin and
nity, and the more abominable, because they had not yet
uite cast away the name of God, but profaned it by taking
in vain upon them. True religion was now almost lost,
ven among the religious party, and hypocrisy became an
pidemical disease, to the sad grief of Colonel Hutchinson,
nd all true-hearted Christians and Englishmen."‡

Even when she is speaking of the most fanatical servants of
at cause to which her husband and herself were so passion-
ely devoted, Mrs. Hutchinson retains perfect freedom of
dgment, accurately observes their weaknesses, and some-
mes stoops to irony in her description of them. " Major-
eneral Harrison," she says, " who was but a mean man's
n, and of a mean education, and of no estate before the war,
d gathered an estate of two thousand a year besides en-
ossing great offices, and encroaching upon his under-officers;
d maintained his coach and family at a height as if they had
en born to a principality. About the same time a great
nbassador from the King of Spain was to have public
dience in the House, and was the first who had addressed
em, owning them as a republic. The day before his au-
ience, Colonel Hutchinson was sitting in the House, near
me young men handsomely clad, among whom was Mr.
harles Rich, since Earl of Warwick; and the colonel him-
lf had on that day a habit which was pretty rich but grave,

* Memoirs of Colonel Hutchinson, p 353.   † Ibid., p. 279.
‡ Ibid., p. 370.

K

and no other than he usually wore. Harrison, addressing himself particularly to him, admonished them all, that now the nations sent to them, they should labour to shine before them in wisdom, piety, righteousness, and justice, and not in gold and silver, and worldly bravery, which did not become saints; and that the next day, when the ambassadors came, they should not set themselves out in gorgeous habits, which were unsuitable to holy professions. The colonel, although he was not convinced of any misbecoming bravery in the suit he wore that day, which was but of sad-coloured cloth trimmed with gold, and silver points and buttons; yet, because he would not appear offensive in the eyes of religious persons, the next day he went in a plain black suit, and so did all the other gentlemen; but Harrison came that day in a scarlet coat and cloak, both laden with gold and silver lace, and the coat so covered with clinquant (foil), that one scarcely could discern the ground, and in this glittering habit he set himself just under the Speaker's chair; which made the other gentle-men think that his godly speeches the day before were but made that he alone might appear in the eyes of strangers. But this was part of his weakness. The Lord at last lifted him above these poor earthly elevations, which then and some time afterwards prevailed too much with him."*

Colonel Hutchinson and his wife were naturally too high-minded and refined in manners ever to fall into the littlenesses practised by some of their party; but they participated in their political passions and infatuation, and endured its mournful destiny. The colonel was one of the judges of Charles I., and signed the sentence of his condemnation—a great moral iniquity, and detestable piece of policy, for which the republic and its partisans suffered a just punishment. Of all the men who took part in this fatal act, no one was more sincere, disinterested, and courageous than Hutchinson. He did not even claim the honour of courage. " It is certain,' says Mrs. Hutchinson, " that all men herein were left to their free liberty of acting, neither persuaded nor compelled; and as there were some nominated on the commission who never sat, and others who sat at first but durst not hold on, so all the rest might have declined if they would."† Hutchinson did not decline to sit, but persevered in the deplorable course on which he had entered. Soon, however, all the power of

* Memoirs of Colonel Hutchinson, pp. 348-349.   † Ibid., p. 335.

the revolution, the Long Parliament, Cromwell, the army, the Rump, had successively failed in their attempts to establish the republic in England. The restoration of Charles II. became a fatal necessity, as well as the evident wish of the nation. "The last remnant of the House of Commons," says Mrs. Hutchinson herself, "was divided into miserable factions, among whom some would then have violently set up an oath of renunciation of the king and his family. The colonel, thinking it a ridiculous thing to *swear out* a man, when they had no power to defend themselves against him, vehemently opposed that oath, and carried against Sir Arthur Haslerig and others, who as violently pressed it, urging very truly that those oaths that had been formerly imposed had but multiplied the sins of the nation by perjuries; instancing how Sir Arthur and others, in Oliver's time, coming into the House, swore on their entrance they would attempt nothing in the change of that government, which, as soon as ever they were entered, they laboured to throw down. Many other arguments he used, whereupon many honest men, who thought till then he had followed a faction in all things and not his own judgment, began to meet often with him, and to consult what to do in these difficulties, out of which their prudence and honesty would have found a way to extricate themselves; but that the end of our prosperity was come, hastened on partly by the mad, rash violence of some that, without strength, opposed the tide of the discontented, tumultuous people; partly by the detestable treachery of those who had sold themselves to do mischief; but chiefly by the general stream of the people, who were as eager for their own destruction as the Israelites of old for their quails."*

In the history of the republicans at this period, I cannot find any other example of so much mental vigour and patriotic disinterestedness, combined with no disavowal of his past conduct or forgetfulness of his personal dignity. Colonel Hutchinson for some time reaped the benefit of his courageous moderation. Several distinguished members of the Royalist party laboured zealously to exempt him from the measures taken against the other regicides; and his wife displayed admirable energy and presence of mind in her efforts to serve him in this emergency. He was allowed to retire to Owthorpe, his patrimonial estate, and to live there in peace for three

* Memoirs of Colonel Hutchinson, pp. 393-396.

K 2

years, in the bosom of his family, and occupied only by the care of his domestic interests. But revolutions are pitiless in their reactions; the vices of the Restoration speedily developed themselves; party animosities and court factions sprang up once more; and popular conspiracies were framed in secret. Notwithstanding the combined efforts of his friends and enemies to bring him once more into public life, Hutchinson kept aloof from all these movements; but he took no pains to conceal his opinions, and perhaps even, his hopes. He was consequently closely watched, subjected to continual annoyances, and, on the 11th of October, 1663, arrested in his house at Owthorpe, and confined, first in that same Tower of London in which his wife had been born, and afterwards in Sandown Castle, on the sea coast, near Deal, in Kent. His wife vainly entreated that she might be imprisoned with him; but being refused, she established herself at Deal, with her son and daughter, and walked to Sandown to dine with the colonel, returning to Deal in the evening. Ten months elapsed, during which Colonel Hutchinson's confinement was aggravated by the dampness of the place, the severity of the winter, the avarice of the governor of the castle, and the society of another prisoner whom he suspected of being a spy upon him. Hutchinson preserved his composure unruffled, spent his time in reading pious books, affectionately sustained the courage of his wife, who was very anxious about his health, and gave these last counsels to his son Thomas, as they walked together on the sea-shore : " The courses which the king and his party take to establish themselves," he said, "will be their ruin; the ill-management of the State will cause discontented wild parties to mutiny, and rise against the present powers; but they will only put things in confusion; it must be a sober party that must then arise and settle them. Let not my son, how fairly soever they pretend, too rashly engage with the first, but stay to see what they make good, and engage with those who are for settlement, who will have need of men of interest to assist them."* How sensible and touching is this anxiety of the father to guard his son against those errors into which he could not help feeling that he had fallen himself!

The winter now drew near; the colonel's health became gradually more impaired; Mrs. Hutchinson was obliged to go

* Memoirs of Colonel Hutchinson, p. 475.

to Owthorpe to fetch her younger children, and some furniture, which she required, for her husband's use. She felt very unwilling to take this journey, for she was a prey to melancholy presentiments. The colonel, on the contrary, was full of hope and gaiety; he gave his wife written instructions regarding his plantations at Owthorpe, and the arrangement of his house and gardens. "You give me," said she, "these orders, as if you were to see that place again." "If I do not," said he, "I thank God I can cheerfully forego it; but I will not distrust that God will bring me back again, and therefore I will take care to keep it while I have it."*

Mrs. Hutchinson went to Owthorpe, leaving her husband under the care of his daughter and his brother, George Hutchinson. A few days afterwards his disease grew rapidly worse, and death became imminent, so that his physician, a pious man like himself, told him of his danger, and asked him if his peace were made with God. "The will of the Lord be done," said the colonel. "I am ready for it. I hope you do not think me so ill a Christian, to have been thus long in prison, and have that to do now!" Then they asked him where he would be buried? He told them in his vault at Owthorpe. His brother told him it would be a long way to carry him; he answered, "Let my wife order the manner of it as she will, only I would be there. I would have spoken to my wife and son, but it is not the will of God. Let my wife, as she is above other women, show herself, on this occasion, a good Christian, and above the pitch of ordinary women." He passed the day, on the 11th of September, 1664, in profound repose, speaking occasionally to those who stood by him. Towards the evening he ceased to speak; one of those present mentioned Mrs. Hutchinson's name to him, and said, "Alas! how will she be surprised!" The colonel moved slightly, fetched a sigh, and expired.†

Mrs. Hutchinson was not overwhelmed by her loss; her soul was as strong as it was passionate, and sustained by that deep religious faith which changes hope into certainty, and converts the pangs of death into the privations of absence. Sure of being once more united to her much-loved husband, her chief care now was to hold him up as an example to her children, and to perpetuate his memory. "They who dote on

* Memoirs of Colonel Hutchinson, pp. 475-476.   † Ibid., pp. 478-480.

mortal excellences," she says, "when by the inevitable fate
of all things frail, their adored idols are taken from them,
may let loose the winds of passion to bring in a flood of
sorrow; whose ebbing tides carry away the dear memory of
what they have lost; and when comfort is essayed to such
mourners, commonly all objects are removed out of their
view, which may, with their remembrance, renew the grief;
and in time these remedies succeed, and oblivion's curtain is
by degrees drawn over the dead face, and things less lovely
are liked, while they are not viewed together with that which
was most excellent. But I, that am under a command not
to grieve at the common rate of desolate women, while I am
studying which way to moderate my woe, and if it were possible to augment my love, can for the present find out none
more just to my dear husband, nor consolatory to myself,
than the preservation of his memory."[*]

It was with these feelings, and in order to discharge this
duty, that Mrs. Hutchinson wrote her Memoirs. They remained unknown for nearly a century and a half among the
family papers of Colonel Hutchinson's descendants; but
were discovered and published, in 1806, by the Rev. Julius
Hutchinson.

Rather less than a century before Colonel Hutchinson and
his wife assumed a place in the annals of their country, France
contained a household similar to theirs, more illustrious in
worldly rank, and assuredly more pious and virtuous in the
sight of God: Philip Duplessis Mornay, long the intimate
friend and ever the faithful servant of Henry IV., and Charlotte Arbaleste de la Borde, his wife.[†] Madame de Mornay,
more fortunate in this respect than Mrs. Hutchinson, had
not the sad fate of surviving her husband; she was the first
to take her departure to everlasting rest. But like Mrs.
Hutchinson, she had wished to write the Memoirs of her
husband, with a view to the instruction of her son. She
addressed them to him expressly in a letter written from
Saumur, on the 25th of April, 1595; he was then scarcely
sixteen years of age, having been born on the 20th of July,
1579. "I see you," she says, "ready to depart to go and

---

* Memoirs of Colonel Hutchinson, pp. 19-20.
† Philippe de Mornay, Lord of Plessis-Marly, was born on the 5th of Novem-
ber, 1549, and died on the 11th of November, 1623. Charlotte Arbaleste de la
Borde, his wife, was born in 1550, and died on the 15th of May, 1607.

ee the world, and make yourself acquainted with the manners of men and the state of nations. You are young, my
on, and diverse fantasies present themselves to youth; bear
n mind always the words of the Psalmist: 'Thy testimonies,
) Lord, shall be the men of my counsel.' But that you may
never be without a guide, here is one that I give you by the
hand, and written by my own hand, to accompany you; it is
the example of your father which I adjure you always to
keep before your eyes, as far as I have been able to know his
ife, notwithstanding that our company has frequently been
nterrupted by the misfortunes of the times. I am infirm,
and I do not think that God will leave me long in this world;
so you will keep this writing in memory of me. And when
God shall please to take me from you, I desire that you
should finish what I have begun to write of the course of our
ife; but above all, my son, I shall' believe that you will remember me when I shall hear it said that, in whatever place
you are, you serve God and imitate your father."*

God imposed on Madame de Mornay the unutterable grief
of concluding her narrative of her husband's life by a record
of the death of that son for whom she had written it. Young
Philip de Mornay, who was serving in the Netherlands, in
the army of Prince Maurice of Nassau, was killed on the
23rd of October, 1606, at the siege of Guelders. His father
received the distressing news on the 24th of November;
and, says Madame de Mornay, " Knowing well that he could
not disguise his countenance from me, he resolved that from
the first we should mingle our griefs together. ' My dear,'
he said, ' God calls us to-day to manifest our faith and obedience; since He has done this, we must be silent.' At this
speech, I, being full of doubts and weakened by long illness, fell
into a swoon and convulsions : I could not speak for some time,
and the first words that I could utter were, ' The will of God
be done! We might have lost him in a duèl, and then, what
consolation could we have taken?' The rest may be best
explained, to any person of feeling, by silence; we felt as if
our bowels were torn away, our hopes cut off, and our plans
and wishes frustrated; we could not for a long while talk to
each other, or think within ourselves, of anything else, for he
was, next to God, our only speech and thought; our daughters,

* Memoirs of Duplessis Mornay, vol. i., pp. 1-3. (Paris, 1824.)

notwithstanding the disfavour of the court, being happily married and removed with much trouble from the house, to leave it in his sole possession, thenceforward all our lines started from this centre, and returned thereto again; and we saw that, in him, God had taken everything from us, doubtless that he might take us together from the world, and that we might no longer feel any regret, at whatever hour he might call us. And here it is reasonable that my book should finish by him for whom it was undertaken, that I might describe to him our pilgrimage in this life; and since it has so pleased God, he has finished his life sooner and more pleasantly. And so, if I did not fear the affliction of M. Duplessis, who, according as mine increases, makes me the more sensible of his affection, it would grieve me extremely to survive him."*

She did not survive him long. "I have no son," said Duplessis Mornay, "and, therefore, I shall soon have no wife." Six months after she had learned the death of her son, Madame de Mornay was seized with a violent illness, and died on the 15th of May, 1607, after eight days of cruel suffering. "In all this agony, M. Duplessis did not leave her; and whenever, either to pray to God for her or from the excess of his grief, he withdrew to some corner of the room, she would ask for him, and immediately give him her hand, saying a few words to show that the grief he felt on her account touched her more acutely than the pain she herself suffered."

I shall add nothing to these quotations: what words of mine could so well describe the admirable union of these two excellent persons, both of whom were finished models of piety, virtue, and good sense? Politics occupy a larger space in the life of Duplessis Mornay than in that of Colonel Hutchinson: and Duplessis Mornay holds a more prominent position in the history of his country and his time. Yet Hutchinson, whose mind was chimerical as well as sincere, allowed himself to be drawn, by politics, into the lowest vortex of factions and revolutions. Duplessis Mornay, on the contrary, constantly resisted their influence, in spite of all the causes and temptations which seemed likely to subject him to their sway. This inflexible Protestant, who had con-

* Memoirs of Duplessis Mornay, vol. i., pp. 486-493.

tributed as largely as any man to raise Henry IV. to the throne—who, next to Sully, had enjoyed the largest share of the confidence of his king—who bitterly deplored Henry IV.'s abandonment of his faith, and who braved all dangers and disgraces that he might preserve and maintain his own— Mornay, though discontented, melancholy, banished from the court, and assailed by the discontents and sufferings of his cause and his friends, never entered into any faction or intrigue against a king whom he blamed, and of whom he had great cause to complain; but remained, on the contrary, unshaken in his fidelity to him, and was incessantly occupied in maintaining or restoring a little order and peace in the Protestant Church of France, and in promoting mutual confidence and friendship between Henry IV. and his Protestant subjects. Mornay was ardently devoted to his religious faith, but his devotedness to his faith never made him forget his duty to his country, or to his king, who had preserved his country from ruin. He continued firmly and actively attached to his belief, but did not fall under the yoke of any fixed and exclusive idea; preserved his patriotic good sense as well as his fervent piety, and endured, with melancholy firmness, the anger of his friends and the ingratitude of his king. His life was laborious and full of sorrow, effort and misapprehension; but it is worthy to serve as an example to men of honesty and sense in times of civil discord and revolution.

Madame de Mornay was at once similar and superior to Mrs. Hutchinson. She resembled her in her domestic affections and virtues, and in her fervent piety; she excelled her, not in mental gifts, but in rectitude of judgment and moral gravity. Mrs. Hutchinson had a strong and lively imagination, her intellectual culture was extensive and varied, but she had a secret taste for striking adventures, both in public and private life, and a self-appreciation which led her into some errors, or, at least, gave her some airs of pedantry and vanity. Madame de Mornay was less highly educated, less brilliant, less rich in learning and art, but her good sense was stronger, and her heart more simple; there was not the least shade of romance in her feelings or desires; not the slightest vain complacency in her language regarding herself or those connected with her; for, from attempting amplification or display, she always shows less than she might, and says less than she thinks. The most important events, when related by her, and the most powerful sentiments, when uttered by her lips, present themselves under a modified aspect, exempt from all fictitious ornament, all superfluous or premeditated display. What she says is the pure truth, reduced to its most simple expression, and related incidentally, in the measure of strict necessity, for the information and edification of that son to whom her narrative is addressed, without any other design, or any personal vanity or emotion.

Though I could bring many proofs of this difference between the characters and writings of the two ladies, I will present only one, which is sufficiently striking to demonstrate the truth of my observation. I have quoted elsewhere Mrs. Hutchinson's narrative of her first acquaintance with the colonel, and the preliminaries of their marriage; I now give Madame de Mornay's narrative of the same occurrence in her own life. She was twenty-six years of age, and had been a widow for seven years; for M. de Feuquières, whom she had married at seventeen, died eighteen months after his marriage. She happened to be at Sedan when Duplessis Mornay was there also. "M. Duplessis," she says, "continued to come to see me, and, for nearly eight months, not a day passed but we spent two or three hours together; he had even written to me since his journey to Cleves. I was then planning a visit to France on business, and wished to hasten my journey, because I feared that our familiarity would occasion evil reports. Whilst I entertained these thoughts, he declared to me that he was desirous to marry me, which I received as an honour, but nevertheless told him that he could not have my answer until I was first informed by letter of the wishes of his mother, Madame de Buhy, and his brother, M. de Buhy, that I might be assured that our marriage would be agreeable to them. . . . After having told him that I should esteem myself happy if God should permit those on whom I depended to give their consent to the matter, I requested time, before I gave him a final answer, to write to Madame de la Borde, my mother, and my other relations, that I might learn their will. So I wrote to them all that it was a matter I ardently desired; but that nevertheless I would not consent without their permission. God so showed us that He had ordained our marriage for my great benefit, that we had a reciprocal con-

sent from all those of whom we asked it. During these
arrangements some time passed; and many at Sedan, seeing
that M. Duplessis contrived to visit me, began to think that
he intended to marry me; some even spoke to him of other
matches, of rich girls and heiresses, and would have desired
to be able to turn his thoughts from me elsewhere, seeing
that, besides the graces he had received from God at his
birth, he was destined to rise higher. But after he had
opened his mouth to me, he would never lend his ear to any
other proposition that was made him. Some even offered,
to learn if he thought of me, in case he wished to marry me,
to inform him of the true state of my affairs. But he answered that when he wanted information he would apply to
myself for it, and that property was the last thing he should
think of in marriage; the first was the character of the person with whom he would have to pass his life, and the fear
of God and a good reputation were far beyond riches."*

The woman who spoke so simply, and with such austere
reserve, of the strongest emotions which had ever filled her
soul, and the most important event that had happened in
her life, was as enthusiastic as she was grave; she followed
her husband in all his dangers, took part in all his labours,
loved for him alone, received from him alone all his joys, and
died of grief at the death of their son.

I shall not carry this comparison any further; this is, I
think, its essential feature. M. and Madame Duplessis
Mornay were not only virtuous and pious, they were modest;
and modesty is a virtue unknown to revolutionaries. This
is the real and chief difference between them and Colonel
Hutchinson and his wife. Revolutions are engendered
by men of presumption, and beget presumption. Even the
best revolutionaries have a vain confidence in themselves,
and in all they think and desire, which urges them blindly
along the course they have chosen, and shuts their eyes to
everything that might arrest or divert them. Modesty is a
great enlightenment; it keeps the mind continually open,
and renders the heart ever docile to the teachings of truth.
M. and Madame Duplessis Mornay, as Christians, and strangers to every revolutionary feeling and action, possessed this
precious safeguard of good sense and virtue. Colonel and
Mrs. Hutchinson did not possess it, for, though Christians,

* Memoirs of Duplessis Mornay, vol. i., pp. 86-89.

they were revolutionaries. Hence arose their blindness, their infatuation, and their misfortunes, which, though worthy of sympathy, were natural, and, I say it with sorrow, deserved. The world, and, if I may be permitted to speak with reverence of the supreme justice, God himself is severe in punishing the faults of the good. They have no right to complain : it is an honour to be thus treated.

SIR THOMAS HERBERT.

[1605—1682.]

In the fact that great men monopolise the interest of history we see one of the chief causes of its errors and omissions. Not only is it true that history cares little for any but great men, but it is from them, their ideas, feelings, conduct, and life, that it describes and estimates the character of the mass, and the general condition of society. This test is not infallible. Men of superior powers, who have taken the lead in their age, are not always the most faithful representatives of that age ; they give us no adequate conception of the state of the people who surround them. That which constitutes superiority in an individual is precisely his native originality, strongly-marked individuality which prevents us from identifying him with the multitude whom he influences. Doubtless he is united to his age by an infinite number of ties and relationships ; doubtless his nature is conformed to the same type and confesses the same sympathies as belong to those who follow in his train ; were it not so, how could they follow him ? Originality which should divorce the individual from the sympathies of his time would not elevate, but isolate him. The great man, however, possesses the same ideas, impressions, wants, as those which belong to the people below him ; but events do not affect him as they do the majority of mankind. Occupying a position different from that which they can command, his judgment is different from theirs ; and that originality which gives him his power, at the same time prevents him from being a just expression of the condition of the masses—a perfect mirror of his nation, his epoch, his party.

Far be it from me to deny to great men any portion of that

honour and supremacy which justly belongs to them. They are the strength and glory of humanity, which must find at once its safety and its dignity in learning to appreciate, respect, and follow them; but in order to become acquainted with an age or a people we must also know something of its second-rate and obscure men. The history of the people, properly so called, is that of men whose life is without event; it is in the beliefs, sentiments, and lot of unimportant individuals and unknown families, that the lot, the sentiments, and the beliefs of the country are to be found; here must we look for the vicissitudes of its opinions and affections, and all the changes in its moral and material existence. We are ignorant of the real nature of events, their causes as well as their effects, so long as no record or memorial is found to transport us into the midst of this unknown public which seems to be recognised only as the stage on which these events are transacted, but which, especially in modern times, influences their course in a manner sooner or later decisive.

Sir Thomas Herbert was not, at first among the Presbyterian party, nor afterwards at the court of Charles I., a man entirely obscure. But he did not distinguish himself there by his talents or by his aptitude for business; neither his career nor his character were marked by any brilliant striking features; he was but little removed from the crowd; and if he had not, by accident rather than choice, taken part in the events which are related in his Memoirs, hardly any trace would have been left of him.

He was born at York, in 1605, and was connected with the illustrious family of the Herberts, Earls of Pembroke. Early in life he found a patron in William, Earl of Pembroke, and head of that house, who furnished him with the means of undertaking a long journey in Asia and Africa, of which, on his return, young Herbert published an account.* The death of his protector, which occurred soon after his arrival in London, did not alter his circumstances; Philip, Earl of Pembroke, showed him the same kindness as his predecessor had done. Engaged in the service of the Parliamentary party, to which he remained attached on account of his aversion to

* " Some years' travels into divers parts of Asia and Africa; describing especially the two famous empires, the Persian and Great Mogul (1626)." It appeared in London in 1634, folio, illustrated. It was reprinted four times between 1634 and 1677.

episcopacy, Thomas Herbert was employed, during the civil war, sometimes as commissary of Fairfax's army, sometimes in some of the negotiations which were entered into with the royal party, such as referred to the lesser incidents of the war, not to the great political interests in agitation. He had filled various posts of this kind when, in 1646, he accompanied the Earl of Pembroke and the other commissioners, whom the Long Parliament sent to carry its proposals to Charles I., that the Scots should give him up. What happened to Herbert at this time; how he left the service of the Parliament, and became (as valet-de-chambre) attached to the person of Charles, who had been deprived of his old servants; the respect and affection which he conceived for the prince, and his devotedness to him; the minor details of their common life up to the period of Charles's execution,—all these facts are related in the Memoirs with a dignified simplicity, without any design of exalting himself, or of attributing to his own actions any political importance. They are the sentiments which a man might entertain who had, from infancy, been devoted to the cause and person of the king.

It was not till 1678 that Sir Thomas Herbert was accidentally induced to publish his Memoirs, under the title of "Threnodia Carolina." Parliament was about to vote 70,000*l.* for the erection of a monument to Charles I. The celebrated antiquary, Sir William Dugdale, wrote to Sir Thomas Herbert, asking him if he had ever heard the late king mention any place where he would wish to be buried. The answer sent by Herbert contained so many curious and hitherto unknown particulars, that Sir William Dugdale requested him to write an account of the last two years of Charles's life. Herbert sent, about the same time, to Anthony Wood, author of the "Athenæ Oxonienses," a detailed account of the trial and death of the king. These letters, when collected, were published as Herbert's Memoirs. They were read with avidity, and have been often since reprinted. They are analogous, both as to the nature of the facts which they relate and the position of the author to the "Journal de ce qui s'est passé au Temple," written by Cléry, valet-de-chambre to Louis XVI.; but although scenes of an equally melancholy character are related in the two narratives with a similarly real and unaffected tenderness, that of Herbert is infinitely less dramatic and pathetic than that of

Cléry. The depth of suffering into which Charles I. was plunged is far less than that endured by Louis XVI. and his family. Herbert had taken it for granted that the misfortunes which he had seen could not be surpassed, and that he had exhausted the catalogue of sufferings in the exhibition of Charles's calamities. I will only indicate two features in this deplorable comparison. Though vanquished, dethroned, condemned, executed, Charles I. remained king up to the last hour of his life; recognised as such by the English people, by his judges, by his executioner. The gross outrages which attended the last scenes of his life were isolated acts, and, we may say, comparatively rare; as he retained his own self-respect, so he retained a kind of courteous treatment at the hands of his enemies, who did not add disgrace to their injustice by wanton insolence. Further, Charles was alone in his imprisonment and condemnation; he mounted the scaffold alone. Neither his wife nor his children fell, after him, into a yet more calamitous condition, and into the hands of still more remorseless executioners. Charles I. experienced the extremity of misfortune as a king; but Louis XVI. and his family drained the cup of *human* woe. The narrative of Herbert fills the mind with a feeling intensely sad, but serious and calm; that of Cléry, on the other hand, overwhelms us with indignation and compassion.

The publication of the "Threnodia Carolina" took place a few years before the death of Sir Thomas Herbert. There is no evidence that he took any part in public affairs after the Restoration. Charles II. had conferred on him the title of baronet, in 1660; and he lived at York, entirely occupied in historical researches into the antiquities of his country. Among other things, he assisted Sir William Dugdale in the composition of the "Monasticon Anglicanum." He died on the 1st of March, 1682, after having given to the public libraries of Oxford and York Minster manuscripts which, it is said, give evidence of considerable erudition.

We may regard Sir Thomas Herbert as the type of a large class of estimable men of his time, who were driven into opposition by the vices of the government and court of Charles I., and who were induced to return to Charles by the vices and evils of the revolution. When the chiefs of the Parliament of 1640, after having bravely exposed themselves to danger in a cause which was truly the cause of the country, allowed themselves afterwards to undertake, at their own risk, and to gratify their own passions, a contest which was directly opposed to the general sentiments and interests of the English people, the attention of the people was again turned towards their king; and disinterested men who, like Herbert, had served, up to that point, in the Parliamentary ranks, then passed over with the same disinterestedness to the ranks of the enemy. In these successive changes in the views of citizens who were strangers to political activity— caused by the conduct of the principal actors—we shall find that which can alone be truly called the public history of revolutions.

JOHN PRICE,

CHAPLAIN TO MONK.

[. . . .—1691.]

WHOEVER has taken any part in events which have de- cided the destinies of nations, is at first struck with the con- trast, so often presented, between the grandeur of the spec- tacle and the insignificance of those who move in it. The contrast is still more remarkable when the event contem- plated is already ancient, and can be known only by reading and study. The reader who gives himself up to this study with a somewhat serious attention, soon forgets that the actors on the scene which he contemplates are no longer living and speaking; he transports himself into the midst of those bygone periods, sees them, listens to them, identifies himself with them in feeling, and thought, and interest; and before his busy fancy, great and small all resume their position, and act over again the drama of their life. But as soon as he seeks a more intimate acquaintance with these shadows—as soon as he attempts to learn what they have been and done apart from the place which they occupy in the annals of history, instantly the illusion vanishes, and a multitude of individuals disappear. In vain does he search chronicles, biographies, dictionaries; hardly a word or a line is to be found that will bring to light any circumstance in the life of most of those who were, a short time since, so vividly before him; they have appeared but for a moment in the rapid

ourse of events, as they move onward to the future; with
his exception they are entirely lost; time has not con-
idered them of sufficient importance to perpetuate their
nemories; and when history has thus incidentally mentioned
heir names, it seems as if it only wished to grant them a
eaceable dismissal to that oblivion in which the particulars
f their personal existence are involved.

The Memoirs of John Price, chaplain to Monk, are cer-
ainly the most curious and authentic documents extant
elating to the restoration of Charles II., and the share
hich Monk had in bringing it about. It is impossible to
ead them without being forced into an acknowledgment of
heir value and evident veracity. A short paragraph in
he "Fasti" of the University of Oxford contains, however,
he only information which I have been able to procure
oncerning the life of John Price; no English biographies
hich I have consulted contain even his name. I do not
onder at this; apart from the influence which, in the
rivacy of domestic life, Price was able to exert over the de-
erminations of Monk, in 1659, he had no share in those
vents. Born in the Isle of Wight at an uncertain date,
ducated at Eton, there is no trace of his existence till the
ime when Monk, then in Scotland, chose him as his chap-
ain. He himself tells us that he should never have held
uch an office had not his father been ruined in the service
f the king; whence it appears that his family, at the out-
reak of the political disturbances, belonged to the Cavalier
arty. This is apparent also from the fact that some of the
'resbyterians warned Monk that he had selected a Cavalier
s his chaplain. But it was not without design that Monk
ad made such a choice. Indifferent, or nearly so, to the
istinctions of religious as to those of political parties, he
as unwilling to destroy the relationships which bound him
o the party which he originally served, to which, in his
eepest sympathies, he was all along attached, and whose
eturn he foresaw. If Price was a Cavalier, Gumble, Monk's
ther chaplain, was a Presbyterian, who co-operated as will-
ngly in the general's machinations by which he was pre-
aring for the Restoration.

When this event appeared above the horizon, the time had
assed in which men, governed by fixed beliefs and energetic
assions, had sought a basis for union or separation only in

L

general principles or party attachments. Sagacity for personal interests, foresight of the future, good sense not fettered to any political creed or combination, had been substituted for the spring of enthusiasm and the unflinching consistency of sect and faction. When revolutions thus come to look upon their principles with distrust, and to doubt their power, union exists between individuals alone; parties quickly dissolve and commingle; opinions which were formerly the standards of adverse sects are no longer the occasions of disunion or aversion; and individuals care to form only those personal connexions which shall secure them adherents or protectors, when the events which they foresee shall have been accomplished.

Such was, in 1659, the state of mind in England. Monk offered to those who considered themselves unbiassed, a chief as unbiassed as they;—they rallied around him with the more confidence in proportion as he conducted himself towards them with reserve, and showed himself indifferent to, and removed from, any engagements or convictions. Cavaliers, Presbyterians, or Independents, members of the Parliament and of the army, those who desired the Restoration or considered it inevitable, hastened to adopt Monk as their patron; "for he was a man," said his own soldiers, "in whose steps we may follow with safety." Price's Memoirs, in fact, give us a great idea of Monk's ability and prudence. They afford a lively and accurate description of a great political manœuvre carried on by a single man, whose constant aim was, without compromising any existing interest, to leave to its own gradual accomplishment an event foreseen by all, but of which no one dared or was willing to speak before the day of success. England still regards, not without reason, the reigns of Charles II. and James II. as one of the saddest periods of history. Yet it is no less true that, in 1660, the follies and crimes of the revolution had rendered the restoration of the Stuart a national necessity. Monk was the clearsighted interpreter of an almost universal wish, and at the same time an instrument in fulfilling that decree of Providence which ordains that, before a nation shall receive the blessing which it seeks for by disorder, it should bear the penalty of those evils which disorder has produced.

After the return of Charles II., Price enjoyed his share of the favours heaped upon Monk and his dependents by the

:ing. On the 10th of May, 1660, he was appointed to preach
t Westminster, before the House of Commons, a thanks-
;iving sermon in honour of the Restoration.   A short time
fter he was nominated member of Eton College ; sub-
equently he obtained a lucrative prebend connected with
ialisbury Cathedral, and lastly the valuable rectory of Pet-
rorth, in Sussex.   It was not until 1680, about ten years
fter the death of Monk, that he published his Memoirs.*
n his dedication to the Earl of Bath, he mentions the in-
ucements by which he was led to publish.   Those who
rished to appropriate to themselves all the benefits of the
testoration, wished also to monopolise the credit of having
ccomplished it.   Monk's chaplain was justly indignant at
he ingratitude of the Royalists to the memory of his former
atron, and the " Life of Monk," by his other chaplain,
łumble, was dictated by the same feeling.   Monk had
oubtless shown greater fidelity in his personal relations than
u his political alliances, for his dependents remained constant
ι their attachment to him.   A sermon, preached at Petworth
n the 9th of September, 1683, to give thanks to Heaven for
he discovery of the Rye-House Plot, is the last trace we have
f Price's continued existence.   Nevertheless, he lived long
nough to see the Restoration bend in its turn under the
·eight of that tyranny which it vainly attempted to impose
pon England.   He died in June, 1691, three years after the
xpulsion of James II.   He probably remained a Cavalier ;
ut the English nation had changed its opinion, and if Monk
ad been in 1688 what he was in 1660, his good sense would
oubtless have led him to coincide with the nation.

EDWARD HYDE, EARL OF CLARENDON.

LORD CHANCELLOR OF ENGLAND.

[1608—1674.]

I HAVE no intention of relating the life of Lord Clarendon,
is written already in the events of history and in his own
orks.   There is no man, if we except Cromwell, who has
·cupied a more prominent position in English history; no one

* Entitled " The Mystery and Method of his Majesty's happy Restoration."

L 2

who has so carefully handed down his own history in that of his time.

Posterity has done him full justice; if his name is mentioned in his own country it is always as " the Great Earl of Clarendon," and perhaps he has secured this high renown by his writings, still more than by his political career.   No one of those crises which determine the destiny of nations was moulded and guided by his influence; many men have served their country with as much ability and success; but there are few men who, after a long exercise of power, have yet so far preserved the depth of their convictions and their esteem of their fellow-men as to feel the want of making themselves rightly understood and appreciated after their death.   Long-continued possession of greatness brings with it indifference; few aged state ministers retain any care either for the public or for truth.   Clarendon however, proscribed, infirm, impoverished, without the expectation of seeing his country again, held firmly to whatever he had said or done, and was anxious that posterity might estimate him aright.   He related his life not only because he had been conspicuous in affairs and delighted to dwell on the recollections of his glory, but in order to show that he had judged and acted wisely, in order to defend and justify not only his actions but also his ideas.   In pursuing this object he displayed greater sincerity, greater energy of mind, and a higher tone of moral feeling, than is usually seen in aged dignitaries who are too often shattered by disgrace and sated by the enjoyment of power.

The fact is, that Clarendon possessed and retained that which is so frequently wanting or soon lost in positions of eminence and activity—determinate opinions and a faith in duty. He was often mistaken, and committed or allowed many iniquities, but truth and honour were not in his eyes mere shadows. In the midst of a revolution and in the heart of a court, he more than once obeyed those stern and disinterested convictions which regulate the thinking of a philosopher and the conduct of an upright citizen.   This is the explanation of that unquestioned superiority which has assigned to him a place peculiarly his own among great statesmen, and has succeeded in giving to his memory a greater estimation than his political weight and personal influence on the government of his country would otherwise justify.

When the Long Parliament met, Clarendon was among

those who, sensible of the real grievances of the nation, were anxious that they should be redressed. In spite of his relations to Archbishop Laud and his well-known zeal on behalf of the Established Church, he joined himself to the Opposition. But with a mind characterised rather by pertinacity than comprehensiveness, and a character severe rather than generous, he believed that a respect for laws already in existence would amply meet the rights of the public, and that no new guarantees were required in order to secure respect for these ancient laws. Convinced that the government ought to reform its conduct, a reform of the government itself never entered his thoughts; he therefore misapprehended, at the very outset, the true necessities of England at this crisis, and the real tendency of the national mind. The day had come when abuses could only be remedied by bold innovations; and Clarendon, on his entrance into public life, was equally hostile to abuses and innovations.

The more the revolution advanced, the more confirmed did he become in his misapprehensions—the more did his opinions seem legitimate. The innovations which arose were often mistaken and excessive. The mistakes offended Clarendon's good sense, the excesses shocked his moral sensibility. He gave himself up from that time to the royal cause, repeatedly maintaining that it was the cause of Old England—of the ancient and excellent constitution of the country.

When, after the expiration of twenty years of lawless triumph, Charles II. ascended the throne, Clarendon regarded the revolution as a failure:—it had trampled on justice, it had issued in defeat; the success of its opponents was complete, Providence had declared itself on their side.

Clarendon did not take any part in the struggle between James II. and his country, in which Providence uttered its final decree; but he lived long enough to witness the dissipation of the hopes and illusions which he had entertained for his cause, as, before him, the Presbyterians, the Independents, and all the revolutionary parties had in their turn experienced the same disappointment.

Raised in 1660, by the revolution, to a pinnacle of power, Clarendon received it with a rooted dislike of all that had transpired during the preceding twenty years, and with the determination to restore all things in State and Church as nearly as possible to that position in which the revolution

had found them.   New men and individual interests appeared
to him alone entitled to attention or regard.   With reference
to institutions and laws, it was only necessary, in his opinion,
to restore what had been lost.   James I. and Charles I., it
is true, had used the royal prerogative imprudently, and
often unjustly, and it was fitting to avoid their faults; but
still it ought to be restored unimpaired ; twenty years of
struggle and suffering were to be endured by the English
people, and issue in nothing but a tardy avowal of its crimes
and its errors.

Such was, and continued to be, Clarendon's theory; but
his probity and good sense did not allow him to conform his
practice to his theory.   Every day brought him into collision
with new features of national life ; every day showed that a
just deference to the claims of men could only be gained by
a compromise of things.   He adopted, on principle, most of
the prejudices and pretensions of the old Royalist party ; but,
when he came to apply them, facts met him which he had not
foreseen, and compelled him to uphold what he had promised
to extirpate ; and thus the first minister under Charles II.,
reinstated together with his master after fifteen years of
absence, was soon the patron of revolutionary interests, and
the abhorred adversary of the court and the Cavaliers.

This position, which brought misery and downfal to Clarendon, has since been his glory.   He supported it with
ability and courage.   Often inconsistent and unjust towards
the national party, he was, towards his own, decided, firm,
and even virtuous.   A severe censor of the dissipated habits
of Charles II.; avowedly Protestant, notwithstanding his
dislike of the Presbyterians, in an ungodly or secretly Catholic court ; grave and upright in the midst of unprincipled
and frivolous courtiers ; attached to the ancient laws of the
country, though utterly opposed to the new spirit of liberty ;
restrained from extravagance by a sense of reason, though his
disposition was naturally hard, and even vindictive ; he continually opposed his influence to that spirit of turbulence,
that wanton and capricious tyranny to which the government of England was at that time incessantly led by the vices
of the king and the passions of the Cavaliers.   When he had
left his country the great Chancellor could not subdue the
evil genius of the Restoration, nor did the thought of so
doing even enter into his mind ; his object was, as attached

to ancient English laws, to oppose the corruptions of his party with all the power, ability, and virtue, which he possessed.

After seven years his virtue became too troublesome, his ability was no longer needed,—his merits and his faults alike conspired against him, and he lost his power. Every one used his influence to promote his downfal; the national party would not sustain him, the king was glad to be rid of him. When Clarendon had with difficulty obtained in France an asylum from the ingratitude of his master and the hatred of his enemies, living in sadness, though undisturbed, at Montpelier, at Moulins, at Rouen, he abandoned every undertaking, except that of transmitting to posterity an accurate account of his times and himself. "The History of the Great Rebellion," and the "Memoirs of his Private Life and Ministry,"* occupied the seven remaining years of his life. He brought to his literary occupations the same notions, the same feelings, and almost the same kind of ability as he had shown in his public career; and his writings correspond singularly with his actions. Consistency, perhaps even immobility, was probably the distinguishing feature of his mind. His opinions and character on his entrance into public life were those which he carried with him when he left it; in him reason had outstripped experience; experience neither enlarged his mind nor gave elevation to his ideas; his antipathy to all innovation was more than a principle, it possessed his whole nature—a nature which was wise, upright, well harmonised, but frigid, inflexible, limited, a stranger to strong spiritual impulses and high intellectual ambition. He had that proud sense of wisdom and integrity, which, when it is not the attribute of a large and powerful genius, is the parent of narrow views and unyielding prejudices. A juris-consult and theologian, he paid regard to rules and forms, but disdained principles —not from any contempt for truth, but because questions of a general and fundamental character never entered into the

---

* "The History of the Great Rebellion" was first printed at London, in 1702, 3 vols., folio, and has been often reprinted since. Many passages were suppressed in the first editions, several of which may appear falsifications; but the text has been completely restored in the edition published at Oxford, in 1845, according to the original manuscripts deposited in the library at Oxford. The "Memoirs of the Private Life" of Lord Clarendon appeared, for the first time, in 1759, under the title of "Continuation of the History of the Great Rebellion." The best edition is that published at Oxford, in 1837.

region of his thoughts.   In spite of his sternness and inflexibility, he possessed some capacity for intrigue, and defended
himself with adroitness against the plots of the court.   His
works have been blamed for reserve and even falsehood; and
doubtless they are not entirely free from these faults, especially
the " History of the Great Rebellion," written in a more
official manner than the " Memoirs."   But considering his
position, Clarendon has, on the whole, the merit of sincerely
aiming at impartiality; and if he has shown this in his judgment of persons much more than in his representations of
public feeling and events, it is because the structure of his
mind fitted him to appreciate and understand men better
than nations.

More than once during his exile, Clarendon asked permission, which was always refused, to return and live in obscurity
in England.   On the near approach of death the desire of
revisiting his native country became a melancholy and passionate longing in the heart of this old man, who had sincerely
loved and laboriously served it.   He established himself at
Rouen in order to be nearer the soil of England; and from
thence, as a last attempt, he wrote in the following manner
to Charles II.:—" Seven years was a time prescribed and
limited by God himself for the expiation of some of his
greatest judgments, and it is full that time since I have with
all possible humility sustained the insupportable weight of
the king's displeasure.   Since it will be in nobody's power
long to prevent me from dying, methinks the desiring a place
to die in should not be thought a great presumption."*

Charles II., insensible to any emotion of gratitude, offered
a cold refusal to these entreaties of a man who had devoted
to him his life.   His refusal was not dictated by the fear of
any hatred which courtiers or his people might entertain for
Clarendon, but by the desire to spare himself the annoyance
of feeling that in England, perhaps within a few leagues of
his residence, there resided a faithful servant and an old
friend whom he had basely abandoned.   Clarendon died at
Rouen on the 7th of December, 1674; his greatest honour
now is that he often resisted that contemptible king whom,
in his last days, he vainly attempted to move.

* Clarendon Papers, iii., Supp. xliv.; Campbell's Lives of the Chancellors,
vol. iii., p. 257.

HENRY HYDE, EARL OF CLARENDON.
[1638—1709.]

DURING his exile on the continent, while attending upon Charles II., as he wandered in poverty from one country to another, according as their governments were at peace or at war with Cromwell, the great Earl of Clarendon, who was as yet nothing but plain Edward Hyde, unable probably to pay for a secretary, did not wish, or could not find any other to act as such, except his eldest son, Henry Hyde, then seven-. teen years of age. He was born on the 2nd of June, 1638, just at the time when the murmurs of that storm were begin- ning to be heard which was to cause his father a life of care and agitation. In early life he was made to share in labour and vicissitude. It was in 1655 that Edward Hyde, then Chancellor of the Exchequer for the proscribed king, began that vast correspondence with Spain, France, and the Lower Countries, as well as with England, from which he probably expected little, but which at least preserved to his master the shadow of royalty, and to himself the shadow of an honour- able connexion with royalty. In this correspondence young Henry Hyde acted as secretary; he employed his days in writing in cipher, or in deciphering letters, and he displayed in these somewhat tedious employments a discretion and in- telligence which won for him the fullest confidence of his father. It appears even that more than once the Chancellor left to him the care of answering, as he judged suitable, the secret communications which reached him from England.

When, in 1660, the restoration of Charles II. had justified the anticipations of the Chancellor, and rewarded his fidelity, his son Henry, the companion of his good fortune as he had been of his reversals, married Theodosia, daughter of the illustrious and unfortunate Lord Capel; and soon afterwards, in 1662, after the marriage of Charles II. with the Infanta of Portugal, was appointed chamberlain to the queen. We may wonder that the Lord Chancellor, instead of seeking for his eldest son important political offices, should be contented with his obtaining a situation at court; and this circumstance suggests a doubt whether he had a very high opinion of the qualifications of his son Henry. Other facts give further reason for this doubt. Bishop Burnet, while doing full justice

to the discretion and fidelity which Henry Clarendon had
shown during exile, in the capacity of secretary to his father,
says, " His judgment was not much to be depended upon, for
he was much carried by vulgar prejudices and false notions.
. . . And the king always spoke of him with great sharpness and much scorn." The English editor of Lord Henry
Clarendon's Memoirs bestows much pains in confuting this
testimony; and it may be that the animosity of Burnet against
the opponents of the revolution of 1688 had some share in
producing this opinion. There is, however, no indication that
the talents of Lord Henry Clarendon deserved any very high
esteem; nor that, if he had had a different name, he would
have obtained any importance in his time, or any place in
history.

In 1667, at the time of his father's disgrace, he was member of the House of Commons, and he entered into the Opposition ranks without losing the situation which he occupied
under the queen. His name frequently appears in the Parliamentary debates of that period; and if his speeches have in
them nothing remarkable, they at all events prove that he had
neither surrendered his mental freedom nor sold himself to
the court,—a rare merit at that time, especially for a man
devoted to the Stuarts by descent, and a courtier by position.
In 1674 he became Earl of Clarendon, on the death of his
banished father, and continued, in the House of Lords, to
vote with the Opposition; with sufficient moderation, however,
to keep a way of reconciliation with the court always open.
He was one of those upright men who, without boldness or
foresight, mourn over the afflictions of their country, but
dread still more the remedies for them; who wish they could
reform power without ever offending it, nor wresting from it
any of those rights which they confess it abuses. Such had
been, in reality, though with far more mental elevation and
vigour, the politics of the Lord Chancellor Clarendon; we
meet with it again in his son, stripped of the talent which
graced it, and also without the plausible reasons which, fifteen
years before, the excesses of the revolution afforded for it.
Towards the close of the reign of Charles II. the vices of the
government were the chief grounds for alarm and antagonism;
Henry Clarendon did not approve of them; but when England
showed itself determined no longer to submit to such rule,
when the struggle between the country and the court

assumed a definite and serious character, he took the side of the court party.

In 1680, the favour of the Duke of York procured for him a place in the privy council, and he was one of the number who rejected the famous Bill of Exclusion. He was also one of the councillors whose dismission was demanded by the House of Commons on the 7th of January, 1681.

In 1685, the accession of James II. redoubled the fears of all who were friendly to the civil and religious liberties of their country. Lord Henry Clarendon, who sympathised with these fears, was nevertheless the object of the new king's favours, as James wished to reward him for having opposed the Bill of Exclusion. He accepted the reward, and was first appointed Keeper of the Privy Seal, afterwards Lord-Lieutenant of Ireland. There he became acquainted with the whole extent of the designs that were being formed against England. Sincerely attached to the Established Church, and respecting, if not the liberties, yet at all events the laws of his country, he saw the government of James II. direct all its efforts towards the establishment of Catholicism and absolute power, and alternately using the one as a means to advance the other. He conducted himself with as much honesty as his position allowed, writing with frankness to the king or his ministers, representing to them the danger as well as the unconstitutional nature of their proceedings, and endeavouring to diminish their criminality or ward off the effect of them, but without ever entertaining the thought of formally refusing concurrence in them. When a spirit of servility has taken possession of a man, his good sense, and even his moral integrity become useless to him; he sees the danger and advances onwards to it; he observes the evil and lends himself to it; he has lost the free disposal of his own conduct, he serves the projects which he abhors, and is ruined with the infatuated men whom he has warned. If James II., annoyed by the continual remonstrances and the timidity of the Lord-Lieutenant of Ireland, had not recalled him and substituted Tyrconnel, an avowed Papist, Lord Henry Clarendon would never have thought of retiring upon his own accord, and the revolution of 1688 would have found him in the service of a power to which he could never give his approval.

When Lord Clarendon returned to England in the beginning of 1687, he gained in private life a little of that independence which he would never possess by native force of character: he has himself related his life from that period: to the details which are contained in his journal, referring to his own conduct as well as to the general events of his time, nothing need be added. On the approach and during the course of the revolution of 1688 he was what he had always been—an honest nobleman and sincere Protestant, convinced that the Established Church ought to be saved and the government of the king reformed; disposed even to accept, in order to obtain a better chance of success, the assistance of the Prince of Orange and the insurrection, but full of nervous apprehension, inclined to halt with indignation as soon as, in order to accomplish the work, the axe was laid to the root of that corrupt tree which, often as it had been assailed, had never ceased to increase. We may smile at the credulity with which he went forth to meet the Prince of Orange, flattering himself that he would confine himself to the office of mediating between James II. and his people; but, the revolution of 1688 once accomplished, we must honour the fidelity which Lord Clarendon showed towards the dethroned monarch; a fidelity the more creditable in that it alienated him from the court to which he was attached, and that, after having quitted the court, he took no active part in the plots of the Jacobites, convinced at once that he was interdicted from serving a new master, and from disturbing the repose of his country, in order to recal a power which he had found to be mischievous whilst he believed it to be legitimate. He died on the 22nd of October, 1709, on his estate at Cornbury.

In 1763, the papers which Lord Henry Clarendon had left, on his death, were published at London, in two volumes, quarto. His correspondence with James II. and his ministers, during his government of Ireland, forms the greatest part of this publication; it is worth reading, but its interest is of an entirely special character, and confined to the affairs of Ireland. The Journal of Lord Henry Clarendon, on the contrary, is one of the most lively and truthful documents which have reached us relating to the revolution of 1688; nowhere can we better trace from step to step, through the familiar and daily details of a nobleman's life, the rapid progress of that memorable event, conducted at first by a few individuals as a conspiracy and an intrigue, but sustained and consummated by the expressed concurrence of the English people, and which has established in England that noble form of government to which it has owned, for more than a hundred and fifty years, its peace as well as its liberties, its welfare as well as its renown.

GILBERT BURNET, BISHOP OF SALISBURY.

[1643—1715.]

REVOLUTIONS commence with infatuation and end with incredulity. In their origin proud assurance is dominant; the ruling opinion disdains doubt, and will not endure contradiction: at their completion scepticism takes the place of proud disdain; there is no longer any care for individual convictions nor any belief in truth. Such is the sad condition of man—faith blinds him and experience corrupts him.

Nevertheless—and this secures the honour as well as the safety of humanity—some minds are always to be found in these grand epochs who escape both these evils; who, in the blind impetuousness of the first period preserve freedom of thought, and, in the unmanly incredulity of the second, retain fixed and sincere convictions. These are minds of a superior order, whatever may be their defects, who know how to trust in truth without forgetting the weakness of man, and to distrust the feeble powers of man without ceasing to believe in the omnipotence of truth.

Bishop Burnet is one of these men. Perhaps he owed this happiness to the favourable combination of circumstances which attended his youth. He was born on the 18th of September, 1643, at Edinburgh, of an ancient and reputable family in the county of Aberdeen, and was brought up in the midst of political parties without being prematurely engaged with or hastily plunged into any. His father, a learned juris-consult, was a sincere and moderate Royalist; his mother was a zealous Presbyterian, and Lord Waristoun, his uncle, was one of the most vehement opponents of Charles I. Burnet thus learned, from his infancy, to understand the language, and perhaps also at different times to sym-

pathise with the aims and sentiments of the most opposite
parties. He says of himself: " As I had been bred up by
my father to love liberty and moderation, so I spent the
greatest part of the year 1664 in Holland and France, which
contributed not a little to root and fix me in those principles.
I saw much peace and quiet in Holland, notwithstanding
the diversity of opinions amongst them, which was occasioned by the gentleness of the government, and the toleration that made all people easy and happy."*

If the persons from whom Burnet had received in his youth
so many contrary impressions had been, like so many others,
undeceived and corrupted by events, he would, perhaps, have
learned to respect no opinion, and, pursuing fortune only
disdainfully, to ridicule all regard for principle. But the
different convictions in the midst of which he lived and
grew from 1643 to 1660, during the course of the first revolution, were and always continued serious and disinterested;
so that he yielded them respect without succumbing to their
authority, and that while his ideas were enlarged, he was
never, even in his most ordinary and intimate relationships,
induced to treat with suspicion or scorn any true earnestness
and faith.

From the restoration of Charles II. to the fall of James II.,
Burnet's life was active and busy, and was spent in close connexion with great personages and great events without being
involved in their destinies. He has given a minute account
of it in his " History of his own Time."   At first sight this
narrative does not give us that impression concerning the
author which I have just indicated; we are even tempted, in
reading it, to render him, if not a small share of esteem, yet
certainly but little attention. He appears fickle, restless,
awkward, indiscreet, continually meddling in intrigues, at one
time with the popular party at another time with the court,
familiarly connected with men on whose conduct he bestows
the greatest blame, keeping up in order to gratify his vanity
relationships the most opposed to his convictions, incon-
siderate in his movements and in his language, setting no
bounds to his activity, which is often without an aim, and of
a character as little becoming the superiority of his mind as
the dignity of his position. These were, so to speak, the
exterior faults in Burnet's character, and he has taken no

* Burnet's History of his own Time, vol. i., p. 207, folio edition.

pains to conceal them. But when we regard him more closely, another man appears and shows himself. Burnet's religious opinions are those of the Episcopalians, and yet we cannot find in him any of the vivid and arrogant passions of the bishops; his political principles are those of the Presbyterians, but he is a stranger to their narrow views, their insurmountable prejudices, their puerile and obstinate antipathies. He is familiar with a number of licentious noblemen, while his true friends, the only ones to whom he remained permanently attached whatever might be their condition, are the most upright men of the time. His life is full of intrigues and vicissitudes, yet nowhere can we perceive that he has yielded or changed in his principles, and his disinterestedness manifests itself on all occasions when his fortune might have been completed by the sacrifice of his freedom; he refuses to be a bishop as long as bishops are made the instruments of tyranny; he preaches tolerance to persecutors and reason to fanatics. Charles II. and his brother, the Duke of York, treated him with favour,—he told them the truth: the favour of the princes is withdrawn,—he speaks of them without disguise, but without anger. Sometimes his language would lead us to believe that the vices of the court were not displeasing to him; yet his manners are quite pure, and the thought which remains with him and governs him, in his familiar intercourse with Charles II., is how he may most impressively represent to the king the faults which have brought disorders into his kingdom, and induce him to return to virtue.   "I had reason to believe," says Burnet, in 1681, "that he (the king) was highly displeased with me for what I had done a year before. Mrs. Roberts, whom he kept for some time, sent for me when she was a-dying: I saw her often for some weeks, and, among other things, I desired her to write a letter to the king, expressing the sense she had of her past life: and at her desire I drew such a letter as might be fit for her to write; but she never had strength enough to write it: so upon that I resolved to write a very plain letter to the king: I set before him his past life, and the effects it had on the nation, with the judgments of God that lay on him, which was but a small part of the punishment he might look for: I pressed upon him that earnestly to change the whole course of his life: I carried this letter to Chiffinch's,* on the 29th of

* Valet-de-chambre to Charles II.

January, and told the king in the letter that I hoped the reflections on what had befallen his father on the 30th of January might move him to consider these things more carefully. Lord Arran happened to be then in waiting, and he came to me the next day, and told me he was sure the king had a long letter from me, for he held the candle to him while he read it; he knew at all that distance that it was my hand. The king read it twice over, and then threw it into the fire; and, not long after, Lord Arran took occasion to name me, and the king spoke of me with great sharpness, so he perceived that he was not pleased with my letter.* Nor was the king pleased with my being sent for by Wilmot, Earl of Rochester, when he died: he fancied that he had told me many things of which I might make an ill use; yet he had read the book that I writ concerning him, and spoke well of it. In this state I was in the king's thoughts when Lord Halifax carried me to him, and introduced me with a very extraordinary compliment, that he did not bring me to the king to put me in his good opinion so much as to put the king in my good opinion,—and added, he hoped the king would not only take me into his favour, but into his heart. The king had a peculiar faculty of saying obliging things with a very good grace: among other things, he said he knew that, if I pleased, I could serve him very considerably, and that he desired no service from me longer than he continued true to the Church and to the law. Lord Halifax upon that added that the king knew he served him upon the same terms, and was to make his stops. The king and he fell into some discourse about religion. Lord Halifax said to the king that he was the head of the Church; to which the king answered that he did not desire to be the head of nothing, for, indeed, he was of no church. From that the king run out into much discourse about Lord Shaftesbury, who was shortly to be tried: he complained with great scorn of the imputation of subornation that was cast on himself. He said he did not wonder that the Earl of Shaftesbury, who was guilty of those practices, should fasten them on others. And he used upon that a Scot's proverb very pleasantly, 'At doomsday we shall see whose a— is blackest.' The discourse lasted half an hour

* The complete copy of this letter, which does credit to Burnet's virtue, and even reflects some honour on Charles II.'s toleration, will be found at the end of this article, p. 167.

very hearty and free, so I was in favour again. But I could
not hold it. I was told I kept ill company: the persons
Lord Halifax named to me were the Earl of Essex, Lord
Russell, and Jones. But I said I would upon no consideration give over conversing with my friends, so I was where I
was before."*

This incident gives us a faithful representation of the
character of Burnet as it appeared at the court of Charles II.
Under a somewhat undignified exterior, and with appearances
of flippancy, we can recognise an independent spirit, a sincere
heart, and one of the most upright, as well as one of the most
enlightened men who have ever lived in times of political dissension, of corruption and frivolity.

When the revolution of 1688 was accomplished, Burnet,
who had very actively and efficiently concurred in it, did not
trouble himself further with it, except only to secure to his
country its salutary results. He divided his life between the
State and the Church, the House of Lords, and the bishopric
of Salisbury. In both these functions he conducted himself
in the same manner as he had before he obtained preferment;
sometimes inconsiderately, and with too great eagerness to
act, or to appear to obtain the ascendency, which he would
have well employed, but always acting with probity, generosity, and consistency; faithful to his political friends, and
discharging with conscientious care the duties of his bishopric; continually occupied at court in his endeavour to protect its former enemies, and the nonconformists in his diocese;
discarding, both as a matter of party and of conscience, all
persecution, every measure of severity, and devoting a portion
of his time and of his revenue to the work of bringing up in
the same sentiments the young candidates for holy orders,
whom he afterwards appointed to livings. His blunders,
his unrestrained speech, and also his frankness, sometimes
brought upon him the contempt of the high clergy, and of
William III., who rather regarded him with confidence than
serious consideration. Nevertheless, whenever the English
Church felt itself threatened by any danger, we cannot but
acknowledge that Burnet had a good right to enforce upon
the bishops the duty of tolerance, of regular residence in
their diocese, of ameliorating the condition of the poorer part
of the clergy; and when, in 1698, William wished to find a

* Burnet's History of his own Time, vol. i., pp. 507-508.

tutor for the young Duke of Gloucester, son of the Princess Anne, he chose Burnet; and the king had some difficulty in overcoming the conscientious scruples of the bishop, who desired either to refuse the charge which had been offered to him, or to resign his bishopric, in order to devote himself entirely to his new duties. Burnet only consented to accept this honour on conditions which allowed him to attend to both offices; and he lived thus till the 17th of March, 1715, alternately brought into difficulties by faults which did little harm to any but himself, and into honour by the talents and virtues by which his patrons and subordinates always profited more than himself. He died, after a few days' illness, of pleuritic fever, and showed, during the short continuance of his disorder, qualities which had been seldom seen during his life—the most unruffled serenity, and a perfectly conscious seriousness. He was married three times, and left behind him a large family, by whom he had been tenderly beloved.

His conversation and familiar life were characterised by a singular, and sometimes very embarrassing absence of mind. The famous Olympia Mancini, niece to Cardinal Mazarin, Countess of Soissons, Prince Eugene's mother, had been, in 1680, imprisoned in Paris on a suspicion of poisoning, excited by her connexion with Mesdames Bruivilliers and Voisin. When her son, the Prince Eugene, came over to England, towards the close of Queen Anne's reign, Burnet requested the Duke of Marlborough that he would procure him an opportunity of meeting a person whose fame resounded through all Europe. "To this the duke agreed, upon condition that Burnet would be on his guard against saying anything that might give disgust. Being accordingly invited to dine at Marlborough House, with Prince Eugene and other company, he resolved to sit silent and *incognito* during the whole entertainment. The prince, however, seeing a dignified clergyman at table, inquired who he was; and understanding he was Bishop Burnet, of whom he had often heard, he addressed his discourse to him, and asked him in particular when he was last at Paris. To this question our prelate answered with precipitation that he could not recollect the year, but that it was at the time when the Countess of Soissons was imprisoned. Scarcely had he pronounced these words when, his eyes meeting those of the Duke of Marlborough, he instantly recognised his blunder, and was so

totally deprived of all remaining discretion, that he redoubled
his error by asking pardon of his highness. The conclusion
was, that seeing the whole company embarrassed, and out
of countenance, he retired in the utmost confusion." On
another occasion, when Mr. James Lindsay, the last Earl of
Balcarras, in his early youth, was introduced to Bishop
Burnet by Lady Stair, the bishop, after the common compliments, asked her in the presence of a large number of
people, " Pray what is become of that wicked wretch, Lady
Wigton?" Now, the Countess of Wigton was the young
gentleman's sister. Dr. Burnet was himself so far sensible
of his weakness, that he sometimes avoided the persons whom
he might offend by it. After Lady Frances Pierpoint was
married to the Earl of Marr, the bishop never went to visit
her, and gave Lady Stair this reason for his seeming neglect,
" That he did not like Lord Marr, and could not answer for
his not babbling out something with regard to him that
might give offence."*

The celebrated Marquis of Halifax, the patron and friend
of Burnet, amused himself with making a portraiture of him
and his character, which he sent to the bishop himself, and
which was found among his papers after his death. Thomas
Burnet, his third son, has published this portrait at the end
of the life of his father, which he wrote,† and I will do myself the pleasure of transcribing it, as it is characterised as
much by truthfulness as by friendship.

" Dr. Burnet is, like all men who are above the ordinary
level, seldom spoken of in a mean; he must either be railed
at or admired: he has a swiftness of imagination that no
other man comes up to; and as our nature hardly allows us
to have enough of anything without having too much, he
cannot at all times so hold in his thoughts, but that at some
time they may run away with him; as it is hard for a vessel
that is brimful, when in motion, not to run over; and therefore the variety of matter that he ever carries about him
may throw out more than an unkind critic would allow of.
His first thoughts may sometimes require more digestion,
not from a defect in his judgment, but from the abundance
of his fancy, which furnishes too fast for him. His friends
love him too well to see small faults; or, if they do, think

* Kippis' Biographia Britannica, vol. iii., p. 33, folio. London, 1784.
† Burnet's History of his own Time, vol. ii., pp. 725-726.

that his greater talents give him a privilege of straying from the strict rules of caution, and exempt him from the ordinary rules of censure. He produces so fast, that what is well in his writings calls for admiration, and what is incorrect deserves an excuse; he may in some things require grains of allowance, which those only can deny him who are unknown or unjust to him. He is not quicker in discovering other men's faults than he is in forgiving them; so ready, or rather glad, to acknowledge his own, that from blemishes they become ornaments. All the repeated provocations of his indecent adversaries have had no other effect than the setting his good-nature in so much a better light, since his anger never went further than to pity them. That heat which in most other men raises sharpness and satire, in him glows into warmth for his friends, and compassion for those in want and misery. As dull men have quick eyes in discerning the smaller faults of those that nature has made superior to them, they do not miss one blot he makes; and being beholden only to their barrenness for their discretion, they fall into the errors which arise from his abundance, and by a mistake, into which their malice betrays them, they think that, by finding a mote in his eye, they hide the beams that are in their own. His quickness makes writing so easy a thing to him that his spirits are neither wasted nor soured by it; the soil is not forced; everything grows and brings forth without pangs, which distinguishes as much what he does from that which smells of the lamp, as a good palate will discern between fruit which comes from a rich mould, and that which tastes of the uncleanly pains that have been bestowed upon it. He makes many enemies, by setting an ill-natured example of living which they are not inclined to follow. His indifference for preferment, his contempt not only of splendour, but of all unnecessary plenty, his degrading himself unto the lowest and most painful duties of his calling, are such unprelatical qualities, that, let him be never so orthodox in other things, in these he must be a Dissenter. Virtues of such a kind are so many heresies in the opinion of those divines who have softened the primitive injunctions, so as to make them suit better with the present frailty of mankind. No wonder, then, if they are angry, since it is in their own defence; or that from a principle of self-preservation they should endeavour to suppress a

man, whose parts are a shame, and whose life is a scandal to
them."

It was not till 1724 that Thomas Burnet, the bishop's third
son, published the "History of his own Time." This work
is divided into two parts,—the first includes the period between the accession of Charles I. to the revolution of 1688;
the second part contains an account of the reigns of William
III. and of Anne, as far as the year 1713. It is, in my judgment, the most instructive and truthful book that we have
with reference to that period; the only one which can be
considered, not as a means of discovering the truth, but as
containing, or nearly so, the truth itself. In most memoirs,
we must disabuse our minds of the colouring under which the
facts are presented, and of the conclusions of the writer; in
the work of Burnet, however, except where he treats of the
Catholics, the facts generally appear under their true aspect,
and the conclusions of the author, whether moral or political, are just. The first revolution, from 1640 to 1660, is
only sketched, and that only to serve as an introduction to
the events which happened after the return of the Stuarts till
their expulsion; but this short sketch gives us a lively and
accurate picture of men and parties drawn by a hand which
combines sagacity and just appreciation of the subject with
an impartiality which we shall in vain seek for in other writers
of this period. As to the restoration, there is no truth in a
remark which has been often made, that it may rightly complain of the history which Burnet has left of it; he writes as
a Whig, undoubtedly, but he has none of that absurd credulity, those selfish and malignant passions which belonged to
his party. In spite of the somewhat gross bluntness of occa-
sional expressions, he has treated Charles ·II., James II.,
their councillors and their friends with an equity and mildness which posterity has rarely accorded. Posterity judges a
government as a whole according to its principles and results,
without minutely examining in order to discover whether this
or that king, this or that minister possessed certain amiable
qualities, whether he had, amidst all that appears scandalous,
some glimmerings of justice and good sense, if some excuse
may not be found which may modify its condemnation of
some of his faults; it has brought the last two Stuarts before
its tribunal and condemned their memory with scorn. This
is also the result to which Burnet conducts his readers; but

at the same time he allows them to see all that can moderate the severity of such a result. He has lived with the men of whom he writes : some of them have treated him with kindness; others have charmed him by the fascinations of their mind; he understands their errors, their faults, even their vices ; and whatever he may say or think of them, we find always, in his feelings and in his words, that there is lurking something of that involuntary indulgence which clings to personal relationships, and which has little in common with that justice which is founded on a more exact knowledge of characters and positions. He was, in other respects, a man whose mind was free and unprejudiced,—capable of entering into the very thoughts of his enemies,—easily detached from the judgment he had formed by impartial and vivid impressions,—a stranger to blind prejudices and bitter hatreds,— whose spirit was too equitable, and whose moral feelings were too sensitive to allow himself to be blinded or enslaved by his own private opinions.

In one point alone do they pervert the natural fairness and candour of his reason,—he sometimes, in his estimate of the Catholics, partakes of the prejudices and passions of his contemporaries. We very soon perceive this in the " History of his own Time," when he gives his account of the famous Popish plot ; and more clearly in his " History of the Reformation of the Church of England." This last work, of which the first volume was published in 1679, procured for Burnet an honour which no other writer had received previously nor has obtained since; he had the thanks of both houses of Parliament, with a desire that he would prosecute the undertaking and complete so valuable a work. There is at first sight ground for suspicion, when we see such a popularity and success in the midst of the excited fanaticism which then possessed all minds, and this suspicion is justified by the work itself. It abounds with ingenious remarks, elaborate research, and eloquent passages ; we must even admit that, taken as a whole, and in the general aspect of the facts which it presents, the author has the mastery over his opponents ; but, notwithstanding all this, it is the work of a partisan, full of narrow views, partial statements, biassed opinions, and which, in spite of its prodigious success, does not now deserve the esteem either of the philosopher or of the historian. All that we can say in favour of Burnet is, that the Catholics whom he controverted were not more enlightened nor more impartial than himself. The second volume of this work was published in 1681, and the third in 1714. Burnet himself published an abridgment of the first two volumes in 1682. There are three French translations of this:—one published in London, in 1683 and 1685, in two volumes, quarto; another at Geneva, in 1685, in four volumes, 12mo; a third at Amsterdam, in 1687. There is also a Latin translation of it by Mittelhorzer, in folio, Geneva, 1686.

Burnet has left a great number of other works, namely: 1st. Fifty-eight sermons; 2nd. Thirteen discourses, or treatises on matters connected with Protestant theology; 3rd. Eighteen controversial writings on the Popish question; 4th. Twenty-five historical treatises,—I have mentioned the most important; his " Memoirs of James and William, Dukes of Hamilton," edited from papers in possession of the family, also contain many curious details with reference to the English revolution; it is, on the whole, a very readable book. 5th. Lastly, twenty-six essays on moral, political, literary, and miscellaneous topics.

The author of the article on Burnet, in M. Michaud's " Biographie Universelle," says, that the son of the prelate, Thomas Burnet, published his " Essays and Meditations on Morality and Religion" at the same time as the " History of his own Time." This is a mistake. I find in an arranged catalogue of Burnet's writings, drawn up in 1753, and appended to a new edition of the " History of his own Time," published at London in 1818, the following passage : " The bishop left finished and prepared for the press a book, entitled, ' Essays and Meditations on Morality and Religion;' with directions in his last will that it should be printed, but I cannot find that this order was ever executed."

The following is the letter which Burnet sent to the king, and which was published by his son Thomas Burnet in his life of the bishop affixed to the " History."*

" 29th of January, 1680.

" May it please your Majesty,
" I have not presumed to trouble your Majesty for some months, not having anything worthy your time to offer; and now I choose rather this way, since the infinite duty I owe you puts me under restraints in discourse, which I cannot so

* Vol. ii., pp. 686-689.

easily overcome.   What I shall now suggest to your Majesty,
I do it as in the presence of Almighty God, to whom I know
I must give an account of all my actions; I therefore beg you
will be graciously pleased to accept this most faithful zeal of
your poor subject, who has no other design in it than your
good, and the discharge of his own conscience.

"I must then first assure your Majesty, I never discovered
anything like a design of raising rebellion among all those
with whom I converse; but I shall add, on the other hand,
that most people grow sullen, and are highly dissatisfied with
you and distrustful of you.   Formerly your ministers, or his
royal highness, bore the blame of things that were ungrateful; but now it falls upon yourself, and time, which cures
most other distempers, increases this.   Your last speech makes
many think it will be easy to fetch up petitions from all parts
of England; this is now under consultation, and is not yet
determined; but I find so many inclined to promote them,
that, as far as I can judge, it will go that way.   If your Majesty calls a new Parliament, it is believed that those who
have promoted the petitions will be generally elected; for
the inferior sort of people are much set upon them, and make
their judgment of men from their behaviour in that matter.
The soberer sort of those who are ill-pleased at your conduct,
reckon that either the state of your affairs beyond sea, or your
exchequer at home, will ere long necessitate your meeting
your Parliament; and that then things must be rectified, and
therefore they use their utmost endeavours to keep all quiet.
If your Majesty has a session in April for supporting your
allies, I find it is resolved by many, that the money necessary
to maintain your alliances shall be put into the hands of commissioners, to issue it as they shall answer to the two houses;
and these will be so chosen, that, as it is likely that the
persons will be very unacceptable to you, so they being trusted
with the money, will be as a council of state to control all
your councils.   And as to your exchequer, I do not find any
inclination to consider your necessity, unless many things be
done to put them into a better disposition than I can observe
in them.   The things that will be demanded will not be of
so easy a digestion, as that I can imagine you will ever be
brought to them, or indeed that it will be reasonable or
honourable for you to grant them.   So that, in this disorder
of affairs, it is easy to propose difficulties, but not so easy to
find out that which may remove them.

"There is one thing, and indeed the only thing in which all honest men agree, as that which can easily extricate you out of all your troubles ; it is not the change of a minister or of a council, but it is (and suffer me, sir, to speak it with a more than ordinary earnestness) a change in your own heart, and in your course of life.   And now, sir, if you do not with indignation throw this paper from you, permit me (with all the humility of a subject prostrate at your feet) to tell you, that all the distrust your people have of you, all the necessities you are under, all the indignation of Heaven that is upon you, and appears in the defeating all your counsels, flow from this, that you have not feared nor served God, but have given yourself up to so many sinful pleasures.   Your Majesty may perhaps justly think, that many of those who oppose you have no regard for religion, but the body of your people consider it more than you can imagine.   I do not desire your Majesty to put on a hypocritical show of religion, as Henry III. of France did, hoping thereby to have weathered the storms of those times.   No ! that would be soon seen through, and as it would provoke God more, so it would increase jealousies. No, sir, it must be real, and the evidences of it signal ; all those about you who are the occasions of sin, chiefly the women, must be removed, and your court be reformed.   Sir, if you will turn you to religion sincerely and seriously you shall quickly find a serene joy of another nature possess your mind than that which arises from gross pleasures ; God would be at peace with you, and direct and bless all your counsels ; all good men would presently turn to you, and ill men would be ashamed, and have a thin party.   For I speak it knowingly, there is nothing has so alienated the body of your people from you, as what they have heard of your life, which disposes them to give an easy belief to all other scandalous reports.

"Sir, this counsel is now almost as necessary for your affairs as for your soul ; and though you have highly offended that God, who has been infinitely merciful to you, in preserving you at Worcester fight, and during your long exile, and who brought you back so miraculously, yet he is still good and gracious ; and will, upon your sincere repentance and change of life, pardon all your sins, and receive you into his favour.   Oh ! sir, what if you should die in the midst of all your sins ?   At the great tribunal, where you must appear, there will be no regard to the crown you now wear ; but it will aggravate your punishment, that, being in so emi-

nent a station, you have so much dishonoured God.   Sir, I
hope you believe there is a God, and a life to come, and that
sin shall not pass unpunished.   If your Majesty will reflect
upon your having been twenty years upon the throne, and in
that time how little you have glorified God, how much you
have provoked him, and that your ill example has drawn so
many after you to sin, that men are not now ashamed of their
vices, you cannot but think that God is offended with you;
and if you consider how ill your counsels at home, and your
wars abroad have succeeded, and how much you have lost the
hearts of your people, you may reasonably conclude this is of
God, who will not turn away his anger from you, till you turn
to him with your whole heart.

" I am no enthusiast, either in opinion or temper; yet I
acknowledge I have been so pressed in my mind to make this
address to you, that I could have no ease till I did it: and
since you were pleased to direct me to send you, through
Mr. Chiffinch's hands, such informations as I thought fit to
convey to you, I hope your Majesty will not be offended, if I
have made use of that liberty.   I am sure I can have no other
design in it but your good; for I know very well this is not
the method to serve any ends of my own.   I therefore throw
myself at your feet, and once more, in the name of God,
whose servant I am, do most humbly beseech your Majesty
to consider of what I have written, and not to despise it for
the meanness of the person who has sent it; but to apply
yourself to religion in earnest; and I dare assure you of
many blessings both temporal and spiritual in this life, and
of eternal glory in the life to come: but if you will go on in
your sins, the judgments of God will probably pursue you in
this life, so that you may be a proverb to after ages; and
after this life, you will be for ever miserable; and I, your
poor servant that now am, shall be a witness against you in
the great day, that I gave you this free and faithful warning.

" Sir, no person alive knows that I have written to you to
this purpose; and I chose this evening, hoping that your
exercise to-morrow may put you into disposition to weigh it
more carefully.   I hope your Majesty will not be offended
with this sincere expression of my duty to you; for I durst
not have ventured on it, if I had not thought myself bound
to it, both by the duty I owe to God, and that which will
ever oblige me to be,

" May it please your Majesty," &c.

JOHN SHEFFIELD, DUKE OF BUCKINGHAM.
[1649—1721.]

Two royal favourites of the name of Sir George Villiers, father and son, have given an unhappy celebrity to the name Buckingham which both bore successively.* But their fatal influence on the government of their country was not the only outrage which they committed on morality and reason; both joined to it that irregular splendour by which, at certain times, the flippant insolence of men attached to the court delights to ornament the flagrancy of their life, and for which it is indebted to the blended display which they make of their accomplishments and their vices.

Vices and accomplishments contributed also to the reputation of a third Duke of Buckingham, who was distinguished rather in literature than in politics; I refer to John Sheffield, born in 1649, at first Earl of Mulgrave, and created afterwards Duke of Buckingham by Queen Anne. The career and the character of this man do not present anything specially worthy of attention, they do not show us that he possessed any strong individuality, he does but embody with some fidelity the leading features of his age. Being of a lively and bold disposition, and gifted with a handsome figure, he went to the wars, gave himself up to women and mirth, conforming thus to fashions which had been introduced in his time to the English court from the court of France, and he several times took part in public affairs without leaving behind him any very obvious traces of his influence. After having as a Tory united with the court in showing respect for Catholicism, so long as the favour of the prince was accessible by means of the Catholics, he joined the nation in its hostility to the Catholics when they on the contrary attempted to exclude from all favour every Protestant, however indifferent he might be to Protestantism. James II. had arrived at that point when he would not accept the assistance of any to his projects, unless they would adopt his beliefs. But in order to gain adherents on these terms, more devotion and

---

* The first, a favourite of James I. and Charles I., was born on the 20th of August, 1592, and was assassinated at Portsmouth by Felton on the 28th of August, 1628. The second, his son, and a favourite of Charles II., was born on the 30th of January, 1627, and died on the 16th of April, 1688.

audacity was required than the king could infuse into his partisans. Of those attached to his person, Lord Mulgrave was considered especially trustworthy. He had been appointed, on the accession of James II., Lord Chamberlain and member of the Privy Council. When the negotiations were being carried on which prepared for the revolution of 1688, one of the agents employed by the Prince of Orange to treat with the disaffected lords proposed that Lord Mulgrave should be admitted into their confidence; upon which the Earl of Shrewsbury said, "If you do, you will spoil all; he will never join with us." After the revolution of 1688, King William, relating this circumstance to Lord Mulgrave, asked him, "Pray, my lord, what would you have done if my agent had acquainted you with the whole business?" "Sir," said Lord Mulgrave, "I should have discovered it to the master I served." He had no fear of losing favour with his new master by giving such an answer. The king replied, "I cannot blame you."* His attachment to the interests of his old master did not carry him beyond the bounds of that resignation which events, when they have been once accomplished, demand. He spoke in the House of Lords in favour of the Prince of Orange, and that he should reign conjointly with his wife. But without committing himself entirely to the new government, voting and speaking often in aid of the opposition, he knew how to keep up the position of a man whose alliance is sought for and conciliated by power, but whose constant adherence can never be reckoned upon. Buckingham had no great liking for William III., and even viewed only with a kind of frivolous disdain that taciturn adroitness, that vigorous circumspection, not to be disturbed by any expressions of flattery, and the frigid exterior of that genius which only betrayed itself by great actions. He consented, however, to accept from the king a pension of three thousand pounds, and a seat in the Privy Council. Under Queen Anne, to whom, it is said, he had made his addresses in his youth, he entered more conspicuously into public life; withdrew, therefore, returned, and took part in all the ministerial movements of a reign directed far more than the preceding had been by court influences. This was the appropriate sphere for the Duke of Buckingham: skilful in ruining his friends, unscrupulous as to the agency he em-

* Biographia Britannica, art. Sheffield, vol. vi., p. 3659.

ployed, but, too proud to lower his own personal position, he
sometimes compromised it by his flippancy, and knew how to
retain it by his audacity.   In his youth the freedom of his
pleasantries with the mistresses of Charles II. had brought
on him the displeasure of the king; and, on one occasion, it
is said the king went so far as to take an opportunity to send
the Earl of Mulgrave to Tangier in a vessel which was unfit
to endure the voyage.   The earl, warned of the danger, and
not having been able to obtain a better vessel, was unwilling
to give up an expedition which he had himself solicited; but
he advised several volunteers, who had engaged to follow him,
not to expose themselves to such dangers, since their honour
was not equally concerned.   Many profited by his advice,
others persisted, as a matter of honour, in their first resolution.   Among these last was the Earl of Plymouth, a natural
son of Charles II.   The weather was so favourable to the
travellers that, notwithstanding the miserable state of the
vessel, which leaked in numerous places, they arrived in
health and safety at Tangier; but during the whole passage
the earl would not allow the king's health to be drunk at his
table.

Literature occupied the time of the Duke of Buckingham
which was not given to intrigues with the world or with the
court.   His rank, his friendships with the literary men of
his time, the eulogies of Pope and Dryden, have given to his
verses far more celebrity than they deserve to possess.   As
to his few writings in prose, none of them are beyond what
we should expect from a man of the world accustomed to be
easily satisfied with the most simple efforts of thought : two
alone still possess any real interest.   The first, entitled " Memoirs in the Reign of Charles II.," seems to have had for its
object merely to relate a fact personal to the author, but
which is not without importance, as bearing upon the history
of the time.   We find in it some details, delicately hinted at,
concerning what takes place behind the scene, which is the
true history for a courtier, and which, under the frivolous,
as well as corrupt government of Charles II., were in fact
the basis and true cause of events.   Such Memoirs, referring
to such a time, are as instructive as they are amusing ; and
it is to be regretted that Buckingham did not extend them
to a greater length.

In the fragment which he has written on the " Revolution

of 1688," we can recognise a seriousness which was reflected from the times which were approaching, and the tone of a man who begins to interest himself in the destiny of his country. Nothing can better demonstrate the necessity of the revolution then accomplished in England, than the almost affectionate feeling of pity for James II., and of enmity for the Prince of Orange, which shows itself without disguise in this short narrative, without being accompanied with the least expression of regret for the government which fell. We might be inclined to say that the author endeavours to represent an historical event long since consummated, and which is no longer able to inspire any sentiment except the desire to form a correct estimate of the conduct of the principal actors. Such was, in fact, the character of the revolution of 1688—it was at the time of its accomplishment as much a necessity as if it already belonged to the past. This rendered its progress so tranquil and easy.

After having enjoyed, rather as a courtier than as a statesman, the uninterrupted favour of Queen Anne, the Duke of Buckingham, on the accession of George I., retired entirely from court life, and died in 1721, aged seventy-two years. He had been married three times; the last was during the reign of Queen Anne, to a natural daughter of James II. The periods of lying-in were generally, it appears, very dangerous to his last wife, the only one by whom he had any children; and the author of a kind of biography, wishing to defend him from the charge of avarice which had been brought against him, says, that during the pregnancy of his wife he was always at the pains to secure for her the services of an excellent physician,—an attention, he adds, in which many of those who passed for being more generous than he were deficient. The corruption of morals leads to a refinement of egotism and coldness which the most distrustful observer of human nature could not of himself discover.

SIR JOHN RERESBY.

SIR JOHN RERESBY would have been entirely unknown had he not undertaken to write his own "Memoirs." The manuscript of this work originally contained long personal details, but the editor did not think them worthy of being laid before the public. "Sir John," he says, "having very minutely acquainted us with his birth, education, and travels, which could neither affect the reader nor be admitted as part of what we promised to print of him, we shall set out from the year 1658." The editor was right. It does not appear that the private life of Sir John Reresby possessed interest of any kind, moral or romantic; and it is only that part of his "Memoirs" which refer to the period between the death of Cromwell and the fall of James II.—from 1658 to 1689—that has a truly historical interest. To listen to the testimony of a member of Parliament employed by the court, as Sir John Reresby was, from 1675 until the revolution of 1688, must be an important help to our comprehension of such an epoch; and the personal interests which occupied him during this period, interchange, in a pleasing and instructive manner, with the recital of public affairs. Among the crowd of men who are introduced into the political arena by means of a representative government, a large number are to be met with possessed of very moderate capacities, but who have shown sufficiently a respectable share of good sense in the ordinary circumstances of life, and are, by local partiality, pushed into a prominence which brings them into connexion with the most important events of the country. Destined to swell the ranks of the party to which they have attached themselves, these men are of little importance to a government, unless it is engaged in a struggle with public opinion, and compelled to seek elsewhere for a power capable of sustaining it. Such a government does not address itself to the public, being usually guided by certain ideas of reason and justice, which it is unable practically to embody, or by general interests, which it is unwilling to satisfy. Accordingly it seeks individual interests, of a varied and isolated character, entirely destitute of the power necessary to procure for themselves obedience, and consequently disposed to serve. Political movement thus transforms itself into a kind of stock exchange jobbery, in which each man has his individual place and history. The history of Sir John Reresby is such as might be expected from the position of a man determined to use, for the advancement of his fortune, such of his opinions as were pleasing to power, and to keep back such as were distasteful to it. A Tory by personal inclination, interest, and vanity, Sir John was naturally disposed to render to power all the devotion which it might ask, and, at the same time, he does not conceal from himself the danger of those false measures to which, however, he never refuses his support. Induced to prefer the discriminating conduct of the Marquis of Halifax to the violent opinions of the Duke of York, dissatisfied with the favour of the Duchess of Portsmouth, but steadily bent on pursuing such favour wherever it might conduct him, he proffered his services while he reserved his judgment; and after the revolution of 1688, being grieved at the downfal of his old masters, he felt himself injured by the small amount of eagerness shown by his patron, the Marquis of Halifax, in employing him in the service of the Prince of Orange, whose accession he deplored. In other respects, Sir John Reresby was an honourable man—using the word in a low sense—wanting only in the feeling of political duties, —a feeling which was obliterated after the periods of revolutionary and despotic violence, during which he remained without occupation. He presents himself before us with all the simple frankness of a man perfectly satisfied as to the propriety of his impressions, because he is conscious they are shared in by all around him. Nothing can be more curious than the details of his relations with Charles II. and his ministers; the advice which he gives; the familiarities which win him; the confidences which he receives; the arguments which convince him. As an intelligent and active man, but habitually vulgar in his feelings and notions, he is a sufficiently accurate type of that class of men who sustain power without hindering its decay, and who may be advantageously employed, so long as they are not the sole prop of a government.

The editor of Sir John Reresby's Memoirs, by closing them at the year 1689, seems to indicate that that year was the last of his public life. A time had arrived when servility, in its turn, was to be dispensed with; and whatever prudence Sir John Reresby might flatter himself he could display in his conduct, the services about which the court of the Stuarts had employed him in Yorkshire, rendered him probably little fitted to become the associate of a government which had been called by and designed to act upon fixed principles.

ON THE "EIKON BASILIKE."

ATTRIBUTED TO CHARLES I.

ONLY a few days had passed since the condemnation of Charles I., when the Eikôn Basilikè appeared as his work and portraiture,—as a triumphant revelation concerning a man who, in the eyes of his party, had by his death taken his place among the noble army of martyrs. The effect was prodigious: forty-seven editions in rapid succession showed that the popularity and admiration which it had secured were proportionate to the excited feelings in sympathy with which the work had been produced. Numerous translations carried the echo throughout Europe; and all the writers of the time, English and foreign, united in the expressions of high esteem and veneration entertained by all Europe for the character and talents of the unfortunate prince, whom all agreed in believing to be the author. Bayle, the least enthusiastic and most sagacious of critics, referring to the passage in which Milton calls in question the authenticity of the Eikôn Basilikè,"* adds, " The mere sentiments of this work would not have made any impression abroad; but every one was persuaded that Charles I. had written the book which appeared under his name. This was so honourable to his memory, and seemed so to establish his claim to be considered a martyr, that Milton, professing his belief that it was a forgery, was thought only to have resorted to the trick of an advocate, who denies whatever tells favourably for his opponent."†

Some modern writers, struck with the unanimity of opinion regarding this work in the seventeenth century, have appeared to think that if the Eikôn Basilikè had been published before the death of Charles I. it would have saved him. We, who are remote from the times and persons involved in a struggle, may easily assent to such a supposition; but whoever has watched their progress and observed how inevitably they are driven forward to the point towards which they started, will attach little importance to such an obstacle. In great epochs the first step determines the goal: the collateral events which happen on the road are comparatively

---

* Preface to " Eikonoclastes." Milton's Prose Works. Vol. i., p. 315. Bohn's Standard Library Edition.
† Bayle's Dictionary, article " Milton," note 11.

N

insignificant. Cromwell and his party, in 1649, were not in a condition to recede, but they were not equally without grounds for alarm, even after their victory. This startling display of the feelings and power of the Royalist party could not but cause their own party some disturbance. They had aimed a blow at it which they hoped would be its ruin; great, then, was their surprise, when they found themselves obliged to argue with it. Their writers set themselves to the task of refuting it. Milton published, in 1649, a bitter reply to the Eikôn Basilikè, under the title of "Eikonoclastes," and in his preface he calls in question the authenticity of the work; the astrologer William Lilly, re-suggested the doubt two years after, in his "Observations on the Life and Death of Charles I." Public indignation rejected this as a blasphemy, and the two Republicans, unable to afford any other support to their opinions than conjecture, were branded with the reproach of having given an impotent exhibition of malignity.

Nevertheless, if they had no means of demonstrating their opinion, neither had their adversaries any more decisive proofs of theirs. Under Cromwell the Royalists exerted themselves in destroying or concealing any proofs that might exist of the royal authorship of the Eikôn Basilikè. After the Restoration, the Republicans were prevented by shame from producing any objections which might revive the controversy and lead to a discovery of the truth. The dominant feeling of the public overruled all doubts, and fashion, which is almost as powerful as interest, consecrated every opinion which was cherished by the Royalists. In vain was it that some voices were raised to protest against this universal assumption; in vain was it that some even of the Royalists had reasons for denying or questioning the authenticity of a work which was regarded as the glory of its author; these hints could not reach further than the narrow circle of conversation. The only result was a kind of uneasiness in those who affirmed the authenticity of the book—an uneasiness which betrayed itself in the efforts of some among them to establish by facts what no one would venture strongly to contest; but their opinion, which they felt was poorly supported, was impatient to attack an incredulity which, though unexpressed, gave them annoyance.

The most positive testimony that can be quoted is that of Royston, the printer, who had, on the 23rd of December,

1648, received the manuscript of the Eikôn Basilikè from the hands of Dr. Symmonds, who said that it was the work of the King, and that he had received it from Dr. Bryan Duppa, Bishop of Salisbury, and chaplain to Charles I. Symmonds died a short time after, poisoned, it is said, on this account. Duppa died, also, in 1662, without having been called upon for a public explanation. With them all evidence which could lead to certainty had disappeared. The widow of Dr. Symmonds confirmed the testimony of the printer Royston. Her husband, she said, had often told her that the king was the author of the Eikôn Basilikè, but would not inform her from whom he received it. As to the existence of the original manuscript, the facts produced were still more uncertain. Sir Thomas Herbert had found, among the books which Charles had left him at his death, a manuscript copy of the Eikôn Basilikè, but nothing had fallen from Charles that could justify the suspicion that he was its author; and the terms in which Herbert expresses his opinion on this point indicate rather the manner of one who wishes to believe, than of one who is really convinced. A work published in 1649, entitled "The Princely Pelican," intended probably as an answer to Milton's Eikonoclastes, relates that the manuscript of the Eikôn Basilikè, taken by the Parliamentarians at the battle of Naseby, with other papers of the king, had been restored to him by an officer of the army, who was found, after the Restoration, to be Major Huntington.* Some other evidences of a less decisive character, and of but little authority, were given in support of this.

* Such, at least, was the declaration of Huntington, who added, that the chapters containing reflections were in the handwriting of Sir Edward Walker, with interlineary additions and corrections by the king, but that the prayers were entirely in the king's handwriting. But Sir Edward Walker, who wrote in favour of the authenticity of the Eikôn Basilikè, says nothing of this fact, which, however, would be decisive; and, on the other hand, he relates that a work of his (Historical Discourse on the Civil Wars), composed at the request of the king, presented by him to the king in 1645, and by the king to Lord Digby, who was ordered to take care of it, was lost at the battle of Naseby, and restored to the king, two years afterwards, by an officer in the army. It appears, moreover, that this work of Sir Edward Walker's contained corrections in the handwriting of the king. Huntington, then, supposing that his testimony was sincere, must have confounded facts, and related, with reference to the work about which he was then writing with some warmth, what his memory supplied concerning another manuscript. Besides, it is not impossible that he should have found among the papers restored to the king after the battle of Naseby some documents afterwards employed in the composition of the Eikôn Basilikè, which might have contributed to Huntington's mistake, and to that of the anonymous author of "The Princely Pelican."

These proofs were sufficient for a public, to which none of a different kind were presented. The Eikôn Basilikè had been printed, *cum privilegio regis,* as one of the works of Charles I The question seemed to have been decided, when, in 1686, at the sale of Lord Anglesea's library, the following note, writter by his Lordship, was found in his copy of the Eikôn Basilikè —" King Charles the Second and the Duke of York did both (in the last session of Parliament, 1675, when I showed them in the Lords' House, the written copy of this book, wherein are some corrections, written with the late King Charles the First's own hand), assure me that this was none of the said king's compiling, but made by Doctor Gauden, Bishop of Exeter, which I here insert for the undeceiving others in this point, by attesting so much under my hand.—ANGLESEA."*

If, at the period of this discovery, distance of time had rendered the truth more difficult to elucidate, it had also rendered it more easy to discuss. The tide of events had turned; the revolution of 1688 was preparing, and opinions obnoxious to the reigning house met with no opposition from the public. Otherwise we might be permitted to doubt whether James II., the Catholic son of Charles I., would place a very high value on any proofs which the king his father might have given of his firm attachment to the Protestant religion. It was not, however, till after the revolution of 1688, that the controversy on the authenticity of the Eikôn Basilikè was rekindled; then only the antagonists of the house of Stuart believed that they could treat the subject with greater freedom, while its partisans attached more importance to the relics of it which still remained to them. Neither Bishop Gauden, nor his wife, nor his son, were living; but Dr. Walker, his friend and confidant, maintained the veracity of the note written by Lord Anglesea: he had seen Gauden at work on the Eikôn Basilikè; he had accompanied him on one occasion to the house of Dr. Duppa, to whom Gauden communicated his manuscript; and on that day, in leaving the Bishop of Salisbury, with whom he had a long private conference, Gauden had said to Walker that Duppa desired him to add to the work he had commenced two chapters, one on " the

---

* It may cause surprise that the note of Lord Anglesea, written evidently thirteen years after the death of Dr. Gauden, should designate him Bishop of Exeter, since he died Bishop of Worcester. But Gauden, as we shall see, was Bishop of Worcester for only three months, and, probably, he had been customarily spoken of under his first title.

Ordinance against the Common Prayer-Book," and another on " the Denying the King the attendance of his Chaplains." Duppa was, in fact, commissioned to write these two chapters while Gauden performed the rest. Lastly, Walker had received from Gauden himself the last part of the manuscript of the Eikôn Basilikè, in a sealed parcel, and had remitted it, on the 23rd of December, 1648, to the person whose business it apparently was to pass it on to the printer (Royston), through the hands of Dr. Symmonds.

The particulars given by Dr. Walker were in part confirmed by a paper by Mrs. Gauden, found, it was said, by Mr. Arthur North, her son-in-law, among the papers of her son, and the object of which seemed to be to solicit the assistance of the court after the death of her husband,—which, however, she never received. According to Mrs. Gauden, the Eikôn Basilikè had been composed by her husband in order to counter-balance the advantage which Cromwell possessed with the public by his reputation for piety, and to produce a corresponding favourable opinion on behalf of the king. He had at first given to his work the title of " Suspiria Regalia," and intended to publish it as a manuscript found in the king's apartment after his removal from Holmsby. This project was communicated to Lord Capel, who approved of it, but thought that the book should not be printed without the consent of the king, who was then in the Isle of Wight. The Marquis of Hertford was secretly charged to carry the manuscript thither, and he brought back as an answer to Gauden, that the king, to whom Bishop Duppa, then attending on his person, had read several chapters of the work, approved it entirely as a faithful expression of his thoughts, and desired its publication, but not under his own name ; and that, having been informed of the project of the author, he had requested time to think over it. Gauden was then determined to print the copy which he had preserved, thinking that its publication might be useful to the king, whose position was becoming every day more perilous ; he only changed the title from Suspiria Regalia into Eikôn Basilikè ; he remitted the manuscript to Symmonds, who sent it to Royston as the veritable production of the king; and they were hastening on its publication when the work, partly printed, was discovered and seized. They were therefore obliged to begin afresh, and were not in a condition to publish the Eikôn Basilikè till a few days after Charles's death.

Such is, in substance, the narrative of Mrs. Gauden. Positive as it appears, its authority alone would not be suficient to decide the question. The personal interest of Mrs. Gauden in the matter was great ; the disappearance of nearly all the witnesses left her a clear stage to make what assertions she pleased; besides, whatever confidence we may place in her testimony, the paper which contained it is known to us only through the medium of Ludlow and Toland, both of them imbued with those party prejudices which make credulity so easy ; and neither of them had seen anything but extracts. But the account given by Dr. Walker, and printed in 1692, that is, a year before Ludlow's pamphlet, leaves but little doubt of the fact that Gauden had at least very much to do with the composition of the Eikôn Basilikè. This narrative, moreover, tended to explain other facts which, if well understood, might lead to a kind of certainty.

Much astonishment was felt when, after the Restoration, Gauden was presented with the see of Exeter. At the commencement of the revolution he was chaplain to the Earl of Warwick, and had embraced with ardour the opinions of his patron, and the opportunities which they gave him of pushing himself forward. A sermon, preached by him in 1640 before the House of Commons, had led to his being presented with a rich silver tankard. In 1641 he was promoted to the valuable rectory of Bocking. The enthusiasm of his Parliamentary sentiments did not, however, so far destroy his prudence as to induce him to trust the preservation of his fortune to the chances of party ; though presented to his benefice by the Parliament, he found means to have his appointment confirmed by Archbishop Laud, who was then in the Tower. He was nominated a member of the Assembly of Divines, he adopted the Covenant, but took care to leave his acceptance doubtful; and having declared himself in favour of, not exactly the abolition, but the reform of the episcopacy, he was returned for the Assembly. Nevertheless, his attachment to · the cause which he had at first chosen remained sufficiently manifest to cause him some alarm respecting his living at Bocking ; but, at the same time, his secret connexions secured to him means of proving, in case of need, his full and sincere return to the most loyal convictions. He composed on the

10th of February, 1649, a "Just Invective against the Murderers of Charles I.;" it was not, however, published till
1662 ; and if, on the 5th of January, 1649, he issued under
his own name a "Religious and Loyal Protestation against
the Proceedings of the Army," the rest of his conduct was
apparently so contrived as to protect his living at Bocking,
for he remained in possession of it under all changes of
government, and it was there that he composed his work in
favour of episcopacy, which, published in 1659, was considered
by far-sighted persons as one of the certain signs of the approaching Restoration.

The public conduct of Gauden was not then such as to
merit any favours from the court of Stuart; it showed him
rather to belong to those men whom the resentment of parties,
always more active than their gratitude, might justly exclude
from any share in the fruits of victory ; therefore Bishop
Sheldon and several other heads of the Anglican Church opposed his promotion. But some secret motive required that
he should be humoured, and he was made Bishop of Exeter.
However, Gauden, who rated his services at a higher value,
complained bitterly of a promotion which, while elevating him
in dignity, diminished, or at least did not sufficiently increase,
his revenues. Several of his letters to Lord Clarendon, inserted in the State Papers of that minister, indicate, more or
less clearly, what claims he considered himself to have on the
royal munificence, and the expectations which he had formed,
that what had been done in a princely manner would be rewarded with equal liberality; at last he demands *in commendam*,
till something better is provided, that a benefice worth four or
five hundred pounds sterling should be added to his bishopric.
His papers, also found by Mr. Arthur North, contain an
answer by Lord Clarendon on this subject, whose writing, it
is said, was recognised by his son. Clarendon, appearing to
approve of the arrangement proposed by the bishop, as a convenient method of delivering himself from his importunities,
adds, " The particular you mention has indeed been imparted
to me as a secret: I am sorry I ever knew it ; and when it
ceases to be a secret, it will please none but Mr. Milton."
If, as has been remarked, doubts rest on the perfect authenticity of Mr. Arthur North's papers, nevertheless the sentiment attributed here to Clarendon is more than proved by
the absolute silence maintained in his History of the Great

Rebellion with reference to the Eikôn Basilikè, a publication which all parties had justly regarded as a great event for the royal cause. Clarendon had been informed concerning the secret of the Eikôn Basilikè by Dr. Morley, his chaplain, to whom Gauden had confided it. This did not prevent Dr. Morley from obtaining for himself, in 1662, the see of Winchester, a prize on which Gauden had fixed his ambition. Gauden was obliged to content himself with the bishopric of Worcester, and so little could he satisfy his cravings that he died, apparently from mortification, at the end of a few months, the victim of that restless ambition and vanity which displays itself in his letters to Clarendon, and having, it seemed, but a small chance of ever attaining to any distinction amidst the crowd of those who were pressing forward, anxious to undertake any kind of service. Gauden was then employed by his new party to establish those principles of toleration which the court had adopted; he had just published a declaration in favour of liberty of conscience, to be extended even to the Papists, and was preparing another, tending to exempt the Quakers from all oaths. Death spared him the peril of another step forward or of a new recantation.

Nothing connected with the life and writings of Dr. Gauden could lead to the utterance of his name, were it not for his connexion with the Eikôn Basilikè; there is every reason to believe that to him we must attribute the editing as well as the publication of that work, but it must remain uncertain whether the entire composition of it belongs to him. On this point his letters give no positive information, and the part which appears to have been taken in the work by Dr. Duppa, the chaplain of Charles I., in whom that prince had the greatest confidence, may warrant us in supposing that the unfortunate monarch was not entirely unaware of the intention thus to portray him, from which his partisans naturally expected considerable assistance to their cause. Perhaps some materials from the hand of Charles I. had formed the basis of the work, and whether Clarendon was aware of the fact or not, Gauden had no reason that could induce him to reveal it, and had great interest in keeping it secret. Of this the narrative of Mrs. Gauden says nothing; but this narrative, which is not in other respects, as we have seen, fully trustworthy, is equally silent as to the connection of Gauden with the Bishop of Salisbury,—a silence which may indicate something which it was prudent to conceal. Walker appears to suppose that the work belonged entirely to his friend ; but if we adopt the narrative of Mrs. Gauden, it is evident that Walker was not cognisant of the whole matter, for he expressly states that Gauden never knew certainly whether the king had seen his manuscript, which is a direct contradiction to Mrs. Gauden's statement with reference to the answer brought by the Marquis of Hertford. Lastly, Sir Philip Warwick and several others have recognised in the Eikôn Basilikè things which they had heard from the king's own lips : the identity of doctrine among different members of the same party might serve to explain these apparent similarities ; but they contribute to sustain a supposition natural in itself, and which—if the controversy had an interest for us now, such as it possessed in England forty years after the events had happened—might receive, by a minute discussion of facts, a sufficient degree of probability.

But our curiosity is neither so patient nor so insatiable ; and out of the numerous dissertations that have been written for or against the authenticity of the Eikôn Basilikè, the two principal considerations which remain for us are the political importance and the literary merits of the work. This merit has been so generally acknowledged that, of all the arguments employed by the partisans of the Stuarts to disavow the co-operation of Dr. Gauden, this is the one to which least has been said in reply. No one of those who have maintained most pertinaciously that the Bishop of Exeter was the author of the Eikôn Basilikè has thought of denying the distance that exists between the doctor's acknowledged works and this which they thus attribute to him. " This is certain," says Burnet, " that Gauden never writ anything with that force, his other writings being such, that no man, from a likeness of style, would think him capable of writing so extraordinary a book as that is."* If, in fact, Gauden deserved the reproach cast upon him by his contemporaries of diffuseness, bombast, and affectation, such faults must have been carried to an extraordinary degree in order to make themselves remarked at a time when they were generally characteristic of the style of the period, and especially of theological writings ; and we must confess that the Eikôn Basilikè is in this respect distinguished by a perspicuity and wisdom of

* Burnet's History of his own Times, p. 51, fol. ed.

which few illustrations are to be found in the writings of the Presbyterian school. Nevertheless, the wisdom of this book is sometimes disfigured by a hunting after metaphors, and a too constant use of antithesis; its perspicuity is more than once obscured by cumbrous and lengthy sentences, by the extent and frequency of parentheses; the learned unwieldiness of the Presbyterian style is sometimes perceptible, and, if we may judge by comparison, the specimen which Charles I. has left us, in his controversy with Dr. Henderson, of his mode of treating theological questions, would do little to establish his claims to the composition of the Eikôn Basilikè, which has still less the appearance of being written by a king, although the Bishop of Exeter says of the former that it does not belong to the royal author. Charles's style, as it appears in his controversy with Dr. Henderson, is simple and devoid of ornaments; the sentences are short and clear, such as generally belonged at that time to the style of the Cavaliers, who, for the most part, made little pretension to theological science.

The composition of the Eikôn Basilikè would also be a strong presumption against the authenticity of the work, at least in the state and form in which it is given to us. We may discover in it a species of artifice but little in harmony with the real nature of the impressions of which it pretends to offer the unvarnished representation. Several chapters, said to be written on the suggestion of the moment, are evidently inapplicable to the position which they are intended to illustrate. Thus, two chapters are devoted to the fatal resolution which Charles took in April, 1646, of proceeding to the Scottish camp. The first, which is supposed to be written at the time of the king's departure from Oxford, expresses the hopes of the unfortunate prince with reference to the last asylum which remained to him; in the second is painted his calm and resigned indignation against the men who had betrayed his confidence. It is highly improbable that, on the eve of such a step, any one would think it necessary to commit to writing, for his own private perusal, an account of the motives which led to it; and we can hardly imagine that the captive monarch, after the event, would occupy his leisure in giving expression to his feelings in a manner most suited to dramatic effect.

As to the character of its ideas, the Eikôn Basilikè, to use

the language of a writer of our own time, "contained
nothing beyond the familiar meditations and the limited observations of a court divine."* Gauden, who was early thrown
into the ranks of the opposition, was not a court theologian;
but we have seen that he planned his work with the aid of
the Bishop of Salisbury, and it was doubtless owing to the
assistance, perhaps also to some original pieces put into his
hands, that the doctor's work acquired that colouring of
royalty which, in some respects, we cannot refuse to recognise in it. The divine right of kings, which is assumed in the
Eikôn Basilikè as an incontrovertible dogma, presents itself
moreover under the form of interior and individual feeling,
expressed with that mixture of dignity and personal prejudice
which such an opinion would necessarily produce in the mind
of a sovereign strongly attached, as Charles was, to moral
ideas, and accustomed to regard his own person as the first
object of his attention. Nevertheless, this disguise is not
always so perfectly preserved but that the religious per-
sonality will sometimes show itself instead of the royal, and
lead the theologian to refer to spiritual interests what the
the king would probably have referred to the interests of his
crown. For instance, the egotism of repentance, if I may
be allowed the expression, which is observable in the chapter
on the death of the Earl of Strafford, shows clearly the habits
of thought belonging to a theologian who often sees in crime
nothing but expiation, nothing but the personal interests of
the sinner, and in whose eyes all traces of evil are effaced
when the offender can believe himself ransomed from punishment.

It is in some prayers, veritably composed by Charles himself, that we must seek for the mode of sorrowful expression
which his penitence would lead him to adopt with reference
to this criminal weakness. If he places in the same rank
the self-reproach which he felt for having consented to the
abolition of episcopacy in Scotland, we must recollect that it
was in defence of that institution in England that the unhappy
prince, up to the last moment, sacrificed the hope of approaching peace, and certainly the hope of liberty. "Was
it through ignorance," says he, in one of his prayers, entitled
" A Prayer and Confession in and for the Times of Affliction;"
" was it through ignorance that I suffered innocent blood

* Malcolm Laing's History of Scotland, vol. iii., p. 407.

to be shed, by a false pretended way of justice, or that I permitted a wrong way of thy worship to be set up in Scotland, and injured the bishops in England? O no! but with shame and grief I confess that I therein followed the persuasions of worldly wisdom, forsaking the dictates of a right informed conscience. Wherefore, O Lord! I have no excuse to make, no hope left, but in the multitude of thy mercies."*

If we compare these prayers with those which conclude the chapters of the Eikôn Basilikè, we shall be struck with the difference between them. In the former we find the natural utterance of a soul trembling under an oppressive sense of its own weakness, in the presence of its Creator; the others seem to have been composed in the presence of the public. Without insisting on the continual abuse of antithesis, we recognise without difficulty the desire to obtain honour and favour in the eyes of men by a mention of Divine mercy, rather than any effort to obtain that mercy. It is not thus that a man prays for himself; and it is evident that the mind of the author, having no concern with heaven, did not think it necessary to raise its thoughts from earth.

We are unable to say whether it was from any regard to the public, or only to his own private opinions, that Gauden sacrificed those of the king with respect to episcopacy: in the prayer, unquestionably attributable to the king, which I have just quoted, the aversion of Charles I. to all measures contrary to episcopacy, is far more strongly marked than it is in the Eikôn Basilikè. But it is in the royal controversy with Mr. Henderson that we shall find the king's principal argument in favour of the episcopal hierarchy. "No one thing," says Charles, "made me more reverence the Reformation of my mother, the Church of England, than that it was done according to the Apostle's defence (Acts xxiv. 18), neither with multitude nor with tumult, but legally and orderly, and by those whom I conceive to have the reforming power."† This is, undoubtedly, such a motive as should actuate a king; and in omitting to avail himself of it, and thus giving to his book a far greater appearance of truthfulness, the author of the Eikôn Basilikè must have been influenced by very urgent reasons.

* Works of Charles I., vol. i., p. 196, folio. London, 1662.
† Charles's first letter to Henderson. Dated from Newcastle, May 29, 1646. Works of Charles I., vol. i., p. 156.

It is not for us now to judge accurately as to the causes of the immense sensation which this work produced at the time of its publication. Undeceived as to its origin, far removed in time from the events which gave it birth, we can no longer appreciate those vivid emotions which would be produced in the hearts of loyal English subjects, in the midst of their sufferings, by the least trace of a prince to whom the public grief was unwilling to attribute anything but virtue. It is needful to pass through and mingle in such an epoch in order to share this feeling in all its intensity. When engaged in these scenes, the excited spirit becomes susceptible to impressions which cannot preserve themselves through any succeeding ages. By the wise arrangements of Providence it has been ordained that the sufferings of humanity should not form a depth of woe destined to increase from generation to generation. But the astonishing reputation of the Eikôn Basilikè—the part which Charles I. himself probably took in it—the knowledge, at any rate, which he had of it before its publication, which is equivalent to an assent to it,—all these things make this work one of the most important monuments of that period, and certainly one in which the feelings and the ideas, the state of mind and heart, of the Royalist and Anglican party, are the most faithfully expressed.

ON THE MEMOIRS OF JAMES II.

KING JAMES II. was born with that activity of mind which is often found united with mediocrity of talent, and which, according to circumstances, renders mediocrity honourable or dangerous. It displayed itself alternately in good and disastrous effects; it was useful to him when an exile, and it deprived him of his throne; it led him to devote to honourable employment in France, under Turenne, those years of youth and adversity which his brother wasted in the dissipations of a court; it urged him on afterwards in England to precipitate that fatal catastrophe of the fortunes of the Stuarts which the indolence of Charles II. would have postponed. Always serious and careful of himself, even in the midst of those disorders which preceded and accompanied his devotedness to the Papacy, James had constantly committed to writing the events of his life; and nine or ten manuscript volumes in his own handwriting—which were the chief objects of his solicitude when, in 1688, he fled from England before the fortunes of the Prince of Orange—were the fruit of this journalising. On his departure he entrusted them to the Comte de Thérèse, the ambassador from Savoy, who transmitted them to Leghorn, from whence they were sent to France, Some months before his death, James placed them at the College of Scottish Jesuits at Paris, in the hands of Louis Innes, the Principal of the college, so often mentioned in the writings of Voltaire as the Jesuit Innes. These manuscripts, which are represented, in a note found among the papers of Mr. Fox, as amounting to ten volumes of Memoirs and four of Letters, remained, after James's death, in the Scottish College, where they were seen by different individuals in a magnificent binding, engraved with the arms of Great Britain. At the time when the French revolution began to threaten establishments of this kind with danger, the manuscripts of King James were removed to St. Omer, whence they were to be sent to England. They were entrusted for a time to a Frenchman, a friend of Mr. Stapleton, the Principal of the Jesuit College at St Omer, and were concealed by him in his cellar; but, before the individual in whose charge they were placed could find an opportunity of embarking them, he was imprisoned upon suspicion. His wife, frightened by the fact of having such a charge, began by destroying the binding, a cause more than sufficient at that period to excite against the retainer of it the most dangerous accusations. She then removed the papers to her country residence, where they were buried in her garden; but soon, her alarm increasing as the state of France became more terrible, she burnt them. Thus perished the original source of the most precious information we could have respecting the interior movements of the English court, after the restoration of Charles II.

However all traces of them were not destroyed; the manuscripts of the "Memoirs of James II.," too voluminous, doubtless too chaotic, and perhaps also too unreserved for the uses for which they were required, had undergone a new arrangement (by whose orders and for what purpose is not known), in which long extracts, literally transcribed from the original manuscript, were united to other portions, extracted either from the Memoirs, or the Letters, so as to form a complete and consecutive work, containing the life of James II., from his birth till his death. After the death of the Duchess of Albany, widow of the Pretender, Prince Charles Edward, which took place on the 29th of January, 1804, this last-mentioned manuscript passed, along with the other papers of the house of Stuart, out of the hands of the heirs of James II. into that of Abbé Waters, procurator-general of the English Benedictines, to whom the duchess had bequeathed them by her will. George IV., then Prince of Wales, entered into a negotiation at Rome with the Abbé Waters to obtain possession of these papers, which he consented to yield on condition of receiving a pension for life, of which he only received one payment, and died very soon afterwards. The war and other circumstances prevented for a long time the removal of these papers, which did not arrive in England till 1810, when they were deposited in the library of Carlton House. From thence was taken the manuscript which was printed in 1816* by Dr. Clarke, chaplain at Carlton House, and librarian of the Prince of Wales, then Prince Regent.

The time when the Memoirs of James II. were re-edited is uncertain. There is no reason, however, to doubt that the last part, at least, reckoning from 1688 inclusive, was not revised after the death of James, nor even of his widow, Queen Mary of Modena. The proof of this is found in a sentence in the manuscript, in which, on the occasion of the birth of the Prince of Wales, the writer speaks of the resemblance which the prince had, as he grew older, " to the late king, his father, and the late queen, his mother." We even find, in the part referring to the year 1685, several interlineary corrections, in the handwriting of James's son, known in France as the Chevalier de Saint George; which indicates that all this part had been corrected under his eyes, and by his orders. Lastly, among the papers deposited at Carlton House, there is to be found registered the authority or injunction given, in 1707, by this same Chevalier de Saint George to Louis Innes, that he should remove to St. Germains, for some months, the portion of the Memoirs and other manuscripts of James II. relating to 1678 and the succeeding years, in order that they might be, says the prince, " examined and investigated by such persons as we shall nominate for the purpose." We

* In 2 vols. 4to. London, 1816.

might infer from this that the persons nominated concerned themselves only with that part of the Memoirs which is alluded to; but still the question remains, whether the work was done under the inspection and by the order of James, or only after his death and by the direction of his son.

Two passages in Burnet's "History of my own Time," leave us little reason to doubt that James himself, before his accession to the throne, had caused extracts to be made from his principal journal and his Memoirs. "The Duchess of York," says Burnet, "was a very extraordinary woman. . . . . She writ well; and had begun the duke's life, of which she showed me a volume. It was all drawn from his journal; and he intended to have employed me in carrying it on."[*] And again: "He entered with great freedom with me about all his affairs: and he showed me the journals he took of business every day with his own hand; a method, he said, that the Earl of Clarendon had set him on. The duchess had begun to write his life. He showed me a part of it in a thin volume in folio. I read some of it, and found it writ with a great deal of spirit."[†]

Another fact may throw some light on this question. There appeared in 1735 in the appendix, and among the authorities to Ramsay's "History of Turenne," the "Mémoires du Duc d'York, contenant le récit de ses campagnes en France, et dans les Pays-Bas." This fragment, printed from a manuscript given by James himself to the Cardinal de Bouillon, with the exception of some slight alterations, which we shall presently indicate, will be found entire in the manuscript of Carlton House. It is accompanied by a preface written by the Cardinal himself, which is as follows:

"James II., King of England, having honoured me by relating to me, in the year 1695, divers particulars, and some considerable actions in the life of my late uncle, M. de Turenne, which were unknown to me, as not being mentioned in those Memoirs I had by me of his own handwriting, I made bold to represent to that prince that I was extremely sorry I was debarred, by the profound respect I had for his Majesty, from most humbly begging that he would be pleased, for the sake of that kindness he had for the late M. de Turenne, to commit to writing, at such hours as would be least incommodious to him, those particulars and those actions of his

* Burnet, vol. i., p. 170.   † Ibid., pp. 459-360.

life to which I was an utter stranger; and I further said that I would not scruple to take the liberty of asking this favour of anybody but his Majesty, whom I ought to respect even more than the memory of the late M. de Turenne, which I had regarded, up to that moment, as the thing in the world that was most dear to me. Upon this his Majesty, out of his unparalleled goodness and generosity, told me he would with pleasure do what I wished, as soon as he possibly could, and even acquainted me, that as he had already written in English, by way of Annals, the memoirs of his own life, he would from them extract and translate into French whatever related to the campaigns he had made in the army of France, commanded by M. de Turenne, and those he afterwards made in the Low Countries, in the army of Spain, till the peace of the Pyrenees was proclaimed, and King Charles II., his brother, restored and placed on the throne of Great Britain. It was an agreeable surprise to me, on the 27th of January, in the next year, 1696, when going to St. Germain-en-Laye, to pay my respects to that great and religious king, he took me into his closet, where he told me he would now perform the promise he had made me the preceding year, and at the same time he put into my hand the sheets hereto annexed, into which, he assured me, he had transferred everything that he had found in his Memoirs concerning the late M. de Turenne, from the year 1652 inclusive, to the year 1660; adding, that he gave it me with gladness, not only on account of M. de Turenne, whose memory, he said, would be all his life long most dear and precious to him, as taking him to be the most consummate general and the greatest man he ever knew, and the best friend he ever had, but also in regard of the personal friendship he had for myself in particular. He, however, recommended to me never to permit these Memoirs to be perused by any person whatever till after his decease. Having returned his Majesty my most humble thanks for this favour, I promised him I would obey his commands, which promise I faithfully kept as long as he lived. This gift, from the hands of so great a king, appeared to me so valuable, and so greatly tending to the honour of the late M. de Turenne and of our whole family, that from that very moment I resolved, as I told his Majesty when I received from him this rich present, I would entail it for ever on the eldest branch of our family, as I accordingly do by these presents, being at Rome, the

16th of February, in the year 1715, and having there, by the providence of God, found again this inestimable book, which I had mislaid, and despaired of ever seeing more.

(Signed)   "THE CARDINAL DE BOUILLON,
"Dean of the Sacred College."*

The preface informs us that the fragment, printed under the title of "Memoirs of the Duke of York," was revised and translated by James II. himself, which is confirmatory of the manuscript at Carlton House, at least so far as its editing is concerned. The extract is given as having been literally transcribed from the original Memoirs in James's handwriting. It appears certain, therefore, that at the end of the year 1695, when James undertook for the Cardinal de Bouillon the narrative of his campaigns, the editing of the manuscript at Carlton House had not commenced; for James would probably have made use of the same hand which he had employed in preparing the rest, to help him in drawing up the manuscript which he wished to give to Cardinal Bouillon. We may remark, perhaps, as a singular circumstance, that this manuscript, which had been lost in some unknown way, was found again at Rome, in 1715, where likewise the Carlton House manuscript, with the other papers of the House of Stuart, except the original Memoirs given to the Scottish College, have been since found. We cannot, however, infer anything from this against the authenticity of the manuscript at Carlton House. It is evident that that is the original version from which the manuscript of the Cardinal de Bouillon is only a translation. This last manuscript is, in the first place, more exact in its use of proper names, which may give us ground for supposing that James II., supposing the translation was his own, had it revised by some French secretary; further, in the Cardinal's manuscript the Duke of York is never mentioned except in the third person, whilst in the Carlton House version of the manuscript he is always alluded to under the form of the first person—a fact the more remarkable in that the third person is always employed in the other extracts derived from the original manuscripts; lastly, the Carlton House manuscript gives in de-

---

* The English translation of this document has been taken, with few alterations, from the translation of Ramsay's History of Turenne, which appeared in London in 1785. 2 vols., 8vo.

tail several circumstances of purely personal interest relating to the Duke of York, which are entirely omitted in
the Cardinal's manuscript. Everything, therefore, favours
the supposition that the Carlton House manuscript is more
immediately the work of James; but at the same time there
is every reason to regard the editing of that part of his
Memoirs as a separate work, undertaken for the first time
in compliance with the wish expressed by the Cardinal de
Bouillon, and altogether unconnected with that complete re-
visal, of which, perhaps, he gave the first suggestion to the
king. We know nothing, certainly, with respect to the
authorship of this work; some attribute it to Louis Innes;
and it has been affirmed to have been superintended by
Dryden, probably the son of the poet of that name, himself
also a poet, but of no reputation.

We cannot but deeply regret the loss of the original manuscripts which gave the first impressions of King James
himself. It is difficult to believe that the Memoirs actually
existing were compiled with equal ingenuousness; experience
had then taught the descendants and partisans of King
James, among other things, the necessity of sometimes with-
holding what they knew. Nevertheless, this last narrative,
incomplete as it may be, contains a great number of fragments unquestionably derived from the original author, and
is in other respects so fully stamped with his ideas and feelings, that it would be difficult to find anywhere else so faithful
a representation of them.

www.ingramcontent.com/pod-product-compliance
Lightning Source LLC
Chambersburg PA
CBHW052345110726
47901CB00005B/1369